THE ADOLESCENT

BOOKS BY DOSTOEVSKY IN
NORTON PAPERBACK EDITIONS

The Adolescent (Andrew R. MacAndrew, Tr.)
The Brothers Karamazov (Ralph E. Matlaw, Ed.)
Crime and Punishment (George Gibian, Ed.)
The Gambler (Andrew R. MacAndrew, Tr.)

THE
ADOLESCENT

Fyodor Dostoevsky

A NEW TRANSLATION BY
Andrew R. MacAndrew

W · W · NORTON & COMPANY
New York · London

Copyright © 1971 by Andrew R. MacAndrew

Published simultaneously in Canada by
Penguin Books Canada Ltd,
2801 John Street, Markham, Ontario L3R 1B4.

First published as a Norton paperback 1981
by arrangement with Doubleday & Company, Inc.

Library of Congress Cataloging in Publication Data

Dostoevskiĭ, Fedor Mikhaĭlovich, 1821–1881.
The adolescent.

(A Norton paperback edition)
Translation of Podrostok.
I. MacAndrew, Andrew Robert, 1911–
PG3326.P6   1981   891.73′3   80–29643

ISBN 0-393-00995-5

W. W. Norton & Company, Inc.
500 Fifth Avenue, New York, N.Y. 10110
W. W. Norton & Company Ltd.
37 Great Russell Street, London WC1B 3NU

5 6 7 8 9 0

INTRODUCTION

The great, all-pervading theme of Dostoevsky's five major novels is man's need for God. Without God, the fragile harmony between man and the outside world collapses, and he becomes a bundle of turmoil surrounded by chaos. This is what Dostoevsky calls disorder, and "Disorder" was his original choice for the title of his fourth major novel, which he finally called *Podrostok* —*The Adolescent*. Actually it is the story of a nineteen-year-old searching for identity amidst the disorder of Russian society of the 1870s. To Dostoevsky, that society was disintegrating as the "unifying idea"—God—became more and more deeply undermined. The dogma of the Russian Orthodox Church, the tsar's autocracy, the rigid social hierarchy, and the absolute loyalty to Russia—all these, along with other time-tested institutions and values, were being coldly examined, questioned as to their usefulness, and increasingly challenged. The very foundations of life, as Dostoevsky saw it, were being thereby shaken loose and the whole structure was beginning to sway underfoot. Those old enough to have been raised before the disorder set in still managed somehow to maintain their footing by sheer habit. But the young stumbled, fell, and tried desperately to discover new ways of keeping their balance. Many of them, however, were only too willing to crawl and scatter in search of the nearest cracks and holes to take refuge in dank darkness.

The metaphysical and social landscape in *The Adolescent* (1874) is essentially the same as in *Crime and Punishment* (1866), *The Idiot* (1868), *The Possessed* (1872), and *The Brothers Karamazov* (1880), although its political overtones may well be, as has often been pointed out, less virulent than in its immediate predecessor, *The Possessed*. But whatever variations in emphasis there may be among these books, they are minor in comparison with the palpable ideological difference between Dostoevsky's late major works and his earlier writings. The dividing line, of course, appears to be his Siberian detention and exile, although the break is by no means as abrupt as it is usually presented.

To understand the motivations of the characters in *The Adolescent* (as in any of its sister novels), one must follow the evolution of Dostoevsky's ideology from the 1840s through the 1870s, keeping a particularly close eye on its shifts and fluctuations relative to the changing intellectual climate in Russia. Ideology played an exceptionally important part in Dostoevsky's own motivation as well as in that of his characters, and he peopled his books with characters who were moved by ideas that, at one time or another in his own ideological evolution, may have commanded his allegiance (enthusiastic or grudged) or his opposition (fanatical, understanding, or even sympathetic). And so, like Dostoevsky himself, all his important characters, consciously or unconsciously, are affected by the ideas floating in the air, blown in, as a rule, from the West, ideas that Dostoevsky sometimes compared to intelligent bacteria. In his later works, these bacteria are a source of dangerous infection, a sort of "rationalitis," to which only those with solid roots in their native, Russian soil are immune.

The setting of every major Dostoevsky novel is Russia at a given stage of ideological infection, from which some characters perish while others, with sufficient immunity, survive to continue their search for salvation.

Dostoevsky's method is like that of a scientist who studies the capacity of an environment to sustain life by watching the changes in the organisms that inhabit it, or, to put it in what might be more Dostoevskian language, it is by looking into man's soul that Dostoevsky searches for God. To Dostoevsky, everything in the final analysis depends upon man's relation to God, which, in his own case, was always emotional and tense, albeit unsteady and fluctuating.

In *The Adolescent*, for instance, it is easy to see how Dostoevsky's own intellectual history is reflected in the two most important characters. Versilov, "a man of the forties," which was Dostoevsky's generation, stumbles upon the same ideas that Dostoevsky had stumbled upon at the time, reasons along much the same lines that Dostoevsky had once reasoned along, and gropes desperately for a faith or a substitute faith, just as Dostoevsky had apparently groped himself. On the other hand, Versilov's illegitimate son, the narrator, is partly an autobiographical transplant of the dreamy, romantic young Dostoevsky of the early 1840s (reminiscent of the narrator in *White Nights*) into the 1860s and 1870s, a projection that enables the author to look at the new generation—the nihilists—through the eyes of their young contemporary.

Before looking into the private circumstances of Dostoevsky's life that may have made him receptive or antagonistic to certain ideas at certain times, one must grasp which ideas were prevalent at what moment on the Russian intellectual scene during Dostoevsky's writing career, i.e., roughly between 1840 and 1880.

The most readily available food for thought throughout the 1840s may be described generically as French social Utopianism.* Although made up of such heterogeneous elements as eighteenth-century rationalism, romanticism, and the neo-Catholic mysticism of the Restoration, these nineteenth-century adaptations of Thomas More's sixteenth-century Utopian prototype all share one striking characteristic—a peculiar form of mystical humanism based on the refusal to condone human suffering, combined with an attempt to establish a religious foundation for that position in the Gospels. Like Jean-Jacques Rousseau, the Utopians held that, being of divine essence, man is good by nature. To them, evil was incompatible with the will of God, and the notion of original sin made no sense in view of God's infinite mercy.

Logical inconsistencies such as these were, in the Utopians' view, flagrant perversions of the original teachings handed down by Christ, distortions introduced by men corrupted by life in their wretchedly organized society, which they called "civilization." If asked how a society made up of naturally good men

* Although the brand of Utopianism that reached Russia was distinctly French, it contained easily recognizable elements from Schelling's *Naturphilosophie* and Hegel's *Phänomenologie*, both works that were popularized in France by Victor Cousin and that had also reached Russia independently at an earlier date. The first Russian contact with Utopian thought was mostly secondhand, through French novels read either in the original or in translated installments carried by half a dozen literary periodicals. The most popular of the French writers were Victor Hugo, Balzac, George Sand, and also Eugène Sue, whose *romans-feuilletons*, beside being inspired by Utopian ideas, also had considerable influence on Dostoevsky's plot construction. Of the more directly theoretical works that were read and discussed in Russia, the most important were Saint-Simon's *Nouveau Christianisme* (1819), Lamennais's *Paroles d'un croyant* (1834), and Etienne Cabet's *Voyage en Icarie* (1834). As for Charles Fourier, whose Utopian, cooperative-like phalansteries are the most often mentioned by and in connection with Dostoevsky, his theories were known in Russia mainly through his disciple, Victor Considérant (*La Destinée sociale*, 1834), a much more readable writer from whom Dostoevsky borrowed many ideas and even whole passages (e.g., the vision of the Golden Age).

could be so evil, the Utopians had a ready answer: by *accident*.

According to them, Christ, whom they worshiped as their greatest teacher, was crucified because of a horrible misunderstanding, because of His contemporaries' dismal failure to grasp the true meaning of His teachings, or, as one would say today, because of a disastrous break in communications. Indeed, with better luck, they claimed, mankind would not have been robbed of so many centuries of bliss. But now at last the disaster could be redeemed by those who finally truly understood Him (they themselves). The age of ignorance was over, and, armed with modern knowledge and science, they knew how to build a society from which evil could be scientifically eliminated. And without evil there would be no scope left for its symbiotic twin —suffering.

Whether they were aware of it or not, their theory of unfortunate misunderstanding robbed Golgotha of its poetry, of its whole mystical and religious meaning, which lies in the union of man and God through the suffering of the God-Man. But they felt confident that they could replace this by the mysticism of Christian love for mankind, a sort of automatic love generated scientifically by a fair and ideally efficient organization of society. The Utopians were well-meaning, altruistic, and practical people whose common sense told them that the Christian mystique would be not only more useful but also more noble if directed toward serving others rather than toward the exclusive preoccupation with personal salvation, which amounts to transcendental selfishness.

These, then, were the ideas Dostoevsky encountered in Petersburg when he arrived there in the early 1840s hoping to become a professional writer. Before that, he had been brought up with a formal respect for the Russian Orthodox Church in a family headed by a father both authoritarian and profligate. He grew up in the crowded staff quarters of a Moscow charity hospital, where his irascible father was a resident physician. Early in life, he witnessed the misery of the charity patients and the harshness with which those in authority abused their power. Judging from his early letters, what the boy saw filled him with compassion and a sort of horrified puzzlement. The bleakness of his surroundings was relieved only by his gentle and intelligent mother, who gave him a taste for reading. She taught him to read using a collection of stories based on the Old and New Testaments, of which his favorite was the story of Job. She also read him aloud Mrs. Radcliffe's Gothic novels, which had been her favorites in her own childhood. Occasionally, she took him to the theater, and Schiller's *Robbers*, which he saw at the age of ten, impressed him the most. Later, however, the death of his mother, whom he loved, affected him relatively little, while the news of the death of his father, whom he didn't love, provoked what may have been his first epileptic seizure. The elder Dostoevsky was murdered by the serfs on his little country estate. They had hated their churchgoing, stern master for his brutality and debauchery, especially for his predilection for very young girls. Much later it was established that among his murderers were at least two fathers of such victims. As he had been suffocated with a pillow from his carriage, there were no marks of violence on his body. The guardians of the Dostoevsky children decided not to report the real cause of the death: the imprisonment of the serfs would have entailed too substantial a depreciation of the estate.

It was the shattering of the paternal image, followed by the perpetuation of a lie and the covering up of a crime for practical considerations, that was such a shock to Dostoevsky. The discrepancy between professed religious morality and actual practice bewildered him. And when he tried to escape from the squalid reality into romanesque daydreams, the contrast only stressed the ugliness of his surroundings.

Much later, after he had written *The Adolescent*, he described in retrospect his feelings at that time (in the January 1876 edition of his *Writer's Diary*): "'The beautiful and the sublime!' During those years that phrase was still fresh and could be uttered without irony. Ah, how many such beautiful phrases were current then! We believed in them passionately. . . ." But further on, in the same entry, he describes how he watched an army officer batter his driver's back with his fists while the poor man was desperately whipping his bony nag. Dostoevsky comments on this gap between the "Schilleresque ideal" and brutal reality and remarks: "I was never to forget that scene."

Thus, quite naturally, Dostoevsky, like most of his sensitive intellectual contemporaries whose views were formed during the 1840s, found abundant food for thought in the French Utopian socialism that reached Petersburg. Perhaps it even contained possible answers to the dilemmas that tormented him. For whatever these Frenchmen might have found objectionable in France was even more conspicuously present in Russia: the regime was even more despotic and cruel, the institutions more rigid and illogical, the people hungrier and more brutalized, and the church even more bizarre and gaudy, watching all these appalling injustices with perfect equanimity.

Inspired by the French Utopians, the young Russians who now started questioning what had been taken for granted ("ours is the age of analysis" is how the leading literary critic Belinsky defined that period) came to be known, in the history of Russian thought, as "the men of the forties" and eventually also as "the fathers" to distinguish them from "the sons," who replaced them on the intellectual scene in the 1860s.

Despite considerable variations in the individual positions of "the men of the forties," they were all reformists rather than revolutionaries, Christian would-be rationalizers of both the church and the state who remained loyal to God and the tsar. Indeed, they repeated after Saint-Simon and the other Utopians that, far from rejecting the teachings of Christ, they were rescuing them from the Byzantine rituals in which they were being drowned. Most of these young Russians not only looked to the West for models for theoretical Utopias but also believed that the immediate adoption of certain existing Western institutions would be a great improvement. These were the "Westernizers." Others, the "Slavophiles," contended that foreign institutions could not be simply grafted onto the Russian soil and insisted that the country had to develop its own social and political system built around the native village commune—the *mir*. Yet even they were influenced, perhaps unconsciously, by the Western Utopian thinkers.

But, while Russia's "men of the forties" were denouncing and ridiculing the inconsistencies of traditional Russia, they were themselves advocating their own brand of inconsistencies inherent in their very attempt to rationalize the irrational tsarist absolutism. The social theories they insisted on applying to streamline Russia's haphazard and illogical system were themselves woven of contradictory strands combining logic and mysticism, Locke's liberalism, and Rousseau's rationalistic totalitarianism. As might be expected, these attempts to correct one illogical system by combining it with another, full of built-in contradictions, led to endless discussions, disagreements, and disappointments. Far from being simple, the devising of a system based on reason to run a country turned out to be a very slippery business.

There is, however, a convenient myth that tidies up Dostoevsky's position in this complicated mess. It simply ignores the inner contradictions and inconsistencies both in Dostoevsky and in the ideas involved. It says that, after toying for a while with "atheistic socialism", being caught red-handed by the tsarist authorities, subjected to a phony execution, and sent off to a Siberian penitentiary, Dostoevsky at long last discovered the true oppressed Russia in whose soul lived the "Russian Christ," who finally led him to God the Father. Then the regenerated Dostoevsky is said to have about-faced and started his crusade against his former allies, whom he now recognized as perpetrators of error and spreaders of harmful, alien (Western) ideas.

Such a neat switch from a clear-cut atheistic materialism to a fanatical Russian fundamentalism, so common in many twentieth-century defectors from Communism, is extremely un-Dostoevskian. The complexity of the religious and existential positions of Dostoevsky's characters, as well as of his constantly recurring themes, should be enough to belie it. One may even say that painful ambiguity of belief is Dostoevsky's creative stimulant, the wind in his sails. Besides, as far as can be ascertained, never in his life could Dostoevsky have been described even as an agnostic, let alone an atheist. Nor, for that matter, did he ever succeed in gaining a total, unquestioning faith in God.

One of the favorite topics of discussion in the clandestine Petrashevsky group Dostoevsky had joined was Fourier's system of social organization. At one point, some members, including the founder Petrashevsky, influenced by Belinsky's shift† toward radical determinism and purely utilitarian ethics, decided that a truly scientific social system had no need of Christ as an example since everybody would behave in his and society's best interests anyway. Others, however, maintained that Christ was indispensable, whereupon the group split. Dostoevsky stayed with the original Fourier, and with Christ.

Furthermore, we have the testimony of Dr. Yanovsky (who lived with Dostoevsky at the time) that Dostoevsky had fasted every year on the Feast of the Ascension up until his arrest in 1849, which is the moment he is supposed to have reached his high-water mark of godlessness.

It is also a fact that, ever since 1846, when Belinsky (who had been enthusiastic about *Poor Folk*) disapproved of Dostoevsky's second novel, *The Double,* for its "lack of social con-

---

† Belinsky had embraced Feuerbach's theory that God was only an abstraction invested with all the ideal human virtues of which man had divested himself for just that purpose. Eventually he also adopted Auguste Comte's mystical worship of humanity under the name of Positivism, which suited perfectly Belinsky's rationalistic ecstasy, made him the precursor of the nihilists of the 1860s, and assured him a niche in the Soviet pantheon.

tent" and its indulgence in "the fantastic," the two had become estranged. Obviously, the split between them was not only personal but also ideological and continued to grow until Belinsky's death in 1848. It was, therefore, an ironic twist of fate that caused Dostoevsky to be arrested at a meeting of the Petrashevsky group while reading aloud a secretly circulating Belinsky letter. That letter was an attack (by a man with whom, by then, Dostoevsky widely disagreed) on Gogol's last book, *Selected Passages from Correspondence with Friends,‡* which happened to be teeming with ideas that were to become Dostoevsky's trademark. But, in attacking Gogol's loyalistic credo, Belinsky was attacking the regime; therefore by reading it, Dostoevsky was, indeed, guilty of a subversive act.

It was, according to Dostoevsky, the ten years he spent in Siberia (1849–1859) that wiped out his social Utopian illusions. In 1873, just about the time he was beginning *The Adolescent,* he offered a double explanation for his change of heart in his *Writer's Diary.* First, and most important, was his first direct contact with what he calls the "simple Russian people." Until then, they had been to him an anonymous crowd that he watched from, as it were, his middle-class balcony. But now he had been pulled down to their level, was surrounded by their sweaty bodies, shared their misery, had to adjust to their ways and to live by their bewildering standards. Second, his reading diet during his four years in the penitentiary was limited to one single book—the Bible—which he read and reread

‡ Gogol, whose marvelous satires, particularly *Dead Souls,* had brought down on him frequent accusations of seeing only the seamy side of Russian life, had tried again and again, and always in vain, to incorporate his "positive message" into a work of art. The sequel to *Dead Souls,* which he wrote and rewrote for many years, satisfied him so little that he burned the final versions, and most of the extant drafts seem to justify his judgment. In despair, close to madness and messianic obsession, he decided to deliver his message to Russia in the form of appropriate passages from his old letters, or letters purposely written for that occasion and deliberately antedated, and to publish them in a volume entitled *Selected Passages from Correspondence with Friends.* As it turned out, his messianic message amounted to a proclamation of his mystical faith in the dogma of the Russian Orthodox Church, a strident appeal for loyalty to the tsar, his belief in the special mission of the Russian people, and other such ecstatically religious and nationalistic ingredients. But he still failed dismally to transmute these into art. Dostoevsky, on the other hand, was to do precisely that, for he was the rare bird—the genuine mystical and religious writer.

again and again and even used as a primer to teach some of the illiterate inmates to read, just as his mother had taught him.

This double-pronged explanation of his shift toward his well-known anti-rationalist position appears quite convincing. A Siberian stockade was certainly an excellent place to observe men moved by irrational impulses. For the Siberian convicts Dostoevsky described as "simple Russian people" were anything but simple. They were complex and brutal criminals, whose twisted minds and unpredictable acts both fascinated and frightened him and, as can be gathered from his autobiographical *The House of the Dead*, filled him with a sort of mystical awe. And, amidst the dreadful discomfort and sudden bursts of violence, the only thing this hypersensitive man had to read was the Bible. For four whole years, it filled every moment he had of relative peace and privacy. The rhythmically flowing words and phrases flooded his mind and blended with his daily thoughts and impressions. Then, gradually, the biblical figures came to life, began to move, and broke out of their stylized ancient confinement, just as in the eyes of an invalid confined to his bed, the patterns on wallpaper come to life, start dancing and skip out of their two-dimensional flatness. It is hardly surprising, then, that seen from Dostoevsky's new, terrifying surroundings and with his ears full of mystical biblical music, the optimistic, rosy creed of the social Utopians would appear hopelessly shallow and artificial. How puppet-like and unrealistic must the Utopians' man, free of original sin, have looked to him! And how pale and unconvincing were the noble and reasonable heroes of George Sand in the stark prison world! Compared with a biblical character like Job, who could accept the unacceptable, Sand's people must have seemed to Dostoevsky like artificial textbook illustrations of the "social code" of Pierre Leroux, while Job's character was not only more real than ever but contained in itself the revelation of a deeper truth.

Moreover, the very concept of "equality," as preached by the Utopians, did not seem at all what Dostoevsky's primitive and rebellious companions wanted. They had, he discovered, a strange and paradoxical respect for the status quo. Although they had an instinctive hostility toward the upper classes, they accepted them as such, reserving their special loathing for the members of those classes who tried to imitate the "people," to pretend that there were no differences between them. In the same way, they accepted the established church and traditional religious practices. It repeatedly struck Dostoevsky how these men, often brutal and callous toward one another, would sit reverently through a service, especially during the big holidays like Christmas and Easter. It was obvious that no practical and rational tenets could ever take the place of these old traditional beliefs.

And, finally, what may have come to be Dostoevsky's later, somewhat elusive, concept of freedom seems also to have originated in Siberia. Time and again he had seen a prisoner, generally well behaved and occasionally about to be liberated, suddenly erupt in apparently quite unmotivated outbursts of rage, become openly violent, and indulge in behavior that, in view of the brutal punishment to be expected, could not only delay indefinitely his release but also be literally suicidal. Dostoevsky explained such outbursts as man's sudden overwhelming need to assert his freedom, to prove that he is alive and not just a number subjected to the artificial prison rules and regulations. And this human need for freedom was what inspired, as we shall see later, the "irrational" behavior of his "underground man."

However, all these ideological reappraisals that Dostoevsky claims began in prison did not immediately become obvious upon his return to Petersburg. Judging from the tenor of his books and polemical articles written during the first two post-Siberian years, he still occupied just about the same social Utopian position as he had before his arrest.*

And so, on top of his Siberian experience, it took Dostoevsky an additional couple of years to reach his final, well-known position. Or, to put it another way, if an ideological time bomb had been planted in him in Siberia, it took a good two years of Petersburg irritations to set it off. For the spectrum of the

* After four years in the penitentiary, Dostoevsky had to serve six years in a regiment stationed in Siberia. It was during his last year there in 1859 that he wrote *Uncle's Dream* and *Stepanchikovo Village*. Ideologically, these stories hardly depart from those written in the 1840s; nor does the novel *The Insulted and the Injured* (1861), which is still full of Utopian ideals and daydreams. Even *The House of the Dead* (1862), which contains many observations that indicate the forthcoming shift, recounts his Siberian experiences without transmuting them into the deep feelings bearing Dostoevsky's personal brand out of which his major novels are made. As to his explicit polemical pronouncements, the magazine Vremya [*Time*], which Dostoevsky published with his brother Mikhail, often sided with Nekrasov's liberal *Sovremennik* [*The Contemporary*] against Katkov's right-wing *Russkii Vestnik* [*The Russian Herald*], where eventually most of Dostoevsky's famous works would be published.

intellectual opposition to the regime had shifted considerably during the 1850s when Dostoevsky had been away from the scene. Religious Utopian socialism was pretty much passé, and the new young generation followed Belinsky. Determinism, scientism, and mechanistic causality left no room for the cumbersome concept of God. And along with determinism came its corollary, a simplified version of English utilitarianism (propounded mainly by Belinsky's successor, Chernyshevsky) that contained the possibility of computing mathematically the best way of organizing human society so that each member's spontaneous desires would merge with his personal interests and these with the interest of society as a whole: it was just a matter of setting down the right equations.

The truculent arrogance and smugness of the Russian nihilists (a word coined by Turgenev in his novel *Fathers and Sons*) was what finally blew up the French social Utopianism that was still lingering in Dostoevsky and hurled him toward the "right." The simplistic phrases and slogans of the "sons," who, in their mechanistic rage, ended by denying what was, as Dostoevsky saw it, the very essence of life, also turned him against his former companions, the "fathers." It was they, he decided, who had started the disastrous trend and must bear the responsibility for nihilism. He remembered how lightheartedly they had all tried to analyze (the "age of analysis," indeed!) the traditional concepts, as if these concepts could be broken down into elements and explained in rational terms. All they had succeeded in doing, in fact, was cutting themselves and their children off from their native soil and vital cultural roots. Oh, they themselves had, early in life, absorbed enough native culture through their umbilical cords to retain their human faces. But their sons had no solid traditional values left to feed on, and they came into the world with nothing to help them withstand the rationalistic germs wafting in from the West which soon turned them into subhuman, robot-like freaks.

Once Dostoevsky had come to the conclusion that the "fathers" were responsible, he set out to repair the damage done by two generations—to close that double generation gap. The diluted, rationalized religion of the Utopians, with its preoccupation with social organization at the expense of transcendental salvation, was not only heretical tampering with the sacred texts; it also made impossible the achievement of its own goal—an ideal social organization. For such a perfect society had to consist exclusively of Christians, while it was impossible to raise Christians on the watery Christianity of Lamennais and Saint-

Simon. And certainly that thin stuff was no food to sustain a
Russian soul. What Russian souls needed, Dostoevsky had
found out in Siberia, was quite a different kind of religion.
They needed something that moved them deeply, and they did
not want anyone to analyze it for them. Actually, it was by
comparing the Russian intelligentsia with his Siberian inmates
that Dostoevsky realized the extent of its alienation. Through
the eyes of the inmates, his former peers looked to him like people from some other country, and he felt that in a few generations their descendants would become complete foreigners. The
"people" around him, on the other hand, had remained true
Russians, for they continued to think and feel like Russians
and to practice the religion of their ancestors. And so, however
wildly and cruelly they might behave, they were closer to salvation than the Westernized men in Petersburg, for a Russian
remains redeemable as long as he has not lost his links with his
people and the God they worship in common.

After Siberia, Dostoevsky never worried about whether his
credo sounded reasonable or not. He tried, and asked others,
simply to accept unquestioningly the whole dogma, with literal
physical resurrection and all. He wanted no proofs, such as St.
Thomas', just acceptance by an act of faith like Rousseau's, but
one that Dostoevsky saw as typically Russian. A man who chose
to have faith should find strength in himself to believe everything, not only in God and Christ but in the miracle-working
power of a Russian icon. Dostoevsky's Siberian companions were
able to believe in that way, while the sophisticated "fathers" of
the 1840s found such beliefs funny and the nihilists became
furious at such crass ignorance.

Russian faith was, therefore, indivisible from the Russian
people and Russian nationalism and, since Russia was to bring
salvation to the world, Dostoevsky's strange formula became:
universal brotherhood through the most uncompromising Russian nationalism.

The first written evidence of the crystallization of the "new"
Dostoevsky appears in a little book he wrote upon his return
from his first trip to Western Europe in 1863 entitled *Winter
Notes of Summer Impressions*. It is obvious, however, that his
change of heart must have reached quite an advanced phase
before he had even left Russia, so it was quite predictable how
he would react to what he discovered during his brief visit to
Germany, France, and England. Indeed, he could just as well
have called his book "Dostoevsky's Visit to the Sources of Con-

tamination." And it was certainly no surprise to him to find that the Western countries he saw had lost God and dehumanized humanity by trying to squeeze man into an artificial order called socialism, bedazzling him with the slogan of "liberty, equality, fraternity," words that were used to mean their diametrical opposites—slavery, inequality, and selfishness—since the socialists enticed their victims to join them with promises of material security in exchange for their freedom and obedience to those in charge.

The ugliness Dostoevsky encountered in his discovery of the West fully "confirmed his suspicions." The old European civilization was moribund. It was dying of its own poison, whose symptoms Dostoevsky knew only too well, having observed them in so many of his own compatriots. But Western Europeans did not have the resilience the Russian people had and could never recover by themselves. Well, just as he had thought, salvation must come from Russia because the Russians were the "God-bearing people." It was time for the current to be reversed and to flow from East to West. Yes, and the Russian "lackeys"† had better take notice.

Although *Winter Notes* is no ordinary travelogue by any standards, neither can it be classified as a work of fiction. Within three months after he had finished it, however, Dostoevsky was busy working on a real novel, the first one since his new views had crystallized. The result was a short novel—*Notes from Underground*—that was the first compact presentation of these views fully transmuted into art. This is a very important work since it marks the turning point of Dostoevsky's career, and it is essential for an understanding of the world in which *The Adolescent* is set or, for that matter, everything Dostoevsky wrote after 1863.

To a student of the Russian intellectual scene of that period, *Notes from Underground* is an obvious parody of Chernyshevsky's novel *What Is to Be Done?*‡ Chernyshevsky, who after Belinsky's death in 1848 had become the leading radical literary critic, was also the main proponent of the Russian version of total determinism—nihilism. In his essay "The Anthropological Principle in Philosophy" (1860), he claimed that the most

† When Dostoevsky uses the word "lackeys" or "flunkeys," he usually means Russians who are undiscriminating admirers of Western culture.

‡ In his essay, *"Mirovaia garmoniia Dostoevskogo,"* Komarovich shows how thorough a parody it is by comparing whole passages from *What Is to Be Done?* and *Notes from Underground.*

intimate feelings, the most subtle moral and aesthetic refinements, could be accounted for, predicted, and brought about by applying the knowledge of physics, mechanics, and chemistry (biology being to him a mere function of these). Then, early in 1863, probably to bring home to people how pleasant and efficient life would be if organized rationally according to scientific knowledge, he wrote the fictionalized pamphlet *What Is to Be Done?* The extraordinary success of that would-be novel among the young intellectuals of the 1860s can be accounted for only by their fascination with all aspects of scientism and their firm belief that *the* solution was just around the corner. Otherwise it would be very hard to explain their enthusiasm for seamstresses' cooperatives organized along the lines of Fourier's phalansteries, or for tone-deaf dialogues between wooden characters about "rational" relations between the sexes. But, while failing lamentably both as a creative writer and as a "futurologist," Chernyshevsky does, albeit unintentionally, give us the foretaste of twentieth-century "social realism" and perhaps of an eventual computer-written literature, filled with robot-like characters responding with clicking noises to the "natural laws" of an appropriately programmed world.

But even if a desire to ridicule Chernyshevsky's literary success was the prime mover that prompted Dostoevsky to write his parody and, to a considerable extent, dictated the structure of the *Notes,* the book's great importance today lies rather in the fact that it is a succinct statement of what was to be Dostoevsky's final position: his rejection of (1) exclusive reliance on reason, (2) determinism, and (3) all attempts to build scientifically computed paradises on earth, inhabited by men with automatically controlled utilitarian ethics (which is really an extension of determinism into man's mind and implies its corollary—the possibility of controlling man's thoughts and feelings).

Unlike Chernyshevsky, Dostoevsky makes his point with artistry, perhaps even too subtly and in too roundabout a way, considering how much this book has been misread, misunderstood, and misinterpreted in the hundred-odd years since its appearance. Actually what Dostoevsky does is to give his story a sort of double twist. The simplest way to an easier understanding would, perhaps, be to restore the book to its proper chronological order, to start with Part II, set in the 1840s when the narrator is a young man, and then proceed to Part I, which takes place in the 1860s when, we are told, the narrator's "generation is rounding . . . out its days."

In Part II (which is actually a flashback), the narrator, a

typical young intellectual infected with Western ideas (Schilleresque romanticism, diluted Christianity of the French social Utopians), loses touch with Russian reality and is uprooted from his native soil to such an extent that, even for his daydreams, he must escape into an unreal, foreign setting and, when he speaks, sounds artificial and contrived as if he were reading a book. In fact, he is so immersed in foreign literature and alien ideas that the Soviet critics would have branded him "an internal émigré."

We meet the narrator twenty years later in Part I. We are in the 1860s and he is middle-aged. This time, he sits in a mousehole under the floorboards, which is his refuge from reality. But now he is no longer a romantic because, being an *uprooted intellectual,* he couldn't help but succumb to the latest intellectual fad that has swept over the young generation. So he has switched from romanticism and Utopianism to determinism and utilitarianism (i.e., the position of Chernyshevsky and his nihilist followers). What makes the underground man different from the *others* (his imaginary audience that he keeps addressing) is, above all, his cumbersome intelligence—his lucidity. In the *Notes,* he alone draws the inevitable conclusions from the philosophical acceptance of the deterministic theory, namely, that all truly voluntary action is impossible since whatever man does is only a part of the causal chain and could even be predicted years in advance. This, of course, also makes meaningless the very notion of transcendental ethics (the Christ of the Utopians) and certainly ridicules the pompous exclamations of the romantics about devoting their lives to the service of "the beautiful and the sublime." The stupidity of the *others,* in their failure to see the incompatibility of the two sets of ideas (of the 1840s and the 1860s) and their continuing indiscriminate chattering about noble ideals in a purely mechanistic world, enrages him. What also sets him apart from them is his pessimism. Unlike them, who welcome enthusiastically a "scientific" explanation of the world, he is horrified by it. He is pinned down only by logical arguments and is forced to accept determinism. But, indeed, he hates it.

In this, of course, Dostoevsky and his protagonist agree: they both hate determinism. So, when the underground man rants and rages and behaves like a lunatic, he is really protesting against the world (as he believes it is) that reduces him, a thinking man, to the status of a lump of matter (totally subjected to "the laws of nature"). Therefore, Dostoevsky, who would have hated the predicament of determinism had he believed in it, cannot possibly be trying to present the underground man's revolt as that of a neurotic, psychotic, or sado-masochistic freak, as has been so often maintained. In fact, under the circumstances, the narrator's behavior may be considered an extremely healthy manifestation of vitality, the assertion of a will to live and a refusal to be assimilated to inert matter, a refusal to submit to *necessity* and to "go gentle into that good night."

Notes from Underground is, then, Dostoevsky's relatively streamlined formulation of the problem of free will vs. determinism, a problem that was to remain from then on in the focus of his thought until the end of his life.

It should go without saying (it doesn't, alas!) that Dostoevsky's own position as he wrote *Notes from Underground* was as distinct from his narrator's as the narrator's was distinct from that of his imaginary audience. *They,* the audience, accept every fad, accept it without understanding its consequences, and are delighted because it makes them up to date; the underground man also picks up all the "latest ideas," but he can understand their implications and, in the case of determinism, is horrified. Dostoevsky, unlike his protagonist, "knows" determinism is not true but, like him, would hate what it implies. Furthermore, he not only despises his former companions of the 1840s but considers their irreverent, liberal drivel responsible for the present spreaders of nihilism (e.g., Chernyshevsky). The advantage Dostoevsky has perhaps over his narrator is that, while he made his narrator just sit in his mousehole under the floorboards ("underground") through the 1850s, he himself was discovering "the true Russia" in Siberia.

Ironically, had it not been for the hypersensitive censors of the Russian Orthodox Church, who failed to recognize its new champion, Dostoevsky's religious alternative to determinism would have been more explicit in the *Notes*. The manuscript submitted to the censors contained a statement to the effect that man can never achieve harmony on earth without believing in Christ and in eternal life. The censors, however, decided that, amidst all that raucous invective, introducing the Sacred Name was unmitigated blasphemy and deleted it.

Despite this deletion, Dostoevsky's answer to the rationalist argument in the *Notes* is of a mystical and religious nature. It is implicit in the artistic structure of the story, built into its very essence. Instead of attempting a refutation of determinism and utilitarianism by rational argumentation, Dostoevsky imagined a man of flesh and blood who believed these theories and understood their implications. Then, by a sort of Bergsonian intuition, he entered that character and watched from inside how he felt and behaved under the circumstances. But, while the explicit mention of Christ failed to appear at the end of Part I, that same answer to the underground man's "deterministic despair" is given at the end of Part II by the prostitute Liza: her answer lies in her infinite capacity for compassion and true love, a typically Dostoevskian answer—the refutation of a logical argument on "another plane."

In general, Dostoevsky's feelings about the world are expressed more through what his various characters are, what they do, how they move, gesticulate, scratch themselves, look, laugh, etc., than by what they actually say (although they do often talk an awful lot!). And, even then, a peculiar use of words or a slip of the tongue may have a deeper meaning than the obvious meaning of the statement. Indeed, one may easily visualize them as method actors whose sneezes, burps, and winks can radically change the sense of the lines they say. But while such a method of expressing one's thoughts describes to a certain extent the usual artistic process of expressing thoughts and feelings "by other means," Dostoevsky has no choice but to use it to be consistent with himself: since he dismisses the purely rational process of thought as false and misguiding, its refutation by an equally rational argument would be meaningless. So he skips to another plane and discredits the argument there.

Thus, in *Crime and Punishment*, the would-be utilitarian Napoleon, Raskolnikov, sees his theories refuted by another meek and inarticulate prostitute, while in *The Idiot* it is the very failures of the Christ-like Myshkin that reflect the sad state of Russia where he descends from his Swiss mountains, moving about so awkwardly in his ill-fitting flesh. Again, in *The Possessed*, the intellectual superman Stavrogin, who goes around spreading abstract ideas that send a whole batch of young uprooted people to their perdition, is recognized as a false prophet by the crazy cripple Maria Lebyatkin. But the simplest and probably the best-known example is the indirect refutation of the long and rationalistic argument of the Grand Inquisitor by the kiss of Christ in *The Brothers Karamazov*, followed by Alyosha's kiss in answer to the arguments of his intellectually superior brother Ivan.

In exactly the same way, throughout *The Adolescent*, rationalistic ideas and arguments find their counterarguments, and sometimes answers, on "another plane," the only one that matters to Dostoevsky.

The setting is typically Dostoevskian. After decades of exposure to alien, Western thought, Russia is losing her unifying idea—God, the traditional God of the Russian Orthodox Church. In the 1840s, God's image had been rationalized and secularized by the Russian followers of the social Utopians and had become depoeticized and anemic. And then, in the 1860s, the nihilists stepped in and tried to sweep that image out altogether.

The main theme of *The Adolescent* is that without God man cannot exist. Without that unifying idea, there can be no harmony between man and the world around him; nor, whatever he may do, can he have any inner harmony, which Dostoevsky calls "beauty" (*blagoobrazie*). And, without it, a man is only a haphazard sequence of unsynthesized impulses and reactions, instinctively searching for a substitute unifying principle. That substitute will most likely be an idol, a false god, a delusion of faith, or perhaps an obsessive passion. But, whatever it is, the result will be a whole built around a false principle, a forcibly synthesized and therefore ugly and unstable identity.*

Since, in Dostoevsky's world, a Russian can achieve harmony, beauty, and salvation only together with and through his people and within the fold of his church, which furnishes him with the concept of Christ a Russian needs (the "Russian Christ"), the prospects for the young narrator in *The Adolescent* appear extremely grim. By the 1870s the church and religion had been too thoroughly discredited among the intelligentsia to satisfy fully the emotional needs of a sensitive and thinking boy. Besides, Arkady Dolgoruky is not just any boy, but a living symbol of the spiritual crisis of his time.

There is, to start with, "disorder" in his very origins. He has no rightful legitimate family, which should be the basic unit within the Russian order under God. He is illegitimate (actually a product of adultery), the offspring of what Dostoevsky calls "an accidental family," the growing number of which are symptomatic of the social decay. Although in many ways the

---

* The popularized Hegelian dialectical process (the "whole" attained through the synthesis of the thesis and antithesis), and its even more popular corollary of the whole occasionally splitting back into its component parts, was probably as much of an obsession with certain nineteenth-century novelists as some popularized Freudian theories are with their twentieth-century counterparts.

adolescent is Dostoevsky's autobiographical portrait, by projecting him into another historical period, he uses him to show the damage suffered by the sons of the intelligentsia of the 1840s. Versilov, who was then a humanitarian dilettante, was also a landowner and, as such, seduced the young wife of his gardener Makar during a visit to one of his estates. Both Sofia and her husband were, of course, his serfs, and Versilov appeared to be quite casual about the whole affair. Thus Dostoevsky makes his young narrator illegitimate and *déclassé* by birth, while giving him strong links with "true" Russia through his mother.

Actually, the symbolism of the adolescent's origins is carried much further and contains the whole theme of the book in a concentrated form. Thus we are told, among other things, what Versilov was reading while seducing his serf's wife. It turns out to be two sentimental novels, strongly inspired by French humanitarian ideas and full of suffering "simple" Russian people. And then we see how much Versilov himself is influenced by these sentimental romantics when, after the consummation of the adultery, he summons his gardener and proceeds to sob melodramatically on his shoulder. Nor does this touching scene inhibit him from offering cash compensation to the cuckolded husband. To all these flippant bookish antics, which have led this uprooted intellectual to moral insolvency, Dostoevsky opposes the unshakable respect for tradition in the two humble summits of the triangle; and he chooses to convey it with warm humor by the conventional form of the ensuing correspondence between Sofia and Makar. Again, to emphasize the difference between Arkady's two fathers—the real and the legal one—Dostoevsky makes both of them footloose travelers, but while Versilov is a restless nomad pursuing an elusive faith throughout Europe, Makar is a religious pilgrim, who, trudging along Russia's roads, gets closer and closer to God. That is why, when Arkady finally meets Makar face to face, he is so struck by the strange grace of the old man's ways (the way he sits, laughs, moves, tells things, the words he uses, etc.) that he spontaneously exclaims, "There is *beauty* in you!" That "beauty" of his is the reflection of universal harmony Makar has found, and thus he occupies in *The Adolescent* the place held by Zosima in *The Brothers Karamazov* or Tikhon in *The Possessed*—the place closest to salvation.

The "disorder" that had manifested itself in Arkady's birth is further felt in his abandonment as a small child, his upbringing among strangers, especially in that little boarding school run, significantly, by a Frenchman (the passages about the school are perhaps the most autobiographical), where all true values are twisted and distorted by that transplanted foreigner. From the constant humiliations inflicted upon him, the sensitive boy finds refuge only in daydreams, which, like the dreams of the narrators in the *White Nights* and *Notes from Underground*, are set in exotic foreign surroundings, for the Russia he knows is certainly no place to build romantic dreams in.

Again, with delicate humor and by a quite unexpected use of daydreams, Dostoevsky takes us back to his theme—the need for a unifying principle, especially in an as yet unformed boy. Young Arkady soon realizes that his reveries never go beyond a certain point; they are fragmented, disconnected, and in the final analysis frustrating. It is only when he decides what his goal in life is (he calls it his "idea") that he succeeds in, as it were, giving his daydreams a definite direction, we might say "coordinating his imagination." Since the great unifying idea (the Russian idea of God) has not been handed down to him as part of his birthright and since traditional values have been discredited, he decides to fill the gap with money (Western-type capitalism is displacing the ancient patriarchal Russian order) and "become a Rothschild." Becoming a Rothschild means not just becoming rich; it must be a mystique, a total subordination of everything to the goal, not the careful thriftiness of a German burgher (the former is to the latter what asceticism is to respectable churchgoing). And then the sheer quantity of money must be so immense as to trigger a qualitative change that will bestow upon the possessor of such capital all human virtues (intelligence, wit, beauty, sex appeal, etc.), place him at the top of the human hierarchy (which is some sort of a substitute for a place in the universal harmony).

But, because of his mother's true Russian blood, the Rothschild of Arkady's daydreams (inspired by Pushkin's "Russian" concept of "The Avaricious Knight") ends up by giving away all his millions, becoming a beggar, and being fully satisfied with the mere knowledge that he once had such power. . . .

When, however, the adolescent, prompted by deeper instincts, sets out to search for his real flesh-and-blood roots—for his family and, through it, his own country, even if only as a setting for his daydreams—his original "idea" is eventually displaced altogether.

With his mother, acceptance, forgiveness, and love are spontaneous, and he admires her now, although as a small boy he had been ashamed of her because of her plebeian ways (she still talks to him "like a servant"). With his father, Versilov, whom he had always admired, idealized, and resented at a distance, filial feelings and moral acceptance are more ambivalent, and it is this tense search for harmony through a wayward, unstable father that makes Arkady's journey doubly difficult and dangerous. At times his behavior resembles the course of a satellite spinning around a whimsically zigzagging planet. It is Versilov who in Dostoevsky's final analysis is responsible for Arkady's outbursts of wild spending, indebtedness, and gambling. These excesses show that Arkady still has no built-in resistance to withstand outer disorder. In his childhood, he received no solid set of beliefs, such as are usually transmitted from generation to generation. And later, even though he talks a great deal to his father, he finds nothing in him upon which he can build solid moral standards. For Versilov himself, ever since the 1840s when he so lightheartedly discarded the traditional values of his forefathers, has been vegetating in a moral vacuum. Not only has he nothing to give his son as standards of conduct, but he himself is thrashing around, desperately looking for something to believe in, if only to hold together the disintegrating elements of his personality. Unable to regain his ancestral faith, he devises all sorts of synthetic, intellectualized, and even ritualized substitutes. But his efforts remain futile as none of these artificial constructs succeeds in penetrating his feelings deeply enough. They remain just "ideas"; they never become "idea-feelings"; and the waves of outer chaos keep sweeping into his barren soul.

Versilov, like Arkady, is a partly autobiographical character: he is of Dostoevsky's generation and has been exposed to the same ideas and intellectual aberrations, and his intellect has processed them very much along the same lines as Dostoevsky's did. Also, like Dostoevsky himself and like many other Dostoevsky characters, he finds it excruciatingly difficult to take the step separating the tangible elements of faith from faith itself. Indeed, in that sense, Versilov, whom Dostoevsky had conceived as a sort of continuation of Stavrogin, is even more like another character in *The Possessed*, Shatov. Shatov, who is generally considered as the closest to Dostoevsky's alter ego, follows, step by step, the path toward salvation prescribed by Stavrogin (and Dostoevsky) and reaches the penultimate step —the belief that the Russians are a "God-bearing" people, even the belief in the "Russian Christ." But when asked whether he believes in God, he has to answer that he hopes he will believe. From Versilov's words about Russia and Europe, it would seem that he too has reached the penultimate step, and from the way

he is disposed of in the Epilogue, he obviously never goes beyond it either. For it is from this penultimate point at the end
of the traditional Russian path that the final leap into the unknown must be taken. This is the ultimate act of faith.

Like Svidrigailov, Stavrogin, and Ivan Karamazov, Versilov
is entangled in his cumbersome intellect and cannot jump. So
he is doomed to live in a world of moral weightlessness,
in which the notions of "good" and "evil" become as meaningless as the notions of "up" and "down." This idea takes us back
to the deterministic world of the "underground man" where
everything is permitted and any attempt to act is senseless. It
is to escape from this bottomless indifference that Versilov seeks
to create an artificial moral gravitational pull by trying first
socialism, then Catholicism (which, to Dostoevsky, is only socialism plus mysticism), and finally mere imitations of religious
practices (when he preaches asceticism and wears chains),
which give him the delusion that he is regaining faith. But self-
deception is impossible for a man of his intellectual lucidity
(again, just as it is with the "underground man") and, since
there is no purely rational basis for an unerring moral compass,
Versilov's behavior remains to the end hopelessly erratic. It is
only his equally erratic love for Arkady's mother that, literally,
holds him together. For, whenever his passion for Katerina
Akhmakov displaces it, he splits into two. Arkady's "medical"
explanation for the appearance of Versilov's "double"† is, of

† Much has been said on the subject of doubles in Dostoevsky.
Indeed, some of Dostoevsky's characters have a tendency to lose their
identity and split. They may do so for various reasons. In *The Double*, Golyadkin's identity collapses because of his insecurity, when he
feels his rightful place in the world is being threatened. First it is his
position in the civil service, and then the danger extends to his private
life (even to his romantic daydreams) and culminates in a total disintegration of his personality. Golyadkin's split is, however, rather
different from that suffered by a Dostoevskian "abuser of pure reason,"
which stems from desperate and futile attempts to translate seemingly
incompatible metaphysical mysteries into rational terms in which they
obviously make no sense. At one point, there is a kind of mental
short circuit (that Dostoevsky usually calls "brain fever") and a
"double" splits off from the rest. In the case of Stavrogin and Ivan
Karamazov, it is the purely rational element of their minds; in
Versilov's case, it is a reflection of the outer "disorder" breaking into
his inner vacuum. Eventually, however, the collecting of Dostoevskian
doubles became a fashionable sport and many critics lumped indis-
criminately under the heading of "doubles" other characters in the
novels who may have borne some resemblance to the protagonist or

course, offered by Dostoevsky with tongue in cheek. As in the case of Svidrigailov, Stavrogin, and Ivan Karamazov, the trouble with Versilov is a sort of ontological instability due to his inner vacuum or, as it is often described, to metaphysical boredom (or, more pompously, *ennui*).

Therefore, with both Arkady and Versilov partly auto-biographical projections of certain aspects of Dostoevsky's thoughts and emotions at various points in his life, it is rather meaningless to say that, because of his "overwhelming" person-ality, Versilov steals the show and throws the novel's structure out of balance. The theme of the novel, after all, is how the dereliction of fatherly duties affects the son.

Arkady's mother and his "other father" (Makar Dolgoruky) are different people altogether. Uncorrupted by *l'esprit du temps*, they worship unquestioningly the God of their ances-tors, love life without trying to understand its meaning, and are in harmony with the world. The elements that constitute their personalities are so powerfully held together by "the great unifying idea" that, as characters, they appear made all of one piece, in fact "simple," and are thus more difficult to describe convincingly and to visualize than the "complex" ones, a point Dostoevsky students hardly ever fail to make. Nor do these sim-ple souls ever split; at least as far as I can ascertain, none of them comes up with a double.

Behind the story about the boy, his "idea," his father, his family, his bewilderment, hopes, humiliations, and discoveries, lurk all sorts of Brueghel-like characters of all ages and back-grounds whom Dostoevsky uses to present a panoramic picture of the surrounding disorder.

Beside Arkady, there is a whole array of young people who, by their behavior, outlook, ethics, aspirations, etc., reflect, each

---

even have simply been influenced by the protagonist's ideas. An ex-ample of what extravagance such a "double count" has sometimes led to can be gathered from the following quotation referring to *The Possessed*: ". . . all but one of the major characters are his [Stavro-gin's] doubles. Pyotr is his social double, Liza the Byroness his emo-tional double, and Marya, the cripple he has married, his double in derangement. Fedka the peasant murderer is a double through the link of the intellectual Kirilov, while Lebyatkin and Liputin are doubles in the dress of burlesque. The most important doubles are Kirilov and Shatov, who act out the two sides of Stavrogin's meta-physical problem." (Irving Howe, "Dostoevsky: The Politics of Salvation," in *Dostoevsky, A Collection of Critical Essays,* edited by Rene Wellek, 1962.)

in his own way, the social disintegration of their time. Three‡ of them, for instance, commit suicide (Kraft, Olga, and *le grand dadais*) under quite different circumstances and for seemingly quite different reasons, but one element is present in each case: the loss of the last solid values. And although the sensitive juvenile delinquent Trishatov does not commit suicide, he kills his dream instead and plunges deeper into crime. As to Lambert, the most villainous member of the young generation, Dostoevsky makes him a young and stupid caricature of the Versilov type. Being a Frenchman and a Catholic, Lambert's slipping into a moral vacuum follows, symbolically, his receiving First Communion. His "all is permitted" reaction is then shown in a rather Ionesco-like scene where he steals five hundred rubles, buys a shotgun, and in Arkady's company goes on an absurd binge that starts with the point-blank firing of the gun at a canary and ends in a strange hotel-room interlude between a prostitute and the two boys. Lambert—whose face is *masklike* as are the faces of Svidrigailov and Stavrogin, the supermen "beyond good and evil"—is, however, operating at an infinitely lower level of rational discourse and is absolutely incapable of imagining that there can be something beyond it. In fact, by using him along with Versilov, Dostoevsky shows how differently, albeit equally disastrously, a loss of faith affects the stupid and the intelligent.

Then there is the subversive Dergachev group,* which, to

‡ Actually there are five suicides in the novel: young Lidia Akhmakov takes poison and the little boy in Makar's story drowns himself. In an earlier version there were several more.

* The Dergachev group is the fictional equivalent of the "Secret Society" headed by Dolgushin. The Dolgushin group was tried in July 1874, while Dostoevsky was writing *The Adolescent*. He followed the trial very closely and most of his characters are replicas of the actual conspirators. The following is the statute of the society written by Dolgushin himself (the prototype of Dergachev) and made public at the trial: "The Secret Society consists of people who intend to change the present order, which is supported by an obsolete administrative apparatus; therefore, as long as that apparatus is not destroyed, a planned people's uprising will be suppressed. The aim of the Society is precisely to prevent the crushing of the uprising. Therefore, inasmuch as the administrative apparatus is controlled by only a few persons (the *de facto* power-holders) these persons have to be eliminated. Moreover, although the imperial family rules only *de jure*, its existence is indispensable to those who hold the actual control in their hands. Hence, if an opportunity should present itself, the imperial family must be eliminated too. . . ."

In an earlier version of *The Adolescent*, Arkady was more deeply judge from Dostoevsky's notebooks, was intended to occupy a much greater space in the novel than it does in the final version. But, as it is, it enables Dostoevsky to show a considerable variety of the ideological positions held by the revolutionaries (all of them, of course, wrong in the context of his world). When Arkady gets into a discussion with various members of the group, Dostoevsky very subtly makes several points at once. With the narrator, we realize that each conspirator is moved by his private revolutionary idea, which makes the spiteful arguments among the members sound like a dialogue of the deaf. Also, for each of the revolutionaries, his private idea of changing the world has only the function that Arkady's "idea" of becoming a Rothschild has for him—filling an inner vacuum. And, finally, Arkady, who was until then afraid of talking to skillful debaters such as these people lest their dialectic should, perhaps even inadvertently, prove to him the absurdity of his "idea," realizes that his "idea" has grown too deeply into him and cannot be affected by logical refutation. For, in Dostoevsky's concept, an "idea-feeling" can be destroyed only by another "idea-feeling," which is what happens to Kraft, whose passionate belief in Russia's uniqueness is destroyed by an equally total conviction that he was wrong. This creates a void that Kraft cannot bear. Although his belief, in Dostoevsky's terms, was heresy (a special form of worship of mankind in the form of Russia instead of God, also somewhat like Shatov's), his faith in it was strong enough to enable him to live by it.

Furthermore, we are made aware that, in the human hierarchy, Dostoevsky places a passionate heretic like Kraft much higher than the superrationalist Vasin. Vasin, a detached, logical, dispassionate analyst, whom Arkady at first greatly admires, is gradually shown to be tone-deaf toward the more subtle aspects of life, and his machine-like precision becomes preposterous in its rigidity. Vasin, of course, is a comparatively mild caricature of a "man of the sixties," a benign nihilist, believing in and satisfied with a deterministic explanation of the world. It is, then, probably because he shares many of Chernyshevsky's views that some otherwise perspicacious Soviet

---

involved with the group and was arrested with the conspirators (just as Dostoevsky was in his day with the Petrashevsky group).

Dostoevsky, who went to pay a visit to Dolgushin's house, found a large wooden cross with the two inscriptions: "In the name of Christ" and "Liberty, Equality, Fraternity." This combination, of course, represented to him by that time the essence of the Utopian fallacy for which he had fallen in his youth.

critics ignore, perhaps intentionally, the fact that Dostoevsky ridicules this character.

But subversive groups such as Dergachev's, with members ranging from Kraft to Vasin, are only one symptom of the disorder. Other symptoms are shown to us in the decay of the Russian aristocracy, represented by the two Princes Sokolsky. Old Prince Nikolai's constant use of French symbolizes the extent of his alienation. His eccentricities, tearfulness, taste for little girls ("featherless chicks"), and sudden changes in facial expressions denote the irresponsibility, debility, depravity, and instability of the older generation of a class that, as Versilov explains, was meant to be the embodiment of the Russian (as opposed to the "Western") concepts of honor, duty, etc. Nevertheless, the old man has retained the old-fashioned grace that he received as part of his heritage and that fills Dostoevsky with warmth. His young relative, Prince Sergei, on the other hand, was born too late of parents probably already half-severed from the old traditions. He is a completely disoriented young man and, even while holding forth incoherently about his aristocratic lineage, he gambles, incurs debts, gets involved with shady characters, becomes an accomplice in a forgery, and finishes by dying insane in a prison hospital. Actually, the two Sokolskys, without being father and son, make a point similar to that made in *The Possessed*, where the likable old Verkhovensky is shown to be responsible for the moral monstrosity of his son Peter.

And even the extravagantly melodramatic and often justly criticized plot, with all its gaudy entanglements, is not just a conventional device to make the story move. Various details are, indeed, used by Dostoevsky to restate his central theme in other ways. It has been often said, for instance, that Arkady's persistent reluctance to give up the compromising letter he has in his possession, the "document," is unmotivated. This letter, however, gives the adolescent power over a proud and otherwise inaccessible adult woman, whom both he and his father are in love with. By using the letter, the boy believes he can discredit Katerina in his father's eyes and make him return to the fold—to Arkady's mother, which is what the boy wants most. At the same time, the move would rid him of a formidable sexual rival (for there is sexual father-son rivalry involved here too). Finally, there is the recurring suggestion of the possibility of demanding of Katerina payment in kind in some dark back room, as Lambert insinuates. Arkady even has an erotic dream to this effect. All this, it would appear, gives him plenty of motivation.

Besides, Arkady's behavior also reflects the general moral disorientation. But his own sound nature, with the help of good solid advice from the very Russian old lady Mrs. Prutkov, finally overcomes his hesitations and sets him on what seems to be the right path.

Of all the women in *The Adolescent*, Tatyana Prutkov is probably the most vivid character, even though she is cast only in a supporting role. She belongs to the species of the hard-boiled, eccentric elderly Russian women who unfailingly do the right thing in Dostoevsky's book. Moreover, she compares well with the better representatives of that species in Dostoevsky's other novels, such as Mrs. Epanchin in *The Idiot* or even "Grandmother" in *The Gambler*. On the other hand, Katerina Akhmakov, whom in his notebooks Dostoevsky called "Versilov's female counterpart," is dwarfed by her sister *femmes fatales* Nastasia Filipovna of *The Idiot* and Grushenka of *The Brothers Karamazov*. The same may be said if we compare, for instance, Anna Versilov with the Katerina of *The Brothers Karamazov* or Arkady's mother Sofia with, say, Dasha of *The Possessed* or Sonia of *Crime and Punishment*.

Since, as a rule, the function of the women in Dostoevsky is primarily to test the men while the men test ideas, the women are more standardized than their male companions and more easily recognizable through their disguises as they migrate from novel to novel. One may actually visualize a Dostoevsky novel as a kind of chess game with a few auxiliary and specialized female pieces scattered over the board. But the outcome depends only on what happens to the male pieces, whether they be pawns or kings. And so, if there is a greater variety of male types and a greater complexity in male characters, it is simply because the mission on which Dostoevsky sends them is that much more subtle and perplexing: for it is not psychology that Dostoevsky's major male types are out to test, it is metaphysics.

The male characters, however, are eminently classifiable too. Thus, Svidrigailov, Stavrogin, Versilov, and Ivan Karamazov may be labeled as the superman-in-moral-vacuum type; Luzhin, Vasin, and Rakitin belong to the despised species of cold-blooded rationalist reptiles; and Tikhon, Makar, and Zosima are the "beautiful" old men in harmony with the world.

There are other species and many subspecies and hybrid forms, with a whole spectrum of rationalists, liberals, religious mystics, etc., each type moving across the chessboard the way his type is meant to move—toward his doom, toward his salvation, or, in most cases, only to be blocked on some square by other pieces and to remain there indecisively as the game ends.

If, however, Dostoevsky's novels are really only games played with incarnated ideas, what is there in them that sets them apart from other *romans à thèse*? The answer may perhaps be suggested as one scans the working notebooks of some of his novels. In the early sketches and drafts of *The Adolescent*, for instance, the characters that were later to evolve into the narrator Arkady and his father Versilov were two brothers, and, still earlier, they represented two periods in the life of a single character. Also, in some earlier versions, Lisa was Versilov's stepdaughter and was seduced and made pregnant by him. Later she also had an affair with Arkady and in the end committed suicide. In the final version, of course, she is Versilov's real daughter and is seduced not by him but by Sergei Sokolsky, who also seduces and makes pregnant Katerina's young stepdaughter Lidia. And instead of Lisa taking her life, it is Lidia who poisons herself by drinking a solution of phosphorous matches. Then, as if that was not enough, another character called Olga, which was Lisa's original name, hangs herself out of disgust and despair: disgust, because, while determined to earn her living honestly by teaching math, she lands in a brothel; despair, because she somehow mistakenly suspects Versilov of "dirty" intentions. And finally—alas, only in a short-lived version!—Arkady finds fleeting gratification by actually being seduced by Mrs. Akhmakov. . . .

Well, what is all this reminiscent of? Are these suicides secret death wishes? Is the sexual gratification of this young boy with his father's lady love Oedipal? What are all these displacements and substitutions? Are they just thinly disguised incestuous impulses between father and daughter, mother and son, brother and sister, a sort of incest by proxy? Perhaps they are all that and perhaps also many other things regurgitated from the depths of Dostoevsky's memories, real or imagined, conscious or unconscious. What is certain, though, is that these sketches and early versions—the raw material of his art—bear a striking resemblance to dreams.

To be sure, even in the final version of Dostoevsky's novels, the dream quality always lingers. But there is a great difference. And it is precisely this difference that escapes those who enjoy subjecting works of art to psychoanalysis, starting with Freud himself. They have dug deeply into the dreamlike texture of Dostoevsky's prose and come up triumphantly with Oedipal complexes, neuroses, guilt for onanistic abuse expressed by gambling bouts, sado-masochistic drives, and other fascinating finds. Like children, they have broken off various parts of a delicate piece of machinery and held up odd cogs, bits of wire, and a rusted exhaust pipe to an appreciative audience. Whether there is a point in using an accomplished work of art, a carefully planned piece of craftsmanship, the way analysts use what a patient stretched out on a couch mumbles to them about his dreams is a matter of opinion. Besides, it is none of our concern here to pronounce on the merits of their clinical analysis. What matters to us is how Dostoevsky succeeded in producing great art out of dreams, not what quirks of his personality integrated into his art can be extracted from it.

A finished Dostoevsky novel is the result of his conscious and deliberate choice as to what raw material to discard, what to use, and how and how much it was to be processed to convey whatever he wished. His novels are important not because they may reveal his secret aberrations but because he knew how to turn these aberrations into effective symbols and to build out of these symbols the beautiful structures that so powerfully present his peculiar *Weltanschauung* and *Weltschmertz*. A long look at these structures and a glance at the raw material that went into them—those wild, unbridled, childish, sensuous, preliminary sketches—suggest that Dostoevsky's novels are what they are because they are the stuff that dreams are made of. But his dream stuff is not thrown at us haphazardly so that, after having dazzled us for a while, it ends by boring us. Dostoevsky's novels have *harmony* in them, for the dreams they are made of are given meaning and life by Dostoevsky's *unifying idea*.

And that, perhaps, is what makes them "beautiful," like Makar's laughter, like the Russia of the future in the private world in which Dostoevsky is god.

ANDREW R. MACANDREW
University of Virginia

PART ONE

Chapter 1

I

I couldn't resist: I sat down and started writing the story of my first steps in life, although I could've managed very well without doing so. One thing I know for certain—I'll never again get around to writing my autobiography, even if I live to be a hundred. A man must be unspeakably conceited to write about himself without embarrassment. The only excuse I have is that my reason for writing about myself is different from other people's—I mean I'm not looking for the reader's approval. I have suddenly decided to write down faithfully everything that happened to me during the past year to satisfy an inner need, so violent.was the impression made on me by these events. I will mention just the facts, avoiding all irrelevancies and, above all, literary embellishments. A writer may write for thirty years without ever knowing why he spent all those years writing. I am not a man of letters and have no wish to be one; I would consider it indecent and despicable to drag my soul onto the literary market and turn it inside out while describing my feelings in beautiful words. Annoying as it may be, though, I foresee that I won't be able to avoid altogether describing feelings and making some comments (perhaps quite commonplace ones too) because any literary pursuit corrupts a man even if he undertakes it solely for his own edification. The ideas expressed are likely to be quite banal and uninteresting because what seems so important to me may be completely unimportant to an outsider. All this is beside the point, but it will do as an introduction. I won't say anything more of that sort. So let's get down to business now. Well, there's nothing more difficult than getting down to this business . . . or, for that matter, to any business. . . .

II

I'll start these notes, that is, I'd like to start them, with September 19 of last year, which is the day I first met . . .

But it would be too cheap and conventional a literary device to say who it was I met without explaining anything beforehand. Indeed, I believe it would be in poor taste. Having promised myself to avoid literary devices, here I am falling for one in the very first sentence. But just wanting to write sensibly is not enough to enable a man to do so. Let me add that, in my opinion, writing in Russian is more difficult than in any other European language. I've just reread my opening lines and I can safely say that I'm much more intelligent than what I wrote. Why is it, then, that what an intelligent man manages to express is much more stupid than what remains in him unexpressed? I've also noticed this discrepancy in my verbal communication with people many times throughout this fatal year and it has worried me a great deal.

So, although I'll still start with September 19, I'll first slip in a few words about who I am and where I'd been until then, and this will explain, at least in part, what I had on my mind on the morning of September 19 and make things clearer to the reader, and perhaps also to me.

III

I'm a high-school graduate and I'm nineteen. My name is Dolgoruky and my legal father is Makar Ivanovich Dolgoruky, a former serf on the Versilov estate. That makes me legitimate, although in fact, of course, I'm as illegitimate as they come without there being the slightest doubt about my origin.

This is how it happened. Some twenty years ago a twenty-five-year-old landowner named Versilov (my real father) went to spend some time on his estate in Tula Province. I don't imagine that at that early date he was the striking personality he is today. It seems rather strange that this man, who has made such a strong impression on me ever since I first set eyes on him, who has molded my very way of thinking, and who has probably affected the course of my life for a long time to come, should be, to this day, in many ways a complete enigma to me. But I'll come back to that later, for it's impossible to explain what I mean at this point. Besides, I'll have a lot to say about him as I go on with my story.

It was around that time that he'd lost his wife. She came from an upper-class family, the Fanariotovs, who belonged to high society although they didn't have much money. Versilov had a son and a daughter by her. Otherwise, I have only very scanty information about that woman, who died after only a few years of marriage and whose trail fades away as soon as I try to follow it back into the past. Besides, many circumstances of Versilov's private life escape me completely, for he always treated me with a certain haughty, distant, and casual reserve, although now and then he suddenly became infinitely humble and gentle with me.

I must also mention at this point, to make things clearer later, that so far in his life he has managed to run through three fortunes, and quite substantial ones too, amounting altogether to four hundred thousand rubles or even more perhaps. But now, of course, he hasn't got one kopek to his name.

"God knows why" he went to his Tula estate at that time, or at least that's how he put it to me later. He hadn't taken his children with him but had left them with the relatives with whom they lived. This has always been his way of dealing with his children, legitimate or illegitimate.

There were lots of serfs on that Tula estate and among them was a gardener by the name of Makar Dolgoruky. Let me mention something at this point, just to get it off my chest, so that I won't have to go back to it again: I cannot imagine anyone who has hated and resented his name as much as I have all my life. I know it's stupid, but I can't help it. Every time I entered a new school or met people who, being my elders, had to be treated with respect—and that means every lousy teacher, every tutor, every village priest—every single one of them would, upon asking my name and being told it was Dolgoruky, for some reason invariably add: "Prince Dolgoruky?" and every time I had to set these busybodies straight by saying: "No, just plain Dolgoruky."

That *plain* started driving me out of my mind. And let me note here, as a curious observation, that I cannot remember one single exception: everybody asked that same question. Some of these people had absolutely no business asking me that, although I can't imagine whose damn business it could possibly be anyway. But all of them, from the first to the last, asked me that. And having learned that I was just *plain* Dolgoruky, the questioner would look me up and down with a blank, stupidly apathetic stare, which proved that he had no idea why he had asked me the question in the first place, and then walk away.

The boys at school were the most insulting of all. You know how a schoolboy grills a new classmate. The new boy, lost and overcome with embarrassment, is everybody's chosen victim on his first day at school, and it makes no difference what type of school it is. The others order him about, tease him, treat him like a flunkey. Some big, stocky boy suddenly plants himself in front of the victim and stares at him point blank with a threatening and scornful expression. He appraises him this way for a few seconds. The new boy stands facing him in silence, watches him out of the corner of his eye if he has the courage to, and waits to see what's going to happen next.

"What's your name?"

"Dolgoruky."

"Prince Dolgoruky?"

"No, just plain Dolgoruky."

"I see, just *plain* fool!"

And he's quite right—there's nothing more foolish than to be called Dolgoruky without being a prince. But I'm not responsible for this foolishness that weighs so heavily on me. Gradually the question made me lose my temper. And so when I was asked "You're a prince then?" I'd always say "No, I'm the son of a former serf." And later, when I really couldn't stand it any longer, I'd tell them:

"No, I'm no prince, I'm just plain Dolgoruky, and I'm the son of my former master, Mr. Versilov."

I'd thought up that answer by the time I was in the tenth grade in high school and, although I soon found out how stupid it was, I persisted in being stupid for quite a while. I remember one of my teachers commenting that I was "filled with the justified resentment of a citizen whose civil rights had been violated," but he was the only one of that opinion. As a rule, my new answer made people stop and give me a puzzled look that offended me no end.

At last one of the boys, one who was noted for his sharp tongue and with whom I had hardly exchanged more than a few words in the course of a year, came over and, looking slightly past me, said very solemnly:

"To feel the way you do is, of course, all to your credit, and I'm sure that there must be something for you to be proud of. I admit that, if I were in your place, I wouldn't go around celebrating the fact that I was illegitimate. . . . But you seem to expect people to congratulate you on it."

That put an end to my "boasting" of my illegitimate birth.

Well, as I said before, it is awfully difficult to express oneself in Russian: here I have filled three whole pages about resenting my name all my life and now the reader will probably conclude that what I really resent is *not* being Prince Dolgoruky but just plain Dolgoruky. But I feel I would be demeaning myself if I went into further explanations on this subject to try to justify myself.

IV

And so I'll go on. On that estate, beside Makar there was also a girl, and she was already about eighteen when Makar, who was fifty, suddenly announced his intention of marrying her. As we all know, under serfdom, marriages between serfs had to be approved by their masters and sometimes were even ordered by them.

In those days, it was Auntie who was running the estate. Actually, she was neither my aunt nor anybody else's, but somehow everyone called her that all her life. As a matter of fact, I'm not even sure that she was related to the Versilovs at all. Her name was Mrs. Tatyana Prutkov and she was a landowner in her own right, owning, in the same district of Tula Province, a property with thirty-five serfs on it. Well, it was not that she was officially in charge of Versilov's estate with its five hundred serfs, she simple kept her eye on it as a neighborly service. But I understand that, under her supervision, the estate was run at least as efficiently as it would have been by any professionally trained steward. But that's neither here nor there, and her ability to run estates has nothing to do with me; still, without trying to flatter anyone or be ingratiating, I'll say that this Mrs. Prutkov was a generous woman and, indeed, quite an unusual person.

When gloomy Makar (they say he was gloomy in those days) announced his wish to get married, far from refusing him her permission, Mrs. Prutkov for some reason eagerly encouraged him. Sofia, the eighteen-year-old serf girl in question—my mother, that is—had lost both her parents six years earlier. Her father, who had also been a serf and was under some obligation to Makar, whom he greatly respected, had asked for him as he lay dying and, in the presence of the priest and the assembled servants, had pointed meaningfully to his daughter and said to Makar: "Bring her up and take her as your wife."

Since, as it turned out, all this happened only fifteen minutes before he breathed his last, these words could be dismissed as delirious raving, although there was no need even for that since a serf had no right to dispose of anything anyway. Still, they all heard what he said.

As to Makar Dolgoruky, I don't really know how he felt when he finally married Sofia, I mean whether he wanted to or was just doing what he considered his duty. Most likely he went through with it with an air of complete indifference. Even at that time he knew how to present a dignified picture of himself to the world. Since he was neither educated nor even very literate (his knowledge of the church service and of the lives of some saints was derived mostly from hearing them), he was not at all one of those home-grown back yard philosophers. In fact, he was an obstinate and at times brash man who talked with self-assurance, was very definite in his judgments, and lived "respectfully," as he put it rather strangely. That's what he was like at the time, and obviously these ways made everyone respect him, although I've heard it said that he was quite unbearable. It was quite a different matter, though, when he was emancipated and left the estate; then he was remembered as some sort of martyr and saint. I know that for sure.

As to my mother, Mrs. Prutkov overruled the clerk in charge of Versilov's serfs who wanted to send her to Moscow as an apprentice. She kept her in her house until the age of eighteen and taught her a few things—that is, sewing, making clothes, ladylike deportment, and even a little reading. My mother never learned to write passably. She looked upon her marriage to Makar Dolgoruky as something settled long ago and believed that whatever happened to her was the best that could happen and was just wonderful. And on her wedding day she was as calm a bride as anyone had ever seen, so that even Mrs. Prutkov described her as a "fish." All this about my mother's character at that time was told to me by Mrs. Prutkov herself.

It was six months after the wedding that Versilov arrived at the estate.

V

I must say I could never find out, or even think up, a plausible explanation of how he got involved with my mother in the first place. I am fully prepared to believe, as he assured me himself last year (his face rather red but his tone casual and if anything amused), that there certainly was no romance and that it happened "just like that." I believe that and I find the expression "just like that" delightful. Nevertheless, I still would like to know exactly what could have started it off between them. I myself have always loathed and still loathe to this day all that filth, so obviously this is not just shameless curiosity on my part. Let me note here that I hardly knew my mother until a year ago. While still a small child I'd been packed off to live with strangers so as not to disturb Versilov's peace (I'll have more to say about that later), so I can't imagine what she looked like at that time. If she wasn't particularly beautiful, it remains quite inexplicable why a man such as Versilov was then should have been attracted to her. This matter is so important to me because it could shed some light on an aspect of his character that intrigues me a great deal. And that's why I'm trying to find the answer, not out of depravity. That mysterious and distant man told me himself once—with that disarming charm of his which he could produce out of God knows where when he thought he needed it—that he was "just a stupid young dog" then who, although not particularly sentimental, happened to have just read *Poor Anton** and *Polinka Sachs,†* two literary works which he considered had exerted an overwhelming humanizing influence on the young generation of his day. And he added, with an air of utmost gravity, that it was perhaps under the impact of *Poor Anton* that he had gone to his country estate in the first place. But I still wonder how the "stupid young dog" approached my mother. . . .

The thought has suddenly struck me that if anyone ever read what I've written here, he would burst out laughing at this ridiculous adolescent who, in his silly innocence, has the presumption to discuss and analyze things of which he knows nothing. Well, indeed, I know nothing about these things, and I'm not proud to admit it because I realize that this sort of innocence may look stupid in a nineteen-year-old oaf. But I'd also like to tell that reader that he knows nothing either, and I'll prove it to him. It's true I don't know the first thing about women, but then I don't want to know anything about them. I've decided— the hell with them, and I've sworn to myself that I'll never change on that point. Nevertheless, I am very well aware that there are women who can, within one second, sweep you off your feet by their beauty or charm, while with others it may take you as long as six months just to make them out and understand what's in them; to decipher a woman like that and fall in love with her, it's not enough just to look at her and be ready for whatever may come; no, a man must have a special gift for that. And although, as I've said before, I know nothing, I'm convinced of what I just said because if this isn't so, then all women should be immediately reduced to the status of do-

* *Anton Goremyka* (1847) by D. V. Grigorovich (1822–99). A short novel describing the hardships and suffering of Russian peasants under serfdom. [A. MacA.]

† *Polinka Sachs* (1847) by A. V. Druzhinin (1824–64). A novella strongly influenced by the ideas of George Sand and advocating women's rights. [A. MacA.]

mestic animals and should be kept around only as such; I'm sure many men would like that very much.

I definitely know from various sources that my mother was no raving beauty, although I've never seen the portrait which was made of her at that age and which still exists. Therefore it was impossible to fall in love with her at first sight. If he'd just wanted a little fun, Versilov could've picked someone else, an available unmarried girl like the housemaid Anfisa Sapozhkov, for instance. But for a man who had arrived carrying a copy of *Poor Anton,* it was quite unbecoming to use his *droit de seigneur* to violate the sanctity of marriage, even of a mere serf, because, as I said, he still spoke of that book with great respect only a few months ago (that is, twenty years later). Why, they only took Anton's horse away from him, while in this case it was the fellow's wife! So something special must have happened and Miss Sapozhkov wound up the loser (or, in my opinion, the winner).

Last year, on a couple of occasions when it was possible to talk to him (for it wasn't always possible), I went all out at him with those questions. I noticed that, for all his urbane polish and the twenty-year distance that separated us from the events, he was extremely reticent and evasive. But I insisted. At one point, although he still looked at me with that expression of worldly superciliousness I was so familiar with, he mumbled in a voice that struck me as strange something to the effect that my mother was one of those *helpless* creatures whom a man would not necessarily love—not at all, in fact—but for whom he could suddenly become *sorry,* because of her meekness or something like that. . . . And he is sorry for her for a long time and then he gets attached to her "so that it becomes impossible for him to break it off, my boy, if you see what I mean. . . ." That's what he told me and, if it's true, I cannot agree that he was at the time just a "stupid young dog," as he tried to describe himself as a young man. And that's just what I was after.

He went on, however, to tell me that my mother loved him "out of humility." Some notion, that! He could just as well have said that her love had its roots in the institution of serfdom! He just said it to show off; it was a mean, dishonorable, ignoble thing to say!

It may look as if I've written all this to defend my mother's reputation, which may seem strange since, as I said before, I knew nothing whatsoever of her as she was then. Besides, I was well aware of the hopeless confinement of her early childhood and the degrading notions in which she had been steeped and which clung to her all her life. Still, the fact must be recognized—the disgraceful thing did happen.

But I must put something straight. I have let my feelings run away with me and have left out something that should have been mentioned first, namely, that it all *started* with the disgrace. (I hope the reader won't be so hypocritical as to pretend he can't imagine what I mean by disgrace.) Yes, although Miss Sapozhkov was passed over, it all began from Versilov's use of his *droit de seigneur*. But here I'll stand up for myself and insist that there's no inconsistency in what I say. Because what could a man like Versilov possibly have to say to a girl like my mother, even if he had felt an overpowering love for her? I've heard depraved people say that men and women may just meet and start the whole thing in complete silence, which, of course, I consider an unspeakable monstrosity. Nevertheless, I can't see how else Versilov could've started with my mother, even if he had wanted to. Could one imagine him starting with a literary analysis of *Polinka Sachs*? As a matter of fact, they had much more urgent things to worry about than excursions into Russian literature. From what I gathered from Versilov directly when he let himself go once, they used to hide in corners, wait for each other on the stairs, bounce away from each other red-faced when someone went by; and many a time the "tyrannical landowner" would tremble at the sight of any lowly servant scrubbing the floors despite all his seignorial rights!

But, although it all started as the usual thing for a landowner, it was that and yet not really that, and after all I have said I see that I can't explain anything at all. In fact, it seems even more mysterious now. Just the length of their affair is quite puzzling because, with men like Versilov, the rule is to discard the object as soon as the objective has been attained. But that was not what happened. To sin with a pretty, playful serf girl (my mother was not playful) was not only natural but well-nigh inevitable for a depraved "young dog" (and every landowner was depraved, whether liberal or reactionary), particularly in Versilov's case with the idle life he led and the romantic figure he cut as a young widower and all that. But to love someone for life—that was too much. So, while I cannot guarantee that he loved her, it is a fact that he has been dragging her along with him ever since.

I asked my mother lots of questions, but I didn't dare ask her the most important one. Despite the fact that we drew very close to each other during the past year, and although I was an ungrateful and ill-mannered puppy, full of self-pity "for having been wronged," and didn't feel I had to spare her feelings, I didn't ask her that important question, and want you to take note of that fact.

The question is this: how could *she*, after six months of married life, inculcated as she was with all the notions about the sanctity of marriage, she, a poor downtrodden girl, weak as a fly, worshiping her Makar like a sort of god, how could she, within the short space of two weeks, bring herself to commit such a sin? For whatever one may say about my mother, she was certainly not a depraved woman! Indeed, let me say now, it would be hard to imagine a purer and more innocent creature than she was then and has remained all her life. It would perhaps be possible to explain her behavior by assuming that she didn't know what she was doing. I don't mean that in the sense used by defense councils in court to excuse thieves and murderers, but in the sense that she was overwhelmed by an emotion, which may have a tragic and fatal effect on a simple and sensitive person. Who knows, perhaps she fell in love until her dying day with the cut of his coat, with his hair parted in the Parisian style, with his perfect French—yes, French, of which she couldn't understand one word—with the romance he sang while accompanying himself at the piano. Yes, she could have fallen in love with a man such as she never knew existed before and had certainly never seen (besides, he was very handsome), fallen in love at once, desperately, totally, with his elegant manners, with his singing, with everything about him. I understand that this used to happen to serf girls in the days of serfdom and sometimes even to the most virtuous among them. I can see that very well and he who puts it all down to the humiliating position of serf girls deserves only scorn! Yet it's strange to think that a man like that should have had in him in his young years such a direct and irresistible power of fascination to sweep off her feet and drive to perdition a girl who was so pure and who was as different from him as a creature of another species from another world. That it was her perdition, my mother must have understood soon enough, although when she first went to him I doubt that she even gave it a thought. But that's just the way these "defenseless" creatures are—they may feel it's the end of them, but they still go ahead regardless.

As soon as they had sinned, they repented. He told me with amusement about sobbing on the shoulder of Makar, whom he had summoned, expressly for that purpose, to his study, while she was lying half conscious in her room in the servants' quarters.

VI

But enough of all these unanswered questions and sordid details. After giving Makar some money to compensate him for the loss of his wife, Versilov soon left his Tula estate, taking my mother along and, as I said earlier, from then on he dragged her about with him everywhere he went, except on rare occasions when he stayed away from her for quite a long time. Whenever that happened, he'd leave her in the care of Auntie Tatyana Prutkov, who'd always turn up when he needed her. They lived in Moscow, in other towns, and in the countryside in various provinces; they even went abroad, and then finally they settled in Petersburg. But I'll come to that later, although no, perhaps I won't, I don't think it's of much interest. I'll only say that I was born about one year after my mother had left Makar, followed a year later by my sister and ten or eleven years after that by our youngest brother, a sickly baby who died a few months after birth. After that last painful confinement my mother lost her attractiveness, or so at least I was told: her health deteriorated and she aged rapidly.

However, during all that time, she never completely lost contact with Makar. Wherever the Versilovs were, whether they stopped somewhere for just a short while or lived there for years, Makar never failed to send news of himself to what he referred to as "the family." Strange relations developed between them, quite formal relations, almost ceremonious. As a rule, landed gentry find something comic about such relations. But that was not so in this case. Makar's letters were received exactly twice a year, not more often nor less, and all his letters bore a striking resemblance to one another. I have seen them. There is hardly anything personal in them. In fact, they consist largely of formalized reports of very commonplace interest, along with the most impersonal expression of feelings, if one can express feelings at all that way. First, there was a report on the sender's health, then an inquiry about the health of the addressees, followed by best wishes, solemn regards, and blessings, and that was just about all. That conventional, impersonal tone seems to be the essence of decency and tact among people of that class: "To my much esteemed and highly respected wife, Sofia, I send my humblest regards. . . ." "To our beloved children, I send my fatherly blessings to accompany them throughout their lives." The beloved children were then listed by name, including me and the latest addition. I must add here that Makar was too subtle to describe his "noble-born, most respected master Andrei Petrovich Versilov" as his "benefactor," though he never failed to send him in every letter his "humblest regards," beg him for "continuance of his favor," and call down upon him the blessing of God.

Makar's letters were answered promptly by my mother in very much the same style. It goes without saying that Versilov took no part in the correspondence. Makar's letters arrived from all parts of Russia, from various towns, often from monasteries where he stayed occasionally for quite long periods.

He had become a sort of pilgrim. He never asked for anything. But once every three years or so he would turn up in town and come directly to my mother's and spend some time with her, for it so happened that she always had a place of her own separate from Versilov. I'll have more to say about that later, but here I'll only note that Makar did not install himself on the sofa in the drawing room but discreetly found himself a corner behind a partition. He never stayed long either, five days or a week at the most.

I forgot to mention that he had a great love and respect for his name "Dolgoruky." This, of course, was stupid and ridiculous. And the most stupid thing was that he liked it so much precisely because there were princes of that name. A strange and crazy notion!

When I said that the family always lived together, I meant, of course, all of them except me. I had been cast out almost from the moment I was born and had to live with strangers. But this was not done for any special reason, it just happened that way. After I was born, my mother was still young and attractive and so was wanted by Versilov, while a screaming baby would obviously be a nuisance, especially traveling. So that was why, until my nineteenth year, I hardly ever saw my mother, except on two or three brief occasions. And this was not due to my mother's lack of feeling for me, but rather to Versilov's haughty disregard for the feelings of other people.

VII

Now for something quite different.

A month earlier, that is, one month before September 19, while I was in Moscow, I made up my mind to break off with them all for good and to devote myself entirely to my idea. I have used the phrase "devote myself to my idea" because it expresses my main purpose in life. What this idea of mine actually is, I will have lots to say about later. During the days of my dreamy Moscow loneliness the seed of the "idea" appeared in my mind while I was still in the second year of high school and has never left me since. Everything else in my life became subordinated to it. Even before it got hold of me, indeed from my earliest childhood, I'd always lived in a dream world, colored by a certain special light, but, after this great and all-absorbing idea came to me, my daydreams acquired a certain unity, took on a well-defined shape, and, instead of being crazy, became rational. School, which had not interfered with my dreams, did not interfere with my idea either. I must note that I graduated from school with rather poor marks, although, until the grade before last, I'd regularly been one of the top students in my class. This drop in performance was also due in part to that idea, or perhaps, to be more precise, to the conclusions I drew from it, even if they may have been false conclusions. So it was not school that interfered with the idea, but the idea that interfered with school, and perhaps also with the university. After graduating from high school, I immediately decided to break off completely with my family and, indeed, if the circumstances required it, with the entire world, although I was not even nineteen at the time. I informed my family in Petersburg in writing through the proper channels that I wanted to be left alone once and for all, requesting that they stop sending me my allowance, that indeed they forget me for good (that is, if they ever remembered me), and finally that there was nothing in the world that would make me enter the university. I was faced with the inescapable choice: to continue my education or to put my idea into practice instead of putting it off for another four years. Without hesitation, I opted for the idea, for I thought I had mathematical proof that it would work.

I hadn't seen my father, Versilov, since I was ten, although during that brief encounter he had managed to leave an indelible impression upon me. And now, despite the fact that my letter hadn't been addressed to him personally, he answered me himself, in his own hand. He asked me to come to Petersburg, promising to get me a job there. My pride was greatly flattered by this letter from that cold and haughty man, who, after bringing me into the world and packing me off to live with strangers, took no interest in me and never even gave a thought to the idea that he might have wronged me. (Possibly he was only dimly and intermittently aware of my existence because, as it turned out, it was not actually he who was paying for my upkeep in Moscow.) And now, by filling me with pride, that letter determined the future course of my life. It may sound paradoxical too that what I liked most about the letter (just a small sheet of note paper) was the fact that there was no mention of my entering the university, no attempt to persuade me to reconsider my decision and to complete my education; in short, he did not indulge in all those paternal pretty phrases that are used in such cases. I liked that, although it obviously showed him in a bad light, proving once more his lack of interest in me. So I decided to go to Petersburg. Besides, it didn't interfere with my main goal.

"I'll see what comes of it," I said to myself. "In any case I'll have only a temporary contact with them, and perhaps a very short one at that. But if I see that this move, as ordinary and minor as it is, takes me further from my main goal, I'll break off with them, leave everything, and withdraw into my shell. Yes, my shell, exactly that—I'll hide inside it like a tortoise!" I loved that comparison.

"I won't be alone," I kept ruminating, darting back and forth like one possessed during those last days in Moscow. "I'll never again be alone as I've been all these awful years. I'll always have *my idea* at my side! I'll never betray it! Not even if I become fond of them, even if I'm happy living near them, even if I stay with them for ten years!"

Let me anticipate here and say that it was precisely this ambivalence about my plans and my goals, all of which took shape in Moscow and remained with me in Petersburg (for I don't know whether a day passed without my setting a final limit when I would break off my relations with them and leave), this ambivalence, as I was saying, that was probably one of the main reasons for the indiscretions, villainies, nastiness, and, of course, blunders I have been guilty of during the past year.

It is true I suddenly had a father, a feeling I had never experienced before. I felt quite elated by that thought while preparing for my journey and in the train that carried me from Moscow to Petersburg. It was not just that he was my father—I didn't go in much for that kind of sentimental stuff anyway —but he was the man who had humiliated me and had refused to have anything to do with me during all those years when I had been breathlessly feeding on daydreams about him, if it is possible to apply such words to daydreams. From my childhood on, every daydream I had was lighted by his presence, was spun around him, and finally converged on his person. I don't know whether I loved him or hated him, but in my thoughts his shadow dominated my future life and all the plans I had for it. And this happened by itself; it grew as I grew.

There was another very strong reason for me to leave Moscow. For three months, that is, before the question of my going to Petersburg even came up, there had been something that would grab my heart and force it to pound wildly in my chest. That uncharted ocean tempted me so much because I felt I could enter it as lord and master of the destinies of other people, and what people! But lest there be any misunderstanding about it, let me state clearly right now that the feelings seething within me were magnanimous, in no way despotic. Besides, if he ever deigned to give a thought to me, Versilov was most likely expecting a young boy just out of high school, still a mere adolescent, gaping at the world in wide-eyed wonderment. In actual fact, however, I had found out certain things about him and was in possession of a certain document for which he would have willingly paid several years of his life (this I know for certain today, for I realize how important that secret was to him).

I realize now that what I have written here is full of riddles. But, then, how is one to convey feelings without first presenting the facts. Everything will be amply explained in its proper place because this was my purpose in writing it all down in the first place. Just writing things down any old way would produce delirious ravings or a cloud of words.

VIII

Now, at last, I can get to September 19. First, let me just say in passing, as it were, that I found them all—Versilov, my mother, and my sister, whom I was seeing for the first time in my life—living in very difficult circumstances, almost destitute or on the verge of destitution. I'd found out about their situation while I was still in Moscow, but I never expected things to be that bad. Since I was a child, I had got used to imagining this man, "who would some day be my father," as all but radiating his own light, and I could not conceive of him except as always occupying the top position. As a rule, Versilov never lived with my mother; he always had his own apartment in order to observe their despicable "proprieties." But now they were all living together in a little wooden cottage in a side street behind the barracks of the Semyonovsky Regiment. They had already pawned everything they could, so without Versilov's knowledge I gave my mother the sixty rubles I secretly owned. I said I owned it secretly because I had saved it in the course of two years from my allowance of five rubles a month. I had started saving the very day I conceived my "idea," and that's why it was important that Versilov not know about the money. The mere thought that he might find out about it made me shudder.

My contribution was just a drop in an empty bucket. My mother worked hard and my sister too took in sewing. But Versilov led an idle life, still indulged in his whims and some of his former extravagant habits. He gave vent to his irritation quite freely, especially at dinner, and, in general, behaved like a real despot. My mother, my sister, Mrs. Prutkov, and the innumerable females of the Andronikov family (the head of that family, a government official who had also managed Versilov's affairs, had died three months before my arrival), all groveled before him as though he were an idol. All that, I had never imagined. I must also remark that when I'd seen him nine years earlier, he was incomparably more elegant. As I said before, he had preserved a kind of luminescence in my daydreams so I couldn't imagine how a man could, within some nine years, have aged so much and slipped so badly. This made me feel very sad, sorry for him, and ashamed of something, all at the same time. When I first saw him, the sight was a painful shock to me. And yet he was certainly not an old man at the age of forty-five. Indeed, as I looked at him, I found in his handsome features something even more striking than what I had carried in my memory. There was less glamor in him now than before, less physical beauty, even less elegance of manner, but, on the other hand, life seemed to have engraved on his face something that made him far more intriguing than before.

I also knew that poverty represented no more than a small share of his misfortunes, a tenth or perhaps only a twentieth of them. There was something infinitely more serious than poverty, especially since Versilov still hoped to win a lawsuit now in the courts for the second year, in which he was contesting an estate worth seventy thousand rubles or more with the Princes Sokolsky. I mentioned before that Versilov had already gone through three inheritances in the course of his life, and now it looked as if a fourth one was about to come to his rescue! The case was to be settled very shortly. That was the situation when I arrived. It is true, though, that at the moment he had to put up with being without money since nobody would lend him any just on his expectations.

But, for that matter, Versilov didn't go around looking for somebody to lend him money, although at times he'd be out all day. For more than a year, he had been ostracized by society. The details of that scandal remained a mystery to me, despite all my efforts to learn everything I could about it during my first month in Petersburg. What was most important to me—indeed, the very reason for my coming to Petersburg—was to find out if Versilov was guilty or not. People had turned away from him, including the influential and prominent people with whom he had until then always skillfully maintained good relations. The reason for this ostracism was something unspeakably vile and, what is worse, something "scandalous" in the eyes of society that he was supposed to have done a little over a year ago in Germany. Also, in connection with that ignominy, he was reported to have been slapped by one of the Princes Sokolsky and to have failed to challenge his offender to a duel. Even his legitimate children, his son and his daughter, had turned their backs on him and now lived separately. It is true that they were received in the best society, thanks to their maternal relatives, the Fanariotovs, and their connection with Versilov's former friend, the old Prince Nikolai Sokolsky.

But, after watching Versilov closely during that whole month, I ended up with the impression that it was not high society that had turned its back on this proud man but rather he who had banned these people from his presence, so great was his air of independence. What actually worried me was whether he really had the right to look down on the world with that proud air! I had to find out the truth and find it out very quickly, for I had come here to judge that man! I was still keeping my secret power hidden from him, as I had to decide first whether to accept or reject him. And since rejecting him would have meant hurting myself very deeply, I was in a constant state of anguish.

Well, I suppose I may as well tell the truth: the man meant a great deal to me.

In the meantime, I lived in their house, worked, and tried not to be too rude to them, although I certainly didn't try too hard. Nevertheless, after having lived there for a month, I felt less than ever prepared to demand a full explanation of him. That proud man remained a complete enigma to me, and that offended me no end. Actually, if anything, he was rather friendly with me and often said amusing and witty things, while I'd have preferred to his pleasant banter some nasty remark that would have brought about a confrontation. There was an ambiguous overtone to all our conversations, or perhaps I should simply say that in a peculiar way he was making fun of me.

From the day I arrived from Moscow, he never took me seriously. I could never understand why. True, thanks to that attitude, he remained inscrutable to me since I couldn't possibly humiliate myself by begging him to take me seriously. On top of that, he could say and do things so unexpected and disarming that they left me quite at a loss. To make a long story short, he treated me as if I were a completely immature adolescent, something I could hardly bear, although I'd anticipated that that was how he'd treat me. As a result, I stopped talking to him seriously myself, and soon I almost stopped talking to him altogether. I waited.

What I was waiting for was a person whose arrival in Petersburg might finally enable me to learn the whole truth. That was my last hope. In any case, I was ready to break off with them at any moment and had prepared everything for that eventuality. I was sorry to leave Mother, but it was "either him or me," as I planned to put it to her and to my sister. I'd even fixed the day when I'd leave.

In the meantime I went to work every morning.

Chapter 2

I

On September 19 I was due to receive my first monthly salary for the job that Versilov had found for me in Petersburg. No one had consulted me about whether I wanted the job—they just took me there, I believe on the very day of my arrival. This was, of course, most inconsiderate and rude and probably I ought to have protested. It turned out that I was to work in the house of the old Prince Nikolai Sokolsky. But if I had refused then and there, it would have meant breaking off relations with them on the spot. It was not, of course, that I was so afraid of that rupture with them, but it would have interfered with my important plans. And so, for the time being, I accepted in silence, that silence saving my dignity.

Let me make it clear that this old Prince Sokolsky, a very rich man and a privy councilor, was no close relative of the Moscow Princes Sokolsky, members of a branch of the family that had been impoverished for several generations, who were engaged in the lawsuit against Versilov. They simply bore the same name. Yet the old prince took a considerable interest in them and was particularly fond of one of the Moscow princes—Sergei—the one who was supposed to be the head of that branch of the family and was now a young army officer. Until recently, Versilov had had a tremendous influence on the old man and had been his friend, albeit a strange friend, for the old Sokolsky was terribly afraid of him, not only now, which I noticed, but even before their rupture, during their friendship.

When I arrived, they hadn't seen each other for a long time because the dishonorable act of which Versilov was accused concerned the old prince's family. But Mrs. Prutkov happened to be around, and it was through her that a job was found for me, for old Sokolsky had been looking for a "young man" to work with him in his study. It also happened that he was anxious to do something to please Versilov, a sort of first step toward reconciliation, and Versilov "gave him the opportunity to do so." The old man made the arrangement in the absence of his daughter, the widow of a general, who would certainly have prevented him from taking that step. I'll come to that later, but I want to note here that it was this peculiarity in his attitude toward Versilov that predisposed me in his favor. I reasoned that if the head of the offended household still treated Versilov with respect, the rumors of Versilov's villainy must be at least partly unfounded, or at least open to another interpretation. This was another reason that prevented me from refusing the job with Sokolsky: I thought I would get a chance there to find out what had actually happened.

Tatyana Prutkov was playing a strange role when I saw her in Petersburg. I'd almost forgotten about her existence altogether and never expected to find her in such an influential position. I had seen her three or four times while I was living in Moscow when she turned up from God knows where and, on someone's instructions, arranged things for me—to get me into Touchard's school and two and a half years later to have me transferred to high school and installed in the house of the late Nikolai Semyonovich. Every time she appeared, she'd spend the whole day with me, inspect my linen and clothes, drive me downtown to the Kuznetsky Bridge, buy me whatever I needed, outfit me thoroughly down to the last pencil case and penknife. And all the time she'd hiss at me, nag me, reproach me for all sorts of things, test me, offer me as examples to follow some other boys, unbelievable ones, whom she knew or was related to, paragons of virtue, all of whom were infinitely superior to me, and while telling me all this, she'd pinch me and even shove me, sometimes actually hurting me. Once she'd installed me safely wherever it was, she'd vanish without a trace and stay away for several years.

And now it was she who, when I arrived in Petersburg, appeared to take care of me, to install me once again. She was a small, dry woman with a little beak-like nose and the sharp eyes of a bird. She was slavishly devoted to Versilov and accepted unquestioningly and with complete sincerity whatever he said as though he were the Pope. Soon, however, I noticed with considerable surprise that everywhere we went everybody knew her and treated her with great respect.

Old Prince Sokolsky treated her with extraordinary consideration, as did his family; and Versilov's proud legitimate children did too; the same was true of the Fanariotovs. And yet she earned her living by taking in sewing, by cleaning some kind of lace, by doing some work for dressmakers.

We had a row a minute after we met because she thought she could start hissing at me again as she'd done six years before, and after that we quarreled every day. But that didn't prevent us from occasionally talking to each other, and I admit that toward the end of the month I'd got to like her in a peculiar way. I suppose I liked her for her independent character. But, of course, I never told her how I felt.

I gathered at once that the job they'd got for me with this sick old man consisted simply in keeping him "amused." Obviously this was humiliating and I decided to do something about it. But soon the old crank affected me in an unexpected way, aroused something resembling pity in me; toward the end of the month I felt strangely attached to him and gave up my plan of being deliberately rude to him.

As a matter of fact, he was not really that old—no more than sixty perhaps. But there had been a big to-do over him a year and a half earlier when he'd had some kind of sudden fit. He had gone on a trip somewhere and, while traveling, had suddenly gone off his rocker; this caused something of a scandal and became a subject of gossip in Petersburg. As is usual in such cases, he was immediately whisked off abroad. Five months later he reappeared completely recovered, although he did resign from his government position. Versilov insisted with visible irritation that there had never been any insanity but simply a sort of nervous fit. I immediately noticed Versilov's irritation, which was unusual for him. I must say, though, that I rather agreed with him. All one could say about old Sokolsky was perhaps that he was rather irresponsible for a man of his age, which, I understand, was not at all the case before his fit. I heard that he used to do some sort of counseling and that on one particular occasion he distinguished himself in his counseling. But, after having been with him for a month, I found it difficult to imagine how he could have had any of the special talents required by a councilor. Some people said (although I never noticed it myself) that, after his fit, old Sokolsky developed a peculiar urge to get married and that he had tried to carry out that intention several times in the past eighteen months. This was talked about in Petersburg society, and those whom it may have concerned took note of it. But since this propensity of his was very much against the interests of certain people around him, he was carefully watched.

His direct family was small: he had been a widower for twenty years and had only one daughter, the widow of a general, who was expected to arrive any day from Moscow, probably a young woman of character, whom he obviously feared. He had, however, masses of distant relatives, mostly through his wife, all of them almost destitute. In addition to them, there were the innumerable male and female protégés, whom he had once helped and who for that reason expected to be mentioned in his will. And so all these people were helping the general's widow keep an eye on her father.

Besides all these difficulties, the old prince had another peculiar weakness (I'm not sure whether to call it ridiculous or not) in which he had indulged even in his younger years—finding husbands for penniless girls. For a good twenty-five years now, he had been marrying off distant young relatives of his or his wife's, cousins, stepdaughters, or perhaps goddaughters. He even married off his hall porter's daughter. He started by taking these girls home while they were still children, had them brought up by governesses and Frenchwomen, then sent them to the best boarding schools, and finally provided them with dowries, and married them off. This way he was always surrounded by females, as his married protégées produced new little girls, who in turn became his protégées. And all the time he had to attend christenings and all these people kept coming to congratulate him on his birthday, all of which he enjoyed immensely.

After I'd been with him a short time, I couldn't help noticing that there was a painful suspicion weighing on the old man's mind, namely, that everyone looked at him strangely now and that he was no longer treated in the same way as before, the way a healthy normal man should be treated. He could never get rid of that impression, even at the gayest and most relaxed social occasions. He became suspicious and thought he could detect something in everybody's eye. The idea that those around him thought he was mad oppressed him. Sometimes he looked with distrust even at me. And I believe that if this kindliest of men became aware that someone was questioning his sanity in public, that man would become his implacable enemy. This is a point I want to emphasize. And let me add that it is this circumstance that prevented me from being rude to him the day I entered his service. Indeed, I was glad whenever I could distract him and cheer him up. I don't suppose that this admission can cast a shadow on my dignity.

Most of his capital was invested. Even since his recovery, he had become a partner in a large joint-stock company, a very well-established one, as a matter of fact. And although he was not a member of the board of directors, he followed the operations of the company with great interest, attended the shareholders' meetings, was elected a founding member, made long speeches, opposed motions, made noise, and obviously had a marvelous time. He particularly liked speaking in public because it enabled everyone to judge his intelligence and sanity. And gradually he acquired, even in private conversation, the taste for profound sayings and *bon mots,* which I can very well understand.

On the ground floor of his house he had set up something like a business office with a clerk to attend to the accounts, keep the books, and also manage the house. This clerk could cope quite adequately with these tasks, even though he worked only part time since he was also employed in a government department. Nevertheless, in compliance with Prince Sokolsky's express wishes, I was officially appointed to assist that clerk. But in no time I was transferred to the prince's private study upstairs and often sat there without any accounts or ledgers in front of me to keep up appearances.

I write this feeling like a sobered man, in some respects almost with detachment. But how am I to describe the feeling of deep sadness that weighed me down then and that I still remember so well and, above all, the fervid excitement which reached such a delirious pitch that I was kept awake at night tormented by my impatience to solve the riddles I had set myself?

II

Asking for money, even if it's a salary that's due you, is quite revolting under any circumstances, but it's even worse if, in the secret recesses of your conscience, you feel you haven't earned it. On the previous night, however, I'd heard my mother whispering to my sister, so Versilov wouldn't hear ("not to worry

Andrei"), that she intended to take to the pawnshop an icon which, for some reason, was particularly dear to her. I was supposed to be earning fifty rubles a month but I didn't know when and how I was to be paid—no one had thought to inform me about that. Three days before, I had found the clerk in the downstairs office and had asked him where I should inquire about my salary. He looked at me, smiling with feigned surprise (he didn't like me).

"Why, you get a salary?"

I expected him to follow up my answer with "But for what?" but he didn't. He just said dryly that he knew nothing about it and stuck his nose back into a lined ledger, into which he was copying the accounts from some invoices.

I know, though, that this man must have been aware that I didn't spend my whole time doing absolutely nothing. About two weeks earlier, I'd been busy for four days working on an assignment he himself had given me—to make a clean draft of something or other—although, as it turned out, in the end I had to practically rewrite the whole thing myself. The "thing" was the result of a brainstorm of the old prince, an avalanche of "ideas" that he was preparing to present to the shareholders' committee. I had to organize his material for him, give it the appearance of unity, and fix up his style. Later the prince and I sat arguing about that paper a whole day, and, although he objected vehemently to certain things I had done, he remained very satisfied with it, though I'm not sure whether he finally did present it. I also wrote two or three business letters for him, but I don't even want to mention that.

It annoyed me also to ask for my salary because I had decided to give up my job, expecting that I'd have to leave the house through unavoidable circumstances. When I got up that morning and was dressing in my little garret, my heart pounded wildly in my chest. I tried to dismiss my excitement scornfully, but it only increased as I entered Prince Sokolsky's house: that was the morning when the person for whom I had been waiting was supposed to arrive, that woman whose presence could provide the answers to all my questions, I mean the prince's daughter, the young widow of General Akhmakov, whom I mentioned before and who was now engaged in a bitter feud with Versilov. At last I've been able to force myself to write down that name! I had, of course, never seen her before and I couldn't imagine how I'd talk to her, if I were to talk to her at all. However, I felt, perhaps for good reason, that with her arrival some of the mystery Versilov presented to me would be cleared up. But, try as hard as I would, I couldn't remain detached. I was furious with myself for showing such weakness and awkwardness from the outset; I felt overcome by curiosity and even more by disgust—all at the same time. I still remember, detail by detail, everything about that day!

The prince had not been informed about the impending arrival of his daughter and didn't expect her for another week or so. I'd found out the previous evening when I overheard Mrs. Prutkov, who had received a letter from Mrs. Akhmakov, telling my mother about it. And although they conducted their conversation in whispers and used only cryptic allusions, I understood. Of course, I was not intentionally eavesdropping on them, I simply couldn't prevent myself from listening when I saw how much the news of the arrival of that woman affected my mother. Versilov was not at home.

I didn't intend to tell the old man of his daughter's arrival because it was all too obvious to me how much he was dreading it. Indeed, two or three days before, he'd even inadvertently allowed himself to mumble something indicating very indirectly and in a roundabout way that he was afraid for me or, to be more accurate, afraid of the dressing down his daughter would probably give him because of me. It must, however, be noted that, in family relations, he still managed to keep a certain independence, especially in money matters. In fact, my first impression of him—that he was just a doormat—had to be revised after a few days: even though something of a doormat, he still had been able to preserve if not real strength then at least some stubbornness on certain points. There were moments when this seemingly shy and yielding man became quite intractable. Later, that trait of the prince's character was explained to me by Versilov.

It seems curious to me now that the prince and I almost never mentioned his daughter, as though we were avoiding the subject; or, to be precise, it was I who avoided talking about her while the prince avoided mentioning Versilov. Indeed, I was quite sure that he would simply refuse to answer me if I ever tried to ask him one of those questions about Versilov that preoccupied me so deeply.

If I were asked now what we'd talked about during that whole month, I'd say about everything under the sun but mostly about rather peculiar things. I enjoyed very much the unaffected simplicity with which he treated me. There were times when I would look at him and wonder how a man like that could possibly ever have sat on government committees or presided at shareholders' meetings. I could imagine him very well as a schoolboy, perhaps an eighth grader, sitting next to me in class—ah, what a wonderful school friend he would have made! I also marveled at his face. It was a very serious and handsomely lean face with wide-open eyes and topped by thick wavy white hair which, together with his spare and tall figure, could have given him an imposing appearance had it not been for something disturbing, almost indecent about his expression: in a peculiar way it could suddenly change from utmost gravity to unbelievable childish playfulness, which anyone seeing him for the first time could not possibly have expected. When I told this to Versilov, he listened to me with curiosity, apparently surprised that I was able to observe such things. Then he told me casually that this was a peculiarity that the prince had developed only since his illness, in fact, quite a recent development.

Our most frequent topics of conversation were God and His existence—that is, whether God exists or not—and then women. The prince was very religious and very sentimental. There was a huge icon stand in his study with a lamp burning in front of it. But at times something seemed to come over him: he would question God's existence and say all sorts of very strange things, obviously challenging me to answer him. I felt quite indifferent on the subject, but still we both always got sincerely involved in these discussions. To this day, our conversations are a pleasant memory to me. What he really preferred, though, was to talk about women, but my reluctance to discuss the subject reduced my contribution to almost nothing. This sometimes disappointed him a great deal.

That was the topic he chose as soon as I arrived that morning. Although I had left him the night before in an inexplicable state of depression, now he was in a very playful mood. I, for my part, was very anxious to settle the question of my salary that day because I wanted it out of the way before the arrival of certain people. I felt sure that we would be *interrupted* in the course of the day (that's why my heart was pounding so), in which case perhaps I wouldn't even dare bring up the matter of money. But since money matters stubbornly stayed out of our conversation, I naturally became furious at my own stupidity and in my irritation I remember answering one of his questions that seemed to me really too flippant by expounding for his benefit my views on women, very heatedly and hardly stopping to take a breath. But this only made him more excited on the subject, so then I couldn't get him off it at all and thus sealed my own doom.

III

" . . . I dislike women because they are uncouth and clumsy, because they cannot stand on their own feet, because they dress indecently. . . ." I wound up my lengthy tirade rather incoherently.

"A pity, my dear boy, a pity!" he cried with great delight, which irritated me even more.

I'm accommodating enough to yield on unimportant things, but I'll never give way on a point that matters. When it comes to trifles, such as social conventions and the like, I'm willing to go out of my way God knows how far, but I always loathe myself for being like that. It is because of this sickening wishy-washiness of mine that I can kowtow to any smug well-dressed gentleman, if only he deigns to address me politely. Otherwise, I am liable to get into a violent argument with some moron, which is even worse. All that, I suppose, comes from lack of self-control, because I've grown up in seclusion, hiding in my corner. After letting myself go like that, I always leave furious and promise myself that I'll never be caught at it again, but the next day I get caught once more. This even causes people sometimes to take me for . . . for a sixteen-year-old! But instead of acquiring self-control, even now I'd rather withdraw even deeper into my corner, however misanthropic that may seem to others, and snarl: "All right, I know I'm awkward, but I don't care, good-by!" I mean it and I say it once and for all. But what I've written just now has nothing to do with the old prince or with our conversation that day.

"I don't see what's so hilarious in what I told you!" I almost shouted at him. "I was simply trying to express my opinion."

"Ah, how did you put it? . . . Women are uncouth and indecently dressed! That's something new and interesting. . . ."

"Yes, they're uncouth. Just go to the theater, or go out for a stroll. Every man, for instance, knows what it means to keep to the right, and when two men meet they step out of each other's way—he to his right, I to my right. But a woman . . . I mean, a lady—because it's ladies that I'm talking about—just forges straight ahead, without even noticing you're there, taking it for granted that you'll jump out of her way and let her pass. I'm willing to yield to her because she's the weaker creature, but why should she take it for granted and consider it my duty? That's what's insulting! I always snort with disgust when I meet one of them. . . . And, after that, they dare to come and yell at us that they're oppressed, that they demand equality. . . . What equality is she talking about when she tramples me underfoot or fills my mouth with dust. . . ."

"With dust, did you say?"

"Yes, because they don't dress decently. And one has to be depraved not to notice it! Why do our courts try cases of indecency behind closed doors while tolerating indecency in the streets where there are even more people to see it? They bolster their behinds quite unashamedly with all kinds of *froufrou* to show people what *belles femmes* they are! Of course I can't help noticing it, any young man notices it, every child, and a boy who's just beginning to . . . That's loathsome. I don't care if depraved old debauchees run after these creatures with their tongues hanging out, but there is such a thing as the purity of youth and that must be protected! All we can do is spit after they've passed. . . . Just imagine one of them walking down the street—she lets out the train of her dress a yard and a half and trails it behind her, raising a cloud of dust. And how do you think it feels to walk behind someone like that? What choice is there? Either you jump aside or you start running to get ahead of her, for if you don't do one of those two things she's sure to pump at least five pounds of dust into your mouth and your nose. And, what's more, the stuff she's trailing is silk, which she's willing to drag three miles over sidewalks just because it's the fashion, while her husband is paid only five hundred rubles a year in the Senate, so you can see for yourself where graft and corruption starts. It's always made me swear aloud and spit in her path, yes, swear and spit!"

Although, as I write this down now, the conversation strikes me as rather funny, especially my style of that period, my feelings on the subject have remained unchanged.

"And your swearing never got you into trouble?" the old prince inquired with curiosity.

"Why, I swear at them and walk away. I'm sure they're aware of it, but they won't let on and continue to forge ahead queenlike, without turning their heads. Once I actually stopped and started berating a couple of those creatures who were dragging their trains along the boulevard. . . . Of course, I didn't use foul language, but I did say aloud that I considered their trains an insult."

"Did you put it just like that?"

"Why, certainly. In the first place, they violate rules of social conduct and, in the second place, they raise dust on the boulevard where everybody is entitled to walk—me, Ivan, Fyodor, everybody. And that's what I explained to them. In general, I dislike the way women walk as seen from behind. I conveyed that to them too, or rather I just gave them a hint of it."

"But listen, my friend, that could land you in a lot of trouble: they might have had you arrested."

"No, they could not. What could they have possibly complained about? That a man walked in the street next to them and talked to himself? Isn't everybody free to say what he thinks to thin air? I was not addressing them, I was expressing my general views on things. It was they who attacked me and who used abusive language, much worse than anything I used: they said I was a nasty little brat and that I ought to be sent to bed without dinner that night; also that I was a nihilist, that they'd call the police, that I was pestering them because they were weak, helpless women but that if there had been a man with them, I'd have immediately put my tail between my legs like a puppy who'd been spanked. I answered very coolly that it was they who were annoying me, that I was now going to cross the street to be rid of them, and that, to show them how little afraid I was of their men, I'd follow them at a distance of twenty steps to the house where they were going, then wait by the outside entrance for their men to come out, and that I was very willing to accept their challenge. And that's exactly what I did."

"Really?"

"Of course. Oh, I can see that it was rather silly of me, but I was annoyed. So I had to drag along behind them for a couple of miles on a hot day, and we walked all the way to the Institute, where they entered a one-story wooden house, a very respectable-looking one, I must say, as I could see through the window lots of flowers, two canaries, three lap dogs, and some framed engravings. For half an hour I waited in the street in front of that house. I saw them peep out of the window surreptitiously two or three times, after which they pulled down the curtains. Finally, a middle-aged man, who looked like a petty official or something, came out of the house. He looked as if someone had just pulled him out of bed, not that he actually wore a dressing gown, but he seemed to have put on in a hurry whatever clothes happened to be within his reach when he woke up. He settled himself by the door, folded his hands behind his back, and started staring at me. I stared back at him. He looked away for a moment, then looked back at me, and suddenly I saw he was smiling. I turned my back on him and left."

"You know, my friend, there's some of that romantic Schiller stuff in you! You've always puzzled me: your cheeks are ruddy, you look the picture of health, and with all that you have such a violent—how shall I put it?—violent revulsion toward women. How is it possible that at your age you should fail to react to women in a certain way? When I was only eleven, *mon cher*, my tutor scolded me for staring too much at the statues in the Summer Gardens."

"I bet you'd be delighted if I paid a little visit to some local *demoiselle* and then came back and reported to you in detail how I made out. Well, there's no need for that. I saw a woman completely naked when I was thirteen, female nakedness in all its entirety, and since then I've felt quite disgusted."

"Is that really so? But, *cher enfant*, a beautiful, fresh woman smells of apples. How can one possibly talk of disgust?"

"In Touchard's school, where I went before high school, there was a boy called Lambert. He beat me because he was three years older than me and made me wait on him, pull off his boots and all. When he was going to be confirmed, a priest called Abbé Rigaud came to congratulate him. With wild gestures, they threw themselves into each other's arms, burst into tears, and the abbé pressed Lambert desperately to his breast. I burst into tears too and was very envious of them. . . . Later, when his father died, Lambert left the school, and I hadn't seen him for two years when I met him in the street one day. He said he'd come and see me. By that time, I was already in high school and living at Nikolai Semyonovich's. He came the next morning, showed me five hundred rubles in a big bill, and told me to follow him. Although he'd been beating me up until two years before, he'd always been dependent on me. I don't mean just for pulling off his boots and things like that. He needed someone to confide in, and that was me. And now he told me that he'd stolen the money that very morning out of his mother's strong box, which he'd opened with a copy of the key he'd had made. He explained to me that all the money there was legally his since it had come from his father, and that his mother had no right to refuse to give it to him.

"The day before Abbé Rigaud had come to lecture him about his behavior: he walked into the room, planted himself in front of Lambert, and proceeded to whimper, throwing his arms in the air, making all sorts of disgusted faces, and reproaching him for his ways. 'So,' Lambert said, 'I pulled out a knife and told him that I'd cut his throat for him' (Only he really said th-gh-oat for, being a Frenchman, that's how he pronounced his r's). Then he drove toward Kuznetsky Bridge, and on the way there he told me that he'd found out his mother was having an affair with Abbé Rigaud, that he didn't give a damn really, but that it showed that everything they said about the sacraments was hogwash. He told me many other things and I was quite frightened. On Kuznetsky Bridge, Lambert went shopping. He bought himself a double-barreled shotgun, a game bag, cartridges, a riding whip, and a pound of candy. Then we drove out of the city gates to do some shooting, and on our way we met a bird catcher with bird cages. Lambert bought a canary off him. When we got to a wood Lambert, reckoning that after having been caged for some time a bird wouldn't be able to fly very far, let the canary out and started shooting at it. Still he missed every time. He was firing a shotgun for the first time in his life, although he'd been longing to have a gun even back in our days at Touchard's; in fact, we both had. He seemed out of breath with excitement. His hair was awfully black; his complexion was fair; his cheeks were red as though they had been painted on a mask; his nose was long with a hump in it, the kind many Frenchmen have; his teeth were very white and his eyes black. He finally got hold of the bird, tied it to a branch with a piece of string, and, from an inch or so away, blasted at it out of both barrels. The bird disintegrated into hundreds of feathers. Then we drove back to town, took a room in a hotel, ordered some food and champagne.

"Then a lady arrived. . . . I still remember how impressed I was by how gorgeously she was dressed in green silk. And finally I saw all that . . . you know, what we were talking about just now. . . . When we started drinking again, Lambert began to bait the woman and insult her. Since she was sitting without her dress on, he snatched it up. She became annoyed, asked him to give it back to her, said she wanted to get dressed now. Then he took his riding crop and started lashing at her bare shoulders. I got up, grabbed him by the hair, and twisted him so that he fell to the floor. He snatched up a fork and stuck it into my leg. We must have made a lot of noise, for people forced their way into our room. In the general uproar I managed to escape. . . . So, since that time, the thought of a naked woman turns my stomach, although I believe that woman was beautiful."

While I was telling him all this, the prince's face changed from excessively playful to very sad.

"*Mon pauvre enfant*, I always thought that you must've had many painful moments in your childhood."

"Don't let that worry you."

"But you told me yourself that you had no one . . . except for that Lambert boy. . . . Ah, the way you've described it all —the canary, the First Communion with tears in the arms of the abbé, and then a year or so later he finds out about his mother and the curate. . . . Oh, *mon cher,* the problems facing a child are really frightening in our day. . . . First, for a while these innocent little faces framed by their golden curls look at you with their innocent eyes and radiant smiles—they're just like God's angels or beautiful birds. . . . But later . . . later it may turn out that it would have been better if they'd never grown up."

"You sound quite mawkish, Prince; one would think that you had small children yourself, although you have none now and never will have."

"*Tiens,* what a coincidence!" His expression changed suddenly and completely. "You know, just the day before yesterday, Alexandra, he-he-he, Alexandra Sinitsky I mean—you must've met her here three weeks ago—well, when I remarked jokingly that if I did get married now, there was one thing at least I wouldn't have to worry about—having children, that somehow seemed to irritate her. 'On the contrary,' she said with a strange spite, '*you* are sure to have children; men like you *always* do, within the very first year, mark my word.' He-he-he! For some reason they all expect that I'll suddenly up and marry. Well, even if it wasn't a nice thing to say, it was quite witty, wasn't it?"

"Yes, witty and offensive."

"Come now, *mon cher enfant,* one can't take offense with everybody. What I most appreciate in people is wit; it seems to be on its way to extinction. But as to what Mrs. Sinitsky may say or think, how could that possibly offend me?"

"How was it, how did you put it?" I said, trying to remember his words. "Ah yes, 'one can't take offense with everybody,' yes, that's it! Not everybody is worth being taken notice of. An excellent rule! Just the rule I need! I'll write it down. You know, Prince, sometimes you say the most delightful things."

He beamed all over.

"*N'est-ce pas, cher enfant?* True wit is becoming extinct, it's becoming rarer and rarer. . . . *Eh bien, moi qui connais les femmes* . . . believe me, whatever she may say or preach, the life of every woman is a perpetual search for someone to submit to. . . . It may be described as a thirst for submission. And, mind you, there are no exceptions."

"Marvelous! You're absolutely right!"

I felt elated. At other times we would have gone on to philosophize on that subject for an hour or so, but now it was as if something had suddenly stung me and I turned crimson, my face, neck, all over. I thought that, by hearing me praise his *bons mots,* he would imagine that I was trying to soften him up before asking him for my salary. I wish to make clear now how I felt at that moment.

"Prince, I request that you immediately pay me the fifty rubles you owe me for one month of my services," I blurted out all in one breath and with an irritation verging on rudeness.

I remember the disgusting scene that followed in every realistic detail, as I remember everything that happened that morning. At first he didn't understand and kept staring at me blankly —he didn't know what money I was talking about. Evidently he had no idea that I was to be paid a salary, and, indeed, one may wonder what I could possibly be paid for. It's true that when he recovered, he tried to assure me that he had simply forgotten about it and, very red-faced, started fishing bills out of his pocket. I realized everything now. I stood up and said cuttingly that, under these circumstances, I could not accept any money from him, that I'd probably been either deliberately or unintentionally led to believe by my family that a salary was to be paid to me so that I wouldn't turn the job down at once; however, I appreciated perfectly well now that no salary should be forthcoming since I had done nothing here to earn it. The prince became very agitated and tried to convince me that I had been rendering him incredibly important services, that he needed me to render him even more important ones, indeed, that fifty rubles was nowhere near enough to pay for them, that he planned to give me a raise because he felt he owed it to me, that he himself had made the original arrangements with Mrs. Prutkov, but that they had completely slipped his mind, oh, quite unforgivably. I felt the blood rushing to my head and declared with finality that I'd feel it degrading to be paid a salary for telling him bits of gossip like the one about my following the two train-dragging ladies for miles, that when I was hired I was under the impression that my duties would not be those of a court jester but to attend to serious business and that since there was no business to attend to, we must put an end to this, and so on and so forth. But I never imagined that what I said could cause him to look so terrified. It goes without saying that, in the end, he managed to slip me those fifty rubles and I dropped my objections to staying in his employ. I blush to this day every time I remember accepting those fifty rubles! Everything in the world seems to end in some disgraceful compromise and what I feel most humiliating is that he almost managed to convince me then that I had an indisputable right to the money, and I was stupid enough to believe him. Besides, I couldn't really refuse—it was somehow quite out of the question.

"*Cher, cher enfant!*" he kept hugging me with tears rolling down his cheeks. (I must admit that, for some idiotic reason, I came awfully close to weeping myself, but immediately checked it, which does not prevent me from blushing as I write this.) "My dear friend," he said, "to me, you're one of the family now; in this single month you've reached very, very deep into my heart. In society there's nothing but cold glamor. My daughter Katerina is a brilliant woman, and I'm proud of her . . . but very, very often, my dear boy, yes, very often, she hurts me. As to those girls—*elles sont charmantes!*—and their mothers who visit me on my birthdays, why, they just sit around with their embroidery and have nothing to say. I have received enough embroidery from them to cover a good sixty cushions with nothing but dogs and deer! I am indeed very fond of them, but with you it's different: I feel at home with you, as with a son, or rather a brother. I like it very much when you disagree with me; you have a literary bent, you've read a lot and you know how to be enthusiastic about things."

"I've read practically nothing and I certainly have no literary bent. Once I used to read whatever happened to be lying around, but in the past two years I've read nothing and I'm not planning to read anything."

"Why won't you read?"

"I have other things on my mind."

"*Cher* . . . it's a shame. Perhaps one day, late in life, you'll say to yourself as I do now: *je sais tout mais je ne sais rien de bon.* I have no idea really why I have lived. . . . But I am so indebted to you. I even wanted . . ."

He suddenly broke off; a look of despondency crept over him and he looked dreamily into the air. After every violent emotion (and he could be moved violently at any moment by anything), he seemed to lose temporarily his grasp of things. But that never lasted long and thus caused him no real inconvenience.

For a minute or so we sat in silence. His lower lip, which was very full, hung down. . . . What had surprised me most was that he had suddenly spoken to me of his daughter, and so frankly too. I ascribed it, of course, to his wound-up, nervous state.

"*Cher enfant*, I hope you don't mind if I address you rather familiarly, as if you were still a very young man, or do you?"

"Not in the least, although I might as well admit that at the beginning I was rather taken aback and was on the point of answering you in the same vein. But I realized how stupid that would be on my part because I felt sure you weren't trying to humiliate me by talking to me like that."

But he was no longer listening. Suddenly he fixed his dreamy eyes on me and said:

"How's your father?"

That made me wince: it was the first time he had ever mentioned Versilov to me directly, and furthermore he referred to him as my father, which a man like him would hardly ever allow himself to do.

"He sits at home without money and broods," I answered curtly, burning with curiosity.

"Speaking of money, by the way . . . that lawsuit he's involved in is going to be heard before the judge today. And I'm expecting a visit today from Sergei, you know, one of the Moscow Sokolskys. He promised to come here straight from the courtroom. I wonder how it will go? Their whole fate is at stake really—it's a matter of sixty or eighty thousand rubles. Of course, I've always wished Andrei—I mean Versilov—well and it looks to me as if he'll get everything while the Moscow Princes Sokolsky will get nothing. Well, that's justice for you!"

"So the case is going to be heard today, is it!" I cried in amazement.

The thought that Versilov hadn't bothered to tell me this struck me as very strange, and I immediately thought: "If he didn't tell me, he may very well not have told Mother either. What a character he is!" And then I remembered something else that might be connected with this business.

"Did you say that Prince Sergei Sokolsky is in Petersburg now?"

"He came in yesterday. Directly from Berlin. He made it his business to be in court on the date set."

A very important piece of news too: the man who had slapped *him* would be in this house today!

"Well, why not, I suppose," the prince said, and his entire face again underwent one of those radical changes, to inappropriate playfulness this time. "He'll be preaching about God just as he did before and . . . and I expect he'll be chasing little girls again, the still featherless chicks. . . . He-he-he! In fact, there may be something very piquant afoot right now, something that would make a pretty little anecdote some day, I'm sure. . . ."

"Who's preaching? Who's chasing little girls?"

"Why, Andrei, of course. I wish you'd heard him in those days when he kept cornering everyone and asking them such things as 'What do you eat?' 'What do you think about?' He'd scare people, and chasten them. 'If you're religious,' he'd tell them, 'why aren't you a monk?' He sort of demanded it of everybody. *Mais quelle idée!* Supposing he was right, wasn't he too demanding? And I was his favorite target: he really enjoyed terrorizing me with Judgment Day."

"I've never noticed anything of the sort in him and I've been living in his house for a month now," I said impatiently, very annoyed at his disconnected way of talking, which was, I suppose, the result of his emotional outburst.

"Well, he may not be talking like that now, but you must believe me that he used to. He is a man of acute intelligence—no doubt about that—and he's very learned too. I'm not sure, however, whether his intelligence is really . . . really sound. He became that way after he had lived abroad for three years. I admit I was very shocked . . . everybody was. . . . *Cher enfant, j'aime le bon Dieu.* I believe in Him, I do my best to believe, but on one occasion I just blew up. I suppose I worded what I said rather flippantly, but I did so by choice, to show my annoyance; nevertheless, the essence of what I said is just as valid and serious today as it has been since the creation of the world. 'Assuming that a Supreme Being exists,' I said to Versilov, 'and exists as a personal entity, not in the form of some diffused creative spirit, a sort of fluid or something (for that would be even harder to imagine), well, if so, where does He reside?' I realize that this may sound stupid, my friend, but all the discussion boils down to that—*un domicile*—it's a very important matter. He was furious. He'd been converted to Catholicism while abroad."

"I've heard that already. I'm sure it's utter nonsense."

"I swear to you by everything that's sacred that it's true. Look at him closely. I know he may have changed, as you told me. But you should've been around when he made everyone's life so miserable. He behaved as if he were a saint whose relics would work miracles. He demanded that we account to him for our behavior, I swear! Talk of relics! *En voilà une idée!* I suppose it would still be possible for some monk or a hermit to make a claim about his relics, but here was a man walking around in his town clothes—and there were all those other things we knew about him—and all of a sudden he starts talking about his relics and sets himself up as a saint! It's quite a strange aspiration for a gentleman from good society and, I must say, quite a strange taste. Well, I cannot speak with final authority, of course; obviously when it comes to sainthood, anything may happen. . . . Besides, all that is *de l'inconnu*, but I do think it was quite improper for a gentleman. If I ever found myself in that position, I mean if I were offered . . . well, I swear I'd reject it. Just imagine me going to dine at my club today and the next thing you know I suddenly make an appearance as a saint with a halo. . . . I'd only make everybody laugh—oh, I can see it now! Well, I told him all that at the time. And, you know, he used to wear chains."

My indignation made me turn beet red.

"And you saw those chains yourself, did you?"

"I didn't see them myself, but . . ."

"In that case, let me tell you that it's all lies and vicious slander spread by his enemies, or rather one single enemy, the worst and the cruelest, because he only has one enemy—your daughter!"

It was the old prince's turn to flare up.

"Listen, *mon cher*, I must ask you—and on this point I must insist—never again to associate the name of my daughter with this sordid story."

I got up. He was beside himself. His chin was quivering.

"*Cette histoire infame!* I didn't want to believe it was true, I never wanted to believe it but . . . they tell me 'believe, it's true, believe,' I . . ."

At that moment the butler came in and announced visitors. I lowered myself back into my chair.

IV

Two young ladies walked in. One was a stepdaughter of a cousin of the old prince's late wife or something like that, in any case a protégée of his for whom he had already set aside a dowry, although she had money herself (I mention this here for future reference). The other young lady was my half-sister Anna Andreyevna Versilov, my senior by three years, who lived with her brother at Mrs. Fanariotov's. I'd seen her only once before, very fleetingly in the street, although I had already had a brief clash with her brother in Moscow, which I may describe later if there's room since it's really quite unimportant. Anna Versilov had been, since her early childhood, the old prince's favorite (for the prince and Versilov had known each other an awfully long time).

I was so intimidated by them that I forgot to stand up when they came in, but the old prince did so, in fact he rushed to meet them. After that, I decided it was too late to get up and so remained seated. I must say I was quite perplexed by my situation at that moment, since a minute earlier the prince had raised his voice at me and I was hesitating whether to walk out or not. But the old man had by now forgotten all about that and was beaming with joy and delight, as he always did in the presence of pretty young girls. His face had changed with the usual speed. Indeed, he was now winking mysteriously at me and even managed to mumble quickly under his breath:

"Look at Olympiada, look closely, watch her. . . . I'll tell you why later."

I gave her a look that I thought was close enough and saw nothing particularly interesting: she was not very tall, rather plump, and her cheeks were a very bright red. I must say that it was a rather pleasant face on the whole, especially pleasing to materialists, I suppose. Her expression was amiable enough but with a furrow of reservation. She didn't look like a person of particular intellectual endowment—that is, not in the higher sense—but she was obviously quite shrewd, as could be seen from her eyes. She was no more than nineteen. At school, such a girl might have been nicknamed "cushion." In a word, there was nothing particularly remarkable about her, and if I've bothered to describe her at such length it's because I think it will be useful later. In fact, everything that I've been describing in such seemingly unnecessary detail will be understood at the proper time. I don't know how to avoid mentioning things in advance. In any case, if you find it makes dull reading, don't read it.

Versilov's daughter was quite a different matter. She was tall, rather on the slender side, with an oval and strikingly pale face framed by luxuriant black hair; her expression was not particularly friendly but very dignified; her age, twenty-two. It would be hard to pick out any one feature and say that it resembled Versilov's, although, as if by miracle, her over-all facial expression bore a striking resemblance to his. It would be hard for me to say whether she was beautiful. I suppose that's a matter of taste.

Both girls were dressed modestly so there's no need for me to go into that. I was expecting Anna Versilov to make some sort of scornful gesture or to give me a humiliating look, as her

brother did in Moscow the moment we met. Although she didn't
know me by sight, she knew I had that job with the old prince.
Whatever the prince did or planned to do immediately became
a matter of great concern to the crowd of relatives and other
people who were "waiting." . . . Everything was important and
was discussed, especially his sudden liking for me. I know from
most reliable sources that the prince was extremely anxious to
assure Anna a happy future and was looking around for a bridegroom for her. But it was much more difficult to find a young
man for Miss Versilov than for the young ladies who did embroidery.

Contrary to all my expectations, Anna Versilov, after having
greeted the prince and exchanged a few light conventional remarks with him, looked at me with marked curiosity. Since I
had been staring at her all that time, she suddenly smiled and
gave me a friendly little bow. It's true that, since she'd just
walked in, there was nothing so extraordinary about her acknowledging the presence of someone already in the room. But
her smile was so warm and friendly that it was obvious she had
planned it that way. Still, I remember very clearly the pleasant
feeling it gave me.

When the prince saw her smile to me, he started introducing
us.

"You've already met, haven't you? This is my very dear
young friend Arkady Versi—" He stopped short, perhaps feeling
uncomfortable at introducing us since we were actually brother
and sister.

The "cushion" bowed to me too, but I suddenly lost my temper, jumped to my feet, and allowed myself to be overwhelmed
by a wave of false pride, utterly senseless, due to my morbid
vanity.

"Excuse me, Prince, you made a mistake—my name is not
Arkady Versilov, but Arkady Dolgoruky," I rasped unpleasantly,
completely forgetting that it was my turn now to bow to the
ladies.

Oh, I wish to God this disgraceful moment could be oblit-
erated from my past.

"*Mais—tiens!*" the prince almost cried out, tapping his forehead with one finger.

"Where did you go to school?" I heard close to my ear the
silly, drawn-out question of the girl who had planted herself
next to me.

"I went to a Moscow high school."

"Really? I understand that Moscow high schools are very good."

"Yes, very good."

I stood there answering the way a soldier on parade ground would answer an officer.

The questions that girl asked me were certainly none too imaginative, but they were helpful in distracting attention from my stupid outburst and alleviating the embarrassment of the prince, who by now was listening with a childlike smile to something cheerful that Anna was whispering into his ear and which, I'm sure, had nothing to do with me. What puzzled me, though, is why a girl totally unknown to me should try so hard to redeem my stupid blunder. On the other hand, it was quite inconceivable that she should ask me all those questions for nothing; there was obvious deliberation in her behavior. She looked at me with a curiosity that seemed to me excessive, and she obviously would have liked me to take as much note as possible of her existence. I gave all this quite a bit of thought later and, as it turned out, my conclusions were correct.

"What, today?" the prince suddenly shouted, leaping to his feet.

"Didn't you know?" Anna asked in surprise. "Listen, Olympe, the prince had no idea that Mrs. Akhmakov was due to arrive today. Actually, we came to see her, we were certain that she'd have come on the morning train and have been here for some time. Our carriages drove up to your gate at the same time. Her train had just come in, she said; she asked us to come to your study and promised to join us as soon as she was ready. . . . Here she is—look!"

A side door opened and *that woman* appeared.

I already knew her face from the amazing portrait that hung in the prince's study, a portrait I had been studying all that month. During the three minutes that I was in her presence in the study, I never took my eyes off her face. But if I hadn't been so familiar with her portrait beforehand and if, after those three minutes, I'd been asked what she was like, I wouldn't have known what to say because everything became blurred before my eyes.

Of those three minutes I only remember the presence of an *absolutely* beautiful woman, whom the old prince hugged and kissed while making the sign of the cross over her, and who, almost from the moment she entered, quickly looked around the room and then fixed her eyes on me. I clearly heard the prince, apparently making a gesture toward me, murmur something about his "new secretary" and pronounce my name. She abruptly threw back her head and I received the full blast of her hostility; then suddenly a scornful smile flashed across her face. I took a few steps toward them and, when I was close enough to the old prince, trembling horribly, I started mumbling without being able to finish a single sentence.

"You understand . . . I have things I must . . . I must go and attend . . ."

I turned my back on them and walked out of the room. No one said a word, not even the prince. They all just stared at me. Later the prince told me that I'd turned so pale that he'd been very frightened.

But there was really no need for him to worry.

Chapter 3

I

Indeed, there was no need for him to worry about me: a more important consideration that gave me a strong feeling of satisfaction easily made up for all these minor unpleasantnesses. I left the room in a strange state of exaltation. I felt like singing aloud when I stepped out into the street. It so happened that the morning was glorious too, a sunny day with many people around, lots of noise, lots of movement, everything cheerful. . . . But how could I not have been offended by the way that woman had treated me? From whom else would I have endured that look and that scornful smile without immediately protesting even in the most absurd way? Before she'd set eyes on me, she'd planned to insult me because she thought I was Versilov's stooge. Also, she was convinced at that time and for a long time afterward that Versilov had her at his mercy and could ruin her by using a certain document. It was, she felt, a struggle to the death. And yet I didn't feel offended! Oh, there certainly was offense, but offended I didn't feel. Far from it—although I'd arrived prepared to hate, I now felt, if anything, ready to love.

Can a spider hate the fly he's preparing to snare? The sweet little fly? I think we like our prey, or at least it's quite possible to like them. I, for one, I like my enemy: I'm delighted to find she's so beautiful. I'm absolutely enchanted, madam, that you are so regal and haughty, and if you were humbler, it would take away much of my pleasure. You have spat in my eye and I feel elated. Indeed, if you'd actually spat real spittle into my face, I honestly believe I wouldn't have resented it for the good reason that you are not *his* prey you are *my* prey! An intoxicating thought! No, the secret realization of one's power is incomparably more enjoyable than overt domination. If I were a millionaire a hundred times over, I think I'd enjoy walking around in a ragged old coat and being taken for destitute, for someone reduced to begging, being despised and pushed around, because the knowledge of what I really was would be enough for me.

This is how I can best convey the way I felt at that moment and explain my elation. I'd like to add, though, that the way I described it makes it all sound rather flippant, whereas in fact it was a much deeper feeling and not at all so smug. Well, perhaps I'm less smug deep down than may appear from what I say and do. I wish to God that were so!

Perhaps I was completely wrong when I decided to write this: there's so much more left inside me beyond what comes out in words. A thought, even a bad thought, is always deeper when it's still inside you; when you put it into words, it may sound dishonest and preposterous. Versilov told me that with bad people it's just the reverse: they always lie and it's easy for them. But I'm trying to write down the whole truth and it's awfully hard!

II

On that September 19 I took yet another step.

For the first time since my arrival I had money in my pocket (as I mentioned before, I'd given my mother the sixty rubles representing my two years' savings). A few days before I received my pay, I'd decided to make the "experiment" of which I'd been dreaming for so long. The day before I had cut out of the paper an address given in an advertisement announcing that the effects of one Mrs. Lebrecht would be on sale under the supervision of the clerk of the municipal court of the Kazan Precinct in Petersburg on September 19 and that the goods could be inspected on that day at such and such address.

It was just after one. I hurried over to the address. I went on foot, for I hadn't taken a cab for more than two years. I had promised myself not to and that's how I'd managed to save money in Moscow. I'd never been to an auction before, I'd never *allowed* myself to go to one. And although my present step was only a *trial* move, I felt that, to take it, I should first graduate from high school, break off relations with everyone, retire into my shell, and thus be completely independent. It's true that I was nowhere near being enclosed in a shell or, for that matter, independent, but then the step I was going to take was just an experiment to try to get the feel of it, to indulge in a bit of fancy, and then I'd stay away from it, perhaps until the day when I'd be able to get down to it in earnest. To everyone else this was just a silly little auction, but to me it was the first rib of the ship that Columbus would sail to discover America. That's how I felt then.

I arrived at the address, entered the yard, and, following the instructions in the advertisement, found Mrs. Lebrecht's apartment. It consisted of an entry and four low-ceilinged rooms. The first room after the entry was packed with people, perhaps as many as thirty persons, half of whom were busy bargaining while the rest looked like auction lovers, Mrs. Lebrecht's representatives, and just plain curious passers-by. There were a few merchants, some Jews eying gold items, and a few members of the well-dressed class. Some of all those faces remain engraved in my memory. In the doorway leading to the room on the right was a table which barred access to that room: the items listed for sale lay on that table. The door leading to the room on the left was closed, although someone inside kept opening it a crack and peeping out, probably a member of Mrs. Lebrecht's numerous family, who naturally enough must have felt very embarrassed by the proceedings. At the table in the doorway sat a man who, judging by his badge, must have been a court official, and he conducted the auction.

When I arrived, the auction was half over. I immediately elbowed my way to the table. They were selling some bronze candlesticks. I took a good look around. And as I was looking, I asked myself what could I possibly buy there. What in the world would I do with bronze candlesticks, for instance. How would they serve my purpose? Was this the right way of going about it? Was my plan correct or just a childish notion? I thought all this and waited. I was like a gambler who intends to place a stake but, before doing it, feels: "If I want to, I'll put it down; if I want to, I can walk out. It's all in my hands." The heart does not pound wildly yet; it simply slows down a bit and then throbs slightly—a sensation that may be quite pleasurable. But soon indecision starts weighing on you and somehow you become blind. You stretch your hand out toward the card, but you do it mechanically, reluctantly perhaps, as if someone else were guiding it for you. And finally you have made up your mind and put down your stake. Now that's a completely different sensation—a tremendous one. . . .

What I've written here is not about auction sales in general;

rather it's about myself, for who else's heart can be expected to pound wildly at an auction?

Some people were chatting excitedly; others were waiting in silence for their opportunity; still others had done their bidding, won, and now were sorry they had. I was not in the least sorry for a gentleman who had bought a nickel-plated milk jug thinking it was silver and who had paid five rubles for it instead of the original bid of three. Indeed, I found it very funny. The clerk, whether to avoid monotony or to comply with the demands of customers, put up the items for sale in a most unpredictable order: after the candlesticks, he offered earrings; after the earrings, an embroidered red leather cushion; then a money box. It was hard for me to remain passive for more than ten minutes. I almost bid for the cushion and then for the money box but stopped myself at the last second: these items seemed to me quite impossible. At last the clerk held up an album:

"A family album in real morocco, very slightly worn. Contains watercolor and pastel drawings. Sold with its carved ivory case, locked by silver clasps, price—two rubles."

I stepped right up to the table: it was quite pretty, although the carving of the case was damaged in one spot. I was the only one to step up and examine it. There was no bidding. I could have undone the clasps, taken the album out of the case, and leafed through it. But I didn't use my privilege. I simply waved my hand, which was trembling now, in a gesture of "never mind."

"Two rubles, five kopeks," I said.

I believe my teeth were chattering.

I got the album. I immediately took out the money, paid for it, and retired to a corner of the room. There, I took it out of the case and examined it in feverish haste. Out of its case, the album was probably as worthless a thing as there can be: it was the size of small notepaper, a thin booklet with rubbed gilt edges, the type of album that in olden days girls used to get upon leaving finishing school. It contained crayon and watercolor sketches of temples on mountain sides, of cupids, of a lake with swans on it, and also some verses such as:

> 'By Moscow! I must tear myself away
> From those I love in so many a way
> Now post-horses will, in endless relay,
> Drive me to Crimea for many a day.

I don't know how these lines managed to stay in my memory. Well, I decided, I'd made a fool of myself: if there was someone who certainly didn't need something, it was me and that album.

"Never mind," I said to myself, "one must lose the first time; it's even a good sign."

I was definitely having fun.

"Oh, damn it . . . I see you have it." I suddenly heard next to me the voice of a distinguished-looking gentleman in a blue overcoat. "I've missed it," he went on. "What a shame! How much did you have to pay for it?"

"Two rubles, five."

"Ah, what a shame. But would you consider selling it?"

"Let's step outside," I whispered to him as my heart missed a beat.

When we were on the landing I said, feeling a cold shiver running down my back: "You can have it for ten."

"Ten! Good Lord, what are you talking about!"

"Please yourself."

He stared at me. I was dressed properly, not at all the way one imagines a secondhand dealer or a Jewish speculator.

"But listen, this is a wretched old album of no use to anyone. And the case is really valueless too; you'll never find anyone to buy it either."

"You're trying to buy it, aren't you?"

"Yes, but I have special reasons. I learned about it only yesterday. . . . And then I'm the only person in the world who'd buy it. No, you're not being reasonable."

"I should've asked you for twenty-five rubles really. I only asked for ten to make sure that you wouldn't give up at once. I won't make it one kopek less."

I turned and started to walk away.

"All right, I'll give you four," he said, catching up with me when I was already in the yard. "All right, you can have five."

I said nothing and kept walking.

"All right, here!"

He produced a ten-ruble bill and I handed him the album.

"But you must admit it's not fair—you bought it for two and sold it for ten."

"Why unfair? It's a free market."

"Some free market!" he said, his anger rising.

"Wherever there's demand, there's a market. If you hadn't asked me to sell you that album, I'd have sold it for forty kopeks."

Although I looked serious, inwardly I was rolling with laughter. But it was not joy that caused my inward laughter, it was something else, I don't know exactly what. I felt rather breathless too. Then, suddenly feeling a great liking for this man, I couldn't resist and spoke to him very warmly:

"Listen," I said, "when the late lamented James Rothschild* —the Paris one, you know, the one who left seven hundred million francs"—he nodded—"heard of the assassination of the Duc de Berry† a few hours before anyone else, he informed certain interested persons and by doing so earned several millions in a few seconds. So you see, that's how some people operate!"

"So what do you think you are, a Rothschild?" he shouted at me indignantly, probably deciding I was some sort of fool.

I walked quickly out of the yard. One step and I'd made seven rubles and ninety-five kopeks. And although I realized that this "first step" couldn't be considered very meaningful, that it was more like a schoolboy prank, I couldn't help being terribly excited because what happened seemed to fit in quite well with my general idea. . . . But why bother analyzing feelings? The ten-ruble bill was in my vest pocket. I thrust two fingers into my pocket to make sure the bill was there and then walked on without taking my fingers out. I walked like that for a hundred yards or so along the street, then took the bill out, looked at it, and felt like kissing it.

At that moment, I heard a carriage rumble by me and then stop by the gate of a house. The house porter opened the door and a lady emerged from the house and started to get into the carriage. She was young, imposing, opulent, all silk and velvet, and dragging a two-yard train. Suddenly I saw a pretty little handbag slip out of her hand and drop on the ground. She got into her carriage and the footman started to stoop down and pick up her handbag. But I rushed up, snatched the bag before the man could touch it, and presented it to the lady, taking off my hat—a top hat, by the way, as I was a rather well-dressed young man. The lady gave me a pleasant, albeit reserved, smile and said: *"Merci, monsieur,"* and the carriage rattled off.

Then I kissed the ten-ruble bill.

* James Rothschild (1792–1868), the Paris financier. Rothschild did not make "millions" by passing on the information about the assassination of the Duc de Berry but rather by being the first to learn about Napoleon's defeat at Waterloo in 1815 and speculating accordingly. [A. MacA.]

† Duc de Berry (1778–1820), second son of Charles X, the heir to the throne, who emigrated with his father in 1789 and returned to France after the Restoration of 1814. He was assassinated outside a Paris theater on February 13, 1820. [A. MacA.]

III

That same day I was to see Efim Zverev, with whom I'd gone to high school and who was now studying at a technical college in Petersburg. He himself is not worth describing and I'd never been a particular friend of his, although I had gone to considerable trouble to trace him in Petersburg. It so happened—I don't think there's any point in explaining how it happened—that he would know the address of one Kraft, whom it was very important for me to contact as soon as he arrived from Vilno. Zverev expected Kraft to arrive either that day or the following one and had sent me a note to that effect. I had to cross all the way to the Petersburg Side, but I didn't feel in the least tired.

I found Zverev, who was about nineteen like me, in the yard of the house of the aunt with whom he lived. He had just finished his dinner and was walking about the yard on stilts. He informed me at once that Kraft had actually arrived the night before, that he lived in the same district not far away, and that he was very anxious to see me because he had an important message for me.

"He's going off somewhere again," Zverev said.

Under these circumstances I had to see Kraft right away and I asked Zverev to take me to his place, which was only a couple of blocks away in a little side street. Zverev, however, told me that Kraft was out because he'd met him about an hour earlier on his way to see Dergachev.

"So let's go to Dergachev's. What's the matter with you, is there something that frightens you?" he said.

I wasn't really scared to go to Dergachev's, but I was rather reluctant, and Zverev had twice before tried to drag me there. But what choice did I have? If Kraft spent hours at Dergachev's, I didn't know where I could possibly wait for him. Zverev had a nasty scornful smile as he asked me whether "something frightened" me there. I must state here and now that it was not a matter of cowardice, that I was really apprehensive of something quite different. But this time I decided to go. Besides, it was also very close by. As we were walking there, I asked Zverev whether he still intended to run away to America.‡

‡ "Running away to America" was a very fashionable idea among the young Russians of the 1860s. There were many articles on American life and mores in various Russian magazines of the period and Dostoevsky used some of this material in *The Possessed* (Shatov and Kirilov in the U.S.A.). [A. MacA.]

"I may have to wait a little while," he answered with a chuckle.

I didn't like him very much, didn't like him at all, in fact. His hair was really too white and his face was round and also too white, indecently so, and his skin was like that of a small child. And although he was taller than me, one would never have given him more than seventeen. There was nothing much one could talk to him about either.

"What's going on there? Is there a whole crowd meeting or something?" I inquired to get some idea.

"I see you're still scared," he said and laughed again.

"The hell with you," I said angrily.

"There's no crowd there. There's nobody we don't know—they're all friends. Relax."

"Why should I give a damn whether they're your friends or not? What about me? What makes you think I'm one of you? Why should they trust me?"

"The fact that I'm bringing you is enough. Anyway, they've already heard of you. Besides, Kraft can vouch for you too."

"Tell me, will Vasin be there?"

"I don't know."

"If he's there, I want you to nudge me and point him out as soon as we get in, do you understand?"

I'd heard a lot about Vasin before and was curious about him.

Dergachev occupied the whole cottage in the yard of a wooden house belonging to a merchant's wife; the cottage had three rooms and in all of them the blinds were drawn. He was an engineer and was now employed in Petersburg. But I understand that he had been offered a very lucrative job with a private firm in the provinces and that he had decided to accept it and would leave soon.

As we went in the tiny entry, I heard loud voices arguing about something, with one voice shouting:

"*Quae medicamenta non sanant—ferrum sanat, quae ferrum non sanat—ignis sanat!*"*

It's true that I did feel rather uneasy. Of course, I was in general unaccustomed to the company of people, whoever they were. Even at school, I had to overcome disgust and force myself to chat familiarly with my classmates and I certainly never became really close with any of them. I built myself a shell

---

* A Latin translation of Hippocrates' Greek motto (What medicine cannot cure, iron will cure; what iron cannot cure, fire will cure) was found in Dolgushin's (Dergachev in *The Adolescent*) summer house where his subversive tracts were printed. [A. MacA.]

and stayed inside it. But that was not what was bothering me right now. To be on the safe side, I decided to stay out of arguments, to say as little as possible, so that no one could say anything about me, but, above all, not to get involved in the discussion.

There were seven men and three women in a room that seemed rather small for ten people. Dergachev was twenty-five and he was married. His wife had a sister and another relative who were living with them. The room was furnished in a haphazard way, adequately, though, and looked quite clean. There was a lithographed portrait on the wall, but a very cheap one. In a corner there was an icon without a setting, but the lamp before it was lighted. Dergachev came over to me and shook my hand:

"Please sit down, we're all friends here."

"Please do," said a rather pleasant-looking, simply dressed young woman, nodding slightly in my direction, whereupon she immediately walked out of the room. This was Mrs. Dergachev and I got the impression that she had been engaged in an argument but now had to go and feed a baby.

Of the two women remaining in the room, one, about twenty, was very small, wore a black dress, and was not bad-looking, while the other one was a thin, sharp-eyed, thirty-year-old lady. These two sat listening intently to the men talk without taking part in the discussion.

All of the men, except for Kraft, Vasin, and myself, were on their feet. Zverev had identified them for me because I had never set eyes on any of them, including Kraft. I got up and went over to Kraft to make his acquaintance. I'll never forget his face. Not that there was anything particularly handsome about it, but it was truly extraordinary how that face was free of the slightest suspicion of wickedness, how considerate his expression was, although at the same time there was a remarkable dignity about every one of his gestures. He was about twenty-six, spare, blond, above average in height, with a serious and at the same time gentle look. Everything about him was very quiet. But if I'd been given the opportunity of exchanging my face, which some people might find pretty commonplace, for Kraft's strikingly attractive one, I wouldn't have accepted because his was somehow too serene in the moral sense, reflecting perhaps a sort of secret, unconscious self-satisfaction. But, of course, that can't be exactly the way I felt then; I couldn't possibly have analyzed it like that; it's only now that I like to think of myself understanding him, now that I have the advantage of hindsight.

"I'm so glad you came," Kraft said. "I have a letter that concerns you. Let's stay here for a while and then perhaps you could come to my place."

Dergachev was a dark-haired, bearded man of average height, powerfully built, and broad-shouldered. His eye was quick, his behavior reserved, and he seemed to be constantly on guard. Although he probably said less than the others, it was obvious that it was he who directed the conversation.

Vasin's face didn't really strike me particularly, although he had the reputation of being a remarkably intelligent man. His hair was fair; his light gray eyes were large; his face seemed very open, although I felt that there was also something needlessly hard about it. One could guess that he was not a very communicative man, but I thought he did look extraordinarily intelligent, more intelligent than Dergachev, with a deeper and more penetrating intelligence than that of any person in the room.

Besides these three, I can only remember two faces, one belonging to a tall twenty-seven-year-old man with black sideburns, a teacher or something, who spoke with great volubility, and a young fellow, my age perhaps, with a peculiar frown, who wore a Russian peasant's coat and mostly listened, saying little. And, as it turned out, he did come from a family of peasants.

"No, that's not the way to present the problem," the teacher with black sideburns said, picking up what seemed to be an interrupted argument that excited him more than anyone else. "I don't want to talk about mathematical proof because I'm willing to accept this idea without mathematical proof. . . ."

"Wait a minute, Tikhomirov," Dergachev interrupted him loudly, "the people who've just arrived can't understand what this is all about." Then he turned toward me—if his intention was to test a newcomer and force me to talk, it was a clever maneuver, but I realized it and was prepared—and went on: "You see, Mr. Kraft here, whom we all know well and for whose character and steadfastness we have the highest regard, has, from a very ordinary premise, drawn an extraordinary conclusion that surprised us all a great deal: namely, that the Russians are a second-rate people . . ."

"Third-rate," someone shouted.

" . . . second-rate people whose destiny is to serve only as raw material for a nobler race rather than to have an independent role in the destiny of mankind. Mr. Kraft says further that every Russian who accepts this perhaps legitimate conclusion will give up all effort, that is, throw up his arms in despair and . . ."

"Wait, Dergachev, that's not the way to put it," Tikhomirov interrupted and Dergachev immediately yielded. "Inasmuch as Kraft has done serious research and based his conclusions on physiological data, which he considers as certain as if mathematically demonstrated, and inasmuch as he has devoted two years of his life to this study (for my part, I'd have readily accepted his first conclusion a priori), in view also of Kraft's special interest in the problem and his well-known scrupulousness, I suggest that the fallacy of Kraft's final conclusion is, in its own right, a phenomenon worthy of study. We must first of all decide whether this is just a clinical aberration or an ordinary phenomenon affecting many people. Determining this point is very important for our cause. As to what he says about Russia, I not only readily believe him, but I welcome it heartily because, if it was generally accepted, it would untie many people's hands, emancipating them from the prejudice of patriotism."

"I wasn't thinking of patriotism," Kraft said with apparent effort, obviously finding the whole argument unpleasant.

"I think we can leave patriotism out of it," said Vasin, who had been completely silent until then.

"But why should Kraft's discovery of Russia's secondary role weaken men's aspirations for a universal human cause?" the teacher shouted (he was the only one who shouted; the others talked very quietly). "Let Russia be doomed to being second-rate. People can still strive for something that doesn't concern just Russia. Besides, how could Kraft be a patriot when he has lost faith in Russia?"

"Anyhow he's a German," the same voice was heard again.

"I'm a Russian," Kraft said.

"This is something that has no direct bearing on the question under discussion," Dergachev said to the interrupter.

"Let's try to get beyond your narrow premise," shouted Tikhomirov, who was ignoring what the others said. "If Russia is really the material for nobler nations, what's wrong with being such material? It's still a pretty respectable role. Why shouldn't we broaden the whole problem and content ourselves with that role? Mankind is today on the eve of its regeneration, which, in fact, has already started. The problem facing us now can only be missed by those who are blind. So, if you are disappointed in Russia, forget it and work for the future, still unknown nation that will be built out of all mankind without regard for race. Even without that, Russia was bound to die one day. Even the most gifted nations survive for, say, fifteen hundred years, at best two thousand. The Romans didn't last for even fifteen hundred years and were turned into raw material. Rome hasn't existed for a long time now, but she left behind an idea that became a component part of mankind's future growth. So how can anyone tell a man that there's no point in him doing anything? I can't even visualize a situation where people will have nothing to do! Just work for mankind and stop worrying about the rest. If you look hard enough for what to do, your life won't last long enough for you to do it!"

"We must live according to the laws of nature and of truth," Mrs. Dergachev said from the doorway. The door was open a crack and I could see her standing behind it, holding her baby to her breast, which was now covered. She had followed Tikhomirov's tirade intently.

Kraft listened with a wan smile and finally said with a pained look, sounding absolutely sincere:

"I don't understand how someone whose heart and head are completely committed to an idea can live by anything except that idea."

"But what if it can be demonstrated to you logically, mathematically, that your conclusion is false, that your whole idea is without foundation, that you have no right whatever to take yourself out of the common, useful effort because Russia happens to be doomed to be a second-rate nation, if it is proved to you that beyond your confining horizon there are infinite spaces, that, instead of the narrow concept of patriotism, there is . . ."

"Eh," Kraft sighed quietly, "but I told you that it's not a matter of patriotism."

"There's obviously some misunderstanding here," Vasin suddenly intervened. "The trouble is that Kraft's conviction is not simply based on logic but rather is a logical conclusion transmuted into an emotional belief. People aren't all the same. In some people a logical conclusion may be transformed into the most violent passion, which often gets hold of the entire personality and becomes very difficult to overcome or even to alter. In order to cure such a man, it is necessary to change that emotional creed, which can only be done by replacing it by another creed, equally absorbing. And that's always difficult to achieve, in many cases impossible."

"Wrong!" the argumentative teacher screamed. "Logical reasoning by itself eliminates prejudice. A conclusion based on reason produces a reasonable feeling. Thought is generated by feeling and when it takes hold of a man it, in its turn, forms a new feeling."

"People vary; some change their feelings easily, others with difficulty," Vasin said, seemingly eager to put an end to the discussion, but I was enthusiastic about the point he had made.

"You've put it perfectly, Vasin!" I suddenly heard myself saying. I'd taken the plunge and started talking. "One must substitute new emotional beliefs for the old ones. Four years ago there was a general in Moscow. . . . You see, I didn't really know him, but . . . Well, perhaps there was nothing in him to inspire respect. . . . Besides, the story itself could've been unreasonable but . . . In short, a child of his died or, to be precise, two little girls, one after another, both of scarlet fever. It was as if something had been killed in him: he dragged himself around, so sad, so depressed, that people couldn't even bear to look at him. Well, he died too—it took him six months. . . . There's no doubt that that's what caused him to die. Therefore, we may ask ourselves what could have kept him alive? Answer—a feeling of equal strength. All that had to be done was to dig up the little girls from their graves and give them back to him. That would've been the only thing in that case, I mean doing something drastic like that. So he died. On the other hand, there were so many excellent arguments to convince him to live: that life is transitory, for instance; that we'll all die one day; or one could show him the statistics on how many children die of scarlet fever. . . . That general had been retired . . ."

I stopped, trying to catch my breath. I glanced around me.

"That's got nothing to do with it. . . ." someone declared.

"The example, although not of the same nature as what we were discussing, still presents certain similarities and sheds some light on the question," Vasin said, turning toward me.

IV

I must now confess why I was so enthusiastic about Vasin's theory of ideas transmuted into feelings. At the same time, I'll have to confess something that I'm horribly ashamed of. Yes, I was afraid to go to Dergachev's, but not for the reason that Efim Zverev imagined. I was afraid to go there because even back in Moscow those people frightened me. I knew that they (or others of their kind—it makes no difference) were great at dialectics and would probably make mincemeat out of my "idea." And although I trusted myself completely not to blurt it out to them, they (or others like them) could, without my even hinting at what it was all about, say something that would shake my faith. There were, of course, unanswered questions in "my idea," but I wanted to find the answers myself and not accept them from anybody else. I had even stopped reading books during the previous two years for fear of stumbling upon some passage that disproved my idea, which would be a shattering blow to me. But now Vasin had cleared things up and had allayed my fears in the deepest sense. What was there for me to fear now and what could they do to me with all their dialectic skills? Possibly I was the only one in that room to understand what Vasin actually meant by ideas-turned-into-feelings. Refuting a beautiful idea is not enough, it must be replaced by something equally beautiful; otherwise I'll be unwilling to part with the good feeling the idea gives me and refute in my heart the strongest refutations they may throw at me. And what could they possibly offer me as a substitute for "my idea"? So, thanks to Vasin, I could afford to be more daring. But while I was enthusiastic about Vasin's words, at the same time I was ashamed of myself, feeling that I'd been childish and despicable.

There was something else that caused me to be ashamed of myself. It was not just the contemptible desire to show off how bright I was that had prompted me to let myself go and talk; there was also in me an impulse to "throw myself into people's arms," a longing to be accepted by them, to be taken for somebody nice, to make them want to hug me or something of that sort (I mean all that nauseating stuff). I consider this propensity that I have long suspected within me to be the most loathsome trait I have. I think it developed while I was hiding myself in my corner for so many years, although I'm not sorry about that. I knew I ought to have assumed a more reserved, a sterner attitude in the presence of those people. I was consoled only by the thought that "my idea" was still with me, that the secret had been kept, and that I hadn't betrayed anything. Sometimes I felt cold shivers running down my spine when I imagined myself explaining "the idea" to someone and, having explained it, suddenly realizing that now I had nothing special left, that henceforward I'd be just like all the rest of them, and that I might as well discard the idea altogether. So that is why I kept it so well hidden and why I was afraid of idle talk. But now, at Dergachev's, I had yielded to the first temptation and, even though I hadn't given away my secret, I had indulged in an inexcusable outburst of words, which was disgraceful. What a painful memory! No, I cannot be allowed to live in human so-

ciety; I am as convinced of that as ever; and I'm sure that it will
be as true in forty years as it is today. My idea is my refuge, my
corner. . . .

V

As soon as Vasin had expressed his approval, I felt an irresistible desire to speak.

"I think everyone has the right to his private feelings . . . if
they are based on his convictions . . . and no one has the right
to reproach him for these feelings," I said, addressing myself to
Vasin and, although the words came out clearly and distinctly,
I had the feeling that it was not I who was speaking but that a
strange tongue was moving in my mouth.

"You don't say!" The same sarcastic drawl that had interrupted Dergachev and had shouted at Kraft that he was a German now interrupted me.

To emphasize my scorn for the man who had said that, I ignored his existence and addressed myself to the teacher, as if
making him responsible for the interruption.

"It is my firm belief that I must not judge anyone," I said,
trembling and feeling that I was about to take a plunge.

"What are you being so mysterious about?" came the voice of
the nonentity again.

"Everyone has his own private idea," I said, my eyes fixed on
the teacher, who looked at me in silence with a smile on his face.

"And what's yours?" the nonentity shouted.

"It's a long story. To some extent, my idea is precisely that I
should be left alone. As long as I have a couple of rubles, I
want to live on my own and depend on no one—don't bother—I
know the arguments against it—and do nothing, not even con-
tribute to the great future of the human race, in which Mr.
Kraft was invited to participate. Personal freedom—that is, my
own, sir—is my main concern and beyond that I'm not interested."

I made a mistake: I lost my temper.

"In other words, you're preaching to us the contentment of a
satisfied cow?"

"Why not? Cows offend no one. I owe nothing to anyone; I
pay society taxes for protecting me from being robbed, beaten
up, or killed and nobody has the right to ask me to do more. I
may have some other ideas on that score and if I choose to serve
mankind, I may do so, and perhaps ten times more effectively
than all these preachers, but still I don't want to give anyone the
right to *demand* it of me, as it has been demanded of Mr. Kraft.

I consider myself absolutely free not to lift a finger if I don't feel like it. As to rushing around and crying on people's shoulders out of love for mankind, well, that's only a passing fad. Besides, why must I inevitably love my neighbor in some future society that I'll never know, none of whose members will ever know my name and which will eventually also disintegrate without leaving a trace (time, therefore, is meaningless in this respect), when the earth will turn into an icy rock and float in airless space amidst an infinite number of other such icy rocks? I cannot imagine anything more absurd! And that's what you preach. Explain to me: why must I behave so nobly when nothing is going to last more than a moment?"

"Blah-blah-blah!" the voice shouted.

I'd fired my tirade in anger, irritatedly, pulling out all the stops. I felt I was falling into a deep hole and was hurrying, afraid of being interrupted. I realized only too well that my words were pouring out like water through a sieve, that I was inconsistently skipping from one thought to another. But I was in a hurry to convince them, to beat them at their own game. It was extremely important to me. I had been preparing myself for this moment for three years!

But what was most remarkable of all was that they suddenly fell completely silent and just listened to me.

I was still looking fixedly at the teacher as I spoke.

"Precisely. An exceptionally intelligent man once said that there's nothing more difficult than to answer the question 'Why must one behave honorably?' There are, you see, three kinds of villains in the world: naïve villains, who are convinced that their very villainy is the highest virtue; shamefaced villains, who are ashamed of their villainy but are determined to go on with it to the end; and, finally, just plain villains, the pureblooded villains. I once went to school with a boy called Lambert who, when he was sixteen, told me that, when he inherited the money that was coming to him, his greatest joy would be to feed his dogs on meat and bread while poor children were starving to death or, when the poor had nothing to keep themselves warm with, he would buy up a whole woodstack, have it laid out in a field, and burn it. Well, that's how he felt about it. Now, tell me, what could I have answered that pure-blooded villain if he had asked me why he should behave generously? And this is especially true in our age, in which you have managed to change so many things for the worse. In our society today nothing is clear, gentlemen. Since you deny God and deny saintly self-sacrifice, I want to know what blind, deaf, or dumb force of inertia could make me act against my own interest? You may argue that behaving reasonably in society *is* to my advantage. But what if I consider all your reasonableness unreasonable, what if I find nothing so reasonable about your communal dormitories and phalansteries? What the hell do I care about all that and about the distant future when I have only one life to live here? Let me decide for myself what's to my advantage—it's much more fun that way, if nothing else. Why should I bother my head about what will happen to your mankind a thousand years from now if, according to your own theory, in any case I cannot be rewarded with love, future life, or even gratitude for my services? No, gentlemen, if that's the case, I'd prefer in the most impolite way to live just for myself and let the rest go to hell!"

"A beautiful sentiment!"

"Besides, if I have to, I'm prepared to go to hell with the rest."

"That's even better!"

It was always the same voice. The others were still looking at me in silence, examining me. But then a faint titter from various parts of the room reached my ears. It was quite subdued, but they were all laughing in my face now—all except Vasin and Kraft, that is. The teacher with the black sideburns was also grinning as he stared at me and listened to what I was saying.

"Gentlemen," I said, shivering, "there's nothing in the world that would make me reveal my idea to you. Instead let me ask you: what is there you can say to convince me to follow you? That is, I want to know what convinced you because, since my love for mankind is perhaps ten times greater than yours, I don't even need the same reasons. And you'd better answer me because you've dared to laugh at me. Tell me, how can you prove to me that it will be better when you have things your way? What will you do if my human dignity revolts against your barracks-like world? I've been wanting to meet you, gentlemen, for a long time. You'll have barracks, communal dormitories, *le strict nécessaire,* atheism, communal wives, and no children—that's your final goal, I'm quite aware of it. And it's for that sort of thing, for the small share of your miserable welfare that will be assured me by your rational organization, for a morsel of food and a small heated corner, that you're asking me to sacrifice my individuality! Imagine, my wife might be taken away from me, so how could you appease my individuality so that I wouldn't want to bash in somebody's skull? You may say that by that time I'll have become more reasonable myself. All right, but what will a wife say about such a reasonable husband if she still has any self-respect left? Why, it isn't natural, gentlemen, you ought to be ashamed of yourselves!"

"So you're a specialist in the field of women too!" the nonentity shouted in a tone of triumphant viciousness.

For a second I was about to pounce on him and pound him with my fists. He was a freckled redhead and wasn't too big . . . but who cares what he looked like anyway.

"I've never known a woman yet," I said, facing him for the first time, "so you may reassure yourself, I'm not a specialist."

"A very valuable piece of information which, however, ought to have been imparted to us more discreetly in the presence of ladies."

At that moment there was a general commotion: the men picked up their hats and prepared to leave. This, of course, had nothing to do with me: it was simply time for them to go. However, the silent treatment I had received from them made me feel crushed. I stood up too, when the teacher came over to me and said with a smile:

"You kept looking at me all the time. . . . May I ask you to remind me of your name?"

"Dolgoruky."

"Prince Dolgoruky?"

"No, just plain Dolgoruky, officially the son of a former serf, Makar Dolgoruky, actually the illegitimate son of my former master, Mr. Versilov. And please don't imagine that I've told you all this to make you fall into my arms and have us all cry like calves over this pathetic situation."

A resounding and uninhibited salvo of general laughter greeted my words. It woke the baby next door, who began to cry. I was shaking with rage. In the meantime, one after another they shook Dergachev's hand and left without paying any further attention to me.

"Let's go," Kraft said, giving me a little push.

I walked over to Dergachev, pressed his hand as hard as I could, and shook it violently.

"I'm sorry that Kudryumov kept bothering you," Dergachev said.

Kudryumov was the redhead.

I followed Kraft out. There was nothing I had to be ashamed of.

VI

There's, of course, a tremendous difference between what I am now and what I was then.

Still "having nothing to be ashamed of," I caught up with Vasin as he was going downstairs. I let Kraft get a little way ahead as I considered him of secondary interest. I addressed Vasin in a casual tone as though nothing had happened:

"I believe you know my father . . . Versilov, that is."

"I don't really know him too well," Vasin answered simply and without any of the emphatic politeness that refined people affect toward those who have just disgraced themselves. "I know him a little, though; we've met and I've heard him talk."

"If you've heard him talk, you must know him, you must! Please tell me what you think of him. Forgive me for asking you that point blank, but I need to know very badly. I want to know what *you* think. What I need is your personal opinion."

"That's quite a question you're asking me. I believe he's a man who can set himself gigantic tasks and perhaps can even carry them out but who refuses to account to anyone for anything he does."

"True, very, very true, he's a very proud man. But is he sincere? Tell me, what do you think of his conversion to Catholicism? Although possibly you haven't even heard . . ."

Had I not been in such a state of wild agitation, I certainly would not have fired such a question at a man whom I had never met before, of whom I had only heard. As a matter of fact, I was surprised that Vasin didn't seem to notice my crazy behavior.

"I've heard something to that effect, but I don't know how much truth there is in it," he said in the same calm and quiet voice.

"No truth at all! It's all lies. Could you really think that he would believe in God?"

"It's just as you said yourself—he's a very proud man and many such proud men, especially those who despise people, like to believe in God. Many strong people seem to have a natural tendency to look for something they can adore. Sometimes a strong man finds it very painful to bear his strength."

"I think that's so terribly true!" I cried enthusiastically. "Only I'd like to understand . . ."

"The reason is obvious. They choose God so as not to submit to their fellow men without, of course, acknowledging the underlying reason, namely, that it's less humiliating to submit to

God. Some of these people become ardently religious, or rather thirst ardently for religion. But then they mistake their desire for faith for faith itself, so some of them are bound to be disappointed in the end. As for Mr. Versilov, I believe that there are in his nature certain elements that are extremely sincere. In general, he interests me very much."

"Vasin!" I exclaimed, "you make me so happy! What amazes me most is not even your intelligence but the mere fact that a man of your integrity, a man so infinitely superior to me, can walk next to me and talk to me with such friendly simplicity as if nothing unpleasant had ever happened."

Vasin smiled.

"I think you're praising me a bit too much. As to what happened, it was simply caused by your excessive fondness for abstract discussion. I suppose that until then you must've been silent for a very long time."

"For three years. I've been preparing myself to speak up for three years. . . . I don't expect you took me for an utter fool because you're so exceptionally intelligent yourself. But you may very well have decided that I'm a pig, because it would have been difficult to behave worse than I did."

"A pig?"

"Yes, a pig. Tell me, do you despise me secretly for saying that I'm Versilov's illegitimate son and bragging that I'm officially the son of a serf?"

"You worry too much about these things. If you think you shouldn't have said what you did, don't say it the next time. You've still got a good fifty years ahead of you to correct your mistakes."

"Oh, I know very well that the best thing I can do when there're people around is to keep my mouth shut. The most despicable vice a man can have is to want to throw himself into other people's arms. I just told them that and here I am throwing myself in yours. But there's a difference, isn't there? If you understand that difference, if you are at all able to feel it, I'll bless this minute!"

Vasin smiled again.

"Come and see me sometime if you feel like it," he said. "I'm very busy just now, but I'd be pleased if you came some other day."

"When I first saw you, I decided that your face looked unnecessarily hard and uncommunicative."

"Perhaps you're right. By the way, I met your sister Lisaveta Dolgoruky in Luga last year. . . . Look, Kraft has stopped and seems to be waiting for you, otherwise he would've turned the corner."

I pressed Vasin's hand warmly and ran to catch up with Kraft, who all the time I'd been talking with Vasin had been walking on ahead of us. We walked all the way to his house in complete silence as I still didn't feel like talking to him. Kraft was very sensitive and considerate of other people. That was his most striking feature.

Chapter 4

I

Kraft held some sort of government job and also did occasional work for the late Andronikov, who had a private law practice besides his official government post. Kraft was important to me because his special relations with Andronikov put him in a position to know many things that interested me very much. But now there was something more urgent involved. Maria, the wife of Nikolai Semyonovich, in whose house I had lived while attending high school in Moscow, happened to be Andronikov's former ward and his favorite niece. And it was she who had told me that Kraft had a special message for me. I had been expecting him for a whole month now.

Kraft had a small two-room apartment in Petersburg and, as he had just returned to the city, he was all alone in it, without even a servant. His trunk stood there half unpacked with his belongings strewn around on chairs and on the table; next to the sofa lay a small traveling bag, a briefcase, a revolver, and various other items.

As we entered, Kraft was so completely absorbed in his thoughts that he seemed to have forgotten all about me. Come to think of it, he probably hadn't even noticed that I hadn't said a word to him on the way. He started searching for something right away, but when, passing in front of a mirror, he caught sight of his reflection, he stopped and for a full minute stared at his own face. Although this did strike me as rather peculiar (and later I thought about it a great deal), at the moment I was too preoccupied and too ill at ease to concentrate on anything. Indeed, there was a moment when I thought of getting out of there and forgetting about the whole business. And, anyway, what was this really all about? Hadn't I imagined all the things that tormented me so? The distressing thought came to me that I might be wasting my time on sentimental trifles when I should have been dealing with a difficult and grave problem. Besides, my inability to cope with serious matters had already been demonstrated by my behavior at Dergachev's.

"Tell me, Kraft," I said suddenly, "do you intend to see these people again?"

He turned slowly toward me, as if my words hadn't reached him. I lowered myself into a chair and waited.

"Forgive them," Kraft said incongruously.

At first I thought he was being sarcastic. I looked at him closely. There was in his face such unbelievable candor that I now felt completely perplexed. He must have been serious when he asked me to "forgive them." He took a chair, put it next to mine, and sat down.

"I'm well aware that I may be nothing but a walking combination of vanities, but I still refuse to apologize to them," I said.

"There's no one you need apologize to," Kraft said very slowly in a low dreamy voice.

"Let's say I owe myself an apology. . . . Maybe I like feeling guilty toward myself. . . . And please forgive me, Kraft, for coming to your house and talking nonsense. . . . But tell me, do you really belong to that group? That's what I wanted to ask you."

"They're neither more stupid nor more intelligent than the rest—they're crazy like everybody else."

"Why, is everybody crazy then?"

I looked at him with curiosity.

"All the better people are crazy. . . . Only the mediocrities, the unimaginative bystanders, are having a great time. . . . But why talk about it. . . ."

While talking, he was looking into space, starting sentences without finishing them. I was particularly struck by the note of hopelessness in his voice.

"But surely you don't include Vasin in what you say?" I said. "Vasin is a great intellect and he is the bearer of a great moral idea!"

"There are no moral ideas now, none at all. Suddenly there's not a single one left. And, what's worse, it now looks as if there have never been any."

"Never been any moral ideas at all?"

"I'd rather drop this subject," he said, sounding infinitely tired.

His sincere hopelessness touched me. I became ashamed of

my selfishness. His mood was contagious. He remained silent for about two minutes, still staring into the air.

"Our time," he said slowly, "is an age of the golden mean and insensitivity, of a cult of ignorance and idleness, of an inability to do anything, and of a longing for the ready-made. No one stops to think; hardly anyone can work out an original thought . . ."

He stopped abruptly and remained silent for a moment.

"They are now stripping Russia of her forests, turning the country into a huge steppe, and making it fit only for Kalmucks. If a man with hope in the future wanted to plant a tree, they'd laugh at him, because, they'd say, he was stupid to expect to live to see it. On the other hand, men of good will argue about how things will be in a thousand years. The one unifying idea has been completely lost. People are living in Russia now as if in a hotel: they plan to leave at any moment, they only hope that it will last as long as they're around."

"Just a minute, Kraft, you've mentioned people who worry about what will happen in a thousand years. But isn't your own despair about what will become of Russia something of the same nature?"

"That . . . that is precisely the crucial question," he said with irritation and got to his feet. His voice now sounded completely different and he looked at me with bewilderment. "I'm sorry. . . . I asked you to come in because I had something important for you. . . . But then we got sidetracked. . . . Please forgive me."

It was as though he'd just been torn out of a dream, as if he were embarrassed at being suddenly surprised. He searched in his briefcase, pulled out a letter, and handed it to me.

"I was asked to give you this. It's a rather important document," he said in a businesslike tone.

Later, when I remembered my dealings with Kraft, I thought with wonderment of his ability to give so much selfless attention to other people's business at a time so critical for him and to explain so clearly and calmly things that didn't concern him.

"This letter was written by the late Stolbeyev himself, whose will gave rise to the lawsuit between Versilov and the Princes Sokolsky. The case is being heard now, and most probably will be decided in Versilov's favor, because the letter of the law is on his side. In this letter, however, written two years before his death, Stolbeyev expresses his real wishes, which would tend to favor the claims of the Sokolskys. In any case, this document would give support to the main points on which the Sokolskys' case is based. Versilov's opponents would have given a great deal to get hold of this letter, although it has no official legal value whatsoever. Mr. Andronikov, who was looking out for Versilov's interests, had this letter in his possession and shortly before his death he gave it to me and asked me to put it into a safe place. Anticipating his death, he was apparently worried about the safety of his files. I have no wish to pass judgment on Mr. Andronikov's motives and I admit that after he died I was painfully hesitant about what to do with this letter, especially since the case was about to be decided. But Mr. Andronikov's niece, Maria, whom he had trusted completely, resolved my dilemma by writing me three weeks ago saying that I should definitely hand this letter over to you, which 'probably'—this is the way she put it— 'coincided with Mr. Andronikov's wishes.' So I'm glad that I can at last get rid of this letter by giving it to you."

I found myself in quite an unexpected position and felt at a loss.

"What," I said, "am I supposed to do with this letter now? Tell me, what would you do in my place?"

"That's entirely up to you."

"I don't agree with you—it's not up to me at all; my hands are tied, don't you see? Versilov has been counting on that inheritance. . . . You know, it'd be the end of him without that money. And now, lo and behold, this document turns up."

"It may have turned up, but so far it exists only here in this room."

"So that's the way out?" I asked, looking at him closely.

"If you don't know how to act in this case yourself, how can I possibly advise you?"

"But how can I turn this letter over to Sokolsky, thus killing all Versilov's hopes and, besides, betraying him in a sense? On the other hand, I know that if I give the letter to Versilov I'll be forcing innocent people to suffer poverty. . . . In any case, I'll be placing Versilov in an impossible dilemma: either to give up the inheritance or to become a thief."

"I think you're exaggerating the importance of the whole thing."

"Tell me one thing: can this letter play a decisive role in the final verdict?"

"No, it can't. I'm not much of a lawyer, though, and I suppose that counsel for the Sokolskys would know how to use this letter to their advantage. But Mr. Andronikov felt certain that the letter didn't have any legal weight and, even if the opposi-

tion presented it as evidence, Versilov could win his case anyway. The document is more relevant to the moral than to the
legal right. . . ."

"But that's the most important," I interrupted him, "because
that would put Versilov in an impossible position."

"He'd destroy the letter and be out of all danger."

"Do you have good reason to assume that he would do that,
Kraft? I want to know—that's what I'm trying to find out from
you."

"I suppose anyone in his position would act like that."

"Would you?"

"I don't stand to inherit from anyone, so I can't tell you what
I'd do."

"All right then," I said, slipping the letter into my pocket.
"For the time being, I consider the matter settled. Maria, from
whom I've learned many, many things, also told me that you
were the only person who could inform me about what really
happened in Ems eighteen months ago between Versilov and
the Akhmakovs. I have been waiting for you, as one waits for the
sun, to light up the darkness for me. You can't imagine the situation I'm in, Kraft, and I beseech you to tell me the whole
truth! I want to know what kind of man he is, and I want to
know now more than ever before."

"I'm surprised that Maria didn't tell you everything herself.
She must have heard it all from the late Mr. Andronikov and
I'm sure she knows more about it than I do."

"But she told me that Andronikov himself was rather unclear
about it. Now I begin to think that no one will ever be able to
disentangle it. The devil himself will trip over his own feet. But
I know that you were in Ems at the time . . ."

"I wasn't there during the whole thing, but I'll be glad to
tell you what I know, although I doubt that it'll satisfy you."

II

I won't try to reproduce his actual words; I'll only convey
briefly the essence of what he told me.

Eighteen months ago in Ems Versilov met the Akhmakovs
through the old Prince Nikolai Sokolsky and soon became a
friend of the family. He impressed General Akhmakov greatly.
Akhmakov had just spent three years losing his wife Katerina's
dowry at cards and, due to various excesses, had already had one
stroke, though he was by no means an old man yet. He had recovered and was staying in Ems with his daughter by his first
marriage. She was a consumptive seventeen-year-old girl, in-

credibly beautiful I understand, but also highly eccentric. She had no dowry, but it was assumed that the old prince would supply her with one, as was his habit. Katerina was reputed to be a very good stepmother to her. For some reason or other, however, the girl had become particularly attached to Versilov.

At that time Versilov was preaching "something impassioned," as Kraft described it: he was calling on everyone to start a new life, as he put it; he was "in a religious mood in some exalted sense," according to Andronikov's words, perhaps ironic, as repeated to me by Kraft. But, curiously enough, soon everyone around began to dislike him. The general was even afraid of him. Kraft did not deny the rumor that it was Versilov who had implanted in the sick man's mind the idea that his wife Katerina was not indifferent to the young Prince Sergei Sokolsky, who had at that time left Ems for Paris. Versilov had said nothing specifically, but rather through hints, implications, and suggestions "in his usual way and with the technique at which he is a past master," Kraft said. I must remark here that, on the whole, Kraft considered Versilov a crook and a born schemer rather than a man with a genuine mystical calling, or even an ordinary crank. On the other hand, from other sources, I know that Versilov had a tremendous influence on Katerina at first and that their relations deteriorated gradually until they reached the final breaking point. What Versilov was after, I couldn't understand from what Kraft told me, just as I hadn't understood it before. One thing is certain, though—that is the mutual hatred that followed their early friendship.

Then something peculiar happened. Katerina's consumptive stepdaughter fell desperately in love with Versilov; perhaps something in him had impressed her violently or maybe his preaching had set her afire, but, whatever it was, at one time Versilov spent whole days in the company of the girl. One day the girl came to her father and declared that she wanted to marry Versilov. This fact is certain since it has been corroborated by Kraft, Andronikov, Maria, and even Mrs. Prutkov, who once let it slip out inadvertently in my presence. It was said that Versilov himself not only was willing to marry the girl but even insisted on it and that there seemed to be complete harmony between two such different creatures—one almost a child, the other almost old. General Akhmakov was horrified by the idea, especially because, since his estrangement from Katerina, whom he used to love greatly, he had turned all his affection to his daughter, and even more so after his stroke. But the greatest opposition to the marriage came from Katerina. There was a succession of unpleasant squabbles and family scenes, which may at best be described as revolting. Finally General Akhmakov began to give in, realizing the determination of his lovesick daughter, who, as Kraft put it, had been mesmerized by Versilov. But Mrs. Akhmakov continued her opposition with unabated fury. And it is at this point that the confusion sets in, which no one has as yet been able to disentangle.

Kraft, however, said that, from what he knew, he could make the following conjecture, which, of course, was nothing but an educated guess on his part. Versilov, "in his usual way," may have subtly and effectively insinuated to the young girl that Katerina Akhmakov refused to consent to the marriage because she herself was in love with him, had pestered him with her jealousy for a long time, pursued him, tried to ensnare him, had declared her love to him and, now that she knew he loved another woman, was bent on destroying him, and so on in the same vein. Even worse, Versilov may have "hinted" something about Katerina's love for him to the general, the "poor" husband, explaining that her interest in the young Prince Sokolsky had been just a fleeting fancy compared with this. It goes without saying that the Akhmakovs' family life became hell. According to some versions of the story, what depressed Katerina even more than the resulting hostility of her sick husband was being disgraced in the eyes of her stepdaughter, to whom she had been so deeply attached. But there is, alas, another version—one, indeed, that Kraft accepted, that I had heard before, and that I believed to be true too. It was said—and Andronikov is supposed to have heard this from Katerina's own mouth—that, when he had learned of the young girl's feelings for him, Versilov himself had offered his love to the stepmother. And Katerina, who had been carried away by him at one time and used to be his friend but then had come to distrust him and argued with him constantly, had met his declaration of love with venomous scorn and an outburst of hatred. Nevertheless, after General Akhmakov had suffered a second stroke, Versilov had openly proposed to Katerina that she marry him, whereupon she had asked him to leave her house and never come back. This would explain Katerina's new outburst of hatred for the man when he openly began trying to marry her stepdaughter. Maria, who told me all this in Moscow, believed both versions. She asserted that they both could be true at once, that this was something called *la haine dans l'amour*, a mutual case of wounded love pride, etc., etc.—some oversubtle romantic nonsense unworthy of any sane and responsible person, spiked, moreover, with a goodly amount of villainy. But then dear old Maria was herself stuffed with romances that she had been reading day and night ever since her girlhood, although by nature she was an excellent person. One was thus left with a general impression of Versilov as villainous, lying, scheming, with something about him that was quite horrible and unmentionable, an impression that was further strengthened by the tragic turn of events: the poor girl, whose feelings he had set afire, poisoned herself, they say by swallowing the phosphorous heads of matches, although to this day I'm not sure whether to believe that detail since they tried to hush things up as much as possible. The girl died after an illness that lasted a fortnight. And so, while it's debatable whether matches were used in this case, Kraft firmly believed they were. The general died soon after his daughter; they even say that it was his grief over her death that triggered his last stroke, which came three months later.

It was after the girl's funeral that the young Prince Sergei Sokolsky, who had in the meantime returned to Ems from Paris, met Versilov in the public gardens and slapped his face in the presence of many people. Versilov did nothing about it. Indeed, the following day he reappeared on the promenade as if nothing had happened. And this was what made everyone turn their backs on him, in Ems as well as in Petersburg. Although Versilov still saw some people, they certainly did not belong to his former world. His old social acquaintances placed all the blame on him, even though they didn't know exactly what had happened and were aware only of a young girl's romantic love and of the slap. Only two or three people had a more or less complete picture of the whole business. The best informed had been the late Andronikov who had had long-standing business relations with the Akhmakovs and, especially on one particular occasion, with Katerina herself. But he had kept most of these secrets even from his family, confiding to his niece Maria and to Kraft only as much as he thought necessary.

"Most important of all is that a document exists which worries Mrs. Akhmakov immensely," Kraft declared, and went on to tell me about that document.

When the old Prince Sokolsky was abroad and had started recovering from his peculiar fit, his daughter, Katerina Akhmakov, secretly wrote to Andronikov, whom she fully trusted, a certain letter that thoroughly compromised her. At that time the convalescing old prince had shown a propensity to spend money at an alarming rate, almost to scatter it to the winds. While abroad he went on a spree of buying expensive and quite unnecessary things, all sorts of paintings and vases, and donating large sums to God knows what charities, even local ones in some foreign town; he also almost paid a huge sum to some ruined Russian rogue for his dilapidated and mortgaged estate without even seeing it, and, finally, he was said to be contemplating marriage. In view of all this, Katerina, who had never left her father's side during his illness, wrote to Andronikov, in his capacity as lawyer and trusted friend, a letter in which she asked him to set her straight on a few points. "Wouldn't it be possible," she inquired, "to place my father under guardianship or to declare him legally incompetent? If this can be done, what would be the best way of going about it so that there would be no gossip, so that no one would accuse me of anything, and so that my father's feelings would be spared. . . ." I understand that Andronikov at once made her see reason and advised her against such action. Later, after the old prince had completely recovered, Katerina's idea became quite inconceivable. Her letter, however, was still in Andronikov's files. So when he died, Katerina immediately remembered that letter, which, if it fell into her father's hands, would, she was sure, make him disown her once and for all, stop her allowance immediately, and disinherit her completely. The mere thought that his own daughter did not believe in his sanity and was plotting to declare him legally incompetent would have turned that lamb into a raging predator at once, while she, penniless because of her late husband's passion for gambling, had only her father to look to for help. Indeed, she fully reckoned on him to provide her with a second dowry just as generous as the first one.

Kraft didn't know what had actually happened to that letter but remarked that Andronikov would never have torn up such an important paper since he was a man not only "with a broad mind but also with a broad notion of the permissible"—a judgment showing surprising independence, in view of Kraft's close attachment to and fondness for Andronikov. Kraft seemed convinced that the compromising document had wound up in Versilov's hands because of his closeness with Andronikov's widow and daughters, and because he knew that they had allowed him to go through Andronikov's files after his death. Kraft was also convinced that Katerina took it for granted that Versilov had the letter and was afraid he would show it to the old prince. As soon as she had returned from abroad, Katerina had searched for the letter all over Petersburg, including at Andronikov's, and was still searching for it, in the vague hope that it might not be in Versilov's hands; she had even gone to Moscow to look for the letter and begged Maria to check whether it wasn't among the papers she had in her house. She had found out about Maria's existence and of her relations with the late Andronikov only recently, after her return to Petersburg.

"You don't think she found the letter at Maria's?" I asked.

I had my own ideas on that score.

"But since Maria hasn't told even you about it, she probably hasn't got it."

"So you think Versilov has the letter?"

"That seems to me the most likely. But I really don't know, anything is possible," he said, sounding quite tired.

I gave up questioning him. What was the use anyway? I had an idea now of what interested me most in this horrible mess. All my fears seemed confirmed.

"It's like a dream, like a nightmare," I said, feeling deeply depressed. I picked up my hat.

"This man is very dear to you, isn't he?" Kraft said, looking at me with enormous sympathy.

"Just as I expected, I didn't find out quite everything I wanted from you," I said. "But there's still Mrs. Akhmakov. As a matter of fact, she's my main hope. I may or may not go and see her."

Kraft looked at me somewhat bewildered.

"Good-by, Kraft. And, by the way, why try and force yourself on people who don't want you? I'm sure you'd be better off if you broke with them altogether."

"And where do I go from there?" he asked with a strange grimness, looking at his feet.

"Go into yourself. You must break off with everything and go into yourself."

"Where? America perhaps?"

"Yes, perhaps America. Somewhere of your own! And that's actually my whole 'idea,' Kraft!" I said enthusiastically.

He looked at me with a strange curiosity.

"So you . . . you have such a place that's *your own?*"

"Yes, I have. Good-by, then, and forgive me for causing you so much trouble. You know, though, if I were you and had a Russia like yours in my head, I'd send them all to hell! 'Be off with you,' I'd tell them, 'do your back-biting elsewhere, cut each other's throats—I don't give a damn!' "

He walked me to the front door.

"Wait," he said suddenly, "stay a little longer."

I was rather surprised, but followed him back and sat down. Kraft also sat down, facing me. I clearly remember us grinning at each other. I also remember how puzzled I felt and how I suddenly said:

"You know what I like about you most, Kraft? It's that you're so well mannered."

"Really?"

"I say that because I'd like to be well mannered too, but I don't succeed most of the time. . . . On the other hand, I wonder if it isn't better to hurt people's feelings. That, at least, saves them the trouble of liking you."

"What time of day do you like best?" Kraft asked, obviously not listening to me.

"Time of day? I don't know. I don't like sunset, though."

"You don't?" he said with a peculiar curiosity, and soon became lost in his thoughts again.

"So you're leaving town again?"

"I'm leaving . . . yes."

"How soon?"

"Soon."

"But why do you need a revolver just to go to Vilno?"

I asked him that without anything special in mind, simply because my eye fell on the gun and I was at a loss as to what to say to him. He turned toward the gun and looked at it fixedly.

"That's just a habit of mine."

"If I had a revolver, I'd keep it locked up. Otherwise, it might be too tempting, I swear! I don't really believe in epidemics of suicides, but if you have this thing in front of your nose all the time, there must be moments when you're tempted to use it."

"Don't talk about it," he said, and got up from his chair.

"I wasn't thinking about myself, I'd never use it." I got up from my chair too. "If I'd been given three lives to live, even then I'd feel it wasn't enough."

"Live as long as you can. . . ." he said. The words seemed to burst out of him spontaneously.

He smiled absentmindedly and suddenly started walking toward the front door, as though to show me out, although obviously he was not aware of what he was doing.

"I wish you success in whatever you do, Kraft," I said to him when I was already on the landing.

"That's a good wish," he said firmly.

"Till we meet again, then."

"That's a good wish too."

I remember his expression when our eyes met for the last time.

III

And this was the man the thought of whom had made my heart pound for so many years! What was it I had really expected from Kraft? What revelations had I expected from him?

I felt very hungry when I left Kraft; it was getting late and I hadn't had dinner yet. While still on the Petersburg Side, I entered a little tavern on the Great Prospect. I was prepared to spend twenty, at most twenty-five, kopeks on my food—I wouldn't have allowed myself to spend more in those days. I ordered a plate of soup, gulped it down, and then sat looking out of the window. The place was crowded and it smelt of burned meat, cheap restaurant napkins, and tobacco. It was quite an ugly dive. Above my head, a silent nightingale was gloomily pecking at the bottom of his cage. There was noise coming from the billiard room next door. As I sat there, I sank deep into thought. The setting sun—why did it surprise Kraft that I disliked sunsets?—gave my thoughts a direction that seemed quite inappropriate to my sordid surroundings. I was haunted by my mother's gentle eyes, which had been shyly watching me during the past month. Lately I had been very rude at home, mostly to her. Actually, I felt like saying unpleasant things to Versilov, but since I didn't dare, in my usual cowardly way I took it out on her. Indeed, because of me, she lived in some kind of terror, as I gathered from the beseeching way she looked at me every time Versilov came into the room: she was afraid of a sudden outburst on my part. Strange to say, it was sitting in this tavern that I suddenly became strongly aware of the fact that, while Versilov treated me as a social equal, my mother addressed me as if she were a servant. Oh, I had noticed it before with some surprise and had decided that it didn't reflect too well on her character, but this time the deeper implications of it struck me, and strange thoughts rushed through my head one after another. I remained sitting there for a long time, as it gradually became dark. I was also thinking of my sister.

It was a fateful moment for me. I had to make up my mind. Was I really incapable of making a decision? What was so difficult about breaking off relations with people who didn't even want me? Oh, not my mother and sister—them, I'd never abandon, however things turned out.

It's true, though, that the appearance of that man in my life when I was a little boy, if only for one moment, had been enough to provide the impact that had awakened me. If I hadn't met him then, my intellect, my way of thinking, and my entire life would have taken a different turn, despite my innate characteristics, which would still have been the same.

But now it looked as if this man were nothing but a figment of my imagination that had been in me since childhood. I had invented him myself and now the real man could not possibly match that imaginary being. I'd come here to find a man with a noble soul, not what I'd found. And why did I have to fall in love with him so irrevocably during that brief moment I'd seen him as a child? No, it mustn't be "irrevocably"! Sometime, if I have an opportunity, I'll describe that first meeting, which was really nothing much and from which it is difficult to make out anything. But in my imagination it grew into a whole pyramid. I started building that pyramid under the blanket of my little boy's bed before I fell asleep at night, during the moments when I was free to dream up things and cry. Why cry? I don't know myself. Perhaps because they had got rid of me? Because I was being oppressed? But I felt oppressed only for two years while I was at Touchard's school, and even then only slightly oppressed. Later, there was no one to oppress me and, if anything, it was I who treated other boys with contempt. Besides, I loathe that poor-dear-little-abandoned-orphan stuff. There's nothing more nauseating than orphans, illegitimate children, foundlings, and all that human jetsam in general, for whom I have no sympathy whatsoever, being solemnly held up to the public eye and simpering plaintively, albeit persistently, "Look what was done to us!" I'd like to whip those orphans! None of that sickening lot will ever understand that it would be ten times more dignified for them to keep their traps shut and not pay society the high tribute of asking for its sympathy. But once they've paid this tribute, I say to them: "You've asked for it, you bastards, so it serves you right." That's what I think about it.

But what struck me as funny now was not the fancies I used to invent about Versilov under my blanket as a child, but that I went to Kraft's today because of him, a mere figment of my own imagination. I was so obsessed with him that I almost forgot my main goal. I had come to help him stamp out the calumny about him and confound his enemies.

The document Kraft had mentioned, the letter written by that woman to <u>Andronikov</u>, in which she now saw such a terrifying threat to herself and which she assumed was in Versilov's possession, actually was not in his hands since it was sewn into the lining of my side pocket! I had sewn it there myself and no one in the world except Maria knew about it. The fact that Maria, who was, I suppose, in her way a sort of romantic and who had been entrusted with the document, had decided to give the letter to me was, on her part, a decision based on reasons that I don't feel it necessary to explain here, although I may later if I see a point to it. But whatever the reasons, once I had that document in my possession, I felt in such a strong position that I was only too tempted to rush off to Petersburg. Obviously, I planned to help that man without his even knowing it, without showing myself, without expecting him to throw himself into my arms and thank me and all that sort of nonsense. And I would certainly never have *paid him the tribute* of reproaching him for anything! Anyway, how could he be responsible for my falling in love with him and building him into some sort of an ideal? Besides, perhaps I didn't really love him at all. Neither his originality nor his fascinating character, neither his complicated scheming nor his strange adventures, not even the presence of my mother at his side could stop me any longer now. It was enough to realize that my fairy tale puppet had been shattered and that perhaps I could no longer love him. So what was there to stop me, to hold me back? That was the question.

When everything was taken into consideration, the upshot was that the only fool around was me and no one else.

But if I demand honesty of others, I must be honest myself and admit that the document sewn into my lining aroused in me other desires than rushing to Versilov's assistance. It's quite obvious to me now, but at that time the mere suspicion of it made me blush. I had visions of coming face to face with a haughty, high-society lady; she would despise me, mock me, treat me as though I were a miserable mouse, never suspecting for a second that her future was in my hands. That thought had fascinated me while I was still in Moscow and had grown even stronger in the train carrying me to Petersburg, as I have confessed earlier. Yes, I hated that woman, but I already loved her too as my destined victim, and all this was true, completely true. But it was also so awfully childish that I wouldn't have expected it even from someone as immature as myself. What I'm describing here is the way I felt in that tavern, I mean the thoughts that went through my head as I sat there under the caged nightingale and decided to break with these people once and for all. The thought of my morning meeting with that woman made me blush with shame. How ignominious! What a disgraceful lack of control! And the worst thing about it was that it showed my complete inadequacy for the task I had as-

signed myself. It proved to me that I was unable to resist even
the most ordinary pitfalls and made all the words sound hollow
that I had just been saying to Kraft about having within me a
place that I could call my own and if I had three lives to live,
I'd still find them not enough. And I said all that so proudly! I
can still find excuses for myself for putting aside my personal
pursuits to help Versilov, but rushing around like a crazed rabbit, sniffing here and there and all over the place, and getting involved in all sorts of extraneous things—that was nothing but
sheer stupidity. What on earth, for instance, could have induced
me to go to Dergachev's and start spouting all those inanities
when I should have known in advance that I couldn't possibly
explain anything to them so that it would make sense and that
the best thing I could do was to keep my mouth shut? And after
that there was Vasin trying to make me feel better by reminding me that I still had perhaps fifty years ahead of me and that
therefore nothing was irretrievably lost. That argument does
honor to this man's indisputable intelligence and is so strong because it brings up the simplest possible reason, and the simplest
reasons are best grasped only in the end when everything else,
wise and absurd, has been tried. But I had thought of that argument myself three years before I heard it from Vasin, and indeed
my "idea" was in part based on it. . . .

Those were the thoughts going through my head as I sat in
that tavern.

Tired from the long walk and all that thinking, I felt disgusted and depressed when I reached the Semyonovsky Regiment barracks near which we lived. It was almost eight and already quite dark. The weather had changed: it had cleared up
but the stinging, wicked Petersburg wind was blowing more
and more strongly in my back, whirling sand and dust around.
Gloomy faces flashed by, faces of working people who had finished their daily chores, and were now hurrying toward their
grimy dwellings. Every one of them was plunged in his own sordid preoccupations and probably there was not one single idea
that they all could share and that could unite that crowd! Kraft
was right—everyone is on his own.

I saw a little boy, so little in fact that I was surprised he was
alone in the street at such an hour. It looked as if he'd lost his
way. A woman stopped next to him for a moment, but apparently she couldn't understand what he was saying because she
shrugged helplessly and walked on, leaving the child alone in
the darkness. I went over to him, but for some reason the sight
of me frightened him and he rushed away.

As I approached our house, I made up my mind never to go and see Vasin again. Then, walking upstairs, I thought how important it was for me at that moment that Versilov not be home so that I could say something warm and pleasant to my mother before he came back and also to my gentle sister, to whom I had hardly talked at all during the month I'd spent in Petersburg. This time my wish was fulfilled: Versilov was out.

IV

Before I bring a new character—Versilov, that is—onto the scene in my chronicle, I must give some brief background information on him, even if it really doesn't mean much. I'm doing this here because I believe it will make my story more understandable and also because I can't think of a better place to work it in.

Versilov studied at the university but then joined a cavalry regiment of the Guards. When he married Miss Fanariotov, he resigned his commission. He traveled abroad extensively and when he returned to Moscow he led a gay social life. After the death of his wife, he went to his country estate where he had that affair with my mother. Then he lived for a long time somewhere in Southern Russia. During the Crimean War, he rejoined the Army but never saw action, indeed, never even reached the Crimea. After the war, he again resigned from the Army and went abroad. He took my mother with him but left her in Königsberg. The poor thing told me with a strange bewilderment, helplessly shaking her head, how she had spent six whole months there alone with her tiny daughter, without speaking the language, feeling like a babe in the woods, and how in the end she had even run out of money. Finally Mrs. Prutkov had appeared, taken her back to Russia, and there whisked her off to some place near Nizhny-Novgorod.

After the emancipation of the serfs, Versilov served as an arbitrator of claims between former serfs and their landlords and, I understand, he performed his duties very well. Soon, however, he resigned, moved to Petersburg, and became a counsel for parties involved in private lawsuits. Andronikov always praised his legal talents very highly, had a tremendous respect for his intelligence although, as he admitted, he could never really understand the man. Then Versilov dropped that too and went abroad again, this time for several years. This was when his close relations with the old Prince Sokolsky began. During that time his financial situation underwent two or three radical changes: he'd go completely broke, then suddenly bounce back and be rich again.

Ah, why not, after all? Having brought my narrative to this point, I've suddenly decided that it's time to explain my "idea." I shall put it into words for the first time since its inception. I have decided to reveal it to the reader so that the rest of my story will make more sense to him. And it's not only for the reader's sake. I myself begin to find it difficult to account for my various actions without presenting my great underlying motivation. By keeping the reader in ignorance, I clumsily fell for the novelistic device that I tried to ridicule at the outset. Before going any deeper into my Petersburg story with all the events in which I am to play a disgraceful part, I consider this preliminary explanation quite indispensable. But it was not considerations of literary "prettiness" that have prevented me from explaining things until now, but the very nature of what I'm trying to say, that is, the difficulty of making it understandable. And even now when it's all in the past, I still find it infinitely hard to describe "my idea." Moreover, I feel I must present it in the original form in which I conceived it at the time rather than the way I see it now, and this presents yet another difficulty. There are things that are almost impossible to convey, particularly the simplest and clearest ideas, for these are the most difficult ones to understand. If, before discovering America, Columbus had tried to explain his idea to other people, I'm sure that it would have taken him an awfully long time to be understood. Besides, he wasn't understood. This doesn't mean I'm trying to compare myself with Columbus, and if anyone infers anything of that sort, he should be ashamed of himself.

Chapter 5

I

My idea is to become a Rothschild. I would like my reader to remain calm and not to laugh. I repeat: my idea is to become a Rothschild, that is, rich like Rothschild; not just become rich, but rich precisely like Rothschild. Why, for what purpose, what do I have in mind? I'll answer all these questions later. First, I want to demonstrate with mathematical certainty that my goal is attainable.

It's all very simple: the two key words of the secret are *perseverance* and *relentlessness*.

"We've heard all that before," you'll tell me; "every German paterfamilias drums it into his children, which doesn't change the fact that there has still been only one Rothschild (that is, the James Rothschild of Paris) while there have been millions of German papas."

This is my answer: You may think you've heard all that before, but you haven't heard a thing yet. One point, however, I'll grant you: when I said that it's all very simple, I forgot to add that it's also the most difficult thing there is. All religions and all moral teachings can be boiled down to the simple maxim: "Love virtue, flee vice." Can there be anything simpler than that? All right, then, try to do something virtuous and discard just one of your vices. Just try. Well, it's the same thing with what I'm saying. And that's why innumerable papas may repeat for centuries on end those two magic key words of the secret without managing to produce another James Rothschild. You must conclude, then, that, although it may sound like the same thing, it's not and your papas may be repeating a different idea.

I'm sure the papas have heard about perseverance and relentlessness before, but what is needed to achieve my goal is not perseverance and relentlessness as understood by German papas.

The mere fact that he is a papa (and not necessarily a German papa)—that he has a family, that he lives like everybody else, that he has expenses and obligations like any other man—is enough to make it impossible for him to become a Rothschild and dooms him to mediocrity. I realize only too well that, by becoming a Rothschild or just by setting out seriously (not the way a papa would do it) to become a Rothschild, a man cuts himself off from society.

A few years ago I read in the newspaper about a beggar dying on board a Volga steamer. The man had been walking around in rags, begging for coppers, and had become a familiar figure in that part of the country. But when he died they found about three thousand rubles on him, sewn in his shirt. A few days ago I read about another man, this one from a respectable middle-class family, who walked around restaurants and taverns begging. He was arrested and they found five thousand rubles on him. From this we may draw two conclusions: one, *perseverance* in accumulating money even by tiny sums eventually yields enormous results (time is of no significance here); and two, even the most uncomplicated way of making money, as long as it is pursued *relentlessly*, is mathematically bound to succeed.

There are, however, many good, respectable, intelligent, and self-controlled people who, try as hard as they may, will never manage to have a few thousand rubles tucked away. Why not? The answer is obvious: although they may want that sum, they don't want it badly enough to go begging for it if there's no other way, and they won't deprive themselves and their families of bread in order to save a few coppers. To save money while begging, a man must eat nothing but bread and salt, or at least that's the only way I can imagine, and I'm sure that's what the two beggars mentioned above did—ate only bread and slept under the open sky. I'm sure neither of them wanted to become a Rothschild; they must have been much simpler types like Molière's Harpagon or Gogol's Plewshkin. But even more will power and desire are required by someone who plans to accumulate money on a completely different scale with the goal of becoming a Rothschild. No German papa can muster such will power. There are many degrees of power in the world and nowhere is the difference in degree greater than in the case of human will and human desire, just as water boils at one temperature and molten iron at another.

To become a Rothschild takes the ascetic self-denial of a monk and the heroic fortitude of a martyr. It's no mere idea—it's a passion. For what? Is it noble or monstrous to wear sackcloth and eat nothing but stale bread all your life while carrying around a fortune? I'll deal with these questions later because my primary concern now is to discuss the possibility of attaining my objective.

When my "idea" occurred to me (it consists in keeping oneself constantly in a state of white heat), I started testing myself: Was I capable of monastic life, or asceticism? To find the answer, I lived for a whole month on nothing but bread and water, about two and a half pounds of rye bread a day, to be precise. I had to do it without the knowledge of Nikolai Semyonovich, who was an intelligent man, and of his wife Maria, who was very concerned with my welfare. I insisted on being allowed to eat alone in my room, which saddened Maria greatly and perplexed the tactful Nikolai. Then I disposed of my dinner by throwing the soup either out the window into the nettles or you know where and feeding the meat to the dog or, wrapping it up in paper, smuggling it out in my pocket and flinging it far away from the house. Since they gave me considerably less bread than I required, I secretly bought more bread. I stuck that month out, suffering nothing worse than an upset stomach in the process. The following month I added a little soup to my diet and allowed myself to drink one cup of tea in the morning and another in the evening. I kept this up for a whole year. Well, let me assure you, I felt very healthy and pleased with life; morally, it gave me a great boost and it was a constant secret satisfaction to me. Not only did I not long for the food I was refusing myself, but I even felt happy not to have it. After a year, when I was convinced that I could stand being deprived of all sorts of food, I resumed having dinner with Maria and Nikolai. But that was not the only test I put myself through. I tested myself by deciding not to spend more than half of the five rubles pocket money that I received every month (my board was paid directly to Nikolai). That was a very hard test, but I passed it too and thus accumulated seventy rubles in just over two years, which, along with some other money, was what I had in my pocket when I arrived in Petersburg. The results of these two tests were tremendously important to me, for I had found out that I could definitely *want* strongly enough, that I would reach my goal. So this is my whole idea, for the rest is just details.

II

Nevertheless, we'd still better take a good look at these details. I have already described my two experiments. Then, in Petersburg, there was that auction sale I have already mentioned when I made in one go seven rubles and ninety-five kopeks profit. That, of course, was no real test; it was just a game, just fun: I wanted to steal a foretaste of the future, to get an inkling of how I would behave and operate someday. But while still in Moscow, I had already decided to postpone the real beginning of my effort until I became completely independent. I knew, for instance, that first I had to get through high school (I had decided to sacrifice my university education, as I said earlier). It goes without saying that I was full of secret resentment at going to Petersburg because, having finally graduated from high school, I realized that now it was Versilov's difficult financial situation that would delay indefinitely the realization of my plans. But, although full of resentment, I didn't worry in the least about reaching my goal in the end.

True, I had no practical experience in life, but I had been thinking about it for three years and never doubted the outcome. I pictured to myself a thousand times how I would proceed. I imagined myself suddenly thrown by a chance wind into one of the capitals (it had to be a capital and, for certain reasons, I gave Petersburg preference over Moscow), completely free, not dependent on anyone, in good health, and with a hundred rubles in my pocket. It's impossible to start without a hundred rubles because that would delay even the first tangible results too much. Apart from the hundred rubles, I would be equipped, as I explained, with courage, perseverance, relentlessness, complete self-sufficiency, and secrecy. Self-sufficiency is the most important: even now I have a violent dislike for contact or association with people. Besides, I had to carry out my "idea" alone—that was a *sine qua non*. People weigh on me, make me feel uneasy, and uneasiness would have prevented me from achieving my goal. In general, although in my imagination I've always managed to handle people pretty well, in real life I have proved rather inept at it. I must admit with disgust that I always give myself away by talking too much, by being overanxious, and that's why I decided to stay away from people. That would give me independence and calm and enable me to keep my goal clearly in view.

Despite Petersburg's outrageous prices, I allotted myself only fifteen kopeks for food a day, and I knew I'd stick to my resolution. I'd given the matter of food lots of thought: I decided, for instance, sometimes to eat nothing but bread and salt for two days in a row and then on the third day spend on food whatever I'd saved from my daily allowance. I thought this would be healthier than a regular, fifteen-kopek daily fare. Then I needed a corner, literally a corner, just to sleep, to have a roof over my head when the weather was really impossible. For I'd live mainly in the streets and, if possible, I'd sleep in flophouses where you can get a piece of bread and a glass of tea as well as a bed. Oh, I'd be able to hide my money in my corner so that they wouldn't steal it from me or even suspect I had any at all— that I can guarantee! "I should worry that they might steal from me?" I once overheard a shady character in the street say cheerfully. "I worry more that I might steal from them!" I have no intention of stealing, of course, but I share that fellow's alertness and cunning. Also, while still in Moscow, I decided that I wouldn't be a pawnbroker or usurer. I leave that to Jews and to Russians without character or imagination. Pawnbroking and usury are for mediocrities.

As for clothes, I decided to have two outfits, one to walk around in and one for occasions when I had to be decently dressed. Once I had gotten myself something to wear, I knew that it would last me a long time. I trained myself to wear the same clothes for two and a half years without letting them look shabby and, indeed, I discovered the secret that brushing them as often as possible, perhaps as often as five or six times a day, preserved their new look. Brushing doesn't hurt clothes, believe me, I know what I'm talking about, it's dirt and dust that hurt them because dust is actually rocks if you look at it through a microscope, while a brush, however hard, is nothing but a sort of fur in the final analysis. I trained myself to wear out my boots evenly, the secret being to put your whole foot down flat on the ground and to be careful to distribute your weight equally. It takes about two weeks to learn to walk like that, but after that you'll do it unconsciously. That way, boots last on the average one-third again as long. This is based on two years of experience.

Now for the essentials of my plan.

My reasoning went like this: I have a hundred rubles and there are so many auction sales, junk shops, flea markets, and people requiring things in Petersburg that if someone buys something it's inconceivable that he won't be able to sell it for a little more. From that album, I made seven rubles and ninety-five kopeks net profit from an investment of two rubles and five kopeks. That disproportionate amount of profit involved no risk since I could tell from the eyes of the customer that he wouldn't back out. Obviously it was just a lucky break, I know that only too well. But then it's precisely for such lucky breaks that I'm on the lookout; that's why I've decided to live in the streets. But even assuming that such opportunities won't come up too often, it's still all right, for my cardinal rule is never to take any risks and my second rule is to earn every day more than I spend, even if only very little more. The accumulation must be continuous, without stopping for one single day.

You may object that this is all pipe dreams, that I know nothing about the streets, and that on the very first day they'll make a fool out of me. My answer is that I have character and will, and that the science of survival in the streets is a science like any other and can, therefore, be mastered by anyone with enough perseverance, concentration, and ability. At high school I was just about at the top of my class until my third year and I was especially good at math. So I don't think there's any justification to making a fetish out of experience, presenting the science of survival in the street as an insurmountable difficulty and predicting my failure on those grounds. That's only what people say who have never tried anything, who have never even started to live, and who have grown stiff from sitting motionless amidst things as they found them. "Somebody tried that before and got a bloody nose," they reason, "so if somebody else tries it, he'll get his nose bloodied too." But I won't, not me! I have will power and, if I concentrate hard enough, I can learn anything. Do you really imagine that a man, endowed with relentless energy, who's always on the alert, who's always thinking and calculating, who's always on the go, watching for an opportunity, that such a man won't acquire enough know-how to earn every day, say, twenty kopeks more than he spends on his upkeep? Above all, I resolved never to go all out for a maximum immediate gain, but always to remain cool. Later, of course, after I'd saved a thousand or two, I'd graduate from secondhand dealing and street peddling. Right now I still know too little about the stock exchange, shares, the banking business, and the whole world of high finance. But what I do know, as well as I know I have fingers on each hand, is that, when the time comes, I'll learn everything about the stock exchange, banking, and all that, and I'll get a clearer picture of it than anybody else simply because I'll have reached a point when I'll have to master that science too. Why, it doesn't take all that much intelligence to master these things; you don't have to have Solomon's wisdom. All it takes is will power; the grasp, the skill, and the know-how will come by themselves. Everything will be all right as long as the desire is there.

The most important thing is not to take risks. And that's what takes character. Recently, just since I came to Petersburg, certain railroad shares were put on the market and the people who bought them made quite a handsome profit. For some time the shares kept rising. And now if someone who had failed to buy that stock saw some of those shares in my hands and offered to buy them off me at so many points above the official rate, well, I wouldn't hesitate to sell them to him at once. People would obviously laugh at me, telling me that if I waited just a little longer, I'd make many times that amount. Perhaps, but then my profit is better because it's already in my pocket while theirs is still floating in the air. They'll tell me that, my way, I'll never make big profits. Sorry, gentlemen, you're dead wrong, like all those Kokorevs, Poliakovs, and Gubonins.* Let me tell you something: relentlessness and perseverance in pursuing gain, above all in accumulating money, is much more effective than accidental windfalls, even if they show an immediate profit of one hundred per cent.

A short time before the French Revolution, there appeared in Paris a man called John Law who thought up a brilliant financial operation (which later blew up with a frightful bang). All Paris was in an uproar. Everyone was after Law's shares: people

---

* Big Russian railroad financiers of the mid-nineteenth century. [A. MacA.]

practically fought to get hold of them. The company that had issued the shares was raking in huge sums of money, but even so the offices couldn't handle the mad demand; people of all ages and walks of life thronged the surrounding streets; bourgeois, noblemen, their children, countesses, marquises, and prostitutes—all melted into a furious, crazy crowd, as if they'd all been bitten by rabid dogs. Rank, class, pride, sense of honor, and simple decency were all trampled in the mud; men and women were ready to sacrifice anything just to get hold of a few shares. They started buying shares in the street and when there was nothing else to write on, they asked a hunchback whether he wouldn't rent out his back as a table. He agreed, and you can imagine at what a price!

Soon, indeed very soon after that, it all blew up in their faces, proved a complete flop, and the shares became worthless. Only one person wound up the winner. Who? The hunchback, of course. Why? Because he was paid not in shares but in hard cash. Well, I'm just like that hunchback. I had enough will power to abstain from eating and to save seventy-two rubles by putting aside one kopek at a time. And I reckon I'll have enough will power also to content myself with a sure profit in the middle of a general mad rush for huge future windfalls. But I'm so petty only in small matters; when it comes to big ventures, I'm different. Even after my "idea" was born, I often gave in on small things that required only a little patience but never on things that really mattered—I always had enough patience for them! When, in the morning before I left for my job, my mother gave me coffee that was not hot enough, I grew angry and was rude to her, although I was the same man who'd gone a whole month only on bread and water.

What I've been trying to say here is that it would be unnatural for a person to be unable to learn how to make money. It would also be unnatural if a man who continuously saved and accumulated money, remained constantly alert, watchful, austere, thrifty, and energetic, failed to end up a millionaire. How did the beggar I mentioned earlier accumulate the money found on him, if not by a fanatical will power and perseverance? And am I not as good as that beggar? Finally, even if I achieve nothing, even if my reasoning is wrong, even if I break my neck and prove a complete flop, I still don't care; I'll go ahead with my plans because that's the way I want it to be. That's what I decided back in Moscow.

They'll tell me that this is not much of an "idea," nothing

new. Well, I'll answer for the last time that it's an immense "idea" and that there's a lot that's new in it.

Oh, I knew very well in advance how trivial all the objections would be and how trivial I would sound myself in explaining my "idea." For what have I actually said? I haven't said even one-hundredth of what there is to say. I realize that it came out sounding banal, superficial, crude, and even somehow younger than my age.

III

There still remain the questions "Why?" "For what purpose?" "Is it right?" etc., etc., that I must answer.

I'm sorry to disappoint the reader straightaway, sorry, but at the same time I feel like laughing. I want it to be understood that there is no element of revenge in my "idea," nothing Byronic, no curses, no resentment for being abandoned by my parents, no tears over my illegitimacy, nothing of that sort at all. Indeed, if a lady with a romantic imagination came across my notes, she'd make a sour face from disappointment. The plain object of my "idea" is self-sufficiency.

"But," it may be objected, "there's no need for you to aspire to be a Rothschild just to become self-sufficient. Why do you have to be a Rothschild for that?"

Why? Because, besides self-sufficiency, I need power. The reader may be shocked at the frankness of my confession and wonder how I could write these things without blushing. The answer is that I'm not writing this for publication and do not expect anyone to read it before ten years or so, by which time everything will be viewed from a sufficient distance, will be settled, and my point adequately demonstrated, so there will no longer be anything for me to blush about. Therefore, if I address myself to the reader now and again, it's only a narrative device. My reader is a purely imaginary character.

No, it was neither my illegitimacy which caused me to be taunted at Touchard's school, nor my gloomy childhood, nor the desire for revenge, nor the need to record my protest that lay at the bottom of my idea—it came to me just because my character is what it is. Since the age of twelve, I believe, when I became fully conscious of things, I have disliked my fellow men. It is not that I actually dislike them, but their presence is somehow painful to me. It makes me feel very depressed sometimes that, at moments when I feel the need for sincerity, I can never express fully what is on my mind, even to the people the closest to me; there's always something that holds me back, that makes me so mistrustful, uncommunicative, and unfriendly. Also, I have noticed in myself, since early childhood, a propensity to suspect others, to blame them for everything. But whenever I suspect others, I immediately ask myself: "Perhaps it is I who am really guilty and not them?" And how often have I blamed myself for nothing! It was to avoid such misgiving that I instinctively began to seek self-sufficiency. Besides, I found nothing worthwhile in the company of others, although I tried hard to find something. All the boys of my age I came across were my intellectual inferiors—yes, all of them, I can't think of a single exception.

Yes, I'm gloomy and I always clam up in the presence of people. Perhaps I shall help people someday, but, as a rule, I can't think of any reason why I should. There's really nothing so marvelous about people to bother much about them. Why don't they come to me frankly and openly? Why should I always be expected to make the first move? That's what I ask myself. I'm a responsive person and I've proved it a hundred times by getting caught like a fool. I respond at once to frankness with frankness and become fond of someone who is open with me. And every time I react like that, they immediately take advantage of me and then reject me with a smirk. The most sincere of them all was Lambert, who beat me mercilessly when we were boys, but then he was just an unabashed thug and bully and his sincerity came mostly from his lack of imagination. Such was my state of mind when I arrived in Petersburg.

When I left Dergachev's—God knows why I went there at all—I latched onto Vasin and started praising him in an outburst of enthusiasm. Fine, but later that evening, I liked him already considerably less. Why? Precisely because, having praised him, I had lowered myself before him. Shouldn't a man's reaction be just the opposite? Doesn't it rather add to a man's dignity to give another his due, even at his own expense? I saw that, of course, but it didn't prevent me from liking Vasin very much less. I have deliberately illustrated my point by bringing in a man the reader has already met. Even Kraft left an unpleasant, sour aftertaste of resentment in me for having practically shown me the door, a hostile feeling that lasted until the following day when everything became clear and it was obvious that it was impossible for me to be angry with Kraft. Ever since my first years at school, whenever another boy would get ahead of me in any academic subject or in physical prowess or if he could best me in a discussion by producing wittier and more telling arguments, I'd immediately break off all relations with him and stop talking to him. I didn't necessarily hate him or wish him ill luck or anything; I would just turn away and ignore him because that's just the way I'm made.

Yes, my whole life I've been longing for power, power and self-sufficiency. I was already longing for it when I was so little that, had anyone been able to decipher what was going on inside my skull, he would have rolled with laughter. That's why I became so secretive. Yes, I went about daydreaming so hard that I had no time to talk to people, which made them say I was unsociable. As to my absentmindedness, they thought up even less pleasant explanations for that, although my rosy cheeks obviously gave them the lie.

I was the happiest when I went to bed at night and could pull the blanket over my head, thus isolating myself from the people around me and from the sounds they made. I became free to re-create my life in a different pattern. Wherever I went, my most extravagant, wild daydreams went with me, until I discovered my "idea." Then all my crazy, silly longings were immediately transformed into rational aspirations and my wishful thinking, which had been spinning a dreamy romance inside my head, was turned into reasoned thought applicable to real life. Everything merged into one single goal.

Actually, I don't really think my old daydreams were all that inane, although there were thousands and thousands of them, which naturally caused considerable confusion. I had some favorite ones among them. . . . But, of course, I wouldn't even think of revealing any of them here.

Power! I can well imagine how funny it would have seemed to many people to think that a miserable creature like me aspired to power. But I have an even greater surprise: perhaps in my very first dreams, dating from sometime in my infancy, I never imagined myself except in the top position in everything. And to make an even more peculiar admission, let me add that I still feel that way today. Nor do I feel I have to apologize for it.

So the whole point of my "idea" is that money is the only road that can take a man to the *top spot*, the only force that can propel him there, even if he's a mediocrity. I, for instance, may not necessarily be a mediocrity, but when I look at my face in a mirror, I realize that my quite ordinary face is definitely a handicap. But if I were as rich as Rothschild, who would stop to look at my face? And if I just whistled, wouldn't thousands of women come rushing to offer me their charms? Indeed, I'm absolutely convinced that in the end they would sincerely think that I was the handsomest of men. I suppose I'm quite intelligent. But even if my brain power were ten times that of an average man, I'm sure there'd always be someone around whose brain power was eleven times the average, and what would become of me then? But if I were Rothschild, that fellow with the brain to the eleventh power would be no competition to me, for they wouldn't even give him a chance to open his mouth when I was around. I may be witty, but if a Talleyrand or a Piron† came along, my wit would appear dull in comparison with theirs. But if I were Rothschild, where would Piron or even Talleyrand be if they tried to outshine me? Money confers despotic power upon a man, but at the same time it is the greatest equalizer and that's where its main force lies: money eradicates all inequalities. I worked all that out while I was still in Moscow.

You may see in this way of thinking just presumptuousness, a wish to impose oneself by force, a way for mediocrity to triumph over talent. I concede that my idea is presumptuous, but that's precisely what makes it so sweet to me. But do you really imagine that I thirst for power just to start throwing my weight around, to punish others for what I've had to bear? Why, that's the way a mediocrity would behave. Actually, I'm sure that thousands of talented and outstandingly clever people would crush everybody and smash everything in their way if they suddenly came into possession of Rothschild's millions, just like unimaginative mediocrities. But that's not true in my case: I'm not afraid of money—money will never crush me or force me to crush anybody.

I don't really need money, or rather it's not money that I'm after, nor power for that matter. What I'm after is something that can be acquired through power and only through power: that is self-sufficiency and a calm awareness of my strength. And this is the most complete definition of the freedom that the world is striving for! Freedom! I have finally written down that great word. . . . Yes, self-sufficiency and awareness of one's power are dizzying and beautiful. I possess power and I'm serene. Jupiter possesses thunderbolts and is serene, for how often does he unleash his thunder? Some fool may conclude that Jupiter sleeps a lot. But try and put a man of letters or a peasant woman in Jupiter's place and you'll have one uninterrupted thunderstorm!

If only I could acquire power, I reasoned, I wouldn't even have to use it. I'm sure that I'd always be content to remain

† Alexis Piron (1689–1773), a French poet, author of satirical verse and songs renowned for their double meanings. [A. MacA.]

modestly inconspicuous. If I were Rothschild, I'd go about in a worn overcoat and carry an umbrella. Why should it bother me if people pushed me out of their way in the street or if I had to keep jumping aside into the gutter and just managed not to wind up under horses' hooves or carriage wheels? The knowledge that I was Rothschild would make even that experience pleasant. And I'd know that if I wanted, I'd be able to have a better dinner than anyone else that night because I had the best cook in the world, and the awareness of it would be enough for me. So if I ate just a ham sandwich, the knowledge of what I could have had if I chose to would satisfy my palate. I even feel this way now.

There would be no need for me to try and be accepted by the aristocracy—it would be the aristocracy's problem to be accepted by me. Nor would I have to run after women—they'd come running after me, anxious to give me everything a woman can give. The vulgar ones would be after money, while the more imaginative ones would be attracted to the strange, proud, and distant man, so inscrutable and detached. I'd be nice to both kinds and perhaps give them money, but I would accept nothing from them. Curiosity sometimes inspires passion, and perhaps I'd inspire that sort of passion in them. But they'd leave with nothing except the presents I might give them, and this would only double their curiosity about me:

> I know my power, and to me
> This knowledge is enough.‡

It's strange but true that this fantasy has appealed to me ever since I was seventeen.

I have no wish or intention to oppress or torment anyone, but I know that if I wanted to do away with an enemy of mine, no one would oppose me; indeed, they would all try to gain my favor by helping me. And, again, that's enough to satisfy me. I wouldn't avenge myself on anyone. I always wondered why James Rothschild ever accepted the title of baron. What did he need it for when he already occupied the most exalted position in the world? Oh, I wouldn't care if some insolent general was rude to me as we waited for relay horses at a post station because I'd realize that, if only he knew who I was, instead of claiming the first available horses for himself, he would run to harness them to my modest carriage and then help me to climb in!

‡ From Pushkin's dramatic sketch *The Miserly Knight* (part of the monologue in which the knight addresses his gold). [A. MacA.]

Once I read that in a train in Vienna a foreign count—or was it a baron?—helped a banker to put on his slippers in front of other passengers, and the banker was vulgar enough to allow him to do it. . . . Oh, I wouldn't mind at all if a frightening young beauty (yes, frightening, for there are such beauties), the daughter of a regal and distinguished aristocratic lady, meeting me on a luxury steamer or some such place, glanced at me scornfully and, screwing up her nose, wondered what this quiet and drab-looking fellow with a book or newspaper in his hand could be doing in this place reserved for the elite. Ah, but if she only knew who he was! And she'd find out; then she'd come and sit down next to me of her own accord, submissive, shy, and tender, hoping to catch my eye, dissolving with joy at the sight of my smile. . . .

I'm purposely describing here scenes from my early day-dreams to convey my idea as clearly as I can. Obviously, however, such fancies are bound to be pale, blurred, and trivial; only transferring them to real life will do them full justice.

Some people would feel that, having achieved such power, this self-imposed austerity would be absurd. Why shouldn't I have a sumptuous mansion, receive the best people, and exert my influence? Why shouldn't I marry? But what would be the point then of becoming a Rothschild just to be like everybody else? All the enchantment, all the spiritual strength, would be drained out of my "idea." When I was a boy, I learned by heart the monologue from Pushkin's *Miserly Knight*. It contains the greatest idea Pushkin ever expressed. To this day, I fully share that idea.

"But your ideal is rather vulgar," people might object scornfully; "all you're after is money and material goods. You ignore noble things—public service, philanthropy, and the like. . . ."

But how on earth do they know how I'd use my wealth? What's wrong or immoral about these millions passing from the hands of various Jews, all sorts of harmful and unscrupulous people, into the hands of a sober, strong, austere man who watches the world vigilantly with wide-open eyes?

Besides, all these dreams about the future, all these conjectures, are still at the stage of romance and perhaps I'm wasting my time mentioning them. I could have left them locked inside my skull. I know that possibly no one will read these lines, but if someone does, he may believe that I would cave in under the weight of Rothschild's millions. But if these millions did crush me, it wouldn't be at all the way he would expect. In my day-dream, I often visualized the moment in the future when my

desires would be oversatiated. Then power would no longer be
enough; I'd give my millions away—not out of boredom or hopeless despair but because I would be seeking something even
greater! So I'd let society distribute my wealth, while I myself
would melt into the crowd and dissolve into mediocrity once
more! Perhaps I'd end up like the beggar they found dead on
the Volga steamer, with the difference that they would find not
a single kopek hidden on my person. The mere knowledge that
once I had millions and had discarded them, as one throws out
garbage, would sustain me in my wilderness. I'm prepared even
today to feel that way. Yes, my idea is my fortress into which I
can always lock myself to escape people, even if I die like that
beggar on the Volga steamer. So this is my poem! It must be my
way *all the way* according to my perverse will just in order to
prove *to myself* that I have the strength to renounce it all.

I'm sure people would tell me that it all may sound great but,
if I did somehow get hold of a few million, I'd never let go of
them again in order to end up as another Volga beggar. Maybe I
wouldn't: I was simply trying to explain the principle underlying my idea. But let me say this quite seriously: if I really succeeded in accumulating enough money to put me into Rothschild's class, it's quite possible that I'd end up tossing it all
away to the public. (With less than a Rothschild-size fortune,
however, I realize it would be very difficult to do.) And if I
were to give it away, it wouldn't be just half of it because that
would only be a show in bad taste, which would make me, so
to speak, twice as poor without accomplishing anything else. No,
I'd give up everything, down to the last kopek; for then, becoming a beggar, I'd be twice as rich as Rothschild! Well, if
they can't understand this, it's not my fault, so why should I
take the trouble of trying to explain it to them?

"Mysticism!" they'd say, "the only poetry accessible to mediocrity and impotence; the triumph of vulgarity, a substitute for
talent!"

Yes, I concede, it may be a triumph of vulgarity, require no
talent, and suit a mediocrity, but there can hardly be any impotence in this case. Indeed, my favorite vision was of an average man, without any particular talents, facing the world and
saying with a smile: "Listen you, Galileo and Copernicus! And
you, Charlemagne, Napoleon, Shakespeare, and Pushkin! And
you, statesmen and generals! Here I am, an untalented bastard,
who is, nevertheless, your superior because you accept the fact
yourselves!"

Indeed, I pushed this fantasy to the limit, even wiping out

retroactively whatever education I had had. I felt that the more crass the hero's ignorance was, the better the picture looked. In fact, it was the daydream in which the idea was pushed to its extreme limit that changed my attitude toward learning during my two last years at high school: I stopped studying because of my fanatical belief that my lack of education would only add beauty to my ideal. Now, however, I've changed my views on that particular point and I no longer believe that education would spoil anything.

Why is it, gentlemen, that even the slightest departure from conventional thinking should be so distasteful to you? Blessed is the man who has his own ideal of beauty, even if it be a wrong ideal! But, in my case, I believe it's the right ideal, although I may have been awkward and simplistic in explaining it. I'm sure I'll be able to explain it better ten years from now. But I'll keep what I wrote here for the record.

IV

That's enough about my "idea." If my explanation sounds commonplace and skimpy, the fault is not with my "idea" but with me. As I said earlier, the simpler an idea, the harder it is to grasp, and now I can add that the simpler an idea, the harder it also is to explain. What made it even harder for me was that I was trying to describe it in its original, primitive form.

The corollary to that rule is that the more commonplace and ready-made ideas are, the more readily they are picked up, always by the whole populace, street by street, and the more quickly they are acclaimed as great, tremendous, and inspired, but these ideas only last a day. Cheap things don't last long and quick understanding by the crowd is a sign of cheapness. Bismarck's idea was at once acclaimed as a stroke of genius and Bismarck was hailed as a genius himself, and it's precisely that speed of recognition that makes me suspicious of the idea's true value. I'd like to defer judgment for ten years and see what's left of Bismarck's idea then or, for that matter, of Herr Chancellor himself. I've brought in this highly extraneous observation obviously not to suggest a comparison of "ideas" but simply for the record. (This explanation is for the particularly ignorant reader.)

And now I'll recount two incidents that will complete what I have to say about my "idea"; then I'll be able to proceed with my story without any further interference.

Last July, a couple of months before leaving Moscow for Petersburg, when I had already finished school, Maria asked me to deliver a message to a friend of hers who lived in Troitsky Posad (the message itself is quite irrelevant to my story). In the train on my way back, I noticed a pimply, sallow-faced, dark-haired young man, short and puny, wearing a rather well-cut but stained jacket. What attracted my attention to him was the fact that every time the train stopped at a station he'd rush out to the buffet and gulp down a glass of vodka. Gradually a cheerful and rather unattractive group of passengers formed around him. A merchant, looking somewhat tipsy himself, loudly praised the young man's ability to hold his liquor without showing any signs of drunkenness. Also highly approving of the young man was a very talkative fellow dressed in German-looking clothes who sounded terribly stupid and smelled very unpleasantly. He was a flunkey, as I found out later, and he became so friendly with the dark-haired vodka drinker that every time the train entered a station he'd help the other to his feet, announce "Time for vodka," and the two of them would stagger out arm in arm. The dark young man said almost nothing to anyone, but this did not prevent more and more people from gathering around him. He just listened to them and grinned with a drooling little snigger, only occasionally emitting something that sounded like "Tu-lu-lu" and each time bringing a finger to his nose with a very comical flourish. It was this ridiculous gesture that delighted the merchant, the flunkey, and the rest of them and made them roll with loud, unrestrained laughter. It's very hard to understand what actually makes people laugh. So I joined in too. And, for some reason, at first I took a sort of liking to the young man, just like the rest of them. Perhaps it was because of his obvious disregard for the generally accepted standards of behavior, for it didn't occur to me then that it could be due simply to his imbecility. Soon we got to talking like a couple of old friends and, when we arrived in Petersburg and were leaving the train, he told me that he would come out for a stroll on the Tverskoi Boulevard sometime after eight that evening.

I met him on the boulevard, and this former university student (as he turned out to be) taught me a new peculiar game. We'd walk around looking for a respectable woman, follow her waiting for an opportunity when no one was close to her, and then, without saying a word, come up, one on each side of her, and, pretending not to notice her presence, we would start having the most obscene conversation across her. We called things by their proper names in the most matter-of-fact way and went into the most complicated refinement of filth and perversion, surpassing, I'm sure, the imagination of the most lascivious debauchee. (I'd learned all these things in boarding school, before I'd even been accepted in high school, my knowledge obviously being purely theoretical.) The woman would become very frightened and try to walk faster to get away from us, but we would speed up too and go on with our conversation. She could, of course, do nothing: crying out for help would have been pointless since we'd made sure there weren't any witnesses around and, besides, she'd have felt rather embarrassed to complain.

I spent eight days playing that game and I cannot understand now how I could have enjoyed it, if, indeed, I ever really did enjoy it. I suppose I did it for no special reason, just for the hell of it. At first I found this sport an original way of breaking out of the cage of dull conventions. The fact that I hated women helped too. I told my new friend that, in his *Confessions*, Jean-Jacques Rousseau tells how, as a youth, he would sit hidden in some corner waiting for women to pass and then suddenly step out and expose certain parts of his body that are usually covered. To which piece of information, the fellow's only comment was: "Tu-lu-lu!"

I noticed that this former university student was surprisingly ignorant and that practically nothing interested him. There was nothing in him, no secret idea whatsoever, as I'd hoped to find. Instead of original views, I found nothing but impenetrable dullness. I liked him less and less. The end of our friendship came quite suddenly.

One evening, when it was already quite dark, we picked out for our usual treatment a very young girl, of sixteen or so, who was walking fearfully along a deserted street. She was dressed very modestly and looked to me like a working girl returning home to her widowed mother, who was waiting for her with her younger brothers and sisters. But there's no need to be maudlin. . . . Anyway, for a while the girl seemed to be listening to our filth, while walking as fast as she could with her head bowed and her veil held tight over her face, frightened and trembling. But suddenly she stopped dead, pulled up her veil, uncovering, as I remember, a thin but pretty face, and with eyes ablaze shouted at us: "You dirty, cowardly swine!"

I expected her to burst into tears, but she did something else. She suddenly lifted her frail little hand and, with breathtaking dexterity, delivered a resounding slap on my companion's face. It really landed with a *plopp!* He swore disgustingly and rushed at her, but I held onto him and this gave the girl a chance to escape. We were left face to face, glaring at each other. I told him then what I thought of him, giving vent to all the accumulated irritation of the past few days: he was, I said, a pitiful mediocrity, a mindless, unimaginative hanger-on, without the seed of an original idea. He let out a string of foul words and called me a bastard (I'd told him about my illegitimate birth). Then we spat at each other's feet and parted, never to meet again.

All the evening after the quarrel I felt very upset, less so the next day, and on the third day I'd forgotten the whole incident. As to the girl, I did think of her for a few days, but only vaguely and if something somehow reminded me of her.

It was only in Petersburg a couple of weeks later that the whole scene came back to me in a flash, and it made me suddenly feel dreadfully ashamed, so dreadfully, in fact, that tears of shame filled my eyes. It tormented me unbearably all night and the whole next day, and it still torments me to some extent now. I couldn't understand how I could have sunk so low and, even less, how I could have dismissed it from my mind so easily at first, without feeling any shame or remorse. Only now do I know the answer: it was because of my "idea." To put it as succinctly as I can, I know now that when a man has something permanently fixed in his mind, something rigid, constant, powerful, that absorbs all his attention, it has the effect of removing him from the world; and anything that happens to him seems to happen in a thick fog and slip past him, leaving him with the only thing that matters. Even the impressions he receives from his senses about the outside world become distorted. Moreover, he has a ready excuse for everything. Ah, how inconsiderately I treated my mother in those days, how thoughtlessly I neglected my sister, dismissing my guilt by saying to myself: "All that doesn't matter in the least, only my idea counts!" Also, when I was humbled and insulted myself and would walk away feeling miserable, I'd suddenly say to myself: "All right, I'm despicable, but then I have my 'idea' and they don't know about it!" My "idea" sustained me in my weakness and misery; it dissolved all my shameful traits, smoothed out everything for me. But then, of course, it also blurred my sight, prevented me from understanding what was going on in front of me. And, aside from all the other inconveniences, that was a great impediment to the realization of the "idea" itself.

Now for the second incident.

Last April 1 a few guests came over in the evening to congratulate Maria on her name day. Suddenly the maid Agrafenya rushed in and told us breathlessly that she'd found behind the kitchen door, on the landing of the service staircase, an abandoned screaming baby. What was to be done about it? This caused quite a stir among us and we all hurried over and saw a bark basket: inside it a three- or four-week-old baby was crying away. I picked up the basket, brought it into the kitchen, and only then noticed the folded note that went something like this:

Dear, kind folks: Be charitable to this little girl christened Arina, who later will join us in the prayers for you that we address to the heavenly throne, and we also congratulate you on your name day.

Persons unknown to you.

Nikolai, a man for whom I had always had the highest respect, disappointed me deeply on that occasion. His face suddenly became very grave and he declared that the baby must immediately be sent to a foundling home. It made me feel very sad. It's true they lived very frugally; they had no children of their own and Nikolai was pleased that they were childless. I picked up the little Arina gently by her tiny shoulders, lifted her out of the basket, and got a whiff of that sour, pungent smell of a baby that hasn't been changed or washed for a long time. I said that I wanted the baby girl to stay with us and that I'd take all the expenses upon myself. Nikolai said I couldn't do that and we started arguing the point. Despite his usual gentleness, Nikolai wouldn't change his mind and stuck firmly to his decision, although he tried to make it easier by ribbing me gently about my notion. Still, eventually the baby was not sent off to a foundling home. In another wing of our house there lived a very poor carpenter, an aging man who drank a lot and was married to a younger woman, a very vigorous one at that, who had just lost her own baby, the only one they'd had after eight years of childless marriage. By a strange and lucky coincidence, that baby had also been a girl and had also been christened Arina. I said lucky because, while Nikolai and I were arguing about the little Arina, the carpenter's wife heard us, stopped, inquired about what had happened, and, when told that Arina was the baby's name, became terribly moved. She said she still had milk, unfastened her dress, and held the baby to her breast. While she was feeding the baby, I pleaded with her to take it and said I'd pay for it every month. She said she wasn't sure whether her husband would agree, but said she'd keep the little

Arina overnight. In the morning, the old carpenter came to tell me that he'd be willing to keep the baby if I paid him eight rubles a month. I immediately counted off eight rubles to pay him for one month in advance. He took the money and spent it all forthwith on liquor. Nikolai, smiling strangely, agreed to guarantee that the man would receive his eight rubles even if I was unable to keep my end of the deal. I wanted to give Nikolai all my sixty rubles of savings, but he refused. He said he knew that I had money and trusted me to pay. That delicate tactfulness made me forget at once the irritation I had felt during our argument. Maria didn't interfere but seemed surprised that I was willing to take upon myself such a responsibility. I appreciated their tact, especially since neither of them made any more flippant remarks about my decision; indeed, they now treated the matter with all the seriousness it deserved. I started dashing over to see the carpenter's wife three times a day and, toward the end of the week, I managed to slip her an extra three rubles without her husband noticing it. I spent another three rubles on a little blanket and on swaddling clothes.

But ten days later, little Arina fell ill. I got a doctor to examine her. He prescribed some medicine for her and we spent a whole night forcing the poor little thing to swallow the foul-tasting stuff. The next day the doctor came and said we had sent for him too late; when I begged him, perhaps with a tinge of reproach, to do something, he gave me that final majestic excuse: "I'm not God, after all, am I?" A minute white rash appeared on the little girl's tongue, lips, and all around her mouth, and toward evening she died, with her dark eyes fixed on me as though she knew what was happening to her. I don't know why it never occurred to me to take a picture of the dead baby. You might not believe me if I told you that what I did that night could hardly be described as weeping: I literally howled like an animal, something that I'd never done before (or since). Maria tried to comfort me as much as she could and, again, she did it with the utmost tact; neither she nor Nikolai showed in any way that they thought there might be something peculiar in my behavior. It was our carpenter who made the coffin. Maria supplied him with some material to line the coffin and a pretty little pillow, while I bought some flowers and strewed them over the dead child; and this is how they carried off my poor little baby whom, believe it or not, I cannot forget.

A little later, however, strange thoughts crept into my mind in connection with the whole episode. Little Arina hadn't really cost me very much. Including the coffin, the burial, the doctor, the flowers, and the money given to the carpenter's wife, I'd say, all told, it came to about thirty rubles. I made up the loss out of the forty rubles Versilov sent me for my trip and from the sale before I left of various possessions of mine, so that in the end my capital was the same as it had been before.

"Still," I thought, "if I continue straying from my path like this, I'll never get anywhere."

So, while the episode with the former university student showed that my "idea" was capable of blurring the messages my brain received from my senses, the episode with the baby Arina showed just the opposite—namely, that no "idea" could capture a man (at least me) so completely as to enable him to ignore something overwhelmingly moving and to prevent him from sacrificing to it the results of years of effort directed toward the realization of his "idea."

And both the seemingly opposite observations were correct.

Chapter 6

I

Although Versilov was out, I didn't find my mother and sister at home alone, as I had hoped. Mrs. Prutkov was there, sitting with my mother, and at that moment the presence of any outsider would have annoyed me. A good half of my generous disposition left me immediately. It's amazing how radically my moods can change—a speck of dust or a hair may be enough to change my mood from benevolent to vicious. And I'm sorry to say that unpleasant impressions linger longer in me than pleasant ones, although I'm not a person to bear a grudge for long.

As I came in, I got the impression that my mother, who had been talking to Mrs. Prutkov with great animation, had stopped in the middle of a sentence. My sister was not in the living room: she'd come back from work a few moments before me but had not yet joined the others.

Our cottage consisted of three rooms: the living room, where we usually gathered, was quite spacious and almost presentable, with its soft red sofas and armchairs, comfortable although well worn (Versilov couldn't stand slipcovers on furniture), with a few decent rugs, and a set of tables of various sizes, some of which were quite useless. The door on the right as one entered led to Versilov's narrow room, which had one window. It had a ramshackle desk strewn with dusty books and abandoned papers. Next to this desk was an equally wretched-looking armchair, with a spring sticking up in one corner that got in Versilov's way when he sat down and made him swear. It was on the old, threadbare sofa in this room that Versilov's bed was made up at night. Versilov hated this room that he referred to as his "study," and I don't think he ever did any work in there, for he mostly sat idly in the living room for hours on end. The door on the left led to another room of exactly the same size that was shared by my mother and sister. From the living room, a passage led to the kitchen where old Lukeria lived and cooked, and one could tell when she was cooking because the whole place reeked of burned fat. That stench sometimes made Versilov swear aloud and curse his existence, and on that point I fully sympathized with him because I too hate bad smells, even though they couldn't get all the way to my attic under the eaves, which I reached by very steep and shaky steps. The only things worth mentioning about that garret were a semicircular window, a very low slanting ceiling, and an oilcloth-covered sofa, on which at night Lukeria spread sheets and put a pillow for me to sleep. The rest of my furnishings consisted of two items: a plain wooden table and a ramshackle wicker chair.

There were, however, still some relics of the relative opulence of former days around the house. In the living room, for instance, there was quite a nice china lamp, and on the wall hung an excellent large engraving of the Sistine Madonna; on the opposite wall was a huge and probably expensive photograph of the bronze gates of the cathedral of Florence. In the corner of the living room was a big stand with the old family icons—one of which (the Icon of All Saints) had the gilded silver setting that they had been about to pawn, while another (the Icon of the Mother of God) had a velvet setting embroidered with pearls. Facing the icons was a little lamp that was lighted on every holiday.

Versilov was evidently quite unreceptive to the spiritual appeal of the icons. He also complained mildly, blinking to make his point, that the lamp reflected in the gilded setting irritated his eyes, but he never suggested that my mother stop lighting it.

When I entered the house, I was usually silent and unsmiling, I avoided looking at anyone and sometimes wouldn't even say hello. Since, as a rule, I returned home earlier than I did that day, Lukeria usually served me dinner in my room.

But today I came in and said "Good evening, Mother"—something I'd never done before, although even this time I couldn't bring myself to look at her and sat down awkwardly in a faraway corner of the living room. I was very tired, but that didn't matter.

"That lout still doesn't know how to behave when he walks in," Mrs. Prutkov hissed indignantly in my direction; "looks as if he'll never learn. . . ."

She couldn't refrain from abusing me whenever we met and by now it had become a sort of tradition between the two of us.

"Hello . . ." my mother mumbled, apparently taken by surprise by my greeting. "Your dinner has been ready a long time. . . . I hope the soup is still hot . . ." she added with embarrassment, "and I'll order the cutlets right away. . . ."

She got up and was about to rush out to the kitchen. Somehow, for the first time, I felt ashamed at seeing her leap up so eagerly to wait on me, although during the month I'd lived there, I'd seemed to expect it of her.

"Thank you very much, Mother, I've had dinner already. But I'd like to sit here for a while if I'm not in your way. . . ."

"Why, of course not . . . please, stay."

"And please don't worry, Mother, I won't be rude to Mr. Versilov again." I got it out all in one breath.

"Isn't that magnanimous of him!" Mrs. Prutkov shrieked. "Sofia, dear," she said, turning to my mother, "how long will you treat this oaf as if he were a little prince? What has he done to earn such consideration from his own mother? Why, you look all flustered in his presence, shame on you!"

"I'd be much happier myself if Mother didn't make a fuss over me."

"All right, I won't . . . I . . . I don't really . . ." Mother said hastily. "But from now on . . . I understand . . ."

Her face became very pink, and I thought that at times it could be a very attractive face. There was a certain charming sincerity about it without it being in the least simple-minded. Usually it was a bit pale, because of her anemia. Her cheeks were very thin, almost sunken, and her forehead was already heavily lined. But there were no lines around her big, wide-open eyes, from which shone a quiet and gentle light, eyes that had drawn me to her from the very first day. What I also liked about her face was that there was nothing sad or hurt in her expression; indeed, it might have been described as gay if it hadn't been for an ever-present note of alarm, which could suddenly turn into fright and make her jump to her feet, often for no reason at all. Sometimes she'd listen with intense apprehension to a conversation on an unfamiliar subject until she was fully satisfied that "all was well, just as before," because to her "just as before" meant that everything was all right: as long as nothing changed, even for the better, she was perfectly satisfied. Something may have frightened her as a child to make her fear any change so much. Besides her eyes, I also liked the oval shape of her face, and I believe that, if her cheekbones had been a bit less wide, one might have called her beautiful even now, let alone in her youth. She was no more than thirty-nine, but there was already quite a bit of gray in her dark hair.

Mrs. Prutkov looked at her with real indignation.

"Come on, Sofia, how can you tremble like that before that young clod! You're really ridiculous! Makes me angry to see you act like that!"

"Oh, Tatyana, why do you say all that about him now . . . you don't mean it seriously, do you?" Mother added, detecting something that might have been a smile on the old lady's lips.

It's true that Mrs. Prutkov's name-calling couldn't always be accepted at face value, but now, if she was smiling at all, her smile was directed exclusively at my mother because she was very fond of her for her kindness and I'm sure she'd noticed how pleased my mother was with my new-found meekness.

"Of course, people are bound to resent it if you attack them without any provocation, Mrs. Prutkov," I felt I had to put in, "and, as a matter of fact, you chose to pounce on me just when I came in with a friendly 'good evening,' which is something I've never done before."

"Can you imagine that—he considers that a feat of heroism!" she cried with a renewed burst of indignation. "Do you expect us, by any chance, to go down on our knees and thank you for having been almost polite for once? Besides, even now your manners are not all that perfect either, for why did you have to avoid looking at anyone and stare into a corner when you came in? And I know how you throw your weight around when you're alone with your mother! Also, you could've said hello to me too—I used to change you when you were a baby and I'm your godmother, after all!"

Obviously I ignored her. At that moment my sister came in and I turned to her at once.

"Lisa," I said, "today I made the acquaintance of Vasin. He asked me how you were. Do you know him?"

"I met Mr. Vasin last year in Luga," Lisa answered with complete simplicity as she sat down and looked at me gently.

Somehow I'd expected that she'd become terribly red when I spoke to her of Vasin. Lisa was very blond, almost towheaded, quite unlike our dark-haired parents. But her eyes and the oval shape of her face were just like Mother's. Her nose was very straight, regular, and just the right length. But her face, unlike Mother's, was freckled. From Versilov she'd inherited perhaps only his slender waist, his tallness, and his characteristic grace of movement. And there was not the slightest resemblance between the two of us—in fact, we were just about opposites.

"I've known the gentleman for three months," Lisa added.

"Why do you refer to Vasin as a 'gentleman,' Lisa? Why don't you just say 'him'? Forgive me for correcting you, but it offends me when you talk like that. They seem to have completely neglected your upbringing."

"And it's even more uncouth to make such remarks in front of your mother!" Mrs. Prutkov flared up again. "Besides, you're talking nonsense—her upbringing hasn't been neglected at all."

"It was no reproach to my mother," I replied sharply and, turning to Mother, went on: "I think Lisa is just like you, Mother—you have given her a nature just as kind and charming as your own. . . . I'm sure you were just as lovely as she is now. . . . I mean you still are and always will be. . . . I was simply talking about varnish, those superficial things, you know, those stupid but socially indispensable graces. . . . What makes me furious is that Versilov never bothers to correct you when you refer to people so humbly, because he's so full of himself and cares nothing about any of us. That's what drives me mad!"

"You're about as graceful as a bear yourself and you're trying to teach people refined manners. To start with, who do you think you're referring to as 'Versilov' in front of your mother? And I won't stand for it myself either, d'you hear me?" Mrs. Prutkov rattled with flashing eyes.

"I got my salary today, Mother, fifty rubles. Here, please take it."

I got up, walked over to her, and handed her the money. She became terribly agitated.

"I don't know if I should take it. . . ."

She seemed afraid to touch the money. I couldn't understand why.

"But I'm one of the family, I'm your son and Lisa's brother. So . . ."

"I'm sorry, Arkady. I wish I could tell you something but I don't know how you'd take it. . . ."

She said that with a shy, beseeching smile, but I still didn't understand and interrupted her.

"Did you know, by the way, that the lawsuit between Mr. Versilov and the Princes Sokolsky is being decided today?"

"Oh, is it?" she cried, clasping her hands in front of her in her characteristic gesture of alarm.

"Today?" Mrs. Prutkov cried with a deep shiver of surprise. "Impossible! He'd have told me! Did he tell you, Sofia?"

"No, not that it was today. But I've been waiting and worrying the whole week. I pray God we lose the suit just to get it over with and then live just as we lived before."

"So he never told even you, Mother?" I said. "Ah, what a man! And this is a sample of his lack of consideration and superciliousness that I was talking about, so you see!"

"So how was it decided, how? And who told you anyway?" Mrs. Prutkov kept hammering at me. "Come on, man, speak up, for heaven's sake!"

"He'll tell you himself because here he is!" I said, hearing Versilov's step in the passage and hastily installing myself next to Lisa.

"For Mother's sake, Arkady, be polite with him," Lisa whispered in my ear.

"Don't worry, I'll behave, I came with that intention," I said, squeezing her arm.

Lisa looked at me with distrust. And she turned out to be right.

II

He was so pleased with himself when he came in that he didn't even attempt to hide it. Besides, lately he had stopped bothering to control himself in our presence and allowed us to see not only his evil side but also his ridiculous side, which most people are afraid to reveal. And we certainly did see it down to the last detail. According to Mrs. Prutkov, during this last year he had increasingly lost interest in his appearance and, although he was still decently dressed, his suits began to look old and he wore them without his former distinction. He had decided, for instance, to change his shirt and underwear only every other day. This made Mother very sad and was considered in the house as a great sacrifice on his part, which the collection of admiring females around him described as "heroic."

In the passage he took off his soft, wide-brimmed felt hat, the kind he always wore, and a shock of thick hair streaked with silver sprang up. I always liked to look at his hair come to life as he took off his hat.

"Good evening, I see you're all here, even including you," he said, turning to me. "I heard your voice from the passage. You were saying unkind things about me, I bet."

When he was in a good mood, he'd always tease me; it was an unfailing sign, in fact. Of course I didn't answer.

Then Lukeria came in with her arms loaded with parcels which she put down on the table.

"Victory, Tatyana!" he cried, looking at Mrs. Prutkov. "The case is won and I don't expect the Sokolskys will appeal the decision. We've won! And now immediately I've managed to borrow a thousand rubles without any difficulty! Put away that sewing, Sofia, don't strain your eyes, there's no need any more. Back from work, Lisa?"

"Yes, Papa," Lisa said, looking at him with warmth.

She called him "Papa" or "Father," which was something I absolutely refused to do.

"Tired, Lisa?"

"A bit."

"Don't go to work tomorrow, you're through with working."

"I'd rather go on working, Papa, I wouldn't feel right without it."

"Please, Lisa. . . . You know, Tatyana, how I hate women to work."

"Why shouldn't women work? What an idea—a woman doing nothing!"

"I know, I know, you may be right, I concede. . . . But I was talking particularly about needlework. I think I feel like that because of a painful impression—morbidly painful perhaps —from my childhood. Out of my dim recollections dating from the time when I was five or six, I can see, more and more clearly now and with infinite loathing, a group of intelligent women with stern and sullen expressions sitting around a table with scissors, material, patterns, and designs strewn all over it. All these women express their opinions, judge, estimate, calculate, shake their heads gravely, measure, and prepare to cut. All these friendly, nice faces that usually radiate love for me are now inaccessible and, if I become the tiniest bit too noisy, too playful, I know I'll be ordered out of the room. Even my poor nanny, whose hand rests on my shoulder as though holding me back, ignores my protests and my tugging at her and gapes at the table with the rapture of somebody watching a firebird. It is that severe and solemn concentration of intelligent faces preceding the cutting that is somehow so painful for me to remember to this day. You, Tatyana, you really love making dresses! Well, it may be a terribly aristocratic prejudice, but I do prefer women who don't work at all. But please don't take it personally, Sofia, why should you after all? A woman wields tremendous power whatever she does, you know that, Sofia, don't you? And what's your opinion, Arkady? I'm sure you disagree with me. . . ."

"No, not particularly," I said. "In fact, I liked the way you put it about a woman wielding tremendous power, although I'm not sure why you had to connect it with her working or not. Besides, you must know perfectly well that a woman can't help working when there's no money in the house."

"But now there's enough money," he said, turning back to Mother, who positively beamed under his gaze (I saw her shiver when Versilov addressed me), "and so, at least for a while, I want to see no sewing around here, please, please, I'm asking this as a personal favor. You, Arkady, being a young man of this generation, you're probably something of a socialist and I'm sure you don't like the idea that idleness is appreciated the most among the toiling masses."

"No, not idleness, but rest perhaps."

"No, I mean precisely idleness—the ideal of doing nothing at all. I once knew a man who slaved all the time. True, he didn't actually come from the 'masses,' being fairly well educated and capable of some abstract thinking. Every day of his life that man longed passionately for total idleness, absolute, infinite independence, eternal freedom of fancy, the perfect passivity of contemplation. And this went on until he broke completely under the strain of work, until he was beyond repair and died in a hospital. I sometimes seriously think that it was idle people who invented the notion of the joy of hard work, although I'm sure they meant well. That's one of those Geneva* ideas of the end of the last century."

He took a folded newspaper clipping out of his vest pocket. "Listen, Tatyana," he said, looking at Mrs. Prutkov, "I cut this out the day before yesterday. It's obviously written by one of those eternal students who know Latin and Greek and mathematics and who are prepared to go anywhere and live in a garret or any place. It says: 'A lady teacher will prepare pupils for all schools and colleges [please note: *for all!*] and will give lessons in arithmetic.' A single line, but a classic! If she'll prepare pupils, as she claims, for all schools and colleges it might be taken for granted that that includes arithmetic too. But no, she has to mention arithmetic specifically. That indicates real hun-

* A reference to Jean-Jacques Rousseau. [A. MacA.]

ger, the last degree of hardship! What is touching is her clumsiness: obviously she never prepared for a teaching career and most likely she's quite incapable of teaching anything to anyone. But, although she's at the point when she may drown herself, she uses her last ruble on advertising herself as preparing students for all schools and colleges and, on top of that, teaching arithmetic. *Per tutto mundo e in altri siti*—all over the world and in other places."

"Oh, Andrei, couldn't we do something for her? Where does she live?" Tatyana Prutkov asked eagerly.

"No, there are too many of them," he said, putting the clipping back in his pocket. "Here are a few little presents I bought for you: here, Lisa, and this is for you, Tatyana. Sofia and I, we don't care for sweet things, you know. I suppose you could do with some candy too, young man. I went specially to Eliseev's and Balle's to get them. I felt we'd been 'sitting and feeling empty with hunger,' as Lukeria says." (N.B. None of us had ever gone hungry, of course.) "Here are some grapes, candy, pears, and strawberry tarts. I got quite a good liqueur. . . . And there're some nuts. It's funny, I've always been crazy about nuts, ever since I was a small child, and I still am—the most ordinary nuts too. Lisa takes after me, you know, Tatyana, she can go on all day cracking nuts like a squirrel. Of the childhood scenes preserved in my memory, to me the most enchanting are those when I see myself in a forest, in a copse, picking nuts. . . . It's almost autumn, the weather is bright, but sometimes there's a crisp edge in the air . . . alone, out of sight of anybody, deep in the woods . . . it smells of leaves. . . . Did I see a look of understanding in your eye, Arkady?"

"I spent my early childhood in the country too, after all."

"Did you, really? If I'm not mistaken, you lived in Moscow. . . ."

"He was living in Moscow at the Andronikovs at the time you went there, but until then he stayed with your late Aunt Barbara at her country estate," Mrs. Prutkov set him straight.

"Sofia, here's some money. Put it away. They promised to pay me five thousand in a few days."

"So the Sokolskys have no hope of getting anything?" Mrs. Prutkov inquired.

"None whatsoever."

"I've been always on your side, Andrei, and I've always concerned myself with the welfare of those close to you, but now, although the Moscow Sokolskys are practically strangers to me,

I assure you, I feel terribly sorry for them, and I hope you forgive me for saying so."

"Still, I have no intention of sharing anything with them, Tatyana."

"Of course, you've known what I thought about it all along: they'd never have gone to court if you'd offered to let them have half the sum from the start. I know it's too late now. . . . However, I've no right to judge anyone. . . . All I'm trying to say is that the deceased would never have left them out altogether."

"Not only wouldn't he have left them out, he'd most certainly have left everything to them and nothing to me, that is, if he'd attended to his business properly and left a valid will. But, as things stand, I have the law on my side, and that's that. There's nothing I can do for the Sokolskys, nor do I have any wish to do anything for them. And that's the end of the matter, Tatyana."

I detected irritation in his voice, which was something he seldom allowed himself. Mrs. Prutkov fell silent. My mother looked sadly at him, then lowered her eyes: he knew she agreed with Mrs. Prutkov.

It occurred to me that the slap in the face he had received at Ems had something to do with his present attitude. I could well imagine now what would have happened to the document Kraft had given me if it had fallen into Versilov's hands! I became acutely conscious of my complicity in this affair if I did nothing, and my irritation grew.

"Listen, Arkady," he said, "I'd like you to order yourself some better clothes. . . . Oh, your suit's perfectly all right, but you may have to be well dressed in the future and I'd like to recommend to you a French tailor who is extremely conscientious and also has good taste. . . ."

"I'd appreciate it if you'd never make me such an offer again," I cut in.

"Why do you say that?"

"It's not that I consider your offer humiliating, but inasmuch as I don't agree with your way of looking at things, or rather since I sharply disapprove of it, I intend to discontinue my employment at Prince Sokolsky's, where there is nothing for me to do. . . ."

"But your service to him consists in keeping him company."

"Such an idea is insulting."

"I don't quite follow you. But if you're so proud, you can still keep him company while refusing to be paid for it. It would be very painful for him if you left him now, I'm sure he's got quite attached to you by this time. But please yourself, after all."

I understood that he didn't like talking about it.

"Well, now you tell me not to accept money from him, but it so happens that just today I had to lower myself to ask him to pay me my month's salary because you never bothered to inform me that there was no need to do so."

"So you've done it already! Well, I admit I thought you wouldn't ask him. But, I must say, you're all so awfully practical nowadays! There're no young people these days, Tatyana, are there?"

He was annoyed. And my anger was growing too.

"Why, I had to settle whatever I owed you. . . . It was you who really forced me to claim for my salary. And now I have no idea what to do about it."

"By the way, Sofia, would you please give Arkady back his sixty rubles. And you, my boy, please don't see anything offensive in such a prompt repayment of our debt. It's written all over your face that you've got plans in your head that require a capital investment, or something of that sort."

"I don't know what the writing on my face tells you, but I must say I never expected Mother to tell you about that money since I'd asked her specially not to say anything to you."

I glared at my mother. I felt terribly offended.

"Arkasha, darling, forgive me, dear, but how could I not tell. . . ."

"Don't be angry with your mother for having told me, Arkady. Besides, she meant well: she felt a mother's pride in her son's fine feelings. Anyway I'd have guessed even without her that you're a capitalist. All your secrets are written plainly on your honest face. He has *his idea*, Tatyana, I told you about it."

"Let's leave my honest face out of it!" I cried out with rage. "And I know that you have the capacity to see through things, although mostly you can see no further than your own nose. Well, I must pay my respects to your ability to penetrate people's secrets. Yes, indeed, I do have 'my idea' and, although it's obviously pure coincidence that that's how you referred to it, I'm not afraid to say it openly: 'my idea' exists and I'm neither afraid nor ashamed to admit it."

"Above all, don't feel ashamed."

"But I'll never tell you what it is."

"You mean, you won't condescend to let me in on it. Well,

you needn't bother, my friend, because I already know the essence of it. In any case, it's something like that line

'Into wilderness I shall withdraw . . .'†

Shall I tell you what I think his idea is, Tatyana? He wants to be a Rothschild or somebody like that and withdraw into his own greatness. Of course, he'll pay us a generous allowance—well, perhaps not me—but, in any case, we won't see much of him any more: he'll be like a young crescent moon—he'll rise only to vanish again."

I shuddered inwardly. Of course, it was sheer coincidence. He knew nothing about my idea and meant something quite different, even though he'd brought in Rothschild's name. But how could he have known of my longing to break off relations with them all and withdraw? He had guessed everything and was trying to despoil the tragic beauty of truth by his cynicism. One thing was sure—he was now furious with me.

"Please forgive my explosion, Mother," I said with an affected laugh, trying to turn everything into a joke, "I was so embarrassed when I realized that nothing could be concealed from Mr. Versilov!"

"I'm glad you're laughing now, my boy," Versilov said, "it's the best thing under the circumstances. It's incredible how much people gain by laughing and it makes them look so much better too. I mean that seriously, you know. Don't you think, Tatyana, he always looks as though he had something so important on his mind that this somehow makes him ill at ease?"

"I must ask you, sir, to be a bit more careful of what you say."

"I'm sorry, my friend, but I feel I must say once and for all what's on my mind so there won't be any need to go into it again. You came here from Moscow with the intention of putting us into our proper place, and so far that's all we know about your plans. Of course, I needn't add that you'd like to amaze us with something, that goes without saying. That's why you've been sitting here for a month snorting at us disdainfully, although an obviously intelligent boy like you could have left that sort of snorting to those who have nothing else with which to punish the world for their own mediocrity. You always avoid looking at people, although your honest face and healthy red cheeks prove that you could perfectly well look people straight in the eye with complete impunity. He imagines things, he's a hypochon-

† The first line of a song very popular in the 1870s in Russia. [A. MacA.]

driac, Tatyana, that's what he is! I don't know why the whole new generation should be a bunch of hypochondriacs!"

"You didn't even know where I lived as a child, so how could you possibly know whether there wasn't reason for me to become a hypochondriac?"

"Is it possible that it should offend you so much that I didn't know where you lived as a child?"

"Certainly not, and I wish you'd stop attributing such asinine ideas to me! Mother, Mr. Versilov was pleased just now when I laughed, so let's all laugh instead of sitting around with such grave faces! Would you like me to tell you some amusing stories about myself? It might be fun, especially since it turns out that Mr. Versilov knows nothing of my past adventures."

I was boiling inside. I felt that we'd never again sit all together like this and that, once I left this house, I'd never come back. And so I couldn't restrain myself. He had provoked me to this parting scene.

"It would be charming," he said, looking at me penetratingly, "provided, of course, your stories are really amusing. You've grown a bit vulgar, my boy, wherever it was you happened to live, although, on the whole, you're still quite presentable. He's very sweet today, don't you think, Tatyana? Ah, at last, I'm so glad you finally seem to be succeeding in opening that box of candy. . . ."

But Mrs. Prutkov was frowning. She didn't even look at him and went on slowly opening the packages and laying out the fruit and the candy on the plates that had been brought in. Mother also looked quite worried, obviously feeling that something had gone wrong between us. My sister touched my arm once more.

III

"I simply want to tell you about a father meeting his beloved son for the first time," I started in as casual a tone as I could manage. "And this meeting took place precisely wherever it was the boy lived as a child."

"Are you sure, my friend, this won't be an awfully boring story? You know, *tous les genres* . . ."‡

"Relax, sir, there's really nothing for you to worry about. I fully intend to make everybody laugh."

"May God help you, my boy, I know how fond you are of

‡ *"Tous les genres sont bons hors le genre ennuyeux,"* from Voltaire's comedy *Le fils prodige.* [A. MacA.]

all of us and I'm sure you wouldn't want to spoil our evening," he said with affected casualness.

"Once again you must have read my fondness for you on my face!"

"That's true: partly I read it on your face."

"Well, for my part, I read on Mrs. Prutkov's face that she's madly in love with me. Please don't glare at me as if you were about to tear me to pieces, Mrs. Prutkov; try to laugh it off instead—that'd be much better."

She had turned toward me abruptly and, for half a minute, her piercing eyes had been fixed on my face.

"Watch out," she said, shaking her finger at me, but with such a serious expression that it certainly could not have referred to my stupid joke but must have been a warning to me "not to start anything now."

"Tell me then, sir, can't you really remember the first time we met?"

"I'm afraid not, my boy, and believe me, I'm really sorry, I've completely forgotten. I only know it was sometime very long ago and it was somewhere . . . somewhere . . ."

"And you, Mother, do you remember coming to the village where I lived until the age of six or seven? Did you really come or did I just dream it up or invent it all in my imagination? Was it there that I saw you for the first time? I've meant to ask you about that for a long time but couldn't bring myself to do it until now."

"Of course, Arkasha, of course, my darling, I went to stay with your great aunt Barbara three times: the first time you were just one, the second you were almost three, and the third time was just after your sixth birthday."

"I've wanted to ask you about that all month."

Mother's face grew all pink from the sudden flow of memories and she asked me tenderly:

"But is it possible you remember that, Arkasha, my darling?"

"No, I don't remember anything, I don't know anything for sure. But there's something about your face that has stayed with me all my life, and a feeling that it was the face of my mother. And I see the whole village and Auntie Barbara's estate like in a dream. I've even forgotten my nanny, who was with me every day. Auntie Barbara I remember mostly because she used to bandage her jaw when she had a toothache. I also remember very tall trees by the house, lime trees, I think, and blinding sunshine pouring in the windows, the little flower garden in front of the house, the narrow path. . . . And of you, Mother,

I have a clear picture only during one second: they took me to church once to receive the sacrament and you picked me up so I could receive the host and kiss the chalice. . . . It was summertime, and a pigeon entered a window of the cupola, flew across it and out the window on the opposite side. . . ."

"Yes, yes, that's right, oh good Lord!" Mother cried, throwing up her hands. "I remember the dove. Just as I lifted you up to the chalice, you suddenly got all excited and started squeaking: 'Look, look, little pigeon, little pigeon! There, up there!' "

"Your face, or something about it, the expression perhaps, became so deeply engraved in my memory that I immediately recognized you five years later in Moscow, although no one told me you were my mother. As to Mr. Versilov, I saw him for the first time the day when I was taken away from the Andronikovs where I had been peacefully and happily vegetating for five years. I remember the Andronikovs' apartment down to the minutest detail, and I remember all the ladies and girls who were there and who look so much older today and Andronikov, how he would go to town to do the shopping himself and bring home fish, chickens, and suckling pigs, how at the table often he would serve instead of his wife, who liked to give herself such airs, and how this made us giggle and how he was the first to laugh at himself. Those young ladies taught me French there, but what I liked best were Krylov's fables. I learned lots of them by heart and recited a fable to Andronikov each time I entered his tiny study, whether he was busy or not. In fact, it was with a Krylov fable that I made your acquaintance, sir. . . . I think something's coming back to you, am I right?"

"Yes, yes, my boy, I remember you reciting me something. . . . Was it a fable or was it a passage from *Woe from Wit*? Your memory is really extraordinary!"

"Memory? No, it's the one thing I've never forgotten."

"Very, very good, my boy, you've helped me to bring that scene back to life. . . ."

He even smiled at the resurrected past and, seeing him smile, Mother and Lisa began to smile too. They seemed to feel reassured. Only Mrs. Prutkov, who had finished laying out the goodies and had settled herself in a corner, kept throwing disapproving looks at me.

"This is how it happened," I went on. "One bright morning the guardian angel of my childhood, Mrs. Prutkov, suddenly arrived. As always she simply appeared, as characters appear on the stage. She got me into a carriage and we drove to a sumptuous mansion—Mrs. Fanariotov's house, the one she'd bought from you, sir. There was no one there at the time because Mrs. Fanariotov was traveling abroad. On that occasion, I had to wear an elegant little blue suit and even a new shirt instead of my usual short jacket. All day Mrs. Prutkov fussed over my appearance and bought me a lot of things. Afterward, I wandered from room to room all over the deserted house, looking at myself in the mirrors. And that's how, the next morning around ten as I again started wandering from room to room, I stumbled by chance into your study. I had already caught sight of you the day before when we'd just arrived, but only for a second as you were on your way downstairs and then you got into a carriage and drove off somewhere. That time, you had come to Moscow by yourself after a long absence, and as you were planning to stay only a short time, you had to see lots of people and hardly spent any time at home. When you noticed us—Mrs. Prutkov and me—you just drawled 'ah-ah!' and didn't even stop."

Versilov turned to Mrs. Prutkov.

"He describes it so lovingly, doesn't he?" he said.

She turned away from him without answering.

"I can still see you, the way you looked then," I went on, "so handsome and the picture of health. It's amazing how much older and less handsome you've grown in these nine years! I hope you don't mind my frankness. Although you were about thirty-seven at the time, I couldn't take my eyes off you and just stood there staring in admiration. Your hair was really amazing, almost jet black and shining, without one gray hair in it. Your whiskers and your mustache were perfect, as though cut by a jeweler—I can't describe it any other way. Your complexion was fair, but not sickly pale as it is today; then it was rather like the complexion of your daughter Anna, whom I had the honor of meeting earlier today. Your eyes were dark and burning and your teeth flashed every time you laughed. And that's just what you did when you saw me—you began to laugh. I was not very discriminating at that time and was delighted by your gaiety. That morning you wore a dark blue velvet jacket, a sulfur-colored scarf around your neck, and a magnificent shirt trimmed with Alençon lace. As I came in, you were standing in front of a mirror with some sheets of paper in your hand and were declaiming Chatsky's closing monologue from *Woe from Wit*,* you know, 'Send me my carriage, send it right away!' "

"Good Lord, he's really amazing! Although I was in Moscow

* Griboyedov's classic play written in 1824. [A. MacA.]

for only a few days, I'd accepted to stand in at short notice for Zhileiko (who'd suddenly fallen ill) in the role of Chatsky. It was for a performance at Alexandra Vitovtov's private theater. . . ."

"You hadn't really forgotten it, had you, Andrei?" Mrs. Prutkov said, laughing.

"I had indeed, but he has brought it back to life now. Come to think of it, those few days in Moscow may've been the happiest in my life. We were still so young then and were still fervently waiting for something. . . . It was during that stay in Moscow that I met so many— But please go on, my boy, I'm so glad that you've brought all these memories back to me."

"I stood gaping at you for a moment and then cried out: 'It's great—just like the real Chatsky!' You suddenly turned toward me and asked: 'Why, have you met Chatsky before?' Then you sat down on the sofa and took a sip of coffee out of a cup on the table. You seemed so cheerful and pleasant that I felt like throwing my arms around your neck and hugging you. Then I told you that they read a lot in Andronikov's house, that the young girls knew a lot of things by heart, that they sometimes acted out whole scenes from *Woe from Wit*, and that last week we'd been reading aloud Turgenev's *Hunter's Sketches*, but that what I liked best were Krylov's fables and that I knew many of them by heart. You asked me to recite you one and I recited *The Fussy Maid*, which starts 'A girl may weigh the merits of her suitor . . .'"

"Right, right, now everything is coming back to me!" Versilov cried with delight. "And now I remember you very clearly, my dear friend—you were such a sweet, bright little boy! I must say that, alas, you too have changed considerably for the worse in these nine years."

They all laughed at that crack, especially Mrs. Prutkov, who let herself go quite unrestrainedly: they thought it was very clever, the way he'd paid me back for my dig at him. Well, I admit he pulled it off quite effectively.

"So I was reciting the fable to you and you were listening smilingly, but before I was halfway through, you stopped me, rang for the servant, and told him to ask Mrs. Prutkov to come to your study. She arrived very quickly, in a hurry and out of breath, but looking so different, so cheerful, and smiling so blissfully that I could hardly recognize her. You made me recite *The Fussy Maid* all over again and this time I got all the way to the end and finished with a flourish that made even Mrs. Prutkov smile at me while you yourself went as far as to shout

'Bravo, bravo!' You even added that if I'd recited *The Grass-
hopper and the Ant* with such good understanding, you
wouldn't have been so surprised, but that fable was quite a different matter. 'Did you hear,' you said, 'how this boy, at his age,
recited the lines

> A girl may weigh the merits of her suitor
> There's no crime in that . . .

the way he stressed the words "no crime in that"?' You were
really full of appreciation. Then you started saying something
in French to Mrs. Prutkov that at once brought a frown to her
brow. She began arguing with you, very heatedly too, but who
can resist Andrei Versilov if he suddenly decides upon something? So she took me by the hand, led me away, washed my
face and hands, made me change my underwear and my shirt,
pomaded and even curled my hair. Then she herself went to
change and came out dressed so gorgeously that I gaped at her
openmouthed. Then the two of us got into the carriage and
drove to the theater. It was the first time in my life that I'd been
taken to a theater, even if only a private performance. The
lights, the chandeliers, the elegant ladies, the dashing officers,
the important government officials, the pretty young girls, the
rows of chairs, the curtain. . . . I'd never seen anything like
that. . . . Mrs. Prutkov installed herself in a very modest seat
in one of the back rows and made me sit down next to her. Of
course, there were also some children of my age, but I had no
time to take a good look at them so impatient was I for the spec-
tacle to start.

"When you came on, sir, I was ecstatic to the point of tears.
Why was I in such a state? I couldn't possibly explain it. Why
did tears of rapture fill my eyes? I don't know and for the nine
years that followed I felt completely overcome every time I remembered it. I breathlessly followed the plot of the comedy, of
which I, of course, only understood that *she* was unfaithful to
him and that stupid people, unworthy of his little finger, were
making fun of *him*. And when *he* delivered his monologue during the ball I gathered that he'd been insulted and humiliated,
that he was denouncing all these wretched creatures, and that
he was truly great! Of course, I'd been well prepared by the
readings at Andronikov's house, but it was, above all, the way
you recited it, yes, your acting, sir! And in the final scene when
the guests were leaving and Chatsky called for his carriage, the
amazing way you shouted 'Send me my carriage . . .' made me
leap to my feet, with the rest of the audience, frantically clap

my hands, and yell 'bravo, bravo' at the top of my voice. I also clearly remember the sensation of a violent sting through the seat of my pants, which turned out to be a furious pinch from Mrs. Prutkov. But I hardly paid any attention to it. Of course, as soon as the performance was over, she whisked me away home. 'Why, you didn't expect that you'd stay for the reception and the dance,' she kept hissing at me in the carriage, 'and it's because of you that I couldn't stay myself.'

"I was almost delirious that night, and the following morning at ten I was waiting by the door of your study. But the door was closed, there were people with you, discussing business matters. Then I heard you all leave the house and you were still out that night when I went to sleep. What it was I wanted to tell you so badly I've forgotten, although I'm sure I didn't even know at the time. All I know is that I was in a great hurry to see you. And the morning after that, it was not even eight o'clock when you left for Serpukhov. Around that time, you had sold your Tula estate to pay off your debts, after which you still had quite a bit of money left over. So now you could show yourself in Moscow without fearing your creditors. There was only that 'ill-mannered clod from Serpukhov' who wouldn't settle temporarily for half of what you owed him instead of the whole thing. . . . When I asked about you, Mrs. Prutkov would just ignore my questions: 'That's none of your business. Better get your books and notebooks in order, for remember, I'm taking you to school the day after tomorrow. And it's time you learned to pack your things yourself; you can't expect always to have someone waiting on you.' And you'd start nagging at me for this or that, Mrs. Prutkov, I suppose to drown me out, whenever I mentioned Mr. Versilov during those two or three days.

"And so, sir, I was whisked off to Touchard's boarding school, completely innocent and full of adoration for you, and although this was nothing but a silly incident—I mean that first meeting of ours—would you believe me if I told you that six months later I was planning to run away from Touchard's to you?"

"You told it all very vividly and brought everything back to me very strongly," Versilov said, pronouncing every syllable with slow deliberation. "And what impresses me particularly in your story is the wealth of certain peculiar details, for instance, about my debts. Disregarding the fact that it may be indiscreet on your part to bring up these facts, it is really quite beyond me how you managed to get hold of this information."

"You want to know how I managed to get hold of all this

information? But I told you—I've spent the last nine years finding out everything I could about you."

"Why do you allow him to talk to you like that, Andrei? Why
don't you kick him out?" Mrs. Prutkov hissed, unable to restrain herself.

"No, wait, Tatyana," Versilov said in a tone that made her
lower her eyes. "I'm sure Arkady has something on his mind, so
let him finish. I can see he's very anxious to get it off his chest.
So go on, my boy, start on the next tale. But, as you can well
imagine, it won't be all that new to me since I already know the
ending."

IV

"My plan to run away and join you was quite simple. Do you
remember, Mrs. Prutkov, the letter you received from
Touchard's school a couple of weeks after I'd been taken there?
Maria showed me that letter much later because it ended up in
Andronikov's files after his death. Touchard had suddenly decided that he wasn't charging enough for me and wrote in a
dignified tone that he had sons of princes and senators in his
establishment, that it lowered the tone of the school to keep a
boy with a family background like mine, and that unless he
received an additional—"

"Really, *mon cher*, couldn't you spare us . . ."

"Oh, that's nothing, nothing at all, and, anyway, it's not so
important what I have to say about Touchard. I remember,
though, how purple his face was when he walked into class that
day. He was a short, thick-set Frenchman of thirty-five or so, a
true Parisian he claimed, although, of course, a former bootmaker's apprentice. He had been in Moscow from time im-
memorial and had taught French ever since his arrival among
us. Eventually, he had been given official sanction as an educa-
tor, which made him inordinately proud. Otherwise he was a
man of crass ignorance. Actually, he had only six boys in his
school and it is true that one of them was the nephew of a Moscow senator; and we all lived like a family under the supervision of his wife, a genteel Russian lady, the daughter of some
minor government official.

"During the first two weeks, I showed off unrestrainedly to
my comrades, boasting of my blue suit and of my papa, Mr.
Andrei Versilov. And when they asked me 'How come, then,
your name is Dolgoruky and not Versilov?' that didn't bother
me at all because I myself had no idea 'how come.' "

"Stop him, Andrei!" Mrs. Prutkov shouted threateningly.

My mother, on the other hand, was looking at me with intense interest and apparently wanted me to go on.

"That Touchard fellow," Versilov said thoughtfully, "I do remember now—a fussy little man. . . . But he'd been highly recommended to me. . . ."

"Well, that Touchard fellow walked in with a letter in his hand, went up to the big oak table at which all six of us were sitting doing our homework, grabbed me by the shoulder, lifted me from my seat, and told me to pick up all my books and follow him.

" 'You shouldn't be here, your place is over there!' he said, pointing to a tiny room that gave onto the passage where there was only an unpainted wooden table, a wicker chair, and a sofa covered with a checkered oilcloth just like the one in my attic here. I was both very surprised and very frightened, for I had never yet been treated so roughly. Later, when Touchard left the classroom, I returned there and exchanged glances with the other boys. They began to laugh and I laughed too, thinking that we were all laughing because it was funny. It never occurred to me then that they were laughing at me. But suddenly Touchard burst into the room, seized me by the hair, and started dragging me all over the place.

" 'You have no right to sit with respectable children! You are of disgraceful origin—you're as low as a flunkey!' And he slapped my rosy, round cheeks resoundingly. It hurt. But he obviously liked the way it felt slapping me, for he slapped me again and then again. I cried and sobbed. I was completely bewildered. For a whole hour afterward, I sat weeping with my face buried in my hands. I couldn't understand what had happened and I still don't understand how a man like Touchard, who was not particularly ferocious, who although a foreigner was so pleased about the emancipation of the Russian serfs, could enjoy beating a stupid child like me. Actually I was surprised rather than offended, for I didn't yet know what being offended was. I thought I must've done something wrong but that I'd mend my ways somehow and would be forgiven. And then everybody would laugh again and we'd go and play outside and would have a better time than ever before."

"If only I had known, Arkady, what a horrible little man that Touchard was," Versilov said, with the tired smile of a man who has been listening for a long time. "However, I still haven't lost hope that someday you'll find enough strength in you to forgive us for everything and then we'll all live happily ever after."

I'm sure I saw him suppress a yawn.

"You've got me all wrong!" I shouted, staring at him in bewilderment, "I'm not reproaching you for anything, nor am I complaining about Touchard! As a matter of fact, he only beat me for a couple of months or so. I remember trying to appease him somehow. I'd try and kiss his hands, did kiss them in fact, and I cried and cried. The other boys laughed at me and despised me because Touchard started to use me as a servant, ordered me to hand him his clothes when he dressed. My instinctive servility was useful in this case: I tried hard to please him and felt not in the least insulted because I didn't understand yet about these things. It still amazes me how stupid I was then not to understand that I was not the equal of all these people. It's true that the other boys contributed quite a bit to my eventual understanding—it was a good school in that respect. Eventually Touchard stopped slapping me and, instead, kicked me from behind with his knee. And six months later, he was occasionally even quite nice to me, hitting me perhaps no more than once a month just to remind me of my place. And eventually he allowed me to sit at the table with the other boys and play with them. But not for one second in the two and a half years I spent at his school did Touchard forget my socially inferior status, and he continued using me occasionally for menial tasks, perhaps to make sure that proper order was respected.

"As for running away, I decided on that only about five months after those first dreadful couple of months. In general, all my life I've been very slow to take action. Every night when I went to bed and pulled the blanket over my head, I'd always go back to making up those romances about you, sir, about you alone, I don't know why. And when I fell asleep, it was you I'd dream of. The scene I liked best to imagine was you arriving at the school, me throwing myself into your arms, and you taking me away, to that Moscow study where we'd met and then to the theater, and things like that. And we would never be parted again—that was the most important!

"But in the mornings I had to wake up and get out of bed. Then the baiting by the boys would start all over again. One of them would beat me up first thing every morning and force me to bring him his boots while calling me disgusting names and explaining the secrets of my birth to the great enjoyment of the others. By the time Touchard came around, I was utterly miserable. I felt that I'd never be forgiven by these people and I began to understand what I'd done wrong. Yes, I finally did gather how I was wrong and why I couldn't be forgiven! And that's when I decided to run away. I dreamed incessantly of running away for two months. Then September came around and I decided it was time to go carry out my plan. I waited for all the boys to leave school on Saturday night to spend Sunday with their families. I had carefully made a bundle of the most indispensable things to take with me. I had two rubles in cash. I thought I'd wait until it got dark enough. I'd go downstairs, go out the gates, and start walking. Where would I go? I knew that the Andronikovs had moved to Petersburg. So I'd find Mrs. Fanariotov's house on Arbat Drive. I'd spend the night walking around or hide myself in a doorway, and in the morning I'd try to find out from someone in the courtyard of the Fanariotov house where Mr. Versilov lived, if not in Moscow, then what town or what country. I was sure they'd tell me. And then I'd go back into the street and ask someone else by which gate I should leave Moscow to get to such and such a town or country and I'd start walking. I'd sleep at night under the bushes and I'd eat nothing but bread because one can buy lots of bread with two rubles.

"But I couldn't manage to slip out of the school Saturday night and had to wait until Sunday. It so happened that Touchard and his wife went out somewhere for the day and I was all alone with Agafia. I waited for night to come in a state of terrible anguish. I remember sitting by the schoolroom window, looking out at the dusty street and the few passers-by. Touchard's school was on the edge of Petersburg and from the window I could see a city gate. Would that be the one for me, I wondered. The sun was so red as it rolled down the horizon and the sky looked awfully cold and the wickedly biting wind was raising clouds of dust just like today. At last it got quite dark. I knelt before the icon and prayed. But I prayed very quickly since I was in a great hurry. Then I picked up my little bundle and tiptoed down the creaking stairs, terrified at the thought that Agafia should hear me from the kitchen. The door was locked. I turned the key and suddenly there was the blackness of the night stretching in front of me, boundless, dangerous, and unknown. A burst of wind almost tore my cap off my head. I stepped out into the street. From across the street I heard a scream, a drunken voice, and a streak of foul oaths. I stood there for a few moments, looking out into the darkness. Then I turned around, went back into the house, walked quietly upstairs, unpacked my bundle, undressed, and lay down flat on my face. I didn't cry, my mind was blank, but it was this incident that started me thinking: it made me realize that, besides being a

flunkey, I was also a coward, and it was with this realization
that my real mental growth began!"

"Ah, now I can see through you once and for all!" Mrs. Prutkov exclaimed, jumping up from her seat with such suddenness
that she took me completely by surprise. "Not only did you
have a flunkey's mentality then, you still have a flunkey's mentality today, the soul of a true lackey! I wonder why Andrei
didn't place you as an apprentice to a bootmaker! That
would've been doing you a favor—at least you'd have learned a
trade. Who could've asked more of him? Your father, Makar
Dolgoruky, begged and even demanded that his children be left
in the social class where they belonged and not be pushed above
their natural station in life. Why, you don't even appreciate
that Andrei gave you the opportunity to study all the way to the
doors of the university and that, thanks to him, you have all
the privileges and advantages of a gentleman. But the little boys
teased you and you swore to wreak vengeance on humankind.
. . . No, you're an ungrateful little beast, that's what you are!"

I admit her outburst took me aback. I got up and stared at her.
For a moment I didn't know what to say.

"Well, I've learned something new about myself again from
Mrs. Prutkov," I said at last, looking fixedly at Versilov. "I
really must have a flunkey's soul for not appreciating enough
that Versilov didn't make a bootmaker out of me. Even the
'privileges of a gentleman' didn't move me to tears of gratitude!
Nothing satisfies me and I keep demanding more and, claiming
Versilov's complete attention . . . as a father! So obviously I'm
a born flunkey! Mother, I've had something weighing on my
conscience for eight years now—it's about the time you came to
see me at Touchard's school and the way I received you then—
but I cannot talk about that now. Mrs. Prutkov wouldn't allow
me to finish. Let's leave it to some other occasion, Mother, because you at least I hope to see again. . . . But perhaps I'm
such a flunkey, Mrs. Prutkov, that I cannot understand how a
man can decide to marry another woman when his wife is still
alive. And that's just what Mr. Andrei Versilov did at Ems.
Mother, if you do not wish to live with a man who may marry
another woman tomorrow, let me remind you that you have a
son who will always treat you with the greatest respect. But
you'll have to choose between him and me. You don't have to
decide right now; I appreciate that it takes time to make such a
decision, and . . ."

I couldn't go on. I was too agitated and lost the thread of my
thought. My mother's face was ashen. Her lips were moving,

but no sound came out of her mouth. It was as if I'd cut off her voice. Mrs. Prutkov was saying something so quickly and loudly that I couldn't even make out what it was, and twice she actually shoved me. I only registered her saying that it was all "sham," "the outpourings of a despicable mind," moreover "deliberately twisted and turned inside out."

Versilov sat without stirring. The smile had gone from his lips and his face was grave. I got up and went upstairs to my attic. The last thing I saw was my sister's reproachful glance. She also shook her head in disapproval.

Chapter 7

I

I have described what happened without sparing myself. I must try to recall every detail in order to re-create everything and re-capture the emotions. When I got to my room I wasn't sure whether to be ashamed of myself or proud, like someone who has accomplished his duty. If I'd had a little more experience, I'd have realized that in such cases the slightest doubt is a very bad sign. Moreover, I was completely disoriented by an unac-countable feeling of joy, although I suspected and was even sure that I'd made a mess of things downstairs. Even Mrs. Prut-kov's furious outburst now struck me as funny and I no longer felt in the least offended by it. Perhaps it was because I'd finally broken the chain that had linked me to them and I felt free.

I also felt that my dilemma of what to do about the letter concerning the lawsuit had become even more difficult to de-cide. Now they'd all think that I was trying to avenge myself on Versilov. Actually, though, even during the argument down-stairs, I'd already made up my mind to put the case before an impartial arbitrator—preferably Vasin or, if I couldn't get him, then a certain other person I had in mind. I'd go and see Vasin just for that purpose and then I'd disappear for several months from the sight of all these people, especially Vasin's. . . . I might, though, occasionally see my mother and sister during that time. . . .

Well, everything was topsy-turvy. I'd done what I had to do, but I hadn't gone about it the right way. . . . Still, I was satis-fied. As I said, I was pleased about I don't know what.

I meant to go to bed early, expecting the following day to be very hectic. I had to find myself another place to live, move there, and also do a few other things I had decided must be done. But before the evening was over, something unexpected happened and Versilov managed to surprise me once more.

He had never yet come up to my attic, but on this occasion I hadn't been there an hour before I heard him climbing up the steps. He called to me and asked me to light the way for him, so I went out with a candle and guided him the rest of the way.

"*Merci, mon ami*, you know, I've never been up here before, not even when I came to rent the house. I suspected what kind of place it was, but I didn't imagine it would be so much like a kennel." He stood in the middle of the room, examining it with curiosity. "It's more like a coffin, though, yes, a real coffin!" was his final verdict.

And, indeed, there was a certain resemblance to the inside of a coffin; I was quite impressed by the aptness of his comparison. It was a narrow box of a room and the ceiling sloped up from about the height of my shoulder on one side to the opposite end where I could still put the palm of my hand flat on the ceiling. At first Versilov instinctively held his head between his shoulders so as not to hit the ceiling, but he soon realized that there was headroom where he stood; he relaxed and sat down on the sofa, now looking quite at ease; it didn't seem to bother him at all that my bed had already been made up.

I remained standing and was staring at him in deep wonderment.

"Your mother tells me she didn't know whether she should have accepted the money you offered to pay her for your monthly board. Well, in view of this coffin, I believe that it's us rather who owe you compensation. As I said, I've never been up here before and I never imagined that anyone could possibly live in such a place."

"That's nothing, I'm used to it. But what I can't get over is seeing you here, with me, after all that happened downstairs."

"It's true you were quite rude just now, but . . . well, I may have some ideas of my own and I'll explain them to you. Besides, there's nothing so extraordinary in my coming here to see you or in the scene that took place downstairs. Such outbursts are not so very unusual. But please tell me this: Is it possible that what you told us today, after preparing us so solemnly for God knows what fantastic revelations, was actually all you had to say?"

"That's all. Or rather let's say that's all."

"It's not very much then, my boy, and I confess that after your preliminaries, your promises to make us laugh, and your obvious eagerness to talk, I had expected more of you."

"But why should it worry you one way or the other?"

"It offends my sense of proportion: if that was all, you shouldn't have made such a production out of it. You kept silent for a whole month, storing up something, preparing yourself, and then . . . nothing!"

"I meant to go on and say more but now I'm sorry I even said that much. There are things that are difficult to convey in words and are better left unsaid. And this seems to be the case here, for I was under the impression I did communicate something but now I find you didn't understand a thing."

"I see that sometimes it exasperates you too that a thought refuses to let itself be molded into words. It's a noble torment, my boy, and afflicts only the chosen few. A fool is always satisfied with what he says and, besides, he says more than he needs, for fools always like to have some verbal slack, just in case, you know."

"Just as I did downstairs. I also said more than I ought to have said when, for instance, I laid claim to the whole of Versilov. That is, of course, much more than I need. Actually I have no use for him at all."

"Listen, my boy, you're trying now to make up for what you lost downstairs. You're angry with yourself, so you feel the need to take it out on someone else and this time you hope you won't miss me. I suppose I came up here too soon—you haven't cooled off yet and, besides, you can't stand being criticized. Sit down, for God's sake! I've come here to tell you something. That's better, thank you.

"From what you said to your mother, it's quite clear that it's best for us to part. I've come to try and persuade you to do it as painlessly as possible and without any scenes so as not to frighten and hurt your mother even more. Even the fact that I came to see you now cheered her up a little, for she still hopes we'll make it up somehow and that our life will go on just as before. I think if she heard us laughing together a couple of times, her gentle and simple heart would fill with joy. There are simple and loving hearts that must be treated with gentle care whenever possible. That was the first thing I wanted to tell you. Now for number two: why must we part with bitter thoughts of revenge, gnashing our teeth, abusing each other, etc.? I agree that there's no need for us to throw ourselves into each other's arms, but, without going that far, couldn't we part with mutual respect, for instance? What do you say?"

"All that's just blabber. But I promise I'll leave without a scene and that should be good enough. Tell me, though, are you really so concerned about Mother? I have the impression that you only pretend to be worrying about her. I don't think you really give a damn."

"So you don't trust me?"

"Stop talking to me as if I were a child."

"Listen, Arkady, I'm prepared to apologize to you a thousand times for everything that you hold against me—for your childhood and all the rest. But, *mon cher enfant*, what good will that do? You are too intelligent and have no wish to be put into such a foolish position. Not to mention the fact that I still don't quite understand what you're actually reproaching me for. Is it because you weren't born a Versilov? Since you're laughing and waving your hands, I suppose I must have guessed wrong."

"Yes, you're very wrong. Believe me, I wouldn't consider it an honor at all to be called Versilov."

"You know, we can leave honor out of this. Besides, your answer was bound to reflect your democratic position. But if that's the case, what is it you're accusing me of?"

"Mrs. Prutkov told me today all I have to know, which explains everything I had been unable to understand until now— namely, that I should be grateful to you for not having made a bootmaker out of me. But somehow, I'm not grateful to you, even now that I've been told I should be. Could it be, by any chance, that it is your blood in me that makes me so proud?"

"I don't suppose so. But tell me this now: why, when you really wanted all this time to strike me down, to crush me, did you have to take it out on your mother instead and bully her so that she was the one to suffer? And her you certainly have no right to judge. How is she guilty before you? And, by the way, would you enlighten me on this point too, my boy: what were you trying to achieve by announcing at school and everywhere else to every person you came across that you were an illegitimate child. I've heard it said that you did it with tremendous zest. But it's nonsense and slander because you're perfectly legitimate; you are the son of Makar Dolgoruky, a highly respectable man of remarkable character and intelligence. And if you were given the opportunity of getting an education, it was, indeed, thanks to the country squire Versilov, on whose estate you were born. And so what of it? Don't you see that by publicizing your illegitimacy, which in itself was slander, you were violating your mother's secret and, for the perverse satisfaction of your own false pride, you were placing her at the mercy of anyone who wanted to throw dirt at her! That's not honorable at all, my friend, especially since your mother has nothing to reproach herself for: she's a woman of the highest respectability and if she's not called Mrs. Versilov to this day, it's only because she's still married to another man."

"That's enough now, you have thoroughly convinced me and I have such a high regard for your intelligence that I hope you won't keep slicing me open with it for too long. You who are so concerned with a sense of proportion, let me point out to you that your sudden love for my mother strikes me as rather out of proportion. Now I'll tell you what you'd better do: since you've decided to spend a quarter or half an hour with me—I still don't know why you came, but let's assume it was for the sake of Mother's peace of mind—and since you seem to enjoy conversing with me despite what happened downstairs, I'd rather you talked to me about my father, Makar Dolgoruky, the pilgrim. I've wanted to ask you about him for a long time, as I'm particularly interested in what you think of him. Also, before we part, I would like very much to hear your answer to this question: how is it that, in the twenty years you have spent with my mother, your civilizing influence has not succeeded in dispelling the dark superstitious beliefs she brought with her from her primitive environment? Yes, and my sister is not free of them either. Oh, I'm not talking about my mother's respectability, for she's always been infinitely higher than you in the moral sense, but she is—if you don't mind my saying so—only a morally superior corpse because Versilov alone is alive and all the people around him are there only for the privilege of having him feed on their life juices. But she too must have been alive once, mustn't she? Surely she must've had something in her that attracted you? She must have been a woman once?"

"She really never was, my boy, if you see what I mean," he said, at once assuming the manner which he'd adopted with me from the beginning and which almost drove me out of my mind. For I couldn't make out how much he really meant what he said; on the surface it was all sincerity and frankness, but underneath lurked a rather contemptuous amusement. "No, she never was. Besides, a Russian woman is never a woman."

"As opposed to a Polish woman or a Frenchwoman? And what about Italian women? Wouldn't a passionate Italian woman be good enough to attract a civilized and upper-class Russian like Versilov?"

This made him laugh.

"This is really something!" he said. "I certainly never expected to meet a Slavophile here!"

Then he spoke with considerable volubility, I'd say even enjoying it, and I remember almost every word of what he told me. It was obvious to me from the beginning that he hadn't come to my attic just to chat with me or to appease my mother's anxiety. He must have had some other object.

II

"The twenty years your mother and I have lived together have been spent in silence," he started off in an affected, unnatural tone, "and all that passed between us happened without words. The main feature of our twenty-year union has been silence. I don't even believe that we ever quarreled. I often went off alone, leaving her behind, but I always came back in the end. *Nous revenons toujours*—that is typical of men and comes from their magnanimity. If marriage depended on women alone, no marriage would last. Humility, meekness, self-deprecation, combined with firmness, strength—yes, real strength —all these make up your mother's character. Let me tell you, she's the best of all the women I've met in my life. As to her strength, I can testify to that, for I saw how that strength sustained her. When it comes, for instance, to standing up for her convictions—I'm not talking, of course, about convictions based on reason which she couldn't have, but rather of the things she holds sacred—she'd face torture for them. And since I'm not much of a torturer, as you can probably gather, I usually preferred to keep quiet. So the reason for my forbearance was not just that it was easier to say nothing, and, I must say, I'm not sorry I didn't interfere. Broadmindedness and tolerance was the easiest way under the circumstances, so I don't claim any credit. I'll say parenthetically, though, that she never trusted my tolerance and lived in fear and trembling. But, in fear and trembling as she was, she still firmly rejected whatever civilizing influence she happened to be exposed to. Humble people know how to reject things and, in general, they're better than we are at getting whatever they're after. They manage to live their lives out under the most unfavorable circumstances and remain true to themselves even when everything around them has become completely unfamiliar and strange. We could never do that."

"Who are *they*? I don't quite follow you."

"*They* are the people, the masses, the common Russian people. They have proved their tremendous historical vitality and adaptability both in the moral and the political sense. But to get back to our subject, let me tell you that your mother does occasionally break her silence, but whenever she does express her opinion on something, it at once becomes obvious that it was a waste of time trying to enlighten her, even if you'd spent five years explaining that particular point to her. And she comes up with the most unexpected arguments. Please note, I'm not saying she's a fool; on the contrary, there's intelligence in her, and quite a remarkable intelligence at that. But it's precisely in her intelligence that you'll probably refuse to believe . . ."

"Why shouldn't I? What I don't believe is that you yourself believe in her intelligence and that you really mean what you're saying now."

"Really? So you think I'm something of a chameleon, do you? Well, perhaps I'm giving a bit too much license . . . to my spoiled son. But, all right, I'll let it go one more time."

"Tell me about my father, and try to stick to the truth if you can."

"About Makar Dolgoruky? Well, Makar was a house serf who had a sort of yearning for glory. . . ."

"I bet that in some respects you envy him at this moment!"

"Hardly, my friend, hardly. But I'm rather pleased to find you in this paradoxical frame of mind. I swear that at this moment I'm in a very penitent mood and I'm helplessly sorry for all that happened twenty years ago. Besides, God knows it happened completely by accident, and afterward I behaved as decently as was within my power, or at least I stuck as close as possible to the standards of human decency as I conceived them at the time. Oh, we were all so anxious to do good in those days, to do our duty as citizens, to serve a higher ideal; we wanted to do away with all class privileges and distinctions, with our family estates, and even with pawnshops, at least some of us did. . . . Yes, I assure you that, although there weren't many of us, we spoke very eloquently and sometimes—believe it or not—we were capable of decent acts. . . ."

"Such as the time you cried on Makar's shoulder?"

"All right, my boy, I concede in advance the absurdity of it all, including the crying on his shoulder, which I told you about myself and which you're now using against me, thus taking undue advantage of my trustingness and confidence. But you must understand that there was nothing so terrible in crying on his shoulder, as may appear at the first glance, especially by the standards of the time. Why, we were just beginning then. Of course it was a pose, but I didn't know it was then. And what about you, don't you ever strike a pose when it serves your purpose?"

"I allowed my feelings to get the better of me just now downstairs, and when I came up here I felt horribly ashamed at the thought that you might imagine I'd been putting on an act. It's true, though, that sometimes we may feel something sincerely and still strike a pose. But I swear that everything downstairs was quite genuine."

"That's just it, you've hit the nail on the head: one may be sincere and still pose at the same time. And that's what happened to me too: I was striking a pose and at the same time weeping quite sincerely. Oh, it's perfectly possible that Makar could have taken it as insult added to injury had he been more perspicacious, but his honesty prevented him from looking too deeply into it. I don't remember whether he was sorry for me then, but I very much wanted him to be."

"Even now," I interrupted him, "you're trying to make a fool out of me, just as you've been doing all month. Why do you feel you always have to talk to me like that?"

"You think so?" he said in a gentle tone. "You're too suspicious; even if I laugh sometimes, it's not at you, or at least not just at you, but I'm not laughing now. . . . Well, I acted in the most decent way I could and it was certainly not to my advantage. We—I mean we the superior people as opposed to the common people—had no idea at that time how to act to our own advantage; indeed, we played dirty tricks on ourselves whenever possible and I suspect that this was just what we considered to be 'to our advantage in the higher sense,' obviously in some mystical interpretation. The present generation of progressives is incomparably more down to earth when it comes to their own interests. Even before anything 'sinful' had taken place, I explained the situation to Makar with the most extraordinary bluntness. Today I'd agree that much of what I told him ought not to have been said, especially not that directly. And I'm not even talking about respect for his human dignity; it would've been simply more polite not to mention certain things. But, then, go and try to stop a dancer who has got all warmed up and enthusiastic from performing some exuberant *pas*. Besides, who knows, after all, perhaps such gestures are dictated by the beautiful and sublime ideals inherent in us. I still have no answer to that, although I've tried to find one all my life. But it's too complex a subject for a superficial conversation like ours. All I can truthfully assure you is that it makes me almost die of shame when I remember now what I did then.

"I offered him three thousand rubles. He said nothing and I went on talking. And would you believe what I thought then? I imagined he was afraid of me, I mean because of the rights conferred on me by the institution of serfdom, so I tried hard to reassure him on that subject. I pleaded with him to tell me frankly and without any fear what he thought I owed to him and I even encouraged him to criticize me if he felt like it. To guarantee his complete freedom of choice, I gave him my word that if he refused my terms—three thousand rubles, freedom for him and his wife, and the price of a fare wherever he wanted to go (without his wife, of course)—he just had to say so and I would immediately give him his freedom anyway, his wife too so she could join him, and money, probably the same three thousand rubles, and then I would be the one to leave, alone for Italy, for three years, while they could stay put if they wished to. And you know, *mon ami*, I wouldn't have taken Miss Sapozhkov to Italy with me either, as I was feeling too idealistic for that in those days.

"And what do you think happened? Well, Makar, who knew very well I'd keep my word one way or the other, remained completely silent, and only when I went up to him to shed some tears on his shoulder for the third time did he move aside, raise his hands in a gesture of exasperation, and leave rather abruptly, his abruptness surprising me somewhat. At that moment I caught sight of myself in a mirror and it made an impression on me that I still remember.

"In general, when those humble people say nothing, that's the worst of all, and he was always a taciturn man anyway, so I confess that not only wasn't I sure of what he'd do when I had him called to my study but I was also very apprehensive: there are characters among them that are walking bundles of unforeseeable reactions and that can be more frightening than a direct physical attack. And I mean it literally. So I did take a considerable risk. What, for instance, if that homemade Uriah had started screaming, what could a small-time David, such as I was then, do about it? And that's why I mentioned the three thousand rubles first: it was an instinctive precaution. But, luckily, I had quite misjudged him—Makar Dolgoruky was something quite different. . . ."

"Tell me, was that after . . . ? You said you summoned the husband you planned to cuckold before the act . . . ?"

"You see, it depends on how you wish to understand it. . . ."

"That means it *had* taken place. Then you said that you'd misjudged him, that he was different. Different, how?"

"I still can't make out to this day exactly what sort of man he is. But he was certainly nothing like what I'd imagined and there was something extremely respectable about him, which, in the end, made me feel three times as guilty toward him as I'd felt before. The very next day, he accepted my offer that he leave the estate. He didn't say anything, but he didn't forget the compensation I'd promised him."

"So he took the money?"

"He most certainly did! In fact, he took me quite by surprise on that point. As you can well imagine, I didn't have three thousand rubles right there in my pocket. I had seven hundred, though, and gave them to him as a down payment. And what do you think—he demanded that I give him a promissory note for the remaining twenty-three hundred payable to a certain merchant, feeling that it would be safer that way. Then, two years later, he sued me for that sum and with the accumulated interest too, and then surprised me again by literally going around and begging coppers for the building of a church. And now for twenty years he has been wandering all over the country. I still don't see why a pilgrim should want to have so much money, which is such a worldly thing. Of course, during the minute I made the offer I was absolutely sincere, overwhelmed, we might say, by my own generous impulse; however, many, many minutes later, it was only natural that I should have second thoughts on the subject and reckon that he'd spare me, or rather *us*—her and me. But he wouldn't even consider waiting."

(I must note here that, if Versilov had happened to die before my mother, she would have been left penniless in her old age had it not been for Makar Dolgoruky's three thousand rubles, long since doubled by accumulated interest, which he had kept intact and had bequeathed to her in his will. This goes to show that already then he understood how precarious a grip on money a man like Versilov had.)

"You told me once that Mr. Dolgoruky came to visit you all a few times and on every occasion he stayed at Mother's."

"That's right, my friend, and I admit that at first I was extremely apprehensive of these visits. But in all those twenty years he has come only six or seven times perhaps and I've always stayed out of his way. In the beginning I couldn't understand what he had on his mind or why he came, but later I thought that, from a certain point of view, it was not so stupid on his part. Once I felt curious and came in to have a look at him and, I assure you, he made a very interesting impression on me. It was during his third or fourth visit, which was around the time I was acting as arbitrator between landowners and emancipated serfs and was trying very hard to learn all I could about Russia. I learned much from him that was quite new to me.

Moreover, I found he had a benevolent attitude toward me and an evenness of temper that I had never expected and, what surprised me most, a kind of gaiety. He never made the slightest allusion to you know what, *tu comprends*. He really made sense when he talked and he expressed himself very well without that peasant profundity, which I confess I could never stand despite all my democratic ideas, and without any of these typical Russian vulgarisms used by 'true Russian people' in our novels and on our stage. And he didn't talk much about religion either, indeed, not unless I took the initiative, and then he told me many charming stories about monasteries and monastic life. And, above all, he was always courteous, modest and courteous, that brand of courtesy without which equality in the highest sense is unattainable and without which, I also think, there can be no real superiority. He was dignified without the slightest trace of aggressiveness, full of self-respect whatever position he was in. And it is very uncommon to be so dignified in his particular position; it takes a deep genuine self-respect. . . . You'll see for yourself if you live long enough. But what struck me most later—I emphasize that it was only later and not at the beginning—was Makar's impressive physique. He was, I assure you, an extremely handsome man; old as he was, he was still 'dark-visaged, tall, and spare,' as Nekrasov's line has it, and, on top of that, unaffected and dignified. Indeed, it set me wondering what made my poor Sofia choose me over him in the first place, you know. Although he was past fifty then, he was such a fine-looking man; compared with him, I was just a city slicker. Perhaps it was because already then his hair was forbiddingly gray and must have been very gray even when they were married. . . . Possibly this affected her choice."

This man Versilov had that very cheap trick typical of people in the "best society"—after having made some very clever or "profound" observations (he never missed an opportunity), he would immediately follow up with some asinine remark, like the one about Makar's gray hair making my mother prefer Versilov to him. I'm sure he did it without knowing why himself; he'd simply acquired that idiotic sophisticated mannerism. You could listen to him and think that he was being absolutely serious when, actually, he would just be putting on an act and laughing at you.

III

I don't know quite why I suddenly felt terribly angry. It was one of those outbursts I had in those days that still give me an unpleasant feeling when I remember them. I leaped up from my chair.

"Come to think of it," I said, "you told me you'd come here to make my mother believe that we'd made it up. Now that you've spent enough time here to convince her of that, I wonder whether you couldn't leave me alone?"

A slight redness suffused his face and he stood up.

"My dear fellow, you do treat me in a rather cavalier fashion, don't you? But that's fine with me, I'll leave you since I can't force you to like me. But, first, I'll allow myself to ask you one question: do you really plan to leave the prince?"

"So there it is! I was sure you were after something or other."

"You mean you thought I'd come up here to try and convince you to stay with the prince because it's in my interest? Or perhaps you even imagine that I asked you to come all the way from Moscow in order to derive some advantage from it myself? You're so awfully suspicious, my boy! On the contrary, I have only your own interest at heart and wish you good in every way. Even now, after all that has been said, I wish you'd allow your mother and me to help you when you're in need since, as you know, my financial situation has improved somewhat."

"I don't like you, Versilov."

"So you call me just 'Versilov' now. . . . By the way, I'm very sorry I couldn't give you that name, because therein lies my guilt toward you, if there is any guilt at all. But, again, what could I do? I couldn't very well marry a married woman, could I?"

"And that's probably why you'd tried to marry an unmarried one."

His face twitched slightly.

"I suppose you're referring to Ems again. You did downstairs and you pointed your finger at me in front of your mother. I want you to know, Arkady, that this was where you were the furthest off the mark. You know exactly nothing about what happened between the late Lidia Akhmakov and me. You don't even suspect how much your mother was involved in it, although she wasn't in Ems at the time. And if I ever saw a good woman in my life, it was then, looking at your mother. I can't tell you more about this because it's still a secret. But you just come out and repeat things somebody happened to tell you."

"Just today the old prince informed me that you go in for featherless chicks."

"The prince told you that?"

"Yes. And now shall I tell you why you really came here? I think I've finally guessed the secret reason for your visit."

He was already in the doorway. He stopped, turned his head toward me, and waited.

"Earlier I mentioned inadvertently that Touchard's letter to Mrs. Prutkov, which had been among Andronikov's papers after his death, later came into Maria's hands. When I said that I noticed your face twitch, and only now, seeing your face twitch again in the same way, it occurred to me that you may think that if one letter could have wound up in Maria's hands, why couldn't any other letter from Andronikov's files also have found its way there. And a rather important letter could have been left in Andronikov's files after his death, couldn't it?"

"So I'm supposed to have come up here to try and pump some useful information out of you?"

"You know very well why you came here."

He turned pale.

"All this, you didn't think it up yourself. It's that woman who's put it into your head. That's why there's so much hatred in what you say and in your insulting assumption."

"That woman? Well, yes, I did see her today. And isn't it to keep my eye on her that you want me to continue going to the prince's?"

"I see now that you'll go places if you continue like this. Could this be your 'idea' by any chance? Keep trying, my friend, you have an unmistakable gift for spying and if one has an inborn gift, it's one's duty to cultivate it."

He paused to take a breath.

"You'd better look out, Versilov, don't make an enemy of me!"

"My dear boy, in such cases, it's not wise to say aloud what one thinks. One's thoughts are better kept to oneself. And now would you please light those stairs for me because, although you may be my enemy, I don't suppose it's so bad that you'd want me to break my neck right here. *Tiens, mon ami*, and to think that all this month I'd taken you for a very kindhearted boy. You're so eager, so anxious to live," he went on, descending the narrow stairs, "that three lives probably wouldn't be enough for you. It's written all over your face. And people with such an appetite for life are usually good-natured. Ah, what poor judgment on my part!"

IV

I cannot describe how my heart contracted when I was left alone in my room—it was as if I'd cut off a part of my living flesh! Why did I turn so vicious, why did I have to offend him so cruelly and calculatingly? I couldn't possibly explain it either then or even now. And he had turned so pale! Perhaps that paleness reflected the most sincere and the purest feelings, the deepest sorrow rather than anger aroused by my insults. I'd always thought there were moments when he really loved me. Why couldn't I believe it now, especially since so much of what I hadn't understood had become clear to me now?

I had flown into a sudden rage and all but driven him away, at least partly because of the idea that he had come simply to find out whether there weren't any more letters of Andronikov's in Maria's hands that might be of interest to him. But I'd known all the time that he must have been looking for those letters. Still, perhaps I was wrong, perhaps he hadn't been thinking of the letters at that moment; perhaps it was I myself, who, by ascribing that preoccupation to him wrongly, had brought to his mind the possibility of Maria having certain letters that were important to him.

And then that strange thing had happened again: he had repeated word for word my thought about living three lives, just as I had formulated it to Kraft the day before, using almost the same words. Of course, it could have been just a coincidence, but it was quite uncanny how he could read my innermost feelings with such a frightening insight and penetration! But if he could see certain things so clearly, how was it that he couldn't see others? Or was he just pretending not to see them? Did he or didn't he see that it was not legitimacy that I needed, not to be legally a Versilov, but Versilov himself, the man, the whole of him, the father, and that this need was now in my blood? How could such a subtle, refined man be so obtuse and insensitive? And if he wasn't obtuse and insensitive, why did he pretend to be? Why did he drive me into such a frenzy?

Chapter 8

I

The following morning I got up as early as I could. Usually we —that is, my mother, my sister, and I—would get up around eight, while Versilov lingered in bed until half past nine or so.

Punctually at eight-thirty, my mother would bring my breakfast up to my room. But this morning I didn't wait for it and slipped out of the house before eight. I had prepared a plan of action for the day. But despite my eagerness to go ahead with my plan, I was aware that many important points in it were still unclear in my mind; and this uncertainty had caused me to spend the night in a state halfway between sleep and wakefulness, thinking, losing the train of my thought, slipping into innumerable dreams, and never succeeding in sinking deeper into proper sleep for any length of time. In the morning, however, I felt more refreshed and energetic than ever.

I was particularly anxious to avoid meeting Mother. I knew that if I saw her, I'd have to talk to her on a certain subject, and I was afraid that that conversation might somehow spoil my mood and divert me from the goals I had now set for myself.

It was a cold morning and a damp, milky mist weighed down on everything in sight. I can't explain why, but I always enjoy the early weekday Petersburg mornings, grim as they may be, with all those hurried self-centered people, each immersed in his own personal preoccupations; they somehow fascinate me at eight o'clock in the morning. What I like most, as I hurry to my destination, is to stop briefly to ask some information of one of those hurrying figures, or to be asked for directions by a passer-by; both the question and the answer are always brief and to the point, indeed, sometimes exchanged without stopping, almost always friendly, the willingness to answer being at its highest point of the day. A Petersburg denizen becomes less and less communicative as the day wears on and, toward evening, is prepared to be rude and even scoff at you at the slightest provocation. But it's quite different in the early morning before work, in those sober and most clear-headed moments. That's what I have observed at least.

Once again I was on my way to the Petersburg Side. I had to be back in Fontanka around noon to see Vasin (that was the likeliest time to find him at home), so I walked very fast, resisting the temptation to stop and have a cup of coffee somewhere. Besides, I also had first to catch Efim Zverev at home and, in fact, I almost missed him. He was finishing his breakfast and was about to leave when I arrived.

"What brings you here this time?"

That was how he greeted me, without even getting up.

"I'll tell you what."

The early morning, especially the Petersburg early morning, has a sobering effect on human nature. Many an ardent night-time longing dissolves completely in the morning brightness and crispness, and I myself have often felt ashamed and embarrassed to recall in the morning light some of my dreams and sometimes even actions of the night before. But let me note in passing that the Petersburg mornings, which may seem the bleakest on our whole planet, have for me a unique poetic quality of fantasy. This is my personal view, or rather I should say feeling, and I'll defend it. On a foul, damp, foggy Petersburg morning, it seems to me that the imaginary world of someone like Pushkin's Herman from the *Queen of Spades* (a colossal, extraordinary, and true Petersburg type) must take an even tighter hold of him. Hundreds of times, as I've walked through the Petersburg morning fog, this strange and clinging thought has cropped up: "What if, when the fog lifts and disperses somewhere high up over the earth, this rotten, slimy city is lifted up with it and vanishes like vapor until only the former Finnish marsh remains and, I suppose in the middle of it as a decoration, that bronze horseman on his panting, exhausted horse?" Well, I can't express all my feelings because they're fantasies, even poetry, and therefore utter nonsense. Still another idea—and this one really absolutely idiotic—has recurred in my mind: "Here are all these people rushing around and hurrying desperately when, in fact, who knows, perhaps it's all only somebody's dream and not a single person here is real, genuine, not a single action is really taking place. . . . What will happen if the dreamer suddenly wakes up and everything just vanishes?"

But I'm getting off my subject.

Let me say this first: every man harbors certain wishes and plans that are eccentric enough safely to diagnose him as a madman. It was with such an eccentric scheme that I'd come to Zverev that morning, to him because there was no one else in Petersburg at that time to whom I could broach the subject. Oh, if I'd had any choice about it, Zverev would have been the last man to whom I'd have gone for that, but I had no choice.

I sat down across the table from him and I had the feeling that I was the incarnation of fever and delirium facing him, the incarnation of the golden mean and common sense. But then I had "my idea" and true instinct on my side, while he had only the practical conviction that my way was not the proper way to do things.

In short, I told him that he was the only person in Petersburg I could ask to act as my second in an urgent matter of honor and that, having known each other since school, he could not refuse to carry my challenge to a duel to Lieutenant of the Guards Prince Sergei Sokolsky, who, just over a year ago in Ems, had slapped my father, Versilov. Zverev already knew all about my family circumstances, my relations with Versilov, and almost as much as I did about the Ems incident. I myself had told him various things on the subject on different occasions, except obviously for certain secret details.

He sat listening to me, looking like a caged sparrow with his feathers ruffled, his eyes fixed and intent, his almost white hair sticking up above his puffy face. A frozen sarcastic grin remained stuck on his lips, which, I'm sure, was unconscious and reflected only his firm belief in his superiority over me, both in intelligence and character. I also suspected that he despised me for my outburst the previous day at Dergachev's. He was bound to. For Efim Zverev reflects the feelings of the crowd, the street mob, which recognizes success and nothing else.

"Does Versilov know about this?"

"Of course not."

"Then what right do you have to meddle in his affairs? That's one thing. And, number two, what are you trying to prove by all this?"

I'd anticipated his objections and explained to him that what I had in mind was not as stupid as might appear. In the first place, the arrogant prince would be taught a lesson that there were people who knew the meaning of honor in our class as well as in his; in the second place, Versilov would be put to shame and would learn his lesson too; and in the third place, even if Versilov had perfectly valid reasons—based on his convictions or some such thing—to bear the insult without challenging the prince to a duel, let him see that there was someone in the world who felt the offense to him keenly, who took it as a personal insult, and who was prepared to risk his life to avenge it . . . even though he may have decided to part from Versilov for ever and ever. . . .

"Stop it, don't yell like that, my aunt can't stand people shouting. . . . Tell me this now: is it the same Sokolsky that Versilov is having that lawsuit with about the inheritance? If so, you may have discovered a new way of winning lawsuits—by having your opponent killed off in a duel."

I spelled it out to him *en toutes lettres:* he was just stupid and nasty, and the sarcastic grin that was spreading over his face only showed how smug and vulgar he was, for the consideration of the lawsuit had never entered my mind all this time while it had immediately germinated inside his ponderous skull. Then I informed him that the lawsuit had already been won by Versilov, that Versilov's opponent was not just this Sokolsky but the "Princes Sokolsky," that, therefore, even if one of the princes was killed, there would still be others left to inherit, but that I would certainly delay the challenge until after the final date to appeal the decision (although I knew there would be no appeal, I'd do it just out of decency). As soon as the time for the appeal had passed, the duel would take place. I had come now bearing all this in mind and only wanted to be sure that I'd have a second when I needed him, for I didn't know anyone else in Petersburg. In any case I'd have time to look for another second if Zverev turned me down. That was why I'd come now, I explained to him.

"So why couldn't you wait and ask me when the time came instead of drowning me in your damned nonsense so far in advance?"

He got up and picked up his cap.

"Will you do it for me then?"

"I certainly won't."

"Why not?"

"For one thing, if I accepted now, you'd be coming and pestering me every day until the time for the appeal had passed. Besides, your whole story is completely idiotic; and also why should I risk my career for your sake? Now suppose Prince Sergei Sokolsky asks me 'Who sent you to me?' and I answer 'Dolgoruky'; he'd ask 'What business has Dolgoruky to meddle in Versilov's affairs?' What am I supposed to do then? Explain to him how you were sired? He'd laugh in my face."

"So you give him a punch in the face."

"More pipe dreams."

"Are you afraid? You're such a big guy. You were the strongest boy in school."

"Of course I'm afraid. Besides, the prince would never accept your challenge to a duel because they fight duels only with equals and you aren't his equal."

"I am a gentleman just like him, I'm civilized and I have all my citizen's rights. If anything, it's he who's not my equal."

"That's not true—you're not even grown up."

"What do you mean I'm not even grown up?"

"Just what I say—you're only a boy, we're both just boys, while he's a man."

"Talk for yourself, you moron! I've been old enough to get legally married for a year now."

"All right, so go and get married, but I still say you're a little twerp and you have a long way to go before you're a man."

Of course, I understood he was trying to pull my leg. I also realize that I could have spared the reader this stupid episode and let it be forgotten. Yes, it was a revolting scene, petty and unnecessary, but it happened to have quite serious consequences. However I'll take all the punishment and tell it to the end. Realizing that Zverev was taunting me, I allowed myself to shove him—or, to be more accurate, to take a poke at him. My fist landed on his shoulder. Whereupon he picked me up in the air and turned me upside down, thus proving that he had, indeed, been the strongest boy in school.

II

The reader may imagine that I was completely dejected as I left Zverev's house, but he'd be quite wrong. I was well aware that what had happened was just schoolboy horseplay that could not in the least weaken my determination to see my plans through. I had breakfast on Vasilievsky Island, deliberately by-passing the tavern on the Petersburg Side where I had had supper the previous evening because the mere recollection of that place with its nightingale had become sickening to me. I have a rather strange trait: I can hate locales and objects just as I hate people. On the other hand, I have a few "happy" places in Petersburg, places where for some reason or other I've once felt happy. And, you know what, I sort of save those places, stay away from them as much as I can, so that some day when I feel really low and lonely, I can go there with my sadness and relive happier memories. While I was having breakfast I thought of Efim Zverev and gave him due credit for his common sense. Yes, he was certainly more practical than me but hardly more of a realist. Realism that refuses to see beyond the tip of its nose is like a sort of blindness and is more dangerous than the most fantastic imagination. But while rendering Zverev his due (he probably imagined me now walking along the street swearing at him), I still did not yield to his arguments; indeed, I haven't to this day. I know enough people who are prepared to renounce their efforts and even their ideas as soon as a bucket of cold water is thrown over their heads and who begin to laugh at things they'd considered sacred an hour earlier. Oh, everything is so easy for people like that! Even assuming that Zverev's view of the whole business was sounder than mine, even conceding that I was very stupid and was just striking a pose—still, deep down, there was a point on which I was right and there was something in my position that was just and correct, and, what is most important, something that they'd never be able to understand.

I got to Vasin's house, which was in Fontanka near the Semyonovsky Bridge, exactly at noon, but he was out. He worked somewhere on Vasilievsky Island and as a rule came home punctually just before noon. Besides, it was some sort of holiday, so I was sure he'd be back soon. And so, although it was the first time I'd been to his place, I said I'd wait for him and sat down.

My reasoning went like this: the letter about the inheritance that I had in my possession was a matter of conscience; by entrusting to Vasin's judgment the decision as to what I should do about it, I was showing him how deeply I respected him, which was bound to flatter him. It was true, of course, that I had been worrying about that letter and had felt the need for an impartial opinion, but I admit that I already felt I could cope with the dilemma without any outside help. The best solution, I thought, was simply to give Versilov the letter and let him decide for himself. It was definitely improper for me to set myself up as a judge in this business. By handing the letter over to Versilov without comment, I would remove myself from the position of judge and thereby place myself in a position of superiority over Versilov, since I'd be renouncing any possible benefits myself, being, after all, Versilov's son and thus likely to inherit some of that money one day. That way I felt I would always be able to look upon whatever Versilov decided to do with lofty detachment. On the other hand, no one would be able to accuse me of having been the cause of the Sokolskys' ruin since the letter had no decisive legal force.

I thought all that out while waiting for Vasin in his room. Indeed, what I had to do seemed clear to me now and I realized I'd really come to Vasin's not for advice but to show him what a noble and disinterested man I was and thus get even with him for my previous day's humiliation.

This new outlook made me feel slighted and aroused my anger. But, instead of leaving, I stayed on and waited, although I felt my anger rising as time passed.

In the first place, I found Vasin's room more and more irritating. There is truth in the statement "Show me your room and I'll tell you what sort of man you are." Vasin rented a furnished room in an apartment. His landlady must have been hard up and only managed to make both ends meet by taking in lodgers, for there were obviously other lodgers besides Vasin. I was well acquainted with this sort of room—poky and poorly furnished yet with pretensions to comfort: there was the ever-present soft sofa fresh from the flea market that was dangerous to move lest it collapse; there was a screen and behind it a washstand and an iron bed. I suppose Vasin was the best and the most dependable lodger in the apartment. All landladies have a favorite lodger whom they treat with special consideration: they clean his room with greater care, sweep his floor more thoroughly, hang lithographs over his sofa, and lay a mangy-looking rug under his table. I never trust people who like that sort of musty tidiness and especially the servile deference of their landladies. I'm convinced that Vasin was flattered by his position of favorite lodger. I don't know why, but the sight of books piled high on two tables infuriated me particularly. The books, the papers, the inkpot— everything was arranged with that oppressive and revolting orderliness that fitted in with the ideas about the world shared by the landlady and the cleaning woman.

There were lots of books around—not just magazines and periodicals but real books—and I imagined the ponderous, precise, and pompous air Vasin must affect when he sat down to do his methodical reading or writing. I can't quite explain why, but I prefer books messily strewn around; I suppose that at least shows that work is not performed as some kind of sacred ritual. I'm sure Vasin is always courteous with people who come to see him, but his expression and every gesture remind the visitor "All right, I'll give you an hour and a half of my time and when you leave I'll go back to my work." I guess one can have a very interesting conversation with him and learn something new but, behind it, the visitor must always be aware of Vasin thinking: "All right, I'll talk to you and tell you very interesting things, but only after you've gone will I get down to serious business. . . ."

Nevertheless I sat and waited. And this seemed to make even less sense since I was now quite convinced that I had no need of his advice.

I sat like that for more than an hour on one of the two wicker chairs that stood neatly by the window. I was also aware that time was passing and I had to find myself a place to live before evening. I was bored and thought of picking up a book, but I didn't: the idea that it would be looking for a way to kill time made me feel twice as uncomfortable.

Suddenly, after the complete silence I'd been immersed in for the past hour, I heard people whispering from behind the permanently locked side door that was blocked by the sofa. The whispering grew louder and more distinct. It sounded to me as if the whispers were being exchanged by two women. I couldn't make out the words, but out of sheer boredom I started listening intently. Obviously it was a lively, excited exchange, so they couldn't be discussing something like sewing. They seemed to be arguing about something, one trying to convince the other, begging perhaps, while the other disagreed and refused to comply. I thought they must be other lodgers. I soon got bored and my ears became inured to the whispering; although I kept listening, I did so mechanically, sometimes forgetting that I was listening and not taking the words in. Suddenly something extraordinary happened: one of the women seemed to have leaped up from her seat, landing on both feet at the same time, and then there was a stamping and a moan, then a cry—or rather a shriek, an animal-like squeal—that must have been emitted by someone who no longer cared about being overheard by strangers.

I rushed to the door leading into the corridor and opened it. At the same second, another door at the end of the passage flew open. It was, as I learned later, the door of the landlady's room. Two inquisitive faces peered out from behind it. The shrieking had suddenly stopped. The door next to me opened and a woman, a young one I believe, rushed out of the room onto the landing and ran downstairs. The other woman, a middle-aged one, who had apparently been trying to stop her, moaned helplessly after her: "Olga, Olga, where're you going? Oh! . . ."

But, noticing the open doors of the other rooms, she quickly closed hers, leaving just a crack through which she listened until Olga's steps could no longer be heard. I went back into Vasin's room and installed myself near the window again. Everything was quiet now. It must have been some unimportant, ridiculous incident, I decided, and dismissed it from my mind.

Perhaps another quarter of an hour passed. Then I heard the loud and unrestrained voice of a man just outside Vasin's door. Someone turned the knob and opened the door enough for me to see a tall man; he obviously saw me and even looked me over but still stayed outside, holding onto the doorknob and conversing with the landlady at the other end of the passage. The landlady spoke in a high-pitched, playful voice by which one could tell that she knew the visitor well, appreciated him as a respectable gentleman and good company. The stranger joked in a loud voice about his bad luck at never finding Vasin at home, that maybe it was his fate always to miss him but that, nevertheless, he'd try and wait for Vasin again. All that seemed exquisitely witty to the landlady, so great was her appreciation. Finally, the gentleman flung the door open wide and stepped into the room.

He was extremely well-dressed, evidently wearing clothes made by first-rate tailors, "dressed like a real gentleman," as the landlady would say, although strangely enough he himself didn't look in the least like the gentleman he was, I suspect, trying to pass for. It's not that he was so ill mannered, but he was one of those naturally aggressive clods whom I find somewhat less offensive than people who cultivate a synthetic arrogance in front of a mirror. Yet somehow his dark brown, slightly grizzled hair, his black eyebrows, his big beard, and rather large eyes, instead of giving him character, seemed, on the contrary, to make him look commonplace and uninteresting. A man like that may be ready to laugh, in fact he may burst out laughing at the slightest pretext, but one never really feels gay in his company. And when from cheerful he turns grave and then suddenly starts winking playfully, all these transformations seem unprovoked, somehow haphazard. But enough said about him for the time being. Since I was destined to get to know this gentleman more closely, I have already said more about him than I could possibly have known when he first stepped into the room. To this day, however, it would be difficult to say anything precise and definite about him since the main characteristic of such people is an unfinished, diffuse, and undetermined quality.

Before he had sat down, it suddenly occurred to me that this must be Mr. Stebelkov, Vasin's stepfather, of whom I'd vaguely heard before, I couldn't remember what except that it was not too flattering. I knew that, after Vasin's father had died, Stebelkov was the boy's guardian, but that they hadn't been close for years now, that they had quite different interests and led very different lives. I also recalled now that Stebelkov had some money, that he was a speculator or something of the sort; in fact, I must have heard something more definite about him but forgotten it.

He looked me up and down without greeting me, put his top hat on the table by the sofa, casually pushed the table out of the way with his foot, and sat down, or rather sprawled out on the sofa that I hadn't even dared sit on. The sofa creaked under his weight. He crossed his legs and spent a while admiring his right patent-leather shoe, which was dangling in the air. At last he turned to me and once again measured me with his big, staring eyes.

"Can never catch him at home!"

He nodded vaguely in my direction. I didn't answer.

"Never punctual. He has his own views on the subject. Did you come all the way from the Petersburg Side?"

"You mean you came from the Petersburg Side?" I asked him back.

"Wait a minute—I asked you that."

"Right. . . . Yes, I came from the Petersburg Side. But how did you guess?"

"How? Hm . . ."

He didn't deign to enlighten me. He just winked slyly.

"Actually," I said, "that's not where I live. But I had to go to the Petersburg Side, so that's where I came from right now."

He remained silent for a while, his face distended into a condescending smile that annoyed me. I also found his winking very stupid.

"Were you at Mr. Dergachev's?" he asked me.

"What Dergachev?" I glared at him as he watched me with a sly triumphant air. "I don't even know who you're talking about."

"Hm."

"You can think what you want."

This fellow was making me sick.

"Hm. I see. But first allow me to say this: suppose you buy something in a shop; in another shop another customer buys another commodity. Now what does he buy? Well, he buys money from a shopkeeper who is known as a moneylender because money is a commodity like any other and a moneylender is a merchant like any other. . . . Do you follow me?"

"I suppose so."

"Now comes a third customer. He points at one of the shops and says: 'This is sound business.' Then he points at the other shop and says 'And that one is unsound business.' Tell me, what am I to think of that customer?"

"I have no idea."

"No, wait a minute, I'll give you a little illustration; a good illustration sets everything straight. Suppose I walk along the Nevsky Prospect and I observe on the opposite sidewalk a gentleman whose character I'd like to investigate. So we walk, each on his side, to the corner of Morskaya Street, where there's that English store. And on that spot we find a third gentleman who has just been run over by a horse. Now please follow me closely: a fourth gentleman arrives and he wishes to determine the characters of the three of us, including the man who has been run over, of course. He wants to find out whether we're solvent and reliable people. Do you still follow me?"

"I must say I find it rather difficult."

"I thought you would. All right, then, let's change the setting. Now I'm in a German spa, mineral springs, you know, never mind what spa, I've been to many. Well, I walk around the spa and I see Englishmen all over the place. As you well know, it's quite difficult to become acquainted with an Englishman. But then, two months later, when we've finished our mineral water cure, the whole lot of us, we walk up one of those mountains— never mind which—using those pointed walking sticks, you know. At the pass, I mean at the place where people rest, just on the spot where monks produce Chartreuse—I want you to note that—I notice a native standing silently all by himself and looking around. Now I would like to find out whether this man is trustworthy. Tell me, do you suppose I could inquire among the batch of the Englishmen I'm with? But I'm with them there for no other reason than that I couldn't get to talk to them down at the spa. So what do I do?"

"I really have no idea at all. Excuse me for saying so, but it's awfully difficult to follow you."

"Did you say difficult?"

"Yes, I find it quite a strain."

"Hm."

He winked slyly and made a gesture with his hand that seemed to indicate that he'd succeeded in putting one over on me. Then, with complete composure, he slowly pulled out of his pocket a newspaper that he must have bought just before coming in and started to read something on the back page. I thought he'd leave me in peace now. Five minutes went by.

"Look at that! The Brest-Graev shares haven't hit the bottom! You see, they're still on the market; people are buying them. I know many stocks, though, that have hit the bottom. . . ."

He gave me a warm, hearty look now.

"I understand very little about stock exchange transactions."

"You disapprove, do you?"

"Disapprove of what?"

"Money."

"I don't disapprove of money, but I think that ideas must have precedence over money."

"Allow me, just a minute. Suppose a man has his own capital . . ."

"What I say is that we must start with an idea. Money comes only after that, for without a noble idea human society is doomed."

God knows why I became excited. He glanced at me blankly, apparently having lost his train of thought, but then suddenly his whole face lit up and was distended into a sly and delighted grin.

"And what do you say of Versilov, hey? He hit the jackpot, didn't he, in that lawsuit?"

I suddenly realized that he had known who I was all along and so probably knew many other things as well. But to this day I can't explain why I turned so red and kept staring into his eyes, unable to look away. He looked triumphant again, as though he had caught me most astutely and exposed me for something shameful.

"No, siree!" he cried, raising both eyebrows. "That's what I'd answer if you asked me about Mr. Versilov. You remember what I was telling you about soundness and unsoundness? Eighteen months ago he could've pulled off a perfect deal with that baby, but he fell on his face, yes, siree!"

"What baby?"

"The baby who's being looked after somewhere out of sight. But that will get him nowhere because . . ."

"What baby? What are you talking about?"

"His own baby, of course, by Miss Lidia Akhmakov—that one. . . . You know that line from Pushkin: 'A beautiful maiden was tender to me. . . .' And what about the phosphorous matches, eh?"

"What damned nonsense and wild lies! He never had a child by Lidia Akhmakov!"

"Are *you* trying to tell *me* something? And where do you think I was all that time? Or don't you know I'm a doctor and a male midwife? My name is Stebelkov. You must surely have heard of me? True, I haven't practiced for long, but I was well qualified to give practical advice on a practical matter."

"So you're a male midwife . . . and you attended Miss Akhmakov?"

"No, I didn't attend her. In the suburb where she was confined, there was one Dr. Granz, a man weighed down by a large family whom they paid half a thaler—that's the position the doctors are in there. . . . Besides, no one knew him, so he was there instead of me. In fact, it was I who recommended him for conspiratorial reasons, if you follow me. I myself gave only one piece of practical advice when Andrei Versilov asked me a most confidential question without any witnesses present. But he was trying to catch two hares at once."

I listened to him in bewilderment.

"If you try to catch two hares at once, you catch neither—so goes the popular, or we may even call it vulgar, saying. But what I say is this: exceptions that keep recurring become the rule. So he went after a second hare, or, in plain language, a second lady, and the result was zero. Once you've caught something, you'd better hang onto it! When he should've attended to business quickly, he dilly-dallied instead. Why, Versilov is the true 'ladies' prophet,' as Prince Sergei Sokolsky so aptly called him in my presence. You should come to me, sir, if you want to find out many interesting things about Versilov. You should really come to me!"

He looked with obvious pleasure at my mouth hanging open in surprise. I'd never heard anything about a baby. At that moment a door slammed and someone walked quickly into the next room. Then an irritated woman shouted so loudly behind the partition that we could distinctly hear every word she said:

"Versilov lives in Litvinov's house, which is on Mozhaisk Street, near the Semyonovsky Regiment barracks. I got the address from the Registry Office myself!"

Stebelkov raised both eyebrows and held up one finger.

"Ah, that man! We just mentioned him here and now they're talking about him next door too," he said, "and that's one of those constantly recurring exceptions I mentioned. *Quand on parle d'une corde . . .*"

He hastily sat up on the sofa, put his ear close to the locked door behind the sofa, and listened.

I was completely dumbfounded. It must have been the voice of the girl who had rushed out of the room before and run downstairs, I thought. But how could Versilov be involved here too?

Then I heard that wild, animal-like shriek again—someone seemed to be trying frantically to do or get something and was being forcibly prevented. Now the shrieking lasted longer than the first time. There were sounds suggesting a struggle and the panting words "No, no, I don't want to. . . . Give it back . . . give it back at once. . . ." or something to that effect, I don't remember exactly. Then, like the first time, someone dashed toward the door and flung it open. The two women rushed into the passage just as they had before, one trying to restrain the other. Stebelkov, who had been on his feet since the noise began and had been blissfully eavesdropping, unabashedly burst out of the room into the passage. Of course, I followed him to the door. But the sight of Stebelkov apparently had the effect of a bucket of cold water on the two women because they both rushed back into their room, slamming the door behind them. Stebelkov was on the point of following them but thought better of it, stopped short, raised one finger, and grinned, obviously having thought of something. And this time I detected something evil, vicious, and sinister in that grin of his.

The landlady again appeared at the end of the corridor and Stebelkov quickly ran to her on tiptoe. They had a whispered exchange that lasted for a couple of minutes, after which, probably having received the necessary information, he walked back, this time with an air of ponderous dignity. He came into the room, picked up his top hat, glanced at the mirror, ran his fingers through his hair, and, without even turning his head in my direction, went out into the corridor and stopped by the door to the room of the two women. He held his ear close to the door, winking triumphantly at the landlady, who was shaking her finger coyly at him as if to say: "Oh, you're so naughty, so terribly naughty!"

Finally, with an air of determination, very tactful determination of course—he even seemed to shrink from tactfulness—he rapped lightly on the door with his knuckles. A voice from inside asked "Who's there?" and Stebelkov answered in a dignified, loud, and clear voice:

"May I came in? It's a very urgent matter."

There was a pause, but finally the door opened, first just a crack, then about a quarter of the way. Stebelkov, however, held onto the doorknob and blocked the door with his foot, making it impossible to close it again. He started talking in a loud voice, all the time trying to push himself all the way into the room. I don't remember his exact words, but it was all about Versilov: he could tell them anything they wanted to know about him, clear everything up for them, "You just ask me; I'm the man you need if you want any information about him," or something to that effect. Soon they let him into the room and I sat down on Vasin's sofa to try to eavesdrop, but I couldn't make out what they were saying, except that Versilov's name kept coming up again and again. From certain intonations in Stebelkov's voice, I gathered that he was now dominating the conversation, for instead of his ingratiating tone of the beginning, he had reverted to his usual loud familiarity and I imagined him sprawling on a sofa, as he had in Vasin's room, telling the women long and involved stories punctuated with "now note this," and "do you follow me?" He must have been trying to be very hearty with the ladies, as I heard a couple of his explosive guffaws, although they must have been quite inappropriate because the voices of the two women that sometimes overlapped with his, and occasionally even rose above it, sounded anything but cheerful, especially that of the younger woman, the one who had let out those shrieks. She broke in often, irritatedly and quickly, apparently complaining, accusing, demanding justice. But this did not seem to affect Stebelkov: he simply raised his voice higher and higher, laughed louder and louder and more and more, because he was organically incapable of listening to anybody.

I got up from the sofa, deciding that eavesdropping was despicable, and took my old place by the window. I was convinced Vasin thought nothing of Stebelkov; but if I told him my own, similar opinion of the gentleman, I was certain Vasin would come to his defense and give me a lecture to the effect that he is a "practical, modern businessman whom we may not judge by our abstract standards." I remember, though, above all else, how full of anguish I was at that moment. My heart was beating unevenly: obviously I was expecting something to happen.

Ten minutes went by and suddenly, in the very middle of one of Stebelkov's resounding broadsides of laughter, someone jumped up heavily from a chair, two female voices started shouting at the same time, and Stebelkov obviously got up from his scat too and spoke in a completely different tone, pleading to be allowed to explain something. . . . But he did not get a chance: "Out! Get out, you! Shameless brute! You dirty schemer!" He was certainly being thrown out. When I opened the door, I saw him literally jumping out into the passage: he must have been physically ejected by the two ladies! When he caught sight of me, he suddenly pointed an accusing finger at me and started to yell:

"Here! Look! Here's Versilov's son! Don't you believe me? Look, he's his son, all right! Here!" and he grabbed me by the arm. "Yes, his own son," he repeated, dragging me toward the ladies without any further explanations.

The younger lady was out in the passage, the older one a step behind her in the doorway. I remember only that the poor girl was rather pretty, although she looked sickly and pale; she was about twenty and her hair was blond with a reddish tinge. Her face reminded me somewhat of my sister's. This resemblance struck me and became engraved in my memory. But, of course, I had never seen nor could I conceive of Lisa in such a state of rage as this girl facing me was: her lips were white, her light gray eyes were sparkling, and her whole body swayed with indignation. I remember also being aware of the stupid and undignified position I was in, all because of that ill-mannered nosy brute, but I stayed there without knowing what to say.

"So what if he is his son! Just the fact that he keeps company with you says enough! And you, if you're really Versilov's son," she suddenly turned on me, "tell your father for me that he's a scoundrel, a contemptible and shameless man, and that I don't need his money. . . . Here, I want you to give this back to him, here, take it!"

She pulled out of her pocket a few bills. But the elder woman (who, it turned out, was her mother) caught her hand.

"Olga, but perhaps it isn't even true, perhaps this is not his son. . . ."

Olga glanced at her, hesitated for a second, gave me a quick scornful look, turned, and went back into her room. But before slamming the door, she looked out once more and shouted at Stebelkov: "Out! Get out of here!" and even stamped her foot. Then the door slammed and I heard the key turn. Stebelkov, who was still holding onto my arm, raised one finger and distended his mouth into a long, thoughtful grin, fixing his eyes on mine.

"I find your behavior most undignified and ridiculous," I mumbled indignantly.

But he paid no attention to what I said and kept staring into my eyes.

"That ought to be investigated," he said thoughtfully.

"How dare you to drag me into this! Who is she? What's all this about? You seized me by the arm and dragged me to her! What's going on?"

"Ah, hell, she's just one more who's been deprived of her innocence. . . . As I said, an exception that keeps recurring. . . . Do you follow me?"

He pressed his finger to my chest.

"The hell with you," I said, pushing his finger away.

Quite unexpectedly he burst into soundless, happy laughter and kept laughing for a long time. When at last he finished laughing, he picked up his hat and, his face now grave and stern, said:

"I ought to tell the landlady. . . . Those two should be kicked out into the street. And the sooner the better, otherwise they may . . . You'll see, mark my words. . . . But what the hell!" he cried, suddenly becoming cheerful again: "You'll wait for Vasin, won't you?"

"No, I won't."

"All right, never mind then. . . ."

And without another sound he turned his back on me and left the apartment. He didn't even deign to look in the direction of the landlady, who was obviously waiting for him to tell her what had happened.

I picked up my hat too and, having asked the landlady to give

Vasin the message that Arkady Dolgoruky had been to see him, rushed downstairs.

III

It had all been just a waste of time and when I left I knew I'd better quickly find a room. But I couldn't concentrate and, after having wandered around the streets for a few hours and entered five or six apartments with "rooms to let," I found nothing suitable and I'm sure I must have passed a score of such signs without noticing them. The fact that it turned out to be much harder to find a lodging than I had imagined added further to my annoyance. The rooms I saw were at best like Vasin's, often much worse, but the rent was enormous, far above what I was prepared to pay. I asked for a corner with just enough room to turn round in and they told me scornfully that if that's what I was looking for I'd have a better chance in a flophouse. Moreover, I caught sight here and there of some peculiar-looking lodgers with whom I'd have hated to live under the same roof, so much so, in fact, that I'd have paid not to live near them. There were some characters walking around in vests and shirt sleeves, with disheveled beards, nosy and ill-mannered. In one apartment, I saw about ten such characters sitting in a tiny room drinking beer and playing cards, while the landlady was trying to rent me the room next door. In other places, I gave such absurd answers to the landladies' questions that they stared at me in surprise and in one particular place it even finished in an unpleasant scene.

I'm certainly not going to describe this squalid search in great detail, but I'll just say that it made me feel terribly tired and, as it was already getting dark, I entered a small café to get something to eat. I definitely decided to go straight back and give Versilov the letter about the inheritance without any explanation; I'd pack my belongings in my suitcase, make a bundle out of the rest, and move to a hotel for the night. I knew that there were some inns at the far end of Obukhov Avenue near the Gate of Triumph where you could get a single room for thirty kopeks and I decided to sacrifice that sum rather than spend one more night under Versilov's roof. But then, as I was passing the Technological Institute, I remembered that Mrs. Prutkov lived just across the street and for some reason I decided to drop in on her. The most tangible reason for my visit was, of course, that letter again, but my sudden overwhelming impulse to go and see her must have been due to other causes that I still cannot quite explain—they had to do with the obscure remarks I'd just heard about a certain baby and about certain exceptions becoming the rule. . . . I don't know whether I was driven by a need to get something off my chest, to show off my noble feelings, to have a fight with her, or perhaps even to have a good cry in her presence, but for whatever reason I went up to Tatyana Prutkov's.

I'd been to Mrs. Prutkov's only once before. It was soon after my arrival from Moscow and I'd gone there on an errand for my mother. I'd just stayed for a minute and left without even sitting down. Indeed, she hadn't asked me to.

I rang the bell and the cook opened the door and let me in without saying a word. I'm afraid I'll have to go into great detail here, for otherwise it would be impossible to understand the crazy scene that followed and that so greatly affected my entire story. And so, first of all, a few words about that cook. She was a nasty, snub-nosed Finn who seemed to hate her mistress, although Mrs. Prutkov obviously couldn't bring herself to part with the woman because of that peculiar attachment some old maids contract toward their drooling dogs or their eternally sleeping cats. The Finnish woman was either cuttingly rude or, after Mrs. Prutkov had finally exploded, silent for weeks on end, thus punishing her mistress for stepping out of line. This must have been a period of silence because when I asked her whether her mistress was in (and I clearly remember asking her that), she just turned her back on me and went straight into the kitchen without saying a word.

Obviously, since she had let me in, I concluded that Mrs. Prutkov must be at home, so I went into the living room and waited for her to appear from her bedroom or wherever she might be. I waited for her two or three minutes, without sitting down. It was getting pretty dark now and Mrs. Prutkov's apartment looked even bleaker to me with all the cretonne hanging all over the place. And now I must say a few words about that dingy little apartment, which was the setting of the action about to take place. Because of her old landowner habits and her stubborn, domineering character, Tatyana Prutkov couldn't possibly have rented a few rooms in a furnished apartment and tolerated the presence of a landlady. So she preferred to rent this excuse for an apartment that at least enabled her to be the mistress of her own home. It was a third-floor apartment with windows giving on the courtyard and consisted of just two small rooms, two canary cages set side by side, one even smaller than the other. You entered the apartment through a narrow—five feet or so in width—passage, from which a door on the left led to the two adjoining canary cages, while at the end was the tiny kitchen. Altogether, the whole place could perhaps hold the five hundred cubic feet of air that a human being needs to breathe every twelve hours, but certainly no more. The ceilings were ridiculously low, and what made things even worse was the absurd way all the doors and windows were draped with cretonne, which made the place very dark and made it look like the inside of a closed carriage.

The room I was waiting in, the larger of the two, had enough space for a person to turn around in, although it was cluttered with furniture. I must say that the furniture was of rather good quality: there were all sorts of little inlaid tables with bronze fittings, a beautiful and even elegant dressing table with pretty little boxes on it. But the next room, the bedroom, from which I expected the mistress of the house to emerge and which was separated from the first room by a heavy curtain, had, as I later found out, literally no space for anything but a bed. All these details are indispensable to understand the foolish predicament I was about to find myself in.

And so I was waiting without any particular misgivings when the bell rang. I heard the Finnish cook's unhurried steps along the little passage and then her opening the door and letting people in, again without saying a word. This time, she let in two ladies as I could hear from their loud voices. I recognized one of the voices as Mrs. Prutkov's. And then I recognized the other voice too. It belonged to the person whom I had least expected to meet, for whom I was especially unprepared under the present circumstances. There was no possible mistake: it was that ringing, strong voice with its special metallic quality . . . the voice that had resounded in my ears for just three minutes the day before but that had engraved itself so deeply in my mind. Yes, it was indeed, "yesterday's woman"! What was I to do?

I'm not asking for the reader's advice; I'm simply trying to relive that moment of anxiety and I'm looking in vain for an explanation of what made me suddenly plunge behind the curtain into Mrs. Prutkov's bedroom. Well, anyway, I hid myself just in the nick of time as they were entering the room. Why, instead of going out to meet them in the passage, I hid myself, I cannot say; it just happened like that, without any planning or thinking whatever.

As I jumped into the bedroom and stumbled against the bed, I noticed to my relief that there was a door connecting that room with the kitchen, which meant that there was, after all, a possible escape for me. But when I tried to open it, I found to my horror that the door was locked and there was no key. Hopelessly I

sank onto the bed. I knew now that I'd be forced to overhear a
private conversation, which, from the few words I'd already
taken in, was obviously a very secret one dealing with matters of
a very delicate nature. Oh, I know only too well that a self-
respecting and honorable man would have come out of hiding,
even if only at the last moment, and warned them in a loud
voice: "Wait, I'm here!" and, however ridiculous his position
may have seemed to them, he would have got up and walked
out right past them. But I didn't get up and I didn't walk out.
I didn't have the courage. I chose the most despicable alternative.

"You're really distressing me, Katerina, my dear," Mrs. Prutkov said in a pleading tone. "There's no need for you to go on
worrying like this—it's not at all like you, you know. Usually
you bring joy with you wherever you go, and now suddenly . . .
I hope, though, that you still trust me at least, knowing how devoted I am to you—at least as devoted as I am to Andrei—and I
make no secret of my undying devotion to him. . . . Well then,
believe me, I give you my word of honor he hasn't got that document in his hands, and it may very well be that no one has it. Besides, he's quite incapable of using any such underhanded tricks;
in fact, I think it's rather wicked of you to even suspect him of
it. And I'm convinced that this feud between you two is all in
your minds, yours and his. . . ."

"I know that the document does exist and I also know that he's
capable of anything. And the first thing I saw upon entering my
father's house was *ce petit espion* whom Versilov has foisted
upon my poor father."

"Come now! In the first place *ce petit espion* is not at all *un
espion,* and it was my own idea to send him to your father's because otherwise he'd have gone out of his mind or starved to
death in Moscow—that's what the people with whom he was
staying warned us was likely to happen to him. But, above all,
the boy is just a silly, uncouth clod, who couldn't possibly be a
spy even if he wanted to."

"Yes, he does look like some sort of moron, although there's
no reason why he shouldn't be wicked as well. If I hadn't
been so furious yesterday, I think I'd have laughed my head off:
he turned pale, rushed up to me, bowed stiffly, and mumbled
something in French. And to think that in Moscow Maria tried
to convince me that he was a rare genius. It was from the expression on Maria's face that I concluded that the letter exists
and that it is now in a place most dangerous for me."

"But, darling Katerina, you told me yourself that Maria assured you she had nothing . . ."

"That's just the trouble because I know she's lying and I've found out how skillful she is at lying too! Before I went to Moscow, I still hoped that there were no such documents left, but now . . ."

"You must be wrong, my dear. I've always heard that she's a kind and most responsible person and the late Andronikov trusted her more than any of his nieces. It's true I don't know her too well, but I'm sure you must have won her over completely with your charm and beauty! I know that no one could resist you and, although I'm a gruff old woman, I couldn't possibly stand up to you; in fact, let me kiss you right now. . . . So I'm sure it would've been only too easy for you to bring her over to your side."

"I did try to charm her, Tatyana, I'm sure she was quite enchanted by my manners, but that didn't help me much. She's too sharp for that! No, she's quite a character, a type peculiar to Moscow. . . . And you know what? She advised me to go and see a man called Kraft, who lives in Petersburg now but used to work for Andronikov once. Perhaps he would know something about it, she told me. I had heard about Kraft and, in fact, I vaguely remembered having seen him once. But when she told me that about Kraft, I became convinced that she knew very well where the letter was and was deliberately trying to deceive me."

"But why, why? I think it would make good sense for you to ask Kraft. He's a German who doesn't usually go around wagging his tongue and, I remember very well, he's extremely honest. Really, why don't you go and ask him about it? Only I'm not sure whether he's in Petersburg right now."

"Oh, he's back in Petersburg all right. I've just been to his place and that's why I've come to you in such a state, shaking all over. . . . What I actually wanted to ask you, Tatyana, my angel—you because you know everyone—is what will happen now to all the documents and letters he left behind. I mean whom will they be given to? What if they fall into dangerous hands? I've come to you to ask what you think about all this."

"What documents?" Mrs. Prutkov said in an uncomprehending tone. "Why, you said you'd just seen Kraft yourself, didn't you?"

"Yes, I did just see him, but he was dead—he'd shot himself last night."

I leaped up from the bed. I had managed to control myself while they'd called me a spy and a moron; indeed, the more of the conversation I had heard, the more impossible it had become for me to reveal my presence. By now it was quite inconceivable! So I had decided to sit it out, holding my breath until Mrs. Prutkov saw her visitor off (just hoping that she wouldn't come into her bedroom for some reason!), and then, after Katerina Akhmakov was gone, I'd come out and be prepared, if Mrs. Prutkov attacked me physically, to fight her off, if need be. But when I heard the news about Kraft, I found myself on my feet and shivering all over. Without thinking any further, without visualizing the consequences, without even clearly realizing what I was doing, I stepped forward, lifted the curtain, and stood in front of the two women. There was still enough daylight for them to see my pale face and trembling figure. They both shrieked, for how could they not shriek under the circumstances?

"Kraft . . ." I muttered, staring at Mrs. Akhmakov, "he shot himself, did you say? . . . Yesterday? . . . At sunset?"

"Where've you been? What have you been doing?" Mrs. Prutkov shrieked and literally sank her nails into my shoulder. "You've been eavesdropping! You've been spying on us!"

"Well, what did I tell you?" Katerina Akhmakov was standing and pointing at me.

The anger seething in me burst out.

"It's all lies and garbage!" I shouted, beside myself. "You called me a spy just now! Oh, God almighty! I don't even know that I want to live in the same world with you, let alone spy on the likes of you! A noble man has committed suicide—Kraft has shot himself for an idea, for Hecuba. . . . But you probably haven't even heard of Hecuba! . . . And here I am doomed to live among your intrigues, to make my way around your lies, deceptions, and underhanded plots! I've had enough of it!"

"Slap his face, slap his face for him!" Mrs. Prutkov shrieked frantically.

But Mrs. Akhmakov did not move; she just glared at me fixedly (I remember her glare very clearly to this day). Mrs. Prutkov was obviously about to carry out the attack herself, so I instinctively raised my hand to protect my face. This gesture of mine was, of course, immediately interpreted as my intention to strike her.

"Go ahead, hit me, hit me! Prove to us once and for all the brute that you are! Since you're stronger than an old woman, what's there to stop you?"

"That's enough of your slander!" I shouted back at her. "I've never yet raised my hand to a woman! But you're a shameless old woman, Tatyana Prutkov, and you've always treated me shabbily. Oh, I suppose it's the most practical way of handling people you despise. . . . And you, Mrs. Akhmakov, you're laughing now! I suppose you're laughing at my appearance. Yes, it's a fact that God hasn't blessed me with an imposing presence like your elegant officer's. But that doesn't place me beneath you—indeed, I feel I'm your better! . . . But never mind that, what I'm trying to tell you is that what happened now was none of my fault. . . . I'm here by accident, Mrs. Prutkov! It's your cook who's to blame for my being here or, to be more precise, your strange fondness for her! Why didn't she answer me when I asked her whether you were in and why did she have to show me in instead? And, after that, you must agree that I couldn't very well leap out of a lady's bedroom, which would be a monstrous indiscretion, so I preferred to bear your insults in silence rather than reveal my presence. . . . I see you're laughing again, Mrs. Akhmakov?"

"Get out, get out of here!" Mrs. Prutkov shouted, almost shoving me. "Please don't pay any attention to his ravings, Katerina; I told you he was described to us as deranged by the people he used to live with in Moscow."

"Deranged? They described me as deranged? I wonder who could've written you that? But enough of this anyway. . . . Listen, Mrs. Akhmakov, I give you my word of honor that whatever I may've heard here I shall never repeat to anyone. It was not through any fault of mine that I happened to overhear your secrets. Besides, I'm severing my connections with your father tomorrow, so there's no need for you to worry any longer about the letter you're looking for."

"What are you talking about? What letter?"

Katerina Akhmakov looked completely stunned. She even went pale, or at least that was my impression. I must have said too much.

I walked out quickly and they watched me leave in complete bewilderment. They were dumbfounded by me now.

Chapter 9

I

I hurried home and, strange to say, I was very pleased with myself. Of course, that was no way to speak to ladies, or rather to a lady like that because for me Mrs. Prutkov didn't count. Perhaps I shouldn't have used words like lies and garbage to a lady of Mrs. Akhmakov's class, but now I was glad I had. Apart from anything else, I felt that, by talking to them in that tone, at least I had compensated for being caught in such a ridiculous position. But all these considerations were soon displaced by the thought of Kraft. Although I was not so terribly distressed by his death, it was nevertheless a violent shock to me. Indeed, the very common human habit of reacting with a certain satisfaction when misfortune strikes someone else, such as when another person breaks a leg, is disgraced, loses someone he loves, or something of that sort—even that beastly reaction in me yielded totally to undivided grief, and compassion for Kraft . . . well, if not compassion, at least a strong feeling of respect. And it pleased me to feel that way too. It's amazing, by the way, how many extraneous thoughts can flit through your head when you've just been stunned by some colossal blow, which, it would seem, should have swept away all other thoughts, especially the unimportant ones; but it is precisely the least important thoughts that keep obtruding themselves. I remember also that I was gradually overcome by a hardly perceptible nervous trembling that persisted as I was walking home and then all the time I was talking to Versilov.

That talk took place under very peculiar and unusual circumstances. As I mentioned before, we lived in a detached cottage in a courtyard. The number 13 was marked on our door. Before I'd even entered the gate to our yard, I heard a woman's voice inquiring with impatient irritation the way to Number 13. She had opened the door to a grocery shop near our gate and had asked the way while standing outside. Apparently, instead of obtaining the information she wanted, she had received a rude answer, for she came down the steps of the shop seething with impatient anger.

"Where on earth is the porter here?" she cried, stamping her foot.

The voice was familiar.

"I happen to be going to Number 13," I said, walking up to her. "Who do you want to see?"

"I've been looking for the janitor for a whole hour," she said. "I've asked everyone and have been up all the staircases. . . ."

"Number 13 is that cottage over there in the yard. Don't you recognize me?" I saw that she did and went on: "I suppose you want to see Versilov; so do I. I've come to say good-by to him, for I don't expect to see him ever again. Well, let's go then."

"You're his son, aren't you?"

"That's quite beside the point. . . . Well, after all, let's say that I am his son, although my name is Dolgoruky, but that's because I'm illegitimate. . . . That gentleman, you see, has millions of illegitimate offspring. Besides, there are times when honor and conscience may force a son to leave his father's house. There is such a case in the Bible, you know. Also, he has just inherited a fortune that I do not wish to have any part of, and I'm going to live on what I can earn by the sweat of my brow. If it comes to that, a generous man must sacrifice even his life. Kraft, for one—he shot himself for the sake of an idea. Yes, Kraft was a young man full of promise and he shot himself. . . . It's this way, please, this way. We live in a detached cottage. As to children leaving their parents to find their own nests, you could read about that in the Bible. . . . If they're guided by an idea . . . if they possess an idea. . . . The idea is the main thing, everything in fact. . . ."

I kept blabbering on like that until we reached the cottage. The reader will, of course, notice that I'm not sparing myself anything, although I do give myself credit when it is due. I want to train myself to stick to the truth.

Versilov was at home. Once inside, I didn't even bother to take off my overcoat. She too kept her coat on, a rather shabby one, on top of which she had tied an odd piece of material as a scarf, and on her head was something that looked like a rain hat, old and battered, which certainly didn't help her looks any. In the living room, my mother was sitting in her usual place and sewing. My sister had come out of her room to see who had arrived and was now standing in the doorway. Versilov, who had been doing nothing as usual, got up from his chair and looked at me questioningly and reprovingly.

"I have nothing to do with it," I hastened to explain, stepping aside; "I simply met this young lady by the gate and, since there was no one around to tell her where you lived, I suggested she follow me. As to me, I came here on a certain business, which I'll have the pleasure of explaining to you later on privately."

But Versilov kept looking at me with unabated curiosity.

"Just a minute," the girl butted in impatiently, and Versilov turned his eyes to her. "I have been wondering what made you decide to leave that money for me yesterday. . . . I . . . you understand . . . Here's your money, here, take it!" she suddenly shrieked, tossing a wad of bills on the table. "I'd have brought it earlier but I didn't know your address and had to inquire in the Registry Office. Now you, madam, listen to me!" she said, turning to my mother, who went pale. "I have no wish to insult you because you look like an honest woman, and I suppose that's your daughter over there. . . . Well, I don't know whether you're his wife or what, but I must tell you that this nice gentleman makes a habit of cutting out newspaper advertisements paid for by the last kopeks of girls looking for jobs as governesses and tutors; he goes to see these poor creatures and suggests to them various dishonorable expedients to earn money, sending them to their perdition. I don't even understand now how I could've accepted that money from him yesterday, but he appeared so honorable then! No, don't say one word, sir, you're a dirty scoundrel, that's all you are! But even if your intentions were most honorable, I still don't need your charity! No, no, I don't want to hear what you have to say! I'm satisfied now: I have exposed you for what you are before your womenfolk! May you be cursed!" She ran to the door but stopped in the doorway for a second and shouted: "And now you've inherited money!"

And she vanished like a ghost. She was, of course, that hysterical girl I'd met earlier in the day. The scene obviously made a deep impression on Versilov. He stood for a while looking deeply immersed in thought and then finally turned to me and asked: "You've never met her before, have you?"

"I did this morning, quite by accident. She was having a similar outburst in the passage outside Vasin's room—she was screaming and cursing you. But I didn't talk to her and knew nothing about her. And now I met her by the gate. Could she be that arithmetic teacher in the newspaper ad, by chance?"

"That's her, all right. For once in my life I try to do a decent thing and see what happens. . . . But never mind. What is it you wanted to talk to me about?"

"About this letter," I said. "I got it from Kraft and he got it after Andronikov died. I have no comment and when you read it you'll know what it's about. I'll only add that no one in the world knows about this letter because, after having given it to me, Kraft shot himself almost at once. . . ."

While I was speaking breathlessly, he took the letter from me and, holding it casually in his left hand, continued to look thoughtfully into my eyes. When I mentioned Kraft's suicide, I watched him closely to see the effect the news would have on him but, believe it or not, it had none at all: he didn't even raise an eyebrow. When I stopped talking, he took his lorgnette which was tied to a black ribbon that he always had on him, went over to the candle, and, after glancing at the signature, started to decipher the letter itself. I cannot even convey how offended I was by this disdainful indifference. He must have known Kraft quite well and, besides, a suicide is unusual enough! Also, of course, I'd been eager for the news to produce an effect on him. I waited for perhaps half a minute but, knowing that it would take him much longer than that to read the letter to the end, I walked out of the living room and went up to my garret. My suitcase was packed, and all I had to do was make a bundle of the few remaining things that didn't fit in. I was thinking of Mother and how I hadn't spoken to her just now. I was ready to leave within ten minutes but, just as I was about to go out and find a cab, my sister came in.

"Here, Mother is giving you back your sixty rubles and another twenty. She asks you to forgive her for having told Papa about the money. Yesterday you gave her fifty rubles for your board, but she says it couldn't possibly have come to more than thirty. So the extra twenty rubles is what you overpaid her."

"Well, thank her very much for me and I hope she's telling the truth. And now good-by, Lisa, I must be on my way."

"Where're you going?"

"Right now I'll go and spend the night in some inn because I don't want to spend another night under this roof. Tell Mother I love her."

"She knows it. And she also knows you love Papa. And you must be ashamed of yourself for having brought that poor girl here!"

"I swear I didn't bring her here. I met her by the gate."

"You did bring her here!"

"I assure you I didn't!"

"Just think it over and ask yourself honestly what happened and you'll see that you were the cause of it all."

"Well, all I can say is that I was rather pleased that Versilov was embarrassed. Now listen to this: did you know that he has a baby by Lidia Akhmakov? But I don't know why I'm telling you this. . . ."

"A baby? His baby? No, it's not his baby at all! Where did you pick up that story?"

"Never mind where. What can you know about it anyway?"

"I'm the one who should know, for I've been looking after that baby in Luga. Listen, Arkady, I've known all along that you had no idea of what was going on and yet you persist in offending Papa and thereby offending Mother as well."

"Well, if he's right, I'm willing to be wrong, and that's all there is to it. But I love you and Mother no less. Why have you turned so red, Lisa? And you're getting even redder! In any case, I'll challenge that stupid princelet to a duel for slapping Versilov in Ems, and if Versilov is not to blame for what happened to the Akhmakov girl, then I have even more reason to fight."

"You're out of your mind, Arkady!"

"Thank goodness, that business has been settled in court. . . . Why, now you've gone completely pale! What's going on, Lisa?"

"But Prince Sokolsky will never accept your challenge," Lisa said. She smiled but was still pale.

"Then I'll insult him in public. What's the matter, Lisa?"

Her face was completely bloodless now. Apparently unable to stand on her feet, she lowered herself onto the sofa.

"Lisa!" I heard my mother calling from downstairs.

Lisa got hold of herself, got to her feet, and smiled at me warmly: "Listen, Arkady, forget all that nonsense for the time being. Just wait a little and there're many things you'll find out: you really have no idea of what's going on."

"I'll remember, Lisa, that you turned very pale when I told you I was going to fight a duel."

"Yes, yes, don't forget that!" she said, and smiled at me once again, a farewell smile now, as she went downstairs.

I went out, found myself a cab, and the cabbie helped me to carry my things down from the attic. No one tried to stop me from leaving and I didn't go into the living room to say good-by to my mother as I didn't want to see Versilov again. When I was already sitting in the cab, a new idea suddenly came to my mind.

"Go to the Fontanka, driver, by the Semyonovsky Bridge," I said.

I had decided to go back to Vasin's.

II

It had suddenly occurred to me that Vasin must have already heard about Kraft and must know much more than I did about the whole business. He did, indeed, and he told me all the facts but quite unemotionally. He looked tired. He'd been to Kraft's apartment in the morning. Kraft had used the gun I'd seen there. He'd shot himself when it was already quite dark—that was obvious from the last entry in his diary, made just before he pulled the trigger. In it he mentioned that he was writing in almost complete darkness, hardly able to see what he was writing, since he didn't want to light a candle lest it should set fire to something after he was dead. "Nor do I want to light it now only to blow it out just before I blow out my life." This strange remark was almost the last line of the entry.

He'd begun this diary only three days before his death, as soon as he had returned to Petersburg just before he'd been to Dergachev's. After I'd left him, he'd written in it every quarter of an hour and, during the last forty-five minutes, there was one entry every five minutes. I told Vasin that it was quite beyond me why he, Vasin, had failed to copy the diary when it had been given to him to read; he'd had plenty of time since it was only a few pages long and the entries were brief.

"You could've copied at least the last page," I said.

Vasin smiled and told me that he remembered it by heart anyway. Besides, he said, Kraft seemed to have jotted down at random thoughts that came to his mind. I tried to argue that this was precisely what made it so interesting but soon gave up and, instead, asked him to try to repeat to me verbatim some of the lines Kraft had written an hour before shooting himself. Vasin then recited entire lines such as "I have chills" and "I thought of drinking a glass of brandy to warm myself up but I'd better not as it might intensify the bleeding."

". . . that kind of thing," Vasin said in conclusion.

"And you don't think that's interesting?" I exclaimed indignantly.

"I didn't say it wasn't interesting. I simply didn't copy it down. But there's nothing extraordinary about these notes or, rather, they're quite natural, I mean just what one would expect under the circumstances."

"But these are the last thoughts of a man, his very last thoughts!"

"And sometimes last thoughts can be quite commonplace. I know of another suicide who complained in the last entry in his diary that not a single 'lofty' idea had come to him during that fateful last hour, that he could think only of insignificant, everyday things."

"And do you think that when he wrote that he had chills, it was a trivial thought too?"

"Do you mean his reference to 'chills' or his worrying about bleeding? It's a well-known fact that many people who are able to face their forthcoming death—whether voluntary or not—are often concerned about leaving their bodies in a decent condition. And that's why Kraft wanted to avoid too violent a hemorrhage. . . ."

"I don't know how well known that fact is or whether it's true at all," I said through my teeth, "but I'm really surprised that you should take it all so casually when we saw Kraft only such a short time ago, sitting and talking to us. . . . Aren't you even sorry for him?"

"Of course I am, but that's quite a different matter. In any case, Kraft himself chose death as a logical solution, which goes to show that everything that was said about him at Dergachev's was justified. He left behind a manuscript full of intricate theories, in which he uses phrenology, craniology, and even mathematics to prove that the Russians are a second-rate people and therefore, being a Russian himself, he does not consider it worthwhile remaining alive. Actually, the only remarkable thing is that he did follow his idea through to its logical conclusion and shoot himself, because usually people work out all sorts of logical conclusions but stop there."

"We must at least pay tribute to his character."

"And perhaps not just to his character," Vasin said evasively.

I assumed he was ironically implying that Kraft's reasoning was faulty or even stupid. All that irritated me.

"But you yourself, Vasin, spoke of emotional beliefs and feelings yesterday."

"I wouldn't go back on what I said then; but there's something so flagrantly wrong in this case that a sober look at the whole affair cannot help but dissipate the sympathy one may feel at first."

"You know what—even before I came here, just by the look I saw in your eyes yesterday, I knew you would say nasty things about Kraft, and, in order not to hear you talk like that, I decided not to ask you for your opinion. But you expressed it anyway and I can't help but agree with you. Nevertheless, I don't like your saying what you just said. I'm sorry for Kraft."

"I think this is getting rather involved . . ."

"You're right, it is," I interrupted him, "but it's quite a comfort for those who stay alive to criticize the dead by saying: 'Of course, a man worthy of compassion and indulgence has killed himself, but as long as we are still alive there's no reason for us to be too unhappy about it.'"

"Yes, of course, if you look at it that way. . . . But you didn't mean that seriously! You put it very cleverly, you know. Listen, I usually have tea at this hour; I must go and order it, and you'll have some with me, won't you?"

As he left the room, he glanced at my suitcase and my bundle.

I had intended to say something unpleasant to him about his attitude toward Kraft and I had done my best. But, curiously enough, he seemed to have taken at face value my remark about the pleasant feeling of those who survive a suicide. Well, however you looked at it, his reactions were probably sounder than mine, even when it came to feelings. I readily admitted this to myself. Nevertheless, I definitely disliked him now.

After tea had been brought in, I asked him whether he could put me up just for one night, but said if it was inconvenient I'd go to a hotel. I explained to him briefly that I'd broken off with Versilov without going into detail. Vasin heard me out attentively but with complete detachment. In general, he only answered when I asked him something, although he did so quite readily and pleasantly. As to the letter about which I had come to seek his advice earlier, I didn't mention it and told him that I'd just come to pay him a friendly visit before. I did this because since I'd given my word to Versilov that no one except me knew about the letter, I felt I had no right to mention it to anyone. Besides, there were certain subjects I could no longer discuss with Vasin without repugnance, although I still could talk to him easily enough about other things. I even managed to arouse his curiosity when I told him about the episode in the room next door, the screaming in the passage, and the final scene at Versilov's. He also listened very attentively when I told him about my meeting with Stebelkov. Indeed, he made me repeat twice about Stebelkov questioning me about the gathering at Dergachev's. Vasin pondered for a while in silence, but finally merely let out a short laugh. I had the very strong impression at that moment that nothing in the world could upset Vasin's perfect balance for long, and at first I rather admired him for it.

"On the whole," I said, "Mr. Stebelkov didn't make too much sense to me. What he said was rather incoherent. . . . He seems sort of muddle-headed too. . . ."

Vasin's face was very serious.

"He certainly is not the most articulate person in the world," Vasin said, "but if you get to know him better you'll hear him make extremely acute observations occasionally. He's one of those men of action who is quick to see a profitable angle in a deal and at the same time is hopeless when it comes to abstract thinking. That sort of person ought to be appraised only from a practical point of view."

He had put into words just what I had felt about Stebelkov!

"In any case he caused an awful to-do with your lady neighbors and God only knows how it might've ended. . . ."

Vasin told me that the two ladies had been living next door to him for three weeks or so and that they'd come from somewhere in the provinces. The room they occupied, he said, was very small, and they appeared to have very little money. They seemed to spend their time sitting there and waiting for something. He didn't know that the younger lady had advertised herself in the newspaper as a teacher. But the landlady had told him that Versilov had come to see the girl while Vasin was out. It was obvious that his neighbors had avoided seeing anyone, including the landlady, and during the past few days Vasin had noticed that they were going through some sort of a crisis, although he had never witnessed such outbursts as I had.

I have brought up this conversation about Vasin's neighbors here because of what was to follow and I must note that, while we were talking about them, we couldn't hear a sound coming from their room. Vasin was particularly interested to hear that Stebelkov had said that he'd have a word with the landlady about the two women and that he had twice repeated warningly something about "you'll see" or "mark my words."

"And you'll see all right," Vasin commented; "he must've detected something—he has a good eye when it comes to that sort of thing."

"So you too think the landlady should kick them out?"

"I don't mean that they should be kicked out; I only think something ought to be done to prevent real trouble. Anyway, those unpleasant scenes are bound to come to an end some day one way or another. . . . So let's drop the subject for now."

As to Versilov's visit to his neighbors, Vasin refused to draw any conclusions from that at all.

"It could be anything," he said. "Anything can come into a man's head when he suddenly finds lots of money in his pocket. . . . But it's possible that he was simply acting out of charity. . . . Charity is part of his aristocratic tradition, or perhaps he even has a personal inclination for it."

I also told Vasin what Stebelkov had said about the baby.

"There Stebelkov is completely wrong," Vasin said with a special emphasis that struck me and that I still remember very clearly.

"There are times," he went on, "when Stebelkov puts too much trust in his common sense and jumps too quickly to what he thinks is the most logical conclusion, which, although superficially clever, may miss the mark. He fails to make an allowance for characters that are too complex or for a story that may have an unexpected or even fantastic twist. He had only incomplete knowledge of that affair and concluded hastily that the baby must be Versilov's whereas, in fact, it is not."

I insisted he tell me what he knew about this whole business and this is what I learned to my immense surprise. The father of the baby was Prince Sergei Sokolsky. Whether because of sickness or because of the eccentric streak in her character, Lidia Akhmakov did at times behave very unpredictably. She had fallen in love with Sergei Sokolsky and, as Vasin put it, the prince "felt no compunction in accepting her love." The love affair was quite ephemeral: they quarreled and she sent him away, which "apparently was just what he wanted."

"She was a very strange girl," Vasin said, "and it's quite possible that she wasn't always in her right mind. But when he left Lidia in Paris, the prince had no idea of her condition and didn't learn about it until the end, until his return. In the meantime Versilov had befriended Lidia and it was precisely because of her condition (which even her parents did not suspect until the end) that he proposed marriage to her. The girl, who was by then in love with Versilov, accepted enthusiastically as she wanted to see in this gesture something more than mere chivalry, although she admired that too. Of course, Versilov knew how to handle it all," Vasin added. "The baby, a little girl, was born a month or six weeks prematurely and was temporarily put into a home somewhere in Germany. But later Versilov had it brought to Russia and I believe it may even be in Petersburg now."

"And where do the phosphorous matches come in, then?"

"I know nothing about that," Vasin said. "Lidia Akhmakov died a couple of weeks after her confinement but I don't know how. Sergei Sokolsky, who had just returned from Paris, was very surprised to learn that there was a baby and at first wouldn't believe it was his. . . . The whole story has been hushed up and to this day many details are not known."

"But what a pig that prince is!" I cried indignantly. "What a thing to do to a poor sick girl!"

"She wasn't really all that sick at the time. . . . Besides, it was she who sent him away, although he may have been a bit hasty in accepting his dismissal."

"So you're justifying that despicable princeling?"

"Not really. I simply don't apply any epithets to him. There could have been many reasons besides wickedness for him to act the way he did. Anyway, there's nothing so unusual about the whole affair."

"Tell me, Vasin, do you know that Sokolsky well? I'd greatly appreciate it if you told me what kind of a man he is; it's very important for me to know for certain reasons."

But on this point Vasin was obviously reticent. He did know

the prince but wouldn't tell me under what circumstances he'd met him. He added that one had to make certain allowances for the prince's character. "He is filled with the best of intentions and is a very sensitive person," Vasin said, "but he is neither reasonable nor strong-willed enough to control his whims. Without being sufficiently educated, Sergei Sokolsky pounces upon various ideas and tries to cope with all sorts of situations that are beyond his capacities. He may, for instance, suddenly decide that a man must do whatever he is fit for and then repeat again and again a statement like 'I'm a prince descended from Rurik, but if I'm not fit for anything else, there's no reason why I shouldn't become a bootmaker and earn my living that way. Indeed, I can even imagine a sign: "Prince So-and-So, Bootmaker." It sounds rather good.' And then he doesn't just talk, he's likely to carry out his ideas—that's more important," Vasin added. "But he's not guided by the force of his convictions, only by sudden impulses. Later he's sorry, he repents, and he's ready to go to the opposite extreme. That's how he lives. Nowadays many people are caught like that," Vasin concluded, "and for no other reason than that they happen to be living at this time in history."

These words brought many thoughts to my mind.

"Is it true that Sergei Sokolsky was kicked out of his regiment?" I asked.

"I don't know whether he was actually kicked out, but he did resign his commission under unpleasant circumstances. Do you know, by the way, that after leaving the Army last fall he spent two or three months in Luga?"

"What I know is that you were in Luga then."

"Yes, I spent some time there too. . . . And the prince also knew your sister Lisa."

"Really? I didn't know that. I must say that my sister and I haven't talked much to each other. . . . But surely my mother didn't receive him in her house, did she?"

"Oh no, he was only slightly acquainted with them, through mutual friends."

"Yes, what was it my sister said to me about that baby? Was the baby in Luga too?"

"For a while."

"And where is it now?"

"In Petersburg most probably."

"I'll never believe," I cried in great agitation, "that my mother could in any way have been involved in this business with Lidia!"

"In all these intrigues, which I'm not qualified to judge, I don't think that Versilov played a particularly reprehensible part," Vasin observed with a tolerant smile. I believe he was finding it difficult to continue talking to me, but he didn't want to show it.

"I'll never, never believe that a woman would want to give up her husband to another woman!" I shouted again. "I'll never believe it and I swear that my mother had no part in it!"

"But she didn't seem to oppose it. . . ."

"If I were in her place, I wouldn't oppose it either, out of sheer pride!"

"As for myself," Vasin said, "I absolutely refuse to judge people in these matters."

It's very possible that, for all his intelligence, Vasin understood nothing about women so that a whole area of feelings and emotions was closed to him. So I dropped the conversation.

I knew that Vasin was now working for a stock company and that he often used to bring work home with him. I insisted he shouldn't stand on ceremony with me and should do his work as usual if he had some to do, and finally he admitted he did have a few things to attend to. I think he was pleased with my suggestion, but before sitting down with his papers and accounts, he made up a bed for me on the sofa. At first he had wanted me to sleep in his bed, but I wouldn't hear of it. I believe he was rather pleased about that too. He got a pillow and a blanket for me from his landlady. Vasin was extremely amiable and friendly, but somehow it weighed on me to see him go to all that trouble for my sake. I had felt much more at ease about three weeks earlier when I had spent the night at Efim Zverev's on the Petersburg Side. I remember how Zverev had devised a bed for me, also on the sofa. He had to do it secretly to keep his aunt, who, he assumed, would be very angry if she found out that he allowed his friends to sleep in her house, from knowing. It made us laugh when, instead of a sheet, we used a shirt and, instead of a pillow, a rolled-up coat. I remember how, after having completed the installations, Zverev had patted the sofa tenderly and said to me:

"*Vous dormirez comme un petit roi!*"

And somehow his fooling and the French sentence, which sounded as incongruous in his mouth as a saddle on a cow's back, contributed to a very pleasant night's sleep in that oaf's house. As for Vasin, I felt immensely relieved when he finally sat down at his table with his back turned to me and got down to work. I stretched out on the sofa and, staring at his back, thought at length about various matters.

III

I had, indeed, plenty to think about. There was general confusion in my mind—things wouldn't fit together. And, although certain impressions stood out, there were too many of them for any one to stand out and give meaning to the whole picture. Things seemed to flash by and vanish at random, and I myself felt reluctant to concentrate on any one thing in particular or try to bring order into the chaos. Even the thought of Kraft had been relegated to the background. It was my present situation that had moved to the forefront—the fact that now *I had broken off* with my past, that my suitcase was with me, that what was ahead of me was something completely new, and that until now all my preparations had been like a game, but now *suddenly* everything was in earnest. This thought gave me courage and, despite the confusion in my mind, cheered me up.

But there were other sensations as well. And one of them was trying hard to break out from among the others and get hold of my entire soul. Strangely, that sensation also seemed to give me strength while promising something breathtakingly exhilarating. At first, I was afraid, though: I worried whether I hadn't in my excitement when caught unawares said too much to Katerina Akhmakov about the letter. "Yes, I did say too much and they'll probably guess," I thought. "And then I'll be in trouble! They'll never leave me in peace once they suspect something. But let them! They may not even find me if I go into hiding. . . . But what if they really set out after me? . . ." And I relived in the minutest detail yesterday's scene when I'd stood facing Katerina with her scornful yet at the same time surprised eyes fixed on me, and I realized that I was thinking of it with growing pleasure. Even as I'd left her, she had still been looking at me with amazement. I recalled now that her eyes were not really black, but the absolute blackness of her eyelashes made her eyes look almost black.

Then suddenly I felt unbearably disgusted at trying to reconstruct the scene; I felt sick and angry, both with them and with myself. There was something wrong with me, I decided, and tried to think of something else. I suddenly thought: Why wasn't I in the least indignant with Versilov for the way he'd behaved with the girl next door? I was quite convinced that he'd gone to her intending to take advantage of her distress and have himself a good time. But it didn't arouse my indignation. I thought that no one could expect anything else of him and, although I was glad he'd been exposed and put to shame, I didn't feel in the least outraged.

What bothered me was not what he'd tried to do but the way he'd looked at me with cold hatred when I'd come in with the girl. And, as my heart missed a beat, I thought: "Now, at last, he looks at me without affectation." Ah, if I hadn't loved him, I wouldn't have been so overjoyed by his hatred!

At last I dozed off and then fell asleep. I remember vaguely waking up when Vasin, having finished his work, got up, neatly put away his papers, glanced at the sofa where I was pretending to be asleep, undressed, and blew out the candle. It was past midnight then.

IV

Almost exactly two hours later, I woke up with a start and sat up on my sofa in a panic. Horrible yelling, weeping, and howling were coming from behind the partition. Our door was wide open and outside, in the passage, which was lighted now, people were running back and forth and shouting. I called out to Vasin but realized he was no longer in his bed. I didn't know where he kept the matches, so I fumbled for my clothes and started dressing in the dark. Evidently the landlady, and perhaps the other lodgers, had rushed to the room next door. In the wailing I recognized the voice of the older of the two women; I didn't hear the voice of the younger one at all. That was the first thing that struck me, I remember. Before I'd finished dressing, Vasin came back. He immediately found the matches and lighted a candle. He had on his dressing gown and slippers. He took them off and started dressing.

"What happened?" I inquired.

"Something extremely unpleasant and bothersome," he answered almost angrily. "That young girl you were telling me about has hanged herself in her room."

I let out a scream. I can't even express how stunned I was. I rushed out into the passage. But I must admit that I didn't dare step into the room next door. I saw the poor girl only after they'd taken her down, and even then I didn't come too close to her. They had covered her with a sheet and just the soles of her shoes stuck out from under it. Somehow I couldn't make myself look into her face. The mother was in a terrible state and the landlady, who had remained quite calm throughout, was by her side. All the other lodgers had gathered there too. They consisted of an elderly seaman, who, although usually peevish and demanding, was now quiet and subdued and an elderly couple from Tver, both of whom looked quite respectable.

I won't describe the remaining hours of that night with all the commotion and the arrival of the police. I was shivering all over until dawn and somehow felt it my duty not to go back to bed, although there was really nothing I could do. I noticed how energetic everybody around me seemed. Indeed, it looked as if what had just happened had somehow recharged them with energy. Vasin even rushed off to town on some errand. The landlady turned out to be a much nicer woman than I had thought. I managed to convince her (and I think I must be given credit for this) that the mother should not be allowed to remain with her daughter's body and that the landlady should take her to her own room. The landlady agreed quite readily and, despite the mother's protests and cries that she wouldn't leave her daughter's body, she eventually followed the landlady, who immediately ordered the maid to light the samovar and make some tea. One by one, the other lodgers went back to their rooms, but I stayed at the landlady's for a long time. She was pleased to have someone else there and, for my part, I could tell her a few things that shed some light on what had happened.

The samovar was most welcome. In general, it is an indispensable Russian institution, especially in times of great stress, when you are struck by something sudden, unexpected, and outlandish. We finally succeeded in making the mother drink two cups of tea, even if it took a lot of pleading, persuading, and almost force. I believe I have never seen a more profound and genuine despair than that of this wretched mother. But after many violent explosions of sobs and hysterics, she started to talk and then even spoke eagerly as I listened to her with interest. There are people, women especially, whom it helps to talk and talk when they are struck by a catastrophe; also there are some people who have been, as it were, worn away by misery, who have been hurt too often during their lifetime, who have suffered terrible disasters and experienced constant hardships, and who, even within the sight of the dead body of a loved one, never forget the dearly acquired art of getting along with others. I don't say that deprecatingly; it is not a matter of egoism with them, nor a matter of having a thick hide and a lack of refinement: there is perhaps more goodness in such hearts than in certain heroes; it is a reflex of self-preservation, acquired from the long experience of being downtrodden, that ends by dominating their behavior. The dead girl was not at all like her mother that way, although there was a physical resemblance between the two of them. But while the girl had been undeniably pretty, the mother, who was not old yet (fifty or so) and was still blond like her daughter, had sunken cheeks and large, uneven yellowish teeth. As a matter of fact, everything about her had a yellowish tinge, from the parchment-like skin of her face and hands to her dress, just from being so old and worn. And for some strange reason, one fingernail on her right hand had been covered over with yellow wax. The poor woman's story was not always coherent, but I'll put down here what I made out of it and remembered.

V

They'd come from Moscow. She was the widow of a government employee. Her husband, she said, "had left us nothing except for a yearly pension of two hundred rubles, but what's two hundred rubles?" Still, she had managed to bring up her Olga on that and had put her through high school, "and you should've seen how well she studied—she graduated with a silver medal, you know!"

At that point, of course, came a flood of tears. Before his death, her husband had invested four thousand rubles with a Petersburg merchant who went broke. Later, she heard the merchant was in money again. "I had all the documents, I asked for advice and was told that if I got hold of him I was sure to get everything back. So I got in touch with him and he seemed agreeable. People advised me to go to Petersburg and talk to him directly. So I came here with Olga, a month ago that was. Well, you can imagine how little money we had, so we took the smallest room we could find, which luckily was in a respectable house. That was very important for us, two inexperienced women whom anyone could take advantage of. We managed to pay one month's rent in advance, but it was hard to stay alive. Everything is so expensive in Petersburg. And then the merchant turned us down flat: 'I don't know you,' he said, 'and have no wish to know you.' I had known my documents were not quite in proper order. So people advised me to go and consult a famous lawyer: 'He's not just a lawyer, he's a former law professor, so whatever he advises you to do is sure to be right.' So I took the last fifteen rubles I had left and went to see him. He received me but wouldn't listen to me more than three minutes. 'I see,' he said; 'I know,' he said, 'your merchant will pay you if he feels like it and he won't if he doesn't, but if you try to sue him you'll only be out of pocket even more. The best thing is to resign yourself.' Then he laughed and reminded me that the Gospel recommended resignation and suggested I resign myself before I lost my last kopek, and he kept laughing as he walked me to the door and showed me out. So I just lost another fifteen rubles! I went home to Olga. We sat there for a while looking at each other; then I told her what had happened and began to cry. But she didn't cry, proud as she was: instead, it made her indignant, my story. That's how she always was, all her life, my Olga, ever since she was a little girl: she never cried, never moaned, just sat glaring so fiercely that it frightened me to look at her. And, you know, the truth is that I was afraid of her, yes, I'd been afraid of her for a long time already. And so often when I felt like moaning and weeping, I didn't dare in her presence. I went to see the merchant for one more try, burst into tears, begged him, but he wouldn't even listen to me. He just kept saying 'I know all that, I know, I've heard it all before. . . .'

"We'd never planned to stay in Petersburg that long, and I admit that we'd been sitting around without money for a long time. I'd pawned practically everything I could, but when Olga brought me her own clothes to pawn, I couldn't contain myself and burst into tears. She became furious, stamped her foot, and ran to see the merchant herself. The merchant—he's a widower —heard her out and said: 'Come back in two days at five o'clock. I'll think up something perhaps.' She came home in a better mood. 'Perhaps he will think up something,' she said. Well, seeing her more cheerful cheered me up too, although my heart was heavy with foreboding. What would he come up with, I kept asking myself, although I didn't dare talk to her about it.

"Two days later, she returned from the merchant's ashen pale. She was shivering all over and threw herself down on her bed. I understood everything and didn't want to ask her. Now imagine this: that bandit had offered her fifteen rubles as an advance. 'And if you turn out to be really pure and virtuous, I'll give you another forty.' He'd said that straight to her face, it didn't bother him at all. She told me she'd gone for him, furiously, but he'd managed to push her off and run to another room where he locked himself in. . . .

"And, by that time, I'm ashamed to admit, we had nothing at all to buy food with. We sold the jacket lined with rabbit fur that we'd brought with us and she used the money to place an ad in a newspaper offering to tutor in all subjects, even arithmetic. 'It'd be fine if they paid me just thirty kopeks an hour.'

"I'd felt really awful looking at her those last few days. She wouldn't say a word for hours; she'd just sit by the window staring at the roof of the house across the street and then suddenly jump to her feet and shout something like 'If only I could get some washing to do' or 'I'd dig ditches if only they offered it to me,' and she'd stamp her foot in rage. And in Petersburg we had no friends, no one to turn to. 'What will happen to us?' I kept asking myself, but I couldn't say that aloud in her presence. Once, when she'd been sleeping during the day, she woke up and looked at me. I'd been sitting on our suitcase and looking at her too. She got up, came over to me in silence, hugged me very, very hard, and this time we both couldn't resist and burst into tears. After that we sat side by side, holding on tight to each other. It was the first time we'd been like that in our lives. Then the maid Nastasia knocked on the door and said there was a lady outside inquiring about Olga. That was just four days ago.

"So a well-dressed lady walked in and asked 'Is it you who advertised about lessons in the newspaper?' She spoke good Russian, but her accent sounded German to me. We were very happy and asked her to sit down. She was very friendly and said laughingly that it wasn't she who'd take the lessons, it was her niece who had very young children. 'If you're interested, come over and we'll discuss it.' She gave her an address, somewhere near the Voznesensky Bridge—the street, the house, the number of the apartment—and left. That same day, Olga hurried over there. Two hours later she was back—in hysterics. Later she told me what had happened. She'd asked the janitor for apartment number such and such. He'd given her a peculiar look. 'What business do you have there?' The way he'd asked her that might have warned her to give up the whole thing, but she was such a headstrong, impatient girl and she wouldn't take such insolent questioning. 'It's over there.' The janitor pointed at one of the staircases in the yard and went back to his little room. So she walked up to the apartment and asked for the lady. And, believe it or not, all kinds of horrible women, rouged and in heavy make-up, surrounded her, laughing, saying, 'Welcome, welcome,' dancing around her, pulling at her, while someone was playing the piano. She said she'd tried to run away, but they held onto her and wouldn't let her go. She got frightened then; her knees became all wobbly, but the women still wouldn't let her loose. They opened a bottle of port and offered her some; they insisted, 'Please have some . . .' She finally tore herself loose from their grip. 'Let me go, let me go!' she screamed and 'Help, help, help!' She rushed to the door, but the others held onto it and wouldn't let her out and Olga just went on screaming. . . . Then the lady who'd come to see us appeared. She walked straight up to Olga, slapped her face twice, and pushed her out onto the landing. 'There's no room for a bitch like you in a respectable establishment like ours!' she shouted after her, and another woman chimed in: 'You came here begging us to take you in because you had nothing to eat, but nobody would even want to look at a mug like yours.'

"She was feverish all that night and kept talking in her sleep, but in the morning she got up, her eyes flashing. She walked up and down the room for a while and suddenly declared: 'I want to lodge a complaint against that creature, I'll take her to court!' I said nothing, only thinking what good could that possibly do and how would she prove her charge. She went on and on, pacing the floor and wringing her hands, tears running down her cheeks, with her lips tightly closed. And from then on, it was as if a shadow of doom had come over her. Still, on the third day, she seemed to have calmed down a little and sat quietly. . . . And it was then, at four in the afternoon, that Mr. Versilov came to see us.

"And now let me tell you this: I still cannot understand why Olga, usually so distrustful of people, listened to him almost from the moment he started talking. What impressed us both at the time was his serious, even stern air, the quiet, effective way he had of expressing himself, while always remaining courteous or, even more than that, considerate toward us without any possible ulterior motive. It was evident that he'd come to see us with the purest intentions.

" 'I have read your advertisement in the paper, ma'am, and I thought I ought to tell you that it wasn't worded properly, that, the way it is, it might even attract undesirable responses.' And he started explaining why. I admit I couldn't follow everything he said, especially what he said about the arithmetic, but Olga went quite red in the face and answered him and sort of livened up as they spoke. She talked to him willingly (he sounded so intelligent!) and I even heard, to my great surprise, her thanking him for coming. He questioned her with interest about our life, and it turned out he'd lived in Moscow for a long time and knew well the principal of the high school Olga had gone to.

" 'I'll find lessons for you here,' he said. 'I'm sure there'll be no problem because I know many people in Petersburg, and some of them are even quite influential. So even if you were interested in a permanent position, I have no doubt that one could be found too. . . . But in the meantime,' he said, 'you must forgive me if I ask you a blunt question: Isn't there anything I could do for you right now? If so, it would be I who'd be obliged to you. Let it be a loan,' he said, 'and you'll pay it back in no time after you start working. I give you my word of honor that if I ever find myself in dire need one day when you're well off, I'll send my wife or my daughter to you to ask for a small loan. . . .'

"Well, I can't remember everything he said, but I couldn't hold back my tears the moment I noticed that Olga's lips were trembling from gratitude too.

" 'If I accept your offer,' she said to him, 'it's only because I trust an honorable and kind man who could have been my father. . . .'

"She put it very well and it came out so dignified when she called him an honorable and kind man!

"He got up immediately: 'I'll find you lessons, you can rest assured of that. I'll get busy on it right away, it won't be difficult at all. You're a perfectly qualified teacher. . . .'

"Ah, yes, I forgot to tell you that earlier he had asked to see Olga's graduation certificate and had even tested her a little in arithmetic and other subjects. 'He examined me, Mother, in every subject,' Olga said to me later; 'he's such a well-educated and intelligent man! One doesn't often have the opportunity to talk to one like him!' She was all radiant now. 'Put this money away, Mother,' she said about the sixty rubles he had left on the table. 'We'll pay him back first thing when I get a job and he'll see that we're as honest as we are proud, which he already understood.' She remained silent for a moment and sighed. 'You know, Mother,' she said after a while, 'if we'd been ordinary, unrefined people, we might have rejected his offer out of false pride, but, by accepting the loan, we have proved our refinement to him, since it shows we trust him implicitly as an honorable, gray-haired man. Don't you agree, Mother?'

"I didn't quite understand her at first. 'Why shouldn't one accept help from an honorable and rich man if, on top of everything else, he also happens to be kind, Olga?'

" 'No, Mother,' she said, and frowned, 'it's not his kindness it's his human understanding that I appreciate. As to his money, I'd really have preferred it if he hadn't offered it to us and perhaps we'd better do without it: it's good enough to know that he's promised to get me a job. I think that would be best, although we do need money. . . .'

" 'Well, you know, Olga, our situation is pretty desperate and I don't think we can afford to refuse the money.' I even laughed a little. Things were looking up now, I thought, but before an hour had passed Olga said to me:

" 'Still, Mother, I want you to wait before you start spending that money.' Her tone was harsh when she said that.

" 'But why, Olga?'

" 'Because that's how it must be.' And she said nothing more all that evening, and, between one and two o'clock in the morning, I woke up and I realized she was not asleep from the way she was turning from one side to the other.

" 'Are you awake, Mother?' she asked, and I said, 'Yes, Olga, I'm awake.' 'Do you know,' she said then, 'he was trying to insult me.' 'But why, Olga, what makes you think that?' 'I'm sure I'm right, he's a despicable man and don't you dare spend one single kopek of his money.' I tried to object, I even cried some, but she turned away from me, to the wall: 'Leave me alone, I'm trying to get some sleep.'

"In the morning she got up and started pacing the room with a face all dead and expressionless. I swear to God, after she'd been to that infamous house, she was never quite the same; something must've cracked in her heart and in her mind when they'd insulted her there! So I looked at her that morning with great anguish and I decided not to contradict her any more, whatever she said.

" 'Do you realize, Mother, he didn't leave his address.'

" 'Oh, come now, Olga—you were here when he came yesterday; you yourself had nothing but praise for him, you almost cried out of gratitude. . . .'

"Ah, the way she screamed when I said that! 'Your way of thinking is unspeakable!' she shouted at me. 'Perhaps it's because you were brought up on the old ideas of serfdom!' And that was all she found to say; she just seized her little hat and dashed out of the room while I called after her, worrying terribly what she would do. Actually, she went to the Registry Office and got Mr. Versilov's address.

" 'I'll go to his house and throw the money in his face because he wanted to insult me, just like Safronov—that was that merchant, you know—except that Safronov is just an uncouth clod while Versilov is a tricky Jesuit. . . .'

"And it was just then that that gentleman knocked on our door and said that he had heard us mention Versilov's name and could tell us whatever we wished to know about him.

"As soon as he pronounced that name, Olga pounced on him and started to talk and talk as if in a frenzy. I could only stare at her in amazement, for she'd always been so silent and reserved and now she was letting herself go like that with a completely unknown man. Her cheeks were blood red and her eyes were burning. And he seemed to agree with her.

" 'You're absolutely right about him, ma'am: Versilov is exactly like those generals who were exposed in the newspapers, the ones who put on their dress uniforms, pin on all their medals, and go and make the rounds of all the governesses who advertise in the papers; they usually find what they're looking for, and if they see it won't work, they just stay for a while, promise God knows what, and depart, feeling satisfied even with that kind of distraction.'

"Olga laughed, but the gentleman didn't understand that she was laughing from rage and so he caught her hand and pulled it toward his heart: 'I dare say, ma'am, I'm also a man of means and I too could easily have offered my services to a beautiful lady, but I'd rather simply kiss her pretty little hand first. . . .' and I saw him pulling her hand toward his lips.

"Ah, the way she jumped to her feet and threw herself at him! I got up too and together we pushed him out of the room.

"Later in the afternoon, Olga took the money from me and left. When she came back, she announced: 'Well, I've punished that despicable man, Mother.' 'Oh, Olga, Olga, you may very well have thrown away our last chance and offended a good and honest man!' I was so outraged at what she'd done I couldn't hold back my tears. Then she started screaming at me: 'No, no, no! I don't want his charity, even if he is the most honorable man in the world! I don't want anyone to be sorry for me! No, no, no!'

"I lay on my bed and my mind was empty: I only remember staring at that nail on the wall where a mirror must've hung once. . . . I never thought she could do it, never expected it of my Olga. . . . I usually sleep very heavily and I snore, I guess it's the blood going to my head, and sometimes, when it goes to my heart, I scream in my sleep and Olga shakes me and shakes me to bring me out of it. 'Why, Mother,' she'd say, 'you sleep so hard sometimes that it's impossible to wake you up.' 'Yes, Olga, I do sleep very, very hard. . . .' And so, I guess, she waited until I started snoring, and got up, feeling quite sure I wouldn't wake up. She used the long strap from our trunk. It had been lying around and just that morning I'd thought I ought to put it away somewhere so it wouldn't get lost. She must've climbed on a chair and then kicked it out from under her and, to prevent it from banging on the floor, she'd put a skirt under it. I think I didn't wake up until at least an hour later. But right away I had a feeling that something wasn't right and I called out 'Olga, Olga!' I don't know what it was, perhaps because I didn't hear her breathing or perhaps because her empty bed looked somehow too flat in the darkness. Then I got up and felt with my hand—the bed was empty all right, and her pillow was cold. My heart sank at once and I didn't know what to do. Maybe she's gone out, I decided, but then I thought I saw her standing there in the corner, by the door. I looked at her and she seemed to be looking back at me in the darkness, without moving. But why should she be standing on a chair? I wondered, and I whispered to her: 'Olga, Olga, can you hear me?' But then somehow I suddenly understood: I stretched out both hands toward her and seized her; I threw my arms around her. She swayed in my arms. . . . I understood everything, but I refused to understand; I wanted to scream but no sound came out of me. . . . 'Ah!' I thought as I was still holding onto her and swaying to and fro. Then, I suddenly let go and fell down on the floor. It was only then that I could scream. . . ."

When Vasin returned in the morning, after five, I said to him: "If it hadn't been for your Stebelkov, perhaps none of this would've happened."

"Who can tell?" he said. "I suppose it would've happened anyway. Everything seems to have been leading up to it even without him . . . although I must say that sometimes Stebelkov is . . ."

He didn't finish, just pursed his mouth in distaste. He rushed off somewhere before seven; he seemed very busy. I was left to myself. It was already getting light outside. I felt slightly dizzy. I was thinking of Versilov. From what the woman had said, he appeared to me in quite a different light. To think things over more comfortably, I lay down on Vasin's bed. I was dressed, boots and all, and intended to lie down just for a few minutes. But, without knowing when it happened, I fell asleep. I slept for four hours. Nobody waked me.

Chapter 10

I

I awoke around ten-thirty and for a long time I couldn't believe my eyes. On the sofa where I'd gone to sleep last night sat my mother and next to her the mother of the girl who'd killed herself. They were holding each other's hands, crying and whisper-

ing to each other, probably so as not to wake me up. I got up
from Vasin's bed, went over to my mother, and kissed her. She
gave me a radiant smile, kissed me back, and made the sign of
the cross over me three times. But before we could exchange a
word, the door opened and Vasin and Versilov walked in.
Mother immediately got up and led the poor woman away. Vasin
said good morning to me while Versilov, without saying a word,
lowered himself into the armchair. Evidently he and Mother
had been here for quite some time. Versilov was frowning and
looked worried.

"What I regret most, Vasin," he said slowly, apparently resuming a conversation they must have started before coming in,
"is that I didn't manage to arrange it all yesterday evening. For
if I had, this horrible thing would probably never have happened. Besides, I had plenty of time—it wasn't even eight o'clock
yet. . . . You know, when she rushed off from my place yesterday, I thought I'd follow her here and try to convince her she
was wrong. . . . But then there was that unexpected urgent
business, which, however, could have waited until today or a
whole week for that matter. . . . Yes, it was that damned business that prevented me from taking care of things and ruined
everything. It had to come up at just that moment!"

"It's not at all sure you would have succeeded in convincing
her," Vasin remarked in a matter-of-fact tone; "I think she had
already reached the breaking point, and it would have happened
whatever you'd done."

"No, I know I could have prevented it. . . . I even thought
of sending Sofia here instead of coming myself, but I didn't
follow up the idea. I'm sure Sofia alone could have overcome
the poor girl's suspicions and she'd be alive now. No, this is the
very last time I meddle in people's private business—'good works'
are not for me! And to think that this was the only time in my
life I tried my hand at it! I imagined I still hadn't lost touch
with the new generation and could understand today's young
people! But I see now that my own generation has grown old
before even reaching maturity. As a matter of fact, there are so
many people these days who still classify themselves as the
younger generation because they feel they were young only
yesterday and they don't notice that they're already on their way
out."

"There was a misunderstanding, an obvious misunderstanding," Vasin said reasonably. "Her mother maintains that it was
the insults of the prostitutes in that house that caused her mind
to crack. And it came on top of the treatment she'd received

from that merchant and her previous humiliations. . . . But all
these things could just as well have happened a generation ago
and they don't shed any special light on the mentality of today's
young people."

"Well, I suppose today's younger generation is rather impatient while its understanding of life is still very vague," Versilov
said. "That, of course, can be said of the young people of any
generation, but I believe it's especially true of this one. . . .
But tell me, what part did Mr. Stebelkov play in this story?"

"Mr. Stebelkov," I butted in suddenly, "is responsible for
everything that happened. Without him, everything would have
been all right. He poured oil on the flames."

Versilov heard what I said but didn't even look at me. Vasin
frowned.

"There's something else, something rather ridiculous, that I
blame myself for," Versilov drawled out unhurriedly. "I think I
succumbed to my usual unfortunate propensity for flippancy,
for a kind of irresponsible lightness; in other words, I was not
sufficiently blunt, impersonal, and solemn, which are the three
qualities particularly valued by the young today. And so I gave
her good grounds to mistake me for a roving seducer."

"Just the contrary!" I interfered again. "Her mother says you
made an excellent impression on the girl, precisely by your serious and dignified attitude and even by your sincerity. I'm just
repeating what the old lady said herself: her daughter had nothing but praise for you right after you left."

"Is . . . is that so?" Versilov mumbled, throwing a cursory
glance in my direction. "Here, take this, it's essential to the
business," he said, handing Vasin a tiny scrap of paper.

Vasin took it and, noticing my curious look, gave it to me. It
had on it two uneven lines, written in pencil and apparently in
the dark, saying: "Mother dear, forgive me for cutting short
the début in life of your daughter who has caused you so much
grief—Your Olga."

"They found it only later in the morning," Vasin explained.

"What a strange note!" I exclaimed in amazement.

"What's so strange about it?" Vasin asked.

"How can anyone use humorous expressions at such a moment?"

As Vasin was still looking at me questioningly, I went on to
elaborate my point. "Besides, it's a peculiar sense of humor: she
uses a conventional, schoolgirl expression—a sort of private joke—
'cutting short the début' . . ."

"I see nothing wrong with putting it that way," Vasin said, still puzzled.

"I don't think it has any pretension to humor," Versilov suddenly said. "I agree, of course, that the expression she used is quite incongruous under the circumstances and the tone is rather unsuitable—it may come from conventional schoolgirl slang or perhaps from something she read. But I'm sure the poor girl wasn't aware of the tone it gave her awful note and used it completely seriously and unaffectedly."

"That's impossible, she graduated with a silver medal!"

"The silver medal has nothing to do with it; lots of people graduate with silver medals these days."

"Here we are attacking the new generation again," Vasin said, smiling.

"Not really," Versilov said, getting up and reaching for his hat. "I'm sure the present young generation has other qualities, even if it may be somewhat deficient in literary taste. Besides, even that is not true of everybody," he added with great seriousness. "Take yourself, for instance: you could hardly be accused of a lack of literary culture, although you may still be considered young."

"But Vasin too sees nothing peculiar in the use of the word *début*," I couldn't resist putting in.

Versilov silently held out his hand to Vasin. Vasin, however, also picked up his cap to leave at the same time.

"See you later!" he called out to me as they left.

As for Versilov, he seemed to have forgotten my very existence and departed in silence.

I myself didn't have any time to waste: I had to find a place to live, even more urgently now than before. My mother was not at the landlady's; she had left and had taken the mother of the girl with her.

When I stepped out into the street, I somehow felt full of energy: something new and important was building up inside me. Besides, everything seemed to favor me that morning: in no time I stumbled on very suitable lodgings. But I'll come back to that later; for now I'll just stick to the essentials.

It was only shortly after one when I came back to Vasin's to pick up my suitcase. He was home. He seemed sincerely delighted to see me:

"I'm so glad you found me here—I was just about to leave! I have something to tell you that I think will interest you."

"I'm sure it will," I said.

"Why, you're looking cheerful today! Tell me, did you know

anything about a certain letter that Kraft had on him and that is now in Versilov's possession? It has something to do with that inheritance suit which was just settled. Well, that letter, written by the person who made the will, can be interpreted in a sense contrary to the decision of the court. That letter was written a long time ago and I don't know exactly what it says. . . . I was just wondering whether you had any idea of what was in it?"

"How could I help having an idea? It was because of that letter that Kraft invited me to his place after we left those people. He gave me the letter then, and yesterday I handed it over to Versilov."

"I see, that's just what I suspected. Now imagine this: the business that Versilov said had prevented him from coming here last night to talk to the girl was something he had to attend to in connection with that letter. He went straight to the Sokolskys' lawyer, handed him the letter, and declared that he refused to accept the inheritance he had just won. As of this moment, his refusal has already been registered in the form of an official document, in which Versilov emphasizes that he merely acknowledges the legitimacy of the Sokolskys' claim and that his gesture should not in any way be interpreted as a present to them."

I was stunned and bursting with admiration. I'd been convinced that he would destroy the letter. And, although I'd told Kraft that it wouldn't be an honorable thing for him to do and although I'd repeated to myself that evening in the tavern that I had come to Petersburg to join an honorable man and not somebody like that, deep down I felt that destroying the letter was the only course open to him. That is to say, if he'd done it, I wouldn't have found anything out of the ordinary in it. And if later I'd reproached him for doing it, I'd have done so only to emphasize my moral superiority over him. But now, hearing what he'd actually done, I was filled with boundless admiration for him, together with shame and repentance for my own cynicism and failure to appreciate his nobility. Ah, Versilov was so infinitely above me! I almost threw my arms around Vasin.

"What a man, what a man!" I cried out enthusiastically. "Is there anyone else in the world who'd have done that!"

"I agree that many people wouldn't have done it and that no doubt it's a very disinterested act. . . ."

"But what, Vasin? There seems to be reservation in your praise."

"Well, there may be: Versilov acted a bit too quickly and perhaps not all that sincerely really," Vasin said with a smile.

"Not sincerely? What do you mean?"

"Just that. There seems to be in his action a concern for his image: he's sort of building a pedestal to himself, because he could have achieved the same results without sacrificing his own interests the way he did. Even taking the contents of the letter into account, if not half then at least a considerable part of the inheritance may still in all justice be due Versilov. And since the document has no legal force and the court has already decided in his favor, even the lawyer of the opposition is of that opinion and said as much to me just now. Versilov's deed would have been just as noble if he hadn't been carried away like that by his pride and rejected everything in such a hurry. Didn't he himself say, as you must have heard, that it could have waited even a whole week. . . ."

"I'm afraid I must agree with you, Vasin, but I prefer the way I understood it at first. I like it better that way!"

"I suppose it's a matter of taste," Vasin said. "It was you who asked me to explain my reservations. I wouldn't have brought them up otherwise."

"Well, even if he is building a pedestal for himself, that's still good enough. Such a pedestal is a very valuable thing. Actually it's just another word for 'ideal' and I don't think that we need rejoice if some of our contemporaries are not concerned with it, even if there is a little freakishness hidden in it—just as long as it exists! Ah, Vasin, you're such a nice, good, and upright fellow! . . . Well, I no longer know what I'm saying but I'm sure you understand what I mean. Otherwise you wouldn't be the Vasin I know. In any case, let me hug you!"

"Why, just out of sheer joy?"

"Yes, out of great joy! For the man 'was dead and liveth and was lost and is found'! I know I am rotten to the core and am not worthy of you and I admit that now only because there are moments when I'm a different person, a much better and wiser one. Since I praised you to your face two days ago—and I did it only because you'd made me feel so low and inferior—I hated you—until this moment. I promised myself never to come and see you, and when I came here yesterday morning, it was just out of spite—yes, try to understand that—*out of spite!* So I sat on this chair and found fault with everything in your room, criticizing every book of yours as well as your landlady, trying to find something ridiculous in you, making fun of you. . . ."

"There's no need for you to tell me all this."

"Last night I concluded from something you said that you didn't understand women and I was delighted to find a weakness I could exploit. Then I was also very pleased that you found nothing strange about the word *début*. . . . And all that because I had once praised you aloud. . . ."

Vasin kept smiling and did not seem in the least surprised.

"Well, it's all quite natural," he said at last; "everybody always feels that way after having overpraised someone—that's the first reaction. But, as a rule, no one admits it. Nor is there any need to. It will work itself off in time and no harm will come from it."

"Does this really happen to others too? Is everyone like me then? And you say that so calmly! How is it possible to go on living with such a view of life?"

"Why, do you agree then with Pushkin when he says that he prefers 'the ennobling delusion' to 'the degrading, dingy truth'?"

"Ah, that's so true!" I cried. "There's a sacred truth in those two lines!"

"I'm not sure and I don't feel competent to judge whether those two lines are true or not. I suspect, though, that the truth lies somewhere between that sacred ideal and the outright lie. All I know is that this dilemma will remain with us for a long time and that people will go on arguing about it for years. But I see that you feel more like dancing around just now than debating such matters. So why don't you go and dance? Exercise is good for you. Besides, I'm terribly busy today. . . . In fact, I think I'm late. . . ."

"All right, all right, I'll make myself scarce! But let me just say this," I said, picking up my suitcase. "If once again I, so to speak, threw myself into your arms, it was only because when I came in you told me the good news with such obvious pleasure and were, as you said, delighted that I got here in time, and all that after the remark I made to you about the word *début*. . . . Well, your sincere joy at once recaptured 'my youthful heart.' So good-by, and I promise to stay away from you as long as I'm able to hold out. I can see by your eyes that you're pleased with this promise and I'm sure that it will be to our mutual advantage. . . ."

I went on chattering away like that, almost wallowing in my joy, until I got my suitcase and other belongings out of Vasin's room and took them to my new quarters. What pleased me particularly was that Versilov had been so obviously angry with me when I had last seen him that he wouldn't talk to me or, for that matter, even look in my direction. When I had moved my belongings, I at once rushed over to my old Prince Sokolsky's. I must say that I had missed him these past couple of days. Besides, he must have heard by now about Versilov's gesture.

II

Just as I'd expected, he was overjoyed to see me, and I swear I'd have gone to see him even if Versilov hadn't done what he had. But before I'd been frightened away by the thought that I might meet Katerina Akhmakov there, whereas now there was nothing for me to fear.

The old man hugged me in his joy at seeing me.

"Have you heard? What do you say of Versilov, eh?" I started right off with what interested me most.

"Ah, *cher enfant*, it was such a noble, such an honorable, gesture that even Kilyan"—that was the name of the scribe in the downstairs office—"even he was completely flabbergasted! Oh, I know, this is quite a reckless thing to do when it comes to his own interests, but it's such an elegant, such a dazzling act! One must admire a man who lives up to his own ideal!"

"That's true, very true. We always agreed on that point."

"We've always agreed, my dear boy, on every point. But where have you been all this time? You know, I wanted to go and find you, but I didn't know where to look for you. Because, as you must understand, I couldn't very well go over to Versilov's, could I? Although, after what he's done now. . . . And shall I tell you something, my boy? I think that it's gestures like that that make him so irresistible to women; it's that quality in him. . . . Yes, there's no doubt about it. . . ."

"Ah, while I think of it, before I forget, let me tell you what a despicable buffoon said about Versilov yesterday to my very face: he said he was a 'ladies' prophet'! What do you think of that? Some phrase, isn't it? I've been saving it for you!"

"'A ladies' prophet,' ha! *Mais c'est charmant!* Ha-ha-ha! That fits him so well. . . . I mean, it doesn't fit him at all, but it does hit a true note. . . . Well, not really, but still . . ."

"All right, never mind; if you like it, why shouldn't you appreciate it just like any other *bon mot?*"

"Yes, you put it just right—it is a *bon mot,* and one that carries a very profound meaning . . . a perfectly true idea. Would you believe me if . . . I mean, I must entrust you with a little secret: you remember that girl called Olympia whom you met here? Well, she has a sort of crush on Andrei; actually she even cherishes the hope . . ."

"Cherishes the hope!" I cried out with indignation. "Why, I could give her a suggestion of what she could do with herself if she asked me for advice."

"Please, *mon cher*, stop shouting. For all I know you may be perfectly right from your point of view. And, by the way, my friend, what came over you the other day when Katerina was here? You were literally swaying so that I thought you were on the verge of fainting. I was about to rush up to you so you wouldn't fall . . ."

"I'll tell you some other time. . . . Well, there was something that made me feel very embarrassed . . ."

"It must have been quite something! Now you've turned red too!"

"And, of course, you immediately have to rub it in! But you must be aware that she's on bad terms with Versilov, that and all the rest, so there's nothing so strange about my feeling ill at ease. But let's drop the subject for now, we'll discuss it some other time. . . ."

"Right, right, let's drop it; in fact, I'd be glad to forget the whole business if it were possible. . . . I'll only say that I feel very guilty toward her and I'd like you to forget everything I said about her to you that day. And I'm sure she'll change her opinion of you too. . . . But here comes Sergei!"

A handsome young officer walked in. I had never seen Prince Sergei Sokolsky before and proceeded to examine him with curiosity. To say he was handsome would simply repeat what everyone said about him, but there was something rather unpleasant in his regular features and young face. That unpleasantness struck me the very first second I saw him and the impression always remained with me. He was lean and very tall; his hair was dark brown and his face looked healthy and tanned. There was a cold and hard intensity in his beautiful dark eyes, even though he seemed perfectly relaxed. I think it was that determined look of his that repelled me particularly, because I felt that his determination didn't cost him any effort. . . . But I don't really know how to explain what I mean. . . . Of course, his face could suddenly shed its coldness and become extremely warm and open, although never gay, not even when he rolled with laughter; even then you could feel that he had never known the real, light, and cheerful abandon of gaiety. . . . But it's very difficult to describe a man's face this way and I simply haven't got the knack.

According to his usual stupid habit, the old prince immediately rushed to introduce me:

"This is my young friend Arkady Vers—"—here he goes again—"Arkady Dolgoruky . . ."

The young prince turned to me with concentrated courtesy, although my name obviously didn't ring a bell.

"He's a . . . relative of Andrei Versilov's," muttered my friend, irritating as only old men can be with their idiosyncrasies.

But now Sergei Sokolsky knew who I was.

"I've heard so much about you," he said, rattling off the words at a great speed. "I've also had the pleasure of meeting your sister in Luga last year. She too had a great deal to say about you. . . ."

His face was beaming. He seemed sincerely pleased to meet me, so much so, in fact that I was rather taken aback.

"Excuse me, sir," I muttered, pulling back both hands, "I must tell you quite frankly—and I'm glad that I can do it in the presence of Prince Nikolai Sokolsky here, who is very dear to me—that, although I had been very anxious to meet you too, until recently, yesterday, in fact, I had very different ideas about our meeting. So let me tell you everything now, even if it surprises you. To make it short, I intended to challenge you to a duel because you insulted Versilov eighteen months ago in Ems. And, although you might have turned down my challenge because I'm a minor, an adolescent, hardly more than a schoolboy, I was still determined to challenge you, whether you accepted or not . . . and, indeed, this is still my intention now."

Later the old prince assured me that I sounded very dignified and noble. But the young prince looked at me with genuine distress.

"I was going to tell you something, but you didn't give me a chance," he said in a grave tone. "When I spoke to you so cordially, it was because now I feel quite differently about Mr. Versilov. I'm sorry that I cannot explain to you all the circumstances, but I give you my word of honor that, for a long time, I have regretted my unfortunate conduct at Ems. When I left for Petersburg, I decided to give Mr. Versilov every satisfaction he might demand of me. I mean to apologize to him in whatever way he considers satisfactory. My change of position was due to the highest and weightiest of considerations. The fact that we were on opposing sides in a lawsuit has not affected my decision one way or the other. As to what he did yesterday, I was completely overwhelmed by his generosity and to this moment I still feel shaken. And I have come here now to inform the prince of the very latest development: three hours ago, while they were drafting that document with my lawyer, a friend of Mr. Versilov's came to me with a challenge to a duel on Mr. Versilov's behalf . . . it was a formal challenge for that Ems affair. . . ."

"So he did challenge you!" I cried, the blood rushing to my face and my eyes glowing.

"Yes, he did, and I immediately accepted his challenge, but I decided to send him a letter first explaining my present feelings about what had happened and my deep regrets for the stupid mistake I had made. . . . Because it was nothing but a mistake, an unfortunate and fateful mistake! I must also call your attention to the fact that, by writing this letter before the duel, I would be jeopardizing my position in the regiment, for my brother officers were certain to disapprove. . . . I'm sure you understand. Nevertheless, I decided to send him such a letter, but before I had time to do it—indeed, only an hour after I had received his challenge—Mr. Versilov sent me another note, in which he apologized for having troubled me, asked me to disregard the challenge, and to forgive him for his 'selfish and petty outburst'—those are his very words. So he has relieved me of the obligation to send that letter. I haven't sent it yet, but I came here because I wanted to discuss certain matters connected with it with the prince. . . . Now I would like you to believe me when I tell you that my conscience has made me suffer much more than any person possibly could have. Well, Mr. Dolgoruky, does my explanation satisfy you, at least for the time being? Will you do me the honor of believing in my complete sincerity?"

I was wholly conquered. I was convinced of his complete sincerity, a sincerity I had never expected of him. Indeed, I had never expected anything of the sort. I just mumbled something or other and held out both hands, and he eagerly took both of them in his.

After that, the two princes Sokolsky had a private five-minute conversation in the old prince's bedroom and, when they emerged, Sergei said to me in a loud voice:

"If you want to do me a great favor, come with me and I'll show you the letter I'm about to send to Mr. Versilov and the letter I received from him."

I consented very readily. The old prince became all excited and asked me to come in to his bedroom for a few words in private with him.

"I'm so delighted, so delighted, *mon ami*. . . . But we'll

discuss all that later. By the way, I have here in this briefcase a couple of letters: one of them must be delivered with a personal explanation and the other must go to the bank, and there too you must . . ."

And he gave me two errands to do that he pretended were very urgent and required great care and attention on my part. I had to deliver the letters personally, get receipts, and so on.

"Ah, you can be so awfully sly sometimes!" I said, accepting the letters. "I could swear that this is all nonsense, that there's absolutely no need for me to deliver these letters, and that you've thought up the whole business just to convince me that I'm really working for you and that I'm not being paid for nothing."

"*Mon enfant*, I assure you that you're completely wrong: these two are most urgent matters. . . . *Cher enfant!*" he cried, overwhelmed by a sudden rush of emotion, "my dear young friend"—he put both hands on my head—"I bless you and the path in life you are going to take. . . . Always be as pure of heart as you were today, as kind and as good as you can. . . . Love everything that is good and beautiful in all forms. . . . Well, *enfin . . . enfin rendons grâce . . . et je te bénis!*"

He couldn't finish and started whimpering with his hands on my head. I even began to whimper too. Anyway, I hugged my eccentric old friend hard and I felt happy. It was a warm embrace.

III

Prince Sergei Sokolsky—or Sergei as I shall refer to him henceforward—drove me in an elegant light carriage to his apartment, which surprised me by its sumptuousness. Well, perhaps to call it sumptuous might be an exaggeration, but it was the "right" sort of a place with large, light, high-ceilinged rooms (I saw two of them, the doors leading to the others were closed), elegantly and lavishly furnished with comfortable and stylish furniture, although it might not have been the best Versailles, Renaissance, or what not. Also there were expensive rugs, carved wood, and pieces of sculpture. It struck me as strange because I'd always heard that this branch of the Princes Sokolsky was penniless. But, on the other hand, this Prince Sergei was reputed to be a show-off who liked to play the role of a young millionaire whenever he could, here as well as in Moscow, in Paris as well as among the officers of his former regiment. Indeed, I'd also vaguely heard that he was a gambler and had debts.

I myself had on a crumpled jacket, which was, moreover,

covered with fluff because I had slept in it on Vasin's sofa, and
it was the fourth day that I was wearing the same shirt. Although my jacket wasn't badly cut, as I entered Sergei's apartment now, I somehow remembered Versilov's suggestion that
I order myself another suit.

"You know, I haven't undressed all night because of a suicide," I remarked in a casual tone and, as he made a proper show
of curiosity, I told him briefly what had happened. But his mind
was obviously on his letter.

I was still quite perplexed by this man's reactions. What had
surprised me most was that he hadn't found it in the least ridiculous when I'd challenged him to a duel: not only hadn't he
smiled but he hadn't shown in any way that such a challenge on
my part might be considered absurd, as might well have been
expected of a man in his social position.

We sat down facing each other across his huge desk and he
passed me the final draft of his letter to Versilov. The letter was
very much what I'd expected from what he'd told me before;
indeed, its tone was very warm and sincere. I still was not too
sure how much to trust his apparent good will and good faith,
but I was more and more prepared to take him at face value, for
I had no reason left not to. Whatever he might have done and
whatever his reputation might have been, deep down he still
could be a decent man. I also read Versilov's seven-line note withdrawing his earlier challenge. And although Versilov did use
such adjectives as "petty" and "selfish" about himself, there was
still something haughty in his apology, something suggesting a
scornful casualness toward the whole business. But I didn't share
this impression with Sergei.

"What do you make of his withdrawing the challenge, for I'm
sure you don't believe he was afraid to go through with it, do
you?"

"Of course not," he said with a peculiarly solemn smile; then
a look of worry appeared on his face. "I know only too well how
fearless he is. He just did what he considered right, what was in
accord with his ideas. . . ."

"Oh, I'm sure of that," I interrupted him. "You know, there's
a man called Vasin who claims that, by renouncing his right to
the inheritance, Versilov was trying, as Vasin puts it, to 'erect a
pedestal to himself.' But I can't believe that a man would do
something like that just for show. I say it must satisfy some inner need."

"I know Mr. Vasin very well," Sergei said.

"Yes, of course, you must've met in Luga. . . ."

Our eyes met and I believe I blushed slightly. He changed the subject. I was still very anxious to have an open and uninhibited talk with him. I was longing to ask him questions about someone I had met the previous day, but I didn't know how to go about it. I was also very impressed by his courtesy, his irreproachable good manners, and the natural polish that people of his class must acquire almost from the cradle. I had, however, found two bad grammatical mistakes in his letter. In general, when I'm in the company of such people, so as not to appear overawed, I tend to become unduly abrupt, which, of course, is not the right way to behave. Besides, in this instance, I was also painfully aware of the fluff stuck on my jacket. This caused me to slip into a vulgarly familiar tone. Yes, I'd noticed that Sergei kept glancing at me surreptitiously.

"Now tell me this, Prince," I suddenly fired at him, "you must find it funny, even if you don't want to show it, that someone like me—a mere adolescent, in fact—should challenge you to a duel for offending somebody else, mustn't you?"

"I think an offense to one's father can be taken as a personal offense. No, I don't see anything funny in it."

"But I myself think it must look terribly funny. . . . Seen from the outside, of course, not from my own viewpoint. Besides, my name is not even Versilov but Dolgoruky. Of course, you may not be telling me the truth to make it easier for me because you have such marvelous manners. If so, however, how can I be sure that all the rest you've told me is true?"

"No, I don't think there's anything funny about it," he repeated with the utmost seriousness. "How could you help being aware of your father's blood in your veins? . . . It's true that you're still very young and I believe one's not allowed to accept a challenge to a duel from a minor. . . . And then there may also be another serious objection—by challenging me for an offense to another person, you show, in a sense, a certain lack of respect for that person, don't you think?"

We were interrupted by a footman who appeared in the doorway. It looked as if Sergei had been expecting him, for he got up and quickly walked over to him. The lackey told him something in a whisper that I couldn't hear.

"Would you please excuse me?" Sergei said to me. "I'll be back in a moment."

He went out and, left alone, I paced the room, thinking. Strangely enough, I both liked and intensely disliked this man. There was something in him that strongly repelled me, but I couldn't put my finger on it. "If he doesn't find me in the least ridiculous, he must be quite guileless; but if he's laughing at me, then . . . then I'd find him more intelligent," was the odd conclusion I finally came to.

I went to the desk, reread Versilov's note, and again got lost in my thoughts. Suddenly I realized that Sergei's "moment" must have lasted a quarter of an hour already. I got worried, I walked up and down the room once more; then I picked up my hat and was about to walk out, expecting to meet a servant in the passage, send him to tell his master I was leaving, and when Sergei came, say good-by to him immediately because I could not wait any longer. I thought that, under the circumstances, this would be the most dignified thing to do, as I felt he was taking me too much for granted in making me wait such a long time.

The two closed doors were at the opposite ends of the same wall. I no longer knew through which door we'd entered and, without giving it much thought, I opened one of them and found myself in a long, narrow room with a settee in it and someone sitting on the settee. . . . I recognized my sister Lisa. There was no one else in there with her and she was obviously waiting. But before I even had time fully to register my surprise, I heard Sergei's voice: he was talking rather loudly to someone in the corridor. I quickly stepped back into the study, closing the door behind me, unnoticed by Sergei, who came in through the other door. I remember him apologizing and mentioning someone called Anna. . . . I was so upset and embarrassed that I didn't take in what he was saying. I just muttered something to the effect that I had to be on my way, insisting that I had to leave at once. I quickly left. The well-bred prince must have noticed the peculiarity of my manners with amused curiosity. He saw me to the door, continuing to make conversation, although I didn't take any part in it, nor, for that matter, did I so much as glance in his direction.

IV

When I got out into the street, without thinking, I turned left and started walking. Inside my head was chaos; nothing made any sense to me. I walked very slowly and I must have walked a good way, perhaps five hundred yards, when suddenly I felt a tap on the shoulder. I turned around and saw Lisa. She had caught up with me and had tapped me on the shoulder with her umbrella. There was something irresistibly gay and perhaps a tiny bit roguish in the way she was looking at me.

"I'm so glad you took this street because otherwise I wouldn't have found you today!" she cried, slightly out of breath from walking so fast.

"Look at you—you can hardly breathe!"

"I had to run to catch up with you."

"But it was you I saw just now, wasn't it?"

"What do you mean?"

"Just now, at Sergei Sokolsky's?"

"Me? Oh no, you certainly couldn't have seen me there!"

We walked about ten yards in silence. Then Lisa burst into a fit of laughter.

"But of course it was me! Why, you were staring me straight in the face and I was staring back at you, so how can you ask me whether it was me? What a character! And, you know, I almost burst I felt like laughing so much: you looked so funny the way you were gaping at me!"

She laughed and laughed. The anguish weighing on me was lifted.

"Tell me, then, how did you get there?"

"I came to see Anna."

"What Anna?"

"Anna Stolbeyev. I used to spend days on end at her house when we were in Luga. Mother went to see her too and she even came to see us, although she almost never went visiting. She's a distant relative of Papa's and is also related to these Sokolskys. I believe she's Sergei's great-aunt or something like that."

"Is she living at Sergei's, then?"

"Uh-uh—Sergei is living at Anna's."

"Why, whose apartment is that?"

"It's hers and has been hers since she rented it a year ago. Sergei is just staying with her. But she, too, has come to Petersburg for just four days."

"Well, I don't really care about the apartment, Lisa, or for that matter about the old woman either."

"You're wrong, she's a great old lady."

"So go and congratulate her for me. And we're great too! What a gorgeous day—look how beautiful everything is! As a matter of fact, you look beautiful today too, Lisa, although you still have the mentality of a small child."

"Tell me about last night, Arkady, about that girl. . . ."

"It was so awful . . . the poor thing!"

"Yes, poor thing! What a life she had! And, you know, I feel guilty, walking in the sun and feeling so gay while her soul is floating somewhere in the darkness, in a bottomless black void, weighed down by her sin and anger. . . . Tell me, Arkady, who's really responsible for her suicide? It's all so frightening! Tell me also, do you ever think about that darkness? I'm terribly afraid of death, although I know how sinful that is. Still, I hate darkness, I love sun. Mamma says it's a sin to be afraid. . . . Arkady, how well do you know Mamma?"

"Very little."

"She's quite an extraordinary woman. You really ought to get to know her; you ought to try and understand her. . . ."

"Sure, sure. Besides, just a short while ago I didn't know you either, but I got to know you well at last. Actually it took me only one minute to understand you completely. So let me tell you this, Lisa: you may be afraid of death, but I'm sure you are brave and bold and proud. You're a much better person than I am, incomparably better, and I'm awfully fond of you. And, you know, let death come when it's time for it to come, but in the meantime let's live, live, and live! Let us be sorry for that poor girl, but let us still praise life. Do you agree, Lisa? And you know —I have my 'idea' . . . No, first, have you heard Versilov has refused the inheritance?"

"How could I not have heard? Mamma rushed to embrace me when she learned the news."

"But you can have no idea what that man means to me. . . ."

"Why shouldn't I? Of course, I know what he means to you."

"I see that you know everything! And no wonder, you're so incredibly intelligent, even more intelligent than Vasin, I think. You and Mother, you have eyes that see through things and are humane at the same time. . . . I mean, not your eyes, but your way of looking at things. Oh, I'm getting all mixed up, I'm no good myself. . . ."

"All you need is taking in hand—that'll do it."

"So take me in hand, Lisa. It's so pleasant to look at you today. Do you realize how terribly pretty you are? I'd never noticed your eyes before. . . . Where did you get those eyes, Lisa? I never saw them until today. Did you buy them? How much did you have to pay? I never had a friend until now, and I used to consider the notion of friendship sheer nonsense. But it would make sense to be friends with you. So would you like us to be friends? Do you understand what I mean by that?"

"I guess I have a pretty good idea."

"Without any conditions, any restrictions, any obligations—just friends?"

"Yes, just friends, but I still think we should agree on one point: even if some day we should disapprove of each other, if we should become spiteful and nasty and horrid, even if we should forget everything else, let us always remember this day and this hour; let us vow never to forget this day when we walked side by side, laughing and feeling so gay and happy. All right? Is it a deal?"

"All right, Lisa, I swear. But it suddenly occurs to me that I've never heard you talk yet. Tell me, have you read much?"

"You never listened to me talk until yesterday when you noticed me using a phrase that was not to your liking. But that's what attracted your attention, most honorable sir, Mr. Sage."

"But you could have taken the initiative and spoken to me first if I was such a fool."

"I was just waiting and hoping that you'd grow more intelligent. I have been watching you ever since you arrived, sir, and I came to the conclusion that you'd end up by coming to me and that I should leave you the honor of taking the first step. Let him look for a chance to talk to me, I decided."

"Ah, how you like to play games, Lisa! Now tell me honestly —have you been laughing at me this whole month?"

"Well . . . you know you are very, very funny, Arkady. . . . But, you must know, if I became so fond of you in that one month, it's because you're such a funny lunatic. But in some respects you're also a wicked lunatic, and I have to say that so you won't be too pleased with yourself. Besides, do you know who else was laughing at you? Your mother; we often laughed together, in fact; 'Isn't he a lunatic,' we'd whisper to each other, 'isn't he funny!' while you'd be sitting there, fancying we were in awe of you."

"Tell me, Lisa, what do you think of Versilov?"

"I think a great deal of him, but I'd rather not talk about him now, not today, all right?"

"All right, all right. . . . Ah, you're so awfully intelligent, Lisa, you're definitely more intelligent than me. . . . But wait, when I finish with the business I'm attending to right now, I'll have something to tell you. . . ."

"Why are you frowning like that?"

"I'm not frowning, it's just that . . . well, I'd better tell you the truth: it's just the way I'm made. I can't stand people putting their fingers on my vulnerable spots. . . . In other words, I can't let certain feelings show so that people can stare at them— it makes me feel embarrassed, see? So sometimes I prefer to frown and keep my mouth shut. You're so intelligent, you must understand what I mean."

"Of course I do and, what's more, I'm just the same. I understand you completely. And, you know, Mother is like that too."

"Ah, Lisa, I'd like to go on living in this world as long as possible! . . . What did you say?"

"I didn't say anything."

"Why are you looking like that?"

"But you're looking exactly the same way. I'm looking at you and I like you."

I saw her almost to the door and gave her my new address. Before I left, I kissed her. It was the first time I'd kissed her.

V

Everything would have been good except for one thing that was bad. One painful thought had been throbbing in my mind and I couldn't get rid of it: when I'd met that girl by our gate, I'd told her that I was leaving that house to find myself another shelter because Versilov was evil and had droves of illegitimate children. Hearing a son say that about his father could only have confirmed the poor girl's suspicions of Versilov's motives and proved to her once more the wickedness of his plans. And so, while I was blaming Stebelkov, it was perhaps I myself who had been the chief culprit in pouring oil on the flames. It was an awful thought, and it horrifies me to this day. . . . On that particular morning, though, even if it had already started tormenting me, I was still able to dismiss it as nonsense. She was already in a bad enough state by then anyway, I tried to reassure myself. Ah, never mind, I'd recover and somehow make up for whatever blame I might have had in this business—I had fifty years before me to do it!

But the thought was still there.

PART TWO

Chapter 1

I

I shall now skip a couple of months, but the reader needn't worry: in due course, everything will be made clear. I'll resume my story on November 15, a date I have all too many reasons to remember. Let me say first that someone who hadn't seen me during these two months would have had trouble recognizing me. Well, I mean, he might have recognized me physically, but he still would have been immensely surprised. For one thing, I was now dressed like a dandy. Not only had that French tailor, whom Versilov had recommended to me for his good taste and conscientiousness, made me a suit but he had already been superseded by really top tailors, from whom I had ordered several suits. Indeed, I had even opened accounts with them. I also had a charge account in a very fashionable restaurant, but I was still somewhat nervous about it and preferred to pay cash whenever I could, although I knew that this was *mauvais ton* and that I cheapened myself in doing so. The French hairdresser at the Nevsky Prospect Gentlemen's Barber Shop gossiped with me while attending to my hair. I must confess I practiced my French with him. For, although I knew French fairly well, I was still too unsure of myself to launch into it in high society and I suspected that my accent was far from Parisian. I went around in a smart turnout driven by a dashing coachman called Matvei, who was at my service whenever I sent for him. He had a sorrel trotter (I disliked grays). . . . But everything wasn't taken care of yet: now on November 15 we were having the third day of cold winter weather and all I had was an old raccoon-lined coat that used to belong to Versilov and that wouldn't fetch more than twenty-five rubles. I had to get myself a new fur coat, but I was broke just then. Besides, I absolutely had to find some money for that night; otherwise I'd be "wretched and lost," as I put it in those days. . . . Oh, what a contemptible creature I was! For where do you imagine the thousands of rubles for my clothes, the trotters, and the fashionable restaurants came from? How could I have suddenly changed like that and have forgotten about everything? What a disgrace! Well, I just have to tell the

story of my degradation, although there's nothing more painful
to me than these recollections.

I speak like a judge, for I know that I'm guilty. Even though I
was caught in a whirlpool and had no one to turn to for guidance and advice, I was fully conscious of my downfall and
therefore cannot be excused. Nevertheless, I was almost happy
during those two months. . . . Why did I say "almost"? If anything, my happiness was excessive because the awareness of degradation that descended on me at certain moments (very frequent moments!) and that made me shudder inwardly—would
you believe it?—intoxicated me all the more with joy! "If I must
descend so low," I felt, "why not go down to rock bottom? I'm
sure I won't lose my footing and I'll climb out of the pit. I was
born under a lucky star!" Or it was as if I were walking on a
flimsy plank over a precipice, enjoying the very absence of
guardrails and experiencing a special pleasure in glancing down
into the abyss. It was risky and it was exhilarating. As to my
"idea," it could wait, I'd attend to it later; this was just a detour,
and why shouldn't I have a little fun now and then? Well, as I
said, that was precisely the weak point of my "idea": it allowed
all sorts of detours. If it hadn't been so rigid and radical, I might
not have dared to deviate from it at all.

Meanwhile I kept on renting the same small room, although
I didn't really live there. It was just a place to keep my suitcase,
my bag, and various other belongings. I actually lived at Sergei
Sokolsky's: I spent days on end there; I slept there for whole
weeks. I'll explain how this came to pass in a moment, but first
I must say a few words about the room I rented. It meant a lot
to me because Versilov came there on his own initiative to see me
after our quarrel and then returned many times. Yes, I repeat,
this period was one of great disgrace but also of great happiness.
. . . Yes, everything seemed to be working out so well; everything seemed so full of promise!

"What was all that former gloom about?" I mused during a
blissful moment. "Why all that morbid self-laceration?" My
lonely, disconsolate childhood, my silly dreaming under a blanket, my vows, my plans, and even my "idea" had all receded
somewhere into the background. Perhaps I had invented all that,
made up an imaginary world, while in reality it was not like that
at all: life was easy and full of joy and I had a father—Versilov
—and a friend—Sergei—and also . . .

But we'll leave that "also" for later.

Alas, while everything seemed to be founded on love, generosity, and honor, it turned out later to be hideous, shameless, and false.

But enough of this.

II

He came to see me on the third day after our quarrel. As I was out, he waited for me. Although I'd been expecting him all that time, when I entered my tiny room and saw him there, everything turned dark before my eyes and my heart began to pound so violently that I had to stop in the doorway. Luckily my landlord was there too, keeping him company while he waited. Apparently he had made Versilov's acquaintance and now was telling him something with great volubility. He was a petty government employee in his forties, very pockmarked and very poor, burdened by a consumptive wife and an invalid child, and of an extremely friendly and gregarious disposition, though not altogether without tact. I was very pleased that he was present, for what could I have said to Versilov without him? For three days now I had known deep down inside me that Versilov would come to me first. Nothing in the world would have induced me to take the first step myself; this was not out of stubbornness but rather out of love, a strange mixture of love and envy that I can't express because of my lack of eloquence, which the reader must have already noticed. And so, although I'd been waiting for him the past few days, constantly imagining to myself how he'd walk in, I was never able to imagine, try as hard as I might, how we would begin talking to each other after what had happened.

"Ah, here you are at last," he greeted me in a casually friendly tone, holding out his hand to me without getting up. "Sit down then and listen to the very interesting story your landlord has been telling me about that rock by the Pavlovsky Barracks or somewhere around there. . . ."

"I know that rock," I said, quickly installing myself next to him. We all sat around the table that occupied a good part of the very small room.

I drew a deep breath. A satisfied gleam flashed in Versilov's eye. Probably he had been worried that I might decide to make some dramatic gesture. But now he felt reassured.

"I suppose you'd better begin at the beginning again," he said to my landlord in a friendly familiar tone as though they'd known each other a long time.

The landlord turned to me and, looking nervous, as though

he were worrying about the effect his story would have on me, began:

"It happened back in the reign of the late Tsar. . . . Well, since you've seen that stone, you know how stupid it looks sitting there in the middle of the street, just getting in the way. . . . The Tsar drove by there many times, and every time there was that stone. In the end, the Tsar became displeased: why must that huge rock sit there like a mountain and spoil the whole street? 'I don't want to see that stone again!' Well, you understand what it meant when he said he didn't want to see it again? You know how the late Tsar was, don't you? But what could be done about the stone? They all lost their heads; they had a whole to-do about it in the city council. And then one of the highest dignitaries of the time—I forget his name now—who had been listening to the argument suddenly got up and said: 'It will come to at least fifteen thousand rubles in silver'—because, as you may know, under the late Tsar they quoted prices in silver rubles rather than in paper rubles as they do now. 'Fifteen thousand in silver?' they cried out, 'what are you talking about?' Well, the first plan was for the English to install rails around it, load the stone onto a wagon, and use a steam engine to pull the whole thing away. But just imagine how much it would have cost since there were hardly any railroads at the time, except the one running to Tsarskoe Selo. . . ."

"All they had to do was break the stone up," I said, beginning to frown.

I felt irritated and was ashamed of my landlord in front of Versilov, who, however, seemed to be enjoying the story. I suppose he was glad the landlord was there because he also felt awkward toward me, and I remember being touched by his embarrassment.

"Right you are," the landlord said, "that was exactly what they decided to do; Montferrant, who was building St. Isaac's Cathedral, said: 'Break it up and then cart the pieces away.' All right, but how much would it cost do you think?"

"Practically nothing," I said, "if they just broke it up and removed it piece by piece."

"Just a minute, just a minute. They still had to bring that steam engine. And, then, where were they going to take all those pieces? It's a whole rocky mountain, remember! 'It cannot possibly come to less than ten thousand,' some high dignitary insisted, 'in fact, I'd say between ten and twelve thousand!'"

"But listen, you're talking nonsense. That's not the way it was at all," I said impatiently but was stopped short by a discreet wink from Versilov, in which I saw such a delicate compassion for the landlord, indeed, a pained sympathy for his silliness, that it moved me a great deal. So, instead of going on, I just laughed.

"Well, you see then," the landlord cried with obvious relief; he hadn't noticed Versilov's wink and was pleased to be allowed to continue his story, hoping there wouldn't be any further heckling. "Well, at that moment, up walks a workman, a young fellow still, with a pointed beard, a typical Russian workman, you know, in a long-skirted coat, a little drunk perhaps . . . well, not really drunk, just, you know. . . . So he stands there while they all discuss what to do—Montferrant, those Englishmen, and that important dignitary in charge who, having just driven up in a carriage, is listening to them and is beginning to lose his temper because they seem unable to agree. And suddenly he catches sight of that worker standing at some distance, just standing there and grinning deceptively . . . no, I don't mean deceptively, I mean . . . What's the word?"

"Derisively?" Versilov suggested discreetly.

"Yes, that's right, derisively, just a little bit derisively, you know, that typical, good-humored Russian smile. That, of course, irritates the dignitary. 'What are you doing here, you with the beard? Who are you, anyway?' 'I'm just looking at this little stone, Your Honor.' Yes, that's what he called the dignitary who might even have been someone like Prince Suvorov himself, the descendant of Suvorov of Italy, the famous general. . . . No, he wasn't really a Suvorov. . . . It's such a shame that I've forgotten his real name, and, although he was a prince, he was a real Russian, a patriot, a cultured man, and so he understood the situation. 'Perhaps you know how to get that stone out of here? Why are you grinning like that?' 'I'm grinning at them English, Your Honor; they charge you much too much because they know how fat the Russian purse is while they have nothing to eat at home. But if you can spare me a hundred rubles, Your Honor, I'll get this little stone out of the way for you by tomorrow evening.' Can you imagine such a proposition! The Englishmen, of course, are ready to eat him up alive; Montferrant laughs. But that high dignitary with the noble Russian heart says: 'Let that man have a hundred rubles. So you'll move it away, will you?' 'It'll be done by tomorrow evening, Your Honor.' 'And how will you do it?' 'That,' he says, 'is my secret, may Your Honor forgive me.' And he says it in such plain Russian that His Honor takes a liking to him. 'Give him everything he asks for,' he orders and departs. So they left the fellow there. Well, what do you think happened?"

The landlord paused and looked at us each in turn with delight.

"I wonder," Versilov said with a smile.

But I just scowled.

"So here's what he did," the landlord said so triumphantly that one would have thought he'd done it himself. "He hired ordinary Russian workers, who came with their spades, and he made them dig a deep hole just by the edge of the stone. They went on digging all night and dug a deep hole, as deep as the stone was high or perhaps an inch deeper. And when they'd done that, the fellow with the pointed beard told his men to start digging the earth slowly out from under the stone. So gradually there was nothing left for the stone to stand on and it started to tip over; when it did, they just pushed it a bit from the other side, one, two, three, and bang, the big stone rolled into the hole! Then all they had to do was shovel the earth on top of it, pack the earth down with a roller, and then pave it over, and everything was smooth and neat and the stone was gone!"

"Just imagine that!" Versilov said.

"So people rushed from all over the place to look at the spot where the stone had been—those Englishmen too, of course, furious, for they had guessed from the beginning what the fellow was up to. And Montferrant arrived and said, 'This is too simple, too uneducated.' But that's just what was so clever about it, that it was so simple! Otherwise, why didn't they think of it themselves, the stupid fools! So let me tell you that the dignitary, that statesman, you know, he hugged that fellow, kissed him, and asked him: 'Who are you and where do you hail from?' 'I come from around Yaroslavl, Your Honor, and by trade I'm actually a tailor, although during the summer we sell fruit too.' When the exploit reached the ears of the authorities, they decided to give the fellow a medal and so after that he went around with a medal hanging on his chest. But later he wouldn't leave the bottle in peace, as happens to many Russians who don't know when to stop. And that's why foreigners are still ruining us to this day, see?"

"Yes, no doubt about it, the Russian mind . . ." Versilov began, but luckily he was interrupted by someone asking for the landlord, who immediately rushed off.

"You know, he entertained me with his stories for an hour perhaps before you came," he said laughing. "That stone! It's one of those awful, shameless patriotic tall tales! But how could you stop a man like that? Didn't you see how he was melting from sheer joy. Besides, if I'm not mistaken, that stone is still sitting there and hasn't been buried in a hole at all."

"Good heavens, of course! How could he . . ."

"Why? What's the matter? I think you even look outraged. Relax! He simply must have got a bit mixed up. I heard a story about a stone somewhat along those lines when I was a little boy. Oh, of course, it must have been a different stone. And the way he said that about the exploit reaching the ears of 'the authorities': everything in him was vibrating with pride: just imagine—'the authorities!' People confined to this fellow's pitiful surroundings cannot live without such legends. There are plenty of stories like that going around because people can't help making them up—it's a sort of incontinence. They've never studied, never learned anything fully, so what can they talk about when they get tired of talking shop or about card games, when they want to speculate on universal themes, when they need something poetic? What sort of a man is your landlord?"

"He's a miserable wretch. . . . In fact, I believe he's a very unhappy man."

"So you see—and perhaps he doesn't even play cards! Maybe, by telling us his nonsense, he satisfies his need for loving his neighbor since he wanted to make us happy too. And his need for patriotism was also satisfied. Another example is that story about the English offering a million rubles to Zavialov not to put his trademark on his products."

"Oh God, I've heard that story too."

"Who hasn't? And the man who tells these stories may know perfectly well that you've already heard them before and he deliberately pretends that you haven't. I believe the story about the vision of the King of Sweden is a bit out of date now, but when I was a boy it was repeated over and over again in enthusiastic whispers. And also the tale about someone having knelt in the Senate before the senators at the beginning of the century. There were numerous tales about General Bashutsky, for instance, the stolen monument. . . . People also love anecdotes connected with the court, like the tales about Chernyshev, a seventy-year-old minister of the late Tsar who managed to make himself look like a man of thirty so that the Tsar himself was amazed. . . ."

"I've heard about him too."

"Of course you have. All these stories are epitomes of poor taste, but I assure you that this type of bad taste is much more widely spread and deeply rooted than we suspect. The desire to say any kind of nonsense just to make one's neighbor happy is common among the best people, for we all suffer from the incontinence of our hearts. Only, of course, we make up a different kind of story. Just think of the tales people tell about America, for instance—it's really quite unbelievable—even from distinguished statesmen! Besides, I must confess that I myself belong to this reprehensible category of people and have suffered from that foible all my life."

"I myself have told the story about Chernyshev on various occasions," I said.

"Really, you too?"

"There's another lodger here. He's quite old and he's pockmarked like our landlord, but, unlike him, he's very down to earth, and as soon as the landlord starts telling one of his stories, that lodger starts heckling him. As a result, the landlord now will do anything to please him, he literally slaves for the old man to get him to listen to his stories."

"Well, that's another product of our disorder, and indeed more revolting than the first. The first type is all enthusiasm: 'Just let me tell my lies and you'll see how nice everything will be!' The second type is all gloom and lack of imagination: 'No, I won't allow you to lie. Be specific: Where did it happen? What year?' In short, a man without a heart. You must always allow people to lie a little. It's an innocent pleasure. Even a lot, sometimes. First of all, it shows that you're tactful and, secondly, it'll enable you to lie too—two tremendous advantages gained at the same time! We must love our neighbor *que diable!* . . . But I must be on my way. I'm glad to see you've found yourself a nice place," he said, getting to his feet. "I'll tell your mother and your sister that I dropped in on you and found you in good health. Good-by, then, my dear fellow."

Was that all he had to say to me? It was not at all what I'd wanted really. I'd expected him to talk to me about *really* important matters. But I resigned myself; he probably couldn't bring them up this time. I picked up the candle and saw him off to the landing. The landlord came running out and was about to join us, but I grabbed him by the arm while Versilov's back was turned and violently pushed him away. He gave me a puzzled look but made himself scarce.

"Ah, these staircases . . ." Versilov moaned, dragging out his vowels endlessly, probably trying to fill the silence so as not to say something he would regret later or to prevent me from saying something he didn't want me to say. "I'm no longer used to stairs . . . that's three floors . . . but don't bother, I'm sure I'll be able to find my way in the dark now. . . . Thank you, go back now, my boy, don't catch cold. . . ."

But I wouldn't leave him. I accompanied him all the way downstairs.

"I'd been waiting for you these past three days," I suddenly heard myself blurting out. It came out by itself. I was panting.

"Thank you, my dear boy."

"I knew you'd come."

"And I knew you knew I'd come. Thank you."

He was silent as I followed him all the way to the outer door. He opened it. A rush of wind blew out my candle. I suddenly seized his hand. It was completely dark. He started but said nothing. I pulled his hand to my mouth and kissed it. I kissed it again and again, many times, fervently.

"My dear little boy, what have I done that you should love me so much?" he said now in a quite different voice. There was a quiver in it and a certain ring that was new to me; it was as if someone else had spoken.

I tried to say something but couldn't. So I ran back upstairs. He must have stood there without moving for quite a while, for I didn't hear the outer door slam until I was back on my floor. I dashed past the landlord, who somehow happened to be around again, slipped into my room, bolted my door, and, without re-lighting my candle, threw myself onto my bed. I buried my face in the pillow and wept. I wept and wept and it was the first time I had wept since Touchard's school. The sobs burst out of my chest with incredible force. I was happy. But why describe all that . . .

I've written all this down without shame because it was perhaps a good thing, although it may sound idiotic.

III

But did I make him pay for it! I became a frightful despot. It goes without saying that never again was any mention made of that scene between us. Indeed, when we met two days later, it was as though nothing had happened. What's more, I was almost rude that evening and he, for his part, was rather cold. The meeting took place in my room again. Somehow I still hadn't been to his house, although I would have liked to see my mother.

During all that time—those two months, that is—we talked only about the most abstract subjects. I think it's rather strange: although our topics of conversation were of general human interest and were very important, they had no bearing whatsoever on our present immediate concerns. Yet there were so many things affecting us directly that had to be cleared up and decided, even urgently. Only we avoided bringing them up. I never even mentioned Mother or Lisa and, of course, never a word about myself and my past. Whether it was because of embarrassment or some stupid notions so common to immature adolescents, I'm not sure. I think it was stupidity because I guess I would have finally overcome my embarrassment had it just been that. In the meantime I treated him abominably, occasionally slipping into outright rudeness that went against my own feelings. But I had no control—it sort of happened on its own. He, for his part, still had that subtle overtone of irony when he spoke to me, although he managed at the same time to sound very warm and affectionate. I also realized with a certain surprise that he preferred to meet me at my place so that I got to see Mother only rarely, at most once a week, especially later when I got involved in too many things. He'd always come in the evening, sit in my room, and chat with me; he also liked to chat with my landlord, which enraged me no end. And I sometimes wondered whether he didn't come to see me simply because he had no one else to talk to. But I knew that there were many places he could go now, for he had of late reestablished his connections with Petersburg high society, which he had severed during the previous year. But obviously he had resumed those ties only formally and really preferred to spend his time with me. Sometimes I was very touched by the way he came in the evenings, looking rather sheepishly at me at first, as though asking "You're sure I'm not disturbing you? I can leave, you know, if you want me to?" In fact, he even said something to that effect out loud on a few occasions.

Once, for instance, toward the end of that period, he arrived when I was all decked out in a new suit just received from my tailor, ready to leave to pick up Sergei and go with him to a certain place (which I'll explain later). Being in one of his strange absent-minded states, he sat down without noticing that I was about to go out. And to make things worse, he mentioned my landlord, which triggered my outburst:

"Damn that landlord!"

He quickly got up.

"Ah, dear me, I believe you were about to go out, my boy. . . . Don't let me stop you. I'm sorry I hadn't realized . . ."

And he meekly hastened to leave. It was precisely that meekness on the part of such a worldly, independent man with so much character that brought back all my tenderness for him, all my trust in him. But if he loved me so much, why didn't he stop me from disgracing myself? If he had said one word then, perhaps I would have pulled myself together, although perhaps not. He certainly must have noticed my ostentatious way of dressing, my showing off, my coachman Matvei (once I offered him a lift in my carriage, but he declined—in fact, several times he declined my invitations to drive him somewhere), the way I was throwing money around! But he never commented on it, never even showed any interest in where the money to pay for it all was coming from. To this day I still can't account for this attitude of his, especially since at that time I never bothered to hide anything from him. I was quite frank about everything, although I never actually tried to explain anything to him. He never asked and I never volunteered.

Yet, to be precise, two or three times we did touch on practical matters. Once, soon after his renunciation of the inheritance, I inquired what he was planning to live on now.

"Oh, I'm sure I'll manage," he said with complete equanimity.

But I have since learned that half of Tatyana Prutkov's five-thousand-ruble capital was used to pay Versilov's expenses in those two years.

On another occasion we spoke about Mother. He said to me sadly:

"You know, my boy, I often used to tell Sofia at the beginning of our life together—actually, I told her at the beginning, the middle, and now toward the end—that I knew I was making her miserable, making her life a hell without even being sorry for her, but that if she happened to die, I'd never forgive myself and it would kill me."

As a matter of fact, I remember he was exceptionally frank that evening.

"I wish I could be a weakling, know it, and suffer for being one. But, instead, I'm immensely strong. And do you know wherein lies my strength? In my great ability to accommodate myself to anything, which is so characteristic of the Russian intellectuals of our generation. There is nothing that can destroy me, wipe me out, or, for that matter, surprise me. I have the survival capacity of a mongrel dog. I can experience quite comfortably two contradictory emotions at the same time, not, of course, because I want to. Nevertheless, I'm aware that it's not honorable to be like that, mainly because it's so practical. I've lived for nearly fifty years now and I'm still not sure whether it's a good thing to have lived so long or a bad thing. Of course, I enjoy being alive, but that has nothing to do with it because it

may be reprehensible for a man like me to love life. Lately
something new has been happening, and people like Kraft cannot accommodate themselves to life and shoot themselves. But
obviously that type of person is stupid while we are intelligent.
Therefore no parallels may be drawn and the question remains
unanswered. But is it possible that the earth exists only for the
likes of us? The most likely answer is yes, but such a notion is
so utterly depressing! No, the question still remains unanswered."

He said this with great sadness, but I wasn't sure whether he
was being sincere or putting it on. There was always something
controlled about him, a control he never seemed to relax.

IV

I kept bombarding him with questions; I pounced on him like
a starving man on bread. He always answered me readily
enough and to the point, but it invariably ended in abstract con-
structions and aphorisms so that I could never extract anything
personal from him. And these were the questions that had tormented me back in Moscow, to which I'd hoped to find the answers when I joined him in Petersburg. I even told him so once
and, instead of laughing outright, as I'd feared he might, he
pressed my arm. Nor could I extract from him much guidance
on political and social problems, which worried me more and
more because of my "idea." Of people like Dergachev, I once
made him blurt out that "They are beneath criticism," although
he immediately added that "he reserved the right of attaching
no significance to his own opinion." For a long time he wouldn't
express any opinion on what would happen in the future to the
nations in existence today and what social changes were forthcoming. But finally I did manage to wrench a few words out of
him:

"Something quite commonplace will happen, I suppose. *Un
beau matin*, despite all their 'balanced budgets' and 'absence of
deficits,' all the governments will get so hopelessly bogged down
in their debts that they'll decide to suspend payment and declare themselves bankrupt. Of course, the conservative elements
all over the world will be opposed to that declaration because
they'll be the shareholders and the creditors of the governments.
Then there'll be what we may call a general fermentation:
Jews will appear all over the place and Jewish rule will begin.
And those who never held any shares, indeed, never possessed
anything, that is, all the penniless beggars, will refuse to accept a liquidation based on former holdings, and the struggle

will begin. . . . Well, then, after seventy-seven defeats, the beg-gars will wipe out the shareholders, take their shares away from them, and, of course, become shareholders themselves. Perhaps they'll introduce some innovations, and perhaps they won't. Most likely they'll go bankrupt too. Well, that's as much as I can guess about the future that will change the face of this world of ours. But I suppose I could refer you to the Apoca-lypse . . ."

"Do you really think, then, that it all depends on such ma-terialistic considerations? Is it possible that the world as it is to-day will come to an end just because of finance?"

"Well, of course, I took only one detail out of the whole pic-ture but, as you know, every detail is compositionally connected with all the others by indestructible links."

"So what should be done?"

"You don't need to worry about it: it's still pretty far away. In general, though, the best course is to do nothing at all, that way at least you'll be able to keep a clear conscience for having stayed out of it all."

"Oh, stop it, for heaven's sake, I'm asking you seriously: I want to know what I should do and how I should arrange my life."

"What you should do, my boy? Well, be honest, never tell lies, don't covet your neighbor's house. . . . Why don't you read the Ten Commandments? You'll find all the answers you need once and for all."

"Oh, come off it—that's so old it's no longer funny. Besides, that's just words—I mean business."

"I suppose if you get unbearably bored you could perhaps try loving someone or even just getting attached to something or other. . . ."

"You're always making fun of everything. Besides, how could I be the only one to obey your Ten Commandments?"

"Just obey them and, despite your questions and your doubts, you'll be a great man."

"Known to nobody."

"There is nothing hidden that shall not become manifest."

"You're still pulling my leg!"

"Well, if you take it so much to heart, you'd better hurry and specialize in something. You could become an architect perhaps or a jurist, and then when you have serious matters to concern yourself with, you'll forget about all that nonsense."

I let it go at that. There seemed nothing I could get out of him. Somehow, however, after every such talk, I was even more worried than before. Besides, I saw clearly that he had a secret he didn't want to share with me, and that drew me to him even more. Once I interrupted one of his evasive tirades.

"Listen," I said to him, "I've always suspected that you talk like that out of sheer bitterness, because something is hurting you inside, while secretly you're fanatically devoted to some lofty idea. But you're just ashamed to admit it."

"Thank you, my dear boy."

"I know that there's nothing more noble than being useful to mankind," I said. "So tell me, how can I make myself most useful right now? I know that there's no simple answer, but all I want is advice. And whatever you advise me, I'll do it, I swear! So tell me, what great problem is facing man and needs a great idea to solve it?"

"Well, I suppose discovering how to turn stones into bread would be a great idea."

"The greatest idea there is? You've just pointed out a new goal to me. But tell me, is it really the greatest?"

"It's very great, very great indeed, my boy, but it's not the greatest. In fact, it is a secondary problem and is only of utmost importance at the present moment, because once man has eaten his fill, he'll say: 'Fine, my stomach is full now, so what am I supposed to do next?' And that question remains permanently unsettled."

"Once you mentioned to me what you called the 'Geneva ideas.' What did you mean by that?"

"By Geneva ideas, I meant virtue without Christ, which is the contemporary concept or, we may even say, the idea underlying today's civilization. It's a very long story and it would be boring to go into it. I suggest it would be better if we picked other subjects for discussion or, still better, picked none at all."

"You always prefer to pass over things in silence."

"But don't you agree, my dear boy, that silence is always good, safe, and aesthetically superior?"

"Aesthetically superior?"

"Certainly. Silence is always beautiful and a silent man is always more pleasing to the eye than a talking man."

"If you talk the way you do now, I agree that you might just as well be silent. I'm not interested in what you call the beauty of silence and even less in whether it's safe or not."

"My dear boy," he said now in a somewhat firmer tone, in which I also detected a touch of emotion, "I assure you I have no intention of selling you on some sort of bourgeois virtue to take the place of your ideals. I'm not trying to convince you that happiness is better than heroism. Indeed, I believe heroism is better than any conceivable happiness because the mere capacity for heroism constitutes happiness. So we agree on that point. And I do respect you precisely for having, in this era of rot and decay, got hold of some 'idea' of your own—I certainly remember that you have your 'idea,' you can be sure of that. Nevertheless, I say you should maintain a sense of measure because I can see that you're spoiling to set something on fire, to smash something, to live explosively right now, to rise above everyone in Russia, to pass through the sky like a thunderbolt, leaving everybody in awe and admiration as you vanish from sight to live in America. I'm sure that something of that sort is going on in your head and that's why I feel I must warn you. The trouble is, my dear boy, I've become sincerely fond of you."

What could I make out of that? Only that he was concerned about me, worried about the practical aspects of my future. He was talking like any other father, with the best of intentions and hopelessly down to earth. What I wanted to hear from him was an idea for which any good father would have been willing to send his son to death, like Horatius, who sent his sons to die for the idea of Rome.

Also I often pestered him with questions about religion, but here the fog was even thicker. When I asked him what position I should take on religious matters, he'd answer in the silliest way, as one would answer a small child:

"You ought to believe in God, my boy."

"But what if I don't believe?" I'd answer with exasperation.

"That's fine."

"What's fine about it?"

"It's a very good sign, the most hopeful, in fact, because a Russian atheist, if he really is an atheist and has a bit of intelligence too, is perhaps the nicest fellow in the world, overflowing with agreeable feelings which he is always ready to lavish on God. The reason he has so much kindness is that he's so pleased with himself, and the reason he's so pleased with himself is that he's an atheist. So our atheists are extremely respectable and dependable people, the pillars of our country, in fact. . . ."

That was something at least, but still not what I was after. Once, however, he said more. He put it so strangely that I was quite surprised, especially in view of all I'd heard about his Catholicism and his wearing those penitential chains. It happened in the street as I was seeing him off after one of our long conversations in my room.

"You know, my boy," he said, "it's impossible to love men

such as they are. And yet we must. So try to do good to men by doing violence to your feelings, holding your nose, and shutting your eyes, especially shutting your eyes. Endure their villainy without anger, as much as possible; try to remember that you're a man too. For, if you're even a little above average intelligence, you'll have the propensity to judge people severely. Men are vile by nature and they'd rather love out of fear. Don't give in to such love: despise it always. There's a passage in the Koran where Allah bids the Prophet look upon those troublesome creatures as upon mice, do them good and pass them by. It may sound rather haughty but it's the right way. Also, you must learn to despise them even if they're well behaved because it's just then that they are most often wicked. You know, my boy, I said that judging from myself. Someone like me, who is not completely stupid, cannot go on living without despising himself, and it makes no difference whether he's honest or not. It's impossible to love one's neighbor without despising him. I believe that man is physically unable to love his neighbor. The very concept of 'love of mankind' is completely misleading from the start, unless 'mankind' is something he has created in his mind (in other words, he invents himself to love himself). But then that 'mankind' has never really existed and never will."

"Never?"

"I agree, my boy, that if I'm right, the whole business looks rather silly, but I can't help it if it does. And since I wasn't consulted when the world was created, I reserve the right to express my opinion on the subject."

"But after what you've just said, how can anyone say that you're a Christian!" I exclaimed. "They even say that you're some sort of an ascetic, a preacher, that you go around wearing fetters. . . . I don't know what to think now!"

"Who says all that about me?"

I told him. He listened attentively but wouldn't say any more.

I don't remember what brought about that memorable conversation, during which he occasionally sounded rather irritated, something very unusual for him. He spoke with heat and there was no mockery in his tone, as though it was someone other than me he was talking to.

But, again, I didn't believe he meant what he said, because why should he speak seriously about these things to someone like me?

Chapter 2

I

On the morning of November 15, I found Versilov at Sergei's. It was I who'd brought them together, although there were many things that would've brought them together without me (I mean all that business between them abroad, etc.). Besides, Sergei had insisted that Versilov should accept at least one-third of the inheritance, which might amount to twenty thousand rubles or more. I remember thinking it rather peculiar that Sergei should insist on a third rather than half the inheritance, but I kept it to myself. Sergei had made that promise of his own accord; Versilov had never suggested any such thing. When Sergei came up with the idea, Versilov listened to the offer without turning it down, but after that he never reminded Sergei of it, indeed, never indicated that he hadn't forgotten all about it. Let me note here that, at first, Sergei was completely spellbound by Versilov, especially by the things he said, and he even told me about his enthusiastic admiration. Sometimes, when the two of us were alone, Sergei would exclaim in despair how ignorant and unworthy he was compared to Versilov. That was when we were still good friends. For my part, I tried to impress Versilov with Sergei's best points and played down his weaknesses, of which I was well aware. But Versilov only smiled as he listened to me.

"Even if he has faults, he has at least as many qualities that make up for them!" I once pleaded with Versilov when we were alone.

"You do flatter him, you know."

"Flatter him? How?"

"Why, he would be canonized if he had as many merits as he has vices!"

But, beyond that, he would not elaborate. In general, he avoided expressing value judgments, except on abstract matters, and that was particularly true when it came to Sergei Sokolsky. I suspected that Versilov and Sergei met occasionally without my knowledge and that their real relations were rather peculiar. But I refused to think about it. Nor was I jealous of Sergei because Versilov seemed to speak to him in a more serious tone than he did to me; he didn't sound quite as flippant and casual. I was not jealous because I was so happy at the time; in fact, this difference rather pleased me. Versilov was obviously making allowance for the prince's intellectual limitations, for his literal interpretation of every word, which made certain humorous implications quite inaccessible to him.

But of late Sergei seemed to be changing, as did his feelings toward Versilov. Sensitive as he was, Versilov at once detected the change. I must say that at the same time Sergei's attitude toward me also changed quite drastically. And soon nothing but the external, by now meaningless, trimmings of our original friendship remained. But I still continued to see him: it had become like an addiction for me and I couldn't just stop going there. Oh, I was still so inexperienced then and I suppose only innocence can lead one all the way to such helpless humiliation! I used to accept money from Sergei, thinking that there was nothing wrong with that, indeed, that it was the proper thing to do. No, that's not quite true—even at that time I knew it wasn't quite right, but I didn't give it much thought. Still, money wasn't the reason I was spending my time with Sergei, although I needed money desperately. No, I didn't go and see him for the sake of money. But each time I went there I accepted his money. My whole life during that period was a continuous whirl and, on top of that, there was something else in my heart, something singing with joy!

So I got to Sergei's at about eleven that morning and found Versilov there, finishing what appeared to be a long discourse. Sergei was listening, pacing the room. Versilov sat in an armchair. The prince appeared somewhat agitated, but then Versilov could throw him into that state at will. Sergei's sensitivity verged on simplicity, which caused me to be rather condescending toward him. But, as I said, lately I'd detected in him something that might be described as an inner spiteful snarl. He stopped short when he saw me and his face twitched. I knew that there were things that were bothering him, but what is awful is that I imagined only about a tenth of what was really weighing on him and never even suspected the existence of the remaining nine-tenths. Yes, it was stupid and awful because I often took it upon myself to reassure him, offer him advice, and I'd even smile condescendingly at his propensity to lose his temper over what I called "such trifles"! He said nothing, but I can imagine how he must have hated me at those moments. I never even suspected in what a false position I was; I swear to God I had no inkling of what mattered to him most!

Despite all that, he greeted me with his usual courtesy, holding out his hand, while Versilov merely nodded to me, without even interrupting what he was saying. I sprawled myself out on the sofa because that was my style at the time, the manner I affected. Indeed, I even exaggerated in the presence of strangers just to show them how much at ease I felt. Ah, if there was a way to relive that period, how differently I'd behave!

So as not to forget, I must mention here that Sergei Sokolsky was still living in Mrs. Stolbeyev's apartment, but now he was all alone because she'd left for somewhere after spending only one month in Petersburg.

II

They were talking about the Russian aristocracy. I must say that this was a subject that aroused Sergei a good deal despite his progressive views. I even suspect that many of his reprehensible acts were caused by his attitude toward his title: he was proud of his ancient name but, having been poor all his life, he had gone deep into debt in order to spend money with what he considered suitable lavishness. Several times Versilov had discreetly suggested to him that a princely title did not consist simply in throwing money around and had tried to implant in him a loftier concept of aristocratic duties. Lately, Sergei had begun to resent being lectured. Well, I gathered that this was the kind of conversation they were having, although I'd missed the beginning. At first, Versilov's position struck me as rather reactionary, but eventually he made up for it.

"The word honor means duty," Versilov was saying (I can only try to reconstruct the meaning of what he said from memory). "As long as a country is governed by a ruling caste, the nation is strong. The ruling caste always has a sense of honor and a code of honor, which may sometimes be unreasonable but which always serves as a bond for the nation and strengthens it. It is useful morally and, even more so, politically. It is the slaves—that is, all those who do not belong to the ruling caste—who must bear the burden. To make it easier for them, they are given equal rights. That's what was done in Russia and it's very good. But all available experience—that is, Europe's experience—teaches us that whenever all citizens are granted equal rights, there is a general weakening of the sense of honor and, therefore, of the feeling of duty. Selfishness displaces the old unifying principle, and the whole system breaks up into a multitude of individuals, each with a full set of civil rights. Then the emancipated individuals, left without the old unifying principle, also lose all connecting links with one another so that they even stop defending their newly acquired civil rights.

"The Russian aristocracy, however, has never resembled its European counterpart: Even now after it has lost its special privileges, the Russian aristocracy has been able to retain its superior status as the repository of honor, enlightenment, learning, and lofty ideals without becoming, as before, an inaccessible caste, which would have meant the end of the unifying principle. On the contrary, the doors of entry into this caste, which have been barely open for a long time in Russia, must now be opened wide once and for all. Let every feat of honor, learning, and heroism confer upon any citizen the right to join the ranks of our ruling caste. Then that caste will become, in the true meaning of the word, a national elite and not just a privileged caste as before. It is in this new altered form that the caste system can be retained."

The prince bared his teeth in a grin.

"What kind of aristocracy would that be? It's some sort of free masonry you're offering us, not an aristocracy!"

I repeat, the prince was quite an ignorant man. His answer made me shift my weight on the sofa, although I didn't quite agree with Versilov either. Versilov immediately saw through the prince's grin.

"I'm not quite sure what you mean by free masonry," he said, "although I suppose, since a Russian prince rejects my idea, it goes to show that the time is not yet ripe for it. The notion that honor and enlightenment should be sufficient qualifications for anyone to join the open and constantly renewed elite caste may seem a bit Utopian, but there's no reason for dismissing it as impossible. As long as this notion is kept alive in a few minds, there's still hope for its realization: it's like a bright spot glowing in the dark."

"You seem to be very fond of phrases like 'lofty ideals,' 'unifying principle,' and 'superior status.' I'd like to know, for instance, what precisely you mean by 'lofty ideals'?"

"I admit I find it rather difficult to answer that question, my dear Prince," Versilov said with a wry smile. "Indeed, I confess I don't really know how to define it myself. A lofty ideal is mostly a feeling that sometimes remains undefined for a very, very long time. All I know is that it has been always the source of 'living life,' not the intellectual and theoretical life, but the sparkling, joyful life. . . . We may say, then, I suppose, that 'the lofty ideal' from which this life flows is absolutely indispensable, which, of course, is most annoying."

"Why is it annoying?"

"Because it's a strain to live by ideas and always more fun to live without them."

The prince swallowed and asked with obvious irritation:

"And what do you mean by 'living life'?"

"I don't know that either, Prince, except that it must be something awfully simple—the most common, obvious thing that we experience every day and every minute but that is so incredibly simple and natural that we've been passing it by without recognizing it for thousands of years."

"And all I want to say is that your idea of the aristocracy amounts to the rejection of the aristocracy," the prince said.

"All right, if you really insist, I'll say that possibly there has never been an aristocracy in Russia."

"Everything you say is vague and obscure. If you want to talk, I think you'd better explain what you mean. . . ."

The prince glanced at the clock on the wall and frowned. Versilov got up and picked up his hat.

"You want me to explain again?" he said. "No, I don't think I'll elaborate any further. Besides, I have the weakness of talking without elaborating. I assure you it's true. And then I have another peculiarity: sometimes I begin to develop a thought that I believe true and then I begin to have doubts about it myself. I don't want to risk that now. So good-by, dear Prince, somehow I always chatter too much when I'm with you."

Versilov left and the prince saw him politely to the door. Still I felt offended.

When the prince came back, he passed by me without looking at me, went over to his desk, and suddenly observed:

"You seem displeased. Is there something you disapprove of?"

"I seem displeased," I said with a tremor in my voice, "at the new tone in which you speak to me, and even to Versilov. . . . Of course, Versilov may have sounded pretty reactionary at first, but he made up for it later and . . . and it's possible that there was a profound meaning in what he said, which, however, you simply didn't understand and . . ."

"I have no wish to be lectured like a schoolboy!" he snapped angrily.

"Look here, Prince, such an undignified . . ."

"Kindly spare me any dramatic gestures. I'm very well aware that I behave in a reprehensible way, that I gamble, scatter money to the winds, that perhaps I'm even a thief . . . yes, a thief because I'm losing money belonging to my family. . . . Still, I don't want anybody to judge me—I won't allow it, I won't tolerate it. I am my own judge. And why all these hints? If Versilov has something to tell me, let him go ahead; there's no need for all these obscure and vague words. And then, to have the right to reproach me for what I'm doing, a man should be honest himself. . . ."

"I don't know what was said before I came in—I missed the beginning, but I'd like to know in what way Versilov is dishonest?"

"Enough of this, please. . . . Yesterday you asked me for three hundred rubles, here!" He put the money on the table, lowered himself into an armchair, and nervously crossed one leg over the other.

I felt utterly embarrassed.

"I really don't know . . ." I mumbled. "I know I asked you for it yesterday . . . but, even though I need the money desperately, I cannot, in view of your tone . . ."

"Forget my tone. If I said something that offended you, please forgive me because, I assure you, I have many more important things on my mind. Let me tell you this: my little brother Sasha, who was still a small boy, died four days ago. My father, who, as you know, has been paralyzed for two years, had a new stroke and now they write me from Moscow that he can't speak at all and no longer recognizes people. When they heard about the inheritance, my family were overjoyed and thought of taking him abroad, but his doctor wrote me it was doubtful whether he'd last two weeks. That means there's only my mother and my sister left and now I'm almost on my own. In fact, I am the only one. . . . Well, that inheritance. . . . In a way, I wish there hadn't been any. . . . But this is what I want to tell you: I promised Mr. Versilov that I'd give him at least twenty thousand of the inheritance but I can't right now because of the formalities. I haven't . . . I mean, my father hasn't even been given the titles to the estate yet. And in the meantime I've lost so much money . . . in the past three weeks. . . . Besides, that horrible usurer Stebelkov is charging me such a high rate of interest . . . I've just given you almost the last . . ."

"Oh, Sergei, if that's the case . . ."

"No, no, that's not what I meant. Besides, I'm sure Stebelkov will bring me some money today so I'll be able to manage for the moment. But damn that man Stebelkov: I begged him to let me have at least ten thousand to pay Mr. Versilov, but he won't do it. My promise to give Versilov one-third of the inheritance is eating me. I gave him my word and I must keep it. I swear, I'm making a desperate effort to free myself of at least these depressing connections. That debt is infinitely painful to me, it's driving me frantic. I can't look Mr. Versilov straight in the face. . . . So why must he take advantage of it?"

"In what way is he taking advantage of it?" I asked, non-plussed. "Has he ever reminded you of your promise by so much as a hint?"

"No, he hasn't and I appreciate that, but I keep reminding myself of it. And finally I'm sinking in deeper and deeper. . . . That Stebelkov . . ."

"Listen, Prince, calm yourself, you're getting more and more worked up about something that may be just in your imagination. Oh, I, too, I have let myself go unpardonably and am deep in debt too, but I know it's only a temporary lapse. . . . All I have to do is to win back a certain sum and then I'll pay back everything and . . . That makes twenty-five hundred I owe you now, including these three hundred, doesn't it?"

"I don't remember asking you for it," he said with an unexpected snarl.

"You said you intended to give Versilov twenty thousand. Well, whatever money I have borrowed from you must be subtracted from what you owe Versilov. I absolutely insist. But do you really imagine that Versilov comes to see you to remind you of the money you owe him?"

"It would have been easier for me if he had come and demanded his money," Prince Sergei said enigmatically.

"You were talking about some 'depressing connections' . . . well, if by that you meant Versilov and me, I take exception to that. And then you said that Versilov does not live the life he preaches to others. So that's your reasoning, is it? But allow me to tell you that it isn't logical because even if he is not perfect himself, he can still preach what he considers right. And, besides, why do you use the word 'preaches'? Wasn't it you who called him a 'ladies' prophet' in Germany?"

"No, it wasn't me."

"Stebelkov said it was you."

"He lied when he said that. I'm not that good at coining derisive nicknames. But I still think that a man who wants to preach honor should be honorable himself. That's my way of reasoning, and if you think it's not logical I couldn't care less. That's the way it is and I won't have people coming to my house to judge me and tell me off as if I were a little boy! Anyway, I've had enough of this!" he shouted, waving his hands at me to show that he wouldn't listen to my objections. "Ah, here you are at last!"

The door opened and Stebelkov walked in.

III

It was the same old Stebelkov, just as dapper as when I'd seen him last, sticking out his big chest, staring just as stupidly into people's faces, although obviously imagining that he was being very clever about something and appearing delighted with himself. As he entered the room, he looked around in a peculiar way with a wary and subtle air as though he were trying to gather something from the expressions on our faces. But a moment later he was reassured, and a self-confident grin appeared on his lips, that half-ingratiating, half-insolent smile that I found so unspeakably repulsive.

I had long known that he was giving Sergei a hard time. He had come in twice before while I'd been there. In fact, I too had had some dealings with him in the past month and, for certain reasons, I was rather surprised to see him walk in that day.

"I'll be right with you," Sergei said without greeting Stebelkov and began to search in his desk drawers for the necessary papers and accounts. As for me, I was very offended by Sergei's remarks about Versilov—the implication was so clear (and so surprising!) that I couldn't let it pass without demanding from him a satisfactory explanation which, of course, was unthinkable in the presence of Stebelkov. So I sprawled on the sofa again and opened a book that happened to be lying around.

"You don't say! Belinsky's *Collected Works,* Volume Two! So you've decided to enlighten yourself, Prince!"

My exclamation must have sounded rather contrived. He was very busy and appeared to be in a great hurry, but he heard and turned his head toward me.

"Please leave that book alone," he said sharply.

Now, that was really too much, especially in Stebelkov's presence. And, to make matters worse, a sly, revolting grin appeared on Stebelkov's lips as he winked stealthily in Sergei's direction. Indignantly, I turned away from the fool.

"Take it easy, Prince, I'll make myself scarce and leave you in the company of the number-one man." I'd decided to adopt a casual tone.

"Who's the number-one man—me?" Stebelkov asked cheerfully, pointing a finger at his chest.

"Of course, you're number one and you know it."

"No, please, just a minute, sir. There's always a number two in the world. I'm that number-two man. There's a number one and there's a number two. Number one produces something and number two takes it. So number two becomes number one and number one becomes number two. Do you follow me?"

"No, I don't, I've lost you as always, although you may be right."

"Just a minute then, let me set you straight. There was a revolution in France and they executed everybody. Then Napoleon came along and took everything. So the revolution was number one and Napoleon number two. But then it turned out that Napoleon was number one and the revolution number two. Now, isn't that true?"

I was very amused by the fact that he felt it necessary to bring in the French Revolution when he spoke to me. For some reason he imagined I was some sort of revolutionary and thought he was being very subtle.

"Come with me," Sergei said to him, and they went into another room.

After they'd left, I made up my mind to give Sergei back the three hundred rubles as soon as Stebelkov departed. I needed the money very badly, but my decision was final.

For ten minutes I heard no sound from the room next door. Then there were loud voices talking at the same time, and the next thing I heard was Sergei screaming in uncontrollable rage. He was sometimes subject to these violent fits of temper, which I couldn't hold against him.

At that moment the butler came in to announce a visitor. I pointed at the door to the other room and, when the butler knocked on it, everything became quiet in there. Sergei emerged, looking worried but smiling. The butler went out and half a minute later returned to show the visitor in.

He must have been an important visitor as he was wearing all sorts of distinguished decorations and a family crest. He moved with the ease of a member of high society and looked extremely dignified, although he couldn't have been more than thirty. I must note here that Prince Sergei still hadn't been completely accepted by Petersburg society, despite his ardent ambitions (of which I was aware), and therefore he must have been highly pleased with this visit. As far as I could make out, they had become acquainted only recently, as a result of great efforts on Sergei's part. This was a return visit, which unfortunately had caught him rather off-balance. I saw the painful look Sergei gave to Stebelkov, who, however, did not seem in the least perturbed by it and, instead of leaving discreetly, sat down unabashedly on the sofa and started to ruffle his hair with both his hands, perhaps to emphasize his independence. He even assumed a pompously important air. In fact, he was absolutely unpresentable.

I, on the other hand, even then knew how to behave and certainly wouldn't have disgraced anyone. That is why I was unpleasantly surprised when I caught Prince Sergei's pained and angry look directed at me as well: it showed that he was ashamed of me too, that he was putting me and Stebelkov on the same footing. This realization drove me wild with indignation, so I sprawled myself out even more insolently on the sofa and started turning the pages of the book to make it clear that I didn't give a damn about any of them.

Stebelkov, however, probably believing that it was the correct and polite thing to do, leaned forward and began to listen intently, his eyes almost popping out, to the conversation between Sergei and the visitor, who glanced in bewilderment at Stebelkov a couple of times. Actually, he also glanced once or twice in my direction.

The visitor inquired about Sergei's family, for, as it turned out, he used to know Sergei's mother, who came from an old and distinguished line. As far as I could gather, despite his pleasant tone and apparent lack of affectation, the visitor was very stiff and conceited enough to feel that when he paid someone a visit, he was doing him a tremendous honor. I'm sure that if Stebelkov and I hadn't been present, Sergei would have been more dignified and resourceful. But, under the present circumstances, his lips quivered as he smiled and he seemed quite unable to focus his thoughts on what he was saying.

Before they'd been sitting and talking five minutes, the butler came in to announce still another visitor, who also was hardly to the prince's credit. I'd heard a lot about him and had seen him many times, although he didn't know me at all. He was still very young—oh, not that young really, around twenty-three maybe—handsome, elegantly dressed, from a good family. . . . But everyone knew that he had very shady associations. A year before, he'd been in one of the most glamorous cavalry regiments but had been forced to resign his commission for unpleasant reasons that had become widely known. His family had even announced in the newspapers that they would not be held responsible for his debts. But he went on living it up, borrowing at ten per cent a month, gambling in special gaming establishments, and spending lavishly on a celebrated Frenchwoman. It so happened that a week before he had won about twelve thousand rubles and felt like a conquering hero. He and Sergei were good friends and often gambled together. But this time Sergei shuddered so violently when he saw him that I noticed it from where I sat. The young man obviously felt at home wherever he went; he spoke in a loud and gay voice about anything that came into his head quite uninhibitedly, and, of course, it would never have occurred to him that Sergei could be so painfully embarrassed in front of his important visitor because of his acquaintances.

He came in and, interrupting the conversation even before he sat down, began telling about his latest gambling adventure.

"Weren't you there too? I believe I saw you," he said, breaking off after two sentences to address the important visitor. "No, sorry, I mistook you for someone else," he added, after having stared at him for a moment.

"Alexei Darzan, Ippolit Nashchokin," Sergei hastily introduced them.

I saw that, despite everything, Sergei considered this young man presentable enough to be introduced. He had a respectable name and came from a good family, whereas Stebelkov and I didn't measure up and had to sit quietly in our corners. I was determined not to turn my head in their direction, but Stebelkov started to smirk gleefully at the sight of the young man and was apparently threatening to open his mouth. I felt it was all becoming rather amusing.

"I saw you often at Countess Verigin's last year," Darzan said.

"Yes, I remember. . . . I believe you were in the Army then," Nashchokin said pleasantly.

"That's right, I was. . . . Hey, Stebelkov's here too! What's he doing here? As a matter of fact, it's because of the likes of him that I'm out of uniform today!" Darzan said, pointing at Stebelkov, and burst into loud laughter.

Stebelkov too laughed delightedly, apparently taking Darzan's words for an amiable opening. Sergei blushed violently and hastily addressed some question to Nashchokin, while Darzan walked over to Stebelkov and they got into a heated, though hushed, conversation.

"I believe you got to know Katerina Akhmakov quite well when you were both abroad," Nashchokin said to Sergei.

"Oh yes, I did."

"I believe we're about to hear a piece of news about her: they say she's going to marry Baron Björing."

"That's right!" shouted Darzan, interrupting his own conversation.

"Are you *sure?*" Sergei asked Nashchokin, peculiarly emphasizing the question.

"That's what I was told and I believe many people have heard about it. But, of course, I'm not absolutely certain it's true."

"Yes, it's true!" Darzan cried, walking over to them. "Dubasov told me yesterday and he's always the first to know what's going on. Besides, Prince Sergei here surely should know."

Nashchokin waited until Darzan had finished and then said to Sergei, "She doesn't go out much these days."

"Her father hasn't been too well this past month," Sergei replied rather coolly.

"Quite an adventurous lady otherwise, isn't she!" Darzan suddenly declared.

I turned toward them and stood up.

"I have the pleasure of being personally acquainted with Mrs. Akhmakov," I said, "and I feel it my duty to tell you that all the gossip about her and all those scandalous rumors are nothing but lies, fabricated by the people who buzz around her like flies and only succeed in boring her. . . ."

They all stared at me after my stupid outburst and I faced them squarely, my cheeks afire. But suddenly Stebelkov let out a chuckle. And Darzan, who at first had been taken aback, also began to grin.

"Meet Arkady Dolgoruky," Sergei said, introducing me to Darzan.

"Please believe me, *Prince*," Darzan said, addressing *me*. "I was just repeating what I'd heard. It may all be nothing but gossip, but I'm not the one who invented it."

"Oh, I didn't mean to accuse you personally!" I said, whereupon Stebelkov immediately burst into loud guffaws all because, it turned out later, Darzan had addressed me as "prince." My revolting name caused me embarrassment even here. To this day I blush when I think that I was, of course, too ashamed and failed to correct his stupid mistake by explaining that I was just *plain* Dolgoruky. For the first time in my life I didn't correct it, and now Darzan was looking from me to the laughing Stebelkov in bewilderment.

"Ah yes," Darzan said, suddenly turning to Sergei. "Who's that bright young thing I passed just now on your landing? You know, very fair, with a sharp little nose. . . . Who is she?"

"I really have no idea whom you're talking about," Sergei said quickly, turning red.

"How can you help knowing?" Darzan said laughingly.

"Well, in fact . . ." Sergei hesitated, "it could have been . . ."

"Yes, and you know it was this gentleman's sister, Miss Dolgoruky," Stebelkov butted in, pointing at me. "Because I also saw her. . . ."

"As a matter of fact, it must have been Miss Lisaveta Dolgoruky," Sergei said with an extremely grave and dignified expression. "She's a very close friend of Mrs. Anna Stolbeyev's, whose apartment this happens to be, and I suppose she'd come to pay a visit to Daria, who is also a good friend of Mrs. Stolbeyev's and who was left in charge of the apartment when she went away."

This was all perfectly true. Besides, Daria was the mother of the poor Olga who had killed herself, and it was Mrs. Prutkov who had found a shelter for her at Mrs. Stolbeyev's, where Mrs. Prutkov came to pay the poor woman a visit from time to time, for everybody had come to like her. Nevertheless, Sergei's sensible explanation, perhaps because it came after Stebelkov's stupid outburst and Darzan's calling me "prince," made me turn very red. Luckily, just then Nashchokin got to his feet to leave and held out his hand to Darzan. As there was no one watching Stebelkov and me for a moment, Stebelkov suddenly pointed at Darzan, who was standing in the doorway with his back turned to us. I clenched my fist and shook it at Stebelkov.

Darzan took his leave a minute later, after arranging to meet Sergei the next day, at some gambling house of course. As he was leaving, he shouted something to Stebelkov and made a slight parting gesture in my direction. As soon as he was gone, Stebelkov walked into the middle of the room and raised one finger.

"Now let me tell you the trick that young gentleman played last week. He turned over to someone a promissory note signed by Averyanov. But it turned out that Averyanov's signature had been forged. Well, that IOU is still around, but no one will honor it. It's a case for criminal court. Eight thousand rubles!"

"And I bet you have it in your possession right now!" I cried, glaring savagely at Stebelkov.

"What I have is a bank, a pawnshop, a *mont-de-piété*, not just a promissory note. You must know what a Parisian *mont-de-piété* is—bread and philanthropy to help the poor. That's the kind of business I own."

Sergei looked at him fiercely and asked rudely: "Who invited you to stay here?"

"But why . . ." Stebelkov blinked several times in succession. "Anything wrong?"

"Of course, something's wrong!" Sergei shouted and stamped his foot.

"Well, if that's the way it is . . . If that's so . . . But it isn't so . . ."

He turned abruptly and, with bowed head and bent spine, quickly walked out of the room. When he was already in the doorway, Sergei called out after him:

"And I want you to know, my good man, that I'm not in the least afraid of you."

Sergei was very agitated. After Stebelkov had left, he was about to sit down, but he glanced at me and changed his mind. His eyes seemed to be saying: "And you, why the hell are you still here?"

"You know, Sergei . . ." I started, but he interrupted me.

"Sorry, Arkady, I'm in a hurry, I must leave now."

"It won't take a minute, Prince, it's very important. . . . But first of all, here, please take back your three hundred rubles."

"Why, what's this now?"

He had been pacing the room, but now he stopped.

"Well, after all that happened and all you said about Versilov—that he's not honorable, among other things—and also your general tone all this time . . . In short, I can't accept this money from you."

"That didn't prevent you from *accepting* it all this past month, though."

He suddenly sat down on a chair. I was standing by his desk, holding my hat in one hand and opening and closing Belinsky's book with the other.

"I felt differently then, Prince. . . . Besides, I hadn't planned to go beyond a certain figure. . . . It was my gambling. . . . In short, I can't go on. . . ."

"I think you're simply annoyed because you haven't been very brilliant today. . . . And would you please leave that book alone!"

"What do you mean by that remark? And do you realize that you as good as put me on the same level as Stebelkov in front of your friends?"

"Now I understand!" he said with a poisonous smile. "And to top it all off, wasn't it embarrassing when Darzan addressed you as 'prince'?"

He laughed spitefully. The blood rushed to my head.

"I didn't even think of it. . . . And I wouldn't accept your princely title even if I could get it for the asking."

"I know you only too well by now! It was really funny the way you jumped up in defense of Mrs. Akhmakov. . . . I told you to leave that book alone, didn't I!"

"Why?" I shouted back at him.

"Leave that book alone!" he roared madly, drawing himself up in his chair as though preparing to pounce on me.

"Now that's more than I'll take from you," I said and started walking toward the door, but before I had even reached it he called:

"Come back, Arkady, come back, come back at once!"

I ignored him, but he jumped to his feet, caught up with me in the passage, grabbed me by the arm, and dragged me back to his study. I did not resist.

"Take it, please take it!" he said, pale and shivering, thrusting at me the three hundred rubles I'd thrown on the table. "Take it, you must take it. . . . Otherwise we . . . please!"

"How can I accept it now?"

"All right, I'll apologize to you if that's what you want. Well, I'm sorry, please forgive me . . ."

"I've always liked you, Prince, and if you feel the same . . ."

"I do feel the same, I do, so please take it."

I took the bills. His lips were quivering.

"I understand very well that you're furious with that horrible crook. But I won't accept that money from you unless we embrace and kiss first, as we did after we quarreled before."

I was trembling all over.

"What sentimental nonsense," he muttered, smiling self-consciously.

But he bent down and kissed me on the cheek. As he kissed me, though, I detected an unmistakable look of disgust in his eye that made me shudder.

"At least he did get you that money, didn't he?" I asked.

"Ah, never mind about that now."

"I asked because I was worried about you. . . ."

"All right, he did bring it."

"Prince, we've been friends. . . . And, really, Versilov is . . ."

"All right, all right, everything's fine now!"

"No, really, I don't know whether I should take this three hundred . . ."

I was holding the money in my hand.

"Take it—ta-ake it for heaven's sake."

He smiled again. But there was something in that smile that was anything but friendly.

I took the money.

Chapter 3

I

I took the money because I liked him. If anyone doesn't believe me, I can tell him that, when I accepted the money, I was firmly convinced that if I wanted to I could've raised that sum elsewhere. Therefore, I'd taken it from him not because I had no other choice but out of delicacy, so as not to offend him by refusing to accept his help. Alas, that was the way I reasoned at the time. And yet I left him with a very painful feeling: I had seen that morning how much he had changed toward me. He had never before spoken to me in that tone. As to Versilov, Sergei was positively in full rebellion against him. Even if Stebelkov had exasperated him, Sergei had been unpleasant before Stebelkov had appeared. I repeat that I'd noticed a change in him a few days earlier, but it was nowhere near as drastic. And that was the big difference.

The stupid gossip about Baron Björing could, of course, have had something to do with it. I was worried about that too, but . . . But there was a bright and glittering spot in the center of my field of vision that prevented me from focusing on many things that passed right before my eyes: I lightheartedly refused to take in anything that was gloomy and threatening, being interested only in that bright spot. . . .

It was not quite one o'clock yet. After I left Sergei's, I had my coachman Matvei drive me straight to—would you believe it, of all places?—Stebelkov's. He had really amazed me that morning, not so much by turning up at Sergei's, where he'd promised to be, but by his winking at me. And although winking was a stupid habit of his, this time he had a rather special reason.

On the previous evening, I'd received by mail quite a puzzling note from him. He asked me to come and see him that day between one and two o'clock because he had something to tell me that would "probably come as a surprise." But when he saw me at Sergei's, he never even made a hint to remind me about that note of his. What possible secrets could there be between Stebelkov and me? The very thought struck me as ridiculous. However, in view of what had happened just now, I felt rather worried as I drove to his place.

I'd tried to borrow money from him once before, of course, a couple of weeks earlier, and he'd been quite willing to oblige me. In the end, however, I hadn't accepted the money and had left. As usual, he'd launched into one of his muddled, lengthy speeches and I'd got the impression that he was trying to lay down certain peculiar conditions for the loan. But, since I'd always treated him with the greatest disdain when we met at Sergei's, I scornfully rejected any special arrangements. I remember him running after me all the way to the door as I was leaving. But I wouldn't listen to him and later borrowed the money from Prince Sergei.

Stebelkov lived alone and in comfort. He had an apartment of four large, very well-furnished rooms and apparently a whole staff of male and female servants, commanded by a sort of housekeeper, none too young, however.

I was in an angry mood and, before even stepping into the room, I began with irritation:

"Look here, my good man! To start with, what's the meaning of that note you sent me? I don't want there to be any correspondence between us. And, anyway, why didn't you tell me what you wanted at Prince Sergei Sokolsky's when you saw me there earlier today? You could very well have said what you had to say then."

"And what about you? Why didn't you ask me yourself?" He stretched his lips into a self-satisfied grin.

"Because it's you who wanted to speak to me, not me to you!" I shouted in a burst of anger.

"But then why did you come here?"

He all but leaped into the air he was so pleased with his answer. I brusquely turned my back on him and started walking away, but he caught me by the shoulder.

"Come now, stay, I was just joking. It's really quite important, as you'll see yourself."

I stayed. I admit I was curious. We sat down facing each other across his large desk. He smiled slyly and raised one finger.

"I'll ask you, though," I said, "to cut out your tricks, to stop raising one finger, and, above all, to do without all those allegories of yours. Get straight down to business or I'll leave at once!"

My anger returned and I shouted the last words.

"You're . . . you're proud!" he said in a tone of stupid reproach, rocking in his chair, as the furrows on his forehead crept upward.

"One has to be with the likes of you!"

"You took three hundred rubles from the prince today. . . . I have money too and my money is better than his."

"How do you know I took money from him? Could he have told you?" I was terribly surprised.

"Yes, he did tell me. But you needn't worry, it just came up when we were talking about something else. He hadn't meant to tell me, but he did. Besides, you didn't have to take it from him. Am I right?"

"But I understand that you're asking exorbitant rates."

"Why exorbitant? I only lend money to friends, never to strangers. For strangers, I have a *mont-de-piété.*"

What he referred to as his *mont-de-piété* was a flourishing pawnbroker's shop that he ran from some other premises under someone else's name.

"And I trust my friends with considerable sums."

"Why, is Prince Sergei a friend of yours then?"

"Well, he's a . . . a friend . . . although he likes to treat me as if I were nothing when he's in no position to do so."

"You sound as if you have him well in hand. Does he owe you very much then?"

"Right, he owes me a lot."

"He'll pay up—he has an inheritance coming to him."

"He won't get any money there. He owes it all and a great deal more. That inheritance isn't enough. . . . But you, I won't charge you any interest at all."

I laughed.

"Because I'm a 'friend'? What have I done to earn that distinction?"

"You're well worth it!"

He was leaning his whole body in my direction and started to raise one finger.

"Don't raise that finger, Stebelkov, or I'll leave."

"Listen," he said, narrowing his left eye diabolically, "he could marry Anna Versilov."

"Look here, you, this conversation is getting disgusting and quite out of hand! How dare you drag Miss Anna Versilov into all this?"

"Please keep your temper."

"It costs me a great effort to sit here and listen to you because I can see that you're trying to pull something off now. . . . But I warn you, I may be unable to control myself, Stebelkov!"

"Don't be angry and don't be so proud. Just forget your pride while you hear what I have to say and then be proud again if you must. But you surely must know about Miss Versilov—I mean that Prince Sergei may marry her?"

"Yes, I have, of course, heard of that possibility, but I've never discussed it with Prince Sergei. All I know is that the idea sprouted in the brain of the old Prince Nikolai Sokolsky, who is

sick now, but I've had no part in it and have never spoken of it
to anyone. Now, having cleared up your misgivings on that
point, I want you to tell me why you've brought up the subject
now? It also seems quite incredible to me that Prince Sergei
should talk to *you* about these things."

"He doesn't talk to me—I talk to him while he refuses to listen. In fact, he was screaming at me today."

"No wonder. I understand him only too well."

"The old Prince Sokolsky will give Anna a big dowry—she's
managed to gain his affection. And that's how the young Prince
Sergei Sokolsky will pay me back what he owes me. And he'll
also pay me back a debt that doesn't involve money. Yes, I'm certainly going to get that back too. But, as things stand now, he has
nothing to pay me back with."

"But what has all that to do with me? Where do I come in?"

"To answer an important question for me. You know all those
people, they all receive you. You could find out everything I
need to know."

"What the hell do you want me to find out for you?"

"Whether the young prince is willing, whether Anna is willing, whether the old prince is still willing. . . . I want you to
find out all that for sure."

"How dare you! So you're trying to make me your spy, your
paid spy!" I jumped up from my chair in indignation.

"Please, please, control your pride, just for another five minutes, it won't take more than that." He caught me and made
me sit down again. He was obviously not taken aback by my indignant gestures and protests. Anyway, I had decided to hear
him out to the end.

"I must find out quickly, very quickly, because . . . because
very soon it may be too late. Didn't you notice how painful it
was for him to swallow when that gentleman repeated the gossip about the baron and Mrs. Akhmakov?"

It was now a definite affront to my dignity to stay here and
listen to this man. I knew it. But my curiosity had become irresistible by now.

"Listen you . . . you miserable wretch," I said sternly. "If I
continue to sit here and allow you to go on talking about the
persons you've mentioned, and even if I answer you, it's not because I grant you that right. . . . I can simply smell some low
scheme on your part. And, besides, what can Prince Sergei hope
for from Mrs. Akhmakov?"

"Nothing at all, but that's just what's driving him crazy."

"That's a lie."

"It does drive him frantic. And so, as things stand now, he has lost the hand and must pass up Katerina Akhmakov. That leaves Anna Versilov. . . . Look, I'll loan you two thousand rubles without interest and won't even ask you for an IOU."

He leaned back in his chair and stared at me goggle-eyed. I stared back at him.

"Your suit comes from Bolshaya Millionnaya Street and suits cost lots of money there. So you need money then. Well, my money is better than Prince Sergei's. And, you know, I can let you have even more than two thousand . . ."

"But damn you, what do you expect me to do for it?"

I stamped my foot under the desk. He leaned toward me and said in a businesslike tone: "So you won't interfere."

"But I don't have anything to do with it anyway!"

"I know that you won't talk and that's good."

"I don't need your approval. I myself am very eager to stay out of the whole thing because it's none of my business and because it would be indiscreet for me to interfere."

"You see, you see—it would be indiscreet!" he said, raising one finger.

"What do you mean by 'you see, you see'?"

"You said 'indiscreet'!" he burst out laughing. "I understand that it would be an indiscretion on your part. . . . So, then, you won't interfere, will you?"

He winked at me and now there was something quite intolerably arrogant in his wink, something mocking, and also conniving. He obviously assumed that I was ready to do something very low and despicable and he was basing his hopes on that. That much was obvious, but I couldn't think of what it could be.

"Miss Versilov is *also* a sort of sister of yours."

He sounded businesslike again.

"That's none of your business. Besides, I won't allow you to mention her name again."

"Come, hold your horses for another minute. Listen carefully: he will receive that money and everybody will benefit from it, *everybody,* do you follow me?"

"So you imagine I'll accept money from him?"

"Why, you're accepting money from him now."

"I'm only taking what is mine by right."

"How is it yours by right?"

"It belongs to Versilov. Prince Sergei owes him twenty thousand."

"But that's Versilov's, not yours."

"Versilov being my father . . ."

"But you're Dolgoruky, not Versilov."

"That makes no difference."

Yes, that's the way I talked then, although I knew it damn well did make a difference. Still, I'd say things like that out of "delicacy."

"Anyway, enough of all this!" I shouted. "I don't understand what you're driving at or how you dared to ask me to listen to all this nonsense!"

"Is it possible that you don't understand? Do you really mean it or are you just pretending?" Stebelkov said slowly, staring at me fixedly with an unbelieving grin.

"I swear I don't understand!"

"But I told you: he will take care financially of everybody, yes, *everybody* just as I said, just as long as you do not interfere and try to dissuade him. . . ."

"You must be crazy—what do you mean by 'everybody'? Does that include Versilov too?"

"Not just you and Versilov but also Anna Versilov, who is just as much your sister as Lisa *Dolgoruky!*"

I was gaping at him in bewilderment and suddenly discerned something that might have been a glimmer of pity in his loathsome look.

"Well, if you really don't understand, that's even better. In fact, it's good, very good, if you don't. All to your credit if . . . if you really don't understand. . . ."

I lost my temper again and picked up my hat to leave.

"To hell with you and your damned nonsense! You're crazy!" I shouted.

"It's not nonsense. So you've decided to leave? Never mind, you'll be back."

"I won't be back!" I rapped out from the doorway.

"You'll be back and then you'll talk differently. We'll do some serious talking then. And remember—there's that two thousand rubles!"

II

He'd filled me with such confusion and disgust that, after I left his place, I just kept swearing and trying not to think. The mere thought that Sergei could have talked to him about me and about the money I owed him caused me stabbing pains. "I'll win some money and pay him back today," I thought desperately.

Stupid and muddleheaded as he was, Stebelkov was obviously a life-size villain and he was certainly plotting some shady maneuver now. But the trouble with me was that I had no time and patience to stop and examine his schemes and that's what accounted for my peculiar blindness.

Suddenly I remembered I had things to do and glanced anxiously at my watch. Luckily it wasn't two yet. That left me enough time to take care of a certain visit. Otherwise, in the state I was in, I'd have worried myself to death before three o'clock.

I drove to see my sister Anna Versilov. I'd come to know her quite well at the old prince's, particularly during his illness. I hadn't seen the old man now for three or four days and that weighed on my conscience. And it was Anna who made up for my failure because the old prince had become extremely fond of her and had even started calling her his "guardian angel." By the way, it was true that the old prince had conceived the idea of marrying her off to Sergei, an idea he had even mentioned to me several times, in confidence, of course. I'd told Versilov about this because I'd noticed that, although Versilov seemed quite indifferent to what was going on around him, he'd become attentive whenever I talked about my encounters with Anna. On that occasion, he'd remarked vaguely that Anna had lots of sense and that she could handle the delicate situation without any outside advice. It was also true, of course, that the old prince fully intended to provide Anna with a dowry. But how could Stebelkov possibly aspire to receive part of it? That morning, Sergei had shouted as Stebelkov was leaving that he wasn't afraid of him. Could Stebelkov, then, have spoken to him about Anna when the two of them were alone together in the study? I can just imagine how furious I'd have been had I been in Sergei's shoes!

Lately I'd been to see Anna rather often. But here I must report a peculiarity in her behavior. She always fixed the day and the hour for my visit herself and she was always there when I arrived. But every time I came, she'd somehow act as though my visit was quite unexpected and had taken her completely by surprise. But, despite that peculiarity, I became quite attached to her. She lived at her grandmother's, Mrs. Fanariotov, who was her guardian, since Versilov never contributed anything to her support. But Anna was in no way in the position of a young ward in the house of a rich and aristocratic lady, as often described in literature, like the young protégée of the old countess in Pushkin's *Queen of Spades*, for instance. Indeed, she was more in the position of a countess herself. And although she lived in the same house and on the same floor as the Fanariotovs, she had her own private two-room suite so that during all the time I'd spent there, I'd never met any of the Fanariotovs. Anna was thus free to receive anyone she wished and to spend her time as she chose. Besides, she was already twenty-two. For the past year or so, Anna had almost entirely stopped going out into society though Mrs. Fanariotov spared no expense for her grand-daughter, of whom I'd heard she was very fond. Actually what I liked most about Anna was the simple way she was dressed every time I came to see her and also the fact that she was never idle but always occupied with something, reading or needle-work. There was something monastic about her, something that reminded me of a nun, that I liked very much too. She was not very talkative, but when she said something it was always to the point. And she certainly knew how to listen, something I'd al-ways been very bad at. Every time I told her that, although she didn't have any features in common with Versilov, she reminded me so much of him, she would blush very slightly. Actually she blushed often, always barely perceptibly, and this trait of hers endeared her to me even more. In her presence I never referred to our father just as "Versilov" but always as Andrei Versilov or Mr. Versilov—something that happened spontaneously, all by it-self. I'd discovered that the Fanariotovs were somewhat ashamed of Versilov, although I'd got that impression solely from Anna and I'm not quite sure that the word "ashamed" is the right one; but I'm sure that it was something of the sort. I also spoke to her about Sergei sometimes and when I did she'd listen to me in-tently and seemed curious about what I had to tell her. But somehow she'd never ask me about him on her own initiative. Nor did I ever hint at the possibility of marriage between the two of them, although I rather liked the idea. But then there were many things I would never have dared to utter in her room despite the fact that I felt immensely at ease there. I also admired her for being very well educated and having read a great number of really serious books. In general, she was incom-parably better read than me.

It was she who had suggested I come to see her once, and at the time I thought there must be something she wanted to find out. Oh, at that time, so many people could wheedle so many things out of me! But why shouldn't she, I thought to myself, since that was not the only reason she wanted me to come to see her. In fact, I was delighted if I could be of any use to her and . . . and when I was with her I felt we were brother and sister, although we'd never even hinted at our relationship as if neither of us even suspected it. Sitting there with her made the mention of it absolutely unthinkable, and sometimes the absurd idea would occur to me that she might after all really know nothing about our blood ties. That's what her behavior with me was like.

III

When I got to Anna's that day I found Lisa there. That surprised me a good deal. I was aware, of course, that they'd met before; in fact, it was in connection with the mysterious baby. If I have an opportunity later I'll relate how Anna—usually so proud and proper—had made up her mind to see the baby and how she'd met Lisa on that occasion. Still, I never expected that she'd invite Lisa to come visit her at home. It was a very pleasant surprise to me. Of course giving no sign of my approval, I greeted Anna, pressed Lisa's hand warmly, and sat down.

They were both engaged in serious business: they'd spread out on the table an evening dress belonging to Anna. It was very elegant but "old" (that is, Anna had worn it two or three times) and they were now trying to alter it. Lisa was an expert in these matters, had very good taste in clothes, and hence was playing the role of the wise woman in this council. I remembered Versilov's words about women sewing and it made me laugh. Besides, I was in a happy state of mind.

"You seem in high spirits today—that's very pleasant," Anna said, articulating her words slowly and clearly. She had a strong, carrying contralto voice, but she always spoke quietly, her eyelashes usually covering her eyes somewhat and a faint smile flitting across her pale face.

"Lisa could tell you how unpleasant I can be when I'm in low spirits," I said cheerfully.

"Most likely Anna knows it too," Lisa needled me playfully.

The poor girl! If only I'd had an inkling of what was on her mind at that moment!

"What are you doing with yourself these days?" Anna asked me. (I must note here that it was she who had asked me to come and see her that particular day.)

"I'm sitting here wondering," I said, "why I find it so much more pleasant to see you reading rather than doing needlework. Somehow I don't feel needlework is right for you. In that sense, I'm just like Mr. Versilov."

"And you still haven't made up your mind about entering the university?"

"I'm very grateful to you for not having forgotten our conversation on that subject because it shows that you think of me sometimes. . . . But as to the university, I still haven't decided. Besides, I have some plans of my own."

"He means he has a secret," Lisa said.

"I don't know why you find it so funny, Lisa. An intelligent man quipped recently that all our progressive movement has achieved in the past twenty years is to prove our crass ignorance. And that, of course, applies to our university men as much as to the rest."

"I bet it was Papa who said that," Lisa remarked; "it's awful how you go around repeating his ideas!"

"Why, Lisa, can't you credit me with a few ideas of my own?"

"These days it may be good to listen to what intelligent people say and try to remember it," Anna said, perhaps in my defense.

"That's right, Anna!" I chimed in enthusiastically. "A person who's not concerned with Russia's present is not a worthy citizen. My own views on Russia may appear peculiar, though: we lived through the Tartar invasion and then through two centuries of slavery, and there's no doubt in my mind that both suited our tastes. But now we've been offered freedom, and we have to learn to live with it. Will we manage to get used to it? Will it also suit our taste? That's the question."

Lisa threw a quick glance at Anna, who immediately lowered her eyes and pretended she was looking for something. I realized that Lisa was trying hard to control herself, but the second our eyes chanced to meet she couldn't hold it back any longer and burst into a fit of laughter. I felt the blood rush to my cheeks.

"You're really impossible, Lisa."

"I'm sorry," she said almost sadly, as her laughter stopped abruptly. "I don't know what's going on in my head. . . ."

I could almost hear the tears in her voice and felt very ashamed of myself. I took her hand and kissed it.

"You're a very kind person," Anna commented quietly, as she watched me kiss Lisa's hand.

"But, in fact, Lisa, I was really delighted to see you laugh today," I said. "Because, you know, Anna, lately every time I meet Lisa, she always has on her face a questioning look as if asking 'Have you found out anything? Is everything all right?' Yes, I'm sure, there's been something bothering her all this time."

Anna looked intently at Lisa. Lisa lowered her eyes. Somehow I realized at that moment that they were much more closely acquainted than I had assumed. That pleased me.

"You just said I was kind, Anna. Well, you can't imagine how much better a person I become when I'm here with you than I am usually. It's because I like being here so much," I said with emotion.

"And I'm delighted to hear you say that," she said rather gravely.

I must note here that she never spoke to me about my disorderly way of life, about the cesspool in which I was now swimming, although I was aware that not only had she heard about it but she was even interested enough to question people about it. But now I felt she was moving closer to talking to me on the subject, and my heart opened even wider to her.

"How is the old prince?" I inquired.

"Oh, he's much better. He's on his feet again. Actually he was out for a drive yesterday and will go out again today. But haven't you been to see him today? He's been awfully anxious to see you."

"I feel very guilty toward him. But now you see him often and you've taken my place. He's very fickle, and you've displaced me in his affections."

She looked at me unsmilingly, perhaps because of the triviality of my jocular approach.

"You know, I went to see Prince Sergei earlier today," I mumbled, just to say something, "and, by the way, Lisa, have you been to see Daria today?"

"Yes," Lisa answered rather curtly, without raising her head. And then, quite unexpectedly, she added: "But I was under the impression that you'd been seeing the old prince almost every day. . . ."

"Well, I do set out to see him every day but I never seem to get there," I said laughingly. "I turn off to the left before . . ."

"Yes, indeed, the old prince remarked on how often you go and see Katerina Akhmakov. That made him laugh yesterday," Anna said.

"Why should that make him laugh?"

"He was joking in his usual way, you know. He said that normally a young and beautiful woman like Katerina can arouse only anger and indignation in a young man of your age. . . ."

Anna suddenly began to laugh.

"That was a terribly shrewd observation!" I cried. "But I bet he didn't make it—it was you who said that to him!"

"Why, what makes you think so? No, it was he who said it all right."

"But what if the beauty turns her attention to that insignificant and 'immature' fellow standing in a corner and seething with rage, and what if she singles him out from the whole crowd of her admirers?" I asked boldly and challengingly, feeling my heart pound in my breast.

"If so, that will be the end of you!" Lisa laughed.

"The end of *me?*" I cried. "Uh-uh—it won't be the end of me, it certainly doesn't look that way. If a woman steps into my path, she'll have to follow me. No one can try to turn me aside from my path without getting hurt."

Much later, casually recalling this conversation, Lisa told me that I'd uttered that statement in a very strange and solemn tone, very ponderously, and I sounded so funny that it was quite impossible not to laugh. And, indeed, Anna again broke into a sudden burst of laughter.

"Go ahead, laugh!" I cried in rapture because I was wildly enjoying this conversation and the turn it was taking. "As long as it is you—I'm delighted when you laugh! I like your way of laughing, Anna: you sit there quietly, and then all of a sudden you're laughing. It happens all at once, and it's impossible to anticipate it from your expression. When I was in Moscow, I used to know a lady . . . oh, from a distance, that is. Well, she was almost as beautiful as you are but she didn't have your laugh. And so her face, which was as attractive as yours, lost all its attractiveness. Yours, on the other hand, is irresistibly attractive precisely because of your way of laughing. . . . That's something I've wanted to tell you for a long time."

When I mentioned the Moscow lady who was "almost as beautiful" as Anna, I tried to make it sound as if these words had slipped unthinkingly from my lips, assuming that such a "spontaneous" compliment would be more appreciated by a woman than carefully thought-up praise. And although Anna blushed, I knew it did please her. So there was a point in my having invented that "Moscow lady," for it goes without saying that she never really existed.

"As a matter of fact, it would, indeed, appear that lately you've been subjected to the influence of a charming, beautiful lady," she said with an enchanting smile.

I had the impression I was flying. . . . I wanted to reveal a secret to them. . . . But I restrained myself.

"But, come to think of it," Anna said again, "not so very long ago your feelings toward Katerina weren't so nice at all."

"If I ever spoke ill of her," I said, feeling my eyes sparkle, "it was because of the monstrous slander spread about her. She was said to be Andrei Versilov's deadly enemy. In fact, he'd been slandered too: they said he was in love with her and had proposed to her and all kinds of nonsense. That notion is just as monstrous as that other piece of gossip that she promised to marry Sergei Sokolsky the moment her husband, who was still alive, died but that when that happened she broke her promise. But I know for certain that there's no truth in it and that it was only a joke. Once, when they were abroad and she was in a laughing mood, she did say to Sergei that perhaps, in the future, who knows. . . . But what can words like those imply except a playful mood of the moment? And I also know very well that Sergei couldn't possibly take such a 'promise' seriously . . . and that he has no intention of doing so," I added quickly, remembering something else; "for I gather he has quite different plans," I put in slyly. "Besides, today I heard Nashchokin tell him that Katerina is about to marry Baron Björing and, believe me, Sergei weathered this piece of news very well."

"Did you say Nashchokin went to see him?" Anna asked with obvious surprise.

"Right. He seems to be a very respectable fellow. . . ."

"And Nashchokin spoke to him about Katerina marrying Björing?" Anna seemed terribly interested.

"He just mentioned the possibility of such a marriage, a rumor going around. But I myself believe it's nonsense."

Anna looked thoughtfully into space for a moment and then bent over her needlework.

"I'm very fond of Sergei!" I suddenly announced with great emphasis. "Of course, I'm aware of his undeniable shortcomings, one of which, as I believe I pointed out to you before, is a certain narrowness of vision. But perhaps even his shortcomings bear witness to his forthrightness. Today, for instance, we almost had an explosion because of his notion that only a man who is honorable himself has the right to talk about honor and that, coming from anyone else, any discussion of honor would be nothing but hypocritical lies. Now is that logical, do you think? It isn't, but at the same time it attests to the high standards of honor and duty he sets for himself. Don't you agree? . . . But, my God, what time is it?" I cried, glancing by chance at the clock on the wall.

"It's ten to three," Anna said matter-of-factly, looking at the clock too.

All the time that I'd been talking about Sergei, she'd had her eyes lowered and a whimsical but charming little smile had slightly twisted her lips. She had obviously guessed why I was praising him. Lisa was listening too, her eyes on her work. She had dropped out of the conversation quite a while ago, I'd noticed.

I leaped to my feet as if something had burned me.

"Why, are you late? Were you supposed to be somewhere?"

"Yes. . . . Not really. . . . Well, actually, I am late and I'll have to rush off, but I want to tell you this first, Anna," I said in great agitation. "I must open my heart to you today! I want to tell you with complete frankness how much I've appreciated your kindness and your delicate feelings that have prompted you to invite me to come and see you. My friendship with you has had a tremendous effect on me. . . . When I come from a visit to you, I feel purified and it makes me feel a better person than I really am. It's true, you know! While I'm sitting near you, not only do I become incapable of saying wicked things, but I cannot even have any unworthy thoughts; they seem to vanish in your presence; and when I remember something that's not nice in your presence, it immediately makes me feel ashamed and I become embarrassed and sort of blush inwardly. . . . And, you know, I was particularly happy today to meet my sister Lisa here with you; that's yet another manifestation of your noble character, of your broad-minded views. . . . In short, there's something . . . *fraternal* about you, if you allow me to finally break that barrier. . . ."

As I was saying all this, she slowly rose from her chair, her face growing pinker and pinker. But suddenly she seemed to become frightened, as though she'd caught sight of a line that couldn't be overstepped, and she cut me off:

"Believe me, I do appreciate your warm feelings. I had guessed them before you spoke . . . for quite some time already."

She paused in confusion, held out her hand, and shook mine.

Suddenly I felt Lisa tugging discreetly at my sleeve. I said good-by. Lisa caught up with me in the next room.

IV

"Why did you tug at my sleeve?" I asked her.

"She's horrid, she's scheming, you mustn't trust her. . . . She's got hold of you to find out certain things from you," Lisa told me in angry whispers with an expression such as I'd never seen on her face before.

"What are you talking about, Lisa? She's such a delightful creature!"

"In that case, it's me who's horrid."

"But what's come over you?"

"I'm very bad then. She may be the most charming creature while I'm no good at all. Anyway, forget it. . . . Listen, Mother asked me to tell you something she 'doesn't dare' mention to you herself—that's the way she put it. Please, Arkady dear, stop gambling, I beg you. . . . And so does Mother."

"I know, Lisa, I know myself, but . . . I know that this is just pitiful cowardice but . . . but actually it's not all that bad. You see, what happened is that I got myself deep in debt, like an idiot, and all I want is to win enough money to pay back what I owe. It's possible to win, but until now I've gambled like a fool, leaving everything to chance. From now on, though, I'll sweat over every ruble I play. . . . I guarantee that I'll win now! I want you also to know that I don't have the passion for gambling, that it's only a passing thing with me, and I want you to believe this! I have enough will power to stop whenever I decide. As soon as I have settled my debts, I'll be forever yours and Mother's. Tell her that I'll never leave you then. . . ."

"That three hundred rubles this morning—it must've cost you something to accept it!"

"What do you know about it?"

"Daria heard everything. . . ."

But at that second, Lisa pushed me behind a curtain and we found ourselves in a little space by a bay window. Before I could gather my senses, I heard a very familiar clang of spurs and recognized the footsteps.

"Prince Sergei," I whispered.

"That's him all right," Lisa confirmed.

"Why were you so frightened that he'd see me?"

"No reason, but I certainly don't want him to see me."

"*Tiens!*" I smiled. "Would he be running after you too by any chance? If so, I'd certainly like to have a word with him. Where are you going?"

"Let's get out of here. You were leaving anyway and now I'm coming with you."

"But did you say good-by to her?"

"I did. And my coat's in the hall."

We left. When we were out on the landing, I was struck by an idea.

"Know what, Lisa? I bet he's come to propose to her!"

"N—no. . . . He's not going to propose to her," Lisa said slowly and quietly. She sounded confident.

"You know, Lisa, although I had words with him this morning—as you may perhaps have heard—I'm still sincerely fond of him and wish him luck. Besides, we made it up in the end. . . . As long as they're happy, people are kind. Believe me, there's much about him that is good. There is kindness in him too, at least the rudiments of kindness. And in the hands of a strong and intelligent girl like Anna, he'd straighten out and be really happy. It's a shame I'm in such a hurry. . . . Still, come for a little drive with me. There's something I'd like to tell you."

"No, go where you have to go by yourself. It's not on my way. Are you coming to dinner tonight?"

"Yes, sure, I'm coming. . . . But let me tell you this at least: there's a low crook, a really revolting creature, one Stebelkov —I don't know whether you know him—who wields considerable power over Sergei . . . through IOU's. . . . To cut a long story short, he controls Sergei sufficiently, is now pressing him so hard, and has made him lose his sense of honor to such an extent that he's looking for a way out of his difficulties by marrying Anna, because neither of them can see any other way of getting the money. Actually, the right thing to do would have been to warn her, but I think it's all nonsense, because she would, indeed, put everything right. . . . But what do you think, will she turn him down?"

"Good-by, I must be on my way," Lisa said cuttingly, and in her look I suddenly saw so much hatred that I cried out in horror:

"Lisa dear, what did I do?"

"It's not you . . . just don't gamble. . . ."

"If it's just my gambling, all right, I won't."

"You spoke before about people being happy: are you happy then?"

"I'm madly happy, madly happy! But my God, it's already after three! So see you soon, Lisa darling, sweet little Lisa! But tell me, is it forgivable for a man to make a woman wait for him? Is it permissible?"

"When you have a date with her?" Lisa asked with a very pale, lifeless, quivering smile.

"Give me your hand for luck."

"For luck? My hand? No sir, I certainly won't give it to you!"

And she quickly walked away. And what made it so disquieting was the serious ring to those last words of hers.

I jumped into my sleigh.

Yes, it was that "happiness" of mine that was making me as blind as a mole: there was nothing except myself that touched or concerned me.

Chapter 4

I

Now I've reached a point when I'm afraid even to go on with my story. It all happened long ago and now it seems like some sort of mirage. How could a woman like her have agreed to meet a crude boy such as I was at that time? Yes, that's how the situation must have appeared from the outside!

When I left Lisa and flew off at full speed with a pounding heart *to meet her*, it suddenly occurred to me that I must be mad, that the whole idea was too absurd, and that I mustn't believe it was real. And yet I had no misgivings at all; indeed, the more obvious the absurdity became, the less I doubted.

The fact that it was already past three o'clock worried me somewhat. "How can I not be there at the time she fixed?" I kept repeating to myself. I also asked myself such foolish questions as "What is better under the circumstances—boldness or timidity?" But all these thoughts just flashed through my mind because there was something real that was making my heart pound, something that I couldn't define. All she'd actually said to me the previous evening was: "I'll be at Mrs. Prutkov's tomorrow at three." That was all. But then she'd received me before in her own place, without anybody else present, and she obviously could have said anything she wanted without having to meet me at Mrs. Prutkov's for that purpose. Also, I had no idea whether Mrs. Prutkov would be at home or not. If it was a tryst, then she wouldn't be there. But how could she arrange that without explaining to Mrs. Prutkov in advance why she needed her apartment? Did that mean that Mrs. Prutkov was in on the secret too? This seemed most unlikely to me. It would have been rather indecent, quite shocking, in fact.

Of course, she might have simply decided to drop in on Tatyana Prutkov the next day and mentioned it to me casually, without any ulterior motive, whereupon I had proceeded to imagine a whole fairy tale. Besides, she'd mentioned it fleetingly, carelessly, following a pretty dull visit during which I'd been somehow at a loss, hadn't even talked properly but had only kept mumbling, not knowing really what to say, paralyzed by shyness and furious with myself. Moreover, she'd appeared to be planning to go out that evening so she'd seemed rather pleased when I'd got up to leave. . . . All these reflections flooded my head. Finally I decided that I'd ring at the apartment door and ask the cook whether her mistress was at home.

If she was out, then it was a tryst all right. But, deep down, I had no doubts whatever that it was a tryst.

I tore up the stairs and by the time I'd reached the door, all my fears were gone. "I'll know in one second, whatever it may be!" The cook opened the door and informed me with her usual ill-mannered apathy that her mistress was out. I was on the point of asking her whether there was any one else waiting for Mrs. Prutkov. I should've asked her, but I didn't and decided instead to find out for myself. I muttered something to the effect that I'd wait, took off my overcoat, and opened the door. . . . Katerina Akhmakov sat by the window "waiting" for Mrs. Prutkov.

"Hasn't she arrived yet?" she asked in what sounded to me like a worried and annoyed tone as soon as she saw me. Her tone and expression were so different from what I'd expected that I stopped short in the doorway.

"Who is it you're waiting for?" I mumbled.

"Why, Tatyana, of course. Didn't I ask you to tell her that I was coming to see her at three?"

"I . . . I haven't even seen her since then."

"So you forgot to do it?"

I sat down, feeling completely annihilated. So that's all there was to it! It was as simple and as clear as could be, so how could I possibly persist in believing . . .

"I don't even remember your asking me to tell her anything. In fact, you never did ask me anything; you simply said you'd be here at three!"

I said all that irritatedly without looking at her.

"Is that so!" she cried surprised. "Then if you forgot to give her my message but knew that I was coming, what are you doing here yourself?"

I looked at her face: there was no sarcasm or anger in it, just a bright, amused smile, and something very mischievous in her expression.

But then I'd often seen a certain childlike playfulness in her on other occasions too. And now her expression seemed to say: "See, I caught you. What do you have to say for yourself now?"

I didn't feel like answering and lowered my eyes. We remained silent for half a minute.

"Have you just come from my father's?" she asked.

"I haven't been there at all. . . . I came straight here from Anna's . . . and you know it very well," I added unexpectedly.

"Did something happen to you at Anna's?"

"Why do you ask? Do I look like a madman or something?

No, nothing happened there. I looked like a madman before even I got there."

"Did you recover your normal state there?"

"No, I didn't. Besides, I learned that you were going to marry Baron Björing."

"Was it Anna who told you that?"

"No, it was I who told her. I heard Nashchokin telling Prince Sergei, whom he'd come to visit this morning."

I still kept my eyes lowered. Looking at her would have meant being flooded with radiance, joy, and happiness when I didn't want to be happy. The sting of indignation was deep in my heart and, within a second, I had made a tremendous decision. After that, I started talking. I hardly knew what I was saying. I muttered something breathlessly, but I was no longer afraid to look into her face. I looked into it and my heart was beating. I spoke about something quite irrelevant, but I believe I was expressing myself quite articulately now.

At first, she listened to me with that usual composed, patient smile of hers, but little by little surprise and even fear appeared in her intent look. The smile was still there, but every so often it seemed to quiver. Then I saw she was trembling.

"What's the matter?" I asked her.

"I'm afraid of you," she said almost in terror.

"Why don't you leave then? Since Mrs. Prutkov is not at home and you know she won't be back for a while, why don't you just get up and go?"

"I thought I'd wait, but now . . . I think you're right. . . ." She made a movement to get up.

"No, no, please stay," I stopped her. "Now I saw you shudder again, but you're still smiling. You always smile, even when you're frightened. . . . But now you're really smiling. . . ."

"Are you delirious?"

"Yes, I'm delirious."

"I'm frightened," she whispered.

"Frightened of what?"

"That you'll start breaking down the walls. . . ."

She smiled again, but I saw she was really afraid now.

"I can't bear that smile of yours. . . ."

I began to talk and I talked and talked. I was flying through the air as if something were pushing me. I'd never talked like that before in her presence because I'd always felt shy with her. Indeed, I felt terribly shy even now as I was talking, but I went on talking. . . . I remember I spoke about her face.

"I can't bear that smile of yours. . . . No, no longer!" I cried out suddenly. "Even when I was still in Moscow I imagined you to be awesome and magnificent, sheltering behind elegant and hypocritical phrases. Yes, back in Moscow, Maria and I used to talk about you, trying to imagine what you must be like. Do you remember Maria? You went to see her. When I was on the way from Moscow to Petersburg, I dreamed of you all night in the train. And before you arrived I was staring at your portrait in your father's study, but it didn't reveal anything to me. The expression in it is that of a mischievous child of infinite artlessness. I marveled at it every time I came to see you. But later I also found out that it could become immensely proud and that it could crush people with one glance, such as the one you gave me at your father's the day you arrived from Moscow. I saw you then, but if someone had asked me afterward what you looked like, I couldn't have answered. I couldn't even have said whether you were short or tall, because the second I saw you I was as though blinded. Your portrait is not at all like you. Your eyes are not really dark; they're light and they only look dark because of your eyelashes. You're of medium height, you're stocky, you have the buxom fullness of a strong country girl. . . . And even your face is the face of a village beauty. Please don't be offended because I think that's good, that's the best way to be. Your face is round and rosy, smooth and smiling, it's a bold and bashful face! Yes, Katerina Akhmakov has a bashful and chaste face! I swear it's true. Even more than chaste, child-like! I've been so astounded by it all this time that I've kept asking myself: could she really be *that* woman? Now, of course, I know how intelligent you are, but at first I decided you were rather simple. And your intelligence is a gay, laughing intelligence that needs no embellishments. . . . Another thing I love about you is that your smile never leaves your lips—that's a joy to me! I also love your cool composure, your calm, smooth, almost lazy way of saying things—yes, it's that very languor that I love. I imagine that if a bridge collapsed under you as you were crossing it, you'd just make some quiet comment in a lazy, casual tone. . . . I'd expected you to be all pride and passion, but for two months now you've been talking to me the way one student would talk to another. . . . I never imagined you'd have that brow: it's a little low like the foreheads of statues, but it's so white and looks as smooth as marble under your luxurious hair. Your bosom is high, your movements are light, your beauty is uncommon, but there's no conceit in you. I couldn't believe that you were all these things until now, but now I believe it!"

She listened to this wild talk with wide-open eyes. She could see I was shivering. Several times she raised her elegantly gloved hand in a charming gesture to try to stop me, but each time she pulled it back, looking dismayed and puzzled. Two or three times a smile broke through her seriousness; at one point she blushed deeply, but toward the end she appeared very worried and turned paler. And, as soon as I stopped, she held out her hand and said in a voice that, though as smooth and calm as usual, had a note of entreaty in it:

"You mustn't talk like that. . . . It's not right for you to talk like that. . . ."

She got up and unhurriedly picked up her scarf and her sable muff.

"Are you leaving?" I exclaimed.

"I'm really afraid of you. . . . You're taking advantage. . . ." she said slowly with sadness and slight reproach.

"Listen, I promise I won't break down the walls."

"But you've already started," she said, failing to suppress her smile. "I'm not even sure that you won't try to physically prevent me from leaving."

She looked as if she might really be afraid.

"I'll open the door for you myself if you want to go. I only want you to know that I've taken a tremendously important decision, and if you want to pour some balm on my soul, sit down and allow me to say a few more words. But if you'd rather not, I'll open the door for you at once."

She looked at me and then sat down.

"Another woman would have left in indignation, but you sat down!" I cried out enthusiastically.

"You've never allowed yourself to talk to me like this before."

"I never dared to before. And even this time I didn't know what to say to you when I came in. And do you think I'm not afraid to talk now? I am very much so. But, all of a sudden, I made a great decision and I felt I'd carry it out. And the moment I made up my mind, I went mad and started talking. . . . Listen, this is what I wanted to ask you: have you been using me to spy for you? Please, answer me!"

The color rushed to her face.

"All right, don't answer me yet, listen instead to what I have to say and only then tell me the whole truth."

Now all the barriers were broken and I was floating in space.

II

"Two months ago, I stood here behind the curtain while you were telling Mrs. Prutkov, you know, about that letter. . . . I couldn't stand it, rushed out, and blurted out things I wasn't supposed to say. You gathered at once that I knew something—you couldn't have failed to. . . . You'd been looking for an important document, you were worried. . . . Wait, don't say anything yet. . . . You were right, your suspicions were well founded: that document does exist. . . . I mean, I saw it: it's your letter to Andronikov, isn't it?"

"You've seen that letter?" she asked me quickly, looking both worried and embarrassed. "Where did you see it?"

"At Kraft's—you know, the man who shot himself."

"Really? You saw it yourself? And what happened to it?"

"Kraft tore it up."

"Were you there when he tore it up? You actually saw him tearing it up?"

"Yes, I was there. He probably tore it up in order to destroy it before he died. Of course I didn't know then that he was going to shoot himself."

"So it has been destroyed! Well, thank God," she breathed slowly, sighed, and crossed herself.

I wasn't lying to her . . . that is to say, I was lying only in the sense that the letter was actually in my hands and that Kraft had never had it. But that was an insignificant detail; I'd told her the truth about what really mattered. And as I was lying to her, I swore to myself that I was going to burn the compromising letter that very evening. I swear that if I'd had it in my pocket, I'd have taken it out and given it to her then and there. But I didn't have it on me; I'd left it at home. Actually, I'm not absolutely sure I would've given it to her because I might have been too ashamed to admit that it was in my possession and I'd waited so long before turning it over to her. But it made no difference: I was determined to burn it when I returned home. Yes, I swear, I was quite pure of heart at that moment!

"And since you know now," I said, almost choking with emotion, "tell me this: is it because you suspected I knew the whereabouts of that letter that you've been so nice and friendly with me and lavished on me your irresistible charm? Wait, don't answer yet, let me finish what I have to say. Every time I came to see you, I suspected that the only reason you received me so nicely was to find out whatever I might know about that document, to reduce me to a state in which I'd have to tell you everything. . . . Just one more second: I suspected that, and it hurt me. The possibility of your duplicity caused me unbearable suffering because . . . because I'd discovered what an extraordinary and noble person you are. This is the truth: I used to be your enemy until I discovered your nobility and was utterly conquered. Still, there was that duplicity—I mean the suspicion of duplicity—that tormented me. But now everything will be cleared up, resolved, the time has come. . . . Wait, before you speak, I want you to know how I feel about all this, I mean right now, this very second. . . . In all honesty, even if that was your purpose, I won't resent it. . . . I mean, I won't feel offended, because it would be only natural, I understand all too well. There would be nothing unnatural, evil, in it: you're worried about that document, you suspect that such and such a person knows something about it, and you wish to find out what he knows. . . . There's nothing reprehensible in that, nothing at all. I mean it. But I want you to tell me now. . . . I want you to admit. Forgive me for using that word. I want to know the truth. I don't know why, but I need it. So tell me, have you been so nice to me all this time because of that document? Is that true, Katerina?"

As I spoke, I felt I was falling into a void. My forehead was burning. She, on the other hand, looked at me without any fear now. Instead, there was a shyness in her, as though she felt embarrassed about something.

"Yes, it was because of the document," she said slowly in a half whisper. "Forgive me, I'm guilty," she added suddenly, half raising her hands.

I hadn't expected that. I had been prepared for anything except these words from her, whom I thought I knew so well.

"You say you're 'guilty'! Just like that: 'guilty' . . ."

"For quite some time I've been feeling guilty toward you. . . . Indeed, I'm rather relieved now that it has come out into the open."

"So you've felt it for some time? Why didn't you tell me before?"

"I didn't know how to tell you," she said, and smiled. "I mean, I couldn't make myself. . . ." She smiled again. "Still, I felt it was wrong . . . because it's true that at first I tried to 'charm' you, as you put it, just for that purpose, but very soon I became sick of this hypocrisy. Please believe me," she added bitterly; "in fact, I was sick and tired of the whole business."

"But why didn't you ask me straight out? You could have said: 'I know that you know about that letter, so why play games?' And I'd have told you everything I knew at once."

"Well, I was rather . . . rather afraid of you. Also, I confess, I didn't trust you too much either. And, anyway, if I haven't been very straightforward with you, neither have you been with me," she added with a quick smile.

"Yes, yes, I've behaved despicably!" I cried. "Alas, you can't even imagine the depth of the abyss of degradation into which I've fallen!"

"Come now—'abyss of degradation'! I recognize your style," she said with a quiet smile. "That letter," she added seriously, "was the saddest and most thoughtless act of my life. It weighed on me constantly. Because of certain circumstances and certain fears, I'd come to doubt my lovable and generous father. Then I was afraid that this letter might fall into the hands of wicked people, and I had good reasons to fear that," she added with heat, "and that they'd want to take advantage of me by showing it to my father. . . . It might have affected him terribly in his state of health. . . . And it might have robbed me of his love too. . . . Yes, indeed," she said, looking me straight in the eye, having perhaps detected something in my look, "yes, I was also afraid of the consequences for myself: I was afraid that, during his sickness, he might deprive me of his favor. . . . Yes, that worry was also a part of it, but I'm sure I did him an injustice there too; he's so kind and generous that I'm certain he'd have forgiven me. . . . Well, that's all there was to it. As for the way I behaved with you, I see now that there was no need for it. . . ." She looked very embarrassed again. "You've made me feel ashamed of myself."

"There's nothing you need be ashamed of!" I exclaimed.

"But I did count on your . . . your warmth and impulsiveness. . . . I admit it," she said, lowering her eyes.

"Ah, Katerina!" I cried out as though drunk. "What made you admit that to me? What was there to prevent you from getting up and subtly explaining in appropriate phrases, as though telling me that two times two is four, that, although there may have been something that led me to believe . . . in reality there was nothing at all—you know, the way they handle the truth in your high society? On top of everything, I'm stupid and primitive and I'd have believed you at once; indeed, I'd have believed anything you chose to tell me! It would've cost you nothing to do it that way. You're not really afraid of me, are you? So why did you have to humiliate yourself like that before an impudent upstart, a mere adolescent like me?"

"In this, at least, I haven't humiliated myself before you," she said with great dignity, probably misinterpreting my enthusiastic outburst.

"Of course not, on the contrary! That's what I was saying. . . ."

"Ah, it was so horrible, so irresponsible of me!" she exclaimed, raising her hand to her face as if to cover it. "I already felt ashamed of myself yesterday, and that's why I was so ill at ease while you were there. . . . The truth is that, the way things stand now, I had to find out what had happened to that unfortunate letter. Otherwise, I might have forgotten about it altogether, for it wasn't really just for the sake of that letter that I was seeing you," she added unexpectedly, and these last words made my heart tremble. "Of course not," she said, smiling faintly, "and just as you observed so shrewdly a moment ago, we talked much the way two students would talk to each other. Believe me, I've often been very bored in the company of society people, especially since my return from abroad and all the troubles that have beset my family. These days I go out very little, and not just out of laziness. I'm longing to go and live in the country and reread my favorite books that I put aside long ago but have never got around to reading again. I've already told you all that. Remember, you even laughed at me because I read newspapers at the rate of two a day . . ."

"I didn't laugh at you for that. . . ."

"Of course not, because you too were worried about what was going on. . . . Yes, as I said to you long ago, I'm a true Russian and I love this country. Remember how we used to look together for what you referred to as *facts*? And although at times you can be a little peculiar, if I may say so, on those occasions you became quite perspicacious; your remarks were very much to the point and you happened to be interested in just the things that interested me most. You know, whenever you assume the role of 'student,' you become extremely charming and original, while many of your other roles don't suit you well at all!" Again that irresistible subtle smile appeared on her lips. "Remember how sometimes we spent hours on end discussing bare statistics, such as how many schools we have and the prospects of education in our country; then we counted murders and other criminal offenses and tried to compare these figures with actual news items. We wanted to know where all this was leading and what would happen in the future. I found you sincere. This was not the sort of conversation gentlemen have with ladies in our society. Last week, for instance, I tried to ask Prince ***ov what he thought of Bismarck because I was very puzzled by Bismarck's moves and couldn't make out on my own what he was after. So Prince ***ov sat down next to me and started to explain the situation in great detail in an ironic and unbearably condescending tone, the tone a wise statesman might use to answer a silly woman who is prying into affairs that should not concern her. But remember how you and I almost quarreled about that same Bismarck! And then you even told me that you had an 'idea' of your own that went quite beyond Bismarck's!" She laughed. "There have been only two people who talked to me with complete seriousness before: my late husband, who was an extremely intelligent and . . . and extremely high-minded man," she said emphatically, "and after him . . . well, you know very well who . . ."

"Versilov!" I shouted. I'd been listening to every word almost breathlessly.

"Yes, I loved to listen to him, and in the end I became quite . . . much too frank with him, and it was then that he refused to believe me."

"He didn't believe you?"

"Nobody ever did."

"But Versilov. . . . He's different."

"It wasn't just that he didn't believe me," she said, lowering her eyes and smiling strangely, "but he decided that I had all the vices. . . ."

"But you don't have any at all!"

"That's not true—I do have some."

"Versilov didn't love you and that's what prevented him from understanding you!" I exclaimed, my eyes flashing.

Something twitched in her face.

"Forget it—never speak to me of . . . of that man," she said with finality. "And it's getting late." She got up. "So what do you say, do you forgive me?" she asked, looking me straight in the eye.

"*Me* forgive *you*? . . . But I wonder if I may ask you something without making you angry: is it true that you're getting married?"

"It's not decided yet." She sounded rather taken aback now. My question seemed to have embarrassed her.

"Is he a good man? Forgive me, I just want to know that."

"Yes, he is—a very good man. . . ."

"Say no more, don't honor me by answering anything further! For I do realize that such questions from someone like me are absolutely inadmissible. All I wanted to know was whether he was worthy of you. But I'll find out on my own."

"No, please, what do you mean?" she said in a frightened voice.

"All right, all right, I won't, I'll step out of your way. . . . Let me say only that I wish you every happiness with whomever you may choose. Because you yourself have given me so much happiness during this past hour! Your imprint will always remain in my soul. I have acquired a treasure—the realization of your perfection. As long as I suspected you of perfidy and crude flirtatiousness, I was unhappy because I couldn't associate these qualities with you. I have thought about it night and day these past weeks. . . . But now everything has become clear. When I came here, I expected to confront the Jesuitical cunning of a prying viper but found instead an honest, honorable, and enchanting 'student'! I see it makes you laugh. . . . All right, go ahead and laugh. Since you're a saint, you wouldn't laugh at sacred things. . . ."

"Oh, it's only that you use such awfully funny phrases. . . . What do you mean, for instance, by 'prying viper'?" And she again burst out laughing.

"You said something yourself that I found beautiful," I went on enthusiastically. "How could you say to my face that you were reckoning on my 'impulsiveness'? Indeed, you are a saint, even if you admit those calculations of yours because you imagine you're guilty of something or other and want to punish yourself for it. . . . But, in fact, you're guilty of nothing and, even if there were something you could reproach yourself for, it would be something saintly since it comes from you, saint that you are. Still, you didn't have to use that particular word. Such frankness is not even natural; it only reveals your supreme purity and shows your respect for me and your trust in me!" I was aware that my incoherent exclaiming was ridiculous but went on. "Oh, don't blush, please don't! I can't imagine how some people can say that you're a woman swayed by passions! Oh, forgive me, for I see the pained expression on your face, so please forgive this overenthusiastic adolescent for his clumsy way of saying what he feels. But are words and phrases really so important now? Aren't you above anything that can be conveyed by words? Versilov once said that the reason Othello killed Desdemona and then himself was not jealousy but because he had been robbed of his ideal. . . . I understood today how true that is because I have been given back my ideal!"

"You're really praising me too much—I don't deserve all that. By the way, do you remember what I said about your eyes?" she added lightly.

"What? That, instead of eyes, I have a couple of microscopes that make me take every fly for a camel? Well, I don't think it's a camel I'm seeing now, definitely not! . . . Why, are you leaving now?"

She was standing in the middle of the room, holding her muff and her shawl.

"No, I'll wait until you're gone. I'd like to write a note to Tatyana."

"All right, I'm leaving at once. I only want once again to wish you happiness, either alone or with whomever you choose. Let God see to that. As for me, all I need is an ideal!"

"Nice, sweet Arkady, believe me that I feel. . . . You know, my father always says that you're a 'sweet and kind boy.' Yes, I'll always remember what you told me about the poor abandoned little boy you were, living in his dreams among strangers. I can understand only too well what made you into what you are. . . . But for the moment, although we may be like a couple of students," she smiled embarrassedly and, gave me her hand, "we can't go on meeting like before. I'm sure you understand that?"

"Why not?"

"No, we mustn't. Not for a long time. . . . And that's my own fault. I know it won't be possible now. But we'll meet occasionally at my father's. . . ."

I wanted to cry out: "So you're afraid of my excessive ardor, you're not sure of what I might do?" But I realized that she'd suddenly become so embarrassed that these words never crossed my lips.

"Tell me," she stopped me as I was reaching the door, "did you see with your own eyes that letter being torn up? Are you sure? And how do you know that it was the letter I wrote to Andronikov?"

"Kraft told me about it and even showed it to me. . . . Good-by now! When I was with you in your study, I felt shy in your presence, but every time you left the room, I longed to go down on my hands and knees and kiss the spot on the floor where your foot had stood. . . ."

I said that without realizing myself what I was saying. After that I didn't look at her again and rushed out in a great hurry.

I set off for home. There was rapture in me: all sorts of things were flashing through my head; my heart was full to the brim. But when I got close to my mother's house, I suddenly remembered the wicked things Lisa had said about Anna. They were so cruel, so ugly, that a painful feeling came over me. "Why all this harshness? What's the matter with Lisa?" I asked myself as the carriage stopped in front of the house.

I dismissed Matvei and told him to come pick me up at my place at nine o'clock that evening.

Chapter 5

I

I was late for dinner, but they had waited for me and weren't at the table yet. Perhaps because I went there so seldom for dinner, some sort of special hors d'oeuvres were served, sardines and things like that. But to my painful surprise, I found everyone rather tense and worried. Lisa hardly smiled when she saw me, Mother was obviously ill at ease, and although Versilov did give me a smile, it was a rather forced one. I wondered whether they'd been having an unpleasant argument. However, dinner started off quite normally, except for Versilov's slightly pursed nose at the soup with dumplings and the wry face he made when handed the meat and rice pies.

"All I have to do is mention that a particular dish doesn't agree with me, and, lo and behold, I'm given it the very next day," he said with annoyance.

"But I really no longer know what to serve, Andrei. . . . I can't think of anything new you'd like for a change," Mother protested timidly.

"Your mother is just the opposite of the newspapers which proclaim that anything new makes news and is good," Versilov said in a lighter and more cheerful tone, trying to joke away the unpleasantness.

He didn't succeed at all, however, and only added to Mother's distress, for she of course could make nothing of his comparing her with the newspapers and was now looking about her perplexed.

At that moment Mrs. Prutkov walked in, announced that she had already had dinner, and sat down on the sofa next to Mother.

I had still been unable to get in her good graces. Indeed, she pounced on me these days more than ever, at the slightest provocation or even without one. She disapproved in particular of my highly fashionable clothes, and Lisa told me that when Mrs. Prutkov had learned that I had at my beck and call a coachman and horses, she had something like a fit. It had got to the point where I started avoiding her as much as I could. When, two months before, I'd dropped in on her to talk to her about Versilov's noble gesture, I'd found no sympathy whatsoever: she was very displeased that Versilov had given up the whole inheritance instead of just half of it. And she added tartly:

"I bet you're convinced that he renounced the money and challenged Sergei to a duel just to regain Mr. Arkady Dolgoruky's esteem, aren't you?"

And her guess was almost correct: actually, I did feel something of the sort at the time.

And now as soon as she walked in, I knew she couldn't fail to attack me. In fact, I had a feeling that she'd come especially with that purpose in mind. And that's what pushed me to adopt a casual, couldn't-care-less attitude, which I did without great effort because I was still inwardly radiating with joy from what had just happened. Let me note, though, that this casual attitude has never sat well on me, never seemed natural to me, and when I affect it I always end up by disgracing myself. And that's what happened that day. I inevitably said something I shouldn't have. I didn't do it with any evil intent, just out of complete thoughtlessness. Having noticed that Lisa looked very gloomy, I blurted out:

"For the once in I don't know how many weeks that I come here to dinner, it's just my luck to find Lisa in such a gloomy mood!"

"I have a headache," Lisa said.

"Who cares whether she's sick or well," Mrs. Prutkov immediately took advantage of the opening, "since Mr. Arkady Dolgoruky has deigned to come to dinner, the poor girl is duty-bound to sing, dance, and be merry!"

"You're really the bane of my existence, Mrs. Prutkov! I'll never come here again when you're around!"

I banged my fist on the table in annoyance. Mother started; Versilov gave me a strange look. I suddenly burst out laughing, apologized to them, and, turning to Mrs. Prutkov, added with easy familiarity: "All right, ma'am, I take back my statement that you're the bane of my existence."

"No, no, don't take it back," she replied cuttingly, "I feel rather flattered at being the bane of your existence. I'd rather be that than the opposite, I assure you."

"You must learn to put up with small irritations in life, my boy," Versilov said softly and smiled; "without irritations, life isn't even worth living."

"There are times when you sound like a terrible reactionary!" I exclaimed with a nervous laugh.

"I couldn't care less, my boy."

"That's not true either. But why don't you just tell an ass plainly that he's an ass?"

"You're surely not speaking of yourself, are you? But, above all, I cannot nor do I want to judge anyone."

"Why can't you and why don't you want to?"

"I'm too lazy and I find it unpleasant. Once an intelligent woman told me that I have no right to judge others because I *don't know how to suffer* and that, in order to qualify as a judge of others, I must first earn that right through suffering. Sounds a bit grandiloquent, but it may well have some truth in it when applied to me, so I agreed quite readily."

"Could it really be Mrs. Prutkov who told you that?" I cried.

"How did you guess?" Versilov said, looking at me with surprise.

"I knew by looking at Mrs. Prutkov's face, by the way it twitched when you said that."

I'd guessed quite by accident. As I learned later, Mrs. Prutkov had expounded that view to Versilov during a heated discussion the previous day. And, in general, I had stumbled upon these people at a very bad moment: I was vibrating with exuberance and joy while each of them was preoccupied with his own troubles, and very serious ones.

"I don't understand that reasoning—it's too abstract for me," I went on. "You love abstractions, sir, and that's a trait indicating egotism. For only egotists enjoy talking in abstractions."

"Not a bad observation. But why must you be so aggressive?"

"Just a minute, please," I insisted, letting myself go. "What does it actually mean to qualify through suffering to sit in judgment of others? I say that anyone who's honest is entitled to judge."

"Even so, you won't find many qualified judges."

"I could name one to start with."

"Who would that be?"

"He's talking to me now."

Versilov snorted in a peculiar way, leaned toward my ear, and, holding onto my shoulder, whispered: "He has always lied to you."

I still don't understand what he meant, but I realize he was in a state of extreme anxiety at that time (I was later to learn the cause of it). These words, whispered so unexpectedly, in such a serious tone, and with an expression that did not at all suggest he was joking, made me start. I was frightened and looked at him perplexed. But now it was Versilov's turn to laugh hurriedly.

"Well, thank God!" Mother said, for she'd become very frightened when Versilov had whispered in my ear. "I was almost thinking. . . . Don't be angry with us, Arkasha—there are plenty of intelligent people without us in the world, but who will there be to love us if we lose one another?"

"That's precisely what makes love between relatives immoral, Mother—the fact that it isn't deserved. One must deserve love."

"It may take you quite a while still to deserve it, but here we love you even so," she said, and everyone suddenly laughed.

"Well, I don't know whether you fired the gun intentionally, Mother," I said laughingly, "but you certainly brought down the bird!"

"So I see you really fancy there's something in you that makes you worth loving," Mrs. Prutkov pounced on me again. "Not only do people love you for nothing, they even manage to love you despite the revulsion you inspire!"

"You may be wrong there!" I cried gaily. "Could you guess, for instance, who found me quite lovable today?"

"You were being made a fool of when you were told that!" Mrs. Prutkov said with strangely intense malice, as if she'd been waiting for these words to multiply her spite. "You know, you could make a sensitive person, a woman especially, really sick with that filthy mentality of yours. You, with your hair so neatly parted on your head, with your fine linen, with your suit made by a French tailor, underneath, you're really nothing but filth! Who's paying for your clothes, who's feeding you and giving you money to play roulette? Just think of whom you're sponging on so shamelessly?"

My mother reddened violently. I'd never seen an expression of such painful shame on her face before. I was outraged.

"The money I'm spending belongs to me and I don't have to account to anyone for it," I snapped, as the blood rushed to my face too.

"What do you mean it's your money? How is it yours?"

"It's either mine or Mr. Versilov's. I know that he won't refuse me. . . . I've been taking money from Sergei Sokolsky on account of the debt he owes Mr. Versilov. . . ."

"My boy," Versilov said firmly, "not one kopek of that money is mine."

These words descended on me with a dreadful heaviness. They cut my breath. Oh, in the absurd, carefree, irresponsible state of mind I was in at the time, I could have wiggled out of this difficulty by some "noble" gesture, by some high-sounding phrase, or something of that sort, had I not suddenly noticed the angry, accusing look under Lisa's frown. I felt it was unfair, I even detected something sarcastic in it. And it was as if some evil force was egging me on:

"It seems to me, ma'am," I said to her, "that you pay rather frequent visits to Daria, who happens to be staying in Prince Sergei's apartment. And so perhaps you would kindly oblige me by paying him back this three hundred rubles, about which you already nagged me earlier today?"

I took the money out of my pocket and held it out to her.

Well, will I be believed if I say that these nasty words were uttered without any particular motive, without alluding to anything? Besides, how could I have been alluding to something since I knew absolutely nothing at the time. Perhaps I simply wanted to needle her a little, to make her see that she was just a young lady who ought to be minding her own business but if she insisted on prying into other people's affairs, well then she could go and meet that young Petersburg gentleman herself, that prince, that dashing army officer, and run that little errand for me. But, to my utter amazement, my mother suddenly got up and, shaking her finger menacingly in front of my face, shouted at me: "Don't you dare, don't you dare!"

I would never have imagined any such outburst from her. I jumped up from my chair too. It was not fright but a painful sensation in my heart that made me realize I'd done something awful. . . . But Mother quickly covered her face with her hands and rushed out of the room. Lisa followed her without even glancing in my direction. Mrs. Prutkov, who had been staring fixedly at me for the last half minute, suddenly exclaimed in a voice that revealed tremendous surprise:

"Could you really have meant what you said?"

And after that enigmatic outcry, without waiting for my answer, she ran out of the room to join them. Versilov got up, looking cold and almost hostile, went to the corner of the room where he'd left his hat and picked it up.

"I never imagined you could be that stupid, although you certainly must be somewhat simple-minded," he said quietly with a sarcastic edge to his voice. "If they come back, tell them not to wait for me for dessert. I'm going out for a short walk."

So I remained all alone. At first I was rather bewildered; then I became filled with resentment, but in the end I felt that it had been all my fault. I sat by the window and waited. After ten minutes, I too took my hat and went up to the attic where I used to live. I knew I'd find Mother and Lisa there and that Mrs. Prutkov would have left by now. And, indeed, Lisa and

Mother were sitting on my old sofa and talking in whispers. They immediately became silent when they saw me. To my surprise they didn't seem angry with me any longer. Mother even smiled at me.

"I'm sorry, Mother," I muttered.

"All right, all right, never mind," Mother said quickly, "all I want is that you should love each other and not quarrel. Then God will send you happiness."

"I'm sure Arkady never meant to hurt me, Mamma," Lisa said.

"If it hadn't been for that Mrs. Prutkov, nothing would have happened. That woman is a real menace!" I cried with relief.

"See, Mamma, did you hear what he said!" Lisa said, pointing at me.

"Let me say this to the two of you," I told them; "if there's someone who is really horrible in this world, it's me. All the rest of the world is just wonderful!"

"Don't get angry, Arkasha," Mother said, "but it would be so nice if you could really stop. . . ."

"Stop gambling? Is that what you mean, Mother? All right, I'll stop after today. But I'll go there one more time. I must, especially since Mr. Versilov has informed me officially that Sergei doesn't have a single kopek of his money. You can't even begin to imagine how ashamed I feel. . . . I must, however, get an explanation from him. . . . Mother dear, the last time I was here, I said something stupid. . . . I didn't really mean it. . . . I was just showing off . . . because I really believe in Christ. . . ."

A week earlier we'd had some sort of discussion about these things and in the end Mother had felt very sad and worried about me. Now, hearing what I said, she smiled at me the way one smiles at a baby:

"Christ," she said, "will forgive everything, Arkasha. He will forgive your blasphemy and will forgive even worse. Christ is our Father, He will never fail us, and His light will reach us even in the blackest night. . . ."

I said good-by to them and left. I was hoping to see Versilov later that evening: I had to talk to him about things I couldn't bring up during dinner. I suspected that he might be waiting for me at my place. I walked home on foot. The temperature had dropped now and, after a warm day, it was beginning to freeze. It was pleasant to walk.

II

I lived near the Voznesensky Bridge in a huge block of flats. My apartment gave onto an inner courtyard. I was almost at the gate leading to that yard when I stumbled on Versilov.

"As usual when I go out for a stroll, I walked all the way to your house. In fact, I even walked up to your apartment, for I thought I'd wait for you in the company of your landlord. But I got bored in the end. People seem to be quarreling all the time up there, and today his wife even retired to her room in tears. When I saw that, I left."

Somehow I felt irritated.

"I begin to think that this is the only place you ever go and that, except for myself and my landlord, you have no one to talk to in the whole of Petersburg."

"What does it matter one way or the other, my boy?"

"And where are you off to now?"

"I don't feel like going back to your place. . . . If you want, though, come for a walk with me, it's such a lovely evening."

"If, instead of all your abstract philosophizing, you talked to me like a human being; if, for instance, you'd said something to me about my idiotic gambling, I wouldn't have allowed myself to sink into it like that," I suddenly reproached him.

"So you regret it now? That's good," he said, articulating his words with deliberation. "Well, I've always thought that gambling was not the main thing with you, but just a temporary deviation. . . . And you're right, my dear boy, gambling is a stupid and piggish occupation. Besides, there's always the risk of losing."

"What's more, losing money that doesn't even belong to me."

"And you've lost money that wasn't yours?"

"I've lost your money. I used to take money from Sergei on your account. Oh, I realize how stupid it was on my part to consider your money as my own . . . but I wanted so much to win back what I'd lost."

"Well, I must warn you once more, my dear boy, that Sergei has no money that belongs to me. I'm well aware that that young gentleman is in dire straits himself and I don't consider that he owes me anything, his promises notwithstanding."

"In that case my position is twice as bad, in fact, it's ridiculous! But what reason could there have been for him to give me money and for me to accept it from him?"

"Well, that's really your problem. . . . But tell me, you

feel now that there wasn't any reason for you to accept money from him, is that right?"

"Except for the fact that we were good friends. . . ."

"Nothing except that? There wasn't anything else that made you feel you were entitled to accept money from him? No particular considerations whatsoever?"

"What considerations could there be? I don't understand."

"I'm glad you don't. I must say, I was sure you didn't. *Brisons-la, mon cher.* Just try somehow not to gamble."

"I wish you'd told me before! But even now, you aren't saying clearly what's what—you seem to be hinting at something, implying something. . . ."

"If I'd told you before, we'd have quarreled and you wouldn't have let me come see you in the evenings. And I want you to know, my dear boy, that all warnings and salutary advice are nothing but gratuitous impositions upon another man's conscience. I've meddled enough with other people's consciences and wound up with nothing but taunts and rebuffs. Of course, I don't give a damn about taunts and rebuffs, but what's important is that such interfering never gets you anywhere: no one will listen to you, however hard you try, and they'll only end by disliking you."

"I'm glad at least that you've decided to talk to me about something other than abstractions. Well, there's something else I've been wanting to ask you for a long time, but somehow you made it impossible for me to bring it up. I'm glad we're out in the street now. Do you remember that evening two months ago, my last evening in your house, when you sat in my garret, my 'coffin,' and I kept asking you about Mother and Makar Dolgoruky? Tell me, do you remember the rather rude way I questioned you? How could you allow a stupid young pup to talk so disrespectfully about his mother? But you never even made a gesture to stop me; indeed, you sort of 'opened yourself up' and thus encouraged me to continue."

"My dear boy, I'm only too pleased to hear that you . . . that you feel that way. Yes, I do remember it very well indeed, and I was waiting to see whether you'd turn red, and if I encouraged you to go on, it was just to bring you to the limit. . . ."

"And, as a result, you only deceived me more, only muddied up further the stream coming from my heart. Yes, I'm nothing but a wretched adolescent who every minute keeps losing the sense of what's good and what's bad. If you'd only hinted to me then what the right course was, I'd have rushed to follow it. But, instead, you just made me angry."

"*Cher enfant,* I always felt that one way or another we'd get to understand each other some day. You did get 'red in the face' in the end, and without my assistance or advice. I assure you it was much better for you that way. I have in fact noticed that you've learned a lot lately. But could it really be due to your friendship with that princeling?"

"Stop praising me—I don't like being praised. Don't make me suspect you of praising me with a Jesuitic purpose in mind, scorning the truth just to keep my affection. Let me tell you, then, that what I've done lately has also included visiting ladies. For instance, I've been well received by Anna Versilov."

"She told me that herself, my dear boy. She's a very nice and intelligent young lady. *Mais brisons-la, mon cher.* I somehow feel rather sick and tired of everything today. I suppose it's due to a general state of depression. Or perhaps I should really put it down to hemorrhoids. What happened at home? Nothing? You all made up, no doubt, and it ended in embraces, didn't it? *Cela va sans dire.* It depresses me to go back to them sometimes, even if I haven't enjoyed being out at all. In fact, there are times when I make a deliberate detour in the rain just to put off the moment of return to the familial hearth. . . . What a bore, oh my God, what a bore!"

"Mother . . ."

"Your mother is the most perfect and the most delightful creature. . . . In fact, I'm sure I'm not worthy of her or Lisa. By the way, what was the matter with them today? They've been rather peculiar lately. . . . You know, I always try to ignore all that, but there's something serious brewing today. . . . Did you notice anything?"

"I know nothing and I certainly wouldn't have noticed anything out of the ordinary if it hadn't been for that horrible Prutkov woman, who can't prevent herself from snapping at me. But you're right, there's something wrong there. Today I met Lisa at Anna's and, even there, she struck me as rather peculiar. She quite surprised me. . . . But you knew that Anna was seeing her, didn't you?"

"I knew that, my boy. But tell me, when did you go to see Anna today? What time was it? I have good reason to ask."

"I was there between two and three. And imagine, as I was leaving, who should arrive but Sergei. . . ."

And I told him about that visit in great detail. He listened in silence, never commenting when I mentioned the rumor about Sergei marrying Anna, and when I repeated my enthusiastic praise of Anna's qualities, he just muttered something to the effect that she was a "nice girl."

Then, to my own surprise, as though someone were pulling the words out of me, I suddenly announced:

"You know, I surprised Anna a great deal today when I told her the latest bit of gossip about the possibility of Katerina Akhmakov marrying Baron Björing. . . ."

"Was she really surprised? But it was Anna herself who told me that rumor this morning, well before noon, which was certainly before you surprised her with it."

"What!" I was dumbfounded. "From whom could she possibly have heard it? . . . But why, after all, why shouldn't she have heard about it from some other source? . . . But then why did she react as if it were a complete surprise to her? Well, never mind . . . long live tolerance. We must be tolerant of people, mustn't we? I, for instance, I'd have blurted out everything right away, but she, she prefers to close up what she knows as if in a snuff box. So let her—that doesn't prevent her from being a most enchanting young lady of the finest character!"

"Oh, no doubt of it—everybody is fine in his own way. And what's most remarkable is that all these fine characters can act in quite unexpected ways at times. Now, just imagine this: my daughter Anna all of a sudden fires this question at me: 'Are you,' she asks me, 'in love with Katerina Akhmakov or aren't you?' "

"What a wild, unheard-of question!" I exclaimed, completely stunned again. Everything began spinning before my eyes. I'd never dared bring up that subject with him and now he himself . . .

"Did she explain why she was asking?"

"She didn't explain anything, my boy; she asked and then closed up her little snuff box even tighter than before. I want you to know that it never even occurred to me that we could talk about things like that, and she herself . . . But you told me you knew her well, so I'm sure you can imagine for yourself how incongruous that question was coming from her. I wondered if you didn't know something about it?"

"I'm just as surprised as you are. Maybe it was just curiosity, maybe she meant it as a sort of joke. . . ."

"Not in the least—she was as serious as she could be, and it sounded more like an interrogation than a casual question. It was as if she had to know for a very important and urgent reason. Are you planning to see her soon? If so, wouldn't you try to find out whether there's something behind it? I'd even ask you if I could to . . ."

"But how could she! How could she even imagine that you're in love with Mrs. Akhmakov! I'm sorry, I just can't get over it! I've never allowed myself to talk to you about such things."

"And that has been extremely sensible on your part, my boy."

"Your past relations and quarrels with her are, of course, quite an unsuitable subject for us to discuss, and I'm sure it would have been just plain stupid for me to try and bring it up. . . . But, lately, several times I've said to myself, that, if indeed you once loved that woman, even if only for one second, you couldn't possibly have been so terribly mistaken about her as you were in fact! As to the results of that mistake, I'm very well aware of them: I know of your mutual hostility and aversion, I heard of it, in fact only too much of it for my liking, while I was still in Moscow. But what is striking about your relations is your obvious grim mutual dislike. So how could Anna suddenly ask you whether you loved that woman? How could she be so poorly informed? There's something absurd in her question. She must have been joking, I assure you, she was joking!"

"But I notice now, my very dear boy, that you yourself are talking about it with rather unusual heat." There was something nervous, something strangely intimate, in his voice that I'd very seldom heard, and his words reached deep into my heart. "You just told me that you've been 'visiting ladies.' Of course, I feel rather awkward asking you questions on that subject, but . . . but, by any chance, would that particular lady be on the list of your recent lady friends?"

"That woman . . ." My voice suddenly started trembling. "Listen, sir, that woman is the 'living life,' as I believe you put it today at Sergei Sokolsky's. You said that 'living life' is something simple and spontaneous, something that stares us straight in the face, and, because of its directness and obviousness, we cannot believe ourselves that it is precisely what we've been looking for all our lives. . . . And it was that refusal to believe that prevented you from recognizing the ideal of womanhood and led you to ascribe to her every conceivable vice! That's what happened to you!"

The reader can guess the state of exaltation I was in.

" 'Every conceivable vice'! Oh, I've heard that phrase before," Versilov said. "And if this phrase has reached you now, perhaps there's something I ought to congratulate you on? If it indicates such an intimacy between you two, perhaps I should also praise you for a discretion and modesty that not too many young men of your age are capable of. . . ."

Charming, gay laughter sparkled in his voice. Even if there may have been a hint of challenge in it, his tone was warm and his expression radiant, at least as much as I could see of it in the darkness. He was vibrating with life. I could not help beaming back at him.

"Oh, no, no, it has nothing to do with discretion—there's no secret!" I cried out, turning deep red and holding onto his hand, which I had seized and forgotten to let go. "No, no, nothing of the sort. . . . Certainly there's nothing to congratulate me about, and nothing of the sort will ever happen. . . ." I felt as if I were floating breathlessly through the air. I enjoyed the flight, I loved it. "You know. . . . Well, I'll let myself go, this one time, my dear, dear Papa—I hope you won't object to my calling you that just this once. It's impossible for a son to talk to his father, or to anybody else, about his relations with a woman, even if they are of the purest kind. Indeed, the purer they are, the more forbidden is the subject. It's a shocking thing to do—it's unspeakably crude. . . . In short, confidences are ruled out! But since there's nothing, absolutely nothing, then, of course, one should be allowed to talk, right?"

"Do as your heart tells you."

"I must ask you a very, very indiscreet question first: of course, during your life you must have known many women, you must have had affairs? I'm not asking anything specific, just in general. . . ." My face was on fire; I was blabbering in my enthusiasm.

"I suppose I have a few sins of that sort on my conscience."

"In that case, you could perhaps clear something up for me, since you have so much more experience than I. Now, suppose a lady who is just saying good-by to you suddenly says: 'I'll be at such and such a place tomorrow at three.' She says that without looking at you and it sounds as if the words had slipped out of her mouth quite unintentionally. . . . Well, let's assume she says she's going to be at Mrs. Prutkov's . . ."

I took off and was floating through the air again. My heart, which had been pounding wildly, suddenly skipped a beat. I couldn't even go on talking. He was listening with frightening concentration.

"And so the following day at three o'clock I'm standing in front of Mrs. Prutkov's door, reasoning as follows: if it's the cook who opens it—I suppose you know her cook, don't you?— I'll ask her: 'Is Madam in?' and if the cook says no, I'll know that Mrs. Prutkov is out and that a certain lady is sitting in her room and waiting. But what conclusions should I draw from that? Tell me if you . . . I mean if you . . ."

"Simply that you had a date with that lady. But obviously it did happen! And it happened today, didn't it?"

"No, no, nothing of the sort, nothing, nothing! It happened, but it was something completely different. It was an appointment, but not of that kind at all. I want to make that clear right from the beginning because I don't wish to be an indiscreet pig, but . . ."

"My dear friend, this is getting so interesting that I suggest . . ."

Suddenly a tall figure barred our way and announced:

"Gentlemen, I used to hand out ten- and twenty-five-ruble bills to anyone who asked me! But now I, a former officer, beg you to give me just ten kopeks for a drink!"

It was quite possible that he was a former army officer. The most curious thing was that the man was rather well dressed, at any rate much too well dressed for a beggar, and yet his hand was stretched out toward us, palm up.

III

I mention that insignificant incident with the wretched former officer intentionally, for in order to understand Versilov thoroughly one must know the minutest details of the circumstances at that moment, a moment that was to prove crucial for him, although I had no idea of it at the time.

"If you don't leave us alone at once, I'll call the police," Versilov said, suddenly planting himself in front of the man. His voice seemed to me unnecessarily loud and harsh. I never would have expected that such an insignificant incident could have made that philosopher so angry. Besides, he was only further delaying the resumption of our conversation that had just begun really to interest him, as he himself had admitted.

"Is it possible that you don't even have a five-kopek piece to spare?" the former officer shouted rudely, waving his hands. "No bastard seems to have a copper these days! Ah, the damned rabble! The stinkers! They go around dressed in beaver and kick up a fuss about five kopeks!"

"Constable!" Versilov called out loudly, although there was no need for him to shout as the policeman on the corner had already heard what was going on.

"I want you to be a witness to this insult. I ask you to come with us to the police station."

"Ha! I don't care—there's nothing you can prove against me. If you do prove anything, it'll be that you don't have much brains!"

"Take note of what he says, Constable, and please escort us to the police station," Versilov said in an imperious tone.

"Do you really want to drag him to the police station? Leave him alone, the hell with him," I whispered to Versilov.

"I certainly intend to go through with it, my boy. Such disorderly behavior in our streets gets unbearable in its ugliness. If every citizen did his duty, we'd all be better off. I know that *c'est comique mais c'est ce que nous ferons.*"

For a hundred yards or so, the man tried to swagger, arguing with heat that the law shouldn't be allowed to drag a man off to the police station because of a five-kopek piece, and so on and so forth. But then he started whispering into the policeman's ear. The policeman, apparently a reasonable man with a distaste for street incidents caused by citizens' irritability, seemed to be on his side, at least to some extent. In answer to the fellow's whispers, he mumbled something to the effect that it was "too late now," that "it had gone too far," "unless perhaps" he apologized and "the gentleman was willing to forget it, then, of course, perhaps it would be possible . . ."

"But, listen to me, please, sir, where are we going, after all? What are we going to prove and what's the point of it all?" the former gentleman cried out. "If an unfortunate man acknowledges his misfortunes and is willing to apologize. . . . If, finally, you feel like humiliating him. . . . Ah, hell, after all we're in the street, not in a drawing room, and I'm sure that my apology should be good enough for the street. . . ."

Versilov suddenly stopped and burst out laughing so that I thought for a moment he'd just been having a little fun. But that was not so.

"I fully accept your apology, Mr. Former Officer, and I'm sure that you're a man endowed with unquestionable abilities. I advise you, in fact, to extend your range of operations to the drawing room and it will soon become quite effective there too. In the meantime here are two twenty-kopek pieces that you can use for a few drinks and a bite to eat. Please forgive me for having bothered you, Constable. I would have compensated you too for your trouble, but you are too public-spirited for that, I'm sure. . . . My dear boy," he said, turning to me, "I know a café around here, a horrible place really, but we could get some tea and I suggest we go there now."

I repeat, I'd never seen him in such a tense state, although his face was all brightness and gaiety. Still, his fingers were trembling as he tried to fish the two twenty-kopek coins out of his purse to give the man. Indeed, they trembled so much that in the end he handed me his purse to extract the coins and give them to the fellow. I'll never forget that.

He took me to a small café on the bank of the canal. There were only a few customers, and a loud barrel-organ that badly needed tuning was playing something. It smelled of none-too-clean napkins. We installed ourselves in a corner.

"Do you know, sometimes out of boredom, out of that horrible kind of boredom that seems to drain my soul, I like to come to this awful sort of dump. These surroundings, the out-of-tune strains of 'Lucia,' the waiters in their impossible Russian shirts, the thick smoke of cheap tobacco, the shouting from the billiard room—all this is so vulgar and dreary that it verges on the fantastic. . . . Well, so what were you going to tell me, my dear boy, when this son of Mars interrupted us just as it seemed to be getting really interesting. . . . Ah, here they're bringing us tea now! I like having tea here. . . . Can you imagine, I heard your landlord trying to convince the pockmarked lodger that during the last century the British Parliament appointed a special committee of jurists to review the entire trial of Jesus by Pilate and the High Priest. The purpose was to find out how the trial would have come out if contemporary laws had been applied and if modern court procedures, with defense counsels, prosecutors, et al., had been followed. Well, they concluded, of course, that the jury would have come up with the verdict of guilty as charged. A really wonderful story! But then that stupid pockmarked lodger began to argue, lost his temper, quarreled with the landlord, and announced that he was moving out of the apartment. The landlady began to weep because she was sad at losing the income. . . . *Mais passons.* . . . Do you know that in some cafés like this one you sometimes find a nightingale? And have you heard the Moscow story that sounds rather like one of your landlord's tales? A nightingale was singing in a Moscow café when a merchant walked in. 'I don't care how expensive it is! How much does this bird cost?' 'A hundred rubles.' 'All right, roast it, and serve it to me.' They roasted the nightingale and brought it to the merchant. 'All right, cut me twenty kopeks worth!' I told that story to your landlord, but he didn't believe it and was even quite indignant."

He talked a lot like that and the bits I have mentioned are just odd samples to give a general idea of the sort of thing he said. And as soon as I opened my mouth to go on with my story, he interrupted me to tell me some peculiar and unrelated non-sense. He spoke excitedly, gaily, laughing at God knows what; he even chuckled, which is something I'd never heard him do before. He gulped down one glass of tea and poured himself another. He was like a man who has just received a long-awaited letter that holds considerable promise for him and who keeps that letter on the table in front of him and deliberately delays opening it—picking it up, turning it between his fingers, examining the envelope and the seal, leaving the room for a moment to see to something or other, in short, putting off the great moment, knowing that it will not escape him, prolonging it to enjoy it all the more.

Of course I told him everything from beginning to end. I talked nonstop for a whole hour, and no wonder since I'd been longing to talk about it all day. I started from the first time I'd met her at her father's, the old Prince Sokolsky, when she'd just arrived in Moscow. Then I told him how gradually things had developed. I didn't leave out anything; I couldn't have, for he himself led me on by his questions to tell him everything; he even guessed much and at times actually prompted me. Now and then I had a strange feeling that there was something uncanny about him: it was as though he'd been eavesdropping behind the door wherever I'd been during the past two months: he knew instinctively everything I felt and thought. I derived boundless delight from confessing to him because I found in him such intimate gentleness combined with a profound psychological understanding and a mysterious gift for knowing what I was going to say before I uttered the first word. He could listen with the tender attention of a woman. Above all, he succeeded in putting me so much at ease that nothing embarrassed me any more. Now and then he stopped me to make me repeat some detail, saying: 'Leave nothing out, I want every tiniest detail; the tinier it is, the more important it may turn out to be." He interrupted me several times to tell me words to that effect.

Oh, of course, at first I began speaking of her in a casual tone, but soon enough I dropped the pose. I reached the point where I told him in all candor that I had impulses to throw myself on the ground and kiss the spot where her foot had rested. The greatest and most glorious thing was his absolute understanding of her being so frightfully worried about the document without that preventing her from being the pure and irreproachable woman she had revealed herself to be earlier that day. He understood very well what she meant by saying that we talked to each other like "fellow students."

As my story was drawing to an end, however, I noticed that under his kindly smile was now an impatient twitch and a vague air of absent-mindedness and impatience. When I came to the actual whereabouts of the "document," I hesitated whether to tell him the whole truth or not, and finally, despite my state of exaltation, I didn't tell him. I'm recording this fact here so that I may remember it as long as I live. I gave him the same version I'd given her—I mean about Kraft destroying the letter. His eyes glowed then. A strange frown appeared on his brow, a very grim and ominous frown.

"Are you sure, my boy, that you clearly remember seeing Kraft burn the letter over a candle? You're sure you aren't mistaken?"

"I'm sure," I repeated.

"The thing is that that piece of paper is most important to her, so that if you had it in your possession, you could have this very day . . ." He never finished telling me what I could have that very day; instead, he added: "But are you sure you don't have it on you now?"

I shuddered inwardly, but outwardly nothing showed. I didn't give myself away, didn't bat an eye; I still refused to believe his question.

"What do you mean by asking whether I have it on me *now* since I told you that Kraft burned it?"

"Really?"

His glowing eyes were fixed on mine. I'll never forget that heavy fixed stare and yet he was smiling. But there was no trace left now of the almost feminine gentleness with which he had looked at me earlier. The atmosphere between us became tense and ill defined, and he appeared more and more absent-minded. If he had maintained his self-control to the end, he would never have insisted about the letter, but since he did insist he must have reached a state of exasperation. But all this is hindsight on my part, for at the time I did not detect at once the change that had taken place in him: I still had the sensation of floating through the air and there was still that same music playing in my heart. But finally I came to the end of my story and looked at him.

"Very peculiar . . ." he commented after I'd told him everything I could think of. "It really seems very strange, my boy. You say that you were there between three and four and that Mrs. Prutkov was out, right?"

"To be exact, I was there from three to four-thirty."

"Now, listen to this: I dropped in on Tatyana at half-past four on the dot, and she met me in the kitchen. You know, I almost always take the service entrance when I go to see her—that gets me directly from the stairs into her kitchen."

"And . . . and she was in the kitchen!" I cried, reeling under the impact.

"And she told me she was sorry she couldn't ask me in. Actually I stayed no more than a couple of minutes—I'd only dropped in to ask her to come and have dinner with us."

"Perhaps she'd just returned home from somewhere?"

"I don't know. . . . But no, she couldn't have: she was wearing her old loose dressing gown. And at exactly half-past four."

"But didn't she tell you that I was there?"

"No. If she had, I wouldn't have asked you about it now."

"Listen, it's very important . . ."

"I suppose it is . . . depending on the point of view. Why, you've turned pale, my friend! But, actually, why is it all that important?"

"She made a fool of me and treated me like a little boy!"

"Perhaps she was simply apprehensive of your excessive ardor, as she told you, and so felt safer with Tatyana there."

"My God, what a dirty trick! Do you realize that she made me reveal everything to her within earshot of another person, of Mrs. Prutkov! So Mrs. Prutkov must've heard every word I said! It's too horrible even to imagine . . . !"

"*C'est selon, mon cher*, it all depends. . . . Besides, didn't you tell me that you had a broad-minded attitude toward women and didn't you even exclaim 'Long live tolerance!'?"

"If I were Othello and you were Iago, you couldn't have. . . . But, actually, it all makes me laugh! How can I be Othello since there's never been anything between us. . . . So how can I help finding the whole incident very funny? All right, but I'm still convinced she's infinitely above me, and she remains my ideal. If she arranged it all as a joke at my expense, I forgive her, for why shouldn't she have fun at the expense of a wretched little adolescent? Besides, I never tried to pass myself off for someone better than I was, and she accepted me as what she called a 'fellow student,' and as such I believe I still remain in her heart and her memory and perhaps always shall. . . . But we've talked of this enough! Only tell me now, should I go over to her place and ask her to tell me the whole truth?"

I was assuring him that I found it funny and wanted to laugh, but in reality there were tears in my eyes.

"Why not? You can if you feel like it."

"Now I feel all dirty inside having told you all that. Please don't be angry with me for saying so, but, as I told you, one should never talk about a woman to a third person—no *confidant* is ever able to understand, and a self-respecting man must do without intimate confidences. Now I have lost my self-respect. Good-by then, I'll never forgive myself. . . ."

"Come, come, my dear boy, you're rather overdoing it, aren't you? Why, you just told me yourself that there was nothing between you."

We left the café and stood facing the canal. We said good-by when he suddenly said to me with an unfamiliar tremor in his voice:

"Will you ever kiss me warmly, as a child, a son, kisses his father?"

I kissed him enthusiastically.

"Dear boy . . . may you always remain as pure of heart as you are now."

I'd never kissed him before. And, of course, I could never have imagined that he'd ask me to kiss him.

Chapter 6

I

"Of course I'll go there!" I decided as I rushed home. "I'll go there right away. Probably I'll find her alone, but if there's someone with her, I'll ask her to come out. She'll receive me, all right, she'll be quite surprised, but she'll see me. And if she refuses to see me, I'll insist and say that it's very urgent. Then she'll think it has something to do with the letter and ask me in. And I'll find out about the role played by Tatyana Prutkov. And then? And then what do I care? If I'm wrong, I'll make it up to her, and if I'm right and she's wrong, then it's the end of everything. So what is there to lose? Nothing! So I'm going, I'm going!"

But I didn't go and I shall always remember with pride that I did *not!* No one will ever know it and the knowledge will die with me, but it's enough for me that I know it and that I was capable of such noble resolution under those painful circumstances.

"This is a temptation, but I'll ignore it," I finally made up my mind. "I was threatened with factual evidence, but I refused to believe and I never lost faith in her purity! And what would be the point of going there and asking her? How could I demand of her that she have as much faith in my 'purity' as I have in hers and that she be certain that I can overcome my 'ardor' and feel she doesn't need the extra insurance of Tatyana Prutkov's physical presence? I haven't yet deserved that much trust on her part. So let her not know yet that I do deserve her trust, that I do not yield to temptations, that I never believed the wicked things said about her! As long as I know it myself, it will give me some self-respect. . . . Yes, yes, but still she allowed me to open my heart within Tatyana's earshot; she allowed that woman to listen because she must have realized that Tatyana wouldn't miss the opportunity to eavesdrop, she knew that Tatyana would laugh at me . . . and that's just terrible, terrible! But . . . but perhaps she couldn't avoid it? Perhaps she had no control over the circumstances and couldn't change them? So how can I blame her? Besides, didn't I lie to her about Kraft? I deceived her because I felt I couldn't avoid it and lied to her in all innocence. Ah, my God!" I suddenly cried out loud, feeling the blood rush to my face. "What have I just done myself? Wasn't that as bad as letting Tatyana eavesdrop on us? Why, didn't I just repeat everything to Versilov? . . . No, not quite, there's a difference. It was all confined to the document—I actually told Versilov only about what concerned that document. Besides, there was nothing else I could tell him, there couldn't possibly be! Wasn't I emphatic from the start in telling him that there was nothing between her and me and couldn't be? And he's a man of great understanding. He has, nevertheless, a deep hatred for her to this day. Something frightfully dramatic must have happened between the two of them! What could possibly have caused it? I'm sure it was all a matter of pride. *Versilov is incapable of any feeling except boundless pride.*"

Yes, that last thought sprang up in my mind by itself, without my noticing it almost. So this was the sequence of thoughts that passed through my head since I was completely sincere with myself. I didn't deceive myself, didn't try to make things different from what they were, and if there was something I failed to take in at that moment, it was simply from lack of brains and not from hypocritical self-deception.

I arrived home in a highly excited and—I don't know why —exuberantly gay, albeit very confused, state. But I was afraid to analyze it and tried hard to distract myself and think of something else. So I went to my landlady's room. It turned out that she really had had a frightful row with her husband. She was in an advanced state of consumption and, like all consumptives, had quite an erratic temper, although otherwise she'd probably have been a good-natured woman. I immediately started reconciling them. I went to the other lodger, an ill-mannered, pockmarked fool named Chervyakov, who was employed in a bank and whom I greatly disliked, although we got along fine because I was despicable enough to join him in taunting our landlord. I easily persuaded him not to move out as he had threatened, for I'm sure he would never have made up his mind to move out anyway. So in the end I succeeded in calming the landlady down completely and I even straightened the pillow under her head. "My husband could never have handled everything the way you did," was her final irritated comment.

Then I went to the kitchen and prepared two tremendous mustard plasters for her. My poor landlord was watching me with obvious envy but I didn't allow him to help and was rewarded by his tears of gratitude.

But then, I remember, I became tired of it all as if it had suddenly occurred to me that I wasn't looking after the poor invalid out of sheer kindness but for some quite different reason.

Actually I was nervously waiting for Matvei. I had decided to try my luck at cards once more that evening. Whether I was to be lucky or not, I felt a powerful need to gamble: I couldn't bear the thought of not going. Without that, I couldn't have resisted and would have rushed off to *her*. Matvei was supposed to come any moment now. But, instead, the door opened and in came an unexpected visitor—Daria, the mother of the girl who had hanged herself. I was very surprised and couldn't help screwing up my nose in disappointment. That lady knew where I lived because she'd come to see me once before to give me a message from my mother. I invited her to sit down and stared at her questioningly. But she remained silent, looking straight back at me with a meek smile.

"Have you come on Lisa's behalf?" I finally asked her.

"No . . . it's nothing special."

I told her I was just about to go out, to which she replied again that she'd come for "no special reason" and that she'd leave right away. Somehow I suddenly felt terribly sorry for her. After her tragedy, she'd received a great deal of sympathy from all of us, especially from my mother and Tatyana Prutkov; however, once she'd been installed in Mrs. Stolbeyev's apartment, everybody had begun to neglect her, except perhaps Lisa, who often went to visit her. The reason for this neglect was her own special faculty for effacing herself and keeping aloof, her meek smile and humility notwithstanding. Personally I disliked that meek smile of hers and the fact that she always seemed to contrive the expression on her face; once I even thought reproachfully that her grief for her dearest Olga hadn't lasted very long. But this time I somehow felt an acute pity for her.

And, lo and behold, all of a sudden, without uttering a word, she rushed over to me with lowered eyes and, throwing her arms impulsively around my waist, hid her face in my lap. Then she seized my hand, and with horror I expected her to kiss it, but instead she pressed it to her eyes and I felt hot tears wet my fingers. She was shaking all over with sobs but in complete silence. My heart shivered responsively, although at the same time I felt a sort of irritation. But she was so completely trusting in her embrace and it obviously never occurred to her that I might become annoyed, although a few seconds earlier she'd been smiling so ingratiatingly at me. I started to try to calm her.

"Dear me, dear me, I don't know what to do with myself. . . . As soon as it gets dark, I can't stand it any longer. I feel drawn into the streets, into the blackness. And it's my fancies that draw me there. Somehow I get the feeling that if I go out into the streets, I'll meet her. And so I walk and I imagine I see her . . . that is, I see some other person and start following her and saying to myself 'It must be her, my Olga!' And I think and think . . . I've become almost crazy now: I go out and butt into people, and some get angry, for they think I'm drunk. I've been trying to keep it all to myself and I no longer see people I know. . . . Anyway, seeing them only makes it worse. . . . But now, as I was walking by, I said to myself: 'I'll try to drop in on him—he's the kindest of the lot and he was there when it happened.' So please forgive me, a useless old woman. . . . I'm leaving now anyway."

She suddenly got up in a hurry.

At that moment Matvei arrived. I made her get into the carriage with me and dropped her off at Mrs. Stolbeycv's house, which was on my way.

II

Lately I'd started going to Zershikov's gambling saloon. Previously I'd been going to three gambling houses always in Sergei's company because it was he who had introduced me to those places. In one of the houses they usually played faro and the stakes were rather high. I didn't like it there, as I realized you needed a lot of money to back yourself up and, besides, there were too many arrogant members of what is called *la jeunesse dorée.* But that was precisely what Sergei liked: he liked gambling too, but he also liked to mingle with those swaggering snobs. I'd noticed that, although we'd arrive together, he'd always manage to slip away from me during the evening and never thought of introducing me to any of the people in his set. And he may have had a point, because I looked out of place there, like some sort of savage, sometimes even attracting people's attention. At the gaming table I did occasionally exchange a few words with those around me, but once, when I tried to say hello the next day to a fellow with whom I had not only exchanged a few words but even joked—indeed, I'd even guessed two cards for him—he acted as though he'd never seen me before or, even worse, he stared into my face with feigned amazement and passed by grinning. And so I soon gave up that house and started frequenting a certain dump, which I cannot describe in any other way. It was a sordid little place with a roulette run by a kept woman who, however, never showed up in the gaming rooms. There everything was extremely free and easy, although there was also a sprinkling of army officers and rich merchants among the customers. Everything took place in an atmosphere of squalor and dirt, which, indeed, must have held an attraction for some people. Besides, in that establishment, I'd often been lucky. But I dropped that place too after a revolting incident that occurred in the middle of a game and ended in a fight between two customers. And it was after that that I started going to Zershikov's, where again I had first been introduced by Sergei. Zershikov was a retired army captain and the tone of his establishment was quite tolerable—militarily curt, businesslike, with a fastidious observance of formalities. There were no inveterate practical jokers there or extravagant merry-makers. Also the stakes were often very high. Both faro and roulette were played. I'd been there only twice before, and already the owner seemed to recognize me. But otherwise I didn't know anyone there. Unfortunately, Sergei didn't turn up until midnight when he appeared in the company of Darzan. They had been until then in the house frequented by "the gilded youth" that I'd stopped patronizing. So all evening I'd felt like a stranger in the midst of an unknown crowd.

If someone should read what I've written thus far of my adventures, he certainly wouldn't have to be told that I'm not well fitted for social life of any kind. Above all, I don't know how to behave in company. Whenever I enter a place where many peoole are assembled, the eyes directed at me give me the sensation of so many electric shocks. It makes me shrivel—I mean it literally, in the physical sense. And it happens to me even if I enter a theater, to say nothing of a private house. In all those gambling houses and dens, I'd been quite unable to acquire poise: either I'd sit still and reproach myself for excessive meekness and mildness or I'd leap up and do something downright rude. At the same time, I realized that people who were unquestionably my inferiors knew how to behave with amazing dignity, and that drove me into a fury and made me lose my self-control even more. So I can truly say that not only now but even then all this crowd and, indeed, the very prospect of winning became, in the end, both repulsive and painful. Yes, actually painful. Of course, I did derive extreme pleasure from gambling, but that pleasure had to pass through much pain before it reached me because the whole process—I mean the gambling itself, all those people, and above all myself—seemed horribly disgusting to me.

"As soon as I win, I'll never do it again—to hell with it!" I would repeat to myself at dawn every time as I was slipping into sleep at home after a night of gambling. And, again, how can I account for my gambling mania since I certainly was not crazy about money? Of course, I'm not going to reel off here the stupid string of clichés so often given as explanations of why people gamble—not for the sake of money but rather for the strong sensations, the thrill of risk, excitement, etc. No, I needed money quite desperately at that time and I decided to try to get it that way, as a sort of experiment. In this I was following the "idea" that dominated me: Since I had already concluded that one can unfailingly become a millionaire provided one has an appropriately strong character, since I had already tested my strength of character, why shouldn't I also test it through gambling? I cannot believe that gambling requires more character than *my idea!* And that was the reasoning I kept repeating to myself. To this day I firmly believe that in gambling complete calm and self-control, which enable one to preserve subtle thinking and careful calculation, will always overcome the crudeness of blind chance. And so, of course, I grew more and more exasperated with myself, realizing that I kept showing a lack of character, losing self-control, and giving in to the excitement like a miserable schoolboy. The thought that I, who had been able to withstand hunger, couldn't remain master of myself during such an easy test of will depressed me no end. Above all, my notion that, however ridiculous and pitiful I might appear, I possessed a hidden strength that one day would force every-

body to change his opinion of me, the notion that had been with
me since my unhappy childhood and my only source of life,
hope, dignity, and consolation, was so indispensable to me that,
without it, I'd have put an end to my life when I was still a little
boy. So how could I help being exasperated with myself when
I realized into what a helpless creature gambling could turn
me? And that's why I couldn't give up gambling. I understand
it very clearly now.

And, of course, to that must be added petty vanity. My constant losing humiliated me, made me feel ashamed before Sergei,
before Versilov (although Versilov never deigned to talk about
it), before everyone, even that woman Tatyana Prutkov! At
least that's how I felt at the time.

Finally, I must admit that, the life of luxury had already
quite corrupted me: I found it hard to forego a seven-course
dinner at a fashionable restaurant, to give up Matvei or patronizing the store selling imported English goods, or to jeopardize
the good opinion of my French barber. I was conscious of this
even at the time, but I dismissed the thought as nonsense and
refused to dwell on it. But now, as I write, my cheeks are red
from shame.

III

Having come to the club alone and finding myself surrounded
by strangers, I installed myself at a corner of the table and began
staking small sums. I sat like that for two hours without budging.
For those two hours everything worked completely haphazardly—no patterns, nothing one way or the other. I let
slip some wonderful opportunities but tried to control myself
and remain calm and self-confident. After two hours I was just
about where I'd started: of my three hundred rubles, I'd lost
perhaps only ten or fifteen. That negligible result irritated
me. Besides, a rather nauseating incident had taken place. I'm
quite aware that one is likely to come across plain thieves at the
gaming tables, not just common pickpockets from the street
but quite well-known gamblers. I'm sure, for instance, that
Aferdov, who is well known in all the gambling clubs, is a thief.
Even now you can see him all over town driving a pair of his
own ponies, but he's a thief because he has stolen from me. But
I'll describe that incident later, for what happened during the
evening in question was simply a prelude.

As I was sitting in my corner, the neighbor on my left during
all that time was a horrible dapper little fellow, I suspect a Jew.
Actually he was a member of some political movement, did

some writing, and was even published. At the very last moment, I won twenty rubles. Two red ten-ruble bills were put in front of me. All of a sudden I saw that wretched Jew stick out his hand and grab one of the bills. I was about to stop him, but before I could make a move he turned toward me himself and, in a calm voice and looking me arrogantly in the eye, informed me that it was his win because he had put down his stake at the very last second. Indeed, he did not wish to pursue the matter any further and turned away from me. Unfortunately, just at that moment, my mind was completely preoccupied with a stupid idea, and I just shrugged in disgust, got up, and left the table, letting him keep the ten rubles. Besides, it would have been difficult to force him to return my bill now, as the gambling had already resumed. I should have put my foot down right away and I hadn't done it. And that turned out to be a grievous mistake with deplorable repercussions. Two or three men at the table had noticed the incident and, realizing how readily I'd given in, took me for an easy mark.

It was exactly midnight. I went to the adjacent room, thought out a new plan of action, came back, changed my big bills into forty-odd half-imperials, divided them into ten piles, and decided to place them ten times in a row on the zero. "If I win—good; if I lose—even better, for then I'll never gamble again," I said to myself. And I want you to note that, during the two hours I had been playing before, the zero had never come up so that no one was even staking on it any more.

I was placing my stakes, standing behind the table. The third time around, Zershikov announced loudly: "Zero!" It hadn't come up all day. A hundred and forty gold half-imperials were counted out to me.

I still had seven of my original stakes left and I went on putting them on zero while the whole world seemed to be spinning and dancing before my eyes.

"Come over here!" I shouted across the table to a gray-headed, mustachioed, purple-faced gentleman in long tails, who had been placing small sums for hours with unwavering patience and losing stake after stake. "Come over here, sir, it's a lucky spot!"

"Are you addressing me?" he replied from his end of the table, in a tone that was at once surprised and threatening.

"Yes, you, because if you stay there, you'll lose everything you have!"

"That shouldn't be any of your business and I'd appreciate it if you'd stop bothering me."

Still, I couldn't restrain myself when I heard a middle-aged officer sitting in front of me mumble to his neighbor:

"Strange—*zero*. . . . No, I'd never dare to stake on the *zero*."

"You'd better dare, Colonel!" I shouted to him, placing a new stake on the *zero*.

"I'd like to be left alone and need none of your advice," he retorted sharply. "Besides, I think you make too much noise."

"I was giving you good advice, but if you wish I'll bet you on the side that the *zero* will come up again. What about ten gold half-imperials?"

And I counted out ten half-imperials.

"Ten gold pieces? All right, I'll take your bet," he said in a dry and stern tone. "So I bet that the *zero* won't come up now."

"So ten louis d'or, Colonel."

"What do you mean—ten louis d'or?"

"It's the same as ten half-imperials. It's just a more elegant way of saying the same thing."

"Let's stick to ten half-imperials; I'd appreciate it if you spared me your jokes."

Obviously I didn't expect to win the bet: the chances were thirty-six to one that the zero was not going to come up. The only reason I offered him that bet was because I felt like showing off and also because I wanted everybody to pay attention to me. I saw only too clearly that, for whatever reason, they didn't like me around here and were only too pleased to let me know it.

The roulette wheel spun. And, to the general amazement, it again came to a halt on the *zero*. Many voices shouted at the same time! And now success completely befogged my sight. Again, one hundred and forty half-imperials were counted out to me. Zershikov asked me whether it would be all right if I was paid partly in bills, but I could only mumble something inarticulate in reply for I had lost the ability to express myself intelligibly. My head was spinning and my legs felt weak. I felt that I was about to take crazy risks. Moreover, I was longing to do something unusual, to make another bet on the side, to count out a few thousands to someone or other. . . . Without having the sense to count them, I scooped up my bills and gold into the palms of my hands. And it was at that moment that I noticed Sergei and Darzan: they stood behind me. They'd just come in from their faro room where, as I learned later, they'd lost every last kopek they had on them.

"Hey, Darzan," I shouted, "here's where the luck is! Bet on the *zero*."

"I've lost all I had and have no money left," he said dryly.

As to Sergei, it was as though he hadn't even seen me.

"Here's some money!" I shouted, pointing at the heap of gold. "Help yourself to whatever you need."

"What the hell's going on?" Darzan said, turning very red. "I didn't ask you for money, did I?"

"Somebody's calling you," Zershikov said, pulling at my sleeve.

It was the colonel who had lost the side bet with me. He'd been trying to catch my attention almost rudely.

"Kindly take this," he snapped, purple with indignation. "How long do you expect me to wait for you to take it? I don't want you to say later that you haven't been paid in full. Count it."

"I trust you, Colonel, I don't have to count it. . . . Only please don't shout like that and don't be angry," I said, scooping up the money.

"I'll ask you not to lavish your hearty advice on me, my good man; keep it for those who wish it," the colonel rasped; "I've never eaten from the same trough with you."

"Why do they let such people in?" a voice said. "Who is he, anyway?" "Some crazy child," I heard other voices.

But then I stopped listening. I was now staking haphazardly, no longer sticking to the zero. I placed a whole pile of bills on the first eighteen numbers.

"Let's get out of here, Darzan," I heard Sergei's voice behind me.

"You going home?" I asked, turning to them. "Wait for me, we'll leave together. I'll call it a night."

I won again. It was a big win.

"That's enough!" I shouted and started raking in the money and stuffing it into my pockets. My hands were trembling as I clumsily crumpled the bills, trying to get them into the side pocket of my coat.

But suddenly a fat hand with a signet ring pinned down three rainbow-colored hundred-ruble bills. It belonged to Aferdov, who had been sitting across the table from me and had also been playing for high stakes.

"Just a minute, sir, these are not yours," he said sternly and emphatically, albeit rather softly.

And that was the prelude that was destined to have such an unpleasant sequel a few days later. Now I swear on my honor that these three hundred-ruble bills were mine, but at the time, although I was quite convinced that they were mine, I unfortunately could still conceive of the outside possibility that I was mistaken, which, for an honest man, is enough to put his claim in question, and I'm an honest man. The most important thing, though, was that at the time I had no idea that Aferdov was just a plain thief. Indeed, I didn't even know his name then, so I could very well conceive of the possibility that I had made a mistake and that these three bills were not among those that had been counted out to me. I hadn't been counting my money, just raking it in in a heap, while, in front of Aferdov, money was also piled up, but his was counted money, arranged in neat piles. Finally, Aferdov was well known around there, considered a rich man, and treated with respect. All that affected me too and, once again, I decided not to protest. And this was a fatal mistake! But the ugliest and most shameful part of it was my being in a state of euphoria.

"I'm pretty sure that they're mine, but unfortunately I can't be absolutely sure," I said, my lips trembling from indignation, and my words immediately aroused a disapproving outcry.

"In such matters people ought to be *absolutely sure* while you admit you are *not* absolutely sure," Aferdov said in an unbearably scornful tone.

"But who is he, after all?" "How can he be allowed to get away with it?" I heard people exclaim.

"That's not the first time for him. A little while ago he had a run in with Rechberg over a ten-ruble note," a sickening voice rasped near me.

"All right, that'll do, take it!" I cried. "Sergei . . . where're Sergei Sokolsky and Darzan? Have they left? Have you seen Prince Sergei Sokolsky and Darzan, gentlemen?"

I grabbed all my cash and, with my hands still full of gold pieces that I hadn't had time to stuff into my pockets, I rushed off to try and catch up with Sergei and Darzan.

I hope the reader will note that I'm not sparing myself, that I'm presenting myself just as I was at that time, in all my repulsiveness, so that what follows will be understandable.

Sergei and Darzan had gone all the way downstairs, completely ignoring my calls. I'd almost caught up with them by the door, but somehow I stopped for a moment by the hall porter and, goodness knows why, thrust three half-imperials into his hand. He gave me a bewildered look and didn't even thank me. But I couldn't have cared less and I'm sure that if Matvei had been around, I would've given him a whole handful of gold coins. In fact, I had full intentions of doing so when I suddenly remembered that I'd let him go until the next day. At that moment, Sergei's sledge drove up and he got into it.

"I'm coming with you, Sergei, I'm going to your place!" I shouted, snatching up the fur cover to get into the empty seat.

But suddenly I saw Darzan jump in past me and the coachman, snatching the fur cover out of my hand, tucked it around him.

"God damn it!" I shouted in indignation, for it might have looked as if I had lifted the cover to allow Darzan to install himself in the sledge, as though I were his flunkey!

"Home!" Sergei ordered the driver.

"Stop!" I screamed, clutching onto the sledge.

But the horse started up and I was sent rolling into the snow. I even had the impression that they laughed. I jumped to my feet, quickly found a cab, and, constantly urging him to whip on his wretched nag, I hurried to Sergei's.

IV

But, as if to annoy me deliberately, the nag moved with desperate slowness, notwithstanding the whole extra ruble I'd promised the driver, who for his part certainly did a good ruble's worth of whipping. My heart was sinking and when I tried to say something to the driver, the words wouldn't come out right and sounded like incoherent mumbling. It was in that state that I ran up to Sergei's apartment. He was alone, having dropped Darzan off on the way. Pale and ill humored, he was pacing his study. It must be remembered that he had lost heavily that evening. He first stared blankly at me, then frowned with exasperation.

"What, you again!"

"I wish to settle our accounts, sir!" I cried out breathlessly. "How dare you to treat me like that?"

He glared at me uncomprehendingly.

"If you meant to drive off with Darzan, you should have said so. But, instead, you just started up the horse and . . ."

"Ah, yes, of course, I believe you fell into the snow. . . ." and he laughed straight in my face.

"Such things are usually answered by a challenge and so, first of all, I want to settle our money accounts."

I proceeded to pull the money out of my pockets and lay it out on the sofa, the little marble table, and even on an open book that happened to be lying there. My hands were trembling as I laid the money out in piles and heaps and handfuls, untidily, so that some gold pieces rolled onto the carpet.

"Yes, of course, I believe you won tonight. One could easily tell that by your tone."

He had never been so insulting with me before. I was very pale.

"I don't know how much there is here. . . . Count off whatever I owe you. . . . Three thousand, isn't it? Tell me how much, is it more or less?"

"I've never pressed you to pay me back as far as I can remember."

"So it's me who's insisting, and you must know why. Here, I know that there's one thousand in this pile of rainbow-colored bills." I tried to count, but my hands were trembling too much and I gave it up. "I know there's a thousand here anyway. So I'll keep that thousand for myself and you can take all the rest in payment of my debt to you or on the account of my debt, whatever it is. . . . I think there must be at least two thousand rubles here. . . ."

"Nevertheless you still wish to keep one thousand for yourself?" he said, baring his teeth in a grin.

"Why, must you have that too? Well, I thought you wouldn't accept everything. . . . But since you need it. . . . Here, take it!"

"No, I don't need it."

He turned away from me contemptuously and resumed pacing the room. But soon he stopped abruptly in front of me.

"What the hell has come over you? How dare you shove your money at me!"

There was an ultimate challenge in his voice.

"I'm paying you back so I can ask you for satisfaction!" I roared back at him.

"Get the hell out of here with your stupid big words and grand gestures!" he screamed, stamping his feet in a real fit of rage. "I've been wanting to kick both of you out for a long time —you and your Versilov!"

"You're mad!" I shouted, and he looked it all right.

"You've made me sick to death, rattling off those phrases of yours, phrases about honor and all that! Damn you—I've been wanting to send you packing for a long time, and now I'm happy to do it at last! I considered myself bound and forced myself to receive you two here, although it made me feel ashamed! But there's nothing to bind me to you any longer, nothing at all! Do you know that your Versilov has been inciting me to attack Katerina Akhmakov and ruin her reputation. . . . So I don't want to hear you mention honor to me! You're people without honor, both of you. . . . Yes, and I really wonder how, in view of everything, you could go on taking money from me!"

Everything became dark around me.

"I accepted money from you as a friend," I said in a sickeningly weak voice; "you offered it to me yourself and I trusted in your friendship. . . ."

"You're not my friend, and if I have lent you money it wasn't out of friendship but for a reason you know very well."

"I was taking money from you thinking that it was from the account of what you owed Versilov. . . . I realize it was stupid on my part, but . . ."

"You couldn't have done that without Versilov's explicit permission and I would never have let you without his explicit orders. I gave you money that belonged to me and you knew it and took it, while I had to bear that loathsome comedy in my own house!"

"What is it I'm supposed to know? What comedy are you talking about? Why did you give me money?"

"*Pour vos beaux yeux, mon cousin!*"

He roared with laughter, looking straight into my eyes.

"Go to hell then!" I screamed. "And take everything, that thousand as well. We're quits now, and tomorrow—"

And I flung at him the roll of hundred-ruble bills I had put aside to keep for myself. The roll hit him on the waistcoat and fell to the floor. He took three huge steps and stopped just short of touching me.

"Are you trying to tell me," he articulated slowly and with fierce deliberation, "that while you were accepting my money during this whole month you didn't know that your sister was pregnant by me?"

"What? . . . What did you say? . . ."

My legs went all weak and I sank helplessly onto the sofa. Later he told me that I "literally turned as white as a handkerchief." Everything became confused. I only remember us staring and staring into each other's eyes. There was something like fright in his expression and he suddenly leaned over me, took me by the shoulders, and held me tight. I remember only too clearly his frozen grin of amazement, verging on disbelief. He never expected that what he said would have such an effect on me, for he had been convinced all along of my duplicity.

Finally I passed out completely, but my fainting spell didn't last more than a minute and, as soon as I came to, I scrambled to my feet. I looked at him and tried to put my shattered world in order. If someone had asked me what I was supposed to do about Sergei now, I'd probably have answered that I should tear him to pieces. But, instead, I did something quite different, something that had nothing to do with my will: I suddenly covered my face with both hands and began to cry aloud like a

child. It came out by itself, and it was as if the little boy broke
through the young gentleman I thought I was. I suppose it
shows that a good half of my soul was still occupied by a child.
I fell back on the sofa, sobbing: "Lisa, Lisa . . . poor, unhappy
little Lisa, poor thing . . ."

Sergei finally became fully convinced.

"My God, how unfair could I be!" he exclaimed with
sincere sorrow. "I've misjudged you so terribly in my stupid
suspiciousness. . . . Please forgive me, Arkady!"

I leaped up. I planted myself in front of him. I wanted to
say something to him but couldn't, so I said nothing and just
rushed out of the room. I walked all the way home, but I remember nothing of that walk. I threw myself onto my bed,
buried my face in my pillow, and thought and thought. Of
course it's never possible to think in an orderly way at such
moments. My thoughts and my imagination kept straying and I
remember catching myself daydreaming about unrelated things,
indeed, about God knows what things. But the stinging pain
of the disgrace always returned and caused me to wring my
hands and cry out "Lisa, Lisa . . ." and weep again.

I don't remember finally falling asleep but I know that I
slept soundly and sweetly.

Chapter 7

I

I awoke at eight in the morning. I got up, quickly locked my
door, sat down by the window, and began to think. I sat like
that until ten. The maid knocked twice on my door, but each
time I sent her away. At eleven there was another knock. Thinking that it was the maid again, I shouted at her to leave me alone.
But this time it was Lisa. The maid came in after her with my
morning coffee and prepared to light the stove. I felt that it
would be awkward to send her away now, so all the time Fekla
was arranging the wood and then lighting the fire, I kept pacing
up and down my little room with long strides, avoiding looking
at Lisa as I couldn't talk to her in the presence of the woman,
who was unbearably slow in her movements, as servants always
are when they feel they can prevent people from talking. Lisa
sat on the chair by the window and watched me.

"You'd better have your coffee before it gets cold," she said
suddenly.

I glanced at her: not the slightest trace of embarrassment, perfect composure, even a smile on her lips.

"Ah, women!" I muttered, unable to restrain myself any longer and shrugging in disbelief.

At last the maid had finished lighting the fire. Then she started cleaning up the room. I told her irritatedly to get out and locked the door after her.

"Tell me, please, why are you locking your door?" Lisa asked me.

I stopped in front of the chair on which she was sitting.

"I would never have believed that you could lie to me like that, Lisa!" I suddenly shouted, never having planned to begin our conversation this way. And I didn't feel like weeping now; instead, a feeling of spite quite unexpectedly got hold of me.

Lisa turned red. She didn't answer, just kept looking me straight in the face.

"How stupid could I be, Lisa!" I went on. "But could it really be called stupidity? How could I have guessed before? It was only yesterday, after all, that all the indications and the evidence suddenly converged and pointed straight at the same thing. Could I have possibly suspected you just because you went to Mrs. Stolbeyev's apartment to see that Daria woman? Besides, I looked up to you like a sort of sun, Lisa, so how could I ever have imagined anything like that? Do you remember when I met you in *his* apartment about two months ago, how we walked together in the sunshine, feeling so happy to be alive? Well, was it already going on then?"

She nodded a mute yes.

"So you were lying to me already then! But it's not my stupidity that made me so easy to deceive; rather it's my egotism, the egotism of my heart and perhaps my faith in the sacredness of certain things. Oh, I was always absolutely sure that you all were infinitely better than me! So now . . . Right up until yesterday, despite all the clues, I was still far from suspecting anything. . . . True, I had other things to think about yesterday. . . ."

I suddenly remembered about Katerina and felt a painful stab in my heart that made me blush. Obviously I couldn't be kind and understanding at such a moment.

"But why are you trying to justify yourself, Arkady? It seems to me that you're in a great hurry to justify yourself—why?" Lisa said quietly in a gentle tone that sounded firm and confident.

"What do you mean? Tell me what I'm supposed to do now?

You ask why I'm trying to justify myself when I'm really trying to think how a brother should act in such a situation. . . . I know that some people go, gun in hand, and demand the man marry her. . . . I'll do whatever an honorable man is meant to do. . . . But I wish I knew what an honorable man does under these circumstances. . . . Why? Because we are not even members of the gentry, while he's an aristocrat and a prince and his career is what matters to him most. So he won't even listen to honest people like us. Why, officially we're not even brother and sister but nameless bastards assumed to be the children of a serf, and who has ever heard of princes marrying even the legitimate offspring of serfs? Disgusting! And to top it all off, you sit here and seem surprised to hear what I'm saying!"

"I know you're very hurt," Lisa said, blushing deeply. "But you seem to be in a great hurry to deliberately hurt yourself."

"You say I'm in a hurry? So you don't think I'm rather late in finding out? Is it really right for you, Lisa, to say that to me?" I was gradually giving way completely to my indignation. "Can you imagine how much ignominy I've had to bear and how much that prince of yours must despise me now? You know, he was absolutely sure that I'd been aware of your affair with him for a long time but that I was saying nothing and turning up my nose at him so as to be able to hold forth to him about honor. And he even imagined that I was capable of accepting his money in payment for your disgrace! And if he found it sickening, I can hardly blame him! How else could he feel about a fellow whom he receives only because he's *her* brother and who keeps talking to him about honor? That would be enough to turn anyone's stomach! And you allowed all that to happen; you never even thought of warning me! He despised me so much that he even told Stebelkov that I was accepting money from him, and last night to my face he declared that he couldn't wait for the day when he'd be able to kick Versilov and me out of his house. And then even Stebelkov reminded me that, after all, Anna was as much a sister to me as Lisa and that his money was *better* than Sergei's. . . . And all that time I was insolently sprawling on Sergei's sofa, playing at being his equal, trying to be familiar with his lousy friends! Well, it was you, you, who allowed all that to happen! I suppose that Darzan knows now, at least judging from his tone last night. . . . Oh, everybody must know it except for me!"

"No one knows anything—he never told any of his acquaintances, *he couldn't* have told them," Lisa interrupted me. "And

I know about Stebelkov, I know that that man is pestering him, but if Stebelkov suspects anything, it's only what he may have guessed on his own. . . . Besides, I've spoken to *him* about you several times and *he* absolutely believed me that you knew nothing. And so I simply can't explain what happened between you two last night."

"At least I paid him what I owed him yesterday—and that's a load off my heart! . . . Tell me, does Mother know? She must because, otherwise, why would she've pounced on me like that yesterday? Ah, Lisa, do you really consider that you're absolutely blameless in all this, that you have nothing to reproach yourself for? I don't know how such behavior is supposed to be judged nowadays, what thoughts you have on the subject, or how you believe it should affect your mother, your brother, your father. . . . Does Versilov know?"

"Mamma didn't tell him and he didn't inquire. He apparently doesn't want to talk about it."

"So he knows and doesn't want to know? That's so like him! All right, you can laugh off the silly reaction of your brother when he brings in pistols and all that, but what about your mother, what about Mamma? All night I've been worrying about her. Her first thought now will probably be: 'It's because I did wrong myself, and now the daughter has followed her mother's example.' "

"What a nasty and cruel thing to say!"

Tears stood in Lisa's eyes. She got up and quickly walked to the door.

"Wait, wait!" I caught her, put my arm around her shoulders, and made her sit down next to me, still keeping an arm around her.

"It's just as I thought. On the way here I felt sure you'd demand that I admit my guilt. All right, then, I admit it. If I didn't say anything before, it was out of pride. And even now I'm much more concerned about having hurt Mother and you than about myself. . . ."

She couldn't go on and burst into tears.

"Don't, Lisa, don't. . . . I don't want anything. . . . I have no right to judge you. Only tell me about Mother—how long has she known?"

"I think for a long time, although I told her only recently how it all happened," Lisa said in a very weak voice and lowered her eyes.

"What did she say?"

"She said have the child," Lisa murmured, now hardly audibly.

"Oh, of course, Lisa, you must have it. Don't do anything horrible to yourself, God forbid. . . ."

"I won't do anything of the sort," she said emphatically, and again looked me in the eye. "You needn't worry about that," she said firmly; "it's not at all the way you think."

"I realize now that I still know nothing about it, but if I've found out anything at all, it's how much I love you, Lisa. There's one thing that is quite beyond me, though: what did you find in him that made you love him so? How could you love a man like that? That question . . ."

"I suppose that also kept you awake all night?" she smiled quietly.

"All right, Lisa, it may be a ridiculous question and I understand that it makes you laugh. . . . But you must see yourself that you and he are such completely different people! I've got to know him very well: he's a gloomy and suspicious man, and, although deep down he may be very kind, he tends to see evil in just about everything—in that, however, he's very much like me. He greatly appreciates chivalry and generosity, but I believe that to him it's only a principle, an abstract ideal. I also know that he's capable of feeling remorse: he goes around constantly reproaching himself for something, regretting what he's done. . . . But he never reforms—again, I'm probably just the same in that respect. He's stuffed with thousands of preconceptions and extraordinary notions, but there's not one original idea in his head. He's looking for an opportunity to do something noble and heroic, but in the meantime he acts with petty nastiness. . . . But please forgive me, Lisa, I'm talking like a fool because I know that I'm offending you, I realize that. . . ."

"Your portrayal could've been true," Lisa said, smiling, "but you were too angry with him because of me and so it's not true at all. He was wary of you from the start and you couldn't possibly have seen the whole of him. . . . But with me, ever since Luga. . . . Yes, since that time he's had eyes for no one but me. . . . Yes, he's suspicious and morbid and he would have gone mad without me. And if he's forced to give me up, he will, indeed, either go mad or shoot himself. I think he's realized that . . . he knows it now," Lisa added dreamily, as though talking to herself. "Yes, he's continually behaving like a weak man, but he's one of those weak people who are capable on occasion of performing real feats of strength. . . . It was so absurd, your mentioning pistols, Arkady; nothing of that sort is necessary, and I know very well what he'll do. There's no need for me to pursue him; it's he who desperately needs me. Mamma says to me: 'If you marry him, you'll be unhappy and he'll stop loving you.' I don't believe that: he'll never stop loving me, although I may very well be unhappy with him. And that's not the reason why I refused to say yes to him—there was something else that stopped me. For two months, I kept saying *no* to him. But today I told him 'All right, *yes*, I'll marry you.' And you know what, Arkasha"—she suddenly became all radiant, jumped up and threw her arms around my neck—"he went to Anna's and told her with utter frankness that he'd never be able to love her. . . . They had a complete explanation and, whatever speculation there may have been on that subject, it's all finished now! Besides, he'd never done anything to encourage the rumors; from the very start it was just a fancy of your old friend Prince Nikolai. And, of course, he was subjected to pressure from Stebelkov and another scoundrel. . . . And so I gave my consent today. . . . By the way, he would very much like you to come see him this evening. Please don't be offended by what happened last night. He doesn't feel well and will be at home all day. . . . Yes, Arkady, he really isn't well, I didn't just invent that for convenience. He asked me to tell you that he *needs* you, that there are many things he wants to tell you, but he'd rather not talk to you at your place. . . . Well, good-by then. . . . Ah, Arkady, I was so terribly worried on the way here, thinking that you wouldn't love me any more. I even kept crossing myself as I walked. . . . But you're so good, so sweet! I'll never forget it, never! I'm going to see Mamma now. . . . Ah, I wish you could get to like *him* too, a little at least, don't you think you could manage it?"

I embraced her warmly.

"I think you're a strong person, Lisa. I also believe that he needs you more than you need him. Still . . ."

"Still, what was it that made me fall in love with him—that's the question!" Lisa interrupted me and her old mischievous smile reappeared on her lips as she pronounced the words "that's the question," making a perfect imitation of my voice and tone, placing her forefinger between her eyebrows in my familiar gesture.

We kissed. But after she left my heart began to ache again.

II

I'll note here for my own edification that, after Lisa's departure, most unexpected thoughts flitted through my head and that I was rather pleased with them. Why worry? What does it really matter to me? Most people are faced with such problems. So what if this happened to Lisa? Why should it be incumbent upon me to "save the honor of the family"?

I note all these despicable thoughts to show how uncertain I still was then in telling good from evil. What made up for it was only my instinct, which told me that Lisa was unhappy and that Mother was unhappy too. I felt it every time I thought of them, and it was that feeling that told me that what had happened was not good.

I may as well say in advance that, from that day on and right up to the catastrophe of my illness, awful things happened in such quick succession that now, as I think of it, I feel surprised that I could have withstood being crushed by them. My ability to reason and even my capacity to feel were drained so that if I'd given in and committed a crime (which I almost did!), the jury might well have acquitted me. But let me try to describe everything in logical sequence, although there was, of course, not much logic in me at the time. Events rushed at me like a violent wind and ideas were spinning around in my mind like dry dead leaves in autumn. And since all my thinking then was based on borrowed ideas, I couldn't produce any of my own to form an independent decision. There was nothing to guide me at all.

I decided to go and see Sergei in the evening so that we could discuss things freely and at length. Until evening, I stayed at home. But, just as it was getting dark, I received a note by mail. It was from Stebelkov. Just three lines: he was asking me "most insistently" to come to his place at eleven the next morning on "most urgent business, as you will realize yourself." I thought I'd wait and see whether I should go or not. Much could happen before then. I didn't have to decide right away.

It was eight o'clock and I should have been gone already, but I was putting off leaving, hoping that Versilov would come; there were so many things I wanted to tell him! But Versilov didn't come. I couldn't very well go to Mother's myself just now and face her and Lisa, and, besides, I doubted very much that Versilov would be there. So I set out on foot toward Sergei's. On the way, I decided to drop in and have a look in that café on the canal and, lo and behold, there was Versilov sitting at the same table we'd occupied the day before.

"I thought you'd come here," he said, giving me a strange

look and smiling the strange, unkind smile I hadn't seen on his face for a long time now.

I sat down at his table and told him everything I'd learned about Lisa and Sergei and about my scene with Sergei the previous night following the session at the roulette table, mentioning, of course, my win. He listened attentively and asked me to repeat what I knew about Sergei's decision to marry Lisa.

"*Pauvre enfant*, I doubt that it would be such a boon for her. Besides, I don't think it will come off. . . . Although he's quite capable of . . ."

"Tell me as a friend: you knew everything, you expected it all to happen, didn't you?"

"My dear boy, there was nothing I could do. It's all a matter of somebody else's feelings and conscience, even if it happens to be a poor little girl. I told you I've interfered enough in other people's consciences in my day and it's a most unrewarding business. Of course, I'll try to be helpful in a crisis, that is, if I can find out what to do. And you, my dear boy, I suppose you never even suspected anything all this time?"

"How could you then!" I cried in indignation, the blood rushing to my face. "How could you—if you had even the slightest suspicion that I was aware of Lisa's affair with Sergei while accepting money from him all that time—how could you talk to me and shake the hand of a man whom you must have regarded as a despicable scoundrel for selling his own sister!"

"Again, it's a matter of personal conscience," he said with a vague smile and then suddenly added with a peculiar emphasis: "And how do you know I wasn't worried yesterday that things might turn out differently so that you might have lost your 'ideal' and I would have had a ruthless villain confronting me instead of my ardent and honest boy? Fearing that, I tried to put off that moment. Why not ascribe to me, instead of laziness and hypocrisy, something less reprehensible, a touch of stupidity perhaps, but high-minded stupidity? *Que diable*, I'm stupid often enough without being high-minded! What use would you be to me if you already had propensities for ruthlessness? Trying to argue with you, to change you, if you'd been like that, would have been cheap, and, besides, you'd have lost all value in my eyes even if I had managed to set you straight."

"But Lisa—aren't you at least sorry about her?"

"Very sorry, my boy. Anyway, what makes you assume that I'm so unfeeling? In fact, I'll do what I can to— But tell me, what about you? How are your own personal affairs?"

"Let's leave my affairs out of this for now. I have no *personal* business that preoccupies me at the moment. You'd better tell me what makes you doubt that he'll marry her. In that case, why did he have to go to Anna's yesterday and tell her definitely that there could be nothing between them? I'm talking about that preposterous notion of the old prince's of pairing them off. He definitely said no to that."

"Really? When was that? Where did you hear about it?" Versilov asked with interest and I told him. "Hm . . ." he said dreamily and became immersed in deep thought. "Hm . . . of course, a conversation like that could have taken place between them and must have preceded by an hour or so a certain other conversation. . . . It's quite possible, although I know that nothing has been settled as yet by either side. . . . But, then, two words would be enough for such an explanation. However, let me tell you something quite extraordinary that will interest you." A strange smile suddenly appeared on his lips. "Even if your friend Sergei *had* proposed to Anna yesterday—something that I, suspecting the truth about him and Lisa, would have prevented from happening by all the means at my disposal, *entre nous soit dit*—Anna would have turned him down. I believe you're very fond of Anna and have great respect for her, right? That's very sweet on your part and therefore you'll be pleased to hear this about her: she's about to marry someone else, my dear boy, and, from what I know of her character, she will, and of course I'll give her my blessing."

"She's getting married? To whom?" I cried, surprised beyond belief.

"Guess! All right, I won't torment you: she's going to marry Prince Nikolai Sokolsky, that dear old man of whom you're also so fond."

I just gaped at him.

"She must have conceived the idea a long time ago, and I'm sure she worked it out with consummate artistry down to the last detail," he went on, drawling his words lazily. "I assume that everything was settled within one hour of Prince Sergei's visit to her—which only goes to show how ill timed his noble gesture was. Well, she simply went over to Prince Nikolai's and proposed to him."

"You mean—he proposed to her?"

"Ah, no, he certainly wasn't up to that. It was she who did all the proposing. And now he's completely ecstatic, they say, and only wondering why such a brilliant idea didn't occur to him first. I even understand that he became a little ill . . . also, no doubt, out of sheer enthusiasm. . . ."

"Why are you being so sarcastic about it all? . . . But I can't really believe you: how could she possibly have proposed to him? What did she actually say?"

Versilov's face suddenly became extremely serious.

"Rest assured, my boy, that I'm sincerely delighted. He's pretty old, of course, but he's fully qualified for marriage by law and by custom. As to her, well, again this is a matter for her to decide rather than for me, as I already told you. Besides, she's competent enough to have her own views and make up her own mind. As to the finer points of it and the exact words she used, I'm afraid I'm not in a position to tell you, my dear boy. But I'm sure she handled everything much better than either of us could imagine. The best of it all is that there's nothing scandalous in the whole business, everything is *comme il faut* in the eyes of Petersburg society. Obviously she wanted a good position in the world, but then she's worthy of such a position. This is a perfectly proper news item in society life. And I'm sure she proposed to him in the most elegant and graceful style. She belongs to the stern type—a 'young nun,' as you yourself once characterized her, or a 'self-possessed maiden,' as I have always thought of her. You know that she was almost brought up by him so that she has experienced his kindness many times. She has assured me so often of her 'respect for him,' her 'high opinion of him,' their 'mutual understanding,' and so on, that I was to some extent prepared for it. Officially, I was informed of the news this morning by her brother Andrei, my son, that is, whom I don't believe you know and whom I see regularly once every six months. Well, he respectfully approves of her move."

"So everything is official already? My God, I just can't believe it!"

"No, no, it's not at all official for the time being. . . . I don't really know when it will be because I'm quite outside the whole business. But I can tell you it's true."

"But then what about Katerina? Do you think Björing will relish this latest development?"

"As for that, I don't really know what he could actually object to. . . . But you can take my word for it, in that sense, Anna is a very decent person. . . . although she really has character, our Anna! Imagine, just before all this happened, yesterday morning, she suddenly asked me: 'Tell me, are you or aren't you in love with Katerina Akhmakov?' Remember, I told you yesterday how surprised I was when she asked me that.

But now I see it would have made it impossible for her to marry the father if I married the daughter.* So you see how her mind works?"

"Yes, yes, I see!" I exclaimed. "But why should Anna get it into her head that you might want to marry Katerina?"

"Apparently she did, my boy. . . . But listen, I think you ought to be on your way now—it's time for you to go where you're going. Besides, I have a wicked headache. I'll ask them to play 'Lucia' for me. I love the solemnity of boredom here. . . . But I've already told you that and I realize I repeat myself quite unforgivably. . . . Or perhaps I'd better just get out of this dump. . . . I do like you, my sweet boy, but good-by for now because when I have a headache or a toothache I always like to be alone. . . ."

A line of suffering appeared on his brow and I believe he really was in pain.

"See you tomorrow," I said.

"Tomorrow?" he said. "What will happen tomorrow?"

"I'll come and see you or you'll come and see me."

"No, I won't come and see you tomorrow. But you'll come running to me all right."

Something unkind appeared again in his face, but I wasn't in a state to give it a thought. I was still under the effect of what he'd told me.

III

Sergei really wasn't feeling well, and he was sitting at home all alone with a wet towel wrapped around his head. But it was mental agony rather than an ordinary headache. He had been anxiously awaiting my arrival. Once again I must warn the reader that, during that whole time and right up until the catastrophe, I somehow had to deal with people who were all in a state of extreme agitation bordering on real insanity, which couldn't help, as it were, rubbing off on me somewhat. I admit that I felt quite antagonistic toward Sergei when I arrived, and I felt very ashamed of having allowed myself to burst into tears in his presence the day before. Besides, he and Lisa had managed to deceive me so thoroughly that I couldn't help feeling like a real fool. In short, when I marched in, all sorts of hostile feelings were churning inside me. But my planned aggressiveness vanished very quickly because, in fairness to him, it must

* The Russian Orthodox Church bars two men from marrying each other's daughters and thus becoming each other's sons-in-law. [A. MacA.]

be said that underneath his morbid suspicions was an almost childlike trustingness and love. Tears stood in his eyes as he hugged me. Then he immediately went on to tell me how much and how badly he needed me. . . . From what he said and how he said it, I could judge his state of inner turmoil.

He informed me that he planned to marry Lisa as soon as possible.

"The circumstances of her birth have never bothered me for a moment," he said. "As a matter of fact, my grandfather was married to a serf girl who sang in a neighboring landowner's private theater. . . . As for my family, even though they may have some ideas about whom I should marry, they'll just have to put up with it and I'm sure they'll do so without too much fuss. . . . Above all, I want to put an end to my present way of life, put an end to it once and for all! From now on, everything must be different! You know, I don't at all understand why your sister should love me, but I can tell you that, if it hadn't been for her, I probably wouldn't even be alive today. I swear to you that, in my meeting Lisa in Luga, I recognize the hand of God. . . . I'm sure she fell in love with me because I'd fallen so low. . . . But I wonder whether you can understand that, Arkady. . . ."

"I can understand it perfectly," I assured him with conviction.

I was sitting in an armchair while he walked up and down the room.

"I must tell you about our meeting without keeping anything back," he went on. "It all started with a secret of mine that she was the first to know, since she was the only person I could bring myself to tell. And to this day, no one else knows it. I came to Luga with despair in my heart and for some reason stayed at Mrs. Stolbeyev's, probably hoping to find solitude there. I'd just left the regiment in which I'd served since my return from abroad where I'd had that encounter with Mr. Versilov. While in the regiment I had some money and spent rather extravagantly, leading a dissipated life. But, although I tried to get by without offending anyone's feelings, my brother officers didn't like me much. Besides, I may as well tell you that no one has ever really liked me, except perhaps for a certain ensign in my regiment by the name of Stepanov, a featherbrained, dull, and altogether unremarkable fellow, whom nobody really respected. . . . But for all that, he was perfectly honest. . . . Well, somehow he latched onto me. I didn't pay much attention to him and he would come to my lodgings and sit in a corner for hours on end without saying a word, trying to look very dignified. He spent day after day like that, but I really didn't mind him sitting there. . . . Once I repeated to him a piece of gossip about myself—adding a lot of embellishments—to the effect that our colonel's daughter was in love with me and that the colonel had his eye on me and that he certainly would do anything to please me. . . . Well, I'll skip the details, but the result was a very complicated and disgusting scandal. My tale was spread around not by Stepanov but by my orderly, who had overheard and remembered it all because he found this disgusting gossip compromising a young lady very funny. And it was that same orderly who, testifying at the regimental inquiry, blamed Stepanov for making the story public. . . . I mean, he said I'd confided in Stepanov. And so Stepanov was caught in a trap since, as a matter of honor, he couldn't very well deny having heard the story. Actually I'd made up two-thirds of the story. The officers were outraged at what they heard. Then the colonel summoned us all to clear up the matter and asked Stepanov whether he'd heard the story from me. Stepanov told the truth. And so what did I, a prince whose line goes back a thousand years, do then? I denied it and called Stepanov a liar to his face. Oh, I did it as politely as I could, saying that he had misunderstood me, etc. I'll skip the details again and just say that since Stepanov had been spending so much time at my place, I managed to present the matter so that it appeared quite likely that he was involved in some sort of a plot with my orderly for motives of his own. Stepanov just looked at me and shrugged in silence. I remember that look of his, I'll never forget it. After that, he immediately put in a request to resign his commission. But guess what happened—all the officers of the regiment, every one of them, paid him personal visits in turns and pleaded with him to take back his request. Two weeks later, it was I who left the regiment. No one had suggested I do so. I alleged family reasons. And that was the end of the story.

"At first I didn't care one way or the other; I wasn't even angry with anyone. I went to Luga and there I met your sister Lisa. A month later, however, I was staring at my revolver and thinking of death. In general, Arkady, I have a gloomy outlook on life. I wrote a letter to my former regimental commander and my brother officers in which I confessed my lies and fully vindicated Stepanov's honor. After that, I wondered which I should do: send the letter and stay alive or send it and die? I couldn't decide. Then an accident, blind chance, brought me close to Lisa. For until then, although I'd met her when she'd come to see Mrs. Stolbeyev, I only knew her enough to say hello and exchange a few occasional words with her. Now I suddenly told her everything and that was when she held out her hand to me."

"And how did that settle your dilemma?"

"I didn't send the letter. She decided I shouldn't. She reasoned this way: if I were to send it, of course it'd be a very noble gesture that would be more than enough to wash off me all the filth left by what I'd done. But would I be able to bear it? She thought I wouldn't because it would completely ruin my whole future and I wouldn't be able to start out on a new career. Besides, there would have been a point if Stepanov had been hurt by me, but since he'd already been rehabilitated by the officers of his regiment without my help it was quite unnecessary. In short, it may have been somewhat farfetched reasoning but it stopped me from sending the letter. I entrusted myself to her without reservation."

"A truly Jesuitical piece of reasoning!" I cried. "So typical of a woman! She must have already been in love with you then."

"Well, that's what brought me back to life, to a new life. I swore to change, to live differently, to be worthy of myself and of her. . . . But what did it all come to? Playing roulette and faro. . . . And then the windfall of the inheritance corrupted me completely. I couldn't resist the temptations offered by money, with all those people around me, racehorses, and so on. . . . I made Lisa miserable. . . . I was a disgrace!"

He rubbed his forehead and walked up and down the room a couple of times.

"You and I, Arkady, we're both stricken by that common Russian fate: neither of us knows what to do with himself. As soon as a Russian finds himself thrown out of the rut of his time-honored routine, he no longer knows what to do. While he's in the rut, everything is clear: income, rank, position in society, horse and carriage, wife, etc. But the minute he gets out of it, he no longer knows what he is. Then he's like a dead leaf blown around by the wind. . . . I don't know what to do now. In those two months I tried to stay in the rut, I'd got to like that rut, and I followed it. . . . But you still can't realize the full depth of my degradation: I loved Lisa, loved her sincerely . . . but at the same time I kept thinking of Katerina Akhmakov."

"You did?" I cried out in distress. "But what was it you were telling me yesterday about Versilov—something about his inciting you to play a dirty trick on Katerina?"

"Well, I may have exaggerated and perhaps I was just as un-

fair in suspecting him as I was in suspecting you. Let's not talk
about it. But is it possible you don't believe that ever since Luga
I have carried an ideal in my heart? I swear it has never left me
and its beauty has never diminished. I've always remembered
the promise I made to Lisa to reform and start a new life. And
so yesterday when Mr. Versilov was holding forth here about
the duties of the Russian aristocracy, I assure you there was
nothing in what he said that I didn't already know. My ideal is
quite simple: a few dozen acres—only a few for I have almost
nothing left from my inheritance—and then a clean break with
society life; a house in the country, a family, and tilling the
soil with my own hands or almost. And I wouldn't be the first to
do that in my family: my father's brother used to plow the fields
himself, and so did my grandfather. Our family goes back a
thousand years and is as aristocratic as the house of the Rohans,
but we haven't got a kopek to our name. And this is what I'd
like to say to my children: 'Remember as long as you live that
you're an aristocrat, that the sacred blood of Russian princes
runs in your veins, and never be ashamed of the fact that your
father used to till the soil with his own hands for he did it in a
princely way.' I'd leave my children nothing except that small
piece of land, but I'd be sure they got a university education because I'd consider that as my duty. Oh, Lisa would help me
with all that. Lisa, children, hard work—oh, how often we've
dreamed together, here in these very rooms, of such a future.
But then . . . at the same time I was thinking about the Akhmakov woman whom I didn't love at all and envisaging the possibilities of marrying a socially desirable and rich woman . . . !
Indeed, it was only after what Nashchokin told me yesterday
about Björing that I decided to go to Anna's. . . ."

"But you went there to tell her you wouldn't marry her,
didn't you? And that, I think, was a very honorable move."

"Was it?" He planted himself squarely in front of me. "No,
you still know nothing about the kind of man I am . . . or . . .
or perhaps there's something else I don't quite understand myself. I'm sincerely fond of you, Arkady, and, besides, I feel very
guilty toward you for my behavior during these past two months.
And therefore I feel that, being Lisa's brother, you ought to
know everything. I went to see Anna not to break off with her
but to propose to her."

"How is that possible? Lisa told me . . ."

"I lied to Lisa."

"Wait. You proposed to Anna officially and she rejected you?

Is that right? Is it? It's very important to me to know exactly what happened."

"No, I didn't actually propose to her but only because I didn't manage to get that far. It was she who made me understand—oh, not directly but plainly enough, God knows—that the very idea of marriage between us was now impossible."

"So it's just as if you'd never proposed. And, besides, that way you haven't had to suffer the humiliation of rejection."

"How can you talk like that! What about my own self-esteem, and what about Lisa to whom I lied and whom I intended to desert? And what about the vow I made to myself and to my forefathers to reform and to atone for my unspeakable past? But please, don't tell Lisa about all this! Perhaps she won't be able to forgive me. . . . Since yesterday I've been a sick man. And now this seems to be the end of everything—the last of my line of the Princes Sokolsky will be thrown into prison. Ah, poor Lisa! I was waiting for you anxiously today, you, Lisa's brother, so I could tell you everything she doesn't know: I'm a common criminal, for I've taken part in the forgery of *** Railway shares."

I jumped to my feet, looking at him in horror.

"Oh, that too!" I cried. "Now it's prison!"

His face wore a look of doom and endless sorrow.

"Sit down," he said, lowering himself into an armchair opposite mine. "First of all, let me tell you this: just over a year ago, during the summer I was in Ems with Katerina and Lidia Akhmakov, and after that when I went to Paris for two months—well, during all that time, I was as usual short of money. . . . It so happened that in Paris I ran into Stebelkov, whom I'd met before. He let me have some money and promised to give me more if, in return, I'd render him a small service. What he needed was a draftsman, an artist, an engraver, a lithographer, and also a chemist and a technician . . . all this for a certain specific purpose. And he gave me a pretty good idea at the very start of what this purpose was. Well, don't you think that was quite a shrewd appraisal of my character? . . . At first, though, it just made me laugh. The point is that when I was at school I had a friend who's now one of those Russian emigrés, although he's actually of foreign origin. He lives, I believe, in Hamburg. In Russia he'd already been involved in a scandal—something to do with forgery of shares. And that was the man Stebelkov wanted. However, he needed someone to introduce him to that man and he decided I could render him that service. So I wrote him a couple of lines of introduction and immediately forgot all about it. Eventually I ran into Stebelkov a couple of times more, and he let me have about three thousand rubles altogether. Then the whole business literally slipped my mind. Later, in Russia, I've always given him IOU's for whatever money I've borrowed and he's always been most servile with me. . . . Then yesterday, all of a sudden, I learn from him that I'm a common criminal."

"When exactly yesterday?"

"Yesterday when he and I had words in my study just before Nashchokin arrived. It was the first time he'd dared to speak quite openly to me about Anna. I raised my hand to hit him, but he quickly got up and told me to remember that I was his accomplice and therefore just as much of a crook as he himself. . . . Oh, he used different words, but that was the general meaning."

"Nonsense, I bet you're imagining things. . . ."

"No, it's not nonsense. He came here today and explained the situation to me in considerable detail. The forged shares have been in circulation for some time now and more of them will be put on the market, even though some have already been recognized as forgeries. Of course, I had nothing to do with it directly, but, as Stebelkov says: 'You did give me that note of introduction to the gentleman, didn't you?' "

"But you didn't know exactly why he wanted to be introduced to that man. Or did you?"

"I knew all right," Sergei said quietly and lowered his eyes, "although, actually, I both did and didn't know. The whole thing made me laugh. I thought it was all very amusing. I didn't give it much thought at the time since I had no use for forged shares myself and had no intention of forging them. Still, the three thousand rubles he'd given me in Paris—he never even claimed it back from me, never even made note of it, and I, I accepted it. Besides, how can you be sure that I'm not a forger too? I couldn't possibly not have understood what was going on —I'm not a child, after all. I knew and found it amusing, so I helped those miserable thieves and crooks to perpetrate their forgery and I did it for money! Hence, I'm a forger just like them!"

"You exaggerate; perhaps you aren't blameless, but you do exaggerate your part in it."

"What makes it worse is that there's someone else involved—a young man by the name of Zhibelsky. He's some kind of clerk in a lawyer's office. He also had something to do with those forged shares: he came to see me on the part of that Hamburg gentleman; oh, it was about something of no importance and shares were not even mentioned. Still, he now has two notes written in my hand, just a couple of lines each, and, of course, that also could be used as evidence against me. I understand that now. Stebelkov says that this Zhibelsky is spoiling everything, that he has misappropriated some public monies and now wants to get hold of more funds to leave the country. What he needs, in fact, is a minimum of eight thousand to emigrate. Stebelkov says that he would consider my personal debt to him settled if I transferred to him my share of the inheritance, but he says that Zhibelsky must also be compensated. . . . To make a long story short, they're demanding my share of the inheritance plus another ten thousand rubles. That's their final word. Only when I've met these demands will they give me back my two compromising notes. It's quite obvious that they're acting in concert."

"What you say makes no sense: if they report you, they'll give themselves away too. They can't possibly do that."

"That's right and I know it. But they never said that they would report me. They say: 'Of course, we won't report you unless the whole business blows up.' That's all they say, but that's bad enough. Besides, it's not just a matter of not being exposed; indeed, even if I had those two compromising notes in my hands right now, still the mere fact that I'm an accomplice of those crooks and have to be one of them forever will weigh on me as long as I live and I'll always be forced to lie, always—lie to Russia, lie to my children, lie to Lisa, lie to my own conscience!"

"Does Lisa know all this?"

"Not everything. She couldn't bear it in her present condition. I'm still wearing the uniform of my regiment and every time I meet a soldier and he salutes me, I feel how unworthy I am to wear it."

"Listen!" I exclaimed suddenly. "I know a way out: go at once to Prince Nikolai Sokolsky and ask him for ten thousand rubles without telling him exactly what for; summon those two crooks, pay them off down to the last kopek, get hold of the two notes, and that will be the end of it. And after that you'll be free to go and till the soil! So stop imagining all sorts of sinister things and have faith in life."

"I was thinking of that," he said in a determined tone. "I've been trying to make up my mind all day and finally I've decided. I was only waiting for you. I will go to him. You know, I've never yet asked Prince Nikolai for anything: He's always been kindly disposed toward our branch of the family, but I personally have never received any favors from him. However, now I've decided to accept. . . . I want you to note, by the way, that our branch of the Princes Sokolsky is older than his; he belongs to a lesser branch, a sort of offshoot, in fact, hardly recognized. . . . There was a feud between our ancestors. At the beginning of the changes introduced by Peter the Great, my great-grandfather—also a Peter—remained an Old Believer and went off to live in the Kostroma forests. That Prince Peter was also married (his second marriage) to a woman of lowly birth. And that's when the second branch of the Sokolskys came to the fore. . . . But what am I talking about?"

He looked terribly tired and was obviously unable to keep his mind on what he was saying.

"Please calm yourself." I got up and picked up my hat. "First of all, you must lie down and get some sleep. As to Prince Nikolai, I'm sure he won't turn you down, especially in his present state of bliss. Haven't you heard the news? You haven't? Really? Well, I've heard the incredible news that he's getting married. It's a secret but of course not from you."

And while standing there, ready to leave and holding my hat in my hand, I told him everything. He hadn't heard about it and asked me for more details, mainly about the time and place that the marriage had been settled. He also wanted to know how reliable the story was. I didn't conceal from him that it had been arranged almost immediately after his visit to Anna. It's hard to convey the painful impression the news made on him. His face became contorted and his lips froze in a twisted grin. Then he turned terribly pale, lowered his eyes, and immersed himself in deep thought. It became only too obvious to me what a blow to his pride Anna's engagement to another man was. Probably he felt he'd been humiliated and made ridiculous by a girl whose acceptance he'd taken for granted. And on top of that, he must have fully understood now how shabbily he had behaved toward Lisa, and all to no avail.

Sometimes I wonder about the standards of behavior of this type of elegant young gentleman and about what his self-respect consists of. Surely it must have occurred to him that Anna might very well have been aware of his liaison with Lisa, since they were after all sisters, or, if she didn't yet know of it, she was very likely to find out about it sooner or later. But that did not seem to prevent him at all from taking for granted that she would accept his proposal!

"How could you imagine that I would consider going to Prince Nikolai and asking him to lend me money after what you've just told me?" he cried out aggressively, fixing his eyes on mine. "The man who's now engaged to marry the woman who rejected me! That would be acting like a beggar, like a miserable flunkey! No, everything is lost now, and if the help of that old man was my only and last hope, let that last hope perish!"

Deep down, I agreed with him. But one could take a broader view of the situation: what sort of a rival was the old prince, after all? Several ideas crossed my mind. Anyway I had already decided to pay a visit to the old fellow. For now, I tried to soften the blow for Sergei. I insisted he go to bed.

"Have a good sleep," I said, "and you'll see that when you wake up things will look less hopeless. It's not really as bad as you think!"

He shook my hand warmly but this time didn't go in for any hugging. I promised to come back and see him the next evening, so that we could talk everything over, since there was so much we had to discuss. He smiled strangely when I said that to him.

Chapter 8

I

All that night I kept dreaming of gambling, roulette, piles of gold pieces, raking in my winnings. . . . And all the time in my dreams I was calculating I don't know what stakes and probabilities, all of which pressed on me and turned my dreams into nightmares. The truth is that during the entire preceding day, despite all my shocking experiences, my thoughts had kept returning to my success at Zershikov's gambling saloon. I tried not to think of it, but I couldn't help reliving the emotion it had aroused in me and the very memory of it made me shiver. My winning had really gone to my head. Could it be, then, that I was an incurable gambler? Well, at least I must have some of the traits of a gambler. Indeed, even now as I write I feel a certain pleasure just at the thought of gambling. I sometimes spend hours absorbed in mental calculations about stakes and chances, visualizing myself as playing and winning. Yes, I certainly have many of the traits of a gambler and my soul is an unquiet one.

By ten o'clock I had decided to go to Stebelkov's on foot and I sent Matvei away as soon as he appeared. As I drank my morning coffee, I surveyed the situation. Somehow I felt pleased. I wondered what I could possibly be pleased about and came to the conclusion that it was the prospect of seeing the old Prince

Nikolai, whom I was planning to visit that day. But that day turned out to be a momentous one in my life and things took quite an unexpected turn from the very start.

At ten sharp, my door was flung open and Tatyana Prutkov burst into the room. If there was anything in the world I least expected at that moment, it was to see her appear and I leaped up in alarm. She looked fierce, she was gesticulating wildly, and if she'd been asked why she'd burst in on me like that, chances are she wouldn't even have been able to say. As I was to find out later, she'd just learned something which had upset her terribly and from which she'd not yet recovered. And, it turned out, it affected me too.

She stayed in my room only half a minute or, at most, a whole minute, certainly no more. But the way she tore into me!

"So this is what you've been up to!" she shouted, glaring into my face and leaning threateningly toward me. "Oh, you nasty little pup! Do you realize what you've done now! Or perhaps you don't know yet? Look at him, drinking his coffee as if nothing had happened! Ah, you miserable babbler! You paper Romeo! What you need is a whipping, a good whipping on your backside!"

"What's the matter, Mrs. Prutkov? Did something happen? Is something wrong with Mother?"

"You'll find out soon enough!" she shouted menacingly, and rushed out of the room.

She was gone. I was about to run after her but was stopped by a thought. . . . Actually, it was more of a foreboding than a thought: I somehow felt that the phrase "paper Romeo" was the keynote in her outburst. Obviously I couldn't guess myself what it was all about, so I decided to attend quickly to my business with Stebelkov and then to go and see the old prince where I felt instinctively I'd find the answer to the new riddle.

To my surprise, Stebelkov already knew everything about Anna down to the last detail. Without repeating his words or describing his gesticulations, I'll simply say that he was elated; indeed, he was in a paroxysm of elation over what he characterized as a "master stroke."

"There's a woman for you!" he cried out. "There's someone who certainly knows what she wants! Ah, she's made of quite different stuff from us who just sit around and do nothing while she, once she's set her sights on something, however inaccessible, she gets it. She's . . . she's a Greek statue of Minerva, with the only difference that she can walk and wears fashionable clothes."

I asked him to get down to business, and the business consisted, as I'd suspected, in asking me to plead with Sergei that he should go to the old Prince Nikolai and beg for his financial assistance.

"Why," Stebelkov said, "Prince Sergei is really in a very, very bad position, and not just because of me. . . . Surely he must see he's in serious trouble. Or doesn't he?"

He watched my expression intently, but I believe he never suspected that I had learned something since our previous meeting. And, in fact, how could he possibly have guessed anything since I never uttered a word or let out a hint that could betray that I knew about the forgeries? Our conversation didn't last long and he soon started promising me money, "a goodly sum, a goodly sum, just for your cooperation, just so that you see to it that Prince Sergei goes to see Prince Nikolai. . . . But it's urgent, terribly urgent; indeed, the whole point is that it's so urgent. . . ."

Having no wish to get into another unpleasant argument with him as I had the day before, I got up and, to be on the safe side, muttered something to the effect that I'd do my best. Then he asked me for something I never expected. I had almost reached the door and was about to open it when he caught me by the waist in a very friendly manner and proceeded to say something I couldn't quite understand at first.

Again I'll skip the details and the whole sequence of what he said, for it may be tiresome, but what it boiled down to was that he wanted me to introduce him to Dergachev since, as he put it, "you frequent his house."

I immediately pricked up my ears, trying hard not to betray myself by some involuntary gesture. I simply said that I wasn't well acquainted with either Mr. Dergachev or anyone else in the family and that I'd been there only on one occasion, and that by sheer accident.

"But since they let you in once, that means they'll let you in again, isn't that right?" he said.

I asked him then point blank, but in a very detached tone, why he wanted to be introduced to Dergachev, and to this day I cannot understand how a man who doesn't seem to be a fool and whom Vasin described to me as a shrewd businessman could be so naïve! For Stebelkov told me quite unashamedly that he suspected that "some forbidden, strictly forbidden, activities" must be taking place at Dergachev's and that therefore, if I found out something about these activities, I could work myself into "an advantageous position." And he winked his left eye at me.

I gave him no direct answer. I pretended to be reflecting for a while and then declared that I'd give it some thought and left in a hurry. Things were getting more and more complicated.

I rushed as fast as I could to Vasin's. This time he happened to be in.

"So here you are too!" Vasin said enigmatically when he saw me.

Without asking him what he meant by his remark, I quickly told him what I'd come about. He was visibly surprised but lost nothing of his ever-present self-control and coolly questioned me about every detail.

"Couldn't it be that you misunderstood him?"

"No, what he meant was plain enough."

"In any case, I appreciate very much your telling me," he added with warm sincerity. "From what you say, I gather he must have taken it for granted that you wouldn't be able to resist the lure of money."

"Besides, he's well aware of my financial position. I've been gambling and behaving very badly. . . ."

"So I've heard."

"What puzzles me most is that he seems to know a lot about your activities and is aware that you go there," I risked remarking.

"Oh, he knows perfectly," Vasin answered readily, "that I'm not involved in anything there. Besides, all these young people do is talk, nothing but talk. But you must've gathered that much yourself, I'm sure."

I got the impression that Vasin didn't quite trust me.

"In any case, I'm very grateful to you," he said again.

"I've heard," I tried again, "that Mr. Stebelkov's affairs are not in very good shape these days. . . . At any rate, I heard about certain shares . . ."

"What shares?"

I had deliberately mentioned the "shares," but I certainly had no intention of telling Vasin about what Sergei had confided to me in secret the day before. All I wanted was to utter the word and then judge from his eyes and his facial expression whether he'd heard something about these shares. And my purpose had been achieved: by a hardly noticeable fleeting twitch, I gathered that he did know something. So I didn't answer his question "What shares?" but lapsed instead into silence. He, for his part, did not pursue the matter any further.

"And how's your sister Lisa?" he inquired with sympathy.

"She's fine. You know, my sister has always spoken of you with the greatest respect. . . ."

There was a sparkle of pleasure in his eye. Just as I had guessed all along, he was not quite indifferent to Lisa.

"A few days ago Sergei Sokolsky came to see me," he suddenly said.

"When exactly was it?" I asked anxiously.

"Four days ago."

"You're sure it wasn't yesterday?"

"No, it wasn't yesterday."

There was a question in his look.

"One day I may tell you more about that meeting, but for the moment I feel I ought to warn you," Vasin went on enigmatically, "that he appeared to me to be in an abnormal state . . . perhaps even mentally ill. But then I had another visit," he said, suddenly dissolving into a smile, "and I was again forced to conclude that that visitor too was in an abnormal state. . . ."

"Was Sergei here again just now?"

"No, not him, I didn't mean Sergei. The visitor I just had was Mr. Versilov. . . . Why, don't you know anything about that visit? Did something new happen to him?"

"No, I don't know although something may very well have happened. But what exactly did take place between you two?" I was anxious to find out.

"I suppose I ought to keep the secret. . . . But you and I, we've been having such an enigmatic conversation . . ." He smiled again. "Anyway, Mr. Versilov never made me promise to keep it secret. Besides, you're his son and, since I believe I know how you feel about him, I'm sure I'm doing the right thing in letting you in on it. Now imagine this: he came to ask me whether, if it happened that one of these days he had to fight a duel, especially if it came up without much notice, I would be his second. I, of course, absolutely refused to render him that service."

I was stunned. That was the most alarming piece of news I'd heard yet! Something must have happened, something that I still hadn't heard about! I suddenly remembered Versilov telling me the previous night that it would be I who'd rush to him, not he to me. I decided to hurry to the old Prince Sokolsky's, feeling that there I'd find the answer to the puzzle.

As we parted, Vasin thanked me once more.

II

A rug wrapped around his legs, the old prince was sitting by his fireplace. He looked at me questioningly when I appeared, as if wondering why I'd come, although he'd been sending people over to my place almost daily to beg me to visit him. Still, he greeted me warmly, but when I started asking him questions he answered with obvious reluctance and also seemed to find it difficult to keep his mind on what he was saying. He'd stop again and again, as if trying to work something out, then look fixedly at me, apparently trying to remember a matter that had some connection with me. Then I told him straight out that I'd heard the big news and that I was very happy for him. A warm and kind smile appeared on his old lips; he became quite animated; his wariness and caution vanished; he seemed to have forgotten that he'd been trying to be reserved. Indeed, he must have forgotten whatever had been restraining him until then.

"Oh, you're such a dear friend! I was sure you'd be the first to congratulate me. . . . You know, only yesterday I was thinking: 'Who'll be the most happy for me? He will!' As a matter of fact, no one else is pleased about it, but never mind. People have wicked tongues, but why worry? Ah, *cher enfant*, it's such a poetic, such a charming story! And let me tell you that Anna has a very high opinion of you. . . . Don't you think she has a severe and at the same time an enchanting face, the face of an English keepsake? . . . She's as lovely as an English engraving. . . . A couple of years ago I had a whole collection of English engravings. . . . I always intended to propose to her; indeed, I'm surprised it never occurred to me to carry out my intention. . . ."

"As far as I remember, you've always been particularly fond of Anna."

"And, my dear boy, we have no wish to hurt anyone. To live among friends, among those who are dear to your heart—that is true paradise on earth, and all the poets . . . Well, I mean to say that it's been a known ideal ever since prehistoric times. You know, we're leaving first for Soden and from there we'll go to Bad-Gastein. . . . But why haven't you been to see me for such a long time? Did anything happen to you, my dear boy? I've missed you so dreadfully! Ah, how many things have happened since then, don't you think! The only trouble is that I can't help worrying: as soon as I'm alone, I worry. And that's why I mustn't stay alone—that's as obvious as two times two is four, isn't it? When she spoke, I understood from her very first word. . . . Actually, she only said very few words but it was . . . it was the most beautiful poem I ever heard. . . . And, come to think of it, you're her brother, almost her brother, aren't you? And so it's not hard to understand why I've been so fond of you from the beginning. . . . I felt that this was destined to happen, I swear I did. . . . I kissed her hand and wept."

He took out his handkerchief and it looked as if he were about to burst into tears all over again. He was in a state of violent agitation, indeed, in one of the worst states I could recall since I'd known him. Usually he was much more cheerful and relaxed.

"I'd like to forgive everybody, my dear boy," he babbled on; "I want nothing more than to forgive them all. It's a long time since I've been angry with anyone. There's art that is the poetry of life, there's the joy of helping those in need, and then there's Her—the biblical beauty! Ah, *quelle charmante personne!* What do you think? *Les chants de Salomon . . . non, ce n'est pas Salomon, c'est David qui mettait une jeune belle dans son lit pour se chauffer dans sa vieillesse. Enfin, David, Salomon,* all that keeps spinning around inside my head—there's a real jumble inside my skull now. Everything, *mon cher enfant,* can be both sublime and ridiculous at the same time. *Cette jeune belle de la vieillesse de David—c'est tout un poème,* while someone like Paul de Kock would have turned it all into *une scène de bassinoire* and made us all laugh. Besides, Paul de Kock has neither a sense of measure nor good taste, although one cannot say that he's altogether without talent. . . . My daughter Katerina keeps smiling. . . . I told her that we won't be in the way. We have started our romance and I want to be given a chance to complete it. . . . Even if it is a pipe dream, I don't want them to take it away from us."

"Why do you call it a pipe dream, Prince?"

"Pipe dream? What do you mean? But whatever it is, a pipe dream or not, I want to be allowed to die with that pipe dream."

"But who's talking about dying, Prince? Now, if ever, is the moment for you to live!"

"That's just what I say, that's just my point. I absolutely cannot understand why life should be so short. I suppose it's short so as not to allow us to get bored because, of course, life is a work of art too, a creation of the Creator Himself in the finished and perfect form of a Pushkin poem. And brevity is the first rule in art. . . . However, if someone is not bored, it would be nice if he were given a chance to live a little longer."

"Tell me, Prince, is it already official?"

"Oh no, not at all! We've all agreed that it's strictly a family matter—absolutely private, absolutely! For the time being I've told only my daughter Katerina because I feel guilty toward her. Ah, Katerina is such an angel, a real angel!"

"Oh yes, she certainly is that!"

"Ah, so you think so too? And I thought that you were her

enemy! By the way, she asked me not to receive you here any longer but—can you imagine?—I forgot all about it the second you arrived!"

I jumped to my feet.

"What did you say? Why? What have I done? When did she say that?"

Well, I'd had a feeling that something like this would happen ever since Tatyana had burst into my room.

"She said that yesterday, my boy, only yesterday, and I can't even understand how you got in here because orders have been given not to admit you. How did you manage to get in?"

"I just walked in."

"That's the surest way: for if you'd tried to slip in without being noticed, they'd have stopped you. Acting openly, *mon cher enfant,* shows really supreme cunning!"

"I don't understand at all what's going on here. I take it that you have decided not to receive me any more in your house?"

"No, no, my friend, I told you, I have nothing to do with it at all. . . . That is, I did give my full assent. But I want you to rest assured, my dear boy, that I'm terribly fond of you. However, Katerina was quite intransigent on that point. . . . And here, you see . . ."

At that moment Katerina appeared in the doorway. She was dressed to go out and, as was her custom, was coming to kiss her father before leaving. When she saw me, she stopped short, looked very embarrassed, then turned around and left.

"*Voilà!*" cried out the old prince, visibly shaken and greatly worried.

"There must be some misunderstanding!" I shouted. "I'm going to clear it up. . . . I'll be right back, Prince!" And I rushed out in pursuit of Katerina.

After that things happened so quickly that not only didn't I have time to make sense out of them but I never even got a chance to prepare myself to face what lay ahead. If I'd been prepared, of course I'd have behaved quite differently. But I lost my head just like a little boy. First I ran to her suite, but the lackey told me that Mrs. Akhmakov had gone downstairs and was about to drive off in her carriage. I rushed toward the main staircase and saw her descending the stairs. She was wearing her fur coat and was accompanied by—or rather was walking arm in arm with—a tall, straight-backed, forbidding-looking officer in full uniform, including sword, while a lackey followed behind, carrying the officer's greatcoat. This was the baron. He was a colonel of thirty-five or so, a dry, spare man, the dashing officer type, with a rather long face, a reddish mustache, and even reddish eyelashes. And although his face was by no means handsome, there was something striking and imperious in it. I have described him sketchily, the way I took him in at first sight. I'd never met him before. I ran after them downstairs, coatless and hatless. Katerina saw me coming first and whispered something to her companion. He turned his head slightly and made a sign to the lackey and the doorman. The lackey came toward me as I was about to open the outside door, but I pushed him aside and rushed out after them just as Björing was helping Katerina into the carriage.

"Mrs. Akhmakov! Katerina!" I shouted stupidly.

Ah, how idiotic, how incredibly idiotic, I must have looked, standing there hatless and shouting! I can see it so clearly today.

Furious, Björing again turned to the lackey and loudly shouted one or two words to him that I couldn't make out. I felt someone seize me by the elbow. At the same instant the carriage started up. I called out to Katerina again and rushed after the carriage. I saw Katerina's face looking out of the carriage window and I got the impression that she was extremely worried. But, in my violent rush toward the carriage, I must have inadvertently pushed Björing and stepped on his foot rather hard, for he let out a muffled cry of pain and clenched his teeth. Then I felt his strong hand catching me by the shoulder and giving me a strong and vicious shove that threw me back about ten feet. At that moment the flunkey handed him his greatcoat, which he threw over his shoulder; he climbed into his sledge and again shouted something imperiously to the doorman and the lackey, pointing at me. This time they seized me and held onto me. A servant threw my coat at me and another one handed me my hat. I can no longer remember what they said, but they did tell me something and I stood there listening to them without understanding a word. Then suddenly I left them standing there and rushed away.

III

Hardly aware of where I was, bumping into people, I ran all the way to Tatyana Prutkov's apartment without it ever occurring to me that I would have got there much faster if I'd taken a cab. . . . It was in Katerina's presence that Björing had shoved me! True, I'd stepped on his foot and he'd pushed me away instinctively as a man would if someone treads on his corn (and, who knows, perhaps he really had a corn!). But, still, she saw him push me and also saw the servants grab me, so *she* was witness to all that ignominy!

When I burst into Mrs. Prutkov's apartment, at first I couldn't even utter a sound because my teeth were chattering as if I were running a high fever. Well, yes, I probably was feverish and, what's more, I was also crying. . . . Oh, I felt so horribly insulted.

"What? So they kicked you out? Well, you asked for it, so it serves you right!" Mrs. Prutkov declared.

I sank into an armchair and just stared at her.

"But what's the matter with you?" She looked at me intently. "Here, drink this glass of water, drink it! And tell me, what have you been up to there this time?"

I mumbled that I'd been thrown out of the old prince's house and that Björing had shoved me in the street.

"Are you in a state to understand something now or not yet? Here, read this, isn't it pretty?"

She picked up a piece of paper from the table, handed it to me, and stood there to watch the effect it would produce on me. I at once recognized Versilov's handwriting. It consisted of just a few lines and was addressed to Katerina Akhmakov. I shuddered and instantly recovered full comprehension. Here is that horrible, monstrous, absurd, and criminal note word for word.

> Dear Mrs. Akhmakov,
>
> As depraved as you may be by nature and as expert as you may be in your depravity, I still thought you would restrain your passions and not deploy your wiles on mere children. But you were too shameless even to stop at that. So let me inform you that the document of such great concern to you was certainly not burned over a candle and, indeed, was never in Kraft's possession, so there is nothing to be gained for you in that respect. Therefore stop depraving an adolescent needlessly. Spare him, he is still a minor, almost a boy in fact, and is not yet fully developed either mentally or physically. So what good can he be to you? I am concerned about him, and that is why I have decided to write you, although I do not really expect that it will do any good.
>
> I have the honor to inform you, madam, that I am also sending a copy of this letter to Baron Björing.
>
> (signed) Andrei Versilov.

As I read it, I turned paler and paler, but when I'd finished, the blood rushed to my face and my lips quivered with fury.

"He writes that about me! After what I told him two days ago!" I shouted in rage.

"That's just it—you told him!"

Tatyana snatched the letter out of my hands.

"But that was not what I told him, it wasn't that at all! Oh, good God, what will she think of me now! Why, he's insane! I saw him only yesterday. . . . When did he send this letter?"

"Yesterday afternoon. She got it in the evening and brought it to me today."

"But I saw him yesterday myself. . . . Yes, he must be mad! Versilov would never have written anything like that. This letter was written by a madman. Who else could write such things to a woman?"

"It's precisely madmen who write like that in their rage when jealousy makes them blind and deaf and turns their blood to rat poison. . . . You still have no idea of what kind of man he is! And now they'll crush him until there's only a wet spot left behind. And it's he who's asking for it. Why, he might just as well go to the Nikolaevsky Railroad and lay his head down on the tracks—that would rid him of his head, since it seems to have become too heavy for him to carry. . . . But you, what pushed you to talk to him? What induced you to taunt him? Unless perhaps you wanted to brag about your success?"

"Ah, how he hates her, how he hates her!" I cried out, striking my head with my hand. "And why, why? . . . To hate a woman so much! What did she ever do to him? What can there have been between them to make him write her such letters?"

"Hates her . . . hates her. . . ." Mrs. Prutkov mimicked me with loathing.

The blood rushed to my head again as I suddenly understood something that I hadn't understood before. I stared searchingly at the old woman.

"Get out of my sight!" she shrieked, turning away from me and waving me away. "I've had enough of looking after the lot of you! But I'm through now and, as far as I'm concerned, you can all drop dead! The only one I'm still sorry for is your mother. . . ."

It goes without saying that I then ran over to Versilov's.

Ah, how betrayed I felt, how terribly betrayed!

IV

Versilov wasn't alone.

At this point I must anticipate my story and explain the position he was in. After he'd sent the letter to Katerina and a copy, just as he'd said (God knows why), to Björing, he naturally expected that what he had done would have certain consequences and had prepared for them. The first thing he'd done that morning was to move Mother and Lisa (who, I learned later, had been ill since she'd returned home and had to stay in bed) into my former coffin-like attic, while the rest of the place, especially the living room, had been cleaned and tidied up with special care.

And, just as he'd expected, at two o'clock in the afternoon he received a visit from a certain Baron R., a forty-year-old colonel, one of those German barons of whom there are so many in the Russian service, who are full of their baronial arrogance though penniless, who have to live on their pay and are the most zealous sticklers for rules and regulations. He was a tall, lean, and powerful-looking man and his hair had the same reddish tinge as Björing's, although this baron's hair was already getting thin on top.

Since I arrived after Baron R. I missed the beginning of their conversation and now they both seemed rather excited, as well they might. Versilov sat at the table and the baron occupied an armchair next to it. Versilov was pale and spoke with restraint, as though pouring his words through a funnel. The baron, on the other hand, kept raising his voice and was obviously a man who could lose his temper without much provocation. Now he was making a visible effort to control himself, still looking supercilious and even contemptuous, albeit rather surprised. When he saw me he frowned, while Versilov seemed rather pleased at my unexpected intrusion.

"Hello, my dear boy! Well, Baron, here is the young—extremely young—gentleman whom I mentioned in my little note. I'm sure he won't be in our way and, in fact, his presence may be very useful." (The baron looked me over with scorn.) "You know, my dear boy, I'm even delighted that you came, so I'll ask you to sit down over there in the corner and wait until the Baron and I are through with our business. . . . Please don't let his presence disturb you, Baron, he'll sit quietly in the corner."

I didn't object. My mind was already made up. Besides, I was quite taken in by what was going on. So I retreated into my corner and sat there without making a sound or stirring until the end of their conversation.

"Let me repeat once more, Baron," Versilov said, pronouncing his words with utmost precision, "I consider Mrs. Akhmakov, to whom I wrote that reprehensible and crazy letter, not only as a most honorable lady but even as the incarnation of all perfection."

"This form of disavowal of your own words sounds too much like a reiteration of them," the baron growled, "and I consider what you say definitely disrespectful."

"Still, you'd come closest to the truth if you took them literally. You see, sometimes I suffer from certain fits and . . . well, all sorts of nervous troubles—in fact I'm under medical care now—and so it happened that during one such moment . . ."

"Such an explanation is not acceptable. I tell you once more that you persist in being irrelevant; indeed, I believe you're being deliberately irrelevant. I told you at the very beginning that whatever concerns the lady in question and the letter you wrote to her must be entirely excluded from our present explanation, but you still keep bringing that matter in. Baron Björing expressly asked me to make it clear to you which of your actions concerned him personally—namely, your insolent gesture in sending him a copy of your letter with a postscript to the effect that you were prepared to answer for this when and how he pleased."

"But that, it would seem to me, is sufficiently plain and requires no further explanation."

"I understand that, I heard you say it. You don't even apologize for what you did but, instead, keep repeating that you're willing to answer for it in any way he pleases. But that would be getting off too easily! And so, in view of the twist you've been trying to give to your explanations, I consider that I'm now entitled to tell you without any restraint my own conclusions—namely, that it is utterly and absolutely impossible for Baron Björing to have anything to do with you . . . on an equal footing."

"Such a conclusion is, of course, the easiest way out for your friend Baron Björing and I must admit it doesn't surprise me at all: I expected something of this sort."

I must observe here parenthetically that, from his very first words and from his expression, it was obvious to me that Versilov was trying to provoke an outburst, that he was deliberately taunting this irascible baron, and that he was trying to test how long his patience would last. And now the baron bristled all over.

"I know you have the reputation of being a witty man, but being witty is not the same as being intelligent."

"An extremely profound observation, Colonel."

"I didn't ask for your approval and I didn't come here to chat with you!" Baron R. burst out angrily. "So be good enough to listen to what I have to say. Baron Björing was in quite a dilemma as to how to act when he received your letter because it

had all the earmarks of a lunatic. There were, of course, ways
. . . of keeping you quiet. But, for certain special reasons, he
decided to treat you with indulgence since inquiries were made
and it was found that once you had belonged to decent society
and had even served in the Guards but that later you had been
ostracized and that your reputation was, to say the least, dubi-
ous. However, despite all available information, I have come here
to ascertain the facts personally and now, after having admitted
yourself that you are subject to nervous fits, you have decided
to display your wit. Enough! Baron Björing's position and his
reputation forbid him from stooping . . . from having any association with you whatsoever. . . . In short, I have been
authorized to warn you that if there is a repetition of your previous action or if you ever do anything of that sort again, steps
will promptly be taken to bring you under necessary control,
and let me assure you that it would be done very quickly. Why,
we're not living in a jungle, after all, but in a modern well-
organized state!"

"Are you really so sure of that, my good Baron?"

"Damn it all!" The baron suddenly leaped to his feet. "Would
you like me to prove to you that I'm not 'your good Baron'?"

"Good heavens, must I remind you again that my wife and
daughter are within earshot and that I have requested you to
lower your voice because your screams may bother them," Versilov said, also getting to his feet.

"Your wife. . . . Ah, hell, if I've sat here all this time and
tried to talk to you, it was only to get to the bottom of that whole
disgusting affair," the baron went on with unabated anger and
without lowering his voice. "That's enough now!" he roared furiously. "Not only have you been ostracized by decent people,
but you are a maniac, a real raving maniac and that's how you
are known! I'm telling you now that you don't deserve any
mercy at all and this very day appropriate measures will be taken
to render you harmless; you'll be taken out of town and placed
in a suitable institution where they'll bring you back to your
senses."

And in long and rapid strides Baron R. left the room. Versilov
did not see him out of the house; he just stood there absorbed in
his thoughts, his eyes fixed on me but probably not seeing me.
Suddenly he smiled, tossed back his hair, picked up his hat, and
was about to leave the room when I caught him by the arm. He
stopped, facing me.

"Ah yes, you. . . . Did you hear?"

"How could you do such a thing! Why did you have to distort everything like that, splatter it with dirt, act in such an underhanded way?"

He looked at me intently, but then his smile spread more and more and finally turned into laughter.

"But it's I who was disgraced!" I shouted, beside myself. "I was disgraced in her presence! . . . He pushed me . . . and she was watching. . . . He shoved me. . . ."

"Did he really? Ah, my poor little boy! I'm sorry that happened to you. . . . So you say they had a bit of fun at your expense?"

"And that makes you laugh! You're laughing at me yourself now!"

He quickly freed his arm from my grip, put his hat on his head, and, laughing in the most genuine way, walked out of the room.

What would have been the point of me running after him now? I had lost everything I'd ever had in that single minute. . . .

Suddenly I caught sight of Mother. She'd come noiselessly downstairs and was looking around warily.

"Has he left?"

"Mother dear, how can you stay here any longer? Come with me, I'll find a shelter for us and I'll work like a slave to provide for you and Lisa. . . . Forget all of them and let's get out of here. . . . We'll live on our own! Mother, do you remember that when you came to visit me at Touchard's school I didn't even want to recognize you?"

"I remember it very well, darling, and I've felt guilty toward you all my life: I brought you into this world but I didn't know you."

"It's he who's responsible for everything, it's all his fault—he never loved us."

"He did."

"Let's go, Mother."

"How can I leave him? You know he isn't happy, don't you?"

"Where's Lisa?"

"Lisa's in bed. . . . She came home not feeling well and I'm afraid she's ill. . . . Tell me, are they very angry with him? What are they going to do to him? Where did he go? What was that officer threatening?"

"Nothing will happen to him. Nothing ever does, for he's the kind of man to whom nothing can ever happen! And if you don't believe me, ask Mrs. Prutkov here. (Mrs. Prutkov had suddenly walked into the room.) Good-by then, Mother, I'll be back very soon and when I return I'll ask you again to do what I just asked you."

I rushed out. I didn't want to see anyone and certainly not Tatyana Prutkov. And I was terribly worried about Mother. I felt I had to be alone, completely alone.

V

But even before I'd crossed the street I felt that I couldn't bear to walk around aimlessly, butting into indifferent strangers. . . . So what else could I do with myself? Who could have any use for me now and what could I want now? Without even thinking of him, I instinctively set out for Sergei's. . . . When I got there, his manservant Peter told me he'd gone out. I said I'd wait in Sergei's study, as I'd often done before. The study was a large, high-ceilinged room, cluttered with all sorts of furniture. I went into the darkest corner, sat down on a sofa, put my elbows on a little table nearby, hid my face in my hands, and wondered: "What am I to do now?"

But although I could still formulate that question, I had absolutely no idea of how to answer it. Besides, I wasn't in a state to think sensibly. As I said earlier, I felt crushed after the events of those few days. So I just sat there with odd bits of thoughts whirling chaotically around in my head: "I never saw what he was really after, never understood him"—the words flashed through my mind again and again. "He laughed in my face just now, but it wasn't at me he was laughing—it was at Björing, it's all Björing and not me. . . . Two days ago at dinner, he already knew everything and looked dejected. In that inn, he got that stupid confession out of me and then distorted it until there was no truth left in it. . . . But what does he care about truth? He himself doesn't believe a single word of what he wrote. All he wanted was to insult, insult wantonly, and all he needed was a pretext and I supplied him with that pretext. . . . He's like a mad dog! Unless he wants to kill Björing? Why? His heart must know why! But I know nothing of what's going on in his heart! . . . No, no, I still don't know! Can it be that he loves her with such a passion? Or hates her with such a passion? I don't know and perhaps he doesn't know himself. . . . Why did I tell Mother that nothing could happen to him? What did I mean by that? Have I lost him? Is there a hope left that I haven't? *She* saw how I was shoved. . . . Did she laugh at me too? Or didn't she? I'd have laughed in her place. . . . Why, they were just giving a snooper what was coming to him. . . . A snooper!" And then suddenly the question flashed through my head:

"What did he mean in that loathsome note when he said that the compromising letter had never been burned and that it still existed? . . . Oh no, he won't kill Björing! I bet that he's sitting right now in that inn, listening to 'Lucia.' But perhaps, after having listened to 'Lucia,' he'll go and kill Björing. . . . Björing pushed me and almost hit me! Did he actually hit me? Since Björing doesn't even consider Versilov as worthy of fighting a duel, he would certainly never consider accepting my challenge. . . . So I may have to kill him tomorrow—wait for him in the street and shoot him down with a revolver. . . ."

This conclusion slipped into my mind all by itself and I didn't stop to examine it.

At other moments I lapsed into a daydream: the door would suddenly open and Katerina would walk in, give me her hand, and both of us would burst out laughing. . . . "Oh, my nice fellow student," she'd say. . . . That's what I imagined, what I was longing for, especially after the room became dark. Ah, it was not all that long ago that I really had stood near her, that she really had given me her hand, and that we'd laughed together! So how could such a horrible distance have grown between us within such a short time? Perhaps all I had to do was to rush to her and explain everything. That's it: just explain everything! Ah, God, how had it happened that all of a sudden I'd found myself in a completely different world? Yes, a completely new world! . . . And Lisa? And Sergei? Oh, that was still part of the old world. . . . And now here I was at Sergei's. . . . But Mother, how could Mother go on living with him the way things were? I could . . . I could stand anything, but Mother, how could she? So what would happen now? . . .

And in a crazy whirl the figures of Lisa, Anna, Stebelkov, Sergei, Aferdov, and all the rest kept spinning around inside my aching head until everything became shapeless and slippery, and I was lucky to manage to hold onto anything, to recognize it. . . .

"No, I have my Idea!" it suddenly occurred to me, but then I asked myself whether it was really true, whether I was not just repeating unthinkingly a familiar phrase. My Idea was obscurity and solitude, but could I, after all that had happened, crawl back into my former darkness? And, oh God, I hadn't burned that letter, had I? I'd forgotten to burn it the day before yesterday. So as soon as I got home I'd burn it over a candle, yes, absolutely over a candle. . . . Only I'm not sure whether that's what I was really thinking. . . .

It was completely dark now and Peter came in with candles.

He stood over me briefly, inquiring whether I had eaten, but I just waved him away. Nevertheless, he reappeared about an hour later with some tea and I eagerly emptied a large cup. Then I asked him the time and he told me it was half past eight and I wasn't the least surprised to find that I'd been waiting there for five whole hours.

"I came in three times before, but I think you were asleep, sir," Peter said.

I didn't remember his coming in. I don't know why but the thought that I might have been asleep suddenly frightened me, so I got up and started pacing the room in order not to fall asleep again. In the end my headache became very bad.

At exactly ten, Sergei came in and I was quite surprised to realize that I'd been waiting for him—indeed, I'd forgotten why I'd come, completely forgotten.

"I see you're here," he said, "while I've been to your place looking for you."

He looked stern and grave. There was not the slightest trace of a smile on his face. One single thing seemed to absorb him.

"I've been rushing around all day; I've done everything I could," he went on, obviously pursuing his inner train of thought, "but nothing worked. . . . Ahead, I see nothing but horror." (N.B.: He still hadn't been to see the old prince.) "I saw Zhibelsky. He's an impossible man. First, we must get the money and then we'll see. But, if even with the money it doesn't work, then. . . . So I've decided not to think of it now: let's just try and get hold of the money and once we have it we'll see. The money you won the day before yesterday is still intact; not one kopek of it is missing: it comes to exactly three thousand—that is, three rubles short of three thousand. It is three hundred and forty rubles more than what you owed me. Now I want you to take that, plus another seven hundred rubles to make it one thousand, and I'll keep the remaining two thousand. Then we'll go to Zershikov's, sit down at opposite ends of the table, and try to win ten thousand. Perhaps it will work and if not . . . well, anyway, there's nothing else left for us to do."

He looked at me with resignation, as if leaving it all up to fate.

"Yes, yes!" I suddenly cried out, feeling as if life were coming back to me. "Let's go right away! I've been waiting for you. . . ."

I must note here that during all those hours I had never even given a thought to roulette.

"And what about the sordid side of it? What about the ugliness of it all?" Sergei suddenly asked.

"Do you mean roulette? Only that?" I said with emotion. "No, money is all important and, in fact, you and I, we are almost a couple of saints! Hasn't Björing sold himself? Hasn't Anna? And haven't you heard that Versilov is an insane maniac? Yes, a maniac, a maniac!"

"Are you all right, Arkady? Your eyes look so peculiar. . . ."

"Are you suggesting that you could go without me? No, sir, I won't leave you now! It's not for nothing that I dreamed about gambling all night. So let's go!" I shouted, as though I'd suddenly discovered the answer to everything.

"All right, let's go, although you look quite feverish. . . . But we'll see how . . ."

He didn't finish. His expression was grim. We were already walking toward the door.

"Know what?" he said, suddenly stopping in the doorway. "There's still another way out beside roulette."

"What is it?"

"The princely way."

"Well, what's that?"

"You'll find out later. For now I'll only say that I'm unworthy of it because I'm late in acting that way. Let's go then, and you'll remember what I've just said. We'll try the flunkey's way out now. . . . Ah, as if I didn't know that I'm acting like a flunkey now, deliberately and in cold blood!"

VI

I pounced on the roulette table as though my whole salvation lay hidden in it, although, as I said before, I'd never given it a thought until Sergei's arrival. Besides, I wasn't even going to play for my own account; I was going to gamble with Sergei's money, risk his life. I still can't understand what it was that drew me there, but it was an irresistible pull. And never did the people, the faces, the croupiers, the excited shouting of the gamblers, the whole gaudy gaming room at Zershikov's strike me as so revolting, grim, vulgar, and depressing as it did then. I remember only too well the sad and painful feeling that kept tugging at my heart during those hours at the table. But why didn't I leave then? Why did I stay and bear it all as if I'd accepted to bear a cross, as if I were ready to perform a feat of heroism? All I can say of myself at the time is that I was insane. And yet never before had I played my stakes as calmly and deliberately as I did that evening. I was silent, concentrated, attentive, and frightfully calculating; I was patient and stingy, although also resolute at critical moments. Once again I installed myself in the vicinity of the *zero*, which happened to be between Zershikov and Aferdov, who always sat on Zershikov's right; that place was distasteful to me, but I had to sit there because I had to be near the *zero* and all the other chairs nearby were taken.

I had been playing for an hour or more already when suddenly I saw Sergei get up from his seat. He took a few steps and stopped just across the table from me. He had lost everything and was now watching me play, although I don't believe he could understand what was going on; indeed, from what I was to learn later, he probably wasn't thinking about gambling at all. At that moment I had just started winning and Zershikov was counting out the money that was coming to me when, all of a sudden, Aferdov quite unabashedly picked up one of my hundred-ruble bills and, before my eyes, added it to the pile of money in front of him. I let out a cry and grabbed his hand. Something quite unexpected happened inside me: it was as if all at once I'd broken loose from the chain I'd been tied to; it was as if all the blows and insults I'd been exposed to lately became concentrated at that second in that hundred-ruble bill, of which I was being robbed; it was as if everything that had been accumulated and compressed inside me had been waiting for just that additional provocation to burst out.

"He's a thief! He's just stolen a hundred rubles from me!" I screamed, beside myself, glaring at everyone around me.

I won't try to describe the hubbub that followed. It was something unprecedented at Zershikov's, where people behaved with dignity, for the place had a good reputation. But I was now beyond the point of controlling myself. Then, above the shouts and the din, I heard Zershikov's voice.

"Well, it's a fact that there were four hundred rubles here just now and the money is missing."

And then something else happened: the money that had been lying in front of Zershikov's very nose and that belonged to the bank—four hundred rubles in all—had vanished and Zershikov was pointing at the spot where it had been just a moment before, right next to me, next to the spot where my own money was piled up, much closer to me than to Aferdov.

"The thief is here—he's the one! He has stolen again! Search him!" I cried, pointing at Aferdov.

"All this happens because they let in unknown, unrecommended people!" roared an imperious voice amidst the discordant cries. "Who allowed him in? And who is he anyway?"

"His name is Dolgoruky or something."

"Prince Dolgoruky?"

"He was introduced by Prince Sokolsky," someone shouted.

"Did you hear that, Prince?" I yelled in a frenzy across the table. "They're trying to accuse me of being a thief when I've just been robbed myself! What are you waiting for? Speak up!"

What followed was worse than anything that had happened that day or, for that matter, in my whole life: Sergei betrayed me. I saw him shrug and heard distinctly his irritated voice answering the questions that were being tossed at him from every side:

"I'm not responsible for anyone and I'd like to be left alone."

Then I heard Aferdov, who now stood in the middle of the crowd, demand in a loud voice that he be searched while turning out his own pockets. But the people around him protested and shouted: "No, no, we know who the thief is!"

Two flunkeys who were summoned seized me by the arms.

"I won't allow them to search me, I won't stand for it!" I yelled, trying to shake them off.

But they dragged me to the next room and searched me publicly down to the last fold of my clothing while I shouted and resisted.

"He must've got rid of it. We ought to look around on the floor," someone decided.

"It's too late now. What chance have we to find it on the floor?"

"Probably he managed to throw it away somewhere under the table."

"I'm sure we'll never find anything now. . . ."

They led me out, but I managed to hold my ground for a moment as they were dragging me through the door and to scream with insane fury so that my voice rang out through the whole gaming room:

"Roulette is prohibited by police regulation. . . . I shall report you all!"

I was led downstairs, given my coat and hat, and . . . the door into the street opened . . .

Chapter 9

I

Thus my gambling ended in disaster, but the night was not over yet and here's what I remember of it.

It must have been somewhat past midnight when I found

myself in the street. It was a clear, quiet, and icy cold night. I was almost running. I was in a great hurry. And I certainly wasn't going home. Why should I go home? How could I have a home now? A home is where people live. Going home to sleep, to wake up there the next morning, and to go on living was unthinkable now. My life was finished and I could no longer go on living. . . . And so I wandered about the streets, quite unaware of where I was going and why I was in such a hurry. It was very hot and I kept flinging open my heavy raccoon-lined coat. At that moment I felt there was nothing I could do that would make any difference. And, strangely enough, I kept feeling as if everything around me, including the air I was breathing, was coming from another planet, as if I'd suddenly found myself on the moon. Everything—the city, the passers-by, the sidewalk under my running feet—was *no longer mine.* "Well, this may be St. Isaac's and that may be Palace Square," flashed through my mind, "but now I have nothing to do with them." And everything suddenly became alien and was *no longer connected with me.* "But I have Mother, I have Lisa . . . ! So what? What is Mother to me now? And what do I care about Lisa? Everything, everything has come to an end except for one thing —that I'm a thief once and for all."

How would I ever be able to prove that I was not a thief? How would that be possible now? Perhaps I could leave for America? But what would I prove by that? Versilov would be the first to believe that I was a thief. What about my "idea"? What "idea"? What meaning could it have now? If I should live another fifty or even a hundred years, there would always be someone to point at me and say: "He's a thief, nothing but a thief. He started realizing his 'idea' by stealing money at a roulette table."

Was I full of bitterness? I don't know, perhaps I was very bitter. But there was a strange feature in me, a feature that had existed since my earliest childhood perhaps: If I was treated badly, absolutely wronged, thoroughly insulted and humiliated, I always felt an irresistible desire to submit passively to my humiliations and to the whims of my humiliator, even to anticipate those whims. "All right, you've humiliated me and now I'll wallow in the dirt even more, so just watch and enjoy the sight!" Touchard used to beat me to prove that I was the son not of a senator but of a flunkey, so I immediately adapted myself to the role of a flunkey. Not only would I hand him his clothes as he dressed but, of my own accord, I'd grab a clothesbrush and start brushing the last specks of dust off him without his order or request; indeed, at times I'd pursue him, brush in hand, seized by a sort of flunkeyish enthusiasm to remove every last particle from his frock coat until he himself would stop me, saying: "That'll do, Arkady, that'll do for now." Sometimes he'd come in and remove his overcoat, and I'd brush it, fold it carefully, and cover it with a checked silk kerchief. I was well aware that my comrades laughed at me and despised me for this, but that was just what gave me special pleasure: "Well, since you wanted me to be a lackey, I became a lackey, and if you wish me to be a pig, I'll be a pig!" Such a passive hatred and underground spite I could keep up for years. And yet, at Zershikov's, I'd yelled frantically, so the whole room could hear me, that I would report them to the police for playing roulette —a forbidden game—on the premises. But the feeling underlying my outburst could be explained by the following reasoning: "You've humiliated me, searched me, called me a thief, crushed me, all right, so you may as well know that you've guessed right and, besides being a thief, I'm also a stool pigeon!" This is the explanation I have to offer now as I look back at that episode, although at the time I had other things to think of than an analysis of my actions. The words I had shouted out hadn't been planned and, in fact, a second before I had no idea of what I'd say; the words came out by themselves; there was in my mental make-up that "trait" I mentioned earlier.

As I was running, I must have already been delirious, although I remember very clearly that I knew what I was doing. Still, I'm sure that a whole set of ideas and conclusions was already out of my reach by then; indeed, even during those minutes I felt that there were certain thoughts I was still able to think, while there were others I could no longer think. The same was true of some of the decisions I made then: although I was perfectly lucid when I made them, it didn't bother me in the least if there was no logic whatsoever in them. Moreover, at certain moments I could be fully aware of the absurdity of an action upon which I had decided and then go ahead with it, fully understanding what I was doing. Yes, I came very close to committing a crime that night, and it was sheer accident that I didn't.

I had suddenly recalled Tatyana Prutkov's words when she'd said that Versilov might just as well go to the Nikolaevsky Railroad, lay his head on the tracks, and let the wheels of a train cut it off for him. For a moment that idea took complete possession of my thoughts and feelings, but very quickly I chased it away: "If I lay my head on the railroad track, tomorrow they'd say I did it because I'd stolen and was ashamed of it. No, no, nothing will force me to do that!" And it was precisely during that moment that I felt a sudden flash of immense bitterness. "Well," the idea flitted through my mind, "since I can no longer prove my innocence and since I cannot just turn a page and start a new life, the right course for me is to resign myself and become a lackey, a dog, a bug, a stool pigeon, a real informer, that is, while at the same time I'll get ready secretly. . . . And when the time comes suddenly to blow up everything, wipe out both the guilty and the innocent, then they'll suddenly learn that it was done by the man who had been branded a thief. . . . Well, and then I could kill myself."

I don't remember how I got into the narrow side street near the Horseguards' Boulevard. For about a hundred paces I followed the high stone walls that enclosed the back yards. Then, behind the wall, on my left, I noticed a big pile of firewood, a huge one such as might be found in a lumber yard, that rose at least six feet above the stone wall. Suddenly I stopped to study the layout. In my pocket I had a silver matchbox full of wax matches. I repeat once more that I was fully conscious of what I was planning to do and I remember it clearly, although I don't know *why* I wanted to do it, I don't know at all. I just remember that I suddenly felt an overwhelming desire: "I could climb up on top of the wall, I could do it very easily," I said to myself when, only a few steps away from me, I discovered a gate that probably remained locked for months on end. "If I step on the plank that's sticking out of the gate," I went on pondering, "I could hoist myself up on top of the wall and no one would notice me, for there's no one around; it's all quiet in there. And, once astride the wall, I could easily set fire to the wood that all but touches the wall. . . . I wouldn't even have to jump into the yard. . . . In this cold, it would burn even harder. I'd just have to reach a birch log with my hand. . . . No, no need even to pull out that log, I could just tear off some bark, light it with a match, and stick it back into the pile. And I'd have a fire going. I'd jump off the wall and walk off. . . . I wouldn't even have to run because it would take quite a while before anyone noticed anything. . . ."

That's how I pictured it all in my mind and then, all at once, I decided to go ahead with it. I felt an extreme pleasure, a peculiar joy, and I started climbing up the wall. I could climb well: I'd been good at gymnastics when I was a boy. But this time I had rubber galoshes on and it proved much harder than I'd expected. Still, I did manage to grab the plank that was sticking out slightly, pull myself up enough to catch hold of the top of the wall with one hand . . . but then I suddenly lost my grip and went flying backward.

I guess I must have hit the ground with the back of my head and remained unconscious a minute or two. When I came to, I instinctively wrapped my coat around me as I felt unbearably cold, and, still hardly realizing what I was doing, I crawled toward the corner of the gateway and crouched in the recess between the gate and the wall. There was chaos in my head and I probably dozed off very soon. I remember, as if in a dream, my ears were suddenly filled with a heavy, deep ringing of bells, to which I began to listen with great joy.

II

The bell struck clearly and distinctly once every two or even three seconds, but it was definitely not an alarm bell but a pleasant, smooth chime, and suddenly I recognized it: why, it was the old familiar chime of St. Nicholas', the red church across from Touchard's school, that old Moscow church I remember so well, the very ornate one with many cupolas and columns, which had been built during the reign of Tsar Alexei. And it also occurred to me that, since Easter week was just over, tiny new leaves must be shivering on the meager little birches in Touchard's front garden. The bright late afternoon sun was pouring its slanting rays into the classroom, while in the small room next door where Touchard had isolated me a year earlier from the "sons of counts and senators," a visitor was sitting. Yes, I, the boy without a family, was unexpectedly having a visitor, the first visitor I'd had since I'd been at Touchard's school. I recognized my visitor the very second she came in, although I hadn't seen Mother since the time she'd taken me to the village church and the dove had flown across under the cupola. So we sat together in my room and I looked at her in wonderment. Many years later I learned that Versilov was abroad at the time, that she had decided to come to Moscow and had used her meager savings to pay for the journey, I believe secretly from the people with whom she was staying in Versilov's absence—all that just in order to see me. The strange thing was that, although she'd spoken to Touchard and must have told him who she was when she'd arrived, she never mentioned to me the fact that she was my mother. She just sat near me and I remember being rather surprised at how little she had to say. She had brought a little package with her and when she opened it I saw that it contained six oranges, some gingerbread, and two quite ordinary French rolls. I felt offended that she had brought me those two ordinary rolls and prissily told her that we were well fed at school and that every boy got a whole French roll for tea.

"All right, my darling, so I was a bit stupid when I said to myself that perhaps they didn't feed you too well at school. Don't be angry with me, sweet."

"But Madame Touchard will be offended and the boys will laugh at me. . . ."

"Still, won't you take them? Perhaps you could eat them sometime?"

"Please don't . . ."

And I didn't even touch her goodies: the oranges and the gingerbread lay in front of me on the table as I sat with my eyes lowered but with a highly dignified air. Who knows, perhaps I was not very anxious to conceal from her how painful her visit was to me and that I was ashamed of her in front of the other boys; perhaps I even wanted to hint to her that she was disgracing me since she didn't seem to realize it herself. Oh, by that time I was already running after Touchard with the clothesbrush to flick the last speck of dust off his coat! I was also imagining the taunts I'd have to suffer as soon as she left, taunts from the boys and perhaps also from Touchard, so there was not a scrap of warmth in my heart for her that day. I only examined out of the corner of my eye her old, dark overcoat, her rough hands (almost the hands of a working woman), her heavy shoes, her face that had grown very thin, and the first wrinkles that had already appeared on her forehead. Nevertheless, later, after her departure that evening, Madame Touchard said to me, "It looks as if you *maman* used to be rather pretty once."

As we sat there, suddenly Agafia appeared with a cup of coffee on a tray. That was the hour when the Touchards always had their afternoon coffee in the living room. But Mother thanked the maid and refused the cup because, as I learned later, she never drank coffee in those days for it gave her heart palpitations. The trouble was that the Touchards felt that, by allowing her to visit me, they were being great liberals and most generous, and the cup of coffee they had sent up to her was a sort of crowning humanitarian gesture that did utmost credit to their civilized European ways and ideas. And now my mother seemed to be pointedly refusing their coffee.

I was then summoned to Touchard's room and ordered to take all my books and papers and show them to Mother "so that she may see for herself the progress you have made while in my establishment." And while I was there, Madame Touchard pursed her lips and said in an offended and mocking tone: "I'm sorry our coffee was not to the taste of *votre maman.*"

I collected my books and carried them to Mother past the classroom full of the staring "sons of counts and senators" who had been spying and eavesdropping on us.

But the fact is that, in a way, I even enjoyed doing what Touchard had ordered me to do and I carried out his orders exactly. I meticulously showed her my exercise books, explaining that "these are lessons of French grammar, this is an exercise, and this a dictation, these are the conjugations of the French auxiliary verbs *être* and *avoir,* and that's geography, the description of the principal cities of Europe, and these are all the parts of the world, and so on." For at least half an hour, I kept droning on like that in a monotonous little voice with my eyes modestly cast down. I realized that Mother couldn't possibly understand anything of my learned explanations; indeed, I even suspected that she could hardly read and write, but that was just what made the part I was playing so sickeningly enjoyable. But I did not succeed in boring her: she listened to me intently with unwavering attention, reverently, never once interrupting me, so that in the end I got tired of it myself and stopped. I noticed, though, that she looked at me with sadness and there was something in her expression that made me a bit sorry for her.

When at last she got up to leave, in came Touchard and, with an idiotically solemn expression, asked her "whether she was satisfied with her son's scholarly achievements." Mother muttered something disconnectedly and thanked him and, when Madame Touchard came in too, Mother started begging them "not to abandon this poor orphan because he is just like an orphan really, so please be good to him . . ." and, her eyes filled with tears, she bowed deeply to each of them in turn just as humble "common people" might bow when they have to ask a favor of the gentry. The Touchards were apparently surprised and Madame Touchard was even visibly touched and quickly revised the conclusions she had drawn when Mother had declined her cup of coffee. Touchard assured her in an affected egalitarian tone that he made no distinction between the boys, that all those who attended the school were just like his own children, and that he was like their father, that I was almost on an equal footing with the sons of counts and senators, that she ought to understand and appreciate that, and so on and so forth in that vein. Mother just kept nodding in appreciation, looking, however, embarrassed; then at last she turned toward me and, with tears glistening in her eyes, said, "Good-by then, my darling boy!"

She kissed me, or rather I allowed her to kiss me. Obviously she would have liked to kiss me more, to hug and embrace me, but whether because she herself felt embarrassed to do so in the presence of strangers, or because she somehow felt hurt, or perhaps because she had guessed I was ashamed of her, whatever the reason, she quickly bowed to the Touchards once more and walked out while I stood still.

"Mais suivez donc votre mère!" Madame Touchard said to me, and added: *"Il n'a pas de coeur, cet enfant!"*

Touchard acknowledged her remark by a simple shrug that meant "See, it's not for nothing that I treat him like a flunkey."

Obediently I followed Mother downstairs and out the front door. I knew that they were all watching me now out of the window. Mother turned toward the church and crossed herself three times while looking at it. Her lips quivered. A bell was ringing resoundingly and evenly from the belfry. She turned her face to me and could no longer control herself: she laid both hands on my head and burst into sobs.

"Mother, please, enough, you make me feel ashamed. . . . Why, they're watching us from the window. . . ."

She made a great effort and said hurriedly, "Well, may God guard you . . . may He look after you. . . . May the heavenly angels and the Holy Mother care for you. . . . May St. Nicholas . . . Ah, my God, my God!" She kept rattling on, making the sign of the cross over me as many times as she possibly could. "Ah, my sweet little boy, my own little darling! Just one second, my sweet child . . ."

She hurriedly put a hand into her pocket and pulled out a blue checkered handkerchief that was tied in a knot. She tried to untie the knot, but it wouldn't come loose. . . .

"Well, never mind, take the hanky too, it's clean and you can use it. . . . There are four ten-kopek coins there; they may come in handy sometime. . . . Forgive me, my darling, I don't happen to have any more right now, forgive me. . . ."

I accepted the handkerchief, although I was about to protest that Monsieur and Madame Touchard provided perfectly for all our needs and that we really lacked nothing. But I restrained myself and took the handkerchief.

She made the sign of the cross over me once more, again muttered some sort of prayer, and then all of a sudden I saw that she was bowing to me too, just as she had to the Touchards, that deep, slow, low bow that I'll never forget as long as I live. It made me shudder somehow; I didn't quite understand why. What did she mean by that bow? Was it an acknowledgment of her guilt toward me, as I once thought several years later? I'm still not sure. But at the moment it only added to my shame and embarrassment: "They're looking at us from up there. . . . As to Lambert, he'll probably give me a beating for a start. . . ."

At last she left. Her oranges and gingerbread were eaten even before I got back upstairs by the sons of counts and senators and the four ten-kopek pieces were immediately taken away from me by Lambert. He used them to buy chocolate and cakes in the pastry shop next door for himself and the other boys without even bothering to offer me any.

Then six months went by. It was a windy and gloomy October. I'd forgotten completely about my mother. Oh, by that time I had become quite permeated by hatred, unmitigated hatred for everybody and everything, and although I still followed Touchard, clothesbrush in hand, now I hated him, hated him more and more with every passing day. And one late afternoon of that bleak autumn I was rummaging around in my personal box when I suddenly came upon something stuck in a corner: it was the blue checkered cotton handkerchief that had been there ever since. I took it out and examined it with a certain curiosity. The corner of the handkerchief still bore the crease marks of the knot that had been tied in it and even the round imprint of a coin. . . . However, I put the handkerchief back into its corner and closed my box. It was the eve of a holiday and the bells were ringing for the all-night service. All the other boys had left for home right after dinner, that is, all except for Lambert, who was staying at school on Sunday since, for some reason, no one had come to pick him up. Although he still used to give me occasional beatings, now he also talked to me a great deal and in some way he needed me.

We spent the evening discussing Lepage pistols which neither of us had ever seen, Circassian sabers and their advantages in slashing, and we mused on how nice it would be to organize a gang of robbers. In the end, however, Lambert switched to his favorite disgusting topic which, without knowing why, I somehow enjoyed listening to. This time, however, I found it quite unbearable and told him I had a headache. At ten o'clock we went to bed. I pulled my blanket over my head and, from under my pillow, I pulled out the checkered handkerchief: an hour earlier I had gone to my box, extracted the handkerchief once again, and shoved it under my pillow. Once under my blanket,

I held it up to my face and then, all of a sudden, I started kissing it. "Mamma, Mamma . . ." I kept whispering, and my whole chest felt as if it were being squeezed in a vise. I closed my eyes and her face was before me; her lips were quivering and she was crossing herself, looking at the church, and then she turned toward me and made the sign of the cross over me again and again as I said to her, "I feel so ashamed—they're looking at us!" "Ah, Mother, Mother, you came to visit me only once, and now where are you, my faraway visitor? Do you still remember your poor son whom you once came to see? . . . Ah, if you could show yourself to me only once more, if only you would appear to me in my dreams so that I could tell you how much I love you, so that I could hug you and kiss your pretty blue eyes, and tell you that I'm no longer in the least ashamed of you and that even then I loved you, and my heart was aching when I just sat there with you like a flunkey. No, you'll never know, Mother, how much I loved you then! Mother darling, where are you now? Can you hear me? And tell me, Mamma, do you still remember that dove in the village church?"

"Ah, hell, what's the matter with him anyhow!" I heard Lambert grunt from his bed. "He won't let me sleep. . . . Wait, I'll teach him a lesson!"

He jumped out of bed, rushed over to me, and tried to pull off my blanket. But I was hanging on desperately to that blanket, which covered me entirely, from head to foot. He shouted, rolling his *r*'s in his throat as the French do:

"Why must you go on whimpering like that, you moron? Here, this will teach you!" He hit me painfully with his fist in the back, then on the side; he hit me again and again, harder and harder, and . . . and suddenly I opened my eyes . . .

The sun had risen almost completely and the hard, crystal snow was glistening on the wall. . . . I sat half frozen, huddled up in my overcoat, with someone standing over me, trying to wake me up, swearing at me and kicking me painfully in the ribs with the toe of his right boot. I raised myself and looked up. He wore an expensive bearskin coat and a sable cap. He had black eyes and dashing pitch-black sideburns; his gleaming white teeth were bared as he grinned at me from under his aquiline nose; his complexion was pink and white and made his face look like a mask. . . . Then he leaned very low over me and I could see the steam spurting out of his mouth with every breath.

"You'll freeze to death, you drunken swine, you moron, you'll freeze to death if you don't get up! So up on your feet then!" he shouted, gargling his r's.

"Lambert!" I shouted.

"Who are you?"

"Dolgoruky."

"What the hell do you mean? What Dolgoruky?"

"Just *plain* Dolgoruky. . . . You know—Touchard's. . . . The one into whose side you once stuck a fork in a tavern. . . ."

"Hah!" he cried with a broad smile of recollection, for he certainly couldn't have forgotten me. "So it's you, you!"

He picked me up and stood me on my feet. As I could hardly stand up, he had to support me as he led me away. He kept peering into my eyes, listening to me intently, trying hard to understand and make sense out of what I was babbling while I was trying hard to tell him everything, talking without stop, delighted to be able to talk and delighted that the man I was talking to was him, Lambert. Whether he appeared to me at that moment as my savior or whether I saw him in a time of crisis as some sort of messenger from another world, I cannot really say, for I couldn't think straight, but I know that I threw myself at him without thinking. What I said to him then I do not remember at all and I doubt very much whether what I said was very coherent. Indeed, I don't suppose that I could articulate my words properly. Still, he listened to me intently. He hailed the first sledge we met and within a few minutes I was sitting in the warmth of his room.

III

Every person whoever he may be must have a memory of something that happened to him that he considers or likes to consider as fantastic, uncanny, extraordinary, almost miraculous—whether it be a dream, a meeting, a prediction, a foreboding, or whatever. And so, to this day, I am inclined to view this meeting of mine with Lambert as predestined, to judge at least from the circumstances surrounding it and its consequences, despite the fact that, in some respects, our encounter had nothing so extraordinary about it. Lambert was simply on his way home from certain nocturnal pursuits (the nature of which will be explained later). He was half drunk and stopped for a moment by a gate in a side street. And there he caught sight of me. He had arrived in Petersburg only a few days before.

The room in which I found myself was a rather primitively furnished, medium-priced *chambre garnie* of a type quite common in Petersburg. Lambert himself, however, was very elegantly and expensively dressed. On the floor were two suit-cases, only half unpacked. The corner where the bed was was screened off.

"Alphonsine!" Lambert called out.

"*Présente!*" a cracked female voice answered from behind the screen in a Parisian accent and, within less than two min-utes, Mademoiselle Alphonsine emerged in person. She had obviously put on whatever had happened to be within reach and came out wearing an open dressing gown. She was a peculiar-looking creature, tall and thin as a matchstick, dark-haired, with a long waist and a long face, dancing eyes and sunken cheeks, and she looked worn out.

"Hurry! (I'm translating now, for he spoke to her in French.) They must have a samovar next door. . . . Quickly, get some boiling water and some red wine and sugar. . . . Get a glass too; hurry, he's half frozen. . . . He's an old friend of mine. . . . He spent all night out in the snow. . . ."

"*Malheureux!*" she cried out, clasping her hands in a theatri-cal gesture.

"Come on, come on!" Lambert shouted at her as if she were a lap dog, shaking one finger threateningly at her. She at once renounced her dramatic pretensions and ran to carry out his orders.

Lambert examined me, felt me all over, took my pulse, touched my forehead and my temples.

"I still can't understand how you didn't freeze to death," he grumbled, "although it may be because you were completely covered by your fur coat; you were huddled in it like in a tent of fur. . . ."

The glass with the hot brew materialized. I greedily gulped it down and at once felt revived. I started babbling again, non-stop, propped up in a half-sitting position on the sofa, words bursting out of me without waiting for their turn, but I don't recall either what I told Lambert or how I managed to tell him anything. Indeed, there are moments and even whole intervals that remain complete blanks in my memory. I repeat again that I have no idea whether Lambert made much sense out of what I told him, but one thing I became certain of later was that he understood enough to decide to try to capitalize on our meeting. I'll explain in the proper place how he thought he could de-rive some personal advantage from it.

I became not merely animated but at certain moments even positively exuberant. I remember the sun suddenly brightening up the room when the curtains were drawn and the crackling of the stove that somebody had lighted, although I have no recollection of who lighted it or when. I also remember a tiny black lap dog that Alphonsine held in her arms and pressed to her heart with theatrical tenderness. The lap dog somehow managed to distract my attention and twice I even reached out to touch it, but Lambert imperiously waved his hand, whereupon both Alphonsine and the lap dog vanished behind the screen.

Lambert himself was extremely silent. He sat facing me, his head bent in my direction, and listened practically without moving. Now and then a broad, slow smile would uncover his flashing teeth and he would half close his eyes as if trying hard to follow me or to work something out. I have kept a clear recollection only of the moment when I started telling him about that letter-document. I couldn't find the right words to convey it all so he would understand, and I could tell by his expression that he couldn't grasp what I was saying but that he was very eager to, so eager, in fact, that he ventured to interrupt me with a question, which was very risky since an interruption was likely to make me forget altogether what I had been talking about and start me off on another subject. How long we sat like that, with me talking and him listening, I have no idea and couldn't even guess, but at one point he suddenly got up and called Alphonsine.

"He needs some rest. . . . Maybe we should call a doctor. . . . Give him anything he asks for . . . or rather you know what I mean—*vous comprenez, ma fille? Vous avez de l'argent?* No? Here's some." He handed her a ten-ruble bill. They discussed something in whispers for a few moments; then he said aloud in his normal voice: "*Vous comprenez! Vous comprenez!*" He frowned and shook his finger menacingly at her. I understood how much in awe of him she was.

"I'll be back," he said, smiling at me, "and you, the best thing you could do is to have yourself a good sleep."

"*Mais vous n'avez pas dormi du tout, Maurice!*" Alphonsine cried out theatrically, turning to him.

"*Taisez-vous, je dormirai après,*" he told her and left the room.

"*Sauvée!*" she whispered pathetically, pointing after him, and then she walked to the middle of the room and started declaiming: "*Monsieur, monsieur, jamais un homme ne fut si cruel, si Bismarck,* que cet être, qui regarde une femme comme une saleté de hasard. Une femme, qu'est-ce que c'est à notre*

* Bismarck is used here as an adjective to convey the supreme degree of cruelty. [A. MacA.]

époque? Tue la!—voilà le dernier mot de l'Académie française!"

I stared at her, my eyes almost popping out, so much so, in fact, that I began to see double and saw two Alphonsines in front of me. Then I suddenly realized that she was crying and it occurred to me that she might have been talking like that for quite a while without my being aware of it because I might have been asleep or unconscious.

"Hélas! A quoi m'aurait servi de le découvrir plutôt," she exclaimed, *"et n'aurais-je pas autant gagné à tenir ma honte cachée toute ma vie? Peut-être, n'est-il pas honnête pour une demoiselle de s'expliquer si librement devant un monsieur, mais enfin je vous avoue que s'il m'était permis de vouloir quelque chose, oh, ce serait de lui plonger au coeur mon couteau, mais en détournant les yeux, de peur que son regard exécrable ne fît trembler mon bras et ne glaçât mon courage! Il a assassiné ce pope russe, monsieur, il lui arracha sa barbe rousse pour la vendre à un artiste en cheveux au pont des Maréchaux, tout près de la maison de Monsieur Andrieux—hautes nouveautés, articles de Paris, linge, chemises, vous savez, n'est-ce pas? . . . Oh, monsieur, quand l'amitié rassemble à table épouse, enfants, soeurs, amis, quand une vive allegresse enflamme mon coeur, je vous le demande, monsieur: est-il un bonheur préférable à celui dont tout le monde jouit? Mais il rit, monsieur, ce monstre exécrable et inconcevable et si ce n'était pas par l'entremise de Monsieur Andrieux, jamais, oh, jamais je ne serais. . . . Mais quoi, monsieur, qu'avez-vous, monsieur?"*

She rushed toward me, for I believe I started shivering violently or perhaps I even fainted. I cannot fully convey the depressing and painful effect that that crazy creature had on me. Perhaps she was under the impression that it was her duty to keep me entertained; in any case she never left me for a minute. Possibly she had once been an actress, the way she went in for that absurd declaiming and gesturing, performing ceaselessly, while now I kept silent. All I could gather from what she said was that she had some close connections with a certain *"maison de Monsieur Andrieux—hautes nouveautés, articles de Paris,"* etc., that, indeed, she might have originated from that *maison,* but that she had somehow been torn away from *Monsieur Andrieux* by *ce monstre furieux et inconcevable,* and that was the point of the tragedy. She was sobbing, but I was under the impression that it was all part of the routine and that she was not really weeping; at certain moments it looked as if she were about to break up into small fragments like a dried-out skeleton. She spoke in a jangling, suffocating voice, so that the word *préférable* came out as *préfé–a–able,* with the middle *a* syllable bleated out as if by a sheep. Once I suddenly became aware that she was doing a pirouette in the middle of the room, but she was not just dancing: her pirouette had a direct connection with her story and she was trying to use it to convey something she was telling me. Then, unexpectedly, she rushed toward a little old piano that was in the room and proceeded to strum on the out-of-tune instrument as she burst into song. . . . I believe that, for ten minutes or so, my mind became completely blank or perhaps I fell asleep, but then the lap dog yelped and I woke up and this time, for a moment, I somehow felt completely lucid and I saw everything in a normal light. I leaped to my feet, quite horrified. "Why, I'm at Lambert's, Lambert's!" flashed through my mind. I seized my cap and rushed toward my overcoat.

"*Où allez-vous, monsieur?*" vigilant Alphonsine cried out at once.

"I want to get out of here and don't try to stop me!"

"*Oui, monsieur!*" Alphonsine assented vigorously and rushed to open for me herself the door leading into the corridor. "*Mais ce n'est pas loin, monsieur, c'est pas loin du tout; ça ne vaut pas la peine de mettre votre manteau; c'est ici, tout près, monsieur!*" she went on exclaiming.

But when I was out of the room I turned right.

"*Non, c'est par ici, monsieur, c'est par ici!*" she shouted at the top of her voice, clutching at my coat with the long bony fingers of one hand, while pointing with the other somewhere to my left where I had no desire whatsoever to go.

I tore myself away and ran toward the door giving onto the staircase.

"*Il s'en va, il s'en va!*"

Alphonsine pursued me furiously, calling after me in a breaking voice: "*Mais il me tuera, monsieur, il me tuera!*"

I was already tearing downstairs and, although she was still trying to catch up with me, I managed to reach the door, run downstairs, jump out into the street, and grab the first cab I saw. I gave the cabby my mother's address.

IV

But the lucidity that had flared up in me for a moment dimmed quickly. I still remember faintly getting to the door of Mother's house and being helped in. But after that everything becomes vague and vanishes altogether as I lapsed into complete unconsciousness. The next day, as I was told later (and of which, moreover, I also have the glimpse of a recollection), my

mind cleared up again for a moment. I remember lying in Versilov's room, on his sofa, surrounded by the faces of Versilov,
Mother, and Lisa. I also remember Versilov talking to me about
Zershikov and Sergei, while showing me a letter and reassuring
me. They all told me later that I kept asking with terror about
someone called Lambert and that I kept telling them I was hearing a lap dog yelping. But then the faint light of consciousness
went out again and by the evening of the second day I was pros-
trate with violent brain fever. . . .

I will, however, anticipate my understanding of the events
and explain what actually happened.

The evening that I had been thrown out of Zershikov's into
the street, after things had calmed down somewhat, Zershikov
returned to the gaming table and announced loudly that
there had been a regrettable mistake, that the missing four hundred rubles had been found in another pile of money, and that
the accounts of the bank had turned out to be quite correct.
Then Sergei, who had remained in the room, went up to Zershikov and demanded that he publicly proclaim my innocence and,
moreover, that he apologize to me in a formal letter. Zershikov
agreed that this was a fair demand and gave his word of honor
in front of everybody that he would send me a letter of apology
the next day. Sergei gave him Versilov's address and on the
following day a letter of apology addressed to me arrived along
with some thirteen hundred rubles that I had left at the roulette
table. Thus the Zershikov incident was closed and this good
news contributed greatly to my speedy recovery once I had regained consciousness.

When, that same night, Prince Sergei returned home from
Zershikov's, he sat down and wrote two letters: one to me and
the other to the officers of his former regiment where he had
had the incident with Ensign Stepanov. Both letters were sent
off the next morning. After that, he wrote a full confession to
the authorities and early in the morning, with this document
in hand, he reported to the officer in command of the regiment
and informed him that he was a common-law criminal and an
accomplice in forgery, that he was giving himself up to the authorities, and that he wanted to stand trial. Then he handed in
the confession where he had explained everything in writing.

He was held pending trial.

Here is the letter he wrote me that night.

My very dear Arkady:
    When I first tried the "flunkey's way" of getting out of

trouble, I lost the right to comfort myself with the thought that I might eventually do what was right and honorable. I, the last scion of an ancient line, recognize myself as guilty toward my country and my family and I want to bear the punishment. I cannot understand now how I could ever have clung to the despicable thought of self-preservation and for some time hoped I could buy myself off with money since in any case I would have remained guilty in my own eyes as long as I lived. Besides, the people who would have given me back the compromising documents would never have left me in peace to the very end. So I would have been obliged to live with them, to be their accomplice all my life, and this would have been my future! I couldn't face that and so finally I managed to muster up enough courage—or perhaps despair—to do what I have now done.

I have also written a letter to the officers of my former regiment clearing Stepanov of all blame. There is and there can be nothing that could redeem me for what I have done: this is nothing but the last disposition of a man who is about to become a corpse. That's the way you must look at it.

Please forgive me for turning my back on you at Zershikov's: I did it because I was not quite sure of you at that moment. Now that I am a dead man, I feel free to make this confession . . . from the other world.

Poor Lisa! She knows nothing about this decision. I hope she won't be angry at me for choosing this way; let her, instead, think it over herself. For I cannot justify myself to her nor even find the right words to try to make her understand. I also want you to know, Arkady, that when she came to me the last time, I admitted that I had deceived her and that I had gone to Anna with the intention of proposing to her. I could not leave that on my conscience after I had made my final decision and, realizing how much she loved me, I told her everything. She forgave me, forgave me everything, but I couldn't believe her—it was not forgiveness. I couldn't have forgiven if I had been in her place.

Don't forget me altogether.

Your unhappy friend and
the last Prince Sokolsky.

I lay unconscious for nine days in all.

PART THREE

Chapter 1

I

Now for something altogether different.

I know I keep promising again and again to talk about "something different" only to wind up speaking about nothing but myself once more. Yet I have declared a thousand times that I had no intention whatsoever of writing about myself and I was determined not to do so when I started out on these memoirs because I realized only too well that there was no reason why the reader should be at all interested in me. I'm doing my very best to write about other people and if, nevertheless, I keep popping up again and again, it's just a regrettable necessity, which, try hard as I may, I find quite impossible to avoid. What peeves me most, in fact, is that by describing my own adventures with such emotion, I give the impression that I'm still the same person as I was in those days. But surely the reader must remember me exclaiming sorrowfully in the course of the narrative: "Oh, if only it were possible to change the past and to relive everything from the beginning!" Well, I couldn't possibly say that unless I had changed radically and become a different man. That should be pretty obvious to anyone and any reader with imagination will appreciate how tired I am of having to offer all these repetitive explanations and apologies, which I'm even forced to squeeze into the stream of my narrative!

But now let's get on with it.

After spending nine days totally unconscious, I came back to myself quite regenerated but not at all reformed. Actually my regeneration was pretty stupid if considered in a broader sense, and perhaps if it had happened to me now, it would have been quite different. My guiding idea, or rather my feelings, simply amounted to leaving them once and for all (just as I had resolved a thousand times before), but this time I was determined really to do it. I didn't have any desire to punish anyone—I give you my word of honor I didn't—although I might have had a legitimate grudge against all of them. I wanted to leave without anger or harsh words; I felt that I needed to build my own personal strength, a strength that would be dependent on none of them and on no one in the entire world but me! I'm noting the longing I had then, which was an overwhelming feeling rather than a clearly formulated thought. Somehow as long as I was still confined to my bed, I was reluctant to put it into words. Sick and feeble, I lay in Versilov's room where they'd put me and was acutely aware of the extent of my helplessness: I lay there more like a piece of straw than a man and the reason for my impotence was not merely my poor physical state . . . And that's what enraged me most! So, from the deepest recesses of my being, a feeling of protest started rising and gaining strength and I began to suffocate from concentrated arrogance and defiance. In fact, I can't think of any period of my life when I was more bloated by arrogance than in those days of my convalescence when I lay like a piece of straw tossed on that bed.

But I said nothing and even made an effort not to think about these matters. I just looked intently into the faces of those around me and tried to guess what I needed to know. It was obvious that they didn't want to question me; indeed, they even tried not to show any curiosity, and when they spoke to me, it was always about unimportant things. I liked that and yet it made me sad, but I didn't try to analyze that ambivalent feeling. I saw more of Mother than of Lisa, although Lisa too came in to see me at least twice a day. From the exchanges between the two of them and from Lisa's expression, I gathered that Lisa was extremely tense, that she spent most of her days away somewhere attending to matters that concerned her personally. The very thought that she could have *personal* preoccupations somehow offended me, although, of course, these were just the purely physiological reactions of a sick man and are certainly not worth describing.

Mrs. Prutkov also came to see me, almost daily in fact, and, although she didn't treat me with anything resembling tenderness, at least she didn't berate me as she had before. That exasperated me so much that I couldn't help telling her:

"You know, Mrs. Prutkov, I now realize that when you don't abuse people you're an awful bore."

"If that's the way it is, I won't come to see you any more," she answered gruffly, and walked out.

I was very pleased: I had succeeded in getting rid of at least one of them.

The person I was most impatient with was Mother, for it was she who irritated me the most. I had developed a tremendous appetite and I kept grumbling that she was always late in bringing me my meals (actually she was never late). Mother couldn't think how to satisfy me. Once she brought me some soup and began, as usual, to feed it to me herself, while I kept finding fault with everything between spoonfuls. And all of a sudden I felt terrible about behaving like that: "Why, she's probably the one person in the world I really love and she's the one I'm trying to hurt the most!" But the spite in me wouldn't let up, and it was that spite that made me suddenly burst into tears. And then the poor thing started kissing me. I managed to control myself and bear her tenderness, but how I hated her at that moment! No, I didn't really; I always loved Mother, I loved her at that moment too, but what happened was the usual thing: one always insults first the person one loves most.

The only person whom I really hated during those first days was the doctor. He was still quite young, looked conceited, and had an abrupt, even impolite manner. All these learned people seem to act as if they've just discovered something, yesterday perhaps, although I know that nothing special was discovered yesterday. But then that's always the way of mediocrities, the way of the average man. I restrained myself for a long time, but suddenly it became more than I could bear and I told him, in the presence of all my family, that he was wasting his time and mine in coming to see me, that I'd recover just as well without him, that, although he pretended to be a realist, he was filled with all sorts of superstitions and prejudices, that he refused to understand that medicine had never healed anyone, that he seemed to be crassly ignorant, and that recently anybody who claimed to be a technician or an expert of some sort in Russia treated people as if they were dirt. The doctor was very offended, which in itself shows the kind of person he was, but continued his visits. Finally, I warned Versilov that if the doctor didn't leave me alone, I'd tell him things ten times more unpleasant than what I'd already told him. Versilov only commented that he couldn't begin to imagine how I'd go about doubling my unpleasantness, let alone multiplying it by ten. I liked his remark.

Ah, what a man! I'm talking of Versilov. He was the one who was responsible for everything that had happened to me, but somehow I didn't feel resentful toward him. And it was not just the way he treated me that won me over. I believe it was because at that point we both felt there were many things we should explain to each other . . . and because of that, the best course was for us never to explain anything. It's awfully pleasant at junctures in life such as the one I was going through to deal with an intelligent person! As I've already mentioned, Versilov had told me briefly about the letter to me from Sergei, who was now in jail, about Zershikov's rehabilitation of my honor, and all the rest. Since I had resolved not to talk, I only asked him a couple of very short questions that he answered clearly and precisely without one unnecessary word and, what was even more valuable, without injecting into his answers any unnecessary feeling. For it was unsolicitated feelings that I was most afraid of.

Although I've said nothing about Lambert, I'm sure the reader must have guessed that he was on my mind all too much. I did mention his name several times while I was delirious, but once I'd come out of my delirium, I became convinced that everything connected with Lambert had remained a secret and that no one, not even Versilov, knew anything about him. This reassured and pleased me at the same time, although it turned out later, to my surprise, that I was quite wrong: Lambert had already come to the house while I was ill. Since Versilov had never mentioned this to me, I thought that, for Lambert, I had vanished into thin air once and for all. Nevertheless I often thought of him, thought of him not only without revulsion and with curiosity but even with a certain sympathy; somehow I had a feeling that he could lead me to a solution to my troubles and this feeling corresponded to the thoughts and plans that were taking shape inside me at that time. To put it as concisely as possible, I had decided to give serious thought to Lambert as soon as I was able to think straight. Let me add a curious detail: I'd completely forgotten where he lived and the name of the street where it had all happened. The room, Alphonsine, the lap dog—all these I remembered so clearly that I could have sketched them, but where it all took place—I mean in what street and what house—had completely slipped my mind. And, strangest of all, I only became aware of this lapse of memory on the third or fourth day after I regained complete consciousness, by which time I was already worrying a great deal about Lambert.

And so these were my first sensations when I came back to life. I have mentioned only the most obvious aspects and have probably failed to note the essential. In fact, though, it was precisely then that the essential was taking shape and crystallizing in my heart because I couldn't really have been kicking up all that fuss and having all those temper tantrums merely because I was served my broth a little late. Oh, I remember very well how sad and depressed I felt then, especially during the interminable minutes when I was left all alone. Unfortunately, the others soon felt that their company weighed on me and that their sympathy only irritated me. So they tried to stay out of my sight as much as possible—which, as it turned out, was an unwanted result of their sensitivity and tact.

II

At three o'clock in the afternoon on the fourth day after I'd regained consciousness, I was lying on my bed. There was nobody in the room with me. It was a clear, sunny day and I knew that sometime before four, when the sun would start setting, a slanting, reddish beam would hit a certain spot on the wall and turn it into a bright, glowing patch of light. I knew it because that was just what had happened on previous days, and the fact that it would happen without fail within the next hour—that I was as sure of it as I was that two times two is four—irritated me to the point of fury. I turned away angrily and, amidst complete silence, I clearly heard the words: "O Lord Jesus Christ, have mercy on us!" These words were uttered in a half whisper and were followed by a deep, full-chested sigh. Then everything became completely quiet. I quickly raised my head.

Even before then, I mean the previous day or two, I'd noticed that something unusual was happening in the downstairs rooms. The small room, which used to be occupied by Mother and Lisa and which was separated from mine by the dining room, was apparently occupied by someone else now. More than once, sometimes during the day and sometimes at night, I'd heard strange sounds coming from it, but since they'd never lasted for more than a few seconds and had been followed by total silence, I'd never paid much attention to them. The evening before, I'd decided it was Versilov who occupied the room now, especially since he'd walked in shortly after I'd heard the sounds, although I'd gathered from what had been said in my presence that, during my illness, Versilov had moved out of the house altogether and was living in another apartment. As to Mother and Lisa, I'd known from the beginning that they had moved upstairs into my old coffin-like attic—I imagined so as not to disturb me—although I wondered how there could possibly be enough room for the two of them. But now it turned out that there was a man living in their former room and that it was not Versilov. With an ease that surprised me (I'd imagined I still had no scrap of strength in me), I lowered my feet to the floor, put them into slippers, threw around my shoulders a gray, astrakhan dressing gown that happened to be close at hand (a contribution from Versilov), and set out across the dining room to Mother's former bedroom.

I was quite stunned by what I saw there. I'd never expected anything of the sort and stopped dead in the doorway. An old man with a huge white beard and entirely white hair was sitting there, and it was obvious that he'd been sitting like that for a very long time. He sat not on the bed but on Mother's little stool with only his back resting against the bed. As a matter of fact, he held himself so straight that his back didn't seem to need any support whatsoever, although he was obviously ill. He wore over his shirt a short fur-lined jacket; his knees were wrapped in Mother's plaid blanket and he had slippers on his feet. His shoulders were broad and one could guess that he was very tall; even though he was sick, pale, and emaciated, and his face was long and drawn, he still seemed quite strong and cheerful. He looked over seventy. His hair was very thick but not too long. Next to him on a little table lay three or four books and a pair of silver-rimmed glasses.

Although I hadn't in the least expected to see him there, the very second I saw him I guessed who he was, while still failing to understand how he could have spent all those days so close to me without my ever hearing a sound from him.

He didn't budge when he saw me but simply looked at me intently in silence just as I was looking at him, with the only difference that, whereas I stared at him with infinite astonishment, he looked at me without any visible surprise. Indeed, after having studied me for five or ten silent seconds, he suddenly smiled and even laughed soundlessly. The soundless laughter stopped almost at once, but it left a sort of gay, cheerful wake in his whole expression, particularly in his eyes, which were very blue and luminous, very large too, although the lids were swollen and drooping from old age and were surrounded by innumerable little wrinkles. It was the way he had laughed that struck me most.

I think that, in most cases, a man becomes revolting to look at when he laughs. When most people laugh, they uncover their hidden vulgarity and thus demean themselves, although they seldom realize the painful impression their laughter produces on others. Laughing people have no more idea of what their faces look like than sleepers have of theirs. Some people look very intelligent when they're asleep, while others, even including intelligent people, may look pretty stupid and ridiculous in their sleep. What I'm trying to say is that, as a rule, a laughing man is no more aware of his face than a man asleep. Moreover, most people don't even know how to laugh. And, although it may appear that there's nothing much to it, it is an innate talent and cannot be cultivated. The only way perhaps to change one's laugh would be by re-educating oneself, by becoming a better person, by developing the better instincts in one's nature and overcoming the worse: such a person would probably then have a more beautiful laugh. A man may sometimes give himself away completely by his laugh: you suddenly know everything that lies beneath his outward appearance. Thus, even laughter that is unmistakably intelligent may have something repulsive about it. Laughter demands, above all, sincerity of people, but where does one find sincerity? Real laughter must be free of malice, while it is malice that makes people laugh mostly. Sincere laughter free of malice denotes gaiety, and how many people are there who know how to be gay in this century of ours? (That remark about gaiety was made by Versilov and I remembered it.) A man's way of being gay is perhaps the most revealing feature about him. A man may seem quite inscrutable, but if he bursts into sincere laughter, you'll see his whole character as though you were holding it in the palm of your hand. Only superior and happy natures can radiate communicative gaiety, that is, be irresistibly and cheerfully gay. And when I say "superior," I don't mean intellectually superior but superior in character, as a whole human being. And so, if you wish to glimpse inside a human soul and get to know a man, don't bother analyzing his ways of being silent, of talking, of weeping, or seeing how much he is moved by noble ideas; you'll get better results if you just watch him laugh. If he laughs well, he's a good man. You must, however, note all the shades of his laugh. Thus, it is not good if the laugh strikes you as in the least stupid, even if it's completely sincere and unaffected. As soon as you notice a trace of stupidity in laughter, it indicates that the man is at least somewhat limited, even if he keeps dazzling you with all sorts of ideas. Or, even if his laugh doesn't sound at all stupid but the man himself somehow becomes ridiculous when he laughs, it is an indication that he lacks, at least to a certain extent, personal dignity. Finally, even if the laugh is communicative but still somehow seems vulgar to you, you may rest assured that the man's nature has vulgarity in it, that all the noble and refined traits you noticed in him before were either deliberately affected or unconsciously imitated, and that he will eventually change for the worse, devote himself to the pursuit of the "useful," and discard without regret his noble aspirations as if they were mere delusions of youth.

I deliberately decided to insert this lengthy dissertation on laughter here, even at the expense of the continuity of my narrative, because I consider it one of the most important conclusions derived from my life experience. I especially recommend it to the attention of young would-be brides who are prepared to marry the man of their choice but are still watching him with misgivings and distrust and cannot take the decisive step. And let no one laugh at this poor adolescent who comes up with advice on matrimonial matters in which obviously he cannot be an expert. All I claim to know is that laughter is the most reliable gauge of human nature. Look at children, for instance: children are the only human creatures to produce perfect laughter and that's just what makes them so enchanting. I find a crying child repulsive whereas a laughing and gay child is a sunbeam from paradise to me, a revelation of future bliss when man will finally become as pure and simple-hearted as a babe.

And that day I perceived something childlike and incredibly attractive in the fleeting laughter of the old man, and unhesitatingly I went up to him.

III

"Here, sit down, I can see your legs aren't holding you up too good," he said cheerfully, motioning me to a chair beside him, still looking into my face with his luminous eyes.

I sat down next to him.

"I know who you are—you're Makar Dolgoruky."

"That's right, my boy. Well, it's great that you're up now. You're young and that's wonderful. The old must think of the grave, but the young must think of life."

"Are you ill?"

"Yes, dear boy, and it's my legs that give me most trouble. They managed to bring me here, my poor legs, but as soon as I sat down they got all swollen. It all started last Thursday when the frost came. . . . I used to rub them with the ointment that Dr. Lichten prescribed for me two years ago in Moscow and it used to help. . . . But now it doesn't help any more. . . . And then my chest feels all stuffed up too. And, since yesterday, my back is aching—as if dogs are gnawing at it. . . . So I can't sleep at night either. . . ."

"Why haven't I heard you here?" I interrupted him, and he looked at me as though trying to think of something.

"Only don't wake your mother," he said, apparently remembering something. "She's been up all night seeing to things but quietly like a mouse so you wouldn't hear her, and now I know she's having a little rest. . . . Ah, it's bad to be old and sick," he sighed. "One wonders why the soul should hang on like that in the body and still enjoy being alive. It seems that, if I was given a chance to start my life all over again, my soul wouldn't mind at all, although I guess that's a sinful thought."

"Why sinful?"

"Because it's a wish, a dream, while an old man should leave life gracefully. Murmuring and protesting when one mets death is a great sin. But I guess God would forgive even an old man if he got to love life out of the gaiety of his soul. It's hard for a man to know what's sinful and what's not, for there's a mystery in it that's beyond human ken. So a pious old man must be content at all times and must die in the full light of understanding, blissfully and gracefully, satisfied with the days that have been given him to live, yearning for his last hour, and rejoicing when he is gathered like a stalk of wheat unto the sheaf when he has fulfilled his mysterious destiny."

"You keep talking about 'mystery'? What does it mean 'fulfilling one's mysterious destiny'?" I asked, looking around toward the door.

I was glad we were alone and surrounded by complete stillness. The sun that had not set yet shone brightly in the window. He spoke somewhat grandiloquently and none too coherently, but with great sincerity and a strange excitement that suggested he was truly glad I was there with him. But I also noticed certain unmistakable signs that he was feverish, very feverish as a matter of fact. But I too was ill and had been feverish myself when I'd come to his room.

"What's mystery? Everything's mystery, my friend, everything is God's mystery. There's mystery in every tree, in every blade of grass. When a little bird sings or all those many, many stars shine in the sky at night—it's all mystery, the same one. But the greatest mystery is what awaits man's soul in the world beyond, and that's the truth, my boy."

"I don't quite see what you mean. . . . Believe me, I'm not trying to tease you and, I assure you, I do believe in God. But all these mysteries you're talking about have been solved by human intelligence long ago, and whatever hasn't yet been completely solved will be, and perhaps very soon. The botanist today knows perfectly well how a tree grows, and the physiologist and the anatomist know perfectly well what makes a bird sing; or at least they'll know it very soon. . . . As to the stars, not only have they all been counted, but all their movements have been calculated with an accuracy down to the last second so that it's possible to predict, say, a thousand years ahead the exact day and time of the appearance of a comet. And now even the chemical composition of the most remote stars has become known to us. . . . Also, take, for instance, a microscope, which is a sort of glass that can magnify things a million times, and look at a drop of water through it. You'll see a whole new world full of unseen living creatures. Well, that too was a mystery once, but science has now explained it."

"I've heard about all that, my boy, people have told me many times about these things. And this is certainly great and glorious knowledge. Whatever man has has been given him by God, and with good reason it was said that the Lord did breathe into man the breath of life to live and learn."

"Of course, of course, but those are just commonplaces. You're not really an enemy of science, are you? You wouldn't be some sort of partisan of a state under church control or . . . But I don't suppose you'd understand . . ."

"No, my friend, you've got me wrong; I've always respected science since I was a boy and, although I can't understand it myself, that's all right: science may be beyond my ken, but it is within the ken of other men. And it's best that way because then everyone has what comes to him, and not everyone is made to understand science. Otherwise every man thinks he can do everything and wants to astonish the whole world and I'd be the worst of them all perhaps if I had the skill to do it. But since I don't have those skills, how can I hold forth before others, ignorant as I am? But you're young and clever and, since you've been given these advantages, go ahead and study. Get to know everything so that if you meet a godless man or a man with evil intentions, you can answer him properly and his wicked and impious words will not befog your young mind. . . . As to that glass you mentioned, I've seen it; in fact, the last time was not so very long ago. . . ."

He took a deep breath and sighed. No doubt about it: he was enjoying talking to me very much indeed. He was very anxious to communicate. Moreover, I'm sure I'm not just imagining things if I say that at certain moments he looked at me with a strange, even uncanny love, as his hand came to rest tenderly on top of mine or as he gently patted my shoulder. I must say, however, that at other moments he seemed to forget altogether that I was there but he went on talking just as eagerly, and I could imagine him sitting all alone in the room and addressing the walls.

"I know a man of great wisdom who's now living in the Gennadieva desert," he went on, "a man of noble birth who was rich and was also a lieutenant colonel in the cavalry. He couldn't face the bonds of marriage and withdrew from the world to seek silent and solitary retreats where he felt sheltered from worldly vanities. And so he's lived—it's almost ten years now—a life of great austerity, practicing the renunciation of all earthly desires, but he still refuses to take monastic vows. . . . Now it so happens that Peter Valerianovich—that's his name—has more books than I've ever seen in any one man's possession; in fact, he has eight thousand rubles' worth of books, he told me so himself; and I've learned many things from him on various occasions, for I've always loved to listen to him talk. Well, one day I asked him, 'How is it, sir, that a man as learned and intelligent as you, who has spent almost ten years living like a monk, who has learned to control his will and has renounced all earthly desires, how is it that you still refuse to take proper monastic vows and so become even more perfect?' 'You just said something about my being so learned and intelligent, old man,' he said to me; 'well, that learning and intelligence may be my trouble; they're still holding me in bondage, instead of my controlling them. As to living like a monk, it may just have become an old habit with me and I'm not even aware of it. And when it comes to my renunciation of worldly desires, let me tell you this: true, I thought nothing of signing away my estates or resigning my lieutenant colonel's commission. . . . But, you know, for more than nine years now I've been trying to give up smoking my pipe and thus far I have failed. So what kind of monk would I make and how could I claim to have mastered my desires?'

"I marveled at such a humility. And then, last summer on St. Peter's day, I again found myself in that desert—God just willed it that way—and when I walked into his cell, I saw it standing there, that thing, the microscope; he had ordered it from abroad and paid a lot of money for it. 'Wait, old man,' he said to me, 'I'll show you something very strange, something that you've never seen before. Here, see this drop of water that looks as pure as a tear? All right then, look at it now and you'll see that scientists will soon explain all the mysteries of God without leaving a single one to you and me.' That was just how he put it and it stuck in my mind. But it so happened that I'd already looked into a microscope thirty-five years before that, Mr. Malgasov's microscope, my old master and Mr. Versilov's maternal uncle, one of whose estates he later inherited. Mr. Malgasov was a very important general and a big landowner, who kept a huge pack of hounds and whose huntsman I was for many years. When he brought home that microscope and installed it, Mr. Malgasov had all his serfs assembled—everybody, men and women—and ordered them to look into it in turn; they were shown one after another a louse, a flea, the point of a needle, a hair, and a drop of water. And it was very funny—they were afraid to look into the thing, but they were also afraid to incur Mr. Malgasov's anger, for he was pretty short-tempered, our master. Some of the serfs didn't know how to look into a microscope and they narrowed their eyes so much that they couldn't make out anything; others were so scared that they cried out from fright, while old Savin Makarov put both hands over his eyes and shouted: 'Do whatever you want to me, I won't come near it!' And there was a lot of stupid laughing. But I didn't tell Peter Valerianovich that I'd already had a glimpse into this wonder thirty-five years before because I saw how much he was enjoying showing it to me and, indeed, I started marveling out loud and pretending to be horrified. He gave me time to recover and then asked: 'Well, what do you say to that, old man?' And I bowed down and answered him: 'The Lord said let there be light and there was light.' To that he answered: 'And shouldn't there be darkness too?' He said these words in such a strange way without even smiling that I was very surprised, but then he seemed annoyed at something and fell silent."

"It all seems very plain to me," I said; "your Peter Valerianovich is eating his rice and raisins in his monastery and bowing to the ground while he doesn't really believe in God. And you simply stumbled upon him at just such a moment. Besides," I added, "he seems to be a rather peculiar man because surely he must have looked into his microscope at least ten times before, so why should the eleventh glimpse all but drive him out of his mind? It's some sort of nervousness or oversensitivity that he must have contracted living in the monastery. . . ."

"He's a man with a pure heart and a high intelligence, and he's not an atheist," Makar said firmly. "His brain is astir with ideas and his heart is restless. There are many people like him nowadays among the gentry and among the learned ones. And let me tell you this: the man is punishing himself. You should leave such folks alone, not annoy them, they're worthy of respect, and you ought to mention them in your prayers before going to sleep because they're searching for God. You do pray before going to sleep, don't you?"

"No, I don't. I consider it an empty ritual. But I'll admit this much: I rather like your Peter Valerianovich. Whatever else he is, he's not one of those puppets but a real man who reminds me rather of someone whom we both know very well."

The old man seemed to register only the first part of what I'd just said.

"It's a pity you don't pray, dear friend; a prayer gladdens the heart before you go to sleep in the evening, when you wake up

in the morning, and if you awake in the night. . . . Now let
me tell you something else. Last summer, in July, many of us pil-
grims, we were hurrying to the Monastery of Our Lady for the
holy day. The closer we came to the place, the more there were
of us, and finally we were almost two hundred, all going to kiss
the holy and miraculous relics of the two great saints Aniky and
Gregory. We spent the night, my friend, in an open field and I
awoke early in the morning when everyone else was still asleep
and the sun hadn't even peeped out from behind the forest yet. I
lifted my head, my boy, and looked around, and everything was
so beautiful that it couldn't be put into words so I just sighed.
It was still and quiet, the air was light, and the grass was
growing. . . . Grow, God's grass, grow! . . . A bird sang. . . .
Sing, you little bird of God! . . . A little babe squeaked in a
woman's arms. . . . God bless you, little man, grow and be
happy, dear child! . . . And for the first time in my life I became conscious of all that was going on inside me. I put my head
down again and went back to sleep, and it was so nice. It's so
good to be alive, my dear boy! If I should get better, I'll go wandering again come spring. . . . And if there's mystery in the
world, it only makes it even better; it fills the heart with awe
and wonder, and it gladdens the heart: 'All is in you, oh Lord,
and so am I, and so keep me. . . .' Do not repine, boy, mystery
makes it even more beautiful," he added with tender fervor.

"You mean it's even more beautiful because there's mystery in
it. I'll remember that. You express yourself very clumsily, but I
understand what you mean. I feel that you know and understand much more than you can put into words. . . . Still you
sound as if you were feverish. . . ."

This last remark slipped from my lips inadvertently as I stared
at his shining eyes and his face, which had grown even paler.

But I don't believe he heard me.

"You know, my boy," he said, as if pursuing a thought that
had been interrupted, "there's a limit to how long a man is remembered on this earth. It's about a hundred years, that limit.
Less than a hundred years after a man's death, he may still be
remembered by his children or perhaps his grandchildren who
have seen his face, but after that time, even if his name is still
remembered, it's only indirectly, from other people's words, and
it's just an idea about him, because all those who have seen him
alive will by then be dead too. And grass will grow over his grave
in the cemetery, the white stone over him will crumble, and
everyone will forget him, including his own descendants, because only very few names remain in people's memory. So that's

all right—let them forget! Yes, go on, forget me, dear ones, but me, I'll go on loving you even from my grave. I can hear, dear children, your cheerful voices and I can hear your steps on the graves of your fathers; live for some time yet in the sunlight and enjoy yourselves while I pray for you and I'll come to you in your dreams. . . . Death doesn't make any difference, for there's love after death too!"

The trouble was that I was just as feverish as he was and, instead of leaving the room, persuading him to calm down, or even forcing him to get into bed since he sounded delirious, I seized his hand and, pressing it hard, leaned toward him and whispered excitedly, shaken by inner sobs:

"I'm happy I've found you. . . . Perhaps I've been waiting for you for a long time. I don't like any of them: there's no *beauty* in them. . . . I won't follow them. . . . I don't know where I'll go. . . . I'll come with you. . . ."

Luckily, just then Mother walked in. She had obviously just awakened and looked alarmed. In one hand she held a medicine bottle and in the other a spoon. She looked at us wide-eyed.

"That's what I was afraid of!" she exclaimed. "I'm late with his quinine and now his temperature's up! I overslept, Makar dear. . . ."

She gave him his quinine and put him to bed. I got up, went back to my room, and lay down too. But I was in a state of great agitation. I tossed about from side to side, wondering feverishly about this encounter. I don't know what I expected from it. No doubt, my thinking was rather disconnected and it was fragments of thoughts rather than whole thoughts that flitted through my head. As I lay with my face turned toward the wall, I suddenly saw in the corner the bright patch of glowing sunlight that I had been anticipating with such disgust. But instead, I clearly remember now, my whole being leaped with joy and a new light flooded my heart. I remember that blissful minute and I don't want ever to forget it: it was a moment of new promise and of new strength. . . . Of course, I was convalescing then, and these emotional transports could have been caused by my weakened nerves. However, to this day, I believe in that strange promise, and I want to record it so I'll always remember it. It goes without saying that I already knew I wouldn't follow Makar Dolgoruky in his wanderings and I realized I didn't understand the nature of the new impulse that had taken hold of me. It was then that I uttered for the first time the important word "beauty." "There's no *beauty* in them . . ." I thought and decided that "from now on, I shall seek *beauty*. . . . And since they don't possess it, I must leave them."

There was a rustling behind my back. I turned around. Mother was leaning over me and, with timid curiosity, was trying to look into my eyes. Impulsively, I took her hand.

"Mamma, why didn't you tell me about our wonderful guest?"

The words came out by themselves, almost without my being aware of what I was saying. But they swept all the uneasiness from Mother's face and caused joy to flash in it. But she only said:

"And Lisa too. . . . You mustn't forget her either. You've forgotten her. . . ."

She said that very quickly, in one breath, her face turning very pink, and she was anxious to get out of my sight because she had a horror of emotional displays, being in that way very much like me, that is, shy and reserved. Besides, for obvious reasons she felt it awkward to talk about Makar with me. What we had said was quite enough, on top of what our eyes had told each other. But then it was I—I who hate slobbery scenes so much—it was I who forcibly prevented her from leaving by holding onto her hand. I looked tenderly into her eyes, laughing gently, and with my other hand stroking her sweet face and her hollow cheeks. She leaned over and pressed her forehead against mine.

"All right, all right. . . . Christ be with you. . . ."

When she straightened up, she was beaming.

"Get well," she said, "I'm counting on you. . . . He's sick, very sick. . . . His life is in God's hands. . . . Ah, I can't bear the thought! No, no, it can't be . . ."

She left the room. All her life she had honored, in fear and trembling, her legitimate husband, the pilgrim Makar Dolgoruky, who had so generously forgiven her once and for ever.

Chapter 2

I

But about Lisa, Mother was wrong. I hadn't forgotten her. Sensitive as she was, Mother had noticed a certain coolness between brother and sister, but if there was something of that sort it wasn't from lack of affection but rather from jealousy. To make further developments clearer, I'd better say a few words about that now.

Ever since Sergei's arrest, there had been in poor Lisa's attitude a sort of proud challenge, an inaccessible haughtiness that was almost unbearable. But we all understood how she felt and how unhappy she was, and if at the beginning I resented her ways and frowned at her, it was only due to my usual petty irritability, made worse ten times by my illness. This is how I explain it now in retrospect. But I never ceased to love Lisa and, if anything, I loved her more than before; only I wouldn't make the first friendly move and I knew she never would either.

What had happened was that when, following Sergei's arrest, his past dealings had come into the open, Lisa immediately adopted an attitude toward us and everybody else that made it unthinkable to show her sympathy, to try and console her, or to find excuses for what Sergei had done. Indeed, while avoiding all discussion of the subject and all argument, she appeared to be proud of her unfortunate fiancé as if there were something supremely heroic in him; it was as if she kept telling us all (without actually uttering a word, as I explained): "None of you would have acted as nobly as he did and have sacrificed everything to the dictates of honor and duty because none of you have his scruples and pure conscience. As for what he actually did, who is not guilty of some evil deed? But while others keep their evil doings hidden, he preferred to ruin himself rather than remain unworthy in his own eyes." Every gesture of hers seemed to imply that idea. I'm not sure but I think that, in her place, I'd have behaved in the same way. Neither am I convinced that inwardly she really believed all that; in fact, I suspect she didn't. The clear reasoning part of her brain must certainly have been aware of her hero's lack of character, for how could one deny that the unfortunate man, although generous in his way, was in fact nothing but a poor mediocrity? Her very sensitivity on the subject, her challenging attitude toward all of us, her constant suspiciousness of what we might be thinking of him—all that indicated that she might herself have formed a different opinion of poor Sergei in the secret recesses of her heart. I hasten to add, however, that, in my personal opinion, she was at least half right: she had more excuses than anyone else to refuse to make a final pronouncement on Sergei. And I confess that even now, when everything is over, I'm completely at a loss as to how to judge that unhappy man who made things so hard for us.

But, be that as it may, Lisa succeeded in turning the house into a sort of little hell. Her love had been great and she was bound to suffer intensely. And, by her nature, she preferred to suffer in silence. Her character resembled mine—proud and domineering—and I've always thought that it was that domineering side in her that made her love Sergei precisely because he lacked character and that, from the very first hour, after their very first words had been exchanged, he had accepted her domination. Feelings like that may spring up spontaneously in the heart without any premeditation, and the love of a strong person for a weak one is often much more powerful and much more painful than love between equals because the strong one instinctively takes upon himself the responsibility for his weaker partner. At least, that's how I see it.

From the beginning, all of us, especially Mother, surrounded Lisa with loving sympathy. But Lisa not only did not respond to our warm concern for her but seemed to be exasperated by the support we were trying to offer her. At first, she still talked quite a bit to Mother, but as time passed she became less and less willing to talk at all, less and less patient, and often even brusque. In the beginning she sought some legal advice from Versilov but soon turned to Vasin for it, as I later learned to my great surprise. In fact, she went to see Vasin every day. She also spent much time in the courts, discussing Sergei's case with lawyers, arguing even with the public prosecutor. In the end, she was hardly ever at home during the day, for it goes without saying that she also visited Sergei in prison. She went daily or even twice a day to the section reserved for the gentry. As I learned later, these visits were also very painful to her. Although, it's almost impossible for a third person to understand fully the relations between two people in love, I know that Sergei was bitterly reproachful all the time, for, believe it or not, he was madly jealous! But I'll come back to that later. And so it's really hard to say which of them made the other more miserable. Thus, Lisa, who in our presence was so proud of her hero, treated him quite differently when the two of them were alone: I'm convinced of this from certain indications. But I'll come back to this point later too.

And so the feelings I showed toward Lisa and our mutual relations were only an affected coolness, a pretended family rivalry, when in reality we had never loved each other more.

Let me note too that, after her first surprise and curiosity about Makar's presence in the house, Lisa somehow began to treat him almost condescendingly, I might even say scornfully. Often she simply ignored him.

Having vowed to remain "silent," as I explained in the previous chapter, I expected to keep my vow. But that was just theory, or perhaps a pipe dream. With Versilov, for instance, I would rather have talked about zoology or Roman emperors than about *her,* or about the most important passage in his letter to *her* where he informed her that the compromising document hadn't been burned and would still show up, a passage I couldn't get out of my mind the moment I'd recovered from my brain fever. But, alas, from my very first steps and, indeed, even before I could take any steps, I realized how difficult and even impossible it would be to restrain myself and stick to my resolutions. Moreover, the day after I met Makar I was greatly perturbed by an unexpected circumstance.

II

The event that perturbed me was a visit from Daria, the mother of poor Olga who had hanged herself. My mother had told me that Daria had come twice while I was ill and had anxiously inquired about the state of my health. I didn't ask whether that "kind woman," as Mother described her, had come especially because of me or simply because it was her habit to come and see my mother. Mother usually kept me posted on what was happening at home when she brought me my soup and fed me (that is, before I could eat by myself). She did that to distract me, although I always stubbornly pretended I wasn't in the least interested in the household news. And that was why I didn't ask her any additional questions about Daria. It was just as if I hadn't heard Mother mention her at all.

It was around eleven in the morning. I was just about to get out of bed to install myself in the armchair by the table when Daria came in. So I stayed in bed. Mother was busy doing something upstairs and didn't come down when the woman arrived, so Daria and I were all alone. She sat down on a chair by the wall facing me, smiled at me, but said nothing. There followed a long silence, which only increased the irritation her intrusion had already provoked in me. I hadn't even nodded to her when she came in and now just stared straight into her face. And she stared back at me.

"I suppose you find life rather dull living all alone in that apartment since Prince Sergei left," I said, finally losing patience.

"Well, no . . . I no longer live in that apartment. . . . Thanks to Miss Anna, Miss Versilov, I'm looking after the baby. . . ."

"Whose baby?"

"Mr. Versilov's," she whispered confidentially, glancing at the door.

"But isn't Mrs. Prutkov there?"

"Yes, Mrs. Prutkov and Miss Anna are both there, and also Lisa and your mamma . . . all of them. . . . They're all help-ing. Mrs. Prutkov and Miss Anna are great friends now."

That was news! Daria grew quite excited as she talked. I looked at her with hatred.

"You look much livelier since the last time you came to see me."

"Well, yes, maybe."

"You've gained some weight, haven't you?"

She gave me a peculiar look.

"I've grown very fond of her, very fond . . ."

"Fond of whom?"

"Of Miss Anna Versilov. Yes, yes, she's such a high-minded young lady, and so very intelligent too. . . ."

"You don't say! So what about her? How are things with her now?"

"She's very calm, very calm indeed."

"She's always been a very calm person."

"Yes, always."

"Now let me tell you this," I cried out, suddenly losing all patience. "If you've come here to try to stir up trouble, you might as well know that I want nothing to do with all this, that I've decided to break with the lot of them and with everything, that none of it is any concern of mine. I'm getting out of here. . . ."

I stopped abruptly: the meaning of what I was saying sud-denly dawned on me. I felt it degrading to explain to this woman the new goals I'd set for myself. She, on the other hand, took my outcry calmly without any apparent surprise.

Nevertheless, another silence followed. Then she suddenly got up, walked quickly to the door, and peered into the adjoin-ing room. Reassured that there was no one around, she calmly resumed her seat.

"You certainly like to take your precautions!" I commented and couldn't help laughing.

"What about the lodgings you were renting from that clerk —are you keeping them?"

She suddenly leaned toward me and lowered her voice as if the answer to that question had been the main object of her visit.

"My lodgings? I don't know. I may move out. . . . I haven't decided yet."

"But your landlord is expecting you. He's very anxious to see you and so's his wife. And Mr. Versilov assured them that you'd be back."

"But what's it to you, anyway?"

"Miss Anna was interested too, and she was very pleased to hear that you'd be staying there."

"But how can she be so sure that I'll stay there?"

I wanted to add "And what business is it of hers?" but I didn't, feeling it wasn't dignified with this woman.

"Because Mr. Lambert also told her you'd keep the lodgings."

"What's that?"

"Mr. Lambert. It was he who told Mr. Versilov that he was certain you'd keep the place, and he also convinced Miss Anna."

That gave me quite a shock. Extraordinary, wasn't it? So Lambert had already met Versilov, had succeeded in getting to him, and in contacting Anna too! I felt hot all over, but managed to hold my tongue. A violent rush of pride swept over me, of pride or something else. But it was as though I said to myself at that second: "I'll ask her nothing, not one word of explanation, for if I do, I'll again get involved in their affairs and will never succeed in cutting myself loose from them." Hatred flared up in my heart. I firmly resolved not to talk anymore and lay there without moving. She too remained silent for a whole minute.

"How's Prince Nikolai Sokolsky?"

I asked this suddenly, like one whose reason has lost control over his actions. Actually, I was simply trying to change the subject of the conversation but, instead, stumbled on the really crucial point, which was the reason for her being here.

"The prince is in Tsarskoe Selo. . . . He wasn't feeling too well, and since there are those bouts of fever going around town now, everybody advised him to go to his house in Tsarskoe where the air is much better."

I said nothing.

"And now Miss Anna and Mrs. Akhmakov drive over to visit him every other day. They drive there together. . . ."

So she—Katerina Akhmakov—and Anna were great friends now and drove to Tsarskoe together!

But I still said nothing.

"They've become such good friends now, and Miss Anna speaks so nicely about Mrs. Akhmakov. . . ."

I didn't stir.

"And Mrs. Akhmakov is going out again a great deal, one ball after another; she is having a great success and they say everybody, even the people at the Imperial Court, is crazy about her. . . . As to Mr. Björing, that's all over, and there will be no wedding—that's what everyone's been saying ever since that letter."

She meant Versilov's letter. I was shivering. But I didn't say a word.

"Miss Anna is so sorry for Prince Sergei! And so is Mrs. Akhmakov. They all say he'll be acquitted while the other man, Stebelkov, will be found guilty."

I glared at her with loathing. She got up and suddenly leaned over me again.

"Miss Anna especially asked me to inquire about your health," she whispered in my ear, "and she begs you to come and see her as soon as you are well enough to go out. . . . Goodby then for now, get well, and I'll tell her. . . ."

She left. I sat up in bed. Cold sweat beaded my forehead, but it was not fear. The unexplainable and distasteful news about Lambert and his intrigues didn't fill me with terror as might have been expected, judging from the almost irrational horror with which, during my sickness and convalescence, I remembered our last meeting. In fact, during that confused moment when I sat up in bed after Daria had left, I didn't even give much thought to Lambert. I was much too absorbed by what the woman had told me about *her*—about *her* break with Björing, her success in society, at all those balls. . . . I suddenly knew that, try as hard as I might, I'd never succeed in making a clean break from that whirlpool, notwithstanding my obstinate silence and my refusal to ask Daria to elaborate on the wonderful things she'd told me. I felt an irresistible craving for that life, for *their* life, such an overwhelming craving that I could feel nothing else. And, along with it, successively sweet and bitter waves of joy and of excruciating torment swept over me. And in my head fragments of thoughts were spinning around, but I didn't mind: "What good would it do to try to reason?" I felt. "Still, even Mother hid from me the fact that Lambert had come to the house," flashed through my mind. "It must be Versilov who told her not to say anything about it. . . . Well, I'll die before I ask Versilov about Lambert!" "Versilov," flashed through my mind, "Versilov and Lambert! Ah, they have so much to tell to each other! It was great of Versilov, though, to manage to scare away that German oaf Björing with his letter! He *did* libel her all right, and that's *la calomnie . . . il en reste toujours quelque chose,* and that courtly German became too frightened of a scandal! Ha-ha-ha! So let it be a good lesson to her! But I wonder whether Lambert hasn't managed to get to her too? Why, of course, why shouldn't she get involved in some plot with him too?"

At this point I gave up all this senseless tangle and my head sank hopelessly onto the pillow. But a second later, I jumped up from my bed.

"No, no, I won't allow it!" I shouted with sudden resolve.

I slipped my feet into my slippers, put on my dressing gown, and went straight to the room where Makar was. Instinctively I hoped to find there something that could free me from all this madness, a quiet harbor where I could drop an anchor that would hold me.

Yes, I must have felt just like that with my whole being, for otherwise why would I have leaped up as I did and rushed to Makar in such a state?

III

Somehow it had never occurred to me that Makar might not be alone, and now I was quite taken aback to find Mother and the doctor there. I stopped, hesitating in the doorway, but before I even had time to frown in disappointment Versilov arrived and he was followed by Lisa. So all of them had to gather in Makar's room just when I least wanted to see them!

"I've come to find out how you are," I said, going straight up to Makar.

"Thank you, my boy, I've been waiting for you, I knew you'd come! I was thinking of you at night."

He looked warmly into my eyes and I thought that perhaps he liked me best of anyone there. But then I noticed that, although his face was cheerful, his state had obviously deteriorated during the night. Just before I'd come in, the doctor had given him a pretty thorough examination. Later I learned that the doctor (the same young doctor with whom I'd quarreled), who had been attending Makar very devotedly ever since his arrival, had now diagnosed all sorts of complications resulting from his original complaints, but I won't try to repeat it all in medical jargon.

By the way, I was struck at once by the friendly familiarity with which Makar and the doctor talked to each other, and it didn't please me at all. But then, in the mood I was in, nothing would have pleased me.

"Well, Doctor, how is our precious patient today?" Versilov inquired.

If I hadn't been so tense, I'd have been anxious to see how Versilov behaved in Makar's presence, something I had tried to imagine before. Now I was particularly struck by Versilov's strangely gentle and warm expression, which I knew was quite unaffected. I believe I've already remarked that Versilov's face was amazingly beautiful whenever he became really sincere.

"As you well may expect, we still can't agree," the doctor said.

"What? You can't get along with our Makar? I can't believe you, Doctor. No one can *not* get along with him."

"Except that he won't do what I tell him and refuses to sleep at night. . . ."

"Ah, stop complaining, Doc," Makar said, laughing, and then, turning to Versilov, asked him: "You tell me, sir, what they've decided to do about our Mrs. Prutkov? This lady here"—he pointed at Mother—"has been going around sighing and moaning and worrying about it all morning. . . ."

"Yes, Andrei," Mother chimed in, sounding really very worried, "tell us quickly, don't torture us—what have they decided to do to the poor old girl?"

"They found her guilty and sentenced her."

"Ah!" Mother cried out in alarm.

"Well, it's not that bad really—they didn't sentence her to hard labor in Siberia, so don't take it so hard. They only fined her fifteen rubles. The whole thing turned into a real comedy!"

He sat down and so did the doctor, apparently eager to hear about Mrs. Prutkov's day in court. I hadn't heard anything about it yet, so I sat down on Makar's left and Lisa installed herself opposite me on his right. I believe Lisa had some new troubles that day and had shared them with Mother. Her face looked worried and irritated. As we sat down, our eyes met for a second and I thought to myself that here both of us were in a mess and that it was up to me to take the first step toward her. Suddenly I felt softened toward her. . . . In the meantime, Versilov had begun to recount what had taken place that morning.

It so happened that that morning Tatyana Prutkov had had to appear before the judge to answer a charge brought against her by her cook. It was nothing much really. I've already mentioned the ill-tempered old Finnish woman's way of getting back at her mistress by refusing to utter a word, sometimes for weeks on end, not even answering the simplest questions. I've also mentioned Tatyana's strange weakness for that woman and her reluctance to fire her. I know that all these psychological whims of old women and old maids deserve to be ignored and should certainly not be dwelt upon. However, if I've decided to mention them here, it's only because that Finnish cook was destined to play a fateful role in my story later.

Well, once, after several days of total silence, Mrs. Prutkov finally lost patience with her cook and slapped her, which was something she'd never done before. Even then the cook still kept her mouth shut, but later that day she got in touch with a man called Osetrov, who had once been a midshipman but now lived in the basement of the house and eked out a living by taking to court complaints on behalf of various citizens, such as the Finnish cook's. So, in due time, Mrs. Prutkov was summoned to appear before the judge and Versilov had to appear in court as a character witness.

He described all this in a very witty way so that even Mother had to laugh. He imitated Tatyana and the former midshipman and mimicked the cook, who from the start declared that she *only* wanted Mrs. Prutkov to be fined "because if they lock Madam up, who will I work for?" As to Tatyana, she answered the judge's questions in a terribly haughty tone, refused to explain her action, and, in fact, ended her statement with the words: "Yes, I did hit her and I'll do it again," which answer caused her immediately to be fined three rubles for contempt of court. Then the former midshipman, a long-legged, thin young man, started on what threatened to be a long speech on behalf of his client. But luckily he soon lost the thread of his argument and made the audience burst out laughing. The case was quickly settled with Mrs. Prutkov being sentenced to pay fifteen rubles to the injured party.

Tatyana took out her purse and proceeded to count out the money, but when the former midshipman stretched out his hand to collect on behalf of his client, she pushed his hand away rather roughly and held out the money in Maria's direction.

"Oh, don't bother about it, ma'am, just add it to our accounts. As to this fellow, I'll settle with him myself."

"You see, Maria, what a long-legged fool you've picked!" Tatyana said, pointing at the fellow and sounding terribly pleased, probably because her cook had agreed to talk again.

"Yes, he's long-legged all right, ma'am," the cook said with a sly wink. "And, by the way, was it cutlets and peas that you ordered this morning? I didn't catch what you said, I was in such a hurry to get here on time."

"No, I said cutlets and cabbage, Maria, and I want you to be careful not to burn them the way you did yesterday."

"I'll do my best today, ma'am. And now may I have your hand please?"

And the woman kissed her mistress's hand as a sign of peace. The audience was delighted.

"She's really something!" Mother said, shaking her head appreciatively. She had obviously enjoyed the story and Versilov's way of telling it, although she'd kept darting worried looks at Lisa.

"Yes, she's been quite a character ever since she was a little girl, our Miss Tatyana," Makar said with a smile.

"It all comes from idleness and bile," the doctor commented.

"That's me, idleness and bile?"

Tatyana Prutkov had suddenly appeared in the doorway, looking very pleased with herself.

"You ought to be the last one, my young friend," she went on, looking at the doctor, "to talk such utter nonsense because you've known me ever since you were a ten-year-old boy and so I'd like you to tell me when was the last time you saw me idle. As for my biliousness, well, you've been treating me for a year now and if you haven't been able to cure me all this time, that's not much credit to you, is it? Anyway, that's enough of making a laughing stock of me. Thank you, Andrei, for taking the trouble to come to court. . . . And how are you, Makar dear, it's only to see you that I've come, certainly not that one!" She pointed at me but then gave me quite a friendly tap on the shoulder, for she was in a chirpier mood than I'd ever seen her. "Well, how is he?" she suddenly frowned and turned again toward the doctor.

"He just won't stay in bed properly; he insists on sitting up and that tires him."

"Let me stay like this for a little longer, at least while I have company," Makar said with an expression of entreaty like a little boy.

"Yes, he loves it, he loves to have a bit of gossip in a close little circle. I know our Makar so well!" Tatyana said.

"Oh, you're so impatient, Doctor!" The old man smiled again. "You won't even listen to reason. Just wait a little and I'll lie down. But the way I feel is that when you stretch yourself out, you may never get up again. I just have that feeling in my bones. I can't help it, Doctor, my friend."

"That's what I suspected," the doctor said, "old wives' tales to the effect that a man who lies down may never get up again. That's what simple folk fear and they prefer to remain on their feet throughout their sickness rather than go to the hospital. But in your case, Mr. Dolgoruky, you're simply missing the dusty roads and the wide-open spaces. Your trouble is that you're not used to staying long in one place. You are a true wanderer, a pilgrim, and wandering is often a passion among our people. I've noticed it. Our nation is essentially a nation of tramps."

"So, according to you, Doctor, our Makar is a tramp?" Tatyana cried.

"Oh, I wasn't using the word in its ordinary meaning. Well, let's say he's a sort of religious tramp. He may be a pious pilgrim but he's still a tramp. A tramp in the best sense. I speak from the medical point of view. . . ."

"I assure you," I suddenly intruded, addressing the doctor, "that the word tramp would apply much better to me, to you, to everybody else in the room than to this old man from whom we could learn so much because he does believe in something solid whereas we have nothing solid to hold onto in life. . . . But I don't suppose you can understand what I mean."

I must have sounded rather rude, but that's just what I intended. Actually I don't know why I remained sitting there. In a way I felt as though I were insane.

"What's come over him now?" Tatyana growled, and then, pointing at me, she said to Makar: "How did you find him, my dear man?"

"He's a sharp one, God bless his heart," Makar said with a grave expression, although everyone in the room burst into laughter at the word "sharp" while I managed to keep a straight face.

I noticed that it was the doctor who laughed the loudest. Unfortunately I didn't know at the time that Versilov, the doctor, and Tatyana had agreed, three days before, to do their best to distract Mother as much as possible from her constant worrying and brooding about Makar, who was in a much worse state than I suspected, quite hopeless in fact. And that's why they all joked and laughed that day. The doctor, however, was naturally a stupid man and had no sense of humor, which is what brought it all on. Had I known of their agreement, I'd never have said what I did. Lisa, like me, also knew nothing about the agreement.

As I sat there listening distractedly to their talk and laughter, I was really more preoccupied by what Daria had just told me. I couldn't get that woman out of my head. I kept seeing again and again in my mind's eye how she'd got up from the chair and walked stealthily to the door to make sure that there was no one in the adjoining room. A sudden burst of laughter, however, tore me from my thoughts: it had been provoked by

Tatyana suddenly calling the doctor "godless"—I don't know for what reason—but I heard her suddenly declare:

"Why, you doctors are all a godless bunch, the lot of you!"

The doctor, very stupidly, decided to pretend to be offended and turned to Makar, as though asking him to pronounce on Tatyana's statement:

"Mr. Dolgoruky, you tell Mrs. Prutkov: am I godless or not?"

"You godless?" the old man said, looking at him cheerfully. "No, thank God, you aren't godless. Your heart is merry."

"So a man who has a merry heart can't be godless?" the doctor asked ironically.

"That's quite a thought," Versilov said, and he was not laughing at all.

"It's a powerful thought!" I exclaimed, full of admiration.

But the doctor kept looking around, sincerely surprised now.

"You see, I used to be terribly afraid at first of those learned people, of those professors," Makar, who must have said something about professors before, went on, with his eyes slightly lowered. "Ah, the way they used to scare me! I didn't dare say anything to them because there was nothing I was more afraid of than an atheist. I have only one soul, I used to say to myself, and if I lose it, I'll never find another. But later I was no longer afraid of them. Why, I thought, they're not gods after all, they're simply men with all the human weaknesses, just like us. And I was curious too: I wanted to know what that godlessness of theirs was really like. After a time, though, even that curiosity passed."

He stopped, although he seemed to want to go on talking; the same serene smile still played on his lips.

There are simple and unaffected souls who trust everybody and are not aware of the ridiculous. Such people are of limited intelligence because they're eager to reveal to any comer their most sacred secrets. But I felt there was something other than just childlike trustingness that prompted Makar to talk: there was something of a preacher in him. I detected with glee a sly little smile he darted at the doctor or perhaps even at Versilov. This conversation was probably the continuation of a discussion they'd been having all week. Unfortunately, the fatal phrase, which had electrified me so much the day before, slipped in again and this time triggered an outburst in me that I regret to this day.

"Perhaps even now, though," Makar went on with concentration, "I'd be frightened to meet a truly godless man, but let me tell you, Doctor, my friend, I've never really met a man like that. What I have met were restless men, for that's what they should really be called. There are all sorts of people like that and you can't tell what makes them the way they are: some are important, others are little men; some are ignorant, others are learned; and they come from all classes, even the lowest . . . but it's all restlessness. For they keep on reading all their lives and, having filled themselves with bookish wisdom, they talk and talk, although they never find answers to what's bothering them and remain in the darkness. Some of them throw themselves in so many different directions that they end by losing themselves; the hearts of others turn into stones, although there may still be dreams in them; still others become drained of thoughts and feelings but still go around sneering at everything. Some people pick out from books nothing but the little flowers, and even then only those that suit them, but they still remain restless because they could never make up their minds in the first place. And I can see that there's too much boredom in them. A poor man may be short of bread, may not have enough to keep his children alive, may sleep on rough straw, may be brutal and sinful, but still his heart may be gay and merry; while a rich man may eat and drink too much and sit on a pile of gold with nothing but gloom in his heart. A man may study all the sciences and never get rid of emptiness and gloom; indeed, I think that the more intelligence he gains, the more his gloom will thicken.

"Or let's look at it this way: people have been taught and taught ever since the creation of the world, but what have they learned in all that time to help them make the world a gayer and happier place where man can find all the joys he's longing for? What they lack, I tell you, is *beauty*. Indeed, they don't even want it. They're all lost and every one of them glories in what has brought him to his ruin. But they never think to face the only truth, although life without God is nothing but torture. What it all comes down to is that, without realizing it, they curse the only source that can brighten our life. But that won't get them anywhere because a man cannot live without worshiping something; without worshiping he cannot bear the burden of himself. And that goes for every man. So that if a man rejects God, he will have to worship an idol that may be made of wood, gold, or ideas. So those who think they don't need God are really just idol worshipers, and that's what we should call them. But there must be true atheists too; only they're much more dangerous because they come to us with the name of God on their lips. I've often heard about them, but I've never come across one yet. There are some people like that, my friends, and there should be."

"There are, Makar," Versilov suddenly said, "there are and 'there should be.' "

"Indeed, there are and 'there should be!' " I couldn't restrain myself from exclaiming eagerly.

I don't know why but I was captivated by Versilov's tone and somehow saw a deep meaning in the phrase "there should be." The turn the conversation had taken was quite unexpected. But at that moment something happened that was even more so.

IV

It was an extremely bright day. The blind on the window in Makar's room, which had been kept down for many days on the doctor's orders, had been replaced by a curtain that did not extend all the way to the top of the window. This had been done because the old man had felt miserable not being able to see the sun at all. And now the moment had arrived when the sunbeam fell directly on Makar's face. He hadn't noticed it at first while he was speaking and had turned his head aside to avoid the glare that hurt his inflamed eyes. Mother, who stood next to him, kept casting worried glances at the window. The most obvious thing to do, of course, would have been to pull down the blind but, reluctant to interrupt the conversation, she tried instead to pull the bench on which Makar was sitting a little to the right—a mere matter of a few inches. Several times I noticed her bending down and tugging at the bench, but under Makar's weight it wouldn't budge. Apparently aware of her efforts but still continuing to talk, Makar made a few instinctive attempts to raise himself from the bench, but his legs wouldn't obey him. And so Mother went on trying to pull the bench out of the sun with him on it.

In the end this provoked an annoyed outburst from Lisa. I vaguely remember having noticed a few of her irritated glances without understanding the reason for them. Besides, I was too absorbed in what was being said. And then suddenly I heard Lisa's shrill voice saying to Makar: "Can't you raise yourself a bit, for heaven's sake! Don't you see how hard you're making it for Mother!"

The old man looked up at her quickly, immediately became aware of what was going on, and made a great effort to scramble to his feet. But all he could do was lift his body a couple of inches above the bench and then fall back on it.

"I can't make it, dearie," he said, looking helplessly at Lisa. He appeared meek and subdued.

"You can talk and talk and talk, but you haven't enough strength to move," she snapped at him.

"Lisa!" Mrs. Prutkov cried indignantly.

Makar again tried desperately to get up.

"Use your crutch. . . . Over there, next to you. . . . You should be able to get up with it," Lisa suggested impatiently.

"That's a good idea," the old man said and hastily reached for the crutch.

"We ought to lift him," Versilov said, getting up.

The doctor followed his example and Mrs. Prutkov jumped to her feet too. But before they got to him, Makar, pushing hard on his crutch, had managed to raise himself and was looking around with a triumphant and laughing expression.

"Well, I made it, see!" he said almost proudly and smiling happily. "And I must thank you, my dear girl, you've talked sense into me, because without you I never would have expected my poor legs could hold me up at all . . ."

But his triumph didn't last long and, before he could finish his sentence, the crutch that was supporting the whole weight of his body slipped on the carpet, and since his "poor legs" were in reality hardly supporting him, he fell heavily full length on the floor. I remember the heartbreaking scene clearly. A moan came out of everybody's lips and we all rushed toward him to help him up. Thank God, there were no broken bones, although he had fallen heavily, both his knees hitting the floor with a loud thud. Still, he had had time to stretch out his right arm and thus soften his fall a little. We lifted him up and sat him on his bed. He was very pale, but certainly not from fright, rather from the shock, because, on top of everything else, the doctor had discovered he had heart trouble as well. Mother was ashen also, but in her case it was from fear.

Suddenly Makar, still white and his whole body trembling, turned toward Lisa and said in an almost tender voice:

"Well, what can you do, dearie, they won't hold me up, my poor old legs, after all."

I cannot express the impression it made on me. I was struck by the absence of any trace of self-pity and of any suggestion of reproach in the poor old man's voice. It was obvious that he had never noticed any irritation or spite in Lisa's interference and had accepted her impatience as something quite natural, something he fully deserved as if he'd misbehaved.

The whole thing had a violent effect on Lisa. When he fell,

she jumped up and remained standing there, looking stunned. She must have felt horrible because she was really the cause of it all. But when she heard the old man's last words, the blood rushed to her cheeks and colored them with the redness of shame and remorse.

"All right, enough!" Mrs. Prutkov suddenly said in a commanding voice. "This is what comes of too much tongue-wagging. Off we go—everyone to his own place! And it's really the end of everything when the doctor himself starts all that silly chatter!"

"Right you are, Mrs. Prutkov!" the doctor, who had been attending to the patient, agreed with her; "he does need a rest and it was my fault all right. . . ."

Mrs. Prutkov was no longer listening to him though. Her eyes were now fixed on Lisa and remained fixed on her for a good half minute.

"Come here, Lisa, and kiss me, old idiot that I am—that is, of course, only if you feel like it," she said quite unexpectedly.

And she herself kissed Lisa. I don't really know why she felt she had to kiss Lisa, but I was sure it was the right thing to do. In fact, I almost rushed toward Mrs. Prutkov myself to kiss her. Her instinct had told her that it would have been completely wrong to crush Lisa further with reproaches at that moment and it was much better to acknowledge the stirrings of a new feeling that must have been born in the poor girl. But instead of saying what I thought, I got up and, articulating my words with utmost deliberation, declared:

"Once again, Mr. Dolgoruky, you've used that word *beauty*. Well, yesterday and last night I couldn't get that word out of my head: it kept tormenting me. . . . Actually, it has tormented me all my life, but I didn't know why. I consider this coincidence—I mean the fact that you should use that word in that sense—as momentous, even miraculous. . . . I felt I had to say that in your presence. . . ."

But at this point I was actually silenced. I repeat, I hadn't been told about their stratagem to protect Mother and Makar. Besides, from my past record, they certainly had good grounds to fear that I might cause yet another scene.

"Shut him up, shut him up!" Mrs. Prutkov hissed with the fierceness of a wild beast.

Mother was shaking. Makar, seeing that everybody around him was horrified by something, became frightened too.

"That's enough, Arkady," Versilov said sharply.

"As far as I'm concerned," I said, raising my voice even more, "seeing you all near this babe"—I pointed at Makar—"is a shocking disgrace. Only Mother, who is a saintly soul, has the right to be next to him but even she . . ."

"You're frightening him," the doctor said firmly.

"I know, I know, I'm the enemy of the whole world," I mumbled (or something to that effect), and I turned my head to give Versilov one more challenging look.

"Arkady," he said again, "a scene exactly like this one has already taken place in this house once before. So I beg you, control yourself this time."

I cannot express the strength of the feeling with which he said that. Great sadness, bottomless and total, flooded his face. The most surprising thing of all was that there was guilt in his eyes too: he'd looked at me the way an accused might look at his judge. That was the last straw.

"Yes!" I shouted, glaring at him. "An exactly similar scene took place here when I was burying Versilov after having torn him out of my heart. . . . But after that there was a resurrection from the dead. But now . . . this time there will be no dawn! And you'll still see, all of you here, what I'm capable of! You haven't the slightest idea of what I can show you!"

I ran to my room. Versilov rushed after me.

V

I had a relapse: my temperature shot up and by nightfall I was delirious, although not continuously. I also had innumerable dreams, an endless succession, and, of them, one dream or rather a fragment of a dream remained engraved forever in my memory. I'll describe it without comment. I must because it was prophetic.

I find myself, full of noble and proud resolve, in a high-ceilinged room. I remember that room clearly and must emphasize that it was not one of Mrs. Prutkov's rooms, for this is important in view of what follows. I have a nagging, uneasy, and alarming feeling that I'm not alone, that I'm being watched, that I'm expected to do something. Somewhere behind the door they are waiting to see what I'll do. It's an unbearable sensation. "Oh," I think, "if only I were here alone!" Then suddenly Katerina appears. She looks at me timidly; she's frightened; she searches my eyes. *The document is in my hand.* She smiles, she tries to overwhelm me with her charm; she puts on caressing airs. I feel sorry for her, but a feeling of disgust rises up inside me. She covers her face with her hands. I toss *the document* on the table and say with infinite scorn: "No need for all that—

there's nothing I want from you. I'm paying you back for all your insults with contempt." I walk out of the room, wallowing in tremendous pride. But in the doorway I'm suddenly grabbed by Lambert. "You *moron, moron!*" he whispers, rolling his French *r*'s in his throat and holding me tightly by the arm, "she's about to open a boarding school for young ladies on Vasilievsky Island, for she'll have to earn her living when her father hears about the document, disinherits her, and kicks her out of his house." (I'm writing down verbatim the words Lambert uttered in my dream.)

"Arkady is searching for *beauty*," I suddenly hear Anna's voice coming from somewhere close by. But she is not praising me—there's an unbearable sneer in her tone. I go back into the room with Lambert. When Katerina sees Lambert, she bursts out laughing. At first I feel frightened, in fact so violently frightened that I stop and refuse to go any further. I stare at her and I cannot believe my eyes. It's as though she's suddenly removed a mask from her face. Her features are still the same, but now every single one of these features seems to have been twisted and distorted by an unimaginable impudence. "The ransom, madam, the ransom!" Lambert shouts to her and they both burst into even louder laughter. My heart goes cold. "Could this really be the same woman whose glance alone could set my heart stirring with virtuous impulses?"

"So you see now what these proud high-society people will do for money!" Lambert shouts.

But that does not seem to embarrass the shameless creature. The very fact that I'm so frightened makes her laugh. Oh, she's certainly ready to pay the ransom! . . . But what's coming over me now? I no longer feel either pity or disgust. I'm trembling as I've never trembled before. . . . I'm gripped by a new sensation that I never even suspected existed; I cannot describe it, but it's so powerful, as powerful as the whole world. . . . Oh, I no longer have the strength to leave now! Nothing would make me leave! And it's precisely her shamelessness that pleases me. I seize her hands. This contact with her hands makes me shake violently, painfully. I draw my lips close to her insolent bright red lips, which are quivering with laughter and inviting me . . .

Oh, be gone, vile memory! Evil vision! I swear that, until I had that filthy dream, there was nothing on my mind even remotely connected with that disgraceful thought. I never even had any such unconscious wish (although I did keep *the* document sewn into the lining of my pocket and I sometimes touched that pocket with a peculiar little grin). So how could it have come to me, complete with all the details, as it did? The answer must be that I had the soul of a spider. All this must have been hatched long before and been stored in my perverted heart; it was all part of my *desire*, although my heart was still too ashamed of it during my waking hours and my brain still did not dare to formulate consciously anything of the sort. But, in my sleep, my soul had shown and explained exactly what was hidden inside me; it had given a complete, absolutely accurate picture and, what is more, in a prophetic form. And could it be that this was what I'd wanted to *prove* to them that morning when I'd rushed out of Makar's room? But enough of this for the time being. I'll only say that this dream is one of the strangest things that has happened to me in all my life.

Chapter 3

I

Three days later, I got up in the morning and suddenly felt that I was through with lying in bed. I felt that a complete recovery was very close. Perhaps there's really no point going into all this, but the few days that followed, during which nothing special actually happened but which have remained in my memory as a pleasant and serene period, should be mentioned because such periods are rare in my past. But I won't describe my mental state because if my reader knew what it actually was, he would refuse to believe me. Eventually everything will become clear by itself. In the meantime I will ask the reader only to remember—the *soul of a spider*. And that in a man who planned to leave all those he knew and retire from the whole world in the name of *beauty!* The longing for *beauty* was there, and it was extremely intense—there's no doubt about that; but how could it coexist with those other, God knows what sort of desires in me? Well, that's a mystery to me. Yes, it has always been a mystery to me and thousands of times I've stopped and marveled at man's capacity (especially a Russian's, I believe) to cherish in himself some infinitely lofty ideal alongside something unspeakably base, and all this quite openly. Is, then, this *breadth* a trait peculiar to the Russian that will take him far? Or is it just base hypocrisy? That's the question.

But let's leave that for now. One way or the other, a lull followed. I plainly realized that, whatever I had to do, first I had to get well quickly so I could get on with my plans. I decided to lead a healthy life and follow the doctor's orders (however little I thought of the man). So I sensibly postponed the execution of my rebellious intentions (the products of my *breadth!*) until I had fully recovered my strength. How the peaceful healthy joys and musings of that restful period could coexist side by side with the intoxicating and restless throbbings in my heart, I cannot explain and can only suggest again that it might be due to that *breadth* of mine. But I was no longer worrying as before: I felt I would be able to cope with everything when the time came; I no longer trembled at the thought of the future as I had until then; I was now like a rich man, confident of his resources and power. I felt more and more defiant of whatever challenge fate held in store for me, more and more arrogant, I might say, which was probably due to my returning health and to the rapid recovery of my vital energies. And so those few days of final and complete recovery evoke extremely pleasant memories in me.

Oh, those people whom I'd called "ugly" to their faces, they forgave me everything, I mean my nasty outburst. Yes, there is a quality in people I appreciate above all, something I call "intelligence of the heart." This immediately attracts me to people, only up to a point of course. To Versilov, for instance, I still spoke like a friend, although with reservations, but whenever one of us would let himself go a little (and this did happen), we would at once both draw back as if ashamed of something. Often it is the one who gets the upper hand who feels embarrassed, precisely for getting the advantage. Obviously, it was I who was now in a stronger position and so I felt ashamed.

That morning—I mean the one when I had recovered from my relapse—Versilov came into my room and it was then that I learned for the first time of their secret agreement about Mother and Makar's illness. He also told me that, although the old man felt a little better, the doctor still absolutely refused to hold out any hope. I promised wholeheartedly that in the future I'd be more careful of what I said. While Versilov was talking, it suddenly struck me how deeply he himself was concerned about the old man, I mean much more deeply than I would have expected from someone like Versilov, and I realized that old Makar was dear to him personally, not just for Mother's sake. It made me very curious, in fact astounded me, and I confess that, had it not been for Versilov, there are many things I wouldn't have noticed and appreciated in that old man, who made a most unusual and lasting impression on me.

Versilov had apparently been worried about how I would behave toward Makar; that is, he didn't have too much trust in my intelligence and my tact. And so he was very pleased when he eventually saw that I too was capable of appreciating a man with a completely different outlook and ideas from my own and that, when necessary, I too could be tolerant and broad-minded. I'll also admit (I believe without lowering myself) that, in this man from the common people, I'd discovered feelings and views that were completely new to me and that shed a much more serene and joyful light on the world. And yet there were times when I could not help losing my temper when faced with certain obvious superstitions which he accepted unquestioningly with the most unabashed simplicity. But that, of course, was only due to his lack of education because, spiritually, his mind was rather well ordered. In fact, I've never met anyone superior to him in that respect.

II

As I mentioned before, the most attractive thing about him was his complete lack of affectation, his total disregard for the impression he might make: one could guess he had an almost sinless heart. There was *gaiety* in his heart and that's why there was *beauty* in him. *Gaiety* was a favorite word of his and he often used it. It's true that at times he was perhaps abnormally exalted, became filled with an unnatural fervor that might have been due, to some extent, to the fever that never really let up entirely all that time. This, however, never once diminished his inner beauty. There were also in him certain traits that seemed contradictory: side by side with his unbelievable trust, which, to my great exasperation at times, prevented him from detecting irony, there was a certain slyness, which showed up particularly during our arguments. For he did enjoy arguing, though not always, and then it had to be on his own peculiar terms. It was obvious that he had covered on foot large parts of Russia and had listened a great deal to what people said. But, I repeat, it was religious fervor that interested him most and that's why he liked to talk about anything that might inspire it. Besides, he obviously enjoyed telling stories with that fervent religious feeling in them. I heard from him much about his own peregrinations as well as various legends about ascetics of the remote past. Although I had never heard any of these legends before, I'm sure there was much in them he'd changed or invented because for the most part he'd heard them himself from simple, illiterate folk. There were things that one simply could not accept. But, underneath his obvious additions and distortions, there was always that amazing organic unity, something expressing a deep emotion of simple people, always tremendously moving. . . .

I recall, for instance, a rather lengthy story "The Life of Mary of Egypt." I'd no idea of that "Life" or, for that matter, of any such "lives" at the time. Let me say right away, I couldn't listen to that story without tears; and these weren't sentimental tears either, they were brought on by a strange ecstasy. I felt a sensation unknown and burning, perhaps like that parched sandy desert through which the saint had wandered amidst her lions. But this is not what I wanted to talk about; anyway I'm really not qualified.

Besides his tender fervor, I also liked in him certain extremely original views on various problems still controversial in our age. Once, for instance, he told me of something that had happened to a former soldier, something that he'd "almost" witnessed himself. The soldier had returned from the Army to his village, only to find that he no longer liked the idea of living among peasants. Nor, for that matter, did the villagers like him. So the man became dejected, took to the bottle, and one day robbed someone somewhere. Although there was no real evidence against him, he was arrested and tried. At the trial, his lawyer had just about succeeded in having the case dismissed for lack of evidence when the accused suddenly interrupted him. "No, just a minute, wait," he said, and went on to tell everything "down to the last little grain of dust," acknowledging his guilt with tears of penitence streaming down his cheeks. The jury retired, returned, and announced: "Not guilty!" Everyone in the courtroom cried out with joy, they were so pleased with the verdict. But the former soldier just stood there as though he'd turned into a post, looking bewildered. He understood nothing of what the presiding judge told him in admonition upon releasing him. He still didn't believe it when he walked away free. He began to worry, brooded all the time, hardly ate or drank, wouldn't talk to people, and on the fifth day hanged himself. "See, that's how it feels to live with sin on your soul," Makar concluded.

I know there's nothing so special about this story and that many stories of the sort crop up in the newspapers, but what I liked about it was Makar's tone and, even more, certain of his phrases and expressions that were imbued with a new meaning. Thus, in telling of how the villagers took a dislike to the returned soldier, Makar said: "And it is well known that a soldier is a *corrupted villager*." And later, speaking of the lawyer, who almost succeeded in having the case dismissed, he remarked: "And what's a lawyer but *a conscience for hire*." Such phrases slipped from his lips spontaneously, without his seeming to notice them. And although they may not have expressed the feelings characteristic of the Russian people, they did indeed express Makar's own original (not borrowed) feelings. Such judgments found among the people are sometimes striking in their originality!

"And how do you look upon the sin of suicide?" I asked Makar after hearing his story about the soldier.

"Suicide is man's greatest sin," he said with a sigh, "but God alone can judge it, for only God knows what and how much a man can bear. As for us, we must pray tirelessly for that sinner. Whenever you hear of that sin, pray hard for the sinner, at least sigh for him as you turn to God, even if you never knew him—that will make your prayer all the more effective."

"But would my prayer be of any help to him since he's already condemned?"

"Who can tell? There are many—oh, so many!—people without faith who just confuse the ignorant. Don't listen to them because they themselves don't know where they're going. A prayer for a condemned man from a man still alive will reach God, and that's the truth. Just think of the plight of a man who has no one to pray for him. And so, when you pray in the evening before going to sleep, add at the end, 'Lord Jesus, have mercy on all those who have no one to pray for them.' This prayer will be heard and it will please the Lord. Also pray for all the sinners who are still alive: 'O Lord who holdest all destinies in Thy hand, save all the unrepentant sinners.' That's also a good prayer."

I promised him I'd pray, feeling this would please him. And, indeed, he beamed with pleasure. But I hasten to note that he never spoke in a lecturing tone, never sounded like a sage talking to an immature youth. Not in the least. In fact, he was interested in what I had to say and at times listened eagerly as I held forth on all sorts of subjects; for, although I was just a "young'un" (as he said even though he was perfectly aware that the proper word was "youth"), he always remembered that this particular "young'un" was incomparably better educated than himself.

One thing he was very fond of talking about was "life in the wilderness," for to him living all alone in the wild was far superior to wandering around the country. I hotly disagreed, arguing that hermits were really egoists who had fled their worldly responsibilities and, instead of trying to be useful to their fellow men, selfishly sought only their own salvation. At first he couldn't see what I meant; indeed, I suspect he didn't understand what I was talking about and he just went on defending the advantages of being a hermit.

"Of course," he said, "at first you feel sorry for yourself in being all alone, I mean in the beginning. But with every day that goes by, you're more and more pleased you're alone, and in the end you feel you're in the presence of God."

Then I drew for him as complete a picture as I could of all the useful things a learned man, a doctor, or anyone devoting his life to the service of mankind could accomplish. I spoke with such eloquence that he became quite enthusiastic and repeatedly expressed his approval: "That's right, my boy, God bless you, it's great the way you can understand these things!" When I finished, though, he still didn't seem quite convinced. "That's all very well," he said, dragging out his words and sighing deeply, but how many people are there who'd stick to their duties without going astray? A man may not look upon money as his god, but money can easily become a kind of half-god and is so often a mighty temptation. And then there're other temptations: women and vanity and envy. So a man may forget the great cause and try to satisfy all these little cravings. But when he's alone in the wild, it's different, for there he can harden himself and be ready for any sacrifice. Besides, my dear boy, what is there in man's world?" he said with intense feeling. "Isn't it just a dream? It's as if men were trying to sow by spreading sand on rocky ground; only when the yellow sand sprouts will that dream of theirs come true. We have a saying like that in our part of the country. What Christ said was, 'Go and give all you have to the poor and become the servant of all men,' for if you do you'll become a thousand times richer because your happiness won't be made just of good food, rich clothes, satisfied vanity, and appeased envy; instead, it will be built on love, love multiplied by love without end. And then you will gain not just riches, not just hundreds of thousands or a million, but it will be the whole world that you will gain! Today we amass material things without ever satisfying our greed and then we madly squander all we have amassed. But a day will come when there will be no orphans, no beggars, everyone will be like one of my own family, everyone will be my brother, and that is when I will have gained everything and everyone! Today even some of the richest and mightiest of men care nothing about how long they have been given to live because they too can no longer think up ways to spend their hours; but one day man's hours will be multiplied a thousandfold, for he will not want to lose one single moment of his life as he will live every one of them in the gaiety of his heart. And then his wisdom will come not out of books but from living in the presence of God, and our Earth will glow brighter than the sun and there will be no sadness, no sighs will be heard, and the whole world will be paradise."

I believe that it was just such fervent outbursts that Versilov liked particularly and on that occasion he happened to be present in Makar's room. I, for my part, suddenly became excited out of all proportion (I remember that particular evening very clearly) and cried out:

"But, Mr. Dolgoruky, what you're preaching is communism, plain communism!"

Since he knew nothing about the communist doctrine and, indeed, had never heard the word communism before, I immediately proceeded to expound to him all I knew on the subject. I must admit that my own notions were scanty and vague, for I was hardly an expert on communism. Nevertheless I described with tremendous heat whatever I knew on the subject. And, to this day, I recall with a pleasant feeling the profound impression I made on the old man. In fact, it was more than an impression, it was a shock. Also, he was extremely interested in the historical details: "Where? How? Who organized it? Who said that?" In general, this is a peculiar feature of simple people: they're never contented with an abstract idea and always demand concrete and precise details. But since I got some of these details wrong and since Versilov was present, I became more and more embarrassed, which in turn made me speak more and more excitedly. Still, in the end, Makar was so moved that he could only accompany every statement of mine with an approving "Right, right!" because by then he'd probably lost the thread of what I was saying and was no longer following me anyway. That rather annoyed me. Still it went on until Versilov finally got up and announced it was time to go to bed. And, true enough, it was getting quite late.

When, a few minutes later, Versilov stepped into my room, I asked him what he thought of Makar's idea and of the man in general. Versilov smiled with amusement (not at my mistakes about communism—he never mentioned them). I repeat again, he was quite fascinated by the old man, and I'd often noticed him smiling delightedly before as he listened to Makar

talk. However, this did not prevent Versilov from having his
reservations.

"First of all, you must understand that Makar Dolgoruky
is no peasant," Versilov answered, obviously quite willing to
talk now. "He is a former house servant born of house servants.
In the old days, serfs employed as house servants used to share
many of the interests of their masters, intellectual as well as
spiritual. Note that, to this day, Makar is very interested in
the life of his former masters and of the upper class in general.
You have no idea how closely he follows certain recent
developments on the Russian scene. And, do you know, he has
a keen sense of politics. He'll forget about eating if you start
telling him who is at war with whom and whether Russia is
likely to go to war too. Long ago I used to delight him with such
conversations. He also has great respect for science and, of all
the sciences, his favorite is astronomy. But, with all that, he's
worked out for himself a view of the world so independent that
you'd never be able to budge him from it. He does, indeed,
have convictions: some he stubbornly clings to; others, fairly
clear-headed . . . and some, very true. Despite his complete
lack of education, he's capable on occasion of surprising people
by his strange grasp of certain subjects that no one would possibly
have suspected in him. And although he keeps praising the
hermitage and life in the wild, he'll never go and live in the
desert or in a monastery because he's an out-and-out nomad,
a real tramp as the doctor called him so aptly—and, by the way,
there's really no reason for you to be irritated by our doctor.
Well, finally, Makar is something of an artist: he has coined
many of his own expressions and words and also uses well others
that he has picked up. He's a bit lame when it comes to logical
exposition, and at times he indulges in excessive generalizations
and fits of sentimentality, but this is a common trait among
simple folk, or, to be more accurate, these are outbursts of
exaltation that constitute such an important share in the
religious manifestations of our people. As to his purity of heart
and the absence of malice in him, I won't mention them, it's
not fit for the two of us to discuss that subject. . . ."

III

To complete my picture of Makar, let me now retell one of
his stories which he had learned firsthand. These stories of his
were rather strange and there was really no one over-all idea
dominating them, no particular moral to be drawn; nor even
was there any special angle to them. The only thing most of

them had in common perhaps was that they all contained a certain exalted element. But some of them were not really exalted at all; some were indeed thoroughly lighthearted and even poked fun at certain muddleheaded monks, so that, in telling these stories to me, Makar was weakening his own argument. Once I pointed this out to him, but he didn't understand what I meant. At times I was perplexed at his garrulousness and ascribed it partly to his age and partly to his feverish state.

"He's not the man he used to be," Versilov once whispered into my ear, "he wasn't like this at all. He'll die soon, much sooner than we expect, and we must be prepared for it."

I forgot to say that we'd got into the habit of having regular evening "gatherings." Besides Mother, who never left Makar's side, they were attended by Versilov, myself (I had nowhere else to go), and, in the later days, Lisa, who came almost every evening although somewhat later than the others. Mrs. Prutkov dropped in often too, and also the doctor, although less often. In the end, the doctor and I somehow managed to get along, and, although we never became great friends, we had no further clashes. The peculiar candor that I finally discovered in him rather pleased me, and the fact that he showed some attachment to my family made me forgive him his superciliousness as a medical expert. Moreover, I succeeded in making him wash his hands and clean his nails, even if he couldn't change his linen often enough. I told him plainly that bodily cleanliness was not just the attribute of a dandy, not just a matter of aesthetics, but that it was essential for a doctor, and I convinced him of it.

Makar's stories also often attracted Lukeria, who would emerge out of her kitchen and stand in the doorway listening to him. Once Versilov invited her to come in and sit down with us. I approved of his gesture, although after that Lukeria never appeared in the doorway again. She had her own idea of her place!

I'll now tell one of Makar's stories. I've chosen it not for any special reason except that somehow I remember it best. It is a tale about a certain merchant and I suppose that such things happened by the thousands in our large and small towns if only one knew how to look for them. Those who wish to skip the story may do so, especially as I'll try to retell it in the old man's own words.

IV

It happened in our town, Afimievsk, and I'll tell you right off it was just like a miracle. A merchant lived there by the name of Maxim Skotoboinikov and there was no one richer than him in the whole district. He'd built himself a cotton mill and had several hundred hands working for him, and his importance went to his head. Everyone was at his beck and call: the authorities never interfered with him; the archimandrite praised him for his religious zeal, for he gave generously to the monastery. Still, at certain quiet moments, he'd think about his soul, sigh, and worry a great deal about life beyond the grave. He was a widower and childless. There was a rumor that he had done his wife in during the very first years of their marriage, because since his youth he hadn't bothered to keep his hands under control. But whatever had happened had taken place long ago and since then he'd never wanted to accept the bonds of another marriage. He also had a weakness for the bottle and during his drinking bouts he would rush outside stark naked and dash all over town hollering. And, although it was not much of a town to speak of, this was still a disgrace. Then, when he sobered up, he'd be in a wicked mood and there would be no arguing with whatever he thought fit and whatever he decided fair. He'd pay his employees just what he decided they should get. He'd put on his glasses, look into his books, and ask a man:

"How much would you say, Foma, is coming to you?"

"Thirty-nine rubles, sir; I haven't drawn nothing since Christmas."

"That's a lot of money, man; you're not worth that much altogether. That won't look right, you know. I'll take off ten rubles. So you can have twenty-nine."

And the poor fellow said nothing: no one dared argue with him so they just kept their mouths shut.

"I," the merchant said, "know how much I should pay a man. That's the only way to deal with these people. They're all corrupt around here and without me they'd all have starved to death, every last one of them. It's also a fact that they're all thieves: they'd like to have whatever they catch sight of; there's no dignity in them. And they're also a bunch of drunkards: as soon as you pay one of them, off he goes to a tavern and he'll stay there until he has drunk all his money and his clothes too and there's not a stitch left on him and he'll come out completely naked. And these folk are so sickening! The nasty naked wretch will sit there on a stone outside the tavern and start moaning and shouting, "Oh, Mother dear, why did you have to bring into this world an unhappy miserable drunk

like me? It would've been better if you'd strangled me at birth."
Do you call that a man? I say he's an animal, not a man. So
first he must be taught to behave and only then should he be
given money. And I know when the right time comes."

That was what Maxim Skotoboinikov had to say about the
Afimievsk people and, although it wasn't kind what he said,
there was truth in it: they were an unreliable lot and couldn't
control themselves.

There lived in the town another merchant. He died young.
He wasn't a serious, responsible man; he squandered his money
and lost everything he owned. During his last year he thrashed
around like a fish thrown up on the sand, but it was no use,
his time was up. He'd never gotten along with Maxim
Skotoboinikov, still owed him lots of money, and cursed him
with his last breath. He left behind a widow, a young woman
still, and five small children. For a poor widow to be left alone
is just like a lonely swallow being chased from her nest: it
was not only that she had nothing to feed her five little children
with, but her last possession, a wooden house, was also being
taken away from her by Maxim in payment for her late
husband's debts. So she gathered up her children, took them to
the church door, and lined them all up. The eldest was a boy
of eight and the rest were all girls; the biggest of the girls was
four and the littlest was still a babe-in-arms who was sucking
at her mother's breast as they all stood there. When Mass was
over, Maxim came out of the church. All the children at once
knelt down before him and, as their mother had taught them,
stretched their arms out toward him, clasping their little hands
together; and then the woman herself, still holding her baby,
bowed deeply to him too.

"Mr. Skotoboinikov, sir, take pity on these orphans, do not
deprive them of their last crust of bread and do not drive them
from their nest!"

With the children all kneeling there exactly as their mother
had taught them, it was so touching that everyone around had
tears in his eyes, and the woman reckoned that, with all these
people watching, he'd want to show his generosity, forgive them
their debts, and allow the orphans to stay in the house. But she'd
reckoned wrong.

Maxim stopped and looked at her.

"You're a young widow," he said to her, "and it's not the
orphans that you're worrying about: what you're after is a man.
Besides, remember that your husband kept cursing me as he
was dying."

And he walked on without giving them back the house.

"If I caper to this whim," Maxim said to himself (Makar probably meant to say "cater"), "she'll keep on pestering me and it'll be no use. And since people gossip anyway, they'd only gossip more wickedly."

And it's true there was a rumor going around that, ten years before, when the widow had still been a young girl, Maxim had sent her a messenger with a big sum of money—that's how beautiful she was!—forgetting that this was a sin just as bad as looting God's church. That time, however, it never got him anywhere. But with other women, he'd indulged in many such filthy deals both in the town and in the surrounding countryside, so many, in fact, that he'd lost all restraint when it came to these matters.

So the mother could only weep as Maxim turned her out of her house with her little orphans. But it was not really out of spite that he'd done it, for often a man doesn't know himself why he insists on doing certain things. Well, other people helped her at first and then she went out looking for work. But what work could she hope to find around Afimievsk except on the cotton mill grounds? There she could scrub the floors, weed the vegetable garden, heat the bathhouse, while still keeping an eye on her baby and the other four children who ran around outside the buildings in their little shirts. When she'd lined them all up by the church door, the children still had some sort of shoes on their feet and jackets that still looked like jackets, for they were not peasants after all but the children of a merchant. However, everybody knows how a child burns up clothes and now they had to run around barefoot with just their shirts on their backs. But you know how children are: they don't mind; as long as the sun is shining, they don't feel their misery; they're happy like little birds and their voices sound like jingle bells. The widow, she kept worrying though: "What will I do with all my little ones when winter comes? I pray God will call them to Him by then." But she didn't have to wait for winter. In our part of the country there's a whooping cough that goes around sometimes and then it skips from one child to another. First it was the baby that died and then, one after the other, the rest of the little girls fell ill and they all died in turns during the fall, although one of them didn't actually die of the sickness but was run over by a cart in the street. So what do you think? She buried them and wept and wailed. She'd cursed her children herself, but now that God had taken them, she missed them badly. That's a mother's heart for you!

Only the oldest one, her little boy, was left to her and she hung over him and trembled lest he should get hurt. He was a weak child, gentle, and his face was pretty like a little girl's. When she had to go to work as a nanny in the family of an official, she took her little boy to the manager of the mill, who happened to be his godfather. So one day the boy was running around the yard of the mill when all of a sudden the master, Maxim Skotoboinikov, drove up on a pair of horses. As he was stepping out of the carriage, the boy came running up from the side, stumbled against the step by the entrance door, slipped, and while falling stretched both hands out in front of him. And, by accident, those two little hands landed right in Maxim's stomach. So he caught the boy by the hair and roared: "Whose is he? Get some twigs. I want him flogged right here and now in my presence!" The boy was half dead with fear and when they started flogging him he cried out in pain. That annoyed Maxim: "So, on top of everything, you're screaming now! All right, they'll flog you until you stop screaming." Whether they went on flogging him for a long time or a short time doesn't matter, but he only stopped screaming when he passed out. They got frightened then and stopped. The boy lay there in a deep faint, hardly breathing. Later they said that they didn't flog him too hard and that he was simply badly scared. Maxim seemed pretty worried too. "Whose child is he?" They told him. "I see," he said. "Take him to his mother and tell her he has no business hanging around the mill."

For two days he said no more about it, but then he asked, "How's the boy?" Well, things weren't going too well with the boy. He'd fallen ill and lay in a corner in his mother's room. She had to give up her job to look after him. It was pneumonia, he had.

"Really?" Maxim said. "How can that be? I'd understand if he'd been flogged real hard, but it was just a little nothing, just to frighten him a bit. I've ordered others flogged and we've never had any of this nonsense afterward."

He expected the mother would complain to the authorities, but he was too proud to do anything about it and just waited. But, of course, she didn't complain—she didn't dare. And so he sent her fifteen rubles and a doctor. It was not that he was afraid of what she might do or anything like that—it just made him stop and think. . . . But soon the time came for him to start

on one of his drinking bouts and he went at it for three weeks
without letup.

By and by winter passed and on Ascension Maxim suddenly
asked: "And how's that boy, you know the one I mean?" He'd
never once inquired about him all winter. "He's still living with
his mother," they told him, "and he's well enough now for her
to go out to work during the day."

That day Maxim drove over to the house where the widow
lived. He didn't get down from his carriage, but just sat there
and sent for her. She came to the gate.

"Well, honest widow," he said to her, "I want to be a real
benefactor to your son, and do everything that can be done
for him. I want him to come and live with me in my house
and if I'm even a little pleased with him, I'll settle a good sum
on him. Now, if by chance I'm fully satisfied with him, I might
make him the heir of everything I own, just as if he were my
own son. There's only one condition: I don't want you, lady,
to come to my house except on high holidays. If that suits you,
bring the boy over tomorrow morning, for you don't want him
to go on playing with those bits of wood all day long, do you?"

He drove off, leaving the mother almost out of her mind
from shock. But people who heard about it told her: "If you
turn this offer down, when the boy grows up he'll never forgive you for having allowed such an opportunity to slip by."
She spent the night crying over her last child and in the
morning she took the boy, who looked more dead than alive,
to Maxim Skotoboinikov's house.

Maxim had the boy dressed up like a little gentleman; he
hired a teacher for him, and from that time on watched over
the boy's studies himself. Whenever the boy would take his
nose out of his books for a second, he would be sure to hear
Maxim shouting: "Hey, boy, read your book! Study! I want
to make an educated man out of you!" The boy, who had always
been delicate, coughed a lot since the flogging. "Why should
he grow even weaker than before?" Maxim wondered. "Why,
at his mother's he had to run around barefoot and live on stale
bread! What better life could he wish for than in my house?"
"But," the boy's teacher said, "a boy needs to play; he can't
just study all the time, he has to have exercise too." And he made
Maxim see reason. "Makes sense, what you say," Maxim agreed.

That teacher's name was Peter Stepanovich—may he rest in
peace!—and he was in a way like one of those simple-minded
village holy men. For one thing, he drank too much, so much,
in fact, that he hadn't been able to get a job any more and had

to live on handouts before Maxim had hired him. But he was really a very learned man and had brains. "This is no place for me," he thought to himself. "It's in a university that I belong, as a professor. For here I've sunk so deep into the mud that my own clothes are ashamed of me."

And so, one day, Maxim came in, sat down, looked at the boy, and suddenly barked at him: "All right, play now!" But the boy just stared at him, hardly able to breathe from fright. For it had got to the point where the boy would start trembling all over whenever he heard Maxim's voice. This time Maxim was really puzzled: "It's no use, he's no good. I pulled him out of the filth he was living in. I put expensive clothes on his back; I bought him an embroidered shirt and nice leather shoes for his feet, and I'm treating him as if he was the son of a general, but I see he still isn't grateful. Why must he act like a little wolf cub? Why won't he talk to me?"

And although the townsfolk had by then grown used to Maxim's ways, he still managed to surprise them once again: they couldn't see how a man could get worked up like that over a little boy. He wouldn't leave the child in peace. "I don't care if it kills me," he said, "but I'll break that boy! His father cursed me as he lay dying, even after he'd taken the last sacraments, and this boy is just like his father." And although, mind you, he never once used the rod on the child—he was afraid after what had happened—he could frighten the wits out of him all the same, even without a rod.

And then something happened. Once, when Maxim left the room, the boy put down his book, jumped up on a chair to get his ball, which he'd thrown on top of the sideboard. As he was reaching for it, his sleeve caught in a china lamp that fell to the floor smashing into a thousand pieces so that the whole house resounded. It was an expensive Saxony china lamp. Maxim, who was two rooms away, heard the crash and roared with anger. The boy, frightened to death, rushed out onto the verandah, then into the garden, and started running, not knowing where he was going. He crossed the garden, went out the back gate, and reached the riverbank where there was a sort of promenade along the river lined with old willow trees, a pretty place. People saw the boy run down to the water, to the jetty where the ferry was tied, stretch his arms toward the water, and then stop dead, terrified. The river was wide at that spot and the current was swift and barges were passing. . . . On the opposite bank of the river there was a square with shops and a church with the sun shining on its golden cupolas.

And it so happened that, just at that moment, the wife of Colonel Ferzing, the commanding officer of the infantry regiment stationed in the town, came down to take the ferry. She had with her a little girl in a pretty white dress, her daughter, a child of eight or so. The little girl held in her hand a basket of the kind the peasants make. In that basket was a hedgehog.

"Mummy, why is that little boy looking at my hedgehog like that?"

"No, darling," Mrs. Ferzing said, "he seems to have been frightened by something. . . . What frightened you like that, nice little boy? (That's exactly what she called him, as all those who heard her repeated later.) Ah, you are such a nice and pretty little boy and you're so beautifully dressed! Whose boy are you?"

The little boy, who'd never seen a hedgehog before, came closer and was staring at it. He'd forgotten all his troubles by now, for that's how young children are.

"What's that you have there?"

"It's a hedgehog," the little girl said; "we just bought it from a peasant who found it in the forest."

"What's a hedgehog?" the little boy said, and he was already laughing and poking his finger into the animal, who put up its bristles, and the little girl was laughing happily, looking at the boy.

"We're going to take him home and tame him," she said.

"Ah . . . Please can I have your hedgehog?" The way he asked sounded as if he wanted it very much, the hedgehog.

But hardly had the boy uttered these words than Maxim appeared on top of the bank above them. "There he is!" Maxim screamed. "Get him, get a hold of him!" He must have rushed out of the house like a madman to catch the boy: he was hatless and in a rage.

Now everything, of course, came back to the boy: he let out a cry, stepped to the edge of the water, pressed his little fists against his chest, looked up at the sky—yes, they all saw him do that—and jumped. Splash! There were cries, shouts, screams; some men dove from the ferry, but the swift current carried the boy off so that by the time they'd pulled him out he'd swallowed lots of water and it was too late. He was too delicate anyway: it'd been more than he could take. Besides, how much does it take to kill a weak little boy like that?

No one from those parts remembered ever having heard of a small child taking his own life. That was a terrible sin. For what can such a young soul tell our Lord in the next world? And it was just that that made Maxim brood ever after. It changed the man so you could no longer recognize him. He always looked dejected. At first, he tried to drink, drank an awful lot, but then gave it up. It didn't help. He stopped going to his mill, stopped listening to people. If someone spoke to him, he'd just wave the man away without answering. That went on for a month or two and then he started talking to himself. He'd walk around all alone talking out loud.

Later there was a fire in the village of Voskova—that's down-stream from the town—and nine houses burned down from top to bottom. Maxim drove over to have a look. Those who'd lost their houses gathered around him, wailing. He promised to help, even gave orders to that effect to his steward. But later he called the steward back. "No," he told him, "no need for me to give them anything." He didn't explain why he'd changed his mind, although he added: "God has sent me here so everyone can hate me like some kind of a monster, so let it be that way. My ill fame has been spread around as if by the wind."

The archimandrite came in person to have a talk with Maxim. He was a severe old man, strict with the monastery community.

"What are you up to now?" the archimandrite asked Maxim sternly.

"Here's what I'm up to." Maxim opened the Bible and pointed out a passage. It was Matthew 18:6, where it says: "Whosoever shall offend one of these little ones which believe in me, it were better for him that a millstone were hanged about his neck and that he were drowned in the depth of the sea."

"That's right," the archimandrite said, "for, although that doesn't refer directly to what you did, it's still connected with it. A man who loses his sense of measure is a lost man, and you, you've come to think you're all important."

Maxim sat there like in a stupor. The archimandrite kept looking at him hard.

"Listen to this," the archimandrite said, "and don't forget it: the words of a man who has despaired are carried away by the wind. And also don't forget that even the angels are not perfect, only our Lord Jesus Christ is. And it is Him that the angels serve. Besides, you didn't want the death of that child; you just didn't think and acted foolishly. There's one thing, however, I can't understand about you. You've done so many things that are even worse. Think how many men you've ruined, how many women you've corrupted, how many people you've destroyed just as surely as if you'd killed them! Take, for instance, the boy's four little sisters. Didn't the poor little babies die almost before your

very eyes, and largely because of you? So why should this one
particular death trouble you so much more than the others?
For I don't believe you grieved much about the others; in fact,
you hardly ever gave them a thought, did you? Why, then,
should you be so crushed by the death of that boy, for which
you aren't even completely responsible?"

"I dream of him," Maxim said.

"Well?"

But Maxim wouldn't say anything more and just sat there in
silence. The archimandrite looked at him for a while, marveling,
but then got up and left. There was nothing more he could do.

When he was gone, Maxim sent for the boy's teacher, whom
he hadn't seen all that time.

"Do you remember?" he asked the teacher.

"I remember."

"You," Maxim said, "painted that picture in oil that's hanging
in the tavern and you also made a copy of the metropolitan's
portrait. . . . Tell me, can you make an oil painting for me?"

"I can do everything. I have talent, there's nothing I can't
do."

"Then paint me the biggest picture you've ever painted, big
enough to cover this whole wall. And I want you to put into
that picture, first of all, the river with the sloping bank by the
ferry and then all those people who were there at that time, including the colonel's wife and the little girl and the hedgehog
too. And I want you to paint the other bank too, with the square,
the church, the shops, and place where the hackney cabs wait—
you must paint everything just as it is. And by the ferry landing
I want the boy, standing exactly in the spot he stood, just above
the river, and be sure that he's holding his little fists pressed
against his chest, that's very important. And in front of him,
above the church, I want you to open up the sky so that the
angels of heaven can be seen flying on their way to meet him.
. . . Well, can you manage all that, do you think?"

"As I told you, there's nothing I can't do."

"If it hadn't been for the fact that you remember his face, I
wouldn't be asking a village dauber to do that painting; for, as
you well know, I could afford to send for the top artist in Moscow or even in London maybe. Now if you don't get the boy's
likeness at all or if you get it just a little bit, I'll still pay you fifty
rubles, but if the likeness is really good, I'll come up with a
whole two hundred. Remember those blue eyes of his. . . . And
the painting must be big as they come, don't forget."

So they agreed, and Peter Stepanovich went to work on the

picture. But then he came back and said to Maxim: "No, I can't paint it the way you told me."

"Why not?"

"Because killing oneself is the worst sin there is. So how can those angels come to meet him after he's committed such a sin?"

"But he was almost a baby, so surely he can't be held accountable."

"No, he was no baby; he was eight when he did it. So in some way he must answer for it."

That was like another blow on Maxim's head.

"But here's what I've thought up," Peter said. "Instead of opening up the sky and painting all those angels, I'll lower a bright ray down from the sky toward the boy, as if to meet him. Perhaps that ray will do."

And so they agreed to lower that ray. And later I saw the picture with my own eyes—the ray and the river and all. It stretched across the whole wall, that painting, with plenty of blue in it and with that sweet little boy pressing his little fists to his chest, and the little girl, and the hedgehog—the teacher had managed to put everything in. But at the time, Maxim wouldn't show the picture to anyone. He kept his study locked so no one could see it. Many of the townsfolk tried hard to get a glimpse of the painting, but Maxim ordered the servants not to let anyone in.

As to Peter Stepanovich, the former teacher, it was as if it all went to his head: "I," he went around saying, "can do anything; my place is really in Petersburg, in fact at the Tsar's court."

He was the nicest man there was, although he did have that weakness for boasting. Besides, he was fated to meet his end very soon: the very day he got his two hundred rubles he got himself drunk and went around bragging and flashing his money so everybody could see it. Well, a fellow from our own town killed him that night and took the money, we found out the next morning.

As to Maxim, everyone in those parts still remembers how he ended up. One day he drove over to the place where the widow lived—a hut on the edge of town where she rented a room. This time he didn't stay in the carriage. He got down and walked into the yard. He saw the woman sitting there, planted himself in front of her, and bowed down to the ground. You see, she'd been ill ever since that other time, so she couldn't move around much.

"Good lady," he said, "honest widow! Marry me, monster that I am, marry me so I can go on living!

"I want us to have a baby boy together and if we succeed that will mean that the boy has forgiven us both, you and me. For that's what the boy told me."

She must've seen that the man was not in his right mind, that he was in a sort of frenzy, but she couldn't hold herself back from saying:

"What you say makes no sense; it's just meanness talking in you. It was because you were so mean that I lost all five of my little ones. Go away, I can't even bear the sight of you, let alone condemn myself to such an everlasting torture as marrying you."

Maxim drove off, but he didn't give up. The whole town was in an uproar when they heard about what he'd thought up this time. He sent for two of his aunts who were shopkeepers somewhere in the province. Well, perhaps they weren't actually his aunts, but they appeared to be some sort of relatives of his, and in any case they were good enough to act as honorable matchmakers in his behalf. Well, those matchmakers did their best to convince her, arguing with her and refusing to leave until she'd said yes. He also sent to her the wives of some local merchants, the wife of our chief priest, a few wives of officials, and they all went to her hut and tried to talk sense into her. Practically the whole town besieged her and pleaded with her, but that only made her more disgusted: "If it could bring my poor little babies back to life, I'd have to accept him at once, but since it won't, what would be the point? It would only be one more terrible sin toward my departed little darlings."

Maxim even managed to get the archimandrite to help him, and the old man went to the widow and whispered in her ear: "You could make a new man out of him." But the mere thought of it horrified her. On the other hand, people around couldn't see how she could possibly turn down such a chance!

In the end, however, Maxim did get his way. Here's how he did it.

"Whatever we may say," Maxim said to her, "he was no babe when he killed himself. He was old enough to receive Communion. So they couldn't admit him there just like that and he must be held at least partly responsible for what he did. Now, if you become my lawful wife, I solemnly swear that I'll have a holy church built to the eternal memory of his soul."

That was too much of an argument. She couldn't resist and they were married.

Well, to everybody's astonishment, from the very first day, they lived in true and rare understanding, jealously observing their marriage vows, just like a single soul in two bodies. That same winter she was with child, and they went from church to church and prayed while waiting in fear and trembling for God's verdict. They made pilgrimages to three monasteries and listened to prophecies. And Maxim built the promised church in our town and also a hospital and an almshouse. He put a sum of money aside to assist widows and orphans. And he remembered all those he had wronged and tried to make it up to them. Indeed, he began giving money away so easily that often even his wife and the archimandrite had to stop him: "You've given enough to him as is," they'd plead with him. Maxim would listen to them and meekly try to explain: "You see, that time before, I didn't pay Foma what I owed him." So now he paid back Foma everything he owed him and more. And Foma wept and said, "No need for that, no need. . . . I'm happy with everything here as is; I'm grateful to you and I'll always pray for you." So, you see, it touched everyone and goes to show that it's true when they say that man can live by good example. And in those parts people are kind, you know.

It was the wife who took over the running of the mill now, and she turned out to be so good at it that they still remember how well she ran it to this day. He didn't give up his drinking bouts, but now she'd watch over him during those days and try to cure him of this habit. When he spoke to people now, he used only decent words and even his voice was different. He'd become sorry beyond measure when he saw someone in pain, even if it was just an animal. Once he saw out of his window a peasant viciously whipping his horse. He sent someone out to buy the horse from the man for twice its worth. And he received his reward in tears, for whoever spoke to him would have tears in his eyes.

And when her time came and God, heeding their prayers, sent them a son, Maxim's gloom lifted at last for the first time and, that day, he gave away lots of money to the poor, forgave many people what they owed him, and invited the whole town to the christening.

But the next morning he came out of the house looking black as night. His wife saw something was wrong with him and held the newborn babe up to him.

"He's forgiven us, the boy, he's seen our tears and heard our prayers for him."

That was the first time, mind you, they'd mentioned the boy

in a year. Each of them had kept his thoughts about the boy to himself. Maxim just gave her a black look.

"Wait," he said, "the boy hadn't haunted me all year until now, but last night he came to me in my dream."

"These strange words filled my heart with terror," his wife told us later.

And it was not for nothing that the boy had come to him. The moment Maxim had spoken, the newborn babe became sick. The sickness lasted eight days. They prayed all that time and called many doctors; they even sent for the best doctor in Moscow. He came by train and was very angry.

"I'm the greatest doctor in Moscow," he said, "so what do you mean by sending for me for such a trifling thing when all Moscow is waiting for me?"

He prescribed some drops, charged them eight hundred rubles, and left in a great hurry. That same evening the baby died.

Do you know what happened after that? Maxim gave all his land and all he owned to his wife, handed her all his money and titles; he did everything in proper legal form. Then he stood before her and bowed down to the ground.

"Let me go, my priceless wife, for I want to try to save my soul while there's still time. If as time passes I see I cannot save my soul, I won't come back. I was hard and cruel and caused many people to suffer, but perhaps God will take into account the woes and the wanderings that lie ahead of me now, for leaving what I leave behind is no small cross and no small sorrow."

His wife begged him and begged him with tears in her eyes:

"You're all I have on earth now, so what will I do if you leave? My heart has learned to feel for you during this past year."

And all the town pleaded with him for a whole month; they beseeched him and even thought to hold him back by force. But he wouldn't listen to them and slipped away secretly one night, and he's never come back. They say that to this day he's still wandering around and bearing patiently all his hardships. And regularly every year his good wife gets word from him.

Chapter 4

I

Now I've come to the final catastrophe of my story. But first I must explain in advance certain facts of which I myself was not aware at the time, facts whose meaning I grasped fully only much later when everything was over. Otherwise, I couldn't tell my story coherently and would have to present it as a series of riddles. So I'll start with a straightforward explanation, not bothering with artistic considerations, do it impersonally without any feelings or emotions, like a sort of newspaper report.

As it turned out, my childhood friend Lambert belonged to one of those gangs of small-time crooks that go in for what is defined as blackmail by the criminal code, which also specifies the appropriate penalties. The gang to which Lambert belonged had been formed in Moscow and had already carried out quite a number of operations there (eventually some of the members were caught). I heard afterward that in Moscow at one time they had a clever and experienced leader, a man considerably older than the rest of them. Some of the operations were carried out by the whole gang, others by smaller units or alone by individual members. They could be anything from unsavory little scandals (some of which, nevertheless, did make the newspapers) to quite complicated and astutely planned coups executed under the direct command of the leader. Later I heard about some of these. Without going into details, I'll only say that the most common method of operation was to find out certain intimate secrets of persons, sometimes quite respectable as well as respected, in order to threaten them with public exposure backed by documentary evidence (which didn't always even exist), and to make them pay for discretion. There are secrets with nothing criminal or even sinful about them whose exposure may terrify the most honorable and even strong-minded people. The gang specialized mostly in family secrets. Just to give you an idea of the astuteness of the leader, I'll describe in very few words, leaving out the details, one of their operations.

In a certain highly respected family, something truly sinful and reprehensible took place: the wife of an important and highly placed official committed adultery with a rich young army officer. The gang got wind of it and immediately got in touch with the young officer, threatening to inform the husband. They had no proof whatever, the officer knew it, and they didn't even insist they had. But their devilish reckoning was based on the knowledge that, in this particular case, the husband would react in the same way whether presented with evidence or not. They knew enough about the man's character and the special family circumstances. The most interesting fact about the story is that one member of the gang was a young man belonging to the best society and it was he who had supplied the rest of them with the necessary information. They managed to extract from the lover a tidy little sum without having to take any risks, for, as they well knew, he was only too eager to keep the whole thing quiet.

Although Lambert associated with these people, he had never been a full-fledged member of the gang. He had simply acquired a taste for blackmail and little by little had started experimenting with small-scale operations on his own. But I might as well mention that he was not really well suited to this type of venture. Although he could on occasion be quite sharp and calculating, he was too impulsive and in a way naïve or, more precisely, he didn't understand well enough people's psychology and the nature of social pressures. Nor do I believe that he ever understood the role of the Moscow gang leader: he imagined it was easy to organize and direct blackmailing operations. Finally, he took it for granted that everybody else was just about as unscrupulous and crooked as himself. Once he had decided that so and so was, or should be, afraid of such and such a threat, he accepted it as a self-evident truth. I'm not sure whether I have made clear what I mean, but I hope it will become clear when I describe what happened. Still, in my opinion, Lambert was a rather primitive person and not only rejected decency and altruism as motives for action but, I venture to say, didn't even suspect such feelings existed.

He'd come to Petersburg because he'd long thought that Petersburg might offer a wider scope for his operations than Moscow and also because in Moscow he'd fallen out with some character who was now looking for him with extremely unfriendly intentions. As soon as he arrived, he contacted a former Moscow colleague of his who told him that the outlook for their activities in Petersburg was very unpromising—"nothing of any scope in sight." Even after he'd enlarged his circle of acquaintances considerably, nothing important came Lambert's way. "People here are third rate—they're just a bunch of young hoodlums," he later complained to me.

So it was amidst all these disappointments that he had stumbled upon me that morning before daybreak as I lay half frozen under a wall, and somehow he had decided that at last he was on the trail of a big opportunity.

Lambert's whole plan was built on the things I'd blabbered in a half-delirious state as I lay thawing out in his room. And, although most of it was just plain raving, he must have gathered from my words that, of all the affronts I had suffered that terrible day, the one that had hurt me the most and that rankled in my mind was the humiliation inflicted by Björing and by *her*.

Why else would I have returned again and again to that scene without also mentioning, for instance, the scandal at Zershikov's? But it is a fact that I talked of nothing else, as I later learned from Lambert himself. Also, in the exalted state I was in that awful morning, both Lambert and Alphonsine appeared to me as saviors and liberators. When, during my later days of convalescence, I tried to guess how much Lambert could have gathered from my disconnected ranting, I never suspected what an awful lot he'd actually managed to put together! Of course, I already had the unpleasant feeling that I'd said many things I shouldn't have, but I never suspected how many! I also reckoned on my poor articulation during my delirium; indeed, I even remember how difficult it was to pronounce words clearly in my weakened state. But then it turned out that my articulation had been considerably clearer than I'd assumed and hoped. I found out about all this only much later, which made things even worse for me.

From my ravings, disconnected utterances, mutterings, and exclamations, Lambert learned all the exact names, family names, and even sometimes the addresses he needed. Then he managed to get a rough idea of the connections between the persons involved (the old prince, *her*, Björing, Anna, and Versilov). Also, he gathered that I wanted to avenge the insults I'd suffered. And finally, most important of all, he knew now of the existence of a certain document, a secret letter, hidden away somewhere, which, if shown to the crazy old prince, would reveal to him that his own daughter considered him abnormal and had already discussed with her attorneys how to put him out to pasture. That would either drive the old man really insane, or make him turn his daughter out of his house and cut her out of his will, or finally prompt him to marry Miss Anna Versilov, whom he wanted to marry but was restrained from by his family's opposition. To make a long story short, Lambert had understood plenty. And although many fine points still escaped him, this apprentice blackmailer was on the right track. That was why, after my escape from Alphonsine's custody, he didn't have much difficulty in finding me (he simply asked for Versilov's address at the Registry Office). Then he also made the necessary inquiries to check whether all the persons whose names I had tossed around in my babbling really existed. They did. After that, he quickly made his first move.

The three facts that interested him especially were: that the document existed, that it was in my possession, and that it was worth a great deal of money. On that score, Lambert had no doubts. I'll explain later, in the proper place, what actually con-

vinced Lambert of the existence and, above all, of the value of
the document. I may say right now, though, that he had stumbled on that information by sheer chance, which I never suspected until the final catastrophe when everything burst wide
open. But, in any case, as soon as he had found out the essentials,
he went to see Anna.

To this day I cannot imagine how Lambert managed not
only to reach the haughty and unapproachable Anna but even
to fasten himself onto her. He obviously must have collected
some information about her, but I still cannot see how that could
have helped him. True, he was very elegantly dressed, spoke
French with a genuine Parisian accent, and bore a French name.
Still, how could she fail to see right away that he was nothing
but a common crook? Unless, perhaps, a crook was just what she
needed? But can that really be true?

I never found out the details of their meeting, but I've often
imagined the scene. Lambert must have presented himself as a
childhood playmate of mine who was now terribly worried
about his dear old friend. But certainly, even during their first
conversation, he must have succeeded in hinting very clearly that
I had a certain letter in my possession, that he—Lambert—was
the only person who knew I had the letter, and that I was planning to use it to avenge myself on Mrs. Akhmakov, and so on
and so forth. Above all, he must have explained to her as plainly
as possible the importance and the value of the document. As to
Anna, she could ill afford not to listen to such information. And
so she swallowed the bait, absorbed as she was by her "struggle
for survival." For just at that time they had succeeded in getting
her fiancé under control and whisking him off to Tsarskoe where
they kept him under supervision while, for good measure, keeping an eye on her too. . . . And now, suddenly, a lucky break!
There was no longer any need for whispered hints, tearful nagging, gossip, and innuendoes! Now there was a letter, a hand-
written document, irrefutable evidence of the perfidy of her fiancé's daughter and the conspiracy of all those who were trying
to keep them apart. Therefore, the old prince would have to make
his move: perhaps run away, join Anna, and marry her within
twenty-four hours. Otherwise, he'd be dispossessed of everything
and locked up in an institution.

It is possible, though, that Lambert didn't even bother to be
that subtle. "Mademoiselle," he may have told Anna without
beating about the bush, "it is up to you whether to remain an
old maid or to become a princess and a millionaire. There exists
such and such a document. I'll steal it from that boy and give it

to you for an IOU for thirty thousand rubles." Actually this is probably exactly what happened. For he couldn't help assuming that everybody was just as rotten as himself: he had, as I said before, that peculiar simplicity, almost innocence, that is sometimes found in out-and-out scoundrels.

But, however he broached the subject, it isn't likely that, even with a cruder approach, Anna would have hesitated: she must have quickly gained full possession of herself, heard him out, and understood the proposition made to her in blackmailer's language. After all, she too possessed that typical Russian "breadth"! Oh, of course, she may have blushed at first, but then she must have made the necessary effort and listened to what he had to offer. Ah, I can just imagine that unapproachable, truly dignified, and highly intelligent girl working hand in hand with a guttersnipe like Lambert! . . . Well, there must be something wrong with such high intelligences. Yes, the Russian intellectual is eager to embrace the broadest possible range of ideas, especially the female intellectual, and particularly when it suits the circumstances!

Let me sum up. I now know for certain that, by the time I was strong enough to leave the house after my illness, Lambert was hesitating between two alternatives. The first was to ask Anna for an IOU of at least thirty thousand rubles for the letter, help her to frighten the old prince, then help him escape from Tsarskoe, and quickly arrange their marriage. The whole operation had been carefully thought out so that they were only waiting for my cooperation, that is, for the letter. The second alternative was to betray Anna and sell the compromising document to Katerina Akhmakov if she was willing to come up with a better offer. In this, Lambert was basing his hopes mainly on Björing. But Lambert hadn't yet approached Mrs. Akhmakov, although he was already watching her. And, of course, in this case too, he depended on me.

Oh, he certainly needed me or, to be more accurate, the letter that was in my possession. As to how to deal with me, for that too he had two alternative plans of action. First, if there was no other way, he would try to act in concert with me, offering me half the profits, having, of course, assured himself beforehand that I was fully under his control, both mentally and physically. But he far preferred to take the second course—to get rid of me by stealing the document or taking it away from me by force. That was his ideal plan and he loved the very thought of it. As I said before, he had a certain lucky break which I won't mention yet that made him almost certain of the success of that second alternative.

In any case, he was waiting for me with nervous impatience: everything depended on me, his further decisions and the next step he was to take.

In fairness to him I must say that, despite his natural impulsiveness and hot temper, he managed to control himself until the very last moment. After he had spoken to Versilov, he never came back to the house during my illness; he did not bother me, did not try to frighten me, and maintained a completely disinterested attitude toward me. As to the possibilities of my destroying, giving away, or using the letter myself in the meantime, he ruled these out completely. From my own words he had gathered how much I valued the letter and how afraid I was that someone might take it away from me. Also, he had no doubts that it would be to him and to no one else that I would go the day I was strong enough to leave the house: Daria had come to see me partly on his orders, so he knew that my curiosity and my fears had already been aroused and reckoned that I wouldn't be able to hold out. . . . Besides, he had taken care of every detail and knew what day I was to be allowed out of the house. So he felt sure that I couldn't possibly avoid him, even if I decided to.

But, however anxiously Lambert may have been waiting for me, Anna's anxiety must have been even greater. I can safely say that Lambert may have had good reason to prepare an alternative plan to betray her, and it was perhaps really her fault. Despite their obvious agreement (I don't know exactly in what form, but there is no doubt whatsoever that they had an agreement), Anna was never completely open with him up to the very last moment. She never really laid all her cards on the table. She hinted that she was willing to go along with all his suggestions, leading him to believe that she was promising him what he was asking for, but it was only an implied agreement: she listened to what he had to say but offered him nothing but an approving silence. I have good evidence for this, and the reason for her behavior was that *she was waiting for me*. To be sure, she would rather deal with me than with a rogue like Lambert. I understood that, but the trouble was that Lambert finally understood it too. It wouldn't have suited his plans at all if, bypassing him, she made a deal directly with me and persuaded me to give her the letter, especially since Lambert had become quite convinced of the "soundness of the business." Another man might still have had misgivings and hesitated, but Lambert was young, impetuous, impatient for gain, and had little understanding of human nature, since to him everybody was just a plain scoundrel. A man like him could have no doubts, especially since his talk with Anna had confirmed all the information he already had and all his hopes were based on that information.

One more important point: was Versilov aware of what was afoot at that time? Could he be abetting, even in the remotest way, Lambert's intrigues? The answer is a definite no: *not at that point!* Although it is possible that even then the fatal word had already been uttered. . . . But enough of this—I'm anticipating too far ahead.

And what about me? Did I know? That is, what exactly did I know the day I was allowed to leave the house? When I started out on this last explanation which I tried to present in the form of a newspaper account, I said that I wasn't aware of anything when I stepped out of the house, that I was to find out about it all much too late, in fact only when it was all over. Well, that's not quite true, because I certainly knew that something was in the air and I knew it only too well. But how could I possibly have known already then? Well, remember the *dream* I mentioned. The fact that I could have had such a dream, the fact that it could have gushed out of my mind formulated as it was, indicated that I was aware of lots of things—not that I actually knew about them, but that I had a *presentiment* of much of what was afoot that I have explained here. But in actual fact, as I said, I knew nothing until everything was over. I had no knowledge, but a premonition made my heart throb and allowed evil spirits to take possession of my dreams. Nevertheless, it was to Lambert that I rushed off, fully knowing what sort of man he was and with a presentiment of what was going to happen, even down to the smallest detail! So why did I rush to him then? Now, can you imagine that, as I'm writing this, I have the impression that even then I knew exactly why I was rushing to him, although in fact I still knew nothing? I hope the reader will understand this.

And now I shall get back to my story and relate fact after fact, in proper order.

II

This is how it started. Two days before I could leave the house, Lisa came home in the evening in a state of great agitation. She felt terribly humiliated and, indeed, something quite intolerable had happened to her.

I've already mentioned her relations with Vasin. She'd gone

to him for advice, not just to show us that she could do without
our help but also because she really had a high regard for him.
They had known each other ever since Luga, and I was under
the impression that Vasin was not indifferent to her. So, in her
misfortune, it was natural that she should seek advice from an
exceptionally intelligent man, always calm and high-minded, as
she considered Vasin to be. Besides, women are never too good at
evaluating correctly a man's intelligence: if they like him, they're
only too eager to accept even his paradoxes for well-reasoned
conclusions as long as they coincide with their own wishes.
What Lisa actually liked in Vasin was his sympathy for her situation and also what she assumed to be his sympathy for Sergei
in his predicament. Guessing how Vasin felt about her, she appreciated all the more his concern for a rival. But when she
told Sergei that she sometimes went to discuss things with Vasin,
he became very worried and soon very jealous too. That offended
Lisa and, if only for this reason, she continued seeing Vasin. Sergei didn't bring up the subject again but looked gloomy whenever she came. Much later, Lisa told me herself that around that
time her liking for Vasin diminished and that his calm detachment, which had impressed her so much at first, now struck her
as rather unpleasant. It is a fact that he appeared to have a cool
and practical head and had given her some advice that seemed
sound enough, but when she had tried to act upon it, she'd
found it quite unworkable. Also, he offered his opinions rather
condescendingly, a condescension that increased as time went
by until it became quite obvious. She interpreted it as his instinctive scorn for her in her present situation. Thus, when she
once told him how much she appreciated his kindness toward
me and his willingness to talk to me as an equal when he was by
far my intellectual superior (that is, she repeated to him just
what I'd said to her), his answer took her aback:

"It has nothing to do with kindness," he said. "I talk to him
because I see no difference between him and anyone else. I don't
consider him any stupider than the clever ones or any worse
than the good ones. I treat everybody the same way because, in
my eyes, people are all the same."

"You really see no difference?"

"Well, of course, there must be certain differences between
people. But I don't see these differences as long as they don't
concern me. To me, all people are the same and that's why I'm
equally kind to everybody."

"But don't you find it rather boring always behaving like
that?"

"Not at all. I've always found this way of treating people quite satisfactory."

"Don't you ever wish for something different?"

"Well, of course I do, but not very strongly. I need almost nothing. I don't need one ruble more than I have. Whether I were all dressed in gold or remained just as I am would make no difference: gold would add nothing to Vasin as he is. Juicy morsels don't tempt me. And how could high positions and honors make me worth more than I'm worth today?"

Lisa swore to me that this was exactly the way he put it. But, of course, we can't judge him by these words without knowing the exact circumstances in which they were uttered.

Little by little Lisa decided that even Vasin's tolerant attitude toward Sergei did not come from his sympathy for her, but simply because he saw no difference between one person and another and everybody was the same to him. In the end, however, he did slip out of his indifference a little and when he spoke of Sergei she detected in his words not only a note of disapproval but even a tinge of irony. That visibly annoyed Lisa, but Vasin persisted. What exasperated her most was that he still never departed from his calm tone and there was no trace of indignation in what he said about Sergei: he simply reasoned logically and arrived at the conclusion that Lisa's hero was worthless, and it was his logical detachment that made his irony so exasperating. And then, one day, he practically proved to her the "irrationality" of her love for Sergei, showing her how and where it violated the law of reason. "You're mistaken about your own feelings," he concluded, "but once you understand where you went wrong, everything can be corrected."

Indignant, Lisa got up and was about to walk out on him. But what do you think that man of reason did then? He assumed a most dignified air and, with something that might have been a hint of feeling, proposed to her. "You're a fool," Lisa said to his face, and left.

To suggest to a woman that she betray a man down on his luck just because he's a poor wretch and doesn't deserve her affection and then offer to marry her when she's carrying the child of that wretch—that's how the brain of these intelligent people operates! This comes from absolute reliance on one's own theorizing, combined with a total failure to understand what life means and, I maintain, with an infinite conceit. And, on top of all that, Lisa was sure that he was very proud of his performance, if only because he knew perfectly well that she was pregnant.

Straight from Vasin, with tears still in her eyes, Lisa rushed to

Sergei's prison; but there Sergei hurt her even more than Vasin. Somehow now, when seemingly Sergei had no reason left for jealousy, he went raving mad. But this is how jealousy is. Sergei made a dreadful scene and insulted her so horribly that Lisa almost made up her mind to break with him for good and never see him again.

She came home barely managing to control herself but couldn't keep from telling Mother what had happened. That was the evening when the layer of ice that had formed between mother and daughter broke; they cried their fill together, holding onto each other, and Lisa calmed down a little, although she still seemed very depressed. When later that evening we all gathered in Makar's room, Lisa stayed to the end without once opening her mouth. She listened intently to Makar. Since that incident with the bench, her attitude toward him was a sort of shy admiration, although she still said very little to him.

But on this occasion, Makar turned the conversation in a strange and unexpected direction. Earlier that morning, I'd gathered from a few words exchanged between Versilov and the doctor and from their frowning brows that they both were very worried about Makar's state. I'll also note that in five days it was Mother's birthday, an occasion we were planning to celebrate and had been talking about quite a bit. And it was in connection with Mother's birthday that Makar suddenly launched into reminiscences going back to the time when she couldn't yet walk.

"She wouldn't let me put her down," the old man reminisced. "I tried to teach her to walk by standing her up in a corner, taking two or three steps away, and then calling her. And she'd totter after me across the whole room as I'd keep stepping backward; she wasn't afraid; she'd laugh, and when she caught up with me, she'd throw her little arms around my neck and hug me. . . . Yes, Sofia, and all the fairy tales I'd tell you because there was nothing you liked better than listening to fairy tales: you'd sit on my knees for two hours and listen and listen. And everybody around was surprised: 'Look at this little thing, how attached she is to Makar,' they said. And sometimes I used to take you to the forest, find a raspberry bush, sit you down next to it while I myself would get busy cutting whistles out of wood for you. And then on the way home you'd get so tired that I'd have to carry you and you'd fall asleep in my arms. And once you thought you saw a wolf; you became frightened and rushed to me all atremble. . . . But there was no wolf around really."

"That, I remember," Mother said.

"Can you really remember that?"

"I remember many things. And ever since I can remember myself, there was always you, watching over me with kindness and love."

She spoke with deep feeling and suddenly turned very red. Makar remained silent for a minute and then said:

"Forgive me, children, I must leave you soon. . . . It's coming to a close, my life. In my old days I have found solace for all my sorrows. Thank you, my dear ones. . . ."

"Come, come, Makar," Versilov interrupted nervously, "the doctor just told me that you were much better. . . ."

Mother was listening, tense with alarm.

"Ah, what does he know, your doctor?" Makar said, and smiled. "He's a nice man, but that's all he is. Don't be like that, my friends, for you don't really think I'm afraid to die, do you? After I said my prayers this morning, I had a feeling that I'd never leave this room again, and I know I won't. So why not, and may the name of our Lord be blessed. My only wish is to have my fill of looking at you all. The long-suffering Job was comforted by looking on his new children. You don't believe that he could have forgotten his dead children, do you? No, he couldn't, for that's impossible! But, with time, grief diminishes as it gets mixed with joy and then you can breathe freely again. That's how it is in this world: every soul is tried and is consoled. I have decided to say a few words to you, my children," he said with a quiet and radiant smile that I will never forget and then, to my surprise, he addressed me personally: "You, my boy, you must always stand up for our Holy Church and if you're called upon one day to do it, die for her. . . . No, no, don't get alarmed, that's not for a long time yet!" he laughed silently. "You may not be thinking much about these things yet, but later perhaps you will. . . . And I also wanted to say this to you too: if you decide to do a good thing, do it not out of envy but for God. And you must be firm and stick to what you've decided is right; don't give up out of weakness; be steady in your effort and don't throw yourself first this way and then that way. . . . Well, that's all I wanted to say to you, except perhaps that you should try to get into the habit of praying every day. . . . Well, just in case you should remember. . . ." Then he turned to Versilov: "I wanted to say a few things to you too, sir, but I'm sure God will find the way to your heart without my help. Anyway, it's a long time since we stopped talking about these things, the two of us, ever since that arrow pierced my heart. So now, as I'm leaving, I'd only like to remind you of your promise. . . ."

He almost whispered these last words and lowered his eyes.

"Makar . . ." Versilov mumbled with embarrassment and got up from his chair.

"Please, please, don't feel embarrassed, sir, I just thought I'd remind you. . . . Because I'm the one who's most to blame in all this and, although you were my master then, I shouldn't have allowed that weakness. And so, Sofia, don't worry your soul too much because your sin is my sin. Also, I don't think you had full judgment yet . . . nor, perhaps, you either, sir. . . ." He smiled and his lips quivered from some sort of inner pain. "And, though I could have given you a lesson then, my wife, even used a rod on you, and perhaps it was my duty, I was only sorry for you as you fell at my feet in tears and hid nothing from me. . . . It's not to reproach you that I've recalled all this, my beloved Sofia, it's only to remind him . . . because you do remember, sir, your promise—the promise of a Russian gentleman—and I know that lawful wedlock will make everything right. . . . I say that before the children, sir, to you, my former master. . . ."

He was terribly agitated and his eyes, which were fixed on Versilov, seemed to be waiting for confirmation of the promise. As I said, all this was completely unexpected to me and I sat there listening without stirring. Versilov seemed no less tense than Makar. Without saying a word, he walked over to Mother and embraced her. Then Mother, also in complete silence, went up to Makar and bowed down deeply before him. It was an unbearably moving scene. On this occasion we were by ourselves —even Mrs. Prutkov was not present. Lisa, who had until then been sitting still with a strange stiffness, suddenly got up and said in a firm voice, looking at Makar:

"Please, bless me too, Mr. Dolgoruky, for I must face a great ordeal. . . . Tomorrow my fate is to be decided. . . . So pray for me today, please. . . ."

And she left the room. I knew that Mother had told Makar everything about Lisa.

That day was the first time I'd seen Mother and Versilov "together." Until then what I'd seen was "Versilov and his slave." I saw then that there still was so much about Versilov that I'd neither seen nor understood, although I'd already condemned him, that it made me feel ill at ease and I went back to my room contrite and confused. I must say that it was just around that time that his various seemingly unaccountable actions had thickened the fog of mystery that surrounded him and never before had he appeared so puzzling and unfathomable to me. But that's part of the whole story I'm trying to tell and I'd better present the facts in proper order.

"It would appear then," I mused as I got into bed for the night, "that he gave Makar his word as a 'Russian gentleman' to marry Mother as soon as she became a widow. He never told me that when telling me about his relations with Makar."

The next day Lisa went out, returned home only in the evening, and went straight to Makar's room. At first I didn't want to go in there so as not to disturb them, but when I realized that Mother and Versilov were already with Makar, I went in too. Lisa was sitting next to the old man. Her head was on his shoulder. She was crying as he silently stroked her hair. He looked sad.

Later, in my room, Versilov told me that Sergei had insisted they should get married if possible right away, without waiting for the trial. It was hard for Lisa to decide, although she felt she no longer had any right to put off her decision. Besides, Makar had told her she must accept. No doubt everything would have taken its proper course and she would have married Sergei without having to be told to do so by anyone and she wouldn't even have hesitated had it not been for the fact that at that moment she felt insulted by the man she loved while also feeling so degraded by that love in her own eyes that deciding just then seemed unbearably hard for her. But, apart from her mortification, there turned out to be another circumstance that I knew nothing about.

"Did you hear about the arrest of all those young people on the Petersburg Side yesterday?" Versilov asked me unexpectedly, after having told me about Lisa and Sergei.

"What! You mean Dergachev?" I cried out in surprise.

"Yes. And Vasin too."

The news of Vasin's arrest stunned me.

"Why, could he really have been mixed up with that lot? My God, what will happen to them now? And just when Lisa was saying all those things about Vasin! Tell me, what do you think they'll do to them? It must be Stebelkov's doing—I swear it must be Stebelkov . . ."

"Well, let's leave it for now," Versilov said, looking at me the way one looks at someone who neither knows nor understands what's going on, "who can tell what they were up to and what will be done to them . . . ? But that's not what I wanted to talk to you about. . . . I heard you were planning to go out tomorrow. I was wondering whether you wouldn't drop in on Sergei?"

"That's the first thing I'll do, although I admit I'm not looking forward to it and I'm sure it will be very unpleasant. Why, do you have a message for him?"

"Oh no, I'll see him myself. I feel very sorry for Lisa. What can Makar really advise her? He himself knows so little about life and people. You know what, my dear boy"—he hadn't called me "dear boy" for a long time—"there are certain other young people around too—among them a former classmate of yours called Lambert—and I'm under the impression that they are quite an unspeakable lot. I only wanted to warn you, although it's entirely up to you what you decide, for I realize I have no right. . . ."

Without thinking I seized his hand, almost fervently (I often act impulsively like that and my room was almost completely dark).

"Andrei Versilov," I said breathlessly, "I have kept silent until now. You must have realized it. And you know why I remained silent? It was to avoid knowing your secrets. I decided never to know them. I'm a coward and I'm afraid that your secrets will tear you out of my heart for good. I don't want that to happen. So why should you know my secrets? Therefore, it shouldn't matter to you wherever I decide to go. Don't you think that's right?"

"Yes, you're right. But please, no more about it, please!" And he quickly walked out of my room.

So, without intending it, we had some sort of an explanation. But it really only added to my tension as I prepared myself for the important step I had to take the next day. And, as a result, I kept waking up throughout the night. Nevertheless I felt good.

III

Although I didn't manage to leave the house before ten the following morning, I did my best to slip out unnoticed, without taking leave of anyone. I'm not sure why I wanted it that way, but I knew that if even Mother had seen me and said something I'd only have growled rudely at her. When I stepped out into the street and took in a chestful of cool fresh air, I shuddered all over with animal delight, I would even describe it as carnivorous. Where was I off to? For what purpose? It was all quite vague, but still I had that carnivorous feeling. I was frightened and joyful all at once.

"Will I or won't I fall on my face today?" I asked myself cheerfully, although I knew full well that what happened today would affect the rest of my life decisively and irreversibly. But there's no point talking in riddles.

I went straight to the prison to see Prince Sergei. Three days before that Mrs. Prutkov had given me a letter for the warden and he received me very well. I don't know whether that warden was a decent man or not, nor do I think the question is relevant here, but I do know that he very courteously put a private room at Sergei's and my disposal after readily authorizing my visit. The room in question was in his private quarters and was just like any other room in the apartment of an official of his standing and I think it would be irrelevant for me to describe it. What matters is that Sergei and I were left there in complete privacy.

He came in wearing a sort of semi-military attire. His shirt was very clean under an elegant tie; his hair was neatly combed. But his features were drawn and his complexion unhealthily yellow. That yellowness could be seen in his eyes too. In fact, he had changed so much that I was quite taken aback.

"My God, how you've changed!"

"That's nothing. Do sit down, Alexei," he said, with what seemed to me affected lightness. "And let's get down to business right away . . ."

"Arkady . . ." I corrected him.

"What? . . . Oh, yes, yes, of course," he suddenly remembered. "I beg your pardon. . . . But let's get down to brass tacks. . . ."

Obviously he was in a great hurry to get down to something or other. He seemed to be completely absorbed in some terribly important plan that he was anxious to explain to me. He spoke very fast and at considerable length, with great intentness, gesticulating, painfully trying to make something clear to me. . . . Nevertheless, for the first few minutes I understood absolutely nothing.

"To make a long story short," he said, and it was probably the tenth time he'd used that cliché, "if I took the liberty of asking Lisa to insist that you come here, and despite the fact that it is an emergency, for me the importance of the decision is so tremendous and final that we . . ."

"Just a minute, Prince. You say you asked Lisa to ask me to come here, but she never mentioned it to me."

"What did you say?" He seemed quite nonplussed, even horrified.

"Well, she never said anything to me. Last night she was too upset when she came home to say a word to me."

He jumped up from his chair.

"Is that possible, Arkady? If so, it is . . . it is . . ."

"Come on, Sergei, calm down, what's so terrible about it?

There's nothing to put you into such a state. She may just have forgotten or something may have prevented her. . . ."

He sank helplessly into his chair. He appeared completely crushed by Lisa's failure to transmit his message to me. Then he again started talking at a tremendous speed, while frantically gesticulating so that I could hardly follow him.

"Wait a minute!" he suddenly said, cutting his own flow of words and shaking his finger. "That must be . . . that must be . . . just a joke . . ." he muttered with the grin of a maniac. "It means that . . ."

"It means absolutely nothing," I interrupted him. "Indeed, I'm quite at a loss to understand why such a minor thing should affect you like that. Ah, Prince, since that night, you remember . . ."

"What night? Remember what?" He was obviously annoyed at my interruption.

"The night at Zershikov's, where we saw each other for the last time. . . . You know, before you wrote that letter? You were very tense then too, but the difference between then and now is so great that, looking at you, I'm quite horrified. Or perhaps you don't remember?"

"Ah, yes, of course," he said, turning at once into a gentleman of the best society trying to remember something that had slipped his mind. "Yes, that evening . . . I heard. . . . Well, how are you, Arkady, how do you feel now after what happened? . . . But first let's talk about the business at hand. Actually, I'm pursuing three objectives; there are three problems I must cope with, and I . . ."

And he set off once again talking about the "business" that was so important to him. I realized then that I was facing a man who should have had a towel soaked in vinegar wrapped around his head or who might even urgently require leeches to draw off some blood. I guessed, though, that his disconnected tirade had to do with his forthcoming trial. And then I gathered that his former regimental commander had come to see him and was trying to advise him not to do something or other, but that Sergei had decided to do it anyhow; also that Sergei had just sent a note somewhere. He said something about the public prosecutor and how he thought he would be deprived of his civil rights and deported to the far north; he also mentioned his plan of settling and farming in Tashkent, of how he would teach his son (Lisa's child) something and pass on to him something or other in Arkhangelsk, in the Kholmogory hills. . . . "The fact that I wanted to know your opinion, Arkady," he said, "shows how much I respect it. . . . Ah, if only you knew, Arkady, my brother, my dear brother, how much Lisa has meant to me during all the time I've spent here!"

He shouted out these last words, clutching his head between his hands in despair.

"Sergei!" I couldn't restrain myself from exclaiming, "are you really going to ruin Lisa's life and ask her to follow you to . . . to Kholmogory?"

I'd suddenly grasped for the first time what it would really be like for Lisa to spend the rest of her life with this maniac. He glanced at me, got up, took a few steps across the room, about-faced, resumed his seat, and again held his head between his hands.

"I keep dreaming of spiders," he said.

"You're in a highly nervous state, Prince. If you want my advice, lie down and demand that they send for a doctor at once."

"We'll see about that later. . . . First, the important thing I wanted to see you about is the wedding. The ceremony, as you know, will have to take place here, in the prison chapel. I've already told you that. The authorities have given us official permission and indeed, they're rather encouraging the marriage. As to Lisa . . ."

"Couldn't you be nice to Lisa and stop torturing her with your jealous scenes? Why don't you leave her in peace at least for now?"

"What did you say?"

He stared at me, his eyes almost popping out of their sockets. His features were twisted into a crazy, questioning smile. I could see that it was the word jealous that had somehow struck him so strongly.

"Forgive me, Sergei, I didn't really mean what I said. . . . You know, recently I've got to know an old man, the one who's officially supposed to be my father . . . I wish you could meet him—he'd make you feel much easier. . . . Lisa too thinks he's wonderful."

"Lisa . . . ah yes, of course. . . . He's your father, isn't he? No, pardon, mon cher, he's something like . . . I remember— she told me something about an old man. . . . Yes, I'm sure she told me. And you know, I also used to know an old man once. . . . Mais passons, the most important thing now is to grasp the full meaning of the moment, we must . . ."

I got up. I wanted to leave. It was too painful for me to see him in that state.

"I don't understand you!" he said sternly, glaring at me, realizing that I was going to leave.

"It pains me to look at you," I said.

"One more thing, Arkady, just a few more words." He seized me by the shoulders with both hands. His expression had suddenly changed completely. He made me sit down again. "You've heard, haven't you, about those people, you know?" He leaned his head toward me.

"You mean Dergachev? It must be all Stebelkov's doing!"

"That's right—Stebelkov and . . . Don't you know?"

He broke off and stared at me with his eyes still popping out and that fixed, crazy, questioning smile spreading wider and wider on his face, which was turning paler and paler. Something suddenly stung me and I remembered the way Versilov had looked at me the day before when he'd told me about Vasin's arrest.

"Is it possible . . ." I cried out, horrified.

"That's just why I wanted to see you, Arkady," he muttered in a hurry, "I wanted to explain. . . . I wanted you to understand. . . ."

"So it was you who informed on Vasin!" I shouted.

"No, you don't understand—you see, there was a certain manuscript. . . . Just the day before it happened, Vasin gave it to Lisa . . . he wanted her to keep it for him. Then Lisa left it here so I could take a look at it. . . . Then, on the following day, they quarreled . . ."

"And you handed it over to the authorities!"

"Arkady, wait!"

"So-it-was-you!" I yelled, spitting out the words, syllable by syllable. I leaped to my feet. "So, without any reason or motive other than your imagining that the wretched Vasin is *your rival*, you turned over to the authorities a document that had been entrusted to Lisa for safekeeping. Whom did you give it to? The prosecutor?"

He just stood there staring at me with that new moronic smile of his, and it seemed quite unlikely that he would have answered me anyway, but, as it happened, he didn't even get a chance. The door suddenly opened and Lisa walked in. She stopped dead when she saw me.

"Why are you here? What are you trying to do? So . . . so *you know?*"

Her features were distorted with anguish. She already knew just by looking at me that *I knew*. On a sudden impulse, I opened my arms and hugged her very, very hard. It was at that moment that I grasped for the first time the full extent of the unmitigated, hopeless misery that had been destined as the lot of this seeker of suffering—my sister.

She tore herself away from me.

"What's the point of trying to talk to him when he's in this state? Or seeing him? Why did you come here? Just look at him! How can anyone judge him?"

Her face expressed infinite pain and compassion as she pointed at the wretched fellow. He was now sitting in an armchair, his face hidden in his hands. And she was right. He was like a man in a delirium, a man not responsible for his actions.

Later that morning, he was hospitalized and on the following day brain fever set in.

IV

I left Prince Sergei with Lisa and went over to my former lodgings where I arrived around one o'clock. I should have mentioned that it was a dull, damp day with a warmish wind bringing on a thaw, the kind of a day that could cause a nervous upset even in an elephant. The landlord was so pleased to see me that he started to fuss and rush all over the place like a madman, which is something I've always detested, especially at moments such as this. I was icily reserved with him and walked straight to my room. But that still wasn't enough to discourage him from following me and, although he didn't dare ask me any questions directly, he kept looking at me with insatiable curiosity. I remembered that it was in my own interest to treat him more or less civilly: there was something I had to find out from him (and I knew I would find it out). Nevertheless, I felt it demeaning to start questioning him. So I first inquired about his wife's health and we went to pay her a visit. She received me politely but was very matter-of-fact and not in the least chatty, which reconciled me somewhat to the place. . . .

Well, in the end, I did get some very interesting information.

As I'd expected, Lambert had been around and had recently returned twice. He'd said he might be interested in renting and had inspected all the rooms. Daria too had come several times but, in her case, I cannot imagine what she could have been after. The landlord said she'd seemed "very inquisitive," but I must have disappointed him by not asking him what she was inquisitive about. In fact, I didn't ask him any questions. I pretended to be unpacking my suitcase (which was almost empty by then) and just listened to him talk. The only trouble was that, when he became aware of my reserve, he suddenly decided to put on an air of mystery and became less voluble.

"That young lady . . . she came too," he said abruptly, giving me a strange look.

"Which young lady?"

"Miss Anna Versilov. She came twice. Made the acquaintance of my wife. A very pleasant and well-mannered young lady. It was a real privilege to make her acquaintance. . . ."

Now he took a step toward me. He was trying hard to make me understand something.

"So she came twice, did she?" I said in a surprised voice.

"The second time she brought her brother with her."

I decided that he'd mistaken Lambert for Anna's brother, but, just as if he'd thrust his eyes inside my soul, he added: "No, sir, it wasn't Lambert, it was her real brother, the young Mr. Versilov—an army ensign, I believe." And, as I felt somewhat embarrassed, he beamed at me with infinite gentleness.

"And then there was also that Frenchwoman inquiring after you—Mademoiselle Alphonsine de Verdun, she said her name was. It's really something, the way she sings and reads poetry. . . . That day, she'd been to visit the old prince Nikolai Sokolsky in Tsarskoe to sell him some very rare kind of dog—all black and, I understand, no larger than a man's fist. . . ."

I said I had a headache and wanted to be alone for a while. He didn't even try to finish what he was saying and walked out. He didn't look in the least offended; indeed, if anything, he seemed very pleased with himself. He waved at me, implying that there was a secret between us, as if to say: "I understand, I understand." And he tiptoed out quietly, this discretion too giving him obvious pleasure. Ah, how irritating some people can be!

Left alone, I sat down to think it all over and I sat without moving for an hour and a half. Only, instead of making sense out of what I'd just learned, I got lost in my thoughts. I felt confused but not in the least surprised. As a matter of fact, I was expecting even stranger things to happen. Perhaps they've already pulled off something, I thought. For quite some time, I'd had the feeling that the machinery of their plot had been set in motion and I thought that by now it must be in full swing. "All they've been waiting for is me!" flashed through my mind, accompanied by a feeling of peculiar, rather pleasant irritation mixed with conceit. The fact that they were waiting for me and that they were planning to organize something or other in my apartment was clear as day. Could it be, by any chance, the

marriage of old Prince Nikolai? Well, would I oblige those
ladies and gentlemen? That's the big question, I mused con-
ceitedly, savoring my importance.

But, if I got involved in it now, would I again be caught up
like a splinter of wood in a whirlpool? In fact, was I still free
now? And when I saw Mother that evening, would I be able to
say to her, as I had during these past days: "I am on my own,
free and independent."

That was the essence of my thoughts, or rather of my heart-
beats, during the hour and a half that I sat on the edge of my
bed, elbows on my knees and head propped up in my hands.
But even then I already knew that all the problems facing me
didn't really matter, that the only thing I was interested in was
Katerina, that outside of *her* there was nothing. In the end, I
openly admitted this to myself, took a pen, and wrote it down
on a piece of paper. And yet, even now, as I write this, I still
don't know what to call that feeling.

Oh, no doubt, I was sorry for Lisa and my heart was full of
the most sincere grief for her. That deep sympathy by itself
should, it would seem, have wiped out, or at least toned down,
that *carnivorous* feeling I had (I remember that word). But I
was driven by an uncontrolled curiosity, a strange fear, and
some other feeling that I cannot define. I only knew (and had
known all along) that it was a wicked feeling. Perhaps I was
longing to throw myself at her feet, but perhaps too I was longing to torture her and was in a great hurry to prove something
to her. No pity, no compassion for Lisa, could stop me now. So
how could I possibly get up and go back home . . . to be with
Makar?

But couldn't I just go and have a look at those marvels and
monsters, find out everything, and then leave unscathed, never
to return?

At three o'clock I suddenly came to my senses. It was almost
too late! I rushed out, hailed a cab, and drove to Anna's.

Chapter 5

I

As soon as the servant announced my arrival, Anna put down
her sewing and rushed out to meet me, something she'd never
done before. She held out both hands and suddenly turned
red. Without a word, she showed me in and sat down with her
needlework, pointing at a chair next to her where she wanted

me to sit. But, instead of resuming her sewing, she went on looking at me with the same fervent sympathy, still never uttering a word.

"So you sent Daria to me." I decided to get straight to the point, feeling the pressure of her exaggerated warmth, although not altogether unpleasantly.

She ignored my remark and suddenly started to talk.

"I've heard . . . I know about everything. . . . What an awful night it must've been! I can just imagine what you went through! Tell me, is it true that they found you unconscious out in the bitter cold?"

"It was . . . was it Lambert who told you that?" I muttered, reddening.

"It was he who told me about it then and I was so anxious to see you myself. . . . Oh, you should have seen how frightened he was when he came here! In the house, you know, where you were put to bed, well, they wouldn't let him in . . . in fact, he was given a rather peculiar reception. . . . I really don't know what happened there, but he told me at great length about that night: he told me the first thing you muttered when you came to . . . was my name. He was impressed by how devoted you were to me. I was moved to tears, Arkady, because I can't think what I've done to deserve such warm affection on your part. . . . Especially that you should think of me when you were in such a terrible state yourself! Tell me, is Lambert your childhood friend?"

"Yes, I admit I may have been indiscreet on that occasion. I may have said too much."

"Oh, I'd have learned about that horrible, sinister intrigue without him! I've always had the presentiment that they'd drive you to that. But is it really true that Björing dared to raise his hand to you?"

The way she talked, one would have thought that it was entirely Björing's and Katerina's fault that I'd wound up under that fence in the snow. Well, she might have been right at that. But I flared up:

"If Björing had raised his hand to me, he wouldn't have left without paying for it and I wouldn't be sitting here with you now bearing an unavenged insult!"

I felt she was trying to taunt me, to arouse my anger against someone (it was not very hard to guess against whom!), but I still fell for it.

"If you say you had a presentiment that I'd be driven to this, Katerina Akhmakov, for her part, was taken completely by sur-

prise. . . . Although I think she was in too much of a hurry—
perhaps because of her surprise—to discard her kind feelings for
me. . . ."

"Yes, she was in rather a hurry!" Anna assented enthusiastically, looking at me with ardent sympathy. "Oh, if only you
knew the intrigue that's being hatched there now! I realize, Arkady," she said, turning pink and bashfully lowering her eyes,
"how difficult it is for you to understand the delicacy of my
present position. Since the morning I saw you last, I have taken
a step that not everybody would understand as well as you, with
your uncontaminated mind and loving, uncorrupted heart. I
want you to know, my dear friend, that I am capable of appreciating your devotion to me and am eternally grateful to you for
it. In society, of course, there are those who will cast stones at
me, and some have already picked up their stones. But even supposing they may be right from their ignoble point of view, even
so who of them would dare to condemn me? I was abandoned
by my father when I was still a child. The Versilovs are an old
Russian family, and yet I've been forced to live on charity as if I
were scum! So wasn't it natural for me to turn to the man who
had replaced my father since my childhood and whose kindness
I had experienced for so many years? How I feel toward him is
for God alone to judge and I refuse to accept the judgment of
society, whether they approve or disapprove of the step I've
taken. And when, on top of everything, I find out about a sinister and sordid intrigue hatched against a kind and trusting father
by his own daughter, who is determined to ruin him, how can
I stand idly by? And I don't care if it costs me my reputation or
not, but I will save him! If need be, I'm prepared to be nothing
but his nurse, to look after him, be at his bedside when he's ill,
but I'm not going to allow their cold, sordid, worldly schemes to
triumph!"

She spoke with great vivacity, partly put on perhaps, but
still sincere enough, for now I could see how deeply she'd
got herself involved in this whole business. Oh, I knew that she
was lying (but she was sincere in her lying because it is possible to lie with sincerity) and that she was not a nice person.
But it's amazing how a woman can befuddle a man sometimes
with her outward respectability, her refined airs, her well-bred
inaccessibility, and her unquestionable propriety. And so, as
long as I was in her presence, I didn't dare to contradict her. Yes,
a man, especially if he's magnanimous, is always in moral bondage to women. A woman like her could convince a magnanimous man of anything! My God, she and Lambert, I thought,

looking at her with bewilderment! But let me say that to this day I don't know what to think of her, for, just as she said, God alone could judge how she felt because a human being is an incredibly complicated machine, the workings of which appear quite impossible to follow, especially if that human being happens to be a woman.

Nevertheless, I asked her quite firmly: "What do you actually expect of me, Anna?"

"What do you mean by that, Arkady?"

"Judging from everything you've said and also from other indications," I mumbled, getting a bit mixed up, "you sent for me because you want something from me. So I'd like to know what it is you want."

She ignored my question and started speaking fast and with great animation.

"But, of course, I'm too proud to make deals with people I don't even know, people like that Mr. Lambert. . . . It was you whom I wanted to see, not Lambert. . . . I find myself in an awful predicament, Arkady, in a horrible predicament! I'm forced to maneuver cunningly to avoid the snares set for me by that unspeakable woman, and I find it all absolutely unbearable! Imagine, I must lower myself to intrigue against her now! And so I was waiting for you to save me! Who could blame me for looking around eagerly and trying to find at least one true friend? And so how could I not have felt elated to find a friend who, even while freezing to death, thought of me and repeated my name, alone among all names, and thus proved to be a truly devoted friend? And that's what I've been thinking all this time and that's why I based such hopes on you."

There was an impatient probing in the way she looked into my eyes. But I still couldn't gather up enough courage to disillusion her by telling her frankly that Lambert had lied to her, that I'd never said a word to him about my devotion to her and, indeed, had never pronounced her name. Thus, by not denying it, I did in a way confirm Lambert's lie. But I'm sure she herself realized that Lambert had at least exaggerated, if not made up everything altogether, just to have a pretext to establish contact with her. And if she could look me straight in the eye as though accepting unquestioningly what Lambert had told her, it was because she knew I would not deny these words out of what might be called delicacy and because of my youth. But whether my guess was right or not, I still have no idea. Perhaps I'm terribly perverse myself.

"My brother will come to my defense," she suddenly declared heatedly, annoyed perhaps by my silence.

"I understand that you and he came to my apartment," I mumbled with embarrassment.

"But don't you see that poor Prince Nikolai has nowhere to escape from that intrigue or, to be more accurate, from his own daughter except your apartment, the apartment of a friend? Why, isn't he at least entitled to consider you his friend? If you want to do something to help him, do it! That is, if you can do something and have the generosity and the courage to do it. . . . Indeed, if you can really do something for him. Understand, it isn't for me, it's for that unhappy old man, who happens to be the only person with a true and sincere affection for you, who became attached to you as if you were his son, and who misses you badly even now. For myself, I expect nothing, not even from you. How could I, since my own father played such a perfidious and cruel trick?"

"But I was under the impression that Mr. Versilov—"

"Mr. Versilov," she interrupted me with a bitter smile, "my dear father, in answer to my direct question, gave me his word of honor that he had never had any intention whatsoever of marrying Katerina Akhmakov, and, of course, I believed him implicitly when I took that step. . . . But then it turned out that he kept quiet only until he heard something about a certain Mr. Björing."

"That's not so!" I cried. "There was a moment when I too believed that he loved that woman, but that was not it. . . . And even if it was, it would appear that now he needn't worry at all . . . after the dismissal of that gentleman."

"What gentleman?"

"Björing."

"Dismissal? Who told you he'd been dismissed? In fact, I don't believe he was ever in a stronger position than he is now." She snorted mockingly and I even had the impression that she gave me a sarcastic look.

"I heard that from Daria," I mumbled, trying to hide my embarrassment, which she, however, noticed only too well.

"Daria is a very nice woman and I cannot, of course, prevent her from liking me, but she's not in a position to know things that are none of her business anyway."

I felt pained: Anna was obviously trying to arouse my indignation, and she succeeded. However, it was not against Katerina that my anger turned, it was against Anna herself.

"As an honorable man," I said, "I must warn you, Anna, that

your expectations . . . concerning me . . . may turn out to be
quite unfounded. . . ."

"I do expect you to come to my defense," she answered firmly,
"I who have been deserted by everybody else and who am, after
all, if you want me to say it, your sister, Arkady." She looked as
if she were about to dissolve into tears.

"In that case, you'd better stop expecting," I muttered with
an inexpressibly painful feeling.

"How am I to understand that?" she asked too hurriedly, thus
revealing how worried she was.

"Simply that I'll just walk out on all of you and that'll be the
end of it!" I suddenly shouted in a fury. "And I'll destroy that
document. Good-by!"

I bowed to her in silence and walked out of the room, not
daring to look at her. But as I was going downstairs, Daria suddenly caught up with me. She had a folded sheet of letter
paper in her hand. I have no idea where she'd come from or
where she'd been while I was talking to Anna. She didn't say a
word, just gave me the folded sheet, and dashed off. I unfolded
it. It had Lambert's address on it, written very neatly and legibly.
I suppose she'd had it ready for me for several days. I remembered now that when Daria had come to see me during my illness, I'd told her that I didn't have Lambert's address but I had
meant it in the sense that I didn't know where he lived and
didn't care. Since then I'd obtained his address from Lisa, who
had gone to inquire for me at the Registry Office. Now, by dis-
patching Daria to me with that address, Anna seemed to have
planned this move in advance and it struck me as quite cynical:
despite my refusal to cooperate with her, she dismissed what I'd
said as mere pretense and was sending me to deal with Lambert
directly. That showed beyond doubt that she knew everything
about the document and that she'd learned it from nobody else
but Lambert, with whom she now wanted me to come to an
agreement. Ah, they were all taking for granted that I was nothing but a little boy without character or a will of his own! "So
she thinks she can twist me around her little finger!" I thought
with indignation.

II

Nevertheless, I did go to Lambert's. My curiosity had been
too aroused. Lambert lived quite far away—on Twisted Lane
near the Summer Gardens. It was the same lodging where he'd
brought me, but when I'd run away from them, I hadn't noticed either the way or the distance. In fact, I'd been quite sur-

prised when Lisa had given me his address and I'd almost refused to believe her.

I was still going up the last flight of stairs leading to the third-
floor landing where he lived when I saw two young men by the
apartment. They must have rung the bell, I decided, and were
waiting for the door to open. When they heard me coming up,
they turned their backs to the door and watched me attentively.
There were probably other lodgers besides Lambert in that
apartment, I thought, frowning under their stares as I approached them. I would have been very displeased to find someone at Lambert's. Trying to avoid looking at them, I reached for
the bell.

"*Attendez!*" one of them shouted.

"Please wait a moment," the other said in a clear and delicate
voice, slightly drawling his words. "We'll finish what we're doing first and then we'll all ring together, all right?"

I waited. They were both very young, between twenty and
twenty-two. They were up to something peculiar, and I became
curious and took a closer look at them. The one who'd shouted
"*attendez*" was very tall, well over six feet, lean and angular but
obviously muscular, with a disproportionately small head and a
comically grim expression on his slightly pockmarked but by
no means stupid face, which was in a way even pleasant-
looking. Still, there was a somewhat unusual intentness and
deliberation in his eyes. The clothes he wore were very shabby:
an old ill-fitting quilted overcoat with a mangy raccoon collar
that was much too short for him and was obviously secondhand,
heavy workingman's boots, and a horribly battered ancient top-
hat that had acquired a rust-colored tinge. There was a general
air of slovenliness about him: his gloveless hands were grimy
and his fingernails were long and black, like the border of a
mourning notice. His companion, on the contrary, was dressed
with refined elegance: a topcoat of lightweight skunk fur, a
fashionable hat, and pale, immaculate gloves on his slender
fingers. He was about my height. The expression on his young,
fresh face was charming.

The long-legged one was taking off his necktie, which looked
more like an old, greasy, shrunk ribbon, indeed, almost a piece
of tape, while the pretty boy, who had pulled a brand-new black
tie out of his pocket, was tying it around the other's neck, a very
long neck that its owner was stretching out obediently, having
pulled his overcoat down over his shoulders. The effort made
the tall fellow's face look incredibly determined.

"No, it's no good, your shirt's too filthy," the smaller one said; "not only does it destroy all the effect of the tie, but it makes it look even dirtier than it is. . . . Didn't I tell you to put on a clean collar? Ah, I can't make it look decent! . . . Look, perhaps you can?" He suddenly turned to me.

"What?"

"Tie his tie . . . Couldn't you manage somehow to hide his filthy shirt? Otherwise, it'll spoil everything. I just bought this tie for him from Philip, the hairdresser, and he charged me a ruble for it."

"Was it . . . that ruble?" the long-legged one muttered.

"Sure, and now I haven't got one kopek left! . . . I see you can't do it either. Well, we'll have to ask Alphonsine to tie it."

"You going to see Lambert?" the tall one asked me with a strange abruptness.

"Yes," I answered firmly, looking him straight in the eye.

"You're Dolgorovki?" he asked in the same tone.

"No, I'm not Korovkin," I answered sharply, having misheard him.

"Dolgorovki!" the long-legged one all but roared, advancing on me with the suggestion of a threat.

His companion burst out laughing.

"He didn't say 'Korovkin'; he said 'Dolgorovki,' meaning Dolgoruky," he explained to me. "You know how the French distort Russian names. I saw in the *Journal des Débats*—"

"In *L'Indépendance*," growled the other one.

"What's the difference, in *L'Indépendance* too. . . . They'd be sure to spell Dolgoruky 'Dolgorovki,' and somehow Valoniev comes out always as le comte Wallonieff. . . ."

"And remember Doboyny!" the long-legged one roared.

"Yes, yes, that made us really laugh: they wrote about some Russian lady living abroad whose name was supposed to be *Madame Doboyny!* . . . But there are only too many such instances and there's no need to bring them all up. . . . But, if you'll forgive me, you are Mr. Dolgoruky, aren't you?"

"Yes, I am Dolgoruky. But how did you know?"

The long-legged one whispered something into the ear of his nice-looking companion, who frowned and shook his head to signify he didn't agree. But the tall one ignored him and said to me:

"Monsieur le prince, vous n'avez pas de rouble d'argent pour nous, pas deux, mais un seul, voulez-vous?"

"You're impossible!" the pretty boy cried.

"*Nous vous rendons,*" the long-legged one promised, doing violence to French grammar and pronunciation.

"He's a cynic, I warn you," his companion said laughingly, "and perhaps you think his French is bad? He could talk pure Parisian if he wanted. But he likes to imitate those Russians who love to show off their French in company but who can't really speak it. . . ."

"*Dans les wagons . . .*" the tall one explained.

"All right, they do it in trains too. What's the difference? What a bore you are! And why must you always play the fool?"

In the meantime I had pulled out a ruble and handed it to the tall one.

"*Nous vous rendons,*" he assured me, pocketing the ruble.

Then he suddenly turned toward the door and, his face remaining perfectly expressionless, started to kick the door violently with his heavy boots. The strange thing was that he did it without the least trace of irritation.

"Ah, you'll have another fight with Lambert," his friend said in a worried tone. "Perhaps, it would be better if you rang the bell, if you would," he said to me.

I rang, but the long-legged one kept kicking the door.

"*Ah, sacré . . .*" I suddenly heard Lambert's voice as he hurriedly unlocked the door. "*Dites donc, voulez-vous que je vous casse la tête, mon ami!*" he shouted at the long-legged one.

"*Mon ami, voilà Dolgorovki, l'autre mon ami!*" the long-legged one said with affectedly solemn dignity, staring straight at Lambert, who turned beet-red from fury. But as soon as he caught sight of me, his face changed: he beamed with joy.

"Ah, Arkady! There you are at last! You're well now, completely recovered, I trust?"

He seized me by the hands and pressed them hard. He was so obviously sincerely delighted to see me! I found it extremely pleasant to be so warmly received and I felt I even liked him now.

"You're the first person I wanted to see!" I said.

"Alphonsine!" Lambert called, and, as she emerged from behind the screen, he shouted: "*Le voilà!*"

"*C'est lui!*" Alphonsine cried out, throwing her hands up in the air to embrace me, which she would have done if Lambert hadn't protected me from her.

"*Non, non, tout-beau!*" he stopped her as one would stop a dog. "You see, Arkady, I and a few fellows arranged to go out to dinner at the Tartars'. So you'll come with us, for I won't let you out of my sight now. Then, as soon as we've had dinner,

I'll send them packing and we'll have a good long talk, just the two of us. . . . But step in while I'm getting ready . . . I won't be a minute!"

I stepped in and remained standing in the middle of the room, looking around and remembering. Lambert went behind the screen to dress. The two fellows followed us in. It was as though they hadn't heard what Lambert had said to me. So the three of us stood there and waited.

"*Mademoiselle Alphonsine, voulez-vous me baiser?*" the long-legged one growled suddenly.

"*Mademoiselle Alphonsine,*" the pretty boy said, moving toward her and showing her the tie.

She pounced on them fiercely.

"*Ah, le petit vilain!*" she shouted at the shorter one, "*ne m'approchez pas, ne me salissez pas! Et vous, le grand dadais, je vous flanque à la porte tous les deux, savez-vous cela!*"

The pretty boy, however, didn't seem in the least put off by her disgusted expression while she tried to wave him aside as if she were really afraid to be dirtied by touching him (it struck me as absurd because he was so neat and pretty and turned out to have an awfully elegant suit on when he threw off his top-coat). He went on insisting that she should fasten his friend's tie and that she should give him one of Lambert's clean shirt collars. She almost attacked him physically when he asked for the collar, but Lambert, who must have heard what was going on from behind the screen, shouted to her not to hold things up and to do what she was asked because otherwise "they'll just keep pestering you." So Alphonsine quickly produced one of Lambert's collars, fastened it around the tall fellow's neck, and proceeded to put on his tie without a trace of her recent revulsion. The fellow stretched out his neck just as he'd done on the landing and remained like that until she'd finished.

"*Mademoiselle Alphonsine, avez-vous vendu votre bologne?*" he asked.

"*Qu'est-ce que c'est que ça, ma bologne?*"

The pretty boy explained that *bologne* was her lap dog.

"*Tiens, quel est ce baragouin?*"

"*Je parle comme une dame russe sur les eaux minerales,*" le grand dadais answered, still holding his neck stretched out.

"*Qu'est-ce que c'est que ça qu'une dame russe sur les eaux minerales et . . . où est donc la jolie montre que Lambert vous a donnée?*" she said, turning suddenly to the smaller of the two.

"What, they don't have the watch again?" Lambert asked from behind the screen.

"We ate it," *le grand dadais* growled.

"I sold it for eight rubles," his companion said reluctantly. "It wasn't really gold, as you claimed, it was gold-plated silver. You can get one like that at a jeweler's for sixteen rubles."

"I'll put an end to this!" Lambert said with rising anger. "I'm not buying you good clothes and giving you expensive things just so that you can sell them and spend the money on your long-legged friend! And what's that tie you've bought for him?"

"It only cost one ruble, and it wasn't your ruble. Besides, he didn't have a tie and he needed one. And now he still needs a hat."

"Nonsense!" Lambert shouted, really furious now. "I've given him plenty as is, enough to buy a hat too; but all he did with it was to gorge himself on oysters and champagne. Look at him: he's a mess, he even stinks! He's not presentable. How can I take him out to dinner with us?"

"You can take me in a cab," the long-legged one growled, *"nous avons un rouble d'argent que nous avons prêté chez notre nouvel ami."*

"You mustn't give them anything, Arkady," Lambert shouted again from behind the screen.

"Just a minute, Lambert," the pretty boy said, suddenly becoming so angry that his cheeks became pink, which made him even prettier. "I demand that you give me ten rubles right now and stop giving Dolgoruky stupid instructions. I want ten rubles now so I can pay back one ruble to Dolgoruky and use the rest to buy a hat for Andreyev."

Lambert emerged from behind the screen, holding three yellow bills in his hand.

"Here're three rubles—that's all you get until Tuesday, not one kopek more, and don't you even dare . . . Otherwise . . ."

Le grand dadais literally tore the money out of his hand: "Here's your ruble, Dolgorovki, *nous vous rendons avec beaucoup de grâce.* Now, let's be on our way, Peter!" he called out to his companion. Then, raising the hand that clutched the two one-ruble bills in the air and waving it, he riveted his stare on Lambert and screamed:

"Ohé, Lambert! Où est Lambert, as-tu vu Lambert?"

"Don't you dare, don't you dare!" Lambert yelled in a terrible rage.

Obviously there was something underlying these peculiar goings-on, and I looked at them in amazement. I saw that the long-legged one was not in the least intimidated by Lambert's anger since he went on yelling even louder *"Ohé, Lambert!"*

and so on. And he was still yelling as he walked out onto the landing. Lambert made a move to rush after him but changed his mind.

"Eh, I'll throw 'em out by the scruff of the neck soon enough anyway! They cost me more money than they're worth. . . . Let's go, Arkady!" he shouted, still angry, with his French *r*'s rolling in his throat. "We're late as is. . . . Someone I must see is waiting for me. . . . Another bastard. . . . They're all bastards, the lot of them. . . . Nothing but scum. . . ." Then he suddenly calmed down. "I'm so glad you did come in the end! So let's be off. . . . And you, Alphonsine, stay here, don't go one step from the house!"

Outside, a smart turnout was waiting for him. We got in and drove off; as we drove, Lambert kept ranting about the two young men. I was puzzled about why he should take them so seriously and I found quite surprising the cavalier way they'd treated Lambert and refused to be intimidated by him. It was, I suppose, the old pattern stamped on my mind from childhood, making me feel that everybody should be afraid of Lambert, for I was probably still afraid of him myself.

"I tell you—they're just scum," Lambert went on and on. "That long-legged bastard—two days ago, he made my life miserable in front of respectable people. He just planted himself in front of me and started shouting: '*Ohé*, Lambert!' Everyone around laughed, because they knew he was doing it to extort money from me. So I gave him money. Damned scum! Just imagine, he graduated from a good cadet corps school, even served briefly as an ensign in a regiment! Of course they kicked him out, but still who'd ever have guessed that he's an educated man? And I tell you, he has quite a few ideas in his head and he could have been— Ah, hell! And he's strong *comme un Hercule*. Sure, he can be of some use but not much. . . . Besides, as you could see, he just won't wash his hands. I recommended him to a certain wealthy lady—I told her that he was full of remorse for his sins, was suffering so much that he'd decided to kill himself. So he came to her house, sat down, and started whistling. . . . And the other one—the little, good-looking fellow—he's the son of a general, but his family is ashamed of him and I was the one who got him off the hook when he was arrested. And now see how he repays me for having saved him! There's no one reliable here, no one! And these two, I'll throw them out by the scruff of the neck!"

"How did they know my name? Did you tell them something about me?"

"Yes, and that was pretty stupid of me. Now please control yourself and sit tight during dinner: there's another frightful bastard who'll be there. Well, this one is really frightening, terribly cunning. Ah, I find nothing but scum in this town, not one reliable man! Well, we'll finish with this business and then— What would you like to eat? The food is really good there. And you needn't worry, I'm footing the bill. I'm glad you're properly dressed. If you need money, I can give you some, for you, you can always count on me. Now imagine, I wined and dined these fellows here for days and days, with them always ordering the most expensive dishes. . . . And the watch I gave that little Trishatov that he sold! Alphonsine gets sick just looking at him and won't let him near her. . . . And then one day, in a restaurant in the presence of several army officers, he suddenly declares: 'I've decided to have pheasant.' Well, I ordered his pheasant for him, but he'll pay for it—I'll see to that!"

"You remember, Lambert, the day you took me to a restaurant in Moscow. . . . You had five hundred rubles on you. . . . It was the day you stuck the fork into me, remember?"

"Sure, I remember! How the hell could I forget that? I like you! And you'd better believe it! No one else likes you except me, keep that in mind always. . . . The fellow who'll be in the restaurant, the pockmarked son of a bitch, he's a real shrewd trickster, so you'd better not talk to him or, if he starts asking you all sorts of questions, answer him any kind of rubbish you can think of. . . . But best of all, keep your mouth shut. . . ."

At least, thanks to his excitement, he didn't ask me any questions during the drive to the restaurant. I was a bit offended that he felt so sure he could handle me and that it never seemed to occur to him that I might suspect something. He still seemed to have the absurd notion that he could order me about. And, besides, as I was stepping into the restaurant, it suddenly struck me how incredibly ignorant Lambert was.

III

I had been in that restaurant on Morskaya Street before, during my period of dissipation and disgrace. So the rooms were familiar and the waiters recognized me as an old customer. The idea that I was now with Lambert and looked like one of his shady gang, combined with the feeling that I was willingly allowing myself to become involved in a sordid intrigue that might end in disaster, suddenly filled me with disgust and, for a moment, I was on the point of just walking out. But that moment passed and I stayed.

The pockmarked man, whom for some reason Lambert distrusted so much, was already there, waiting for us. He had one of those serious, business-like, and at the same time stupid airs that I've always loathed ever since I can remember. He was about forty-five, of medium height, with hair turning slightly gray. He was very closely shaven except for neatly trimmed whiskers that looked like two thin sausages suspended on each side of his flat and evil-looking face. It goes without saying that he was dull, solemn, taciturn, and, as this type often is, arrogant.

He looked me over with great interest but didn't utter a word. Lambert stupidly didn't introduce us although we were to dine at the same table, so the pockmarked one could easily have taken me for one of Lambert's assistant blackmailers. Nor did the pockmarked man exchange a word with the two young fellows who joined us almost at once, although it was quite obvious that he knew them very well. The only one he addressed was Lambert himself, and even then it was Lambert who did most of the talking while the pockmarked man confined himself to abrupt, gruff, and peremptory remarks, the whole exchange being conducted in harsh whispers. While Lambert, apparently very excited, seemed to be urging the other to take part in some venture, the man's attitude remained disdainful, irritated, and sarcastic.

But at one point, when I reached for the bottle of red wine, the pockmarked man suddenly seized the bottle of sherry, handed it to me, and, although he hadn't spoken a word to me until then, said:

"Why don't you try this instead?"

I suddenly realized that he must have known everything there was to know about me—my name, my life story, and probably what Lambert wanted from me. The thought that he might take me for one of Lambert's flunkeys made me furious. I also noticed a stupidly worried expression on Lambert's face the moment the man spoke to me. The pockmarked one must have noticed it too and it made him laugh. "Ah, Lambert cringes before everybody," I thought and at that moment I really hated him.

And so, although we were all dining at the same table, it was as if we were split into two groups: on the side closer to the window, Lambert and the pockmarked man facing each other; and on the other side, myself, next to the grubby Andreyev, facing the young Trishatov. Lambert seemed to be anxious to get on with the dinner and kept urging the waiters to hurry.

When the champagne was served, he held out his glass to me:
"To your health, Arkady, let's clink glasses!" he invited me,
interrupting his whispered conversation with the pockmarked
man.

"Will you allow me to clink glasses with you too?" the pretty
boy Trishatov, who until then had been silent and brooding,
asked me, holding up his glass across the table.

"With pleasure," I said, and we clinked glasses and drank.

"But I won't drink to your health," the long-legged Andreyev,
who had been busy eating, suddenly said loudly and distinctly,
turning abruptly toward me. "And not because I wish you would
drop dead but because I don't think you should drink any more
now—three glasses of champagne are enough for you. . . . Ah,
I see you're looking at my unwashed fist," he went on, putting
his fist on the table. "I don't wash it and I hire it out, unwashed
as it is, to Lambert to bash in the faces of various parties whenever Lambert finds himself in a tight spot."

And, as he said that, he slammed his fist down on the table so
hard that all the plates and glasses jumped up in the air. Besides
us, there were people eating at the four other tables, all of them
respectable-looking gentlemen, army officers, and the like, since
it was, after all, quite a fashionable restaurant. All these people
now interrupted their conversation and looked over at us. As a
matter of fact, I believe we'd attracted their curiosity from the
beginning. Lambert turned crimson.

"Ha, there he goes again! Didn't I ask you to behave, Andreyev?" he whispered furiously, glaring at *le grand dadais,* who sul-
lenly stared back at him.

"I don't want my new friend Dolgorovki to drink too much
wine."

Lambert's face became even redder. The pockmarked man
listened to them in silence. He was obviously enjoying himself.
He looked approvingly at Andreyev. Apparently I was the only
one there who didn't understand why I shouldn't drink any
more wine.

"He's just trying to extort more money from me. . . . All
right, you'll get seven more rubles after dinner; just let's finish
eating in peace without any scenes," Lambert hissed in rage.

"Ha, ha!" the big Andreyev growled triumphantly, which
delighted the pockmarked man and elicited a spiteful chuckle
from him.

"Listen, you're overdoing it a bit," Trishatov said to his friend
in a worried tone, almost with pain, and Andreyev quieted down
for a moment.

But only for a moment, because being quiet was not in his plans. Two tables away from us, that is, five or six yards away, two diners were engaged in a lively conversation. They were both middle-aged and dignified-looking gentlemen, both very fat, one very tall, the other quite short. They were talking Polish and were discussing the latest developments in Paris. Andreyev had been glancing at them curiously for some time and trying to overhear what they were saying. Probably at first, he found the shorter Pole comical, but soon he conceived a violent aversion for him, as bilious and liverish people are often prone to do without any provocation. At one point the Pole pronounced the name of the French parliamentarian Madier de Mongeot but, as many Poles do, he stressed the penultimate syllable, which made it sound like Má-dier de Mónge-ot. That was enough to set off *le grand dadais*. He sat up straight in his chair and stared in the direction of the Poles.

"Má-dier de Mónge-ot?" he pronounced loudly and deliberately.

The Poles turned toward him furiously.

"What do you want?" the big, heavy Pole asked him threateningly in Russian.

Andreyev waited for a moment.

"Má-dier de Mónge-ot?" he repeated suddenly, and this time loud enough for everybody in the room to hear. He didn't give any further explanation, just as he hadn't when he'd repeated "Dolgorovki!" and moved toward me on the landing in Lambert's house. The Poles stood up. Lambert jumped up from the table. He made a move toward Andreyev but then, changing his mind, rushed up to the Poles and started apologizing to them profusely:

"They're just clowns, just clowns!" the little Pole kept repeating scornfully, his face the color of a carrot. "Soon it will be impossible to come here to eat!"

There was a stir at the other tables, some disapproving noises too, but mostly chuckles. Lambert went over to Andreyev and tried to persuade him to leave the room:

"Please, come, let's go . . ." he kept muttering.

Andreyev looked probingly into Lambert's face and, deciding that now Lambert was prepared to part with some money, agreed to follow him. Obviously he had used such shameless tricks before to extort money from him. Trishatov was about to follow them, but glanced at me and somehow decided to stay.

"Brrr, how ugly . . . !" he muttered, covering his eyes with his slender fingers.

"Yes, it's pretty ugly," the pockmarked man whispered, sounding really annoyed this time.

Lambert soon reappeared. He was very pale and at once started explaining something in whispers to the pockmarked man, who, after having listened to him for a while, called a waiter and told him to bring us our coffee. Then he listened to more of Lambert's explanations with an air of distaste, apparently impatiently waiting to get out of there. It looked as though the whole incident were just a schoolboy prank. Trishatov took his cup of coffee, walked around the table, and sat down in Andreyev's place next to me.

"I'm very fond of Andreyev," he said to me in a relaxed and confidential tone, as though we'd often talked about this before. "You know, it's quite impossible to imagine how unhappy he is. He squandered his sister's dowry on drinking and wild life in the year he was in the Army, and not just the dowry but everything his family owned. I know how miserable he is about it now, and if he's stopped washing, it's out of sheer despair. Sometimes he comes up with the most peculiar ideas. He says that he's a crook and an honest man at the same time, that it all comes to the same, that there's no need to do anything either good or bad, and also that if one feels like it it's all right to do either good or bad, but that the best thing is to lie down without undressing for a month or so, just eating, drinking, and sleeping. But, believe me, he doesn't really mean all that. And, you know, I think that the fuss he just kicked up here right now was all because he decided to break off with Lambert for good. Yesterday he said he'd had enough of him. It may sound incredible, but sometimes at night or when there's no one around he suddenly starts weeping and he weeps like no one else—he sort of howls in an awful way, and, strangely enough, it just breaks your heart from pity. . . . Just imagine someone big and strong like him bawling like that. Ah, the poor fellow! I'd like so much to help him. I myself, though, I'm rotten and nasty through and through, you have no idea to what extent. . . . Tell me, Dolgoruky, would you allow me into your house if I came to pay you a visit?"

"I'd be glad if you came. . . . As a matter of fact I rather like you."

"What can you like me for? Still, thanks, I appreciate it. Well, let's drink another glass of champagne to that. . . . No, wait, you'd better not drink any more. He was right, you shouldn't drink now, but I will." He winked at me meaningfully. "For me, it doesn't matter and, besides, I can never restrain myself anyway, would you believe it? If you told me, for instance, that I could no longer afford to eat in good restaurants, I'd do anything just to be able to dine well. Oh, we all want most sincerely to be honorable people, I assure you, only we keep postponing it. . . . You know the line 'And the years fly by, the best years of our lives. . . .' I'm terribly afraid that he'll hang himself. He'll do it without warning, that's how he is. Nowadays everybody hangs himself! Who knows, perhaps there're lots of people like us! I, for instance, I can't live without money to spend on whims. Money for whims is much more important to me than money for the necessities of life. . . . Tell me, do you like music? I'm crazy about music. I'll play you something when I come to see you. I've studied piano for years seriously, and I can play really well. If I were to compose an opera, I'd choose a theme from *Faust*. I love *Faust*. I keep composing music for that scene in the cathedral—oh, just in my head, of course. . . . The interior of that Gothic cathedral, the choir, the hymns. . . . In comes Gretchen . . . the choir is medieval—you can hear the fifteenth century at once. Gretchen is in despair. First, a recitative, played very softly, but full of suffering and terror, while the choir thunders grimly, sternly, and impersonally, *'Dies irae, dies illa!'* And then, all of a sudden, the devil's voice sings the devil's song. You can't see him, there's only his song mingling with the hymns, almost blending into them, although it's completely different from them—I must manage to convey that somehow. The devil's song is long, persistent. A tenor—it absolutely must be a tenor. It begins softly and tenderly: 'Do you remember, Gretchen, when, still an innocent child, you came here with your mother and lisped your prayers from the old prayer book?' But the devil's voice grows louder, more passionate, more intense, it floats on higher notes that contain despair, tears, and infinite, irretrievable hopelessness: 'There's no forgiveness, Gretchen, no forgiveness here for you!' Gretchen wants to pray but only cries of pain come from her breast—you know, the breast shaken by sobs and convulsions. . . . And all this time the devil's song continues and pierces her soul deeper and deeper like a spear—the notes get higher and higher and then, suddenly, it all breaks off in a shriek: 'Accursed one, this is the end!' . . . Gretchen falls on her knees, her hands clasped in front of her. And then comes her prayer. Something very short, a semi-recitative, but completely simple, without ornamentation, again very medieval, only four lines—Stradella has a passage with a score a bit like that. . . . And then, on the last note, she faints! There's general confusion, they pick her up, and suddenly the choir thunders forth. It must sound like an explosion of

voices, an inspirational, triumphant, irresistible outburst, somewhat like 'Borne on high by angels . . .' So that everything is
shaken to its foundations and it all merges into one single overwhelming, exalted 'Hosanna!'—like an outcry from the whole
universe. . . . And they carry Gretchen off, and just at that
moment the curtain must fall . . . ! Ah, I wish I could do it!
But I'm afraid I'll never be able to write it now, so all that's left
to me is to dream. . . . Yes, I just dream and dream; my whole
life has become nothing but a daydream until I daydream even
at night. . . . Tell me, Dolgoruky, have you read Dickens' *Old
Curiosity Shop?*"

"Yes. Why?"

"Do you remember, there's a passage—wait, I'll have another
glass of champagne first—there's a passage toward the end in
which the crazy old man and his charming, thirteen-year-old
daughter, after their fantastic escape and wanderings, settle
down somewhere in a remote corner of England near some
Gothic cathedral, and the little girl gets a job as a sort of guide,
taking visitors around the church. . . . Well, one evening, the
sun is setting and the little girl stands by the church entrance,
basking in the last rays of the sunset, and looks at the sinking
sun, her young soul plunged in deep contemplation as though
puzzled by something, and, indeed, there is a double mystery:
the sun is God's thought and the cathedral is man's thought.
. . . Well, I don't know how to explain it, but I just know that
God loves such first thoughts in children. . . . And next to the
little girl there's that crazy grandfather of hers, his eyes fixed on
her. . . . Well, there's nothing so special about the scene, nothing much to it really, but you'll never forget it as long as you
live, and it has survived throughout the whole of Europe. Now
why? Because it's beautiful. Because there's innocence in it.
Actually, I don't know what's in it—I only know it's good. I
never stopped reading novels while I was at school. You know, I
have a sister who's only one year older than me. She's out of
town, in our country house, although it's been sold now and
we own nothing there really. Once she and I were sitting on our
terrace under the old lime trees, reading that novel, and the sun
was setting too. We stopped reading and promised each other
that we too would be good and decent people. I was preparing
for my university entrance examination then. . . . Ah, Dolgoruky, we all have our memories, you know. . . ."

His pretty head suddenly fell on my shoulder and he wept. I
felt terribly sorry for him. I was fully aware that he'd had quite

a bit to drink, but he sounded so sincere and trusting as if I were his brother.

At that moment we all heard shouts coming from the street. Then there was a loud banging on the windowpane (these were large pane-glass windows and, since the room was on the ground floor, it was easy to reach them). It was Andreyev who was making all that noise.

"*Ohé, Lambert! Où est Lambert? As-tu vu Lambert?*" his wild yell resounded from the street.

"So he's here, he hasn't left!" Trishatov cried, leaping up.

"I want the check!" Lambert called out to the waiter, his jaw trembling from rage. I noticed that his hands were trembling too as he counted out the money.

The pockmarked man, though, would not let Lambert pay for him.

"But why? I invited you and you accepted my invitation."

"No, no, please." And he took out his purse and settled his bill separately.

"You're offending me, Semyon."

"No, I just prefer to pay for myself," Semyon answered dryly; he picked up his hat and, without taking leave of anyone, walked out of the restaurant by himself.

Lambert threw the money on the table and rushed after Semyon in such a hurry that he forgot about me. Trishatov and I were the last to leave. Andreyev was standing in the street like a tall lamppost, waiting for Trishatov.

"Son of a bitch!" Lambert couldn't keep himself from shouting.

"Uh-uh!" Andreyev roared back at him, and with one wide swing knocked Lambert's round hat off his head. The hat rolled along the sidewalk and, humiliated, Lambert had to run after it to pick it up.

"*Vingt-cinq roubles!*" Andreyev waved at Trishatov the twenty-five ruble bill he'd extorted earlier from Lambert.

"Stop it," Trishatov said. "Why must you always make trouble like this? And why did you take twenty-five rubles from him? It was only seven he owed us, remember?"

"Why? Don't *you* remember that he promised us dinner with Athenian women and then, instead of women, all he had to offer us was pockmarked Semyon. And, to top it all off, I didn't finish eating and had to wait out here in the cold. Well, I reckoned that he owed me at least eighteen rubles for that alone. So, added to the seven he owed us, that makes exactly twenty-five, doesn't it?"

"Get the hell out of my sight, both of you!" Lambert screamed. "I'm through with you. I'll wring your neck if I ever see you again!"

"Wait, Lambert, it's me who's firing you and I may even decide to wring *your* neck!" Andreyev roared. "*Adieu, mon prince*, don't drink any more! Let's go now, Trishatov. So, *ohé, Lambert, où est Lambert? As-tu vu Lambert?*" he cried out for the last time, walking away with incredibly long strides.

"So I'll come and see you, is that all right?" Trishatov said quickly, as he took off after his friend.

I stayed alone with Lambert.

"Let's go then," he said with an obvious effort. He seemed stunned and was breathing with difficulty.

"Go where? I have no intention of going anywhere with you!" I said challengingly.

"What do you mean?" He recovered his senses at once and now sounded extremely alarmed. "Why, I've been waiting all this time so I could talk to you alone!"

"So why must we go anywhere?"

I confess that I did feel a slight buzzing in my head from the three glasses of champagne and two glasses of sherry I'd drunk.

"Why don't we go in there, see?"

"Where the sign says 'French Oysters'? But it doesn't smell too good. . . ."

"It doesn't to you because you just had dinner. Besides, I wasn't suggesting that we order oysters; we're going to have some more champagne."

"I don't want any. You're trying to make me drunk."

"That's what they told you? But don't you see they were just pulling your leg? You don't really believe that scum, do you?"

"Trishatov is no scum. Besides, I'm capable of taking care of myself without anyone's advice."

"What are you trying to do? Impress me with the strength of your character?"

"I'm not trying to impress you, but I certainly have more character than you have. Why, you act like a flunkey with everybody you come across. I was ashamed to be with you, the cringing way you apologized to those Poles! I bet you've received your share of beatings in public!"

"But we must have a serious talk, you idiot!" he exclaimed in a scornful and impatient tone, implying something like "Perhaps you'd like to imitate Andreyev?" And he added: "Why, would you be afraid of me by any chance? Can't you recognize a friend when you see one?"

"You're not my friend. You're just a crook. But I'll come with you just to show you how little you scare me. . . . Oh, it really stinks in here. It smells of rotten cheese. Disgusting!"

Chapter 6

I

I repeat, my head was buzzing from what I'd had to drink, and if it hadn't been for that, I'd surely have spoken and acted quite differently. In the back room of the little café, they really were serving oysters and we installed ourselves at a little table covered with a stained, greasy cloth. Lambert ordered champagne and soon a glass of the cool, golden drink stood in front of me, as if inviting me to pick it up. I felt angry.

"What annoys me most, Lambert, is that you fancy you can still order me about as you used to at Touchard's when, in fact, it's you who cringes before everyone."

"I don't know what you're talking about, you idiot. . . . But never mind, bottoms up!"

"See, you're not even trying to disguise your intentions from me. I wish at least you didn't make it so obvious that you want me to get drunk."

"You're talking nonsense and you're already drunk. So drink some more and that'll cheer you up at least. Come on then, pick up that glass!"

"The hell I will! I think I'll just walk out on you."

And I made a gesture to get up. He suddenly looked terribly worried.

"It was Trishatov who put all this into your head: I saw you two whispering over there. . . . Well, that only goes to show how stupid you are. He even disgusts Alphonsine so she won't let him come close to her. . . . He's a nasty little vermin. I could tell you a few things about him. . . ."

"I think you've already told me: you measure everything by Alphonsine's reactions—it makes you awfully limited, you know."

"Limited? What do you mean?" He stared at me, puzzled. "What I know is that both of them are now working for Semyon. That I can tell, and that's why I sent them packing. They have no loyalty. Now Semyon is really vicious and he'll corrupt them completely, whereas, as long as they were working for me, I always insisted that they behave."

I remained seated. Without thinking, I picked up the glass and took a sip.

"I'm infinitely more cultured than you are and much better educated," I said challengingly, but he was obviously pleased that I'd given up the idea of leaving and poured more champagne into my glass. "You're afraid of them, aren't you?" I went on, taunting him; at that moment I was probably even nastier than he was. "Andreyev knocked your hat off and you didn't do anything to him except give him twenty-five rubles."

"I gave it to him, but I'll make him pay for it. They became troublesome, but I'll show them yet what's what."

"And you're very worried about Semyon. . . . You know, I begin to think that you have no one in the world but me. All your hopes and expectations are centered on me. Or am I wrong?"

"Sure, Arkady, you're the only friend I have left, you're absolutely right there!" And he slapped me affectionately on the shoulder.

What could I do with such a creature, so primitive as to accept my irony at its face value?

"You know, Arkady," he went on, looking at me fondly, "if you really are a good friend, you could get me out of all my troubles."

"How could I do that?"

"You know very well how yourself. Without me, you're sure to mess it all up and spend the rest of your life a penniless fool. But if you cooperate with me, we'll go halves and you'll get thirty thousand rubles. And you know very well how. What are you today? Just think, you have nothing, no position, not even a name, but if you do what I say, we'll hit the jackpot right now and you know what a career you could make with such a capital!"

I was rather caught off balance by such a direct opening. I'd felt sure he'd try to be cunning, try some sly maneuvering first, but here he'd come straight to the point, almost innocently. I decided to listen to him, just because of that "breadth" of mine, and even more . . . because of uncontrollable curiosity.

"I'm sure you won't understand what I mean, Lambert, when I tell you that I'll listen to your proposition because of my 'breadth,'" I declared in a steady voice, and he at once filled up my glass.

"Now let me tell you something, Arkady: if somebody like Björing dared to insult me and strike me in the presence of the lady I loved, I know what I'd do to him! But you, you just took it and did nothing. You make me sick—you're a doormat!"

"How dare you sit here and tell me to my face that Björing hit me! If anything, it was I who struck him," I said, feeling the blood rush to my face.

"No, it was he who struck you."

"You're lying—I'd stamped on his foot!"

"But he shoved you with his hand and, on top of that, ordered his lackeys to drag you away while the lady was sitting in the carriage watching all that and laughing at you. For she knows very well that you have no father and that anyone who feels like it can push you around."

"This is beginning to sound like one of those conversations back at school, Lambert. You're trying to get a rise out of me and you go about it as crudely and stupidly as if I were a sixteen-year-old or something. I can see that you're in cahoots with Anna Versilov!"

I was almost shouting, shaking with anger, and unthinkingly took a long drink of champagne.

"Anna is a bitch—she'd sell you and me and the whole world if she got a chance. I've waited for you because you're in the best position to handle that other woman. . . ."

"What other woman?"

"Madame Akhmakov, of course. I know everything, I assure you. Anyway, you told me yourself that she was afraid of the letter you have. . . ."

"What letter? You must be raving. . . . Did you see her?" I muttered in complete confusion.

"Yes, I saw her. . . . She's really beautiful—*très belle*—you have quite good taste, I must say."

"I know you saw her, but I know too that you didn't dare talk to her. . . . I wish you also had the decency not to bring up her name. . . ."

"She thinks you're just an immature moron and laughs at you—you can take my word for it! We had a lady like that in Moscow, just as virtuous, who also would turn up her nose just like this one. But as soon as we warned her that we could make public various details about her private life, you should've seen how she started to tremble and she gave us just what we asked her for, which was, of course, money plus something else. . . . You do understand don't you? And now she's once again the proud and unapproachable lady she was before, and when she goes for a drive in her beautiful carriage, you wouldn't even dare stare at her. . . . And it's really very hard to imagine her in that little back room where it all took place. . . . You haven't lived much and you have no idea what sort of things ladies will do in little back rooms if they have to!"

"I've thought of that. . . ." I blurted out unintentionally.

"They're corrupt down to their fingertips and they're capable of anything. . . . Alphonsine used to live in such a house and she found it so disgusting. . . ."

"I've thought of these things," I repeated.

"Then why do you stand being pushed around and why are you afraid to hurt them?"

"Lambert, you're horrible and disgusting! You're a bastard, Lambert!" Somehow I only now fully grasped what he was driving at and I began to shiver all over. "I saw it all in a dream—you and Anna. . . . Oh, you damned, filthy crook! But how could you ever have imagined that I was as low as you? I had that dream, and I knew that you'd say all this. . . . Also I still don't believe that you are telling me the truth even now. I know it can't be that simple."

"Tut-tut-tut! That really got you excited, didn't it?" Lambert drawled with a satisfied laugh. "But that's good, my friend, I've now found out everything I needed to know. That's why I had to see you first. Now I know that you're in love with her and that you'd like to get even with Björing. That's just what I was trying to find out. I rather suspected something of the sort, though. *Ceci posé, cela change la question.* Actually, it's better this way because she loves you too. So you could marry her right away. That's the best move for you; I'd even say, you have hardly much choice. Also, I want you always to remember, Arkady, that you have a true friend, whom you can saddle and ride if you have to—that's me, of course. And now that friend will help you and will see to it that you do marry her. I'll get her for you, from the entrails of the earth if I have to! Well, later, to reward that old friend, I'm sure you'll be willing to make him a little present for his efforts—say, thirty thousand rubles?—and he'll see you through, don't worry! I know all the ins and outs of this type of business: I'll get that dowry for you and you'll be a very rich man and make a brilliant career!"

My head was spinning. I stared at Lambert in bewilderment. Could he mean what he was saying or, at least, did he really believe in the possibility of marrying me off? He seemed to be quite enthusiastic about the idea. For my part, I saw, of course, that he would have said anything to entice me into dealing with him (I'm sure I was aware of that then too); but the thought of marrying *her* pierced me so violently that, although I realized how fantastic Lambert's notion was, I came to accept it. And yet

at the same time my reason told me that it could never material-
ize. . . . Somehow all these contradictory notions managed to
accommodate themselves to one another.

"B-but how would that be possible?" I stammered.

"Why not? All you have to do is show her the letter and she'd
be scared and marry you rather than lose the money that's coming to her."

I decided to let Lambert talk and reveal his plans without interrupting him. He sounded completely frank now since it never
occurred to him that I might be outraged. Still, I couldn't prevent myself from remarking that I didn't want to force anyone
to marry me.

"I couldn't do that," I said; "what do you take me for? How
can you even suggest such a deal to me?"

"Ah, come off it! Besides, you won't even have to force her—
she'll be only too anxious to marry you because she'll be too
afraid of losing everything. And the other reason she'll want to
marry you is that she's in love with you," he added hurriedly.

"As if you really believed that! You're just laughing at me.
. . . What makes you say she loves me?"

"I'm sure she does. I know it. And Anna thinks so too. I promise you Anna thinks that. And there's another reason that proves
she loves you; I'll tell you all about it when you come home
with me, and then you'll know that it's true. And Alphonsine,
who went to Tsarskoe, she also learned . . ."

"What could she possibly have learned there?"

"Why don't you come home with me? She'll tell you herself
and that'll make you feel really good. Besides, there's nothing
wrong with you: you're quite nice-looking, rather well educated. . . ."

"Yes, I am a well-educated man . . ." I whispered hardly
audibly. It was difficult to breathe. My heart was pounding.
And it was certainly not simply the wine.

"Yes, as I said, you're nice-looking and you dress well."

"Right, I dress well."

"And, you're kindhearted."

"Yes, I'm kindhearted."

"So why shouldn't she want to marry you? Besides, Björing
won't take her unless there's money coming with her and it is
within your power to deprive her of money. So she'd obviously
be frightened of being left without anything and she'd marry
you. And that way you would settle your account with Björing.
Why, you told me yourself that night when you almost froze to
death that she was in love with you."

"Did I really tell you that? I'm sure that's not what I said."

"Yes, it is."

"I must have been raving. I suppose it was then that I told you about the document too?"

"Yes, you said you had that letter and that surprised me very much. If he really has that letter, I thought, why doesn't he take what's his for the asking?"

"All that's just a pipe dream and I'm not stupid enough to take it seriously," I muttered. "First, there's the difference in age and, secondly, I haven't even got a real name. . . ."

"Don't you worry, she'll be willing to marry you rather than let all that money slip away. In any case, I'll see to it that she does. Besides, she loves you. You must also remember that that old prince of yours is very fond of you and that, through him, you could build up marvelous connections. As to not having a proper name, that doesn't mean anything nowadays: once you get hold of that money, you'll go on to make more and more and within ten years you'll be famous from one end of Russia to the other, so what kind of name will you need then? Or you could go to Austria and buy yourself the title of a baron—they sell them, you know. . . . Besides, once you're married, you'll take her well in hand: a woman in love even likes to be treated roughly. What women admire in men most is character. So the moment you give her a good scare by threatening her with the letter, she'll see that you have character: 'Here's a young man with character,' she'll say."

I sat there and listened and felt as if the whole world were topsy-turvy. What a conversation! Never before had I sunk to such an idiotic level. But there was a sweetish craving in me that prompted me to go on talking to him. And, with Lambert being so stupid, primitive, and all, there was no need for me to be ashamed. . . . Still, I couldn't help saying to him, "You know, Lambert, whatever you may say, we're talking a lot of rot. I'm talking to you like this only because we've known each other since we were boys and there's no need for us to put on airs with each other. With anybody else, I'd consider such talk insulting. But, first of all, I want to know what it is that makes you so sure she loves me. What you just said about the power of money is fine, but you don't know very much about society and I can tell you that it still measures a man by his origins, by his family tree and all that. . . . Therefore, since she still knows nothing about my abilities and doesn't suspect the heights I'll reach some day, as things stand now, she'd only be ashamed to marry someone in my position. Now, having said all that, I won't hide from you, Lambert, that there's something that may give me hope: she might be willing to marry me out of gratitude because that way I might save her from the hatred of a certain man whom she fears a great deal."

"You mean your father? Tell me, is he in love with her too?" Lambert suddenly became tense and looked at me with immense curiosity.

"Oh no!" I cried. "You're really frightening, Lambert, and at the same time so incredibly stupid! How could I think of marrying her if I thought he loved her? After all, we *are* father and son, and it would be too disgusting for words. . . . Besides, he loves Mother, I saw how he embraced her. . . . I too used to think that he was in love with Katerina, but now I'm certain that, even if he did love her once, he hates her now, and has hated her for a long time. He's planning to avenge himself on her and she's afraid of him because—let me tell you this, Lambert—he's really terrifying when he's out to destroy someone. He turns almost insane. When he hates a person, there's nothing that can stop him. Theirs is an old-style feud caused by disagreement on ideals. Nowadays people don't give a damn about general principles but are only concerned with their own particular cases. Ah, Lambert, you can't understand a thing; you have no more brains in your head than in your little toe. You're terribly primitive. Do you remember how you used to beat me up? Well, I'm stronger than you now, did you know that?"

"Come home with me, Arkady, we'll sit down, empty another bottle of wine, and Alphonsine will sing for us and play her guitar. What do you say?"

"No, I have no intention of going to your place. . . . Did you know, Lambert, that I have my own *idea*? So if it doesn't work, if she won't marry me, I'll retire and live with my idea. But you, Lambert, you have no idea of your own!"

"All right, all right, you'll tell me all about it later. . . ."

"I'm not going with you!" I said and stood up. "I don't want to and I'm not going to. . . . I'll come and see you, but still you're a horrible crook. . . . I may give you thirty thousand rubles, but I'm a better man than you, more honorable. . . . I can see very plainly that you're planning to doublecross me all the way. As to *her*, I forbid you even to think of her—she's superior to all of us—and your plans are more revolting and despicable than anything I might have expected even from you. It's true I'd like to marry her, but I don't need any capital, I despise capital. . . . I wouldn't accept money from her if she went down on her knees and begged me. . . . But, when it comes to marriage, that's a different matter. And, you know, I agree with what you said about keeping one's wife in hand. It's great to love passionately, to love with all the generosity that exists in a man and of which a woman is incapable, but it's also great to be able to bully her. Because a woman likes to be bullied. You understand women, Lambert, although you're remarkably stupid in every other respect. And you know what—you're not really quite as repulsive a character as you may seem at first glance. You're really quite a simple soul. I'm sort of fond of you, Lambert. But why are you such a crook? If you were a bit less crooked, we could've had so much fun together! And, you know, I think Trishatov is a nice boy. . . ."

We were already in the street by the time I'd uttered the last disconnected sentences. I'm recounting all this in such detail to show the reader how, despite my frequent vows and solemn resolutions to reform and strive for "beauty," I could so easily slip into such vulgarity. And I swear that, if I weren't absolutely certain now that I'm no longer the same man, that I've gained strength, and that my character has been forged by life, I could never make such a confession to the reader.

As we left the café, Lambert put his arm around my shoulders to steady me. Suddenly, glancing at his face, I recognized in his expression the same fixed, desperately intent, and perfectly sober eyes riveted on me as that morning when I'd almost frozen to death. Then, supporting me just as he was now, Lambert had led me to a cab, eagerly listening to every word I had babbled. I realized all this in one of those flashes of complete lucidity that often come over people who are slipping into a completely drunken oblivion but who haven't quite reached it.

"Nothing in the world will make me go to your place!" I told him firmly and clearly. I pushed his arm away and even looked at him mockingly.

"Come on, don't be silly. Alphonsine will make us some tea. . . ."

He was absolutely confident that I wouldn't escape him now. He put his hand back on my shoulder and held onto me with relish as his prey: I was in just the state he wanted me in; that's how he wanted me in his power. It will become clear later why he felt that way.

"I'm leaving you," I said again. "Hey, cabby!"

A cab that was passing by drove up to the curb and I jumped in.

"What are you doing? Why?" Lambert shouted, panic-stricken, grabbing me by the sleeve of my coat.

"And don't you dare follow me!" I yelled.

At that moment the driver started up and Lambert's fingers lost their grip on my coat.

"You'll come to me yourself, you'll see!" He roared after me in a voice filled with rage.

"I'll come if I feel like it. I'm the one who'll decide!" I retorted and turned around, presenting my back to him.

II

If he didn't follow me, it was simply because there didn't happen to be any other cab around. And in no time I was out of his sight. As soon as I reached Haymarket, I stopped the cabby, got out, and dismissed him. I felt an irresistible urge for exercise. I didn't feel at all tired now, nor did I feel the effect of what I had drunk. In fact, if anything, my trouble now was an excess of energy, a huge influx of energy that made me ready to face anything. And at the same time my head buzzed with lots of very pleasant thoughts. My heart was thudding so powerfully that I could distinctly hear every heartbeat. Ah, how nice and easy everything seemed to me! As I was passing the Haymarket watchman's box, I felt an impulse to embrace the guardian of the peace! It was warm, the snow was melting and had turned dark and ugly, and unpleasant smells wafted from the market square. But that too pleased me.

I'll go toward Obukhov Avenue, I thought, then I'll turn left and walk all the way to Semyonovsky Regiment barracks. It's not the shortest way, but it's so nice, so pleasant. . . . My coat is completely unbuttoned, but no one is trying to snatch it off me although there're supposed to be muggers all around Haymarket. Let them come. I may even offer them my overcoat myself; what do I need it for? An overcoat is property and *la propriété, c'est le vol*. . . . But who cares really because everything is so awfully nice. I'm glad it's thawing. Why should it freeze? . . . Ah, isn't it pleasant to think all sorts of rubbish. . . . What was it I said to Lambert about ideals? I said that there is no such thing as general principles but only particular cases. That was rot, utter rot! I just said that to impress him. Pretty stupid, but never mind, I'll make up for it. So don't worry, don't torment yourself, Arkady Dolgoruky—I like you anyway. Yes, in fact, I like you very much indeed, my young friend! It's only a shame that you happen to be such a nasty little bastard . . . and . . . ah! I suddenly stopped. A new wave of exaltation set my heart beating even faster. Oh, my God, didn't he say it. . . . He said *she* loves me. I know he's a schemer and he lies all the time. He just said that to persuade me to come to his house. But maybe . . . He told me that Anna thinks that too. . . . Also Daria might've got wind of something while poking her nose into everybody's affairs. But why didn't I go to Lambert's house as he wanted? I'd have found out what's really going on! He has a plan, though. . . . Yes, I had a presentiment of everything. . . . I saw it all coming, everything. . . . My dream. . . . Well, you have a pretty ambitious scheme there, Monsieur Lambert, but I'm afraid it's all wishful thinking on your part and things are not going to happen as you expect! Although they just may go your way. . . . Lambert is naïve and takes things for granted. He's stupid and bold, like all men of action, and stupidity and boldness combined make a great force. But admit, Arkady Dolgoruky: you were still scared of Lambert, weren't you? . . . But what can Lambert do with honorable people? He solemnly declares that there's no such thing as an honest man around here. . . . But what am I? Don't scoundrels have to have some honest people? For a swindle, honest people are more indispensable than anything else! But you hadn't realized that, Arkady Dolgoruky, not till now! You were so innocent! . . . But, oh God . . . what if he could really arrange for me to marry *her!*

I had to stop again. And now I must confess to something pretty stupid. Well, since it was all so long ago, I'll admit it: I'd been dreaming of getting married for a long time; I mean, I didn't want to really and I never would have (and I never will, I'm sure), but more than once I had mused about how nice it would be to be married, actually many, many times, especially just before falling asleep at night. . . . It had started when I was sixteen. . . . At school I had a friend about my age named Lavrovsky, a very nice, quiet, pretty boy, although that's all that could be said for him. I didn't have too much to say to him. Once we sat next to each other. There was no one else around. He seemed lost in thought. . . . And all of a sudden he said to me: "Dolgoruky, don't you think it would be nice to be married right now? Why, I don't believe there's a better moment to be married than now! But it so happens that it's absolutely impossible." And he said it so simply, so sincerely. And, to my surprise, I agreed with him wholeheartedly because I too had some kind of dreams of one sort or another. For a few days after that, we'd get together and talk about it, secretly as it were, and that was all we talked about. Eventually, I don't know how, we drifted apart and stopped talking to each other. And that was when I started daydreaming about it. All this was probably hardly worth mentioning except to show how far back that sort of thing can be traced.

I started to walk again and resumed my train of thought: There is a serious objection. . . . Oh, I don't mean the age difference—that's quite unimportant, that's nothing—but . . . she's an aristocrat and I'm *plain* Dolgoruky! That's pretty bad! But couldn't Versilov marry Mother and petition the government for me to be legitimized? Couldn't he, for instance, mention the services he's rendered the country? Why, he has served in the Army and later he was an arbitrator between the landowners and their emancipated serfs, so there must be something he could claim the government's gratitude for. . . . But hell, what a disgusting thought!

These last words came out as a loud exclamation and I stopped. For the third time. But this time I felt as if I'd been run over by something. The painful realization that I could wish for such a shameful, degrading thing as changing my name by being legitimized now seemed like a betrayal of my whole childhood and in a single second my pleasant state of joy was swept away.

No, this is something I'll never tell anyone, I thought, my face on fire; the reason that I've lowered myself to this point is that I'm . . . well, terribly stupid and terribly in love. And if there's something Lambert is right about, it's that all these silly conventions are unimportant nowadays; what counts is only the man himself and then money. Or, rather, not actually money, but the man's potential. With such a capital, I'll launch myself toward the realization of my *idea* and in ten years the whole of Russia will be repeating my name, and I'll have my revenge on all of them! Why should I stand on ceremony with her? There again, Lambert is right: she'll be frightened by the threat and consent to marry me. She'll accept me, plainly and abjectly. . . . I suddenly remembered Lambert's words about "the little back room where it all took place." Yes, I suddenly felt, Lambert is right, a thousand times right, and he understands life infinitely better than idealists like Versilov and myself. Lambert is a realist! When he realizes that I have character, he'll register: "Dolgoruky has character." He's as stupid as his own big toe and is only interested in getting that thirty thousand rubles with my help, but nevertheless he's the only friend I have. There's no other kind of friendship; there can't be; it's just a myth invented by impractical people. . . . But I won't even be humiliating *her*. Why would that humiliate *her*? Nothing of the sort—women are all like that. There's no such thing as a woman without abjectness. And that's why she needs a man to obey: she's a subservient creature by nature. A woman stands for vice and seduction and a man for generosity and magnanimity. And that's how it will always be. And if I intend to use that letter, there's nothing wrong with that. It won't prevent me from being generous and magnanimous. There are no pure Schillers in the world—they're an invention. What does it matter if the means are none too clean as long as the goal is sublime. Eventually everything will be smoothed out and washed clean. All this is only the "breadth" of my nature, life itself, the life truth—yes, that's what it's really called!

Let me apologize once more for reporting all my drunken thoughts in such detail. Of course, all this is only the essence of what was going through my mind then, but now I'm under the impression that I was talking to myself at the time in those exact words. I had to try to remember my exact words because my purpose in writing all this down in the first place was to enable people to judge me. But what would there be to judge me by if not this? As if there could be anything more important than this in life? The wine in me was no excuse—*in vino veritas*.

Absorbed as I was in all these thoughts, I didn't notice that I'd finally reached home, that is, Mother's house. Nor do I remember how I entered the house; indeed, I remember nothing until I was standing in our small entrance hall. But then I suddenly became acutely aware that something very unusual had happened. I heard loud voices inside and my mother's clearly audible crying. I was almost knocked off my feet by Lukeria, who emerged from Makar's room and rushed into the kitchen. I threw off my overcoat and went into Makar's room where they were all gathered. Mother and Versilov were there, standing together. She was leaning limply against him and he was supporting her firmly with his arm. Makar sat on his bench as usual, but he seemed completely drained of strength and Lisa had to make an obvious effort to keep him upright by holding onto his shoulders. I noticed that his body was slipping sideways and that he was about to fall. I quickly stepped toward them and realized that the old man was dead.

He had died just a minute or so before I'd come in, but only ten minutes before he'd been his usual self. Only Lisa had been in the room at the time. She had been sitting next to him, telling him about her troubles, and, as on the previous day, he had been listening to her, gently stroking her head. But suddenly, Lisa told us, he had begun to shiver, tried to get up, made an effort to say something, but instead had started slipping to

the left in silence. (Versilov said that it was a heart attack.)
Lisa had let out a scream that had resounded all over the house
and everybody had come running. As I said, it had all happened
perhaps one minute before I'd entered the house.

"Arkady," Versilov shouted to me, "run over to Tatyana's
quickly. I'm sure she's at home. Ask her to come here at once.
Hurry, get a cab, for heaven's sake be as quick as you can!"

I remember clearly how his eyes shone. There was no trace of
real compassion in his expression. His eyes were completely dry.
Mother, Lisa, and Lukeria were crying. Indeed, what struck me
was the extraordinary agitation, almost elation, reflected in Versilov's features.

So I rushed out to fetch Tatyana Prutkov. I didn't take a cab
because Mrs. Prutkov lived quite close by. Instead, I ran all the
way without stopping. I felt all mixed up and perhaps also in a
way elated. I knew that something momentous had happened.
Every trace of drunkenness in me, together with my impure
thoughts, had vanished by the time I rang Mrs. Prutkov's bell.

The Finnish cook opened the door.

"No one home!"

She was about to slam the door.

"She's not home?" I jammed my foot in the door and forced
myself in. "She must be! Makar's dead!"

"What!" Mrs. Prutkov's cry resounded through the closed
door of her room.

"He's dead! Yes, Makar is dead, and Mr. Versilov would like
you to come over right away."

"What are you talking about? Wait!" I heard a bolt click, but
the door opened only a crack. "Explain what happened!"

"I don't know myself. I just got there and he was already
dead. Mr. Versilov said it was a heart attack."

"I'll be over in a minute. Run along, tell him I'm coming.
. . . Well, go on, go on, what are you waiting for?"

Through the half-opened door, I suddenly caught sight of
someone emerging from behind the curtain that separated Mrs.
Prutkov's bed from the rest of the room. Instinctively, I
grabbed the doorknob and wouldn't let her close the door.

"Is it really true that he's dead, Arkady?"

The quiet, harmonious, ringing voice with that metallic quality about it! Everything inside me began to spin. In that question, there was a stirring note; *she* was deeply moved too.

"Well, if that's the way it is," Mrs. Prutkov cried impatiently,
suddenly letting go of the door, "you'd better manage your affairs yourself! You've asked for it now!"

And, grabbing her scarf and fur coat, the old lady burst out onto the landing, putting on her coat as she ran downstairs.

Katerina and I were left alone in the apartment. I took off my overcoat and closed the door. . . . Just like that other time, *she* was looking at me with those bright eyes and, just like then, she held out both hands. . . . It was as if the ground I was standing on had suddenly been pulled out from under me and I literally fell at her feet.

III

I don't know why, but I was on the verge of tears. I don't know what happened, but the next thing I remember is the two of us sitting side by side. This is my most treasured memory: we sat there side by side, hand in hand, and talked and talked. She asked me about Makar and his death; I told her and one might have assumed it was over Makar's death that I was crying, although at this point that would have been quite ridiculous and she couldn't possibly have thought me capable of such childish sentimentality. When suddenly I realized I *was* crying, I became frightfully embarrassed. But now when I think back, I believe I was crying from elation and, since I assume she understood that, this recollection is not really painful.

At one point it struck me as rather strange that she should be asking me all these questions about Makar.

"Did you know him?" I asked her.

"I've never met him. But I've known of him for a very long time and he has played a certain part in my life too. I heard much about him from a man whom I now fear. You know who that man is."

"All I know is that the man in question was much closer to you than you admitted to me," I said, not quite sure myself what I meant by that, but I felt I was frowning and there was deep reproach in my tone.

"You told me just now that he embraced your mother, that he kissed her. You saw it, did you?" She kept bombarding me with questions. Obviously, she hadn't taken in what I'd just said.

"Yes, I saw it, and I assure you he was absolutely sincere and was full of concern for her!" I hastened to confirm when I realized that she liked hearing what I was saying.

"Well, God grant that it be true!" She crossed herself. "You know, he was completely tied down because of that wonderful old man. . . . But now, with the old man dead, his feeling of duty and his dignity will spring back, as they did once before.

. . . Oh, he's a generous man and, first of all, he will restore peace to your mother's heart because, to him, she's the dearest creature on earth. After that, he will find peace himself, and thank God, for it's high time he did."

"Is he so important to you?"

"Yes, very important, although not in the sense that he would have liked and that your question implies."

"Tell me, who are you worrying about now—him or yourself?" I asked her.

"Ah, you ask me such complicated questions! Let's forget all that."

"All right, although there're many things I knew nothing about, I suppose too many things. But you're right, it doesn't matter now, and if anybody has come back to life, it may be me. I had evil thoughts about you, Katerina, and perhaps less than an hour ago I also acted contemptibly. But here I am sitting next to you and I want you to know that I feel no remorse whatsoever. Because all that has vanished, everything is different, and because I want nothing to do with the man who was plotting against you."

She smiled. "Wake up, you sound a bit delirious."

"Besides, what's the point of trying to judge myself when *you* are involved?" I went on. "Whether I'm base or noble makes no difference since you are, in either case, as inaccessible as the sun! . . . Tell me, why did you come out and talk to me just now after all that had happened? And if you only knew what went on just one hour ago and what sort of prophetic dream came true!"

"I suppose I do know everything," she said, with a gentle smile. "You wanted to punish me by any means you had; you swore to ruin me, but at the same time you would have attacked and even killed anyone who said an evil word about me."

Oh, she was smiling and her tone was light. But, as I realized later, it was out of her great generosity and kindness because at the time she was in the throes of immense personal anxiety and of a powerful feeling that caused her to speak to me and answer my questions mechanically, rather the way an adult keeps up a conversation with a small child who prattles on and on. This suddenly dawned on me and I felt foolish, but I could no longer stop.

"No!" I cried out, unable to control myself. "Not only did I not kill a man who spoke evil of you but, on the contrary, I encouraged him!"

"For heaven's sake, don't tell me, there's no need. . . ." She pressed my hand and a shadow of pain appeared in her expression.

But I had already leaped to my feet and stood facing her. I was prepared to tell her everything and if I'd been given that chance it would have prevented what happened afterward. Probably I would have confessed to her my schemes and returned the letter to her. . . .

But she suddenly began to laugh.

"Please spare me all the details: I already know about all your crimes. I'd guess you were plotting to force me to marry you or something of that sort and you worked out a whole scheme with some accomplice, an old classmate of yours perhaps. . . . Well, it looks as though I must have guessed right, doesn't it?" she exclaimed, looking intently into my face.

"How . . . how could you have known about it?" I muttered foolishly, feeling quite bewildered.

"Anything else you want to know? But enough of this! I forgive you for everything, just as long as you stop talking about it!" she said, now with unmistakable impatience, dismissing the matter with a wave of her hand. "I am a dreamer too and you cannot even imagine what means I'm willing to use in my imagination when I let myself go! So enough of this—you only confuse me. I'm very glad that Tatyana left, for I very much wanted to see you alone; with her around we wouldn't have been able to speak to each other as we now are. I believe I'm to blame for what happened that time, don't you think so?"

"Who can blame you? That time I betrayed you to *him*. So what could you have thought of me then? I've been thinking of that ever since, every minute, thinking and feeling . . ." (I was telling the truth.)

"You could've spared yourself all that worrying. I know only too well how it all came about. You simply blurted out to *him* that you were in love with me and that . . . and that I was willing to listen to you. . . . Well, why not, you're not even twenty after all, so it is quite excusable. Besides, isn't he the most important person to you in the world, one whom you longed to have as your friend and whom you looked up to as an ideal? I understand it all too well. And then I was at fault too. I ought to have called you right away and set your mind at rest once and for all. But I was annoyed and ordered that you not be allowed into the house. And that led to the scene by the house entrance, and then that night. . . . Also, let me tell you that all this time I've been wanting to see you and talk to you secretly; only I didn't know how to arrange it. And what do you think I feared more than anything else? It was that you would believe the things he said against me."

"Oh, I'd never. . . ."

"I did enjoy our past meetings. I like your youth and perhaps your frankness too. . . . With others, you know, I am the most stern and unsmiling of women! I want you to remember that—" She laughed. "Well, we'll talk about it some other day, for now I don't feel too well, I'm overexcited and . . . and I believe I'm close to hysteria. . . . But now, at long last, *he* will allow me to live in peace!"

That last exclamation slipped out of her mouth unintentionally, as I at once felt. I tried not to show it, but it set me trembling violently all over.

"He knows I have forgiven him!" she cried out, again sounding as if she were talking to herself.

"Could you really forgive him for that letter? And how could he know you've forgiven him?" I said, no longer restraining myself.

"How could he find out? Oh, I'm sure he knows. . . ." She still seemed to be talking to herself and to have forgotten my presence altogether. "He's come to his senses now. Besides, how could he not know when he knows me inside out. . . . Why, he also knows that I'm a little like him in a way. . . ."

"You're like him?"

"Oh yes, and he knows it. Oh, I'm not as ardent as he is; I'm calmer, but, like him, I want everybody to be good. . . . For there must be something in me that attracted him."

"Then why does he say that you have all the vices?"

"He just says that. . . . And he has another secret, a personal one. . . . But don't you think he worded that letter in an awfully funny way?"

"You find it funny!"

I was eagerly catching every word she said. I suppose she really was in a state close to hysteria and quite unaware of my existence even while answering me. And I couldn't stop myself from throwing questions at her.

"Of course it was funny, and I can just imagine how I'd have laughed if . . . if I hadn't been so frightened. . . . I'm not so easy to scare, but that night I couldn't go to sleep. . . . I felt as if that letter had been written in blood, a sort of unhealthy blood. . . . And what's left after such a letter? . . . I love life; I'm horribly afraid for my life; in that respect I'm an awful coward. . . . Ah, listen," she suddenly focused her attention on me, "go to him. He's alone now. He can't still be there. He must have left, gone away all by himself. Find him quickly. Yes, you must hurry to find him. Run. Show him that you're a loving son, prove to him that you're a nice, kind boy, that you're my 'fellow student' whom I— Oh, may God send you happiness! I don't love anyone, and I think it's best that way, but I want everybody to be happy, everybody, and him above all, and I wish he knew it, knew it right now. . . . I'd like him to know it. . . ." Tears were glistening on her face, hysterical tears that had come in the wake of her laughter.

She got up and the next thing I knew she was gone, she'd vanished behind the heavy curtain. Alone there, I felt at a loss. I couldn't understand her emotional outburst; I'd never suspected her capable of anything like that. It was as if someone's hand had clutched at my heart.

I waited—five minutes, ten minutes. Suddenly I became aware of the total silence. I stuck my head out the door and called. The Finnish cook appeared and informed me in the most matter-of-fact tone that the lady had put on her fur coat and left through the service entrance a long time ago.

Chapter 7

I

That was all I needed! I grabbed my overcoat and rushed off. She wants me to go to him, I was thinking, struggling into my coat while running downstairs, but where was I supposed to look for him? And above everything else loomed the question: What had made her decide that something had changed and that he'd leave her in peace now? Apparently it was because he was going to marry Mother . . . but perhaps, on the contrary, that was just what made her feel miserable. Couldn't that have been the reason for her hysteria? Why couldn't I get to the bottom of this?

I note this last thought as it flashed through my mind because it is important. That evening had momentous consequences. Yes, there are things that seem to be preordained: before I had walked a hundred yards, toward Mother's house, I stumbled into the man I'd been looking for. In fact, it was he who stopped me, seizing me by the shoulder.

"There you are!" he exclaimed joyfully but at the same time quite surprised. "Just imagine, I've been looking for you at your place and elsewhere, wondering where I could get hold of you —you're the one person I wanted to see in the whole world!

Your landlord was blabbering something, but since he couldn't
tell me where you were I left in such a huff that I even forgot
to leave a message with him that you should come to the house
as quickly as possible. Nevertheless, I was absolutely certain
that fate could not fail to send you my way when you were indispensable to me. And now, lo and behold, you're the first person I see! Come with me to my place—you've never been there
before."

We'd been looking for each other and fate had brought us
together, giving both of us a similar strange feeling. We set off
rapidly toward Versilov's private quarters. On the way he only
told me that he'd left Mother with Tatyana. He lived quite
close by and led me to his place, his hand on my arm. It was
true I had never been to this small, three-room apartment he'd
rented, or rather that Mrs. Prutkov had rented, to house "the
baby." The apartment was still under Mrs. Prutkov's supervision. After the nurse and the baby had been installed, Daria
had come to live there too. But a room was always kept for Versilov, the one nearest the entrance door, a quite spacious and
adequately furnished room that looked like a study where a
person could read and write in comfort. There were many
books around, on the bookshelves, on the desk, all over the
place (there were practically no books in Mother's house), and
I also saw sheets of paper covered with writing and many letters
tied in bundles. Indeed, it looked like a well lived-in place and
I remembered that Versilov sometimes used to move in here from
Mother's house and occasionally (seldom) remained here for
weeks at a time.

The first thing that attracted my attention was a portrait of
Mother hanging over the desk. It was a huge photograph, obviously taken abroad, in an exquisitely carved wooden frame.
Judging by its size, it must have been very expensive. I had not
known of the existence of this portrait and I was struck by the
extraordinary likeness, I mean spiritual likeness, that made it
more like a painting than a mechanically produced print. When
I walked in, I couldn't help stopping in front of it.

"Isn't it . . . isn't it just . . . ?" Versilov came up behind me.

Probably he meant "Isn't it just like her?" I turned around
and was struck by his expression. He was rather pale at that
moment, but his eyes were glowing and intense. There was
great strength in his look. And happiness too. I'd never seen
that expression before.

"I had no idea you loved Mother so much," I blurted out,
also feeling overwhelmed with joy.

He smiled happily. I detected, however, a shadow of suffering in that smile, or rather something compassionate, reflecting feelings of a higher order—I don't know how to express it, but it is a fact that highly sophisticated people are incapable of having triumphantly happy and exultant faces. Instead of answering me, he took the portrait down from its hooks, brought it close to his face, kissed it, and gently hung it back on the wall.

"Observe," he said. "A photograph very rarely resembles the person. That stands to reason since the person only rarely resembles himself. It is only for brief moments that the human face expresses a person's most characteristic thought, a person's essence. An artist studies a face and discovers in it that essence so that, while he's painting, his model's features needn't express that essence at all. The photograph, on the other hand, catches a person at a random moment so chances are that, on some photographs, Napoleon may look stupid and Bismarck may look tender-hearted. Now, when this picture was taken, it luckily caught Sofia in one of those moments when her face, lighted by the sun, expressed her deep inner feelings: her timid, gentle love combined with her diffident, fierce purity. And she was so happy that day when she finally realized how much I wanted to have her portrait! And, although this picture isn't so very old, she does look younger and more beautiful in it. But you can already see those sunken cheeks and those wrinkles on her forehead, and that frightened, timid look—all these traits that have now been accentuated by the years and are growing even more pronounced as time goes by. Do you know, my dear boy, I can't imagine her with a face any different from what it is now, although it used to be so young and charming once. . . . Russian women lose their beauty quickly, it flashes past. And I'm sure this isn't because of any racial peculiarity but simply because they can love without any reservations. If a Russian woman loves a man, she'll give him everything at once: the present and the future, this particular moment and her whole life. She doesn't keep anything in reserve but throws everything into her love, and her beauty passes into the one she loves. And those hollow cheeks of hers, they're also part of that beauty that was consumed by me, during my short-lived infatuation. . . . You're glad I loved your mother and perhaps you didn't even believe I ever loved her? Yes, my boy, I did love her, although I haven't done anything for her except hurt her. . . . Here's another portrait you may want to look at. . . ."

He picked it up from the table and handed it to me. It was also a photograph, a much smaller one, in a narrow wooden oval frame. It was the portrait of a girl with a thin, consumptive face, but strikingly beautiful. The face looked lost in thought but at the same time somehow strangely blank. The regular features seemed to belong to the representative of a race pampered for generations, but the general impression it made was disturbing: it was as if something heavy and painful were weighing on the girl, painful because its weight was too much for her to bear.

"Is she the girl . . ." I muttered shyly, "the one you were to marry . . . but who died of consumption . . . is she *her* stepdaughter?"

"Yes, I was going to marry her, she died of consumption, and she was *her* stepdaughter. I knew you'd heard all those rumors. But I realize that, aside from those rumors, you couldn't possibly have found out anything. Put that picture down, my boy, she was just a poor mad girl and nothing more."

"Was she actually mad?"

"Yes, or perhaps just simple-minded . . . but I believe she was mad too. . . . She had a baby by Prince Sergei Sokolsky—a child of her insanity and not of her love, a consequence of one of Prince Sergei's most despicable deeds. Well, that child is here, in the next room, and I've been wanting to show it to you for a long time. Sergei has never been allowed to see the baby—that was the agreement we reached while we were both abroad. I decided to take care of the child with your mother's permission. And it was also with your mother's permission that I was going to marry that poor girl."

"How could she possibly have consented to such a thing?" I said with heat.

"She did. A woman can be jealous of another woman, but this poor creature was not a woman."

"She may not have been a woman for anybody else, but for Mother. . . . I'll never believe that Mother wasn't jealous of her!"

"Well, you're right. I realized that after everything was settled, after she'd given her consent. But let's drop that for now, since anyway there was no marriage because of Lidia's death. . . . Besides, even if she hadn't died, perhaps it wouldn't have worked out. As is, I still won't allow your mother to see the baby . . . But that was only one episode among many. . . . Ah, my boy, I've waited so eagerly for you to come here. I've been dreaming of this moment for a long time. . . . Shall I tell you exactly how long? Two years."

He looked at me with complete openness and sincerity and also with infinite warmth. I seized his hand.

"Why did you have to wait all that time? Why didn't you bring me here before? Ah, if only you knew all the things that would have happened and all the ones that wouldn't have if you'd brought me here sooner!"

At that moment a servant came in carrying a samovar, followed by Daria with the sleeping baby in her arms.

"Look at him," Versilov said. "I love him and I asked that he be brought in so you could have a look at him. All right, Daria, you may take him away now. . . . Come, move closer to the samovar. Let us pretend that we've always lived like this, without ever having been parted, and that every evening we get together as we're doing now. Let me look at you. Here, turn this way. Right. I want to see your face. If only you knew how often I tried to imagine what you looked like when I was waiting for you to arrive from Moscow! Now, you want to know why I didn't send for you long ago? Wait, perhaps you'll understand."

"How is it possible that Makar's death should suddenly have loosened your tongue? I find that very hard to understand."

But even as I was saying that, I was looking at him with love. We were talking like two friends, in the true, best meaning of the word. He had brought me here to clear up some misunderstandings, to justify himself, to find out something, but now everything had been cleared up and justified without any need for words. Whatever he chose to say to me now, the result was already achieved, and we both knew that, as we looked at each other.

"It was not really Makar's death, not just that. There's something else. . . . And may that moment and our lives be blessed for many years to come! . . . I want to talk to you, my boy; there's something I want to tell you but I keep wandering off the point and losing myself in mazes of irrelevant details. That's always how it is when the heart is too full. . . . But let's talk seriously now; the time has come for that and I have loved you for a long time, my boy. . . ."

He leaned back in his armchair and looked me over once again.

"It's so strange, I can't believe it, I can't believe it. . . ." I repeated in ecstasy.

But at that instant I suddenly saw that usual frown of his, a frown of sadness with a tinge of mockery in it, a frown I knew so well. Then he made an effort and began, perhaps a bit stiffly.

II

"You see, Arkady, if I'd called you here before, what could I've said to you? That question is my answer."

"Are you saying, then, that now you are Mother's husband and my father, while before . . . you didn't know before what to tell me about my legal status in society, is that it?"

"Not just that. I wouldn't have known what to tell you about many things and I'd have had to pass them over in silence. There's even much that is ridiculous and humiliating in it because it looks a bit like a trick, the sort of trick performed by a conjurer. But how could we have understood each other when I have been quite unable to understand myself until five o'clock this afternoon, which was exactly two hours before Makar died. I see you're looking at me as if you were unpleasantly surprised. Don't worry, I'll explain what I mean, but what I just said is absolutely true: a whole life is spent in doubt and perplexity and then suddenly the solution arrives on such and such a day at five in the afternoon! It's even vexing, isn't it? Not so very long ago it would have made me quite furious."

I was listening to him just as he'd said, with unpleasant surprise, looking at that familiar frown on his face that I'd hoped not to see after what had been said earlier in the evening. And suddenly a thought flashed through my head and I almost shouted:

"Good God! Did you hear something from *her* today at five?"

He looked at me fixedly. He was obviously amazed at my outcry and perhaps also at the way I'd said "from *her*."

"You'll learn about it in time," he said with a faraway smile, "and you may rest assured that I'll tell you everything you need to know because that's why I brought you here. I won't keep anything secret from you. But, just now, that can wait. You see, my friend, I've known for a long time that there are children who, from their very early years, brood about their parents and feel insulted by the ugly behavior of their fathers and the moral ugliness of their environment. I discovered such brooding children back in my own school days and I decided they were like that because they were prematurely envious. . . . But perhaps I decided that because I myself was a brooding child. . . . Forgive me, my boy, I keep wandering off the subject. . . . What I was trying to say was that I was worrying almost constantly about you during all that time. I'd always imagined you were one of those young creatures who are aware of their rich endowments and who try to withdraw into themselves. Just like

you, at school, I never liked other boys. So I know how hard life
is for those young creatures left to their own resources and daydreams and possessed by a passionate, precocious, and almost
vengeful longing for 'beauty,' yes, *vengeful*. But now I've
slipped off the subject once more. Even before I got to love you,
I imagined your solitary, wild daydreams. . . . Ah, I forgot
again what I was going to say. Still, I had to tell you that too.
. . . But what could I possibly have said to you before it happened? Now I can feel your eyes on me and I know that it's my
son who's looking at me. But only yesterday I couldn't believe
that one day I'd be sitting and talking with my own son. . . ."

Indeed, he appeared quite unable to fix his attention on any
particular line of thought. At the same time, he sounded
deeply stirred by something.

"There's no need for me to imagine things and to dream any
more. I have you and that's enough. I'll follow you wherever
you go," I said, giving myself to him totally.

"Follow me? But my wanderings are over. They just came
to an end today. You're a little late, my boy. Today is the finale
of the last act and the curtain will come down. That final act
has been going on for quite a while. It started long ago when
for the last time I rushed off abroad. That day, I swept aside everything that could hold me back, and I want you to know that
I'd decided to break off definitely with your mother and
told her so. Yes, I want you to know that. I told her that I
wouldn't be back and that she'd never see me again. But the
worst of it was that I even forgot to leave her money. Nor did
I give a thought to you. I left with the intention of settling in
Europe and never returning to Russia. I emigrated, you see."

"You went to join Herzen? To help spread revolutionary
propaganda from abroad? I bet you've been involved in political
conspiracies all your life!" I cried out, unable to restrain myself.

"No, my boy. I've never taken part in any political conspiracies. Ah, the way your eyes flashed at me! I do love your
way of exclaiming, my dear Arkady. But no, I left simply because I felt terribly depressed here and a moment came when
it was more than I could bear. It was the kind of deep depression
that's liable to afflict members of the Russian gentry. I really
don't know how to explain it any better—it was a gentleman's
depression, just that."

"Was it because of serfdom . . . of the emancipation of the
serfs?" I mumbled breathlessly.

"Serfdom, did you say? Do you really imagine that I couldn't
bear the emancipation of the serfs? Oh no, *we* were the

emancipators. I emigrated without any rancor. I had worked as an arbitrator between the landowners and their freed serfs; I devoted myself to that job quite disinterestedly and I certainly didn't leave the country because I felt that my liberalism had been insufficiently rewarded. None of us—I mean the people like myself—had anything to show for his efforts. I left out of pride more than because I regretted what had been done and, believe me, it never occurred to me to end up in life as a modest shoemaker. *Je suis gentilhomme avant tout et je mourrai gentilhomme!* But I did feel sad. There were only a thousand-odd people like me in Russia, I don't think there were more of us, but still that was quite enough to prevent the idea from dying. We are the bearers of the idea, my dear boy! Perhaps it is unreasonable of me to hope that you'll understand all these incoherent ravings of mine. I've brought you here because of a whim of my heart. For days and days I've longed to tell you certain things; yes, it had to be to you! Although I suppose that after all . . ."

"No, please go on! I can see by your face that now you're being sincere again. . . . So what happened then? Did Europe bring you back to life? And, anyway, what does it mean, a 'gentleman's depression'? Forgive me, but I don't quite follow you."

"You ask whether Europe brought me back to life. No, since I went there to bury it."

"To bury it?" I repeated, perplexed.

He smiled.

"My dear Arkady, my heart was weakened and my spirit perturbed. I'll never forget those first moments in Europe. I'd been to Europe before, but that time the circumstances were very special and never before had I gone there filled with such infinite sadness and . . . and such love. I'll tell you about one of the first impressions of that journey and of a dream I had then, I mean a real dream. It happened while I was still no further than Germany. I was about to leave Dresden, but in my absentmindedness at the railroad station I took the wrong train. The train stopped at about three in the afternoon at a station. I got off. It was a small German town. They recommended a hotel to me, since the train I was to take was not due until eleven o'clock at night. As it was a nice bright day and I was in no particular hurry to get anywhere, I felt pleased by that little adventure. I went wandering around the town and then went to the hotel, which was small and none too prepossessing but with plenty of trees and lots of flower beds all around, as the Germans always have. The room was small too. Having been up most of the previous night, I lay down on the bed and went to sleep at around four in the afternoon.

"I dreamed something completely unexpected. I'd never had such dreams before. In the Dresden museum there's a Claude Lorrain painting listed in the catalogue as 'Acis and Galatea,' but I somehow always called it 'The Golden Age.' I'd seen it before and had noticed it again three days earlier while walking through the museum. It was that painting that I saw in my dream but as a reality, not as a picture. I'm not quite sure, however, exactly what I dreamed about, but I saw a corner of the Greek Archipelago and time seemed to have moved back three thousand years or so. Blue, gentle waves, isles, rocky cliffs, a flowery coastline, the caressing sun setting in the background—the whole formed a fairy-tale scenery that words cannot convey. This was the cradle of Europe and that thought filled me with love and kindred feelings. This was the earthly paradise where gods descended from the heavens to mingle with men. . . . And what a beautiful race of men lived here! They rose in the morning and went to sleep at night, happy and innocent; the woods and meadows resounded with their joyful cries and songs; the great surplus of their untapped energy was spent on love and simple joys. The sun lavished its light and warmth on them, watching lovingly over its beautiful children. . . . A wonderful dream, the noble delusion of mankind! The Golden Age is an aspiration completely beyond the reach of men, but it's one to which they have devoted all their energies, for which they have willingly died, in the name of which they have killed their prophets, and without which they have no wish to live and do not even know how to die!

"And in that dream it was as though I myself had known all these feelings of mankind as I looked at the cliffs, the sea, and the slanting rays of the setting sun. And when I woke up, my eyes were actually wet with tears. I remember how elated I was. A feeling of happiness such as I'd never known before penetrated my heart so violently that it even hurt—it was the sensation of universal love encompassing all mankind. It was already late by then and penetrating through the flowers and the greenery outside my window was a cluster of slanting sunrays sprinkling me with light. And suddenly, my boy, the sun that in the dream was setting on the first day of European civilization turned, upon my awakening, into the sun setting on the last day of our era! Indeed, just then, things seemed to have reached a point when the death knell was about to resound all over Europe. Oh, it was not just the war that was going on, nor what had happened at the Tuileries— I'd always known that all that was fated to go, that the whole old European world would vanish sooner or later. But, being a Russian and a European myself, I couldn't accept the thought. . . . Besides, they'd only just set fire to the Tuileries. . . .

"Oh, you needn't worry, I knew that their act was 'logical' and I understood all too well how unassailable the current theories appeared to them. But, being the bearer of Russian culture and thought, I couldn't accept these theories because Russia's supreme intellectual contribution lies in the general reconciliation of all existing ideas. But who else in the world could possibly understand such a thought at that time? I was all alone. I'm not talking about myself, but about the Russian idea. Over there, there was nothing but logic and bickering. A Frenchman was just a Frenchman, a German nothing but a German, and more intensely so than ever before in history. And never had a Frenchman harmed France or a German Germany more than right then. At that moment, you couldn't find a single European in the whole of Europe! I was the only one who could've told those arsonists that setting fire to the Tuileries was wrong. And I was also the only one who could've explained to the conservatives, bent on revenge, that, although burning the Tuileries was a mistake, it was nevertheless a logical act. And I was in that position, my dear boy, because, being a Russian in Europe, I was the only European there. Understand, though, I'm not talking just of myself, I'm talking about the whole Russian way of thinking. I myself was roaming around from place to place, saying nothing, for I knew I had to remain silent and just wander around. But it did sadden me. You know, my boy, I can't help feeling respect for the Russian gentry of which I'm part. . . . That makes you laugh, I suppose, doesn't it?"

"No, it doesn't make me laugh," I said with feeling. "Not at all! I'm immensely impressed by your vision of the Golden Age, and I assure you I'm beginning to understand you now. Above all, though, I'm pleased that you have so much respect for what you are. Let me tell you also that I never expected that from you!"

"I do love your way of exclaiming, as I already told you," he said, smiling, obviously amused by my naïve enthusiasm. He got up from his armchair and started pacing up and down the room, apparently unaware of it himself. I got up too. He went on talking, deeply immersed in his thoughts but still putting things in that peculiar way of his.

III

"That's right, my boy, just as I said, I cannot fail to live up to my position as a member of the gentry. After generations and generations a certain cultural type has come into existence among us, a higher cultural type than has ever existed in the world before, a type filled with universal concern, a feeling for the whole world. This type is purely Russian, but since it is still confined to the upper cultural layers of the Russian nation, I have the honor of belonging to it. There are, perhaps, at the present time no more than a thousand representatives of that type, well, give or take a few; but, so far, Russia has existed in order to produce that thousand men. Some may say that it isn't very much to show for all those millions of people wasted throughout the centuries, but I believe it's not so negligible."

I listened to him with concentration. I was beginning to understand his position, his entire conception of what life was about. What he'd said about the "chosen thousand" revealed strikingly what he really was. I sensed that it was some external shock that had caused his present expansiveness with me. All this burning flow of ideas was being hurled at me in love, but I still couldn't understand what it was that had suddenly caused him to open up like this and why he'd chosen to speak of all people to me.

"So I emigrated," he went on, "without regretting anything that I'd left behind. As long as I'd been in Russia, I'd served my country to the utmost of my capacities and, after I left, I went on serving her, only in a different, broader sense. But that way I served Russia much better than if I'd remained just a Russian, like a Frenchman who can only be a Frenchman and a German who can only be a German. They still cannot understand that in Europe. Europe has produced noble types of Frenchmen, Englishmen, and Germans, but it still knows almost nothing about the man of the future. And apparently it doesn't even want to know. Well, it stands to reason: they aren't free in the sense we are. Filled with my Russian concern for the world, I was the only man in Europe then who was free.

"It's a strange fact, my boy: in order to serve mankind as a whole, and even just France for that matter, a Frenchman must remain thoroughly French. And the same goes for an Englishman or a German. Only a Russian—even as of today, that is, long before the existence of the ideal of universality—can reach

his utmost Russian essence solely when he also feels completely
European. And this is the most important difference between
us and all the others, for we are different from the rest. In
France I'm a Frenchman; with a German I'm a German; and
faced with an ancient Greek, I would feel like a Hellene. And
this way I, a true Russian, am serving Russia best by incarnating
her basic idea. I'm a pioneer of that Russian idea. Yes, I
emigrated, but did that really mean that I deserted Russia? No,
I went on serving her. Even if I did nothing in Europe but
roam around (and I knew that was all I was going to do), the
fact that I carried with me my Russian idea and my Russian
view of the world was a sufficient contribution in itself.

"I bore within me my Russian anguish about Europe. Oh, it
wasn't just the blood that was being shed at that time that depressed me, nor the burning of the Tuileries, but rather all the
things that were to follow. Those nations are doomed to go on
fighting for years to come because they're still too German and
too French and they haven't yet finished playing these roles. But,
in the meantime, I'm sad about the destruction that's going on.
To a Russian, Europe is just as dear as Russia and every stone
there is precious to him. Europe has always been our homeland
as much as Russia. In a way, even more so! I believe no one
loves Russia more than I do, but I've never felt guilty for feeling
that Venice, Rome, and Paris—with all their treasures of art
and human achievement, with all their history—are dearer to
me than Russia. Oh, how dear are those ancient foreign stones,
those marvels of God's world, those relics of holy miracles to the
Russians! Indeed, they are dearer to us than to them, the natives
of those lands. Their thoughts and feelings are no longer the
same and they no longer treasure their own ancient stones. . . .
Over there, the conservative merely fights back to preserve his
existence while the revolutionary incendiary acts only in the
name of his right to his share. Of all the countries in the world,
only Russia exists not just for her own sake but for the idea she
embodies, and I want you to note, my dear boy, that, for almost
a century now, Russia has lived not for herself alone but for
Europe as a whole! And the other nations? The rest of them
are doomed to go through dreadful ordeals before they gain
the Kingdom of God."

I must admit that I was rather confused. His tone too
frightened me, although I was certainly struck by his ideas.
The thing is, I was morbidly sensitive to false notes. Suddenly
I said sternly:

"You just mentioned the Kingdom of God. Is it true, then,

what I heard about you going around preaching and wearing chains?"

"As for the chains, that's another story and there's no need to go into it now." He smiled. "And I didn't actually preach anything, although it is true that I missed their God. For it was the time when they were proclaiming atheism. Of course, there were only a handful of them, a small advance party, still it was the first official manifestation, and that's why it was important. It was again the result of their logical thinking, but then logic always leads to despair. Being a product of another culture, however, my heart didn't accept it. Their callous scorn for the time-honored ideas they were discarding amidst catcalls and mudslinging was repulsive to me. The crudeness of the whole process frightened me, for stupid brutality will always be present, even among men striving for the loftiest ideals. Of course, I was aware of it. But I was different from them—I had the freedom of choice they did not have. So I could weep and I wept for their old idea, and, indeed, I may have actually wept real tears and I'm not saying this just to be dramatic."

"Is that how strongly you believed in God?" I asked incredulously.

"I don't think the question is very relevant, my dear boy. Even assuming my faith was not so very strong, I still couldn't help grieving for the loss of the idea. At times, I couldn't imagine how men would live without God or whether they'd be able to bear it. My heart always said they wouldn't, although they could probably survive for a limited period. . . . Well, I don't doubt that such a period is at hand. But, in this connection, I always imagined another picture. . . ."

"What picture?"

It's true that he himself told me that day that he was feeling happy and elated and that he was aware he was talking with great abandon. Well, that's just how I took much of what he said. Of course, out of respect for him, I will not repeat here everything he said, but I will jot down an outline of the strange picture I managed to obtain from him. What I most wanted to find out was about those chains he was supposed to have worn and that's why I kept insisting. But some of his rather fantastic and peculiar utterances will always remain engraved on my memory.

"In the picture I imagined," he said with a faraway smile, "all the battles have been fought and the struggle is over. After the curses, the mudslinging, and the catcalls, quiet has descended on the world where men have been left on their own, just as they wished. Their former great idea is no longer there and the great source of strength that till then nourished and warmed them is now sinking away like the majestic sun setting in Claude Lorrain's painting. But in my own picture this may well be mankind's last day. Men have suddenly realized that they have been left on earth completely alone and they feel like abandoned children. You know, my dear boy, I have never been able to imagine men turning into ungrateful and stupid animals. Abandoned, they immediately draw together more closely and more lovingly; they clutch one another's hands, realizing that now they are all that is left to one another! With the great concept of immortality gone, they have to replace it with something, and the immense reserves of love that before were lavished on Him who *was* immortality are now directed toward nature, the world, fellow men, every blade of grass. The more clearly they come to realize how transitory and finite their own existence is, the more ardently they grow to love the earth and life, and that special love is different from anything they've felt before. They start noticing and discovering in nature moments and secrets that they never suspected until then, because now they look at it with different eyes, with the eyes of a lover looking at his beloved. On awaking, they rush to kiss one another in their haste to love, constantly aware that the number of their days is limited and that there is nothing left for them when these days are spent. They work for one another and each of them gives up all he has, and this giving is happiness in itself. Every child knows and feels that everyone on earth is like a father or mother to him. 'Let this be the last day of my life,' every one of them thinks, gazing at the setting sun; 'it doesn't matter, for after I die they'll still be here, and after them there'll be their children. . . .' And the thought that those who will be left behind will always be as loving and as concerned for one another will take the place of the idea of everybody meeting again beyond the grave. Oh, they're in a hurry to love in order to stifle the great sadness in their hearts. They're proud and brave in exposing themselves to danger, but worried and full of concern for their companions, because everyone is anxious for the life and happiness of everyone else. They're tender with each other and they're not ashamed to express that tenderness, as people now are—they stroke and kiss one another like little children. When they meet they look at one another with deep, thoughtful understanding and in their eyes there is always love and sadness. . . ."

Suddenly he stopped and looked at me with a smile.

"Of course, all that's just a fantasy, my dear boy," he went on, "indeed, a rather wild fantasy. But I have imagined it all so often during my life that I don't think I could have gone on living without it. . . . Now I wasn't trying to tell you anything about my religious faith. As a matter of fact, my faith is quite limited: I'm a deist, a *philosophe*, I suppose, like the rest of our 'thousand' . . . although . . . Well, strangely enough, my fantasy almost never stopped there. It mostly ended with Heine's vision of 'Christ on the Baltic Sea.' I realized I couldn't manage without Him altogether and so, in the end, He appears in the midst of the abandoned men. He comes to them, holds out His hands to them, and says: 'How could you forget!' And at once, it's as if the scales fall from their eyes and they break out in a stirring hymn of their new and final resurrection. . . .

"But enough of that, my dear boy. As to those 'chains,' that's nonsense, you needn't even think about it. . . . And let me also tell you that, as a rule, I'm rather sober and reserved in what I say and that, if I let myself go this time, it's because of the state I am in and because I'm with you. I would never have spoken like this to anyone else. I'm just telling you that to reassure you. . . ."

I was deeply touched. There was nothing false in the way he said it and I was particularly pleased to know that throughout his life he had really grieved and suffered and had also loved a great deal. That was the most important to me, and enthusiastically I told him so. But then for some reason I added:

"But, you know, I still have the feeling that, despite your anguish and all that, you must've had a great time."

He laughed gaily.

"You keep hitting the bull's eye with your remarks today," he said. "Sure, I was having a great time, for how could I possibly have been unhappy with this anguish! No one can be freer and happier than a Russian wanderer belonging to the 'chosen thousand.' I really mean that, it's not just a joke. Besides, I would never have exchanged that anguish of mine for any other form of happiness. In that sense I've always been happy, my boy, always. And it was by being happy in that particular way that I came to love your mother. . . . It was the first time in my life . . ."

"What do you mean by the first time?"

"Just what I say. I was roaming around, filled with that anguish, and suddenly I knew I loved her in a way I'd never loved her before. So I immediately sent for her."

"Oh, tell me about that too, tell me about Mother!"

"But that's just why I've brought you here," he said with an amused smile. "As a matter of fact, I was afraid you'd forgiven me for your mother because of my attitude toward Herzen or my imaginary involvement in some sordid political conspiracy. . . ."

Chapter 8

I

Since we sat talking together late into the night, I won't attempt to repeat all that was said and will restrict myself to noting down the facts that shed light on a facet of Versilov that until then had remained a mystery to me.

Let me say first that I don't doubt for a moment that he loved my mother, although at one point he did desert her ("unmarried" her, as he put it). I suppose he'd become somewhat bored, which may happen to anyone but which is nevertheless always hard to analyze. After living quite a long time abroad, far away from Mother, his love for her suddenly came back, *in absentia* as it were, and he sent for her. I suppose some people would describe this as a whim, but I see it differently: I believe it was as important to him as anything can be in a man's life, and that despite his apparent self-indulgence, which I suppose I must acknowledge, at least partly. But I swear I have no doubts about his gift of feeling anguish for Europe's turmoils and in my eyes that capacity in itself is infinitely more important than any kind of practical competence put to use in such modern activities as, say, the construction of railroads. I recognize his love for mankind as an absolutely sincere and profound feeling, without any pretense, and his love for Mother as something beyond dispute, albeit perhaps somewhat implausible. And so, living abroad in "anguish and happiness" and, as I later learned from Tatyana Prutkov, in strict monastic chastity, he suddenly remembered my mother, particularly her "sunken cheeks," and at once sent for her.

"At one point I suddenly realized," he announced unexpectedly, talking about something else altogether, "that the fact that I was serving an idea did not release me, as a moral and rational creature, from my duty to make, in the course of my life, at least one person truly happy."

"Is it possible that such a literary notion was all there was to it?" I asked with disappointment.

"That's no literary notion," he said, "although I suppose you

may be right. Well, it was many different things at the same
time. . . . But I did love your mother really, sincerely, and it
was no literary love. If I hadn't, I wouldn't have sent for her
and, instead, would have tried to make happy any native
German, man or woman, who happened to be close at hand.
To make at least one fellow creature happy, I mean truly happy,
during one's lifetime—I would make that the binding duty of
every civilized person, just as I would make it the binding duty
of every Russian peasant to plant at least one tree in his lifetime
to counteract the deforestation of Russia . . . although one tree
in a lifetime might not be enough, so I'd rather make it one tree
a year. . . . But a highly educated man striving for a lofty ideal
may sometimes completely lose sight of what is around him and
become ridiculous, whimsical, and callous—not only in his
practical life, but ultimately even in his own theories. And so
the obligation to accomplish something real, such as making at
least one live person happy, would bring him back to his senses
and reset him on his proper course. As a theory, this may sound
quite preposterous now, but it wouldn't have been bad at all if
it had been put into practice and had become part of traditional
behavior. I have experienced it myself. As soon as I started for-
mulating my theory about that new commandment—at first,
of course, just as a joke—I suddenly realized the strength of my
love for your mother, of which I'd been quite unaware. Until
then, I'd never even known that I loved her. While I'd lived with
her, I'd enjoyed her as long as she was pretty and then I'd behaved like a spoiled brat. It was only in Germany that it dawned
on me that I loved her. It all started from her sunken cheeks that
I could not think of, or sometimes even look at, without pain,
I mean a real physical pain located in my heart. You know, my
boy, there are painful memories that cause us real physical pain;
almost everyone has such memories, but most people lose them.
. . . Still, it may happen that they suddenly remember perhaps
only one particular detail, but after that they cannot get it out
of their minds.

"I began to recall many details of my life with Sofia and
gradually they came back by themselves, invaded my mind by
the thousands, and almost smothered me while I was waiting
for her to arrive. What distressed me most was the recollection
of her constant submissiveness to me, of her deep-seated feeling
that she was my inferior in every respect, even—imagine—
physically. She felt embarrassed and would blush whenever I
happened to glance at her hands, which, true enough, were anything but aristocratic. But it was not only her hands that she

was ashamed of; she was ashamed of everything about herself, although it was her beauty that I loved. She'd always been fiercely modest with me, but what was worse was some sort of peculiar fear that I detected behind her modesty. In fact, she always felt that I couldn't possibly consider her as a human being and that it was almost indecent for her to be in my presence. At first, I thought that what frightened her was that she still looked upon me as the master and herself as the serf girl. But that wasn't it at all. At the same time, I assure you, I knew she could see my failings better than anyone else and, in general, I've never met a woman with a more perspicacious and subtle understanding. Oh, how miserable it made her when, while she was still beautiful, I demanded that she dress well. That made her suffer in her pride, of course, but above all because she felt she'd never be a lady whatever she put on and wearing elegant clothes would be like masquerading and would only make her look ridiculous. And, as a woman, she didn't want to be ridiculous, for she knew that every woman has her own style—something that hundreds of thousands of women cannot understand, apparently satisfied as long as they're dressed in the latest fashion! I'm sure it was my sarcastic look that she really feared.

"I recall with particular sadness the deep bewilderment I often saw in her eyes, a bewilderment that showed clearly how she felt about what was happening to her and how she feared the future; sometimes I myself would be depressed by that look in her eyes, although, I admit, I never talked to her about such things, for I never treated her as an equal. But let me tell you that she was not always as shy and retiring as she is today, although even now she may all of a sudden cheer up, turn pretty, and behave like a twenty-year-old. When she was young, she often liked to chat and laugh, in her own company, of course, with maids or the old ladies who inhabited the house. But whenever I happened to surprise her laughing, she'd invariably turn very, very red and look at me fearfully!

"Once, shortly before I went abroad, almost the day before 'unmarrying' her, I walked into her room. She was all alone, sitting at a little table. She wasn't doing anything. Her elbows were resting on the table and she was deep in thought. I'd never seen her sitting like that without work before. . . . By that time, I'd stopped showing her any affection at all. I succeeded in tiptoeing up to her so she didn't hear me and then suddenly I threw my arms round her and kissed her. She jumped to her feet and, you know, I'll never forget the rapture, the happiness, with which she looked at me. Then suddenly it all vanished, deep color rose to her cheeks, and her eyes flashed. Do you know what I read in those eyes of hers then? It was: 'This is just a handout, just like giving a kopek to a beggar!' And she burst into hysterical sobs, explaining later that it was because I'd surprised and frightened her, but even at that time it made me think.

"Yes, Arkady, my friend, this sort of memory is always painful. It is like certain 'painful' scenes in the works of great writers that throughout our lives hurt us when we think of them—for instance, the final monologue of Shakespeare's Othello, Pushkin's Eugene Onegin at the feet of Tatyana, or the scene in Victor Hugo's Les Misérables where the escaped convict meets the little girl. Once they have clawed at your heart, the scar will always be there. . . .

"Oh, how I waited for Sofia, how I longed to hold her in my arms! With what wild impatience I planned a whole new life for us—how, gradually and methodically, by patient effort, I'd dispel the constant fear she had of me, how I'd make her become aware of her own real worth and point out to her the many aspects in which she was my superior! Oh, I knew only too well that I always began to love your mother as soon as we parted and turned cold toward her the moment we were together again. But this time it was not that, it was something quite different."

I found it all very strange and kept wondering how she felt.

"So how did you and Mother meet that time?" I asked cautiously. "What happened?"

"That time? That time we didn't meet at all. She just got as far as Königsberg and stayed there while I was on the Rhine. I didn't join her where she was. Instead, I asked her to wait for me there. We saw each other again only much later, very much later, when I went to ask for her consent to my marriage. . . ."

II

I shall explain only the most essential facts, that is, facts that I was able to put together myself from Versilov's later account, which became strangely incoherent. Indeed, when he passed this point, his narrative suddenly all but disintegrated.

It was when he was waiting so impatiently for Mother to arrive that Katerina Akhmakov appeared on the scene. They were all on the Rhine, at some spa or other, all taking mineral water cures. Katerina's husband was already almost dying or, at any rate, he'd been sentenced to death by his doctors. The very first time Versilov saw her, he was under her spell. It was "fate." What strikes me now as I try to remember how he described it all to me is that he never used the word "love," never spoke of "falling in love." But the word "fate," I remember very well.

And certainly it was fate. It was *not his choice,* he did not want to love. I'm not sure I can make it clear, but his whole being was outraged that such a thing could have happened to him. All the freedom he'd had before he met her was destroyed and he was chained to a woman who had no particular interest in him. He did not choose to be a slave to his passion. I'll say plainly: Katerina is a rare species of aristocratic woman, a species so rare that perhaps it no longer exists in high society: a completely straightforward and natural woman. I've heard it said about her and I know myself that this is what made her so irresistible in society, that is, on the occasions when she chose to appear there (because she stayed away from society for long periods at a time). Of course, after their first meeting, Versilov refused to believe that she was all that; indeed, he suspected just the opposite, namely, that she was a hypocrite and a Jesuit. Here, anticipating, I will quote what she herself said about that judgment of his: "He couldn't help thinking the way he did. Like every idealist, as soon as he knocks his head against reality, he assumes at once that there's some horrid trick behind it." Well, I don't know whether her words really apply to all idealists, but I'm sure they fit him perfectly. I may also add here the thought that flashed through my head while I was listening to him: I assumed that he loved Mother with the abstract, humanitarian love that one feels for mankind as a whole rather than with the simple love that a man must feel for a woman; so that the moment he met a woman for whom he felt that simple love, he refused to recognize it, probably partly from lack of experience. But perhaps I was wrong and, of course, I didn't express any opinion. It would have been indiscreet to start with. Besides, he was so wound up that I had to be careful not to hurt him now: his agitation was so violent that, at certain points in his narrative, he suddenly stopped and remained silent for several minutes, pacing the room with a spiteful expression on his face.

Very soon Katerina divined his secret. Indeed, perhaps she deliberately led him on because even the noblest of women can be underhanded in such cases. Such is their incurable instinct. It ended in exasperation and an explosion. I believe he wanted to kill her and gave her an awful fright. . . . In fact, he might have killed her, but then, in his words, "it just turned into cold hatred." After that he went through a strange period: he suddenly decided to subject himself to a regime of suffering.

"You know, the way monks do—the systematic practice whereby they gradually learn to control their will. They start with the most ridiculously trivial things, but in the end they conquer their will and thus gain their freedom."

He explained to me that this monastic practice is an effective method, evolved in the course of a thousand years of experience, and that it can now be considered a science.

What is remarkable, though, is that he did not decide to subject himself to discipline in order to rid himself of Katerina, because by then he was fully convinced that he not only didn't love her but indeed felt a violent hatred for her. Moreover, he believed in that hatred so thoroughly that he decided to fall in love with her stepdaughter, who had been seduced by Sergei, and to marry her. He succeeded in convincing himself of that new love of his and in conquering the heart of the poor simple-minded creature so thoroughly that he made the last months of her life unmitigated bliss. However, it still remains unclear to me why, instead of devoting himself to the poor imbecile, he didn't give a thought to my mother, who was waiting for him in Königsberg. In fact, he must have forgotten Mother altogether, since he even stopped sending her money to live on so that Tatyana Prutkov had to rush to her rescue. When, finally, he did go to Königsberg to see Mother, it was only to ask her consent to his marriage to the girl, explaining that "such a bride is not a woman." Well, possibly all this was behavior typical of a "literary intellectual," as Katerina later characterized him. But then how could these "paper people"—if that is really what they were—suffer so deeply and work themselves into such tragic predicaments? That evening I felt somewhat differently on the subject and suddenly a thought struck me:

"Why is it," I said, "that you had to pay for your moral regeneration, indeed, for your very soul, with a life of struggle and suffering whereas Katerina, she got her perfection for free, without having to pay anything for it? That's quite unfair. That's revolting. . . ." I hadn't meant to please him in saying that; I'd spoken with heat, even indignation.

"Perfection? Her perfection? But there's nothing perfect in her at all," he said, apparently surprised at my evaluation. "She's just an ordinary woman, and perhaps even a rotten one at that. . . . But it's her duty to be perfect in every sense."

"Why is it her duty?"

"Because, with the power she has, it's her duty to be perfect," he said impatiently.

"What's so terrible is that it makes you miserable even now," I blurted out. I hadn't intended to say that.

"Miserable? Even now?" he repeated my words. He ceased pacing up and down the room and stopped, looking at me with surprise. Gradually a slow, distant smile lighted up his features and he held up one finger as if working something out. Then, snapping out of it completely, he picked up an open letter from his desk and tossed it to me.

"Here, read this. I want you to know everything. . . . Ah, why did you have to make me rake up all that old muck? It only brought out the nastiness and spite in me."

I'm quite unable to convey the astonishment I felt. It was from *her* to him. He'd received it earlier that day, around five in the afternoon. As I read it, I almost shivered with emotion. It was only a brief note and it was written with such directness and frankness that, while reading it, I felt as if I were looking at her and hearing her voice. Most unaffectedly, and hence most touchingly, she admitted her fear of him and begged him: "Leave me in peace." She concluded by informing him that she had definitely decided to marry Björing. This was the first time she'd ever written to him.

And this is what I was able to make out of his explanations.

When he'd read the letter upon receiving it earlier that day, he'd suddenly realized with surprise that, for the first time in those two turbulent years, he did not feel any hatred for her, nor anything like the shock that had all but driven him out of his mind when he'd first heard about Björing. "As a matter of fact, I sent her my best wishes and my blessings with complete sincerity," he told me with deep feeling. I registered his words with elation. This meant that all the passions and torments that had been inhabiting him until then had vanished, like a two-year-long obsessive dream. Still unable to believe altogether in his liberation, he rushed to see Mother and arrived at the house precisely at the moment she too became *free,* when the old man who had bequeathed her to him died. And it was the coincidence of these two events that had shaken him to his very foundations. Shortly after that, he'd gone out to look for me, and I'll never forget that he thought of me so soon.

Nor will I ever forget how that evening ended. Again, here was a complete change in him. We sat up until very late. Later, I'll recount how all this news affected me personally, but now I must say a few more words about him. When I analyze it now, I see that what charmed me most in him was his humble sincerity with me, a mere adolescent!

"It was a delusion," he said, "but may that delusion be blessed! Without it I would never have found out how totally and eternally my heart belongs to my sole ruler, to my long-suffering beloved—your mother."

I record literally the passionate words wrung out of him by emotion, because of what was to happen later. But at that moment he gained my undivided love and admiration.

I remember that gradually we became exuberantly happy and he sent for some champagne and we drank to Mother and to the happy future. Oh, how full of vitality he was and how ardently he was looking forward to a new life! And our exuberant happiness was brought on not by what we drank because we only had a couple of glasses each. Still, it got so that we couldn't stop laughing. We talked about all sorts of extraneous things; then he began to tell me funny stories and I told him some too. There was nothing wicked or even sarcastic about the stories we told each other that night; they were just funny and made us laugh. Every time I said it was time for me to go home, he insisted I stay a little longer and I stayed on. And when I finally decided to go home, he came to see me off a little way. It was a beautiful night, brisk, just below freezing. As I was taking leave of him at a street corner, still holding his hand in mine, I asked him quite casually:

"You've already sent *her* the answer to that letter, haven't you?"

"No, not yet, but it makes absolutely no difference. . . . Come back here tomorrow. Come early. . . . And also send Lambert to hell and destroy that 'document' of yours, destroy it at once. Good night."

He turned away abruptly and walked off. I remained standing where I was. I was too confused to think of running after him. His use of the word "document" had given me a jolt. Where could he have heard of it except from Lambert? I arrived home in a state of utter turmoil. Besides, it now seemed incredible to me that his "two-year-long obsessive dream" could have vanished so suddenly like a mirage, a phantom.

Chapter 9

I

Still, I woke up in the morning feeling refreshed and cheered. I couldn't help reproaching myself a little for what seemed to me now the smugness and even condescension with which I'd listened the night before to certain passages of his "confession." What if it had all sounded rather disconnected, at times even incoherent, and some of his "revelations" downright confused? Why shouldn't they, since he certainly hadn't prepared himself to deliver a smooth piece of oratory? Indeed, he had done me a great honor by confiding in me at such a moment as his only friend, and that is something I'll never forget. As a matter of fact, his confession had "touched me" (and let them laugh at me for using this sentimental expression) and, if there were overtones of cynicism or even sarcasm in it here and there, there was enough of that "breadth" in me to make me understand and accept his "realism" without it in the least detracting from his idealism. What was important is that I had finally gained insight into the man, although, paradoxically, I felt almost disappointed that it all turned out to be simple. In my esteem, Versilov dwelled high, beyond the clouds, and that communicated a mystery to everything touching him. So it was, after all, natural that I should find it a little disappointing that unwrapping the enigma had proved no harder than it had. From what I gathered, however, his relations with *her* and the two years of ordeal that had followed had had their share of complexity: he had refused to submit to the bondage of fate; what he'd wanted was not submission to his fate but freedom; it was this bondage to fate that had forced him to hurt my mother who had been waiting for him in Königsberg. . . . Moreover, I saw in him a man with a message: he carried the Golden Age in his heart and he *knew* where atheism could lead. But the moment he'd met Katerina, everything in him had been shattered and distorted. Oh, it's not that I was betraying her, but I had to be on his side. Mother, for instance, I reasoned with myself, would not have interfered with his "fate," nor for that matter would it have changed anything if he'd been married to Mother. That much I understood. But his meeting with *her*—that was something else. It's true that Mother would never have left him in peace either, or allowed him to be calm and contented, but that's as it should be, since people like him must be judged by different standards and they're destined to live differently from others. I'm not saying that their lives are bound to be disorderly and ugly; on the contrary, I feel it would be improper and ugly if they settled down and wound up resembling ordinary people. Versilov's high opinion of the social elite and his words *"je mourrai gentilhomme"* did not disconcert me in the least; I realized what sort of *gentilhomme* he considered himself to be—a man ready to give up everything to become the herald of universal citizenship and the disseminator of the Russian idea that "unites the ideas of every nation." And even if all that turned out to be utter nonsense (I mean the uniting of all national ideas, which appears quite unthinkable), even then I find it admirable that all his life he worshiped an idea rather than worshiping the stupid golden calf! And, thank God, when I myself conceived *my idea,* it was certainly not the worship of the golden calf, for it was obviously not really money that I was after! I swear, all I wanted was the idea! I swear that even if I had a hundred million rubles I would never have one single armchair or sofa upholstered with velvet and would eat the same meals of soup and beef as I do now!

I dressed in a hurry because I was impatient to see him. And let me add that the fact that he'd used the word "document" didn't worry me nearly as much as it had the previous night. In any case, I hoped to discuss everything with him, even if Lambert had managed to get to him and had told him about certain things. I no longer saw why I should be so upset by whatever Lambert may have told him. But the main source of my joy was located in one momentous fact: he did not love *her.* I believed that unquestioningly and it was as though someone had lifted a horrible weight off my chest. I remember a thought that flashed through my mind as I was dressing: the ugly and senseless fury of his explosion upon learning about *her* engagement to Björing and his sending of that insulting letter, indeed the very violence of his reaction, all could have been a sign of the forthcoming radical change in his feelings and of his rapid return to sanity. It was almost like an illness, I thought, just a pathological episode, and now the reaction must be coming. . . . That thought filled me with joy.

"Let *her* do what she wants with her life, let her marry her dear Björing, just as long as he—my father and my friend—doesn't love her!" I kept exclaiming aloud.

I also had certain other, private feelings, but I don't care to enlarge upon them here. Well, enough of this. I'll just give now, without any further comment, the ensuing sequence of events that culminated in the horrible scene.

II

At ten, when I was just about ready to go out (to see Versilov, of course), Daria appeared with a message for me. I asked her hopefully whether it was from him, but to my great disappointment I learned that it was from Anna and that Daria herself had "left the house at daybreak."

"What house?"

"Why, the one where you were yesterday. That apartment, you know, was rented in my name and it's Mrs. Prutkov who's paying the rent."

"Well, all that's none of my concern," I said impatiently, "all I want to know is whether Mr. Versilov is still at home so I can find him there."

To my great surprise, she told me that he'd left even earlier than she had, which must have been very early indeed since she herself had left at "daybreak."

"So he may be back by now."

"No, I'm pretty sure he's not back, and he may very well never come back at all," she said, watching me with that same sharp and furtive expression that she'd had when she'd come to see me while I was ill.

What infuriated me most was all these idiotic secrets and intrigues, without which these people apparently couldn't live.

"What makes you say he probably won't be back? What do you mean by that? I bet he just went to see my mother."

"I . . . I don't know . . ."

"And what have you come for?"

She said it was Anna who'd sent her to tell me that she was at home, waiting for me, that I must come right away "because otherwise it might be too late." That mysterious warning made me lose my temper completely.

"Too late for what? Suppose I don't feel like seeing her? I have no intention of letting them use me again! Just tell her that I don't give a damn about Lambert and that if she sends him to me, I'll kick him out. Tell her just that."

Daria looked horrified.

"No, no, please . . ." She took a step toward me and clasped her hands beseechingly. "Please, don't be so hasty; it's very important—for you and for Miss Anna and also for Mr. Versilov and for your mother too, it's important for everyone. . . . So be so good as to see Miss Anna right away, for she can't wait much longer. . . . You'd better go, I swear you'd better. . . . After that you can decide for yourself what to do next."

I stared at her in astonishment and disgust.

"Rubbish! Nothing will happen! I'm not going!" I shouted stubbornly, almost enjoying her worried face. "Everything is different now! So good-by, Daria. I'm not going, just to show her I'm not at her disposal, and if I'm not asking you for any explanations, it is because I couldn't care less. Your silly stories only create confusion and I have no desire to know your secrets."

Since she made no gesture to leave but just stood there, I grabbed my coat and hat and rushed out of the room, leaving her behind. As a rule, I never kept any letters or papers in my room, for I always left it unlocked while I was out. But before I'd even reached the ground floor, I saw my landlord, hatless and coatless, rushing downstairs after me.

"Mr. Dolgoruky! Mr. Dolgoruky!"

"What is it now?"

"Don't you have any instructions for me before you leave?"

"No."

He looked extremely worried. His eyes were riveted on me.

"Concerning your room, for instance?"

"What about my room? I paid you the rent in time, didn't I?"

"I wasn't thinking about money. . . ." He suddenly smiled broadly, although his eyes were still fixed on me.

"What is it, then, you wish?" I shouted, wild with fury. "What the hell do you want of me?"

He withstood my blast and waited a few seconds more as if still expecting me to say something to him.

"Well, I suppose you're not in the right mood, so you'll give me instructions later," he muttered, as his smile widened even further. "Go in peace then; in the meantime I'll attend to things myself."

He ran back upstairs. No doubt, all this should have made me stop and think. I'm deliberately reporting every detail of all that nonsensical sequence of events, for every detail was like one more line added to a drawing whose importance would become apparent only in the final picture. But at the time these details seemed to make no sense whatsoever. And if I became so excited and irritated, it was because I detected behind certain words the implied existence of secrets and intrigues which reminded me of the past and with which I was fed up to the teeth. But let me get on with my story.

Just as Daria had said, Versilov was out, and it was also true that he'd left while it was still dark. "I'm sure he went to see Mother," I decided stubbornly. I didn't bother to question the nurse, who was an extremely stupid woman, and she was the

only adult there. I rushed off to Mother's, and I was so full
of anxiety that, when I was already halfway there, I jumped
into a cab to get there a little sooner.

I learned that he hadn't been at Mother's since the day before. I found only Mrs. Prutkov and Lisa with Mother, and
as soon as I arrived, Lisa said she had to leave. They were sitting
in my former attic, "the coffin," because in the living room
Makar was laid out on a table and over him some old man was
reading from a psalter in a singsong voice. Although I decided
not to describe anything unless it had a direct bearing on my
story, I will nevertheless remark that the black coffin, which
was already there, was not at all a plain one despite its color—
it was upholstered with velvet—and also that the pall was of a
sumptuousness not at all in keeping with the convictions or the
character of the deceased. But that was in compliance with the
insistent wishes of both Mother and Mrs. Prutkov.

Obviously I hadn't expected to find them in a cheerful mood,
but the oppressive atmosphere, which could be felt at once,
and the despair I read in their eyes warned me that probably
there was something besides sadness about Makar. As I said, I
remember all this with absolute clarity.

I embraced Mother tenderly and at once inquired about Versilov. She gave me an alarmed, questioning look. I told her that
I'd been with him the whole evening till late last night, that
he'd asked me to come back today, *as early as possible,* but
that today I found he'd left before dawn. Mother said nothing
and Tatyana, after a minute or so, only shook her finger at me.

"I must go now, Arkady, good-by," Lisa said suddenly. She
got up and walked out of the attic. It goes without saying that
I rushed out after her. She stopped by the front door.

"I hoped it would occur to you to follow me," she said in a
hurried whisper.

"What's going on, Lisa?"

"I'm not sure, but it looks like all sorts of things. . . . I
suppose it's still that same old story. He hasn't been here. They
seem to know something. But if you're wise, you won't ask them
any questions. Anyway, I'm sure they won't tell you. All I know
is that Mother is completely shattered. I myself didn't ask them
anything. . . . Well, I must be on my way."

She opened the door.

"And what about you, Lisa, has anything new happened?"
I asked, rushing after her.

There was so much misery and hopelessness in her that it
broke my heart. She looked at me with something like spite,

perhaps with callousness; a jaundiced smile twisted her lips, and she waved her hand in despair.

"I wish to God he were dead!" she flung at me from outside and was gone.

She'd said that about Sergei, who was then lying unconscious in the prison hospital. . . . "What same old story?" I thought angrily, and suddenly I felt an impulse to tell them all how I felt about Versilov's confession I'd heard the night before and, indeed, perhaps repeat what he'd told me. "If they think evil of him now," the thought flashed through my head, "let them know the whole truth!"

I remember that, very cleverly, I found a good pretext and started telling them what I wanted. They listened with intent curiosity. This time Mrs. Prutkov bore into me with her eyes. Mother was more restrained. Grave as she was, a faint, delicate, but somehow utterly hopeless smile appeared at one point on her lips and remained there almost all the time I was talking. I'm sure I spoke with eloquence, although I knew they wouldn't understand much of what I was saying. Against all expectations, Mrs. Prutkov didn't heckle me, didn't ask me to stick to the point, and didn't try to trip me with tricky questions, as she usually did whenever I opened my mouth. She just kept pressing her lips together and screwing up her eyes as if following what I was saying demanded a considerable effort on her part. At certain moments I had the impression they understood everything, but that was well nigh impossible. I told them, for instance, about his views on the world, about the state of elation he was in last night, about his admiration for Mother, about the kind of love he had for her, about his kissing her portrait. Now and then, they'd exchange quick glances and Mother's face would flush, but neither of them said anything. Then . . . then, of course, I couldn't talk *in Mother's presence* about his meeting Katerina and all the rest up to the most important point, that is, the letter he'd just received from *her* and his moral regeneration that followed. . . . Yes, that was certainly the most important, but since I couldn't mention it, everything he'd confessed to me about his feelings, which I was sure would make Mother happy, obviously remained beyond her understanding. Well, it was certainly not through any fault of mine: all I could tell in her presence, I told well and eloquently.

When I'd finished, they still said nothing. At first I found their silence perplexing. Then their very presence began to weigh on me.

"Perhaps he has come back from wherever he was and is waiting for me in my room," I said and got up.

"Why, of course, go ahead, go," Mrs. Prutkov eagerly encouraged me.

"Have you been in the living room?" Mother asked in a whisper, as I was taking leave of her.

"Yes, I've paid my respects to him and prayed for him. He looks so calm, so beautiful. . . . I also want to tell you how much I appreciate your not sparing any expense for his coffin. At first it struck me as inappropriate, but then I felt I'd have done the same thing. . . ."

"Will you come to church tomorrow?" she asked, her lips quivering.

"How can you ask me that, Mother? I'll be back here today, for the requiem service, and again after that. Obviously I'll come tomorrow. . . . Besides, it'll be your birthday. . . . Ah, he didn't quite make it, he died three days before. . . ."

I was painfully surprised. What a question—whether I'd be present at the funeral service in the church! If that's what they think of me, what must they imagine about Versilov!

I knew Mrs. Prutkov would come out after me, so I deliberately stopped and waited for her at the front door. As I expected, she appeared soon enough, but, instead of stopping there, she pushed me all the way through the door, followed me out, and closed the door behind us.

"What's happening, Mrs. Prutkov? Don't you expect to see him either today? Or even tomorrow? I'm so worried. . . ."

"Shut up. Who cares whether you're worried or not! Now I want you to tell me whatever you kept back upstairs in your great stories about last night."

There was no reason for me to hide anything from her and, feeling somehow unaccountably irritated with Versilov, I told her about the letter he'd received from Mrs. Akhmakov, about the moral regeneration it had brought about in him, and about the new life he'd resolved to begin now. To my amazement, I saw she didn't react at all when I mentioned the letter and realized she must have known about it already.

"You do talk a lot of rubbish, don't you?"

"No, I don't."

"So he's morally regenerated, ha!" she said with a venomous smile, as if weighing what I'd told her. "Regenerated, indeed! I wonder what he'll come up with next! But is it true that he kissed that portrait?"

"It's true."

"Did he seem sincere or was he putting on an act?"

"Putting it on? As though he ever tried to put on an act! You ought to be ashamed of yourself, Mrs. Prutkov—you have a crude mind, a typical woman's mind!"

I spoke with heat, but she didn't even seem to hear what I said; she seemed to be completely immersed in her thoughts and calculations, unaware even of how drafty and cold it was. I, at least, had an overcoat on whereas she had nothing but a dress.

"I'd ask you to do something but I'm afraid you're too stupid," she said with scorn and annoyance. "Still, listen, run over to Anna's and find out what's happening there. . . . No, perhaps better not, ah, you dummy, you! . . . Well, what are you waiting for, standing there like a post? Get going!"

"I have no intention of going to Anna's! Besides, she already sent for me herself."

"She sent for you herself? Who did she send—Daria?" Mrs. Prutkov, who'd already opened the door to go back into the house, quickly turned around, closed the door, and faced me again.

"I don't want to go to Anna's," I repeated, enjoying my rebellion, "and I won't go if only because you just called me a dummy when, in actual fact, I've never been so perspicacious as today. I can see through you as if you were transparent, ma'am, and still I'm not going!"

"I knew it all along!" she cried out again, ignoring my last words, taking in only what interested her. "They'll get her completely entangled in their nets and then just tighten the noose around her neck. . . ."

"Who? Anna?"

"Idiot!"

"Who are you talking about then? Could it be Katerina by any chance? And what do you mean by the noose around her neck?"

I felt terrified. A vague but horrible thought flashed through me. Tatyana was digging into me with her eyes.

"I'll tell you, I'll tell you a frightful secret, Mrs. Prutkov, but not just now, because there's no time now. . . . I'll tell you everything tomorrow, just you. But then you must tell me the truth, everything, and what you meant by that noose . . . because . . . because I can't get hold of myself, you see I'm trembling. . . ."

"Who cares whether you're trembling or not! And what's this new secret you're planning to tell me tomorrow? Do you really not know then?" She glared at me probingly. "You swore to her yourself that you'd burned Kraft's letter, didn't you?"

"Stop it, Mrs. Prutkov, stop torturing me," I went on, like her, ignoring what I didn't choose to answer because I was beside myself with worry. "Look, Mrs. Prutkov, if you persist in keeping something from me, you may only make things worse . . . because . . . because last night he was like a completely regenerated man. . . ."

"Ah, get out of my sight, you clown! I can see that you're in love up to your gills with Katerina yourself! Who's ever heard of such a thing—father and son sharing their love object! You're disgusting, both of you!"

She rushed inside and slammed the door behind her. Enraged by the shameless, crude cynicism of her last words, a cynicism so typical of a woman, I ran off, swallowing the insult. I won't describe all the misty thoughts and feelings inside me but shall content myself with reporting facts because the facts will make everything clear.

Of course, I stopped over at his apartment and the nurse again told me that he was out.

"Isn't he ever coming back?"

"God knows," she said.

III

I know I promised to stick to facts, but what about the reader? How much will he understand of what's going on? I still remember how puzzled I was myself by those facts, how little sense I could make out of them from the start, and how eventually I became completely befuddled by them. Therefore I guess I'd better set a few things straight in advance.

The thought that was tormenting me was this: If he was really spiritually regenerated and now free of his passion for *her*, where would he most likely be at this moment? The obvious answers would be: either with me, whom he was hugging last night, or with Mother, whose portrait I had seen him kiss. But he was neither with Mother nor with me. Instead, he'd left the house before daybreak, vanished into thin air, and that woman Daria even said that he probably wouldn't be back at all. On top of that, Lisa had let me understand that finally "that same old story" was coming to some sort of a denouement and that Mother might know something about the very latest developments. I also gathered they all knew about Katerina's letter to him and, although they'd listened with interest when I'd told them about his regeneration, they had not believed in it: Mother still looked drained of all hope and Mrs. Prutkov nastily poked fun at the very phrase "moral regeneration." But if they were right, that could only mean that the catharsis and spiritual exaltation I had witnessed had been followed later that night by some sort of diabolical upheaval, that his "regeneration" had burst like a soap bubble, and that he might be roving around seething with hatred, as he had when he'd first heard about *her* engagement to Björing. If so—what would become of Mother? And of me? Yes, of all of us, and also of . . . of *her*? And what was that noose Mrs. Prutkov mentioned when she was trying to send me to Anna's? Did she mean that "the noose" was at Anna's? Why at Anna's? Anyway, I had to go and find out! It was only because I was so annoyed that I had refused to go to Anna's before. Now I'd run there as fast as I could! But what had Mrs. Prutkov said about the "document"? And hadn't *he* himself told me the night before to burn it?

So these were the thoughts that were choking me too like a noose. But, above all, I felt I had to see *him,* for between the two of us we'd immediately know what to do, we'd understand each other with few words. . . . I'd seize his hands and I'd find the right words in my heart. . . . These heart-warming thoughts poured out of me irresistibly. Oh, I was sure I could have helped him overcome his madness! But where was he now, where . . . ?

Ah, damn it, why did I have to stumble on Lambert just then when I was feeling overcome by all these thoughts? Just a few steps from my door, I saw Lambert. He let out a joyful yell and seized my hand.

"*Enfin!* This is the third time I've come looking for you. Come on, let's go and have lunch together!"

He was rolling his French *r*'s in his throat.

"Wait! Were you upstairs in my room? Was Mr. Versilov waiting for me?"

"There was nobody waiting for you. Anyway, you can forget the lot of them! What came over you yesterday? Why did you suddenly get mad at me, you fool? Well, I guess you were just drunk. . . . I have some important news for you today, very good news, you know, connected with those things we were talking about. . . ."

"Listen, Lambert, if I stopped now, it was only to tell you that I'm through with you." I was in a terrible hurry and had difficulty in controlling my breathing. Nevertheless I detected something theatrical in my own tone. "I told you yesterday, although you still don't seem to understand, that you've never grown up, Lambert, you stupid Frenchie. You still imagine that things are just the same between us as they were at Touchard's and that I'm still as naïve as I was then. I wasn't drunk last night, it was not the wine. I had my own reason to feel excited and if I pretended to agree with you it was just a stratagem on my part—to find out what you had on your mind. I was leading you on and you were taken in and poured it all out. Now let me tell you this: your attempt to convince me that you could make Katerina marry me was a stupid piece of nonsense that even a schoolboy would never take seriously. It was quite unlikely that I'd fall for it. But you did. And you could only believe such nonsense because you've never had any contact with high society and have no idea what they think and how they feel. Things are not done so simply there and it's absolutely impossible for a woman like her to just say: yes, fine, marry me off to him. Now I'll tell you what you're after: you want to get hold of me, make me drunk, get that document away from me, try to blackmail Mrs. Akhmakov on your own. Well, you're just letting your imagination run away with you, Lambert. I'm not going anywhere with you, and you may as well know that by tomorrow or at the latest the day after tomorrow the document will be in Mrs. Akhmakov's hands: it is her property because she wrote it. I will give it to her myself and, if you want to know where, I can tell you: it will take place at the apartment of a friend of hers, one Mrs. Prutkov, and in the presence of that same Mrs. Prutkov. I will give Mrs. Akhmakov the document without asking her for anything in exchange. And now, off with you, and don't ever come near me again. Otherwise, Lambert, you won't get away with it as easily as this time."

I was shaking all over by the time I had finished—a sort of high-frequency tremor. The worst habit one can have is going in for dramatic effects; it always gets you into trouble. God knows why I let myself get so excited that, in the end, I told him with immense relish—indeed, almost shouted at him—the unsolicited piece of information: my plan to give Katerina the document in Mrs. Prutkov's apartment. I was trying too hard to humiliate him at that moment! And when I blurted out so casually about "the document" and saw his stupid, frightened look, I felt an irresistible urge to crush him under a wealth of detail. It was this bumptious chatter that was the main cause of the succession of disasters that followed, because what I told him about Mrs. Prutkov's apartment engraved itself on Lambert's mind, the practical mind of a small-time crook, who, although unable to cope with vast, complex operations, still had a flair for petty crime. Without my mention of Mrs. Prutkov's apartment, nothing very grave could have happened. Still, I remember Lambert looked very upset and could only mutter:

"No, no, wait. . . . Come to my house—Alphonsine will sing us something. . . . Alphonsine has been to see *her*. . . . Listen, I have a letter, almost a letter that is, in which Mrs. Akhmakov mentions you. . . . The pockmarked Semyon got hold of it for me—remember him?—and you'll see. Come!"

"You're lying! Show me that letter if you have it!"

"It's at home with Alphonsine."

Of course he was lying, trying to invent anything, because he was terrified of losing me again. I turned and started walking away from him, and when he made a gesture to follow me I stopped and shook my fist at him. He didn't insist; he just stood there and I saw that he was already thinking up something: a substitute plan was probably taking shape in his mind.

But that was not the last surprise or unexpected meeting in store for me that fateful day, and when I look back on it, I have the impression that all these surprises and coincidences had been deliberately prepared by fate and then hurled at me one by one as if from some accursed horn of plenty.

No sooner had I opened the door of the apartment where I lived than I saw in the entrance hall a tall, pale, long-faced, elegant young gentleman. His fur coat was really magnificent and he wore a pince-nez. When he saw me come in, he raised his top hat and also removed his pince-nez from his nose— probably as a sign of special courtesy—and then, with the most graceful smile, although without stopping, uttered a very warm "Ha, *bonsoir!*" and, passing close by me, went out onto the landing. I recognized him at once and he obviously recognized me too, although I remember having seen him only once before in Moscow and only for a second. He was the young Versilov, Anna's brother, that is, my half-brother. The landlady was seeing him off to the door as the landlord hadn't yet returned from work. When the young Versilov was gone, I pounced upon the woman:

"What did he want? Did he go into my room?"

"Certainly not, he didn't go near it. He came to see me . . ." she said in a dry and unpleasant tone, turned away, and was about to go back to her room.

"That won't do!" I shouted. "I want to know: what did he come here for?"

"Good Lord!" the landlady said. "Since when is it my duty

to give you an accounting every time somebody comes to see me!
I think I have the right to receive anyone I please without asking
your permission. Suppose that young man wanted to borrow
money or find out an address, or something like that? Perhaps
I'd already promised him the last time he came. . . ."

"When was the last time he came here?"

"Good Lord, you know very well this isn't the first time he's
come here!"

She left. I realized now that she'd spoken to me in a different
tone. They were no longer as polite with me as before. There
was obviously some reason for it, a new mystery. Ah, those
mysteries! They were piling up and up. The young Versilov
had first come with his sister Anna during my illness. That I
knew only too well. Also, I remembered what Anna had made
me understand the day before to my great surprise—namely,
that the old prince might make use of my apartment to get
married. But it was all so strange and incongruous that I didn't
even know what to think of it. I slapped my forehead and, without even sitting down for a short rest, I started off for Anna's.
There, the hall porter told me that Miss Versilov had gone to
Tsarskoe and wouldn't be back before "perhaps this time
tomorrow at the earliest."

"It's all quite plain then: she went to Tsarskoe to join the
old prince, and in the meantime her brother was inspecting my
apartment! But I won't allow it!" I muttered under my breath,
gnashing my teeth. "And if they really plan to put that noose
around *her* neck, I won't allow them to harm that defenseless
woman!"

From Anna's I didn't go home. It flashed through my inflamed mind that Versilov, especially when he felt despondent,
would occasionally stop at that little inn near the canal. I was
suddenly filled with hope and rushed there. It was already well
after three o'clock and getting dark. At the inn, I was told that
he had been there, had stayed for a short while, and had left
but that he might be back later. I somehow decided to wait for
him. I ordered a whole dinner. At least now there was some
hope of seeing him.

I ate my dinner; in fact, I ate more than I needed so as to be
able to keep the table longer. Altogether, I remained there for
almost four hours. I won't try to describe the alternating periods
of feverish hope and deep despair: it was as if the world inside
me were rocking and spinning. The organ that was playing, the
people who were drinking and eating around me, and the bleak
lighting have probably left a mark on my soul that'll be there as

long as I live! I won't describe the thoughts whirling around in my head like dead leaves in the autumn wind, except to say that at moments I really felt as if dry leaves were blowing around inside my skull. I confess that once or twice I thought I was going insane.

And there was something else tormenting me (an additional torment, of course, not connected with the main one): it was a nagging poisonous feeling, as poisonous as a vicious autumn fly of whose existence you're hardly aware but which keeps buzzing around you, pestering you, until suddenly you feel its painful sting. It was a recollection of an event that I'd never mentioned to anyone. Well, here it is, since I'll have to tell it sooner or later anyhow.

IV

When I was still in Moscow and it had been decided that I was to go and live in Petersburg, Nikolai Semyonovich notified me that the money for my train fare would be sent to me. I never asked him who was to send the money, since I took it for granted that it would be Versilov. And since at that time I was imagining all sorts of dramatic scenes about our meeting, I was quite unable to mention Versilov's name at all, not even to Maria. Although I had enough money of my own to buy myself a ticket to Petersburg, I still decided to wait.

Then, one evening when he came home from his office, Nikolai informed me in his usual style, briefly and without going into unnecessary explanations, that I was to call on a certain Prince V. at his apartment on Myasnitskaya Street the following morning at eleven o'clock. There I would meet Versilov's son, who had just arrived from Petersburg and was staying with Prince V., a friend of his from boarding school days. It was the young Versilov who would hand me the money I'd been expecting. There didn't seem to be anything so special about that: there was no reason why Mr. Versilov shouldn't ask his son to deliver a sum of money instead of sending it by mail. However, when I heard about the arrangement, I became worried and depressed out of all proportion. I decided that perhaps Versilov wanted to use the occasion to make me meet his son, in fact, my brother. This was how I interpreted the intention of the man about whom I was thinking so intensely. I was very worried as to how I should behave during that quite unexpected meeting without demeaning myself.

The next day at eleven sharp I presented myself at Prince V.'s Moscow bachelor apartment, which, as far as I could judge,

was sumptuously furnished and staffed with lackeys in livery. I
was asked to wait in the hall. While there, I could hear the
sounds of laughter and loud voices coming from the drawing
room. Obviously, Prince V. had other guests beside the young
Versilov. I believe that when I ordered the footman to announce
me I did it in a rather haughty way, and I got the impression
that, upon leaving the room, he gave me a rather peculiar look. I
thought it was not quite as respectful as it should have been.
It seemed to take him an awfully long time to announce me,
perhaps as much as five minutes, while the laughter and the
conversation didn't seem to abate in the least.

Obviously while waiting I was standing, since it would have
been unthinkable for a gentleman to sit down in a hall in the
company of footmen. And, of course, I was too proud to go
into the drawing room without being shown in; it was perhaps
too refined on my part, but I was sure that it would have been
highly improper. To my surprise, the two other flunkeys who
were in the hall had the gall to sit down in my presence. I
turned away, pretending not to notice it, but I could not suppress an unpleasant nervous tremor. Abruptly turning to one of
them, I *ordered* him to go in *at once* and announce me again.
Despite my stern expression and my excitement, the flunkey
glanced at me lazily without saying anything. It was the other
one who answered for him:

"You've already been announced, all is in order."

I decided to wait one more minute at the most and then to
walk out. I felt I was dressed very decently: my suit and my
overcoat were quite new and my linen was perfectly clean
(Maria had seen to that especially for this occasion). But, as I
learned much later in Petersburg from unimpeachable sources,
these flunkeys had been told beforehand by the young Versilov's
servant that his "illegitimate brother," a student, was coming
to see him. This I now know for a fact.

One minute passed. It's a peculiar feeling when you've made
up your mind to do something but can't make yourself get up
and do it. "To go or not to go?" I kept asking myself at one-
second intervals, feeling almost chilled. At last the footman
who'd gone in to announce me came back. Between his fingers
were dangling four red ten-ruble bills.

"Here, sir, please, accept forty rubles."

I boiled over. What a terrible insult! All the preceding night
I'd visualized "the meeting of the two brothers" that Versilov
had arranged; I'd anxiously tried to work out how I should behave so as not to cheapen my personal dignity and the world

of ideas I had built in my solitude, of which, I felt, I could be proud in any company. I'd made up whole scenes in which I was dignified, proud, and a little sad, and I'd hoped perhaps to meet Prince V. too and thus gain direct access to high society. . . . Oh, I'm not sparing myself: since this is how I imagined it, I'm writing it down, truthfully, exactly, with all the implications. . . . And what happened in reality? After having been made to wait for ten minutes, they sent forty rubles out to me by a flunkey, who handed me the money not even in an envelope or on a plate but directly from his lackey's fingers!

I shouted at the man so loudly that he started and reeled back. I told him to take the money back and tell his master to bring it to me himself. I'm sure I spoke quite incoherently and it must have been quite beyond the flunkey's understanding. But since I shouted loudly enough, he went. Besides, they must have heard my shouting in the drawing room, for their voices and laughter suddenly quieted down.

Almost at once I heard dignified, unhurried, light steps: a tall, handsome, and arrogant young man appeared in the doorway and stopped a yard or so short of it (that time he struck me even as paler and leaner than when I met him the second time). He was wearing a gorgeous red silk dressing gown, slippers, and a pince-nez. Without saying a word, he stared at me through his pince-nez and started examining me. Like a wild beast, I took one step in his direction, stopped, and glared challengingly into his face. But he studied me like that for only a few seconds and then a very slight mocking grin twisted his lips, whereupon he slowly turned away and walked back into the inner rooms just as lightly and smoothly as he'd come. Oh, these people learn from childhood, from their mothers' knee, how to offend others! Of course, I felt completely lost. . . . Oh, why did I have to lose my head just then!

Almost immediately the same lackey reappeared with the same bills.

"Please take this. It was sent to you from Petersburg. You cannot be received just now. I was told to tell you that perhaps some other day when there is more time. . . ."

I sensed that the fellow had added these last words on his own initiative. But I still hadn't recovered from the shock so I just took the money and walked toward the door. Yes, I accepted the money because I was still in a daze, when obviously I should have refused it. But then the flunkey, apparently wanting to compound my disgrace, indulged in a typical flunkey's insult: he rushed ahead of me, opened the apartment door, held it

open all the way, and, as I stepped out onto the landing, said
with exaggerated emphasis:

"Good day, sir!"

"You low scoundrel!" I yelled and swung back my fist ready
to hit him. But I didn't hit him. "And your master is a low
scoundrel too, and I want you to tell him that from me!" I
added, walking quickly across the landing.

"Don't you dare! If I told the master, he could write a note to
the police and we could take you right off to the police station,
for you aren't supposed to swing at people. . . ."

I walked down the stairs. It was a beautiful, wide staircase and
they could see me from above as I went all the way down the
red-carpeted stairs. Indeed, the three flunkeys came out on the
landing and stood there, leaning over the banister and watching
my descent. Obviously, I decided not to answer them because it
was out of the question for me to exchange abuse with flunkeys.
But I did manage to walk down the stairs without speeding up
and, indeed, I believe I even slowed down my pace a little toward the end.

Oh, there must be philosophers (shame on them!) who
would dismiss all this as nonsense and adolescent oversensitivity.
Maybe so, but in me it left a wound that is still unhealed even
as I write this now, although everything has been settled long
since and I've even been avenged. Oh, I swear I'm not one to
hold grudges for long, for I'm not at all vindictive. True, I always want to get my revenge whenever I'm insulted, morbidly
so perhaps, but only by overwhelming my offender with my
magnanimity. That's how I want to pay him back for his insult
and, as long as he realizes it, I feel avenged. So I may say that,
without being vengeful, I do remember insults. And I *am* magnanimous. I wonder whether there are other people like that.
On that particular day I had come to the meeting full of magnanimity, although I was perhaps somewhat ridiculous at the
same time. Well, why not, it's better to be ridiculous and magnanimous than not to be ridiculous and full of vulgar, ordinary
feelings!

That meeting with "my brother" remained a secret, even from
Maria, even from Lisa later in Petersburg, because to me it was
like a disgraceful slap in the face. And now, lo and behold, this
gentleman turned up when I was least prepared to meet him,
smiled at me, doffed his hat, and greeted me with a friendly
"*Bonsoir.*" Something to think about certainly! But in the meantime the wound was reopened.

V

I sat in that inn for over four hours. Then, as though some-thing had suddenly stung me, I jumped up and raced back to Versilov's apartment. Again, of course, he wasn't there. He hadn't been back at all, the nurse told me worriedly, and she asked me to send Daria home, as if I had nothing else to worry about! I stopped at Mother's house but didn't go further than the entrance hall where I saw Lukeria and was told that Ver-silov hadn't shown up and that Lisa wasn't in either. I saw that Lukeria wanted to ask me something, perhaps even send me on some errand or other, but that was really the last thing I needed! There was only one hope left: he might have gone to my lodgings, but I no longer thought that very likely.

As I've said, I was already almost out of my mind. And now, on top of everything, whom should I find in my room talking to my landlord but Alphonsine. True, she was leaving and he was seeing her off, carrying a candle.

"What's this!" I screamed stupidly at the landlord. "What right did you have to allow this slut into my room!"

"Tiens!" Alphonsine exclaimed, *"et les amis?"*

"Get out!" I hollered.

"Mais c'est un ours!" she skipped into the passage, pretending to be frightened, and disappeared into the landlord's quarters. Still holding the candle in his hand, the landlord came over to me, looking stern and offended.

"You'll just have to control your temper, Mr. Dolgoruky. And, with all due respect, Mademoiselle Alphonsine is not a slut, just the contrary, and she came here not to see you but to pay a visit to my wife, with whom she is acquainted."

"But who authorized you to take her to my room?" My head immediately began to ache again and I seized it in both hands.

"It was just by accident. I went in to close the window that I'd opened earlier to air the room while Mademoiselle Al-phonsine and I were engaged in conversation. So she came in with me while we were talking. . . ."

"That's not true: Alphonsine is a spy and Lambert is a spy, and maybe you're a spy too! She came here because she's trying to steal something from me."

"You may think whatever you please. Anyway, you often say one thing one day and just the opposite the next. Besides, my wife and I are moving into the little back room for a few days because we've rented out our personal quarters, and that makes

Mademoiselle Alphonsine just about as much our lodger as you."

"Did you rent your rooms to Lambert?" I asked in horror.

"No, sir, not to Mr. Lambert." Suddenly that broad smile of his reappeared on his face, but this time he was looking at me firmly, no longer puzzled as before. "I'm sure you know perfectly well whom I rented the rooms to; you're just pretending you don't for appearances' sake, and that's why you're so irritated. Well, good night, sir."

"Yes, go, leave me alone!" I said, waving him away, feeling on the verge of tears. He gave me a surprised look, but said nothing and left. I fastened the door with the hook and threw myself down on the bed, my face buried in the pillow.

And that's how that first awful day finished, one of the three fateful days with which this story ends.

Chapter 10

I

Again I must anticipate the course of events because too many chance happenings that interfere with the logical unfolding of the story require advance explanation, without which it would be impossible to understand what actually went on. I must therefore explain right now what Mrs. Prutkov meant by "the noose" when she blurted out that word. She was referring to the desperate step Anna had decided to take, the boldest move she'd made in her present desperate position. What character that young woman had!

As things stood, the old prince, under the pretext that it was good for his health, had been whisked off to Tsarskoe. The real reason for his removal from Petersburg was to try to prevent rumors being spread about his engagement to Anna, to stifle them in the embryo, so to speak. However, the otherwise weak-willed old man, with whom one could do anything, now categorically refused to break his promise to marry Anna, who actually had taken the initiative of proposing to him. On that score he was a paragon of chivalry who sticks to his promises at whatever cost, thus displaying the strength of will that often appears unexpectedly in otherwise weak characters when they are pushed beyond a certain limit. Besides, he was well aware of the precarious position of the woman whom he respected infinitely, and he could anticipate the rumors and society gossip that would result if the marriage didn't take place and the harm it would do her reputation. What had reassured him until then was the fact that his daughter Katerina had never allowed herself to say one bad word about Anna in his presence and had never displayed any opposition to the marriage. On the contrary, she always behaved in the warmest and friendliest manner with her father's fiancée. Therefore, with her subtle feminine instinct, Anna realized the awkward position she'd been maneuvered into: if she said anything against Katerina, whom the prince also held in very high esteem (perhaps more now than ever precisely because she had agreed to his marriage plans with such warmth and consideration), if Anna made the least attempt to discredit Katerina, she'd hurt the prince's tender feelings for his daughter, arouse his distrust of her, and perhaps even provoke his indignation. And so the two women were trying to outdo each other in their display of mutual respect and refined kindness, until in the end the poor old man didn't know who was the more admirable of the two and, as weak and tenderhearted people usually do, ended by blaming only himself for whatever difficulties arose that made him miserable. Gradually that feeling of despondency led to illness; his nerves became really shattered; and, instead of his stay in Tsarskoe being profitable to his health, it had weakened him to such a point that he almost had to take to his bed.

Here I'll note parenthetically that much later I learned that Björing had suggested to Katerina that she somehow or other convince her father to go on a trip to Europe with her, meanwhile letting the rumor be spread in Petersburg society that he had become completely mentally irresponsible, and have him certified as such by doctors abroad. But Katerina categorically refused to do that, or at least so I was told later. Indeed, she supposedly rejected this scheme indignantly. All that is hearsay, but I believe it.

And it was just when Anna felt that her position was hopeless that she learned from Lambert of the existence of the letter and became convinced that Katerina had already consulted a lawyer about how to certify her father as insane. Her proud and vindictive temperament was aroused to the utmost. Remembering her previous conversations with me and putting together various facts, she didn't doubt that such a document existed. So a bold plan took shape in her strong and inflexible mind: she would face the prince with the brutal truth without any preparation, frighten him, give him a shock, tell him that he was threatened with a lunatic asylum, and, if he still refused to believe it, if he indignantly accused the accuser of lying, she

would produce his daughter's letter, which, at least, should be
evidence enough. Since they had already once before planned
to certify him as insane, now they had even better reasons to do
so, if only to prevent his marriage. And then she would take the
frightened and crushed old man to Petersburg, *directly to my
lodgings*.

It would be terribly risky, but she had complete confidence in
her own powers. Here I'll anticipate even further and say that
she didn't overestimate the effect produced by the letter; indeed, if anything, it even surpassed her expectations. The letter
affected the old prince much more violently than she or any
of us had thought it would. I hadn't known that the prince had
already vaguely heard of the existence of that letter, but, like the
weak and timid person he was, he refused to believe it, trying
to brush aside the disturbing thought in order to preserve his
peace of mind; in fact, he even went so far as to accuse himself
of baseness for listening to these accusations. I may also add that
the news that the letter still existed was a much stronger shock
to Katerina than I had expected. In fact, the scrap of paper I
was carrying in my pocket was a much more powerful explosive than I had ever imagined. But now I think I've run too far
ahead. . . .

I may be asked now why they had to bring him to the apartment where I rented a room. Why did they have to bring the
old prince to this miserable tenement house where he might
be even more depressed by the surrounding shabbiness and poverty? For, if it was really dangerous to take him to his own
house where their plans might immediately be thwarted, why
couldn't they take him to a "sumptuous" place, as Lambert had
suggested? But that's precisely why Anna's maneuver was so
bold and clever.

The main point was to show the letter to the prince the moment he arrived. But since I wouldn't give her the letter and
since she felt she couldn't wait, Anna decided to go ahead without the letter. Her plan was to take the prince directly to my
apartment, reckoning that such a sudden confrontation would
throw both of us off our guard, thus, as they say, killing two
birds with one stone. She was sure that I'd be so shocked to see
him so enfeebled and terrified that I wouldn't be able to withstand their combined pleas to surrender the document she was
after. I admit that it was a cleverly planned move, based on
good psychological insight, and, as a matter of fact, it almost
worked. Besides, what finally convinced the old prince and
made him agree to follow her was Anna's assurance that they

were all going straight to join *me*. All that I learned later. Indeed, only when he heard that I was the one who had the letter did the prince really believe that there must be some truth in what he was being told—that's how great was his trust in me!

I'll note here that Anna never doubted that I still had the letter and was sure that I hadn't allowed anyone else to get his hands on it. Also, her trouble was that she didn't really understand me all that well when she cynically based her calculations on my innocence, simplicity, and even sentimentality. On the other hand, although she foresaw a possible impulse on my part to give the letter back to Katerina, she felt sure I'd do that only under a very special circumstance. Therefore, she thought, all she had to do was to forestall that circumstance and beat Katerina to it by subjecting me to that sudden, overwhelming confrontation.

Finally, her plan had been approved by Lambert. I've already mentioned that Lambert's position was quite shaky at the time. That double-dealer had had his mind set on luring me away from Anna so that he and I could sell the letter to Katerina, a deal he somehow considered more profitable. But since he couldn't get the document from me, he resigned himself to working with Anna rather than losing all prospect of gain, and that's why he kept offering her his services until the very last moment; he even told her he could deliver a priest for the marriage ceremony if need be, an offer that Anna declined with a scornful smile, telling him not to bother. She found Lambert much too crude and felt a strong distaste for him, but, being a practical woman, she thought it wiser to accept his services, which consisted largely in spying for her. By the way, to this day, I do not know whether they had to bribe my landlord, whether he benefited from it at all, or whether he played along for the sheer joy of conspiring. All I know for certain is that he did spy on me for them and that his wife did her share of spying too.

Now the reader will understand that, although I was to some extent forewarned, I still couldn't possibly have guessed that in a day or two I would find the old prince in my apartment and, what's more, under extremely shocking circumstances. How could I ever have imagined such audacity on Anna's part? For while anyone can talk about and think up all sorts of plans, carrying them out is quite a different matter. No, I must say, Anna really had character!

II

And now to go on with my story.

The next morning I awoke late. I had slept exceptionally soundly and without dreams, a fact I find surprising. I felt unusually confident and full of energy as if nothing had happened the previous day. I decided not to go to Mother's but, instead, directly to the church at the cemetery and then spend the rest of the day with Mother. I was sure I'd meet Versilov sooner or later that day at Mother's. I had no doubt about it.

Alphonsine and the landlord must have long since left the house. I didn't want to talk to the landlady. In fact, I'd made up my mind to cut all communications with them and to move out of there as soon as I could. And so, after they'd brought me my morning coffee, I bolted the door again. But soon someone knocked on the door and when I opened it, to my great surprise, I saw Trishatov.

I was delighted and invited him to come in. He hesitated.

"I only wanted to tell you something, just a couple of words. I can do it from right here. . . . Well, I suppose I'd better come in, after all, for I'm sure it would be safer to whisper in this place. But I won't even sit down. . . . I see you're looking at my horrible overcoat—I have to wear it because Lambert took back the fur coat I was wearing the other day. . . ."

The overcoat he had on this time was shabby and much too big for him. And Trishatov's expression was gloomy and sad as he stood looking at me, with his hands in his pockets and without taking off his hat.

"No, no, I won't sit down. . . . Listen, Dolgoruky, I don't know any precise details, but I can tell you for sure that Lambert is plotting something against you and he is just about to carry it out. So you'd better be warned. I got it from the pockmarked Semyon, remember him? He didn't tell me exactly what Lambert was going to do, so I can't tell you anything more. I've only come to warn you. Good-by then."

"Please, Trishatov, sit down. True, I'm in a bit of a rush, but I'm terribly glad to see you."

"No, no, I'm not staying. But I still appreciate your welcome and I'll remember it. Ah, Dolgoruky, why should I lie? I have knowingly agreed to take part in something so disgustingly despicable that I'm ashamed to tell you. My friend and I are now working for the pockmarked Semyon. Good-by, I don't feel worthy to sit down with you."

"Nonsense, Trishatov . . ."

"No, no, Dolgoruky, I'm selfish, I don't care about anyone and soon I'm going to have myself a great time; I'll order a fur coat even more expensive than the one I had when we met last and I'll drive around with the fastest trotters. But at least I'll remember that I refused to sit down with you because I was still aware of my moral degradation that made me unworthy. Despite everything, it will be good for me to remember that much in the state of corruption I'm in. Good-by, Dolgoruky, and I don't even want to give you my hand. Why, even that horrible Alphonsine refuses to touch mine. And please don't come out with me now and don't ever come to see me. I'm bound by a contract. . . ."

The strange boy turned away and went out. I had no time then, but I decided that when I'd taken care of the urgent business ahead of me I'd find him.

I won't describe everything that happened in the course of that morning, although much of it was notable. Versilov never showed up at the church for the funeral and, judging from their faces, they didn't seem to expect him. Mother prayed with ardent devotion and seemed to be completely absorbed in her prayers. Only Lisa and Mrs. Prutkov stood by the coffin. But, again, I refuse to go into details. Then, after the funeral when we all came back and sat down at the table, once more I felt that they didn't expect him to come. When we got up, I went over to Mother, put my arm around her, and kissed her warmly, wishing her a happy birthday. Lisa did the same. Then she came over to me and whispered into my ear: "They *are* expecting him."

"It doesn't *look* as if they were. . . ."

"I know he's coming."

So they obviously must've heard something that made them so certain. I didn't ask any further questions. And although I didn't intend to describe my changing feelings, I must say that, despite my cheerful, confident mood, I suddenly felt oppressed by the atmosphere of secrecy.

We all sat down around Mother in the living room, and I remember how good it felt to look at her. At one point she asked me to read something from the Bible and I read a chapter from St. Luke. Mother didn't cry. Nor for that matter did she look too sad. Actually, what struck me was the spiritual radiance of her face. Her gentle eyes were dreamy and she didn't look like someone waiting with apprehension for something to happen. We never stopped talking about Makar, and Mrs. Prutkov told many things about him I'd never heard before, much of which would be very interesting for its own sake if I retold it here. I was quite struck by how different Mrs. Prutkov was from her usual self: she was very quiet, very gentle, and above all uncharacteristically calm, although she talked a lot to distract Mother. There is one detail that engraved itself so strongly on my memory that I must mention it: Mother was sitting on the sofa and close by, to her left, stood a little round table on which an icon lay, apparently put there for some special purpose. It was an ancient icon without a setting. It represented two saints with little halos around their heads. I knew that the icon had belonged to Makar and also that he had never parted with it, believing it to be miracle-working. Mrs. Prutkov kept glancing at it again and again.

"Listen, Sofia," she suddenly declared, interrupting whatever she was saying, "rather than leave the icon lying there like that, shouldn't we stand it up, perhaps lean it against the wall and light a lamp under it?"

"No, I prefer to leave it as it is," Mother said.

"Well, you may be right at that. It may look too solemn otherwise."

I didn't understand at the time what it was all about, but I learned later that the icon had been bequeathed by Makar to Versilov and Mother was to give it to him when he came in.

After five we were still talking away when suddenly I saw Mother's face quiver. She drew herself up and started listening to something while Mrs. Prutkov, who was speaking at the time, went on talking, unaware of anything. I turned and looked at the door. A second later, Versilov appeared in the doorway. He had entered the house by the back stairs, through the kitchen and the passage, and only Mother had heard his steps.

Now I shall describe the mad scene that followed, move by move, word by word. It was brief.

To begin with, I didn't notice any change in his face, not at first glance anyway. He was dressed as usual, that is, almost too elegantly. He had in his hand a small but obviously expensive bouquet of fresh flowers. He went up to Mother and smilingly handed it to her. She looked at him in frightened perplexity, but after she took the flowers, color brightened her pale cheeks and joy gleamed in her eyes.

"I hope you'll accept these flowers, Sofia," he said.

Since we had all got up when he came in, he took the armchair on Mother's left that happened to have been Lisa's. But he did not realize it and installed himself there. This way he found himself next to the little round table with the icon lying on it.

"Hello, everybody! You see, Sofia, I was absolutely determined to bring you these flowers for your birthday and that's why I didn't come to the funeral. I didn't want to come with this bouquet to the grave. Besides, I know you didn't expect me to attend the funeral and I'm sure that the old man won't resent me offering you these flowers since he himself bequeathed us joy. Don't you agree? I believe he's somewhere around here now, in this room."

Mother gave him a strange look. Mrs. Prutkov's face twitched violently.

"Who's in this room?" Mrs. Prutkov asked sharply.

"Why, Makar, of course. But never mind; a person who doesn't accept the miraculous unquestioningly is the most likely to fall for superstitions. . . . Let me go back to these flowers: I really don't know how I finally managed to get them here safely: three times I had to overcome a violent impulse to throw them into the snow and trample on them."

Mother started.

"The impulse was awfully strong. Ah, Sofia, take pity on me and on my poor head. I wanted so badly to trample on them because they're so beautiful. What is there more beautiful than a flower in this world? And here I was carrying these flowers and all around me was snow and icy cold. Icy cold and flowers—what a contrast! . . . But that's not really the point. I simply wanted to crush the bouquet because it was beautiful. . . . Listen, Sofia, I'm about to disappear again, but I'm sure I'll be back very soon because I'll get frightened and where else could I find another angel to cure me of my fright? There's only you, Sofia. . . . Tell me, what's this icon here? Ah, I remember, it belonged to Makar. It was in his family a long time; his grandfather had it, and Makar never parted with it all his life. I remember he wanted me to have it after he died. I believe it's an icon of a schismatic sect. . . . May I have a look at it?"

He picked up the icon, held it close to a candle, and examined it for several seconds. Then he put it back on the table. I was taken aback by the wild things he was saying, but he tossed them off so unexpectedly and so casually that I never had time to recover my balance and try to make sense of it all. I can only remember the terror that gradually filled my heart. Mother had looked frightened too, but soon her fear changed to puzzlement and then compassion: she understood that, more than anything else, he was unhappy. She had heard him say things just as peculiar before. Lisa, who had turned very pale, looked at me and motioned toward him with her head. But it was Mrs. Prutkov who looked the most frightened of us all.

"Tell me, what's the matter with you, Andrei, dear?" she asked him cautiously.

"I really couldn't tell you, Tatyana. I still remember that you're Tatyana Prutkov and that you're a dear woman. . . . But, you know, I just dropped in for a minute; I wanted to say something nice to Sofia and I'm looking for the right words. But, although my heart is crowded with such words, I don't know how to say them. For they are really strange, peculiar words. You know, I have the impression that I'm splitting into two." He looked at us very gravely, obviously trying hard to tell us something. "Really, I'm sort of split into two, mentally that is, and I'm terribly afraid of it. It feels as though my double is standing here next to me. And while I myself am perfectly lucid and reasonable, my double wants to do something incongruous, sometimes something extremely funny. . . . Then I realize that I too am longing to pull off that absurd prank. God knows why I want it; in fact, I want it without wanting it; I resist my wanting with all my strength. . . . Once, I knew a doctor who, during his father's funeral, suddenly began to whistle in church. And the truth is I was afraid to come to the funeral today because I got the idea in my head that I too might suddenly start whistling in church. Or perhaps burst into a fit of laughter, just like that poor doctor, who, by the way, came to a very sad end. . . . Somehow—I don't really know why—I've been thinking of that doctor all day and can't get him out of my mind. And now, Sofia, watch: I've picked up this icon again"—he was holding it once more in his hands, turning it around—"and I feel terribly like smashing it against this corner of the fireplace. I'm sure it would immediately split into two pieces—two, no more and no less."

The worst of it was that he said all that without the slightest suspicion of affectation. Nor did he sound in the least whimsical: he spoke with complete simplicity, which was precisely what made it so awfully depressing. He seemed to be very afraid of something and I suddenly noticed that his hands were trembling.

"Andrei!" Mother cried out, clasping her hands.

"Put it down, put that icon down, Andrei. Leave it alone!" Mrs. Prutkov jumped to her feet and snatched the icon from him. "You must get undressed and go to bed at once! And you, Arkady, run and call the doctor!"

"But . . . but you really got worried. Why?" he said quietly, and looked searchingly at every one of us in turn. Then he put both elbows on the little round table and leaned his head on his hands. "Oh, I've got you worrying about me. But here is what I'd like you to do, my dear friends: just calm yourselves and sit down for one more minute at least. But that's not what I've come to talk about, Sofia. I wanted to tell you something else: I'm going off on my wanderings again, leaving you once more, as I've left you several times before. You can be sure that I'll come back to you some day—in that sense, for me you are . . . inevitable. To whom else could I come back when everything's over? Believe me, Sofia, I've come now to you as to a guardian angel and not at all as one comes to his enemy, for how could you possibly be my enemy, Sofia, how? And don't think that I've come especially to smash this icon, although, you know, Sofia, I still feel like smashing it quite badly. . . ."

Suddenly he was back on his feet. In a flash he tore the icon from Mrs. Prutkov's hands and, with a fierce backswing, hurled it against the corner of the tiled fireplace. The icon smashed into two. . . . He turned toward us. From pale, his face had turned red, almost purple, and every feature in it was quivering and twitching.

"Please don't imagine this is a symbolic gesture, Sofia: it is not Makar's legacy that I have smashed—I just felt like smashing the icon, that's all. . . . But even so, I'll come back to you, to you, my last angel . . . Although, if you insist, you may think it was symbolic. . . . In fact, I'm pretty sure it must have been."

He rushed out through the door leading to the kitchen where he'd left his hat and coat. I won't try to convey Mother's state. She stood there with a terrified expression holding her clasped hands in front of her. But when he opened the door, she screamed:

"Come back, Andrei! Come back at least to say good-by!"

"He'll be back, Sofia, he'll be back, you needn't worry!" Mrs. Prutkov shrieked, shaking all over in a paroxysm of wild fury. "You heard him say he'll be back! Let the irresponsible fool sow his wild oats once more, for the last time. He's getting on, you know, and you can rest assured that he won't find anybody except you to look after him when he gets really too old to run around, nobody but you, his old nanny. . . . And he's not even ashamed to say so openly, the rat!"

As to us, Lisa had fainted and I, after my first impulse to run after him, rushed to Mother instead. I threw my arms around her and held her tight in my embrace as I watched Lukeria come in with a glass of water for Lisa. Mother soon came to her senses, sank down onto the sofa, covered her face with her hands, and burst into tears.

"Still . . . Arkady, you'd better run after him and try to catch him!" Mrs. Prutkov yelled at the top of her voice, as if suddenly emerging from total blankness. "Yes, yes, go, hurry, and don't let him out of your sight, go!" She stood there, tugging hard at my clothes to get me away from Mother. "Or perhaps I'd better run after him myself. . . ."

"Arkady darling, go and catch him!" Mother asked me too.

I rushed off like a madman, through the kitchen, down the back stairs, across the back yard in a flash. But there was no sign of him anywhere. In the street I saw the dark shadow of passersby in the distance and I took off in their pursuit, looking into the face of every shadow I passed and then, disappointed, resuming my pursuit of the next. And so I got all the way to the crossroads.

Suddenly this peculiar line of reasoning, complete and ready-made, presented itself to me:

"Since it is impossible to be angry with a madman, the fact that Tatyana was wild with rage at him proves he cannot be mad."

So, after all, it *was* a symbolic gesture: he was absolutely determined to put an end to something and he felt the need to convey it to Mother and to the rest of us. . . . But what about that *double* of his? . . . Yes, the double must have been with him just then. No doubt about that. . . .

III

He was nowhere to be found and I thought it quite pointless to look for him in his apartment, since it would really have been incredible, after that terrible scene, for him simply to have gone home. Suddenly I got a hunch and took off full speed toward Anna's.

Anna was home and I was shown in at once. As I walked in, I tried hard to control myself. Without sitting down, I told her about the scene I'd just witnessed, especially what he'd said about his "double." I'll never forget the eager, albeit unemotional and detached, interest with which she heard me out, nor the self-assured expression she had during all that time. She didn't sit down either.

"Do you know where he is now, by any chance?" I asked her sharply. "Yesterday Mrs. Prutkov sent me to you. . . ."

"I sent for you yesterday myself. Yesterday he was in Tsarskoe and then he came to see me. And now, now he must be"—

she looked at her watch—"he must be at home since it's seven o'clock. . . . I'm sure he's there."

"I can see that you know everything, so tell me, tell me!" I cried out.

"I do know quite a few things, but not everything by any means. Of course there's no reason for me to hide anything from you." She measured me with her eyes as a strange smile played on her lips, apparently she was calculating something. "Yesterday, in answer to Katerina's letter, he made her a formal proposal of marriage."

"That's a lie!"

My eyes felt as if they were popping out.

"I had that letter in my hands: it was I who delivered it to Katerina. It was unsealed. That time he acted like a true gentleman and didn't conceal anything from me."

"I no longer understand anything, Anna . . ."

"Why, of course, it isn't very easy to understand. But I suppose he acted like a gambler who puts down his last stake, fully prepared to use the loaded revolver he has in his pocket. This is more or less the meaning of his marriage proposal. He realizes that the odds are ten to one that she'll reject him but it shows he feels he still has that one-in-ten chance. . . . I confess I'm quite fascinated with that sort of reasoning, but then perhaps it was all just an aberration on his part, an act prompted by that double of his, as you put it so well just now."

"I'm glad it amuses you. Only I find it hard to believe that, of all people, he would ask you to deliver his letter of proposal when you yourself are engaged to marry Katerina's father.* . . . Ah, Anna, just out of pity, tell me the truth!"

"Why, he asked me to sacrifice my happiness for his. Well, he didn't actually say that in so many words, but he conveyed it to me quite effectively with his eyes. Besides, why should it surprise you so much? You must've heard, for instance, about him going to Königsberg once to ask your mother's consent to marry Katerina's stepdaughter. Don't you think that's very much like making me his *confidante* and entrusted representative?"

Anna was only slightly pale. Her complete calm and detachment brought out the irony of what she was saying. Oh, there was much that I forgave her when I gradually grasped the situation. For one whole minute, I tried feverishly to sort things out. She waited, watching me in silence.

* As previously noted, the Russian Orthodox Church bars two men from marrying each other's daughters and thus becoming each other's sons-in-law. [A. MacA.]

Suddenly, it all struck me as very funny and I began to laugh.

"I'm sure you transmitted the letter: you knew full well that it didn't threaten you at all: there's no chance of this marriage taking place. . . . But what I'm interested in is what will become of him . . . and of *her* too. . . . There's no doubt that she'll spurn his proposal. . . . And what will happen then?—Anna," I cried out with anxiety, "where is he now? Tell me! I feel something awful could happen at any moment!"

"I've already told you—he's at home. In that letter I delivered to Katerina yesterday, he asked her to meet him *whatever her answer* to his proposal. She agreed and will be at his apartment at seven o'clock this evening."

"She'll go to his apartment? How's that possible?"

"Why not? The apartment actually belongs to Daria, doesn't it? So why couldn't they meet there as, say, Daria's guests?"

"But she's afraid of him . . . he may kill her. . . ."

Anna only smiled at that.

"Despite her fear of him, which I've also noticed, she's always had a great trust and admiration for his code of behavior and his high-mindedness, ever since they first met. And this time she has put her full trust in him in the hope of getting rid of him once and for all. In the letter, he gave her his solemn word of honor that she had nothing to fear. . . . Well, I don't remember exactly how he put it, but she trusted him once more, responding for the last time, so to speak, to his chivalrous promise by her heroic decision. Possibly there is a sort of competition—to see who will act the most nobly—between the two of them . . ."

"But . . . but what about the double, the double!" I exclaimed. "What if he's insane?"

"When she promised to meet him yesterday, Katerina probably never envisaged that additional risk."

There was no time to waste: I rushed off immediately. Obviously I had to get to him, to them, as quickly as I could. . . . But before I had even reached the second room on my way out, I rushed back to her:

"Perhaps that was just what you were hoping for—that he'd kill her!" I shouted and ran out again.

By the time I reached the house where he lived, I was trembling all over as if in a nervous fit. Nevertheless, I managed to control myself and entered the apartment quietly through the back door. In the kitchen, I asked the maid in a low voice to fetch Daria, but before she could leave the room, Daria appeared in person and, without uttering a word, fastened her questioning and distrustful stare on me.

"He—Mr. Versilov's not at home. . . ."

I ignored what she said and, in hurried whispers, told her what I'd just heard from Anna.

"Please, Daria, tell me—where are they?"

"They're in the drawing room, you know, where you sat with him yourself two days ago."

"Daria, dear, let me go in, quickly, please!"

"How could I possibly do that?"

"All right, then, if not in the drawing room, let me into the room next to it. Don't you understand, Daria, that's probably what Anna wants! If she didn't, she wouldn't have told me that they were meeting here. And I promise they won't hear me. . . . Yes, I'm sure Anna wants me to be there!"

"And what if she doesn't?"

Daria's eyes were still riveted on mine.

"Daria, you remember, I was there when your Olga . . . Please let me in!"

I saw her lips twitch and her chin quiver.

"Ah, my dear boy! . . . Well, perhaps I'll let you in, for Olga's sake. . . . For feeling kindly about her. . . . But, you mustn't betray Anna, my boy, you mustn't. You won't betray her, will you?"

"I won't."

"And you must give me your solemn promise that, if I let you in, you won't go bursting into the drawing room screaming!"

"I swear on my honor I won't do that, Daria!"

She held me by the sleeve as she led me to the small dark room adjacent to the drawing room where Versilov and Katerina were sitting. We entered noiselessly on the soft carpet and she made me stop by the doorway which separated the little room from the drawing room by a heavy curtain. She pushed the curtain aside a tiny fraction of an inch and I saw them.

Daria went away and I remained there alone. Yes, of course, I stayed there fully realizing that I was eavesdropping, violating other people's secrets! But how could I not have stayed with that double in there, that double who had smashed the icon before my very eyes!

IV

They were sitting facing each other at the table at which Versilov and I had so recently drunk to his "regeneration." I could see them clearly. She wore a plain black dress and looked as beautiful and composed as ever. He was talking and she was listening to him with great deference and intentness. Well, there may possibly have been a trace of fear in her. He, on the other hand, seemed very wound up.

I'd come in in the middle of the conversation and for some time couldn't make too much sense out of it. The first thing I registered was her asking him: "So it was I who was the cause of it all?" To which he answered:

"No, it was I who caused it all while you were guilty only without guilt. For you realize it *is* possible to be guilty without guilt, don't you? This is the least forgivable way of being guilty. And it almost always bears a punishment," he added with a strange laugh. "But, for a moment, I really thought that I'd finally succeeded in getting you out of my mind and in being able to laugh at my stupid passion . . . but you already know all that. So there seems no reason why I should care about the man you're planning to marry. Anyway, yesterday I proposed to you and I beg you to forgive me for that. I realize how absurd it was, but there was nothing else I could do—I don't know what else there was left for me to do. . . ."

He let out a mirthless little laugh, looking sort of sideways, away from her. Then he looked straight at her. If I'd been in her place, I'd have taken that sad laugh as a danger signal.

"But what made you agree to come here?" he said, suddenly getting up, as if remembering something very important. "My suggestion that you come was just as preposterous as my letter. . . . No, wait, I think I can guess the reason why you're here. . . . Still, I want to hear it from you: what was the real reason? Was it fear alone that brought you here?"

"I came to see you."

She was watching him timidly, very much on her guard. They remained silent for half a minute. Versilov sank back into his chair and started talking again. His tone was gentle but his voice was highly emotional, almost quavering.

"It's an awfully long time since I've seen you, Katerina, so long, in fact, that I couldn't imagine I'd ever sit next to you like this again, look at you, and listen to your voice. . . . We haven't talked to or seen each other for two years. I certainly never expected to talk to you again. Well, so be it—what's passed has passed and what is will also have vanished tomorrow like smoke. Good, let it be that way. I accept that because I have no choice. But please, when you leave now, don't just leave like that, with nothing!" He sounded almost imploring now. "Since you've come out of charity, do something charitable and answer me one question."

"What question?"

"As we'll never meet again, I don't see why you should care anyway . . . so give me the true answer to a question sensible people never ask: Did you, at any time, ever love me or did I just imagine it?"

She blushed.

"I did love you."

Oh, I knew she'd say that—truthful, sincere, and honorable as she was!

"And now?" he asked.

"Now, I don't love you."

"And you find it funny?"

"No, I don't, and if I couldn't help smiling it was only because I knew that you were going to ask 'And now?' I think we always smile when we find we've guessed something right."

I had never expected that she could weigh her words so carefully and at the same time be so shy and self-conscious.

He was devouring her with his eyes.

"I know you don't love me. In fact, you have no love for me at all?"

"Perhaps I have no love for you at all. . . . I don't love you," she added firmly, no longer smiling or blushing. "Yes, I did love you, but for only a brief moment. I stopped loving you almost at once."

"I know you soon realized that I was not what you needed. But what is it that you actually need? Explain it to me once more. . . ."

"Why, have I already explained to you before what I needed, what I was looking for? Well, I'm just an ordinary woman and I like . . . I like gay, joyful people."

"Gay? Joyful?"

"You see, I don't even know how to speak to you. I have the feeling that if you could have loved me a little less, I'd have fallen in love with you."

She smiled timidly. A note of total sincerity vibrated in her voice. Ah, could she really not see that her answer contained the very essence of their relations that explained everything? But he, he must have understood it. . . . And yet he was looking at her with a strange smile.

"And Björing is gay and joyful?" he asked.

"He shouldn't be any of your concern," she said rather hastily. "Still, I can tell you that I'm marrying him because with him

I know I'll feel the most at peace. And my soul will remain completely my own."

"I've heard that you've become fond of society again, resumed social life?"

"It's not society. . . . Well, although I know that there's just as much disorder in society as elsewhere, I still find its external forms quite beautiful, so that, for a person who goes through life casually, it is better to belong to society than to anything else."

"I keep hearing that word *disorder* again and again. Tell me, was it my 'disorder' that put you off then—you know what I mean: the chains, my peculiar ideas, all that nonsense?"

"No, it wasn't quite that."

"So what was it? For God's sake, tell me plainly what it was!"

"All right, I'll tell you plainly and you'll understand because I believe you have a really superior intelligence. . . . Well, I always had the impression that there was something ridiculous about you."

She suddenly turned bright crimson, as if realizing she'd done something foolhardy.

"I could forgive you many things for having said that."

His voice sounded strange.

"I haven't finished explaining what I meant," she resumed hurriedly, turning even redder. "Really I'm the one who's ridiculous . . . if only because I sound like an idiot when I talk to you."

"No, not at all, you aren't ridiculous, you're just a depraved society woman." He had turned frightfully pale. "Well, I hadn't finished what I was trying to say either when I asked you earlier what made you come. Shall I finish now? All right—there's a certain document, a certain letter, that you're very much afraid your father might see, for if he does, he may curse you and have good reason to cut you out of his will. I believe you're afraid of that letter and you've come here to try to get it." He was shaking all over. I thought I could even hear his teeth gnashing.

She heard him out with a sad and pained expression.

"I know that you could make things quite unpleasant for me," she said, sounding as if she were brushing aside something minor. "Still, I've come here not to convince you to stop persecuting me but just because I wanted to see you. Indeed, I've been wanting to see you for a long time. . . . But now that I've seen you, I realize you're still the same as before."

She added the last sentence in a different tone, apparently swayed by a sudden thought or perhaps even emotion.

"Were you hoping to find me changed then? After that letter I wrote about your depravity? Tell me, weren't you afraid as you were coming here?"

"I came here because I loved you once. But please stop threatening me as long as I am here; don't remind me of my bad feelings and thoughts. . . . I'd be so happy if you could talk to me about something else. And if you must threaten me, do it later, but for now I'd like something else. I've come to look at you and to listen to you for a few minutes. But if that's too much for you, you may as well kill me right away rather than threatening me and torturing yourself in my presence."

She looked at him and waited. Strangely enough, it seemed as though she really had conceived the possibility that he might kill her. He got up, looked at her with burning eyes, and said in a firm voice:

"You'll leave here absolutely unharmed."

"Yes, of course, you gave me your word of honor." She smiled.

"Not just because you have my word in writing, but above all because I want to and shall think of you all night. . . ."

"To torture yourself?"

"Whenever I'm alone, I always imagine you by my side and I never do anything else but talk to you. I go and lose myself in slums, bury myself in some sordid hole, and, as if by some law of compensation, you're always there with me in my imagination. But, just as now, you're always laughing at me. . . ." His voice was like a stranger's. I didn't recognize it.

"I've never laughed at you, never!" she said, her voice trembling with emotion and she was looking at him with deep compassion. "If I decided to come here, it was to try hard to convince you that there's nothing left that should offend you. . . . I've come to tell you," she suddenly added, "to tell you that I almost love you. . . . No, you must forgive me, perhaps I didn't put it right," she hastened to correct herself.

He laughed.

"It's such a shame you don't know how to pretend. . . . Why do you have to be so simple and straightforward, instead of being like everybody else? It's quite something to say to a man you're dismissing that you *almost* love him!"

"I simply didn't know how to put it," she muttered hurriedly. "I expressed it so clumsily because I've always felt self-conscious and embarrassed when I speak in your presence, since our very first meeting. But even if it did sound silly when I said that I almost love you, that happens to be very close to the way

I feel, and that's why I said it. Besides, I love you with such a —how shall I put it?—such a *universal* love, the way one loves everyone, so one shouldn't be embarrassed to admit to that."

He listened to her with his glowing eyes fixed on her.

"Perhaps I'm being unfair to you," he said, still not sounding like himself. "My feeling must be of the species they call passion. . . . One thing I know for sure: without you it's the end of me, and with you it's also the end. It makes no difference where you are: far or near, you're always present. I also know that I could hate you a good deal more than I could love you. . . . But I haven't been thinking about any of that for a long time—I don't really care. I'm sorry, however, that I had to fall in love with someone like you. . . ." He broke off as if he was having difficulty in controlling his breathing. "Why, do you find it strange that I should talk like this?" he went on with a faint smile. "I think if I knew it would impress you, I'd be willing to try to spend thirty years standing stiff as a post, even on one foot. . . . I can see now that you're sorry for me and your face says 'I'd love you if only I could, but I can't.' Am I right? I have no pride. I'm like a beggar: I'll be grateful for anything I'm given, anything at all, understand? How can a beggar have pride?"

She got up and walked over to him.

"Dear . . ." she said, lightly touching his shoulder, her face reflecting a variety of inexpressible feelings. "I can't bear to hear you talk like that. All my life, I'll think of you as the best man, the noblest, as a bearer of something sacred, something I can respect and love. Please take in what I'm saying, Andrei, for I did want to come and see you now; you've always been and still are infinitely dear to me. I'll never forget the violent intellectual upheaval you set off in me during our first meetings! So let us part good friends and you'll remain the most precious and the most meaningful memory in my whole life."

"What you're saying is that you'll love me, provided we part first. . . ." Then he went really ashen pale. "Listen," he said, "I want one more charitable handout from you: you don't have to love me, or live with me, or ever see me or hear of me unless you need me for some specific purpose in which case I'll appear, do what you want me to like a slave, and again vanish out of your sight like a slave. . . . There's only one thing I ask of you in exchange: *do not marry anyone.*"

My heart contracted painfully when I heard that. That naïve, humiliating begging was all the more pitiful and heartbreaking to me in that it was so shameless and so obviously futile: he was begging for an impossible charity! And, although he never expected her to do what he was asking, he was willing to humiliate himself so abjectly—just in case! It was unbearable to witness this man's ultimate degradation. And she—all her features now contorted—she was about to say something, but before she could utter a word, he suddenly regained his pride.

"I'll *destroy* you," he said in a strange wooden voice.

And her answer was just as peculiar, also delivered in a voice unfamiliar to me, a strange woman's hard and determined voice.

"If out of charity I did what you asked me, you'd only make me pay for it even more cruelly later; for you'd never forget that once you stood before me like a beggar. . . . But I'm not going to stand here any longer and listen to you threatening me!" she added with indignation, looking at him challengingly.

"You mean you won't stand for threats from a beggar like me? Well, I was only joking." He smiled faintly. "I won't do anything against you; you needn't worry. You may go in peace now. . . . Yes, I'll do everything in my power to send you that compromising document—just go away, go away! I wrote you a stupid letter and you consented to what I asked and came here. . . . So now we are even. . . . This way, please," he said, showing her the door, for she'd made a move to go out through the little room where I was hiding behind the curtain.

"Forgive me if you can," she said, stopping in the doorway.

"Of course, for who knows, perhaps we'll meet some day as good old friends and remember this scene with nice, jovial laughter?"

Every feature in his face was twitching convulsively.

"I wish to God that would happen!" she cried out, clasping her hands and looking at him searchingly and worriedly as if trying to guess what he really meant.

"Go now. There's enough intelligence in either of us, but you happen to be one of my own kind—you agreed to come here in answer to a crazy letter I wrote you just because you felt like telling me that you *almost* love me. Well, whatever else one may say, we are both possessed by the same madness. So, remain always just as insane, never change, and some day we shall meet as friends. I promise that's what will happen, I swear it will!"

"And then I know I'll love you, I'm certain, because I feel it now!"

It was the woman in her that couldn't resist tossing these last words at him from the doorway as she was leaving.

Quickly and stealthily I slipped into the kitchen and, hardly glancing at Daria who'd been waiting for me there, I left the apartment by the back stairs, crossed the back yard, and went out into the street. But I got there only in time to see her getting into a sleigh that had been waiting for her by the main entrance. Then I set off at a run.

Chapter 11

I

I ran all the way to Lambert's. Oh, I'd have so liked to give an appearance of logic and discover be it only a trace of common sense in my behavior throughout that evening and night! But, alas, even today I cannot offer a clear, understandable explanation of my conduct. I was guided by feelings, or a whole raft of chaotic feelings, in which naturally enough I couldn't fail to get lost. True, there was a dominant feeling among these that exerted tremendous pressure on me in propelling me in one direction. . . . But need I really confess that, especially since I'm not even absolutely certain . . . ?

Obviously I was in quite a state when I reached Lambert's. I even frightened them both, him and Alphonsine. I've often noticed that even the most dissolute of Frenchmen are excessively addicted to their bourgeois routine when it comes to their domestic life, to a sort of daily, dull ritual of life established once and for all. Lambert, however, soon recovered, realized that this was a lucky break for him, that finally he had me there, in his lair, *at his mercy!* Oh, he hadn't thought of anything else throughout the past few days! He needed me desperately! And now, when he'd practically lost all hope of getting hold of me, here I was suddenly turning up of my own accord, moreover in a quite abnormal state. What more could he want?

"Hey, Lambert, get me some wine!" I shouted. "Come on, let's drink, let's have a wild time! Where's your guitar, Alphonsine?"

No need to describe the scene that followed. We drank wine and I spoke. I told him everything. It was I, without any prompting, who proposed a whole plan of action that was to set everything afire. First of all, we would summon Katerina Akhmakov here, by writing to her. . . .

"We could do that," Lambert assented, hanging onto every word I said.

Secondly, to convince her, I suggested we should send along

a copy of the "document" so she could see we weren't bluffing but really had her compromising letter.

"That's right, that would be the best way!" Lambert kept nodding approvingly, repeatedly exchanging quick, understanding glances with Alphonsine.

Thirdly, I told them that it was Lambert who should ask Katerina to come, in his own name, as if he had just arrived from Moscow, while I, for my part, would bring along Versilov.

"Right, we could get Versilov too," Lambert agreed readily.

"It's not a question of whether we could—we must get him!" I shouted at him. "He must be here since we're doing all this for his sake!" I kept taking one sip after another out of my glass (I think Lambert and Alphonsine were only pretending that they were drinking with me—in reality, I must've drunk almost the whole bottle of champagne by myself). "You must ask your landlady, Lambert, to rent us another room, and it's there that I'll be waiting with Versilov. . . . And so when *she* agrees to everything, I mean when she pays up the money as well as the other ransom—*in kind,* you know (she's sure to agree, being vile like all women)—just at that moment, Versilov and I will burst in to witness her ignominy. And Versilov, realizing how contemptible she is, will be cured of his passion for her and will throw her out. . . . It would be even nicer if we could get Björing here too; I'd like very much to see the face he'd make!" I added, abandoning myself to my exuberant fantasy.

"No, I don't think we want Björing," Lambert tried to object.

"We do want him, we do!" I hollered at him. "You don't understand anything, Lambert, you're so stupid! What I want is a big society scandal and that way we'll avenge ourselves on society and on her and she'll get what's coming to her! She'll give you that money, Lambert, because I, I don't want any of it. I'll spit on her money, Lambert, and throw it away, but I know you'll bend down, pick it up, and put it in your pocket covered with my spit and all. But I'll be satisfied because I'll have broken her!"

"Right, right, right you are!" Lambert kept encouraging me. "You really have something there!" and he exchanged glances with Alphonsine.

"You know, Lambert, she has a tremendous admiration for Versilov. I've just found out how much she admires him," I went on mumbling.

"It's really great how you found out about everything: I'd never have thought you were so good at spying and had so much brains," he said, obviously believing he was flattering me.

"You're lying, you Frenchie—I'm no spy, although I do have plenty of brains. And let me tell you this: she loves him all right, but she won't marry him because she'd rather marry an officer of the Guards like Björing than a magnanimous humanitarian like Versilov, who, because of that, is just some sort of comic character in their eyes. Oh, she's aware of the passion she inspires in him, she enjoys flirting with him, leading him on, but she won't marry him! Every woman is a snake and every snake is a woman! We must help him to exorcise the spell that makes him so sick, we must tear the scales from his eyes and make him see what she's really like. Then he'll be saved. I'll bring him here, Lambert."

"Yes, that would be just fine," Lambert agreed, pouring me some more wine. He was filling up my glass every minute.

He was very much afraid that I might somehow take offense at something, so he agreed to anything as long as I went on drinking. It was all so unsubtle and obvious that, even in the state I was in, I couldn't possibly fail to be aware of it. However, I could no longer leave him, even if I'd wanted to: I kept drinking and talking, feeling an irresistible need to pour out everything I had in my heart. At one point, when Lambert went out to get a new bottle, Alphonsine played me some Spanish-sounding tune on her guitar and I could hardly control my tears.

"I tell you, Lambert," I cried with deep emotion when he came back, "we absolutely must save him because . . . because there's a spell on him. If she'd agreed to marry him, he'd have kicked her out the day after the wedding. . . . That happens sometimes, you know. . . . Because such an imposed, wild love is more like a noose, or like a fit or a disease, and as soon as the victim is gratified in his desire, the scales fall from his eyes and his feeling changes to the opposite—disgust and loathing, the impulse to crush and to destroy. Do you know the story of Avisage,* Lambert? Have you read it?"

"I don't think so. . . . I don't remember. Is it a novel?"

"You really know nothing, Lambert, you're incredibly ignorant! But never mind, I don't give a damn about you. . . . I'm sure he loves Mother, I saw him kiss her portrait. . . . I'm sure he'd kick that other woman out the next morning and come back to Mother. . . . But this time it may be too late. . . . And that's why we must save him now. . . ."

Later I was weeping bitterly but I kept talking and drinking an awful lot. The most noteworthy fact is that during the entire

* One of the concubines of the aging King David. [A. MacA.]

evening Lambert never mentioned the "document," never asked me where it actually was, never suggested I show it to him or put it on the table. As things stood, since we'd agreed to act together, nothing would've seemed more natural than if he'd demanded to see it. And there was also another curious fact: we had agreed that we had to do something, and would do it without fail, but we never settled the exact time and place, never came around to specifics. All Lambert did was to fill my glass and to exchange glances with Alphonsine. And if I was in no state then to make anything of it, at least I did notice it.

It ended by my falling asleep on his sofa just as I was, all dressed. I slept for a very long time and it was late when I woke up. I remember that, after having wakened, I lay for a while on the sofa pretending I was still asleep. I realized that Lambert wasn't in the room. It was after nine o'clock. The fire in the stove was crackling just as it had crackled that time when I'd been brought here after that icy night. I soon became aware that I was being watched: A couple of times I noticed Alphonsine's face peeking at me from behind the screen, but each time I quickly closed my eyes pretending I was still asleep. I did that because I felt I was in a tight spot and needed time to grasp the situation. I was aware of the unspeakable stupidity and loathsomeness of my confessions to Lambert and of the latest arrangements with him. What a terrible mistake it had been for me to come running here! Thank God, though, I still had the "document" on me, sewn into the lining of my jacket pocket! I could feel it with my hand, it was still there! All I had to do, therefore, was get up and run. Certainly there was nothing to prevent me from breaking my agreement with Lambert—he wasn't worthy of any consideration at all.

But now I was ashamed of myself. As my own judge, I looked into my heart and, oh God, the things I found in it! But why dwell on that hellish feeling, on the new acute awareness of my own filth and loathsomeness? Still, I must confess it here, because I believe the time has come for me to do so and I feel it must be recorded. And so let everyone know that if I wanted to disgrace her and witness her degradation when she paid off Lambert (oh, base thought!), it was not really to save Versilov from his madness and give him back to Mother, but rather because . . . because I was in love with her myself and jealous. . . . Jealous of whom? Björing? Versilov? Jealous of everybody, of every man she looked at during a ball, of every man she talked to while I was standing in a corner ashamed of myself! Oh, how ugly it was!

Well, I don't really know whom I was jealous of. But after that night, I felt that I'd lost her—as surely as two times two is four—and I knew that she'd reject me now and laugh at me for my hypocrisy and idiocy! Ah, she who was so honest and truthful, and I, a blackmailing spy trying to take advantage of a compromising document!

All this has been buried in my heart ever since then and now the time has come for me to account for it. But I'll say once more and for the last time: perhaps a good half or even as much as three-quarters of what I'm writing here is libel against myself. That night I hated her: first with a raving madman's hatred, then with that of a disgusting sensuous drunkard. As I've already said, my feelings were in such a state of chaos that I couldn't disentangle them myself. Still, I had to record at least some strands of these feelings that I could identify.

Overwhelmed by disgust, I jumped up from the sofa. I had an irresistible urge to make up for what I'd done. But the second I was on my feet, Alphonsine skipped out from behind her screen. I grabbed my coat and hat and told her to tell Lambert that what I'd said last night was all nonsense, that I was raving, that I'd slandered an honest woman, that I was just joking, and that Lambert, if he knew what was good for him, had better stay away from me. . . . All this I told her disjointedly, in a hurry, in French, certainly not too intelligibly. But, to my surprise, Alphonsine understood everything perfectly and—what really astounded me—appeared rather pleased.

"*Oui, oui,*" she agreed readily, "*c'est une honte! Une dame. . . . Oh, vous êtes généreux, vous! Soyez tranquille, je ferai voir raison à Lambert!*"

That sudden switch in her feelings, therefore probably in Lambert's too, should have made me stop and think. But I left without saying anything more. My head didn't work too clearly; I couldn't reason. And later, when I'd thought it all out, it was already too late. Ah, what a horrible mess resulted from all this!

But I'd better interrupt my narrative here and anticipate a little, because otherwise the reader may find it hard to follow.

I've mentioned that during that earlier meeting with Lambert, the time he'd brought me home to thaw out, I'd blurted out like a moron that the document was sewn into the lining of my pocket. When, that time, I dozed off for a few seconds, sitting on the edge of his sofa, he immediately felt my pocket and became convinced that the letter was there. Later, in the course of the evening, he again felt my pocket on various occasions to make sure I still had the letter. Then, again, I clearly remember him putting his arms around me several times when we had dinner at the Tartar restaurant. Once he'd made up his mind that he could derive enormous profit from the letter, he made a plan of his own that I never suspected. Like an idiot, I'd always assumed that if he kept inviting me so insistently to his place, it was to convince me to become his partner and act jointly with him. But, alas, he'd wanted me to come to his place for quite another reason! It was to get me dead drunk that he'd wanted me in his lair, and then, when I was lying there snoring, he'd rip open my pocket and get hold of the document! And that was exactly what he and Alphonsine had done that night. She had unsewn my pocket, got out Katerina's letter that I'd carried ever since I came from Moscow, and then sewed, in its place, a sheet of writing paper of the same size so one couldn't tell the difference. And I never suspected it. And so, after Alphonsine had sewn that blank piece of paper into my lining, for a whole day and a half after that, almost to the very end, I went around convinced that I was in possession of Katerina Akhmakov's secret and that I was holding her destiny in my hands.

Let me just add this: it was that theft of the document that brought about all the disasters and everything else that followed.

II

Now I have reached the last twenty-four hours of my story, the closing scene of the final act.

I reached my lodgings at about ten-thirty. I felt excited and strangely dazed. But I didn't feel in any special hurry: I had decided what my next move was to be.

But no sooner had I stepped into the apartment than I realized that there was new trouble; something extraordinary and unexpected had happened to complicate matters further: the old prince was there. He had just been brought from Tsarskoe. Anna was with him.

They had installed the old man not in my room but in the landlord's two private rooms next to mine. They had prepared them, it turned out, the day before by rearranging the furniture and making some improvements, which, however, I think, were hardly noticeable. The landlord and his wife had moved into the little garret that had been occupied by the pockmarked lodger I mentioned earlier, while he himself was temporarily banished I don't even know where.

As I came in, my landlord saw me and followed me quickly to my room. He looked less self-assured than he had the day before but was in a state of great excitement like a man who finds himself at the center of very important events. Without saying a word to him, I went into a corner, clutched my head between my hands, and just stood there like that for a whole minute. At first he thought I was putting on an act, but then he became worried.

"Why, is anything wrong?" he mumbled and, since I didn't answer, added: "I waited for you to ask you whether you wanted me to unlock this door here so that you could have direct access to the prince's rooms rather than have to go through the passage?" He pointed at the permanently locked side door between my room and my landlord's quarters, now occupied by the old prince.

"What I'd like you to do," I said sternly, "is to go and tell Miss Anna Versilov that I want to see her at once: there are a few things we have to settle. How long have they been here?"

"I'd say almost an hour."

"Fine. Then please go and ask her to come in here."

He went out and came back with a peculiar answer: Miss Versilov and the prince were anxiously waiting for me themselves. That meant that Anna didn't wish to pay me a private visit.

So I brushed and smoothed out my coat, which was all creased since I'd slept in it all night, washed and combed my hair. I did everything very deliberately and unhurriedly, for I realized how careful I had to be now. And when I was ready I went in to see them.

The old Prince Nikolai Sokolsky was sitting on the sofa near a little round table while, at another table covered with a cloth, Anna was making tea, pouring the boiling water out of the landlady's glittering samovar, which I'd never seen so beautifully polished before. I came in still maintaining my stern expression, which the old man noticed at once. He started, his friendly smile vanished, and suddenly he looked frightened. Unable to keep a straight face, I began to laugh and held out my hands to him, whereupon he flung himself happily into my arms.

I saw at once how much he had changed. It was obvious that the vigorous old man with at least some common sense and character that I'd known had, since the last time I'd seen him, turned into some sort of a mummy with the mentality of a frightened and distrustful child. Let me add that he knew perfectly well why they'd brought him here, for everything had been done exactly as I've already explained. They had given him a real shock by suddenly revealing to him his daughter's betrayal and her intention of having him certified insane. So he'd allowed them to whisk him off, in his terror hardly realizing what he was doing. They'd told him that it was I who had the irrefutable proof of the plot against him. As it turned out, it was the final proof of the plot and the need for him to make an irrevocable decision that had frightened him most. So he'd expected me to march in sternly with doom in my eye and the terrible document in my hand. That's why he was so relieved and pleased that, for the time being at least, I seemed willing to laugh and talk to him about other things.

As soon as we were in each other's arms, he began to weep. I admit that I too wept a little, but that was because I suddenly felt so awfully sorry for him. . . .

Alphonsine's tiny lap dog started yapping at me furiously, an extraordinarily shrill yapping that sounded a bit like jingling bells. It looked as though it were going to pounce on me from the sofa. The old prince had never parted from it since he'd bought it from Alphonsine. He even slept with it.

"*Oh, je disais qu'il a du coeur!*" he cried, addressing Anna and pointing at me.

"Oh, you look so well, Prince; you look so rested and vigorous," I said, although, alas, just the opposite was true. But I wanted very much to cheer him up.

"*N'est-ce pas, n'est-ce pas?*" he repeated joyfully. "Oh, it's a fact, I do feel so much better!"

"Please, Prince, have your tea, and if you'd allow me, I'd like to have a cup with you."

"Wonderful! As they say, let's drink and be merry, or how does it go? . . . Anna, please give him some tea, *il prend toujours par les sentiments!* Do pour us some tea, my dear. . . ."

Anna poured us some tea; then, turning toward me, she said in a most peculiarly solemn tone:

"My dear Arkady, Prince Nikolai and I have taken refuge here with you. I consider that we are here under your protection. We both beg you to help us. You must understand that the future of this saintly, this most noble man, who has been injured by ingratitude, is now in your hands. And so we await the decision that will be dictated by your just heart. . . ."

She couldn't finish because the prince looked horrified and, trembling from fear, held out his hands to her:

"*Après, après, n'est-ce pas? Chère amie!*"

I cannot even convey how unpleasantly struck I was by Anna's solemn speech. I didn't answer her, contenting myself with a cool, dignified nod. Then I sat at the table with the old man and deliberately talked about other things, told him some silly stories, tried to joke and make him laugh. At first he seemed grateful, but then he cheered up and became genuinely amused. However, it was obvious to me that his gaiety, enthusiastic as it may have been, was very brittle and could at any moment turn into complete despondency.

"*Cher enfant,* I heard that you were ill. . . . *Ah, pardon,* I was told that you'd been going in for spiritualism lately. Is that true?"

"It never even occurred to me."

"No? So who told me something about spiritualism?"

"It was the landlord of this apartment," Anna put him straight, "who's a very amusing man and who seems to know so many amusing stories. . . . Would you like me to call him?"

"*Oui, oui, il est charmant,* he knows so many amusing stories. . . . Still, I suppose we'd better wait a bit before calling him in. Later we'll ask him in and he'll tell us his stories, *mais après.* You know, when we first came in, they were setting the table, so he turned toward us and said: 'You needn't worry, this table won't fly away—we're no spiritualists.' Do you really believe that spiritualists can make tables fly?"

"I really don't know. But they say that all four legs get off the ground . . ."

"*Mais c'est terrible ce que tu dis!*" He looked at me, horrified.

"Ah, don't worry, I'm sure it's all nonsense."

"Well, that's what I say. You must know Mrs. Salomeyev. . . . No, I don't suppose you've met her. . . . Well, never mind, but she too goes in for spiritualism these days. . . . And just imagine, *ma chère enfant,*" he turned toward Anna, "one day I said to her, 'And what about the tables in government offices: there are eight pairs of officials' hands on each of them as they work on their papers, so why shouldn't these tables dance too?' And just imagine what would happen if those tables started to dance! A riot of tables in the Ministry of Finance or in the Ministry of Public Education! That's all we need these days!"

"You still say such charming things, Prince!"

I felt sad but laughed as convincingly as I could.

"*N'est-ce pas? Je ne parle pas trop, mais je dis bien.*"

"I'll go and get the landlord," Anna said, getting up. She beamed. She was delighted to find that I was being so nice with the old man. But no sooner had she walked out than the old man's face changed. He glanced quickly at the door, looked around him, and, leaning toward me from the sofa, said in anxious whispers:

"*Cher ami,* if only I had a chance to see both of them here together and to talk to them. . . . *Oh, cher enfant!*"

"Please, Prince, you mustn't worry like this. . . ."

"I know, I know, but we'll reconcile them, won't we? This is just a silly, small misunderstanding between two wonderful women, *n'est-ce pas?* You're the only one I can rely on now. . . . We'll set everything straight here . . . But what a strange apartment!" He looked around worriedly. "And that landlord of yours. . . . He has such a peculiar face! Tell me, he's not dangerous, is he?"

"The landlord? Why, no, how could he be dangerous?"

"*C'est ça.* So much the better. *Il semble qu'il est bête, ce gentil-homme. Cher enfant,* for heaven's sake, don't tell Anna that I'm so apprehensive of everything: I told her that I loved everything here when we arrived and that I also found the landlord very nice. . . . Listen, do you remember the story of *von Sohn?*"†

"Why?"

"*Rien, rien du tout.* . . . *Mais je suis libre ici, n'est-ce pas?* Do you think something could happen to me here? And if so, what sort of thing?"

"But I assure you, my dear Prince . . . please believe me . . ."

"*Mon ami! Mon enfant!*" He clasped his hands together, abandoning himself to his inner terror. "If you really have something . . . some document, that sort of thing . . . well, I mean if you really have something to tell me . . . don't, don't tell me anything in the name of God, don't tell me for as long as possible. . . ."

He was on the point of throwing himself into my arms; tears were streaming down his cheeks. I cannot express how it broke my heart. The poor old man looked like a helpless, frightened child stolen by gypsies from his parents' home and sold to strangers. But before he had time to embrace me, the door opened and Anna appeared. But, instead of the landlord, she was followed by her brother, the young Andrei Versilov. I was stunned and outraged. I walked toward the door.

"I'd like to introduce you, Arkady," Anna said in a very loud voice. I stopped.

† Von Sohn, an elderly civil servant, was murdered in a Moscow brothel in 1869; his body was stuffed into a wooden crate and shipped to Petersburg. Dostoevsky refers again to this incident in *The Brothers Karamazov.* [A. MacA.]

"I know your brother only *too well* as is," I rapped out, stressing the "too well."

"Ah, that was a terrible misunderstanding and I'm awfully sorry for what happened, Mr. Dolgoruky, my dear An . . . Andrei . . ." the young man drawled with a casual air, seizing my hand, which I couldn't make myself pull back. "It was really all Stepan's fault: he announced you so stupidly that I thought you were someone else. . . . That was in Moscow," he explained, turning to his sister. "But after that," he went on, addressing me, "I looked for you everywhere to explain what had happened, and then I was sick. . . . You can ask Anna. . . . *Cher prince, nous devons être amis même par droit de naissance.* . . ."

The impudent fellow dared even to try and put his arm around my shoulder, which was the height of insulting familiarity. Outraged, I drew back and, overcome by embarrassment and unable to utter a word, I simply walked out. Back in my room, I sat on my bed, feeling offended and befuddled. This whole intrigue depressed me horribly, but I somehow felt I couldn't just cut Anna down and leave her there. I suddenly realized that she too was somehow dear to me and that now I was pretty deep in it myself.

III

Just as I expected, Anna soon came to my room, leaving the prince with her brother, who proceeded to tell him the latest society gossip and thus distracted and delighted the impressionable old man.

I got up from my bed and looked at her questioningly.

"I've told you everything, Arkady," she went straight to the point; "so you understand that whatever happens to me now depends entirely on you."

"But I warned you that I couldn't do it. . . . Every principle I consider sacred prevents me from doing what you expect me to do."

"Is that your final answer? If so, this will be the end of me. But never mind that, what matters is that poor old man! Do you realize that he may go mad before this day is over?"

"I believe that the fastest way to drive him mad would be to show him the letter in which his daughter consults her lawyer about certifying him insane!" I said with heat. "That would really finish him off, for to this moment he doesn't really believe that such a letter exists. He told me so himself."

He'd never told me any such thing, I lied to her, but that was helpful.

"He told you that already? I thought he would. Well, in that case, I'm lost. That's why he's been crying all the time and begging me to take him home."

"I want you to tell me exactly what your plan is," I demanded.

She turned red, wounded in her very insolence, so to speak. But she made an effort and controlled herself.

"If I can produce that letter written by his daughter, I'll be justified in the eyes of society. I would show it at once to Prince V. and to Mr. Pelishev, who have been his friends since childhood and are both extremely influential men. I know that, for two whole years now, they've been watching the maneuverings of his greedy and callous daughter. Of course, they'll reconcile him with her—I'll see to that myself—but the whole situation will be completely changed. Besides, then my relatives on my mother's side—the Fanariotovs—will also, I am sure, come to my support. . . . Still, it is his happiness that I am most concerned about. I want him to know who is truly devoted to him and to appreciate it. For that too, Arkady, I have to rely on your influence on him, and I know how fond of him you are. . . . And, as a matter of fact, who else is there who cares about him except you and me? These past few days he's spoken of nobody but you. He's missed you so much. He refers to you as 'my young friend.' . . . And I needn't tell you that I myself will remain grateful to you as long as I live. . . ."

Was she trying to promise me a reward? Perhaps money? I interrupted her impatiently.

"Whatever you may say, I can't do it," I told her with unshakable determination. "But, in appreciation of your frankness, I'll tell you just as candidly what I've decided to do. I shall return that fateful letter to Katerina in exchange for her promise neither to make a public scandal out of what has taken place here nor to interfere with your happiness. But that's as much as I can do for you."

"That's out of the question."

She again turned very red. Obviously the thought of being at the mercy of Katerina's "discretion" was quite unbearable to her.

"Nevertheless, that's just how it will be, Anna, I won't change my decision."

"Perhaps you will."

"You'd better try to deal with Lambert."

"You can't even imagine the horrible consequences that may

result from your obstinacy, Arkady," she said with grim exasperation.

"There will be horrible consequences, I'm sure. . . . But I feel dizzy. . . . We have talked enough—I have decided and that's that. And, for God's sake, don't bring your brother to me."

"But he's very anxious to make up . . ."

"There's no need for him to make up for anything: I simply don't want to have anything to do with him, I don't!" I shouted, seizing my head between my hands (I wondered whether I hadn't treated her in too cavalier a way). "Tell me, though, where will the prince spend the night? He certainly won't spend it here, will he?"

"He'll spend the night here, in this apartment, with you."

"In that case, I'm moving out this evening."

And after that ruthless announcement, I took my hat, put it on, and began getting into my coat as Anna watched me in sullen silence. Oh, I was sorry, terribly sorry, for that proud girl, but still I rushed out of there without uttering one word that might give her some hope.

IV

I'll try now to sum up what followed. I'd made up my mind and I went directly to see Mrs. Prutkov. Had I found her home, a great calamity might still have been averted, but, alas, she was out. Bad luck seemed to be pursuing me all that day. From there, I went to Mother's, both to see her and in the hope of finding Mrs. Prutkov there. But it turned out Mrs. Prutkov had just left. Mother was sick in bed and Lisa was looking after her. Lisa wouldn't let me into her room, for she didn't want me to wake her.

"She hasn't slept all night worrying. . . . Thank God she's managed to fall asleep now. . . ."

I hugged Lisa and told her only that I'd just made a momentous resolution and that I was going to carry it out that day. She didn't seem to be particularly impressed and took it as just another of my usual statements. Oh, they were quite used to my "momentous resolutions," followed, as a rule, by faint-hearted retreats. She didn't know that this time it was quite different!

Then I went into the café on the canal. I decided to kill some time there before going back to Mrs. Prutkov's, expecting that by that time she'd have returned home. But I suppose I'd better explain why I needed to see that woman so badly: I wanted to ask her to go to Katerina's and bring her back with her, so that I could return the letter to Katerina in Mrs. Prutkov's presence.

That would settle everything: I'd have done my duty and be rid of the whole business. Then, having settled that, I was determined to say a few words on behalf of Anna. I hoped to convince Katerina and Mrs. Prutkov to come with me to my apartment (I needed Mrs. Prutkov as a witness), talk to the old prince, and, in front of him, effect a reconciliation between the two feuding women, thus bringing the prince back to life and . . . and thus making at least this small group of people happy. After that I'd only have to worry about Versilov and Mother. . . . I didn't doubt that my plan would work because Katerina, grateful to me for returning the letter without demanding anything of her in exchange, would certainly not refuse to grant me such a modest request. . . .

Alas, I still assumed that I had the document in my possession! Oh, what a stupid and undignified position I was in, without even suspecting it!

It was about four and getting dark when I returned to Mrs. Prutkov's. Maria, the Finnish maid, snapped rudely "She isn't back yet," giving me a peculiar look from under her brows that I remember very clearly now, although at the time I didn't see any sinister omen in it. Actually, what I was thinking as I was going downstairs was about the poor old prince stretching out his hands toward me earlier that day, and I felt guilty for having deserted him, perhaps just to vent my personal irritation. Then I started imagining various sinister things that could have happened to him during my absence. I sped home. But what had happened was only this.

When Anna had left my room in a rage, she hadn't by any means given up all hope. I must mention that she'd already sent for Lambert earlier. Later she sent for him again, but then, since he still wasn't home, she dispatched her brother in search of the Frenchman. The poor girl, faced with my resistance, was now, as a last resort, reckoning on Lambert to exert his influence on me. She was waiting for Lambert anxiously and was surprised that he, who had been turning around her until recently, had suddenly vanished into thin air. Alas, it certainly couldn't have occurred to her that Lambert, who was now in possession of the document, had switched his plans and was deliberately avoiding her to the point of going into hiding.

Thus, worrying and trying hard to control her own nerves, Anna was hardly in a state to distract, reassure, and cheer up the old prince, whose anguish and depression quickly reached critical proportions. He kept asking strange and frightened questions, several times even looked at Anna with noticeable suspicion.

Once or twice he burst into tears. The young Versilov hadn't stayed long and, after he left, Anna had brought in the landlord, who, she hoped, would distract the old man. But the prince didn't enjoy the landlord's company; indeed, the man only annoyed and revolted him; and somehow the prince felt more and more suspicious of the fellow. To make things worse, the landlord once again started holding forth about spiritualism and described some unexplainable trick that he'd witnessed himself at a seance when a touring medium had chopped off people's heads so that the blood gushed out in front of the audience; then the medium had pressed the heads back onto the necks until they became grafted again and everyone present had seen that too. It had all happened, the landlord specified, in 1859. . . . The story terrified the prince and, for some inexplicable reason, made him so furious that Anna had quickly to send away the witness to these miraculous happenings. Luckily, they brought the prince his dinner, which had been ordered beforehand somewhere in the vicinity by Lambert and Alphonsine from a remarkable French chef who was now unemployed and looking for a position in a club or an aristocratic household. The dinner with champagne cheered up the old man; he ate with a good appetite and joked lightheartedly. After dinner, of course, he felt drowsy and decided to have a nap as he usually did. Anna prepared a bed for him. While falling asleep, he kissed her hands, assuring her that she was his hope, his houri, his "golden flower," his vision of paradise; indeed, he slipped into the most oriental exclamations. Finally he fell asleep. And that was just when I came back.

Anna came to my room, clasped her hands beseechingly before me, and implored me—not for her sake but for the prince's —not to move out of the apartment, to stay there, and to go and see the prince the moment he woke up because otherwise he'd have a nervous fit and might not be able to preserve his sanity even until evening. She added that she absolutely had to go out for two hours or so and that I was the only one to whom she could entrust the prince. I readily promised that I'd stay until evening and that I'd do my best to distract him when he awakened.

"And so I'll be able to do my duty," she declared with determination.

She left. Anticipating a little, I may add that she went to look for Lambert, who represented her last hope. She also went to see her brother and their maternal relatives, the Fanariotovs. I needn't describe the mood in which she came back.

The prince awakened about an hour after she'd left. I heard him groaning through the wall and rushed to his room. He was sitting on his bed in his dressing gown. He was obviously nervous to find himself alone in a strange room lighted dimly by one lone lamp, so that when I walked in, he started violently, jumped up, and let out a frightened cry. I rushed to him and when he realized who I was, tears of joy appeared in his eyes and he threw his arms around me.

"But they told me that you'd moved to some other apartment, that you'd become frightened and ran away?"

"Who could have possibly told you that?"

"Who? . . . Well, perhaps I imagined it all myself. . . . But maybe someone did tell me that. You know, I just dreamed that a bearded old man walked in here carrying an icon, an icon broken into two halves. . . . And then suddenly that old man said to me: 'That's just how your life will be split—into two halves.' "

"Good heavens! But I'm sure you must have heard that Versilov broke an icon into two yesterday. . . ."

"N'est-ce pas? Yes, yes, I did hear that. I heard it from Daria this morning. She told it to me when she came here with my suitcase and the little dog."

"And so that explains your dream."

"Maybe so, but you know that old man kept shaking his finger at me . . . but where has Anna gone?"

"She'll be back very soon."

"Back from where? Did she move out of here too?" He looked at me piteously.

"No, of course not, she'll be back in a moment. She asked me to stay with you while she's out."

"Oui, she asked you to come here. . . . And so I understand Mr. Versilov has gone mad, and he was so 'casual' and 'agile' about it!‡ I always said that was how he'd end up. . . . Wait, my dear boy, come closer!" He suddenly clutched at my jacket and drew me closer toward him. "Your landlord," he whispered, "brought me some pictures, some disgusting photographs of women, naked women in various oriental positions, and started showing them to me through a magnifying glass. . . . At first, I did violence to myself and made some approving noises, although I know that women of that same disgusting type were brought to that wretched fellow to encourage him to drink. . . ."

‡ These two adjectives are taken from Griboedov's comedy *Woe from Wit* where a character describes how one goes mad. [A. MacA.]

"Ah, there you go again thinking about von Sohn! Forget it, Prince, the landlord is nothing but a fool."

"Yes, he's nothing but a fool—*c'est mon opinion!* My dear friend, if you can manage it, get me out of here!" He clasped his hands imploringly.

"I'll do everything within my power, Prince; I'm completely devoted to you. . . . But please be patient, my dear Prince, perhaps I'll be able to put everything right. . . ."

"*N'est-ce pas?* You know what? Let's just run away leaving the suitcase behind, so he'll think we're coming back. . . ."

"But how could we do that? What about Anna?"

"No, of course, we must take Anna with us. . . . Ah, *mon cher*, there's such an awful muddle in my head. . . . Wait, see that traveling bag? In the right compartment there's Katerina's portrait; I slipped it in there on the sly so that Anna, and particularly Daria, wouldn't notice it. Get it out quickly and be careful, I don't want them to catch us with it. . . . Wait, wouldn't it be better if you fastened the door with the latch?"

I found a framed, oval photograph of Katerina in the traveling bag. He took it and held it up to the light of the candle, and suddenly there were tears streaming down his hollow, yellow cheeks.

"*C'est un ange, un ange du ciel!*" he exclaimed. "I'm guilty toward her, I've never acted toward her as I should have. . . . This time again! *Cher enfant*, I don't believe a word of it, not a word! My dear boy, how could it be true that anyone is contemplating having me locked up in a madhouse? *Je dis des choses charmantes et tout le monde rit* . . . and now suddenly a man like me is to be whisked off to a madhouse?"

"Never!" I cried out. "It's all a misunderstanding. I know how she feels about you!"

"So you too know how she feels about me? I'm very glad. You've brought me back to life, my boy! So what are all these nasty things they've been telling me about you? My dear friend, bring Katerina here, let them kiss right in front of me, and I'll take both of them home with me! And that way we'll be rid of the landlord too."

He got up, clasped his hands again, and the next thing I knew he was kneeling before me.

"*Cher*," he whispered now in mad anxiety, trembling like a dry leaf in the autumn wind, "tell me the whole truth, my dear boy—where are they planning to hide me away now?"

I picked him up and sat him on the bed.

"My God," I said, "you won't even trust me now! You even

imagine that I too am conspiring against you! Believe me, I won't let anyone lay a finger on you!"

"*C'est ça*, don't let them," he faltered, clutching my elbows tightly with both hands. "Don't let anyone take me away! And don't ever lie to me yourself! Is it really possible that they're planning to take me away somewhere? Listen, that landlord, whatever his name is, isn't he a doctor?"

"Doctor? Why? What makes you say that?"

"Perhaps I'm already in a madhouse. . . . Isn't this room here in a madhouse? . . ."

The door suddenly opened and Anna came in. She must have been listening for some time behind the door and then, losing patience, she opened it too suddenly so that the prince, who trembled at every sound, let out a cry and flung himself face down on the pillow. He had some sort of a fit that was followed by sobbing.

"See, this is all your doing!" I said, pointing at the poor old man.

"No, it's *your* doing!" she raised her voice harshly. "I'm asking you for the last time, Arkady: are you going to expose an infernal plot against this poor helpless old man and give up those childish romantic dreams of yours to save *your sister?*"

"I'll save you all, but I'll do it my way, as I explained to you before. . . . I'm leaving now and in an hour or so I may be back here with Katerina. I'll reconcile you all and you'll all be happy," I ended almost with inspiration.

"Yes, yes, bring her here," the prince cried out, suddenly recovering his gift of speech. "Or else take me to Katerina! I want to see her right now, I must give her my blessing!"

He was flailing his arms about, trying to get up from the bed.

"See, Anna, you heard him yourself just now. There's no 'document' in the world that can help you now!"

"That may be so," she said, "but it would still justify what I've done in the eyes of society whereas now I'm irremediably disgraced. But what more is there to say about it—my conscience is clear; I've been deserted by everybody, including my own brother, who refused to stick by me the moment my chances of success appeared too poor to him. . . . Nevertheless I'll do my duty and remain with this poor man, happen what may. I'll look after him, simply be his nurse if it comes to that. . . ."

I had no time to listen further and rushed out of the room.

"I'll be back in an hour, and I won't be alone," I shouted from the doorway.

Chapter 12

I

At long last Mrs. Prutkov was at home. I told her everything: about the "document," as well as about all the goings-on in the apartment where I lived. Although she already had a pretty good idea of the situation and probably could have understood everything after the first few words, I went on explaining it to her for a good ten minutes. She let me talk and I told her the whole truth without any embarrassment. She sat in her chair, motionless, straight as a knitting needle, her lips pressed tightly together, her eyes glued on mine, avidly taking in my every word. But as soon as I'd finished, she leaped up, so explosively, in fact, that I jumped up too.

"Ah, you nasty little pup! So it was you who had that letter sewn up inside your pocket! And it was that idiot Maria who sewed it in for you! What shameless, disgusting fools! So you came here to conquer hearts, take elegant society by storm, and avenge yourself on God knows whom for being illegitimate? So that's it, is it?"

"You have no right to insult me, Mrs. Prutkov, and you'd better stop! In fact, perhaps it was you, with your constant insults and nagging, who is responsible for my vindictiveness. As to my being illegitimate, yes, perhaps I would have liked to avenge myself for that, but, as you've just said, God knows on whom it would be because it's impossible to judge who's to blame. . . . But now I want to make you understand that I've broken with the blackmailers and crooks and have overcome my passions and daydreams. I'll give up the document to her in silence and leave without saying a word or waiting for her to thank me. And I want you to be the witness. . . ."

"Come on, give me that letter at once. Here, put it on the table now! Unless you were just lying. . . ."

"It's sewn up inside my pocket; Maria sewed it in herself. . . . Then, when I had a new jacket made here in Petersburg, I took it out of the old one and sewed it into the new jacket. . . . Here it is, feel it! See, I wasn't lying!"

"Go on then, get it out, give it to me!" she continued storming.

"Nothing doing, not like that. I repeat: I'll lay it on the table in your presence as soon as you bring her here and then I'll leave at once, without waiting for her to say a word. But I want her to see with her own eyes that I'm handing the letter over to her without being forced to, without expecting any reward. . . ."

"Are you trying to impress her again, you silly pup? You're still in love with her, ha!"

"Say as many nasty things as you like. . . . I may've deserved them, but you can't offend me. Let her think that I'm a horrid young fool who's been spying on her and scheming, but I want her to recognize that in the end I've conquered myself and put *her* happiness above everything else in the world. . . . No matter what, Mrs. Prutkov, I'll keep repeating to myself: 'Keep up your courage and hope!' This may've been the first real test in my life, but I have come through well in the end, come through honorably! And even if I do love her, what of it?" I exclaimed in some kind of a trance, my eyes sparkling wildly. "I'm not ashamed of it! Mother is an angel while *she,* she is an earthly queen! Versilov will go back to Mother, and I . . . There's nothing for me to be ashamed of when I face her because I heard from behind that curtain what she and Versilov said to each other. . . . Oh, all three of us, we *share the same madness.* Do you know whose phrase that is? It's Versilov's. . . . And you know what? Perhaps there are others beside the three of us who share that madness. . . . Listen, maybe you yourself are the fourth one? I'll tell you something: I bet anything that you've been in love with Versilov all your life and that probably you still are. . . ."

As I said, I was in some sort of trance, in a strange state of elation, but before I could finish Mrs. Prutkov suddenly seized me by the hair with a quickness I'd never have suspected her capable of and violently jerked my head down. . . . Then, just as suddenly, she let go of my hair, retreated to a corner, turned away from me facing the wall, and covered her face with a handkerchief.

"You puppy, you! Don't you ever dare say that again!"

She was crying. It had all been so unexpected that I stood there in complete bewilderment. I just stared at her, not knowing what to do next.

"Ah, you young idiot! . . . Well, all right, come here, and give a kiss to an old idiot!" she said, laughing and crying at the same time. "And never, never say that again, never. . . . And you may just as well know that I do love you and have always loved you, you little idiot."

I kissed her, and let me add parenthetically that since that day Mrs. Prutkov and I have always remained pretty good friends.

"But what am I doing here!" She slapped her forehead as though she'd just remembered something. "What was it you

said about old Nikolai Sokolsky being at your apartment? Are
you sure?"

"Of course I'm sure. . . ."

"Ah, my God, it makes me sick!" In her agitation, she started
scurrying around the room. "I can just imagine how they're
pushing him around there! Seems there's nothing that can beat
sense into some cretins! . . . And you say they've been there
since early morning? She's really quite something, that Anna!
Talk of a nun! But I take it that Militrisa knows nothing about
it?"

"Who's Militrisa?"

"Why, the earthly queen, of course, that ideal of yours! So
what are we supposed to do now?"

"Mrs. Prutkov!" I suddenly shouted, remembering why I'd
come to her in the first place. "Here we've been talking about all
kinds of things and I forgot to tell you the most important: I
came here to fetch Katerina—they're all waiting for us back
there."

And I told her that, before giving Katerina the letter, I'd
ask her to promise to make peace with Anna and even consent to
their marriage.

"Quite right too," Mrs. Prutkov agreed impetuously. "I've
tried to persuade her to do just that myself, a hundred times!
Besides, he'll die before the wedding anyway, but, even without
being married, he's sure to leave Anna money in his will. . . .
Both of them are in his will as is. . . ."

"Surely it's not just money that worries Katerina?"

"No, but she was afraid that it was Anna who had the letter.
. . . And I was afraid of that too. So we were watching her.
Katerina didn't want to give her father a shock. . . . But that
sausage-eater, Björing, I bet he must've been worried to lose a
tidy sum if that letter surfaced at a wrong moment."

"And, knowing that, she still wants to marry Björing?"

"What can you do with a crazy woman? Just as they say,
once a fool, always a fool. He will, she says, give her something
she calls peace of mind and, she says, since she's likely to get
married some day anyway, Björing looks like the most suitable
man around. . . . Well, we'll see how suitable he turns out to
be. I bet she'll kick herself for it some day, but it'll be too late
then."

"So why don't you do something about it? I know you love
her. I even heard you tell her to her face that you loved her."

"Yes, I do love her, and perhaps more than I love all the rest of you put together. But that still doesn't prevent her from being a stupid, crazy woman."

"Please go and get her and we'll talk everything over and then take her to her father."

"But it can't be done, you little idiot; it's impossible now, and that's just the trouble. Ah, what are we going to do? It all makes me feel sick!" She snatched up her shawl and started darting around the room again. "Ah, if only you'd come four hours earlier! But now it's after seven and she must have left: she's dining at the Pelishevs' this evening and then going to the opera with them. . . ."

"But couldn't we run over to the opera? No, I suppose that's impossible. . . . So what will happen to the old prince? Why, he may die tonight . . ."

"Listen to me: don't go back there. Go to your mother's and spend the night there. Then tomorrow morning . . ."

"No, no, I won't desert the old man for anything on earth."

"You're right—don't desert him. And, in the meantime, I'll go over to Katerina's and leave her a note. . . . I'll use our special language to make her understand that the document is safe and that she must be here tomorrow morning at ten, at ten o'clock sharp. You needn't worry—she'll be here if I ask her to. And then we'll settle everything. So now you run back there and do your best to keep the old man happy: put him to bed, calm him, anything, and perhaps he'll last out until tomorrow. And try not to scare Anna either, for I love her too and you're unfair to her because you can't understand her; if she's embittered, it's because she's been neglected since her early childhood. . . . Ah, what a sad lot you are, all of you, and what a burden you are to me! And don't forget to tell Anna that I'm handling everything myself now, that she can rely on me, and that I'll see to it that her reputation remains untarnished. . . . For I'd better tell you that lately the two of us—Anna and I—we've had words, quarreled, and all but spat into each other's eye! So off with you, run along! . . . No, wait a second—let me feel your pocket. . . . Are you quite sure it's there? You're absolutely certain? Listen, give me that letter. . . . What difference would it make to you if I kept it overnight? I promise I won't eat it! Otherwise you may let it slip out of your hands during the night . . . or perhaps change your mind. . . ."

"No, that's out of question! But here, feel it! All right? But there's nothing in the world that would make me give it to you now!"

"All right, I can feel there's some paper in there. . . . Ah,

so you won't give it to me. . . . Well, all right, be on your
way. And I'll go over to Katerina's and then perhaps even to the
opera. . . . Just as you said, it was a good idea. So what are you
waiting for now?"

"Mrs. Prutkov, tell me first: how is Mother?"

"She's alive."

"And Versilov?"

She waved her hand impatiently.

"He'll still come to his senses."

I dashed off, cheered up and filled with a new supply of energy, although what had taken place was rather different from
what I'd planned. But, alas, there were more surprises in
store for me. I do not doubt now that there is such a thing as
fate!

II

While still walking upstairs, I heard noise coming from the
apartment where I lived. The door giving onto the landing was
wide open. A footman in livery whom I'd never seen before was
standing just inside the door. The landlord and his wife, looking frightened, were also standing in the passage, apparently
waiting for something to happen. The door to the old prince's
room was open too and a thundering voice was coming from
there. I immediately recognized it: it was Björing's voice. Before I'd had time to take two steps, I saw Björing and his friend
Baron R.—the gentleman whom I'd seen at Versilov's—emerging
from the room, leading between them the trembling and sobbing
prince. I saw the old man clutch at Björing and kiss him. . . .
As to Björing's roars, they were addressed to Anna, who followed them into the passage. I gathered that he was threatening
her. In his rage, he stamped his foot. The uncouth brutal German soldier was showing under the disguise of the society man.
As it turned out, he had somehow become convinced that Anna
was guilty of a legally criminal act and had decided to take her
to court. Not knowing all the facts, he had exaggerated her role
and now felt he could afford not to stand on ceremony with
her. Actually, he hadn't even had time fully to grasp the meaning of a certain piece of information he'd received anonymously
(I'll get to that later), and he'd arrived there in a state of rage in
which even the most distinguished gentlemen of his nationality
are prepared to fight like the commonest street sweepers. Anna
had faced his first assaults with the utmost dignity (but that was
before I came). What I saw was Björing suddenly leaving the

prince in Baron R.'s hands, turning to Anna, and roaring at her, probably in response to something she'd said:

"You're a vile schemer! What you're after is his money! You've disgraced yourself in the eyes of society and you'll answer for your actions before a court of law!"

"It's you who are trying to take advantage of a poor invalid and you've driven him out of his mind. . . . And if you allow yourself to shout at me like this now, it's only because I'm a woman and there's nobody around to stop you. . . ."

"Ah, you . . . the fiancée! The prince's fiancée!" Björing burst into shrill, spiteful laughter.

"Baron, Baron, please. . . . Chère enfant, je vous aime . . ." the old prince whimpered, stretching his arms out to Anna.

"You'd better keep going, Prince, there has been a plot against you, perhaps even a plot against your life!" Björing shouted at him.

"Oui, oui je comprends, j'ai compris au commencement . . ."

"Prince," Anna said, raising her voice, "now you're insulting me and allowing these people to insult me!"

"Get out of here, you!" Björing roared at her, losing all restraint.

That was more than I could stand.

"You low scoundrel!" I yelled at him. "I'm here, Anna, I'll look out for you!"

I cannot, nor do I wish to, describe in great detail what happened then. It was a horrible, vulgar scene. It seems to me I suddenly went berserk. I remember rushing at him and hitting or at least shoving him violently. Then he struck me awfully hard on the head and I went down. When I came to, I rushed after them downstairs. I noticed that I was bleeding from the nose. There was a carriage waiting for them outside. While they were getting the prince into the carriage, avoiding the footman who was trying to hold me back, I managed to get at Björing once more. The next thing I remember, there were police all around us and Björing, holding me by the collar, was ordering them to take me to the police station. I screamed that he had to come too, that each of us had to make a statement, and that they had no right just to drag me off to the station practically from my home. . . . But unfortunately all this was taking place not at my domicile but in the street, and since I was screaming, fighting like a drunk, and guilty of disorderly behavior, and since Björing was wearing a colonel's uniform, they decided to take just me to the police station. This aroused me to a paroxysm of rage: I resisted desperately and as far as I remember, I hit a policeman.

Then, I believe, two of them led me off to the station. I have only vague recollections of finding myself in a smoke-filled room with lots of people sitting and standing all around, people waiting and writing things, and myself shouting and protesting that I demanded to be allowed to make my deposition. . . . But it was no longer just a matter of making a statement; my case had become aggravated by disorderly conduct and resisting arrest. Besides, I was very ugly to look at. Suddenly someone hollered at me. The arresting police officer was accusing me of assaulting a colonel . . .

"What's your name?" I was asked.

"Dolgoruky."

"Prince Dolgoruky?"

That was really too much. Beside myself, I answered with an obscenity and they dragged me off into a dark cell "until he sobers up." Oh, I'm not complaining because I know that recently the papers had carried a story about a complaint lodged against the police by a gentleman who had been kept all night handcuffed in such a cell, also "until he sobered up," although he hadn't done anything at all, whereas I, at least, had done something. So I found myself lying on a sort of communal bunk on which already lay two unconscious bodies. My head ached, my temples throbbed, my heart was pounding. . . . Then I believe I lost consciousness and started raving. I remember waking up in the middle of the night, sitting up, and suddenly visualizing clearly all that had happened. I sat up and remained sitting for a long time, my elbows propped up on my knees and my head resting on the palms of my hands, immersed in thought.

Oh, there's no point describing how I felt then, nor do I wish to take the time to do so, although I will say this: perhaps never before in my whole life had I known a more blissful moment than when I sat there in the cell of the police station, thinking hard in the middle of the night. This may sound rather peculiar or at least like an effort to shock the reader and to impress him by my originality. But it is the absolute truth. It was one of those moments, familiar to most people, that happen only very rarely, perhaps only once in a lifetime. At such moments a man's future is determined, his final views on life forged. "The truth is there and that's where I must pursue it!" he says to himself. Yes, it was that night that I saw the light. I'd just been insulted by the arrogant Björing and expected to be insulted the following day by Katerina. But, although I was in a position to avenge myself on them, I decided not to take advantage of it. As tempting as it may have seemed to me then, I was not going to make the "document" public, nor cause a scandal in society. (I couldn't help, though, toying with the idea.) I repeated to myself again and again that I'd put the letter down on the table in front of her and, if need be, accept her sarcastic smile instead of gratitude without a word of protest; and then I'd step out of her life forever. But that's enough on the subject. As to my present trouble with the police and the possible consequences when I would have to answer the charges, I simply forgot to think about that.

Finally, I crossed myself and, with my heart filled with love, I stretched out on the wooden bunk and fell into a happy, childlike sleep.

It was already daylight when I awoke. I was all alone in the cell now. I sat up and waited. It was a pretty long wait, an hour perhaps, for it was close to nine when they finally came to fetch me. I could, of course, report in detail what happened, but since it has no direct bearing on my story, I won't go into it and instead will get on with what I'd set out to tell in the first place. All I'll say is that, in the morning, to my great surprise, everybody was extremely polite to me. They asked me some questions, I answered something or other, and they allowed me to leave. I left in silence and was gratified to detect in the way they looked at me a certain admiration for a man who, even in my present situation, managed to preserve his dignity. This is a fact, for if I hadn't noticed it I wouldn't have made note of it.

Outside the police station, Mrs. Prutkov was waiting for me. And now I must explain briefly why they let me off so easily. Early that morning, perhaps at eight or so, she'd arrived at my—I mean my landlord's—apartment, hoping that the old prince would still be there. Then they told her about the scandalous things that had happened during the night and that had led to my arrest. She rushed to Katerina (upon returning from the opera that night, Katerina had found her father who'd been brought home), woke her up, and demanded that she see to it that I be released immediately. Katerina gave her a note for Björing, and Mrs. Prutkov drove over to see him. She made him write a letter "to whom it may concern," which said that it had all been a misunderstanding and urgently requesting that I be released forthwith. She presented that letter at the police station and Björing's request was granted.

III

And now back to really important things.

Mrs. Prutkov pushed me into a cab, took me to her place, ordered her Finnish maid to light the samovar, took me to her kitchen, and herself scrubbed my face and brushed my clothes. In the kitchen, she announced loudly that Katerina would be there at eleven-thirty to meet me, as the two of them had agreed. Maria, the maid, overheard that and a few minutes later brought in the samovar. But, when a little later Mrs. Prutkov called her, the Finn didn't answer: it turned out she'd gone out for some reason. The maid's failure to answer is important; the reader must remember it. It happened, I believe, at quarter to ten. Mrs. Prutkov, although irritated at the maid's silence, decided she must have gone out to buy something and forgot all about her. Besides, she had other things on her mind since we kept talking all the time with all we had to say to each other. I, for my part, hardly paid any attention at all to Maria's absence (reader, please note this too).

There is hardly any need for me to say that I felt as though I were floating on a cloud. My feelings were pouring out of me. Katerina was going to be here in an hour or so and the thought that I was about to see her at such an important moment in my life set me atremble and aquiver. Still, I managed to drink two cups of tea before Mrs. Prutkov got up and said, picking up a pair of scissors:

"All right, now let's see that pocket of yours. You certainly don't want me to rip out your lining in front of her, do you!"

"Here," I said, unbuttoning my jacket.

"What a mess! Who sewed it in like that?"

"I did."

"It looks like it too. Ah, here it is . . ."

She took out the envelope that I recognized. She opened it and pulled out a blank sheet of notepaper.

"What's this?" Mrs. Prutkov cried out, turning the white sheet over in her hands. "Hey, what's the matter with you?"

I stood ashen and speechless and then suddenly my knees buckled under me and I sank helplessly into a chair. I was on the verge of fainting.

"What does all this mean?" she screamed at me. "Where's the letter?"

"Lambert . . ."

I slapped myself on the forehead. I guessed everything. I leaped to my feet and hurriedly, breathlessly, told her about the night I'd spent on his sofa, about our conspiracy before I fell asleep, although I'd already confessed to her on the previous day that I'd been plotting with him.

"So they've stolen it, stolen it!" I screamed, stamping my feet madly and tearing my hair in despair.

"We're really in trouble now!" Mrs. Prutkov summed up the situation after having weighed it for a moment. "What time is it?"

It was close to eleven.

"And Maria isn't in. . . . Hey, Maria, Maria! Where on earth can she be?"

"What is it, ma'am?" Maria's voice suddenly answered from the kitchen.

"So you're here. . . . What are we going to do now?" She glared at me. "Ah, you helpless moron, you! Well, I guess I'd better rush over to Katerina's."

"And I'm off to Lambert's!" I shouted. "I'll strangle him if I have to."

"Ma'am!" Maria's grating voice suddenly came from the kitchen. "There's a woman here. She says she wants to see you. . . ."

But before Mrs. Prutkov could answer, the woman who wanted to see her had evaded the Finn and broken into the room with a deafening wail. It was Alphonsine. I won't try to describe the scene that followed at any length: it was all pretense and fake, but I must pay Alphonsine her due: she acted her role very convincingly. With tears of repentance and gesticulating wildly, she rattled on and on (in French, of course) confessing that it was she who'd ripped the letter out of my jacket while I was asleep, that Lambert now had it in his possession jointly with *"ce bandit, cet homme noir,"* that they were planning to lure Madame Akhmakov to their lair and to shoot her there, all this within the next hour. . . . They'd told her of their plan and she'd become terribly frightened because she'd seen a pistol in their hands—*"un pistolet!"*—and that had made her decide to rush here and warn us so we could warn Madame Akhmakov . . . because *"cet homme noir . . ."*

"What *homme noir*?" Mrs. Prutkov interrupted her in exasperation.

"Tiens, j'ai oublié son nom. . . . Un homme affreux . . . Tiens, Versiloff. . . ."

"What? Versilov? . . . Impossible!" I screamed.

"Oh yes, it is possible!" Mrs. Prutkov cried shrilly. "And you, my good woman, try to tell us what happened sensibly without jumping around and waving your arms. What is it they want? Talk sense because, after all, they don't intend to shoot her, do they?"

Alphonsine then gave us the following explanation (which, I hardly need to say, was all lies): Versilov was to wait behind the door, and, as soon as Madame Akhmakov came in, Lambert would show her *cette lettre*. . . . Then Versilov would rush in and . . . *oh, ils feront leur vengeance!* . . . and she—Alphonsine—was terribly worried that something really awful could happen *à cette dame*, and that she herself might be accused of being an accomplice. Now she was sure that Madame Akhmakov would come at once because they'd sent her a copy of that letter to prove to her that they really had it in their possession. It was Lambert who had written to Madame Akhmakov, representing himself as someone who'd just arrived from Moscow, *de la part d'une dame de Moscou* (N.B.—my old friend Maria!) and never mentioning Versilov.

"Ah, how sickening, how sickening!" Mrs. Prutkov kept exclaiming.

"*Sauvez-la, sauvez-la!*" Alphonsine urged us shrilly.

Despite the almost palpable inconsistencies in Alphonsine's crazy tale, we accepted it because we had no time to analyze it and because somehow it struck us then as extremely plausible. Still, we could have assumed that, upon receiving Lambert's message, Katerina would first have come to Mrs. Prutkov's to discuss the matter, but then she might also have decided to go there directly, in which case she was lost! It was, of course, rather unlikely that she'd rush, at the first summons, just like that to Lambert's, whom she didn't know, but then again that couldn't be ruled out either, for the copy of the document would have convinced her that they really had it, and their trick would have worked! Anyway, we had no time to weigh all the possibilities.

"Versilov will kill her!" I cried. "If he could stoop so low as to make use of Lambert, he could very well murder her too! It's all the work of that double of his! . . ."

"Double, double!" Mrs. Prutkov repeated, wringing her hands in despair. After a while, however, she regained her calm.

"All right," she said, "we've no time to waste: Put on your hat and coat and off we go. And you'll take us there at once, my good woman. . . . Ah, it's quite a long way, I see. . . . Hey, Maria!" she called out to the maid, "if Mrs. Akhmakov should come, tell her I'll be back very soon and ask her to wait. If she refuses to wait, lock the door and don't let her out. Tell her that I've ordered you to keep her here. There'll be a hundred rubles for you if you manage to hold her."

We rushed out of the apartment and ran down the stairs. Certainly Mrs. Prutkov's plan appeared to be the best under the circumstances, since it was at Lambert's apartment that the worst

could happen; for if Katerina did decide to go to Mrs. Prutkov's first, Maria could always detain her there. Nevertheless,
after we'd found a cab, Mrs. Prutkov suddenly had a different
idea.

"All right, you go with her!" she told me, leaving me behind
with Alphonsine. "And, if need be, die there, understand? I'll
follow you right away, but first I'd better rush over to Katerina's.
I may still find her at home. . . . It all still sounds rather fishy
to me."

And so, while Alphonsine and I went on our way to Lambert's, Mrs. Prutkov rushed off to Katerina's.

I kept constantly urging on the cabby while trying to find
out more from Alphonsine, who, however, confined herself to a
variety of exclamations and eventually took refuge in tears.

But, just as we were plunging into the jaws of disaster, we
were suddenly saved. Before we'd driven a quarter of the way
to Lambert's, I heard my name called out behind me. I looked
back and saw another cab catching up with us. The passenger in
it was Trishatov.

"Where're you off to? What are you doing with Alphonsine?" he shouted in a frightened voice.

"You were right, Trishatov!" I shouted back. "Just as you
said, there's trouble! I'm going to Lambert's. The bastard! Come
along, the more people, the better!"

"Stop, turn back, don't go there! It's a trick. This slut lied to
you. It was pockmarked Semyon who sent me: there's no one
at Lambert's. He and Versilov have gone to Mrs. Prutkov's—I
just met them. . . . They must be there now. . . ."

I stopped my cab, got out, and jumped into Trishatov's. I still
don't know why I accepted unquestioningly what he told me. I
made up my mind at once. Alphonsine screamed and squealed
desperately, but we paid no attention to her, and I'm not sure
whether she turned her cab around to follow us or drove on
home. I never saw her again.

During our drive, Trishatov told me rather breathlessly that
there had been some sort of a deal between Lambert and pockmarked Semyon but that the pockmarked one had changed his
mind at the last moment and had now sent Trishatov to Mrs.
Prutkov to warn her not to believe what Alphonsine might tell
her and to beware of Lambert. Trishatov said that this was all
he knew because Semyon had had no time to tell him more,
that he had been in a tearing hurry to get somewhere else. "But
when I saw you, I felt I had to catch you and tell you," he said.
Obviously, then, Semyon knew everything since he'd sent Trish-

atov directly to Mrs. Prutkov's. But that was a new mystery. In order to avoid confusion, before I describe the catastrophe, I'll explain what had really happened, once more and for the last time anticipating the events.

IV

After stealing the letter from me, Lambert had immediately contacted Versilov. I won't attempt to analyze here what prompted Versilov to make such a deal with an individual like Lambert except to remind the reader of that "double" of his. But I'll get back to that later.

To keep his end of the bargain, Lambert still had to entice Katerina to his place. Versilov didn't believe he'd succeed and told him he was sure Katerina would never come. But for two days now, since the time I'd met him in the street and had announced theatrically that I'd return the letter to Katerina at Mrs. Prutkov's, Lambert had organized a sort of surveillance of Mrs. Prutkov's apartment or, to be more precise, he'd enlisted the Finnish maid to spy for him. He'd given her a down payment of twenty rubles, and the following day, after he'd stolen the letter from me, he'd had a second meeting with Maria, promising her another two hundred rubles for her further services. And that's why, when she heard that Katerina was expected at Mrs. Prutkov's at eleven-thirty that morning and that I'd be there too, Maria had rushed out of the house, hailed a cab, and driven over to Lambert's to pass the information on to him. This was precisely what he'd expected of her. It so happened that, at that very moment, Versilov was there, and it took him less than one second to devise the whole diabolical scheme. It must be true that at certain moments madmen are capable of extraordinary Machiavellian cunning.

His plan was to lure both Mrs. Prutkov and me out of the apartment before Katerina was due to arrive, if only for a quarter of an hour. He and Lambert were to wait outside until we'd left and then rush upstairs, be let into the apartment by Maria and wait for Katerina. In the meantime, Alphonsine was to do her best to detain us downstairs if we should come back too soon, using her imagination to keep us busy for as long as possible. In any case, Katerina was expected to arrive at half past eleven, which was long before we could possibly be back.

Needless to say, Lambert had never summoned Katerina to his place as Alphonsine had told us: the whole thing down to every last detail had been invented by Versilov, including the role of the frightened accomplice that Alphonsine was to play. Of course there was some risk involved in the plan, but it was based on sound reasoning: If it worked, fine; if not, nothing was lost since they still had the document.

And it did work: We had to follow Alphonsine as long as there was the slightest chance that she was telling the truth. Besides, as I said before, we were given no time to think.

V

Followed by Trishatov, I rushed into Mrs. Prutkov's apartment through the kitchen where we found the terrified maid, who, when letting Versilov and Lambert in, had noticed that the Frenchman had a gun in his hand. Although she'd accepted his money, the gun was not part of their bargain. Now she had strong misgivings, and the second she saw me she rasped with distress:

"Mrs. Akhmakov's here. . . . And they . . . they've got a gun!"

"Wait here, Trishatov," I said, "I'll call you if I need you. Then come quick."

Maria let me into the passage and from there I slipped quietly into Mrs. Prutkov's tiny bedroom, where there was just enough room for a bed and where I'd been forced to eavesdrop on a conversation once before. So I sat down on the bed and quickly made myself a tiny opening in the curtain.

The conversation was already quite heated and was being conducted in loud voices. While still in the kitchen, I'd heard Lambert's voice. He was shouting. Katerina, who'd arrived just after them, was sitting on the sofa and Lambert was standing in front of her and shouting as only a fool would. Now I know why he was behaving so stupidly: he was in a tremendous hurry to close the deal and get out of there because he was terrified of being caught (by whom, I'll explain later). He was holding the letter in his hand. Versilov was not in the room. I was ready to rush in at the first sign of danger. I'll try to convey just the gist of what I heard, for the chances are that I missed many details: I was too excited to take in everything.

"This letter will cost you thirty thousand rubles! Why do you look surprised? I know it's worth a hundred thousand! But all I ask you is thirty!"

Lambert's voice was very loud. He seemed terribly wound up.

Katerina, although apparently frightened, still managed to behave with composure, her attitude expressing a mixture of scorn and surprise.

"I realize that I've been caught in some sort of trap," she said, "but if you really have that letter . . ."

"Here it is, see! Don't you recognize it? Now start writing that promissory note for thirty thousand rubles—not one kopek less!"

"But I have no money."

"Just write that IOU. Here's some paper. After that you can go and find the money. I'll give you just one week, no more. When I get the money, I'll give you back the IOU and the letter."

"You're talking to me in such a peculiar tone. . . . I think you're making a big mistake: this document will be taken away from you no later than today, as soon as I lodge a complaint. . . ."

"Who are you going to complain to? Ha-ha-ha! What about the scandal that would cause? And what if I showed this letter to your father? Also, how will they take it away from me? You don't suppose that I keep such documents at the place where I live, do you? I'll have the letter shown to the prince by a third person. You'd better not be so obstinate, madame, and be grateful that I'm not asking for much more. You may also realize that somebody else might have asked you for another form of payment . . . in kind, you know, a payment that no pretty woman can afford to refuse when she finds herself in such an embarrassing situation! He-he-he! *Vous êtes belle, vous!*"

Katerina's face had turned very red. She got up and impulsively spat into his face. Then she quickly walked toward the door.

It was then that that idiot Lambert pulled out his gun. Being just an unimaginative small-time criminal, he had blindly based all his calculations on the document, without bothering to try to understand what sort of person he was dealing with. As I said before, he simply went around assuming that everyone else was guided by the same motives as he was. His rudeness at once aroused her anger and disgust, and perhaps if he had behaved differently she might conceivably have considered paying him something for the letter.

"Don't move! Stay right where you are!" he roared.

Her spitting in his face had made him mad with rage. He seized her by the shoulder, pointing the gun at her (obviously just for the effect).

She let out a cry and sank back onto the sofa. I leaped out of my hiding place. . . . But that very same second I saw Versilov burst out from behind the door leading into the passage. Before I could blink an eye, the gun was in his hand and Lambert was swaying and falling unconscious as Versilov struck him on the head with it. Blood gushed from Lambert's head onto the rug.

When she saw Versilov, Katerina went deathly pale. For a few seconds she stared at him and then, her face contorted in undescribable horror, she fainted. He rushed toward her. I can still see it all as though flashing before my eyes. I remember my fright upon seeing his dark red, almost purple face and his bloodshot eyes. He must have seen me, but he didn't appear to register my presence or recognize me. He picked up the unconscious Katerina as if she weighed nothing; he held her in his arms the way a nurse holds a baby and, carrying her, started pacing senselessly up and down the room. In that rather small room, he moved from corner to corner with surprising speed, obviously not knowing what he was doing. I'm sure that during those seconds his mind was quite blank. His eyes never left her face. I was trotting behind him, for I was afraid of the gun he was still clutching in his right hand; he'd forgotten all about it, and it was awfully close to her head. But when I got too near him, he pushed me away with his elbow, and when I tried again, he kicked me. I thought of calling Trishatov, but I was afraid it might cause the madman to go berserk. In the end I pulled aside the curtain that screened off Mrs. Prutkov's bedroom and started pleading with him to put Katerina down on the bed. To my surprise, he did just that and stood over her, still looking into her face for perhaps a whole minute. Then he bent over her, quickly kissed her pale lips, and then kissed her once more. By that time I could see clearly that he was no longer himself.

Suddenly the gun flashed through the air: he'd swung at her with it. But he broke his motion in mid-air. Something seemed to have dawned on him: he turned the gun and pointed it at her face.

I seized his hand and shouted for help. Trishatov came running in and the two of us tried to disarm him. But he succeeded in shaking us off and, as soon as his right hand was free, he turned the gun on himself and pressed the trigger. Probably he'd intended to shoot her first and then shoot himself, but since we'd interfered with his original plan, he'd pointed the gun at his heart. . . . Still, at the last moment I somehow succeeded in pushing his hand upward and the bullet hit him in the shoulder. . . .

Just then, Mrs. Prutkov rushed in screaming at the top of her voice. But Versilov was already lying unconscious on the floor next to Lambert.

Epilogue

I

It is almost six months now since all that took place. Much has changed since then. Things are quite different now and, as for me, I've started on a completely new life. . . . But I suppose I must now release the reader too.

At the time, as well as for quite a while afterward, what puzzled me most was how Versilov could have brought himself to associate with someone like Lambert and also what he had been trying to achieve by the association. Gradually, I found some sort of explanation. I don't think that, during the final scene at Mrs. Prutkov's or even on the previous day, Versilov could have had any clear objective in mind at all. I'd even say that he wasn't reasoning but was acting directly under the impact of a whirl of emotions. However, I definitely deny that he was ever really insane, especially since today he may be described as anything but insane. But I do accept fully the hypothesis of the presence of a "double."

What does it actually mean, a "double"? According to a medical treatise that I read later while doing some research on the subject, such a "double" is the first stage of a specific nervous disorder, a rather serious disorder that may lead to a very tragic end. Moreover, Versilov himself had explained to us with terrifying frankness the split between his feelings and his will when he'd broken the icon at Mother's. But, on the other hand, I must repeat that his smashing of the icon, although certainly done under the influence of his "double," still was loaded with—I always felt—a sort of wicked symbolism, a spiteful irritation at these women who expected him to act in a certain way, an impatience with them for making certain claims on him and with their right to judge him. And so, acting jointly with his "double," he picked up the icon and smashed it in two! Or, to put it simply, even if a "double" was involved, it was, at the same time, also a whim. . . . But all this is only conjecture; I have no definite explanation.

It is a fact that, for all his passion for Katerina, Versilov had always been highly skeptical of her moral qualities. I'm convinced that, while he was standing in the passage during her exchange with Lambert, he fully expected her to accept Lambert's disgraceful demands. But did he want her to accept them? As I said, I'm convinced he wanted nothing, he wasn't even thinking: he just felt he had to be there, perhaps to leap out of hiding, say something to her, maybe insult her, and perhaps . . . perhaps kill her. Anything could happen, but when he first arrived in Lambert's company he had no idea of what it was going to be. I also want to emphasize the fact that the gun belonged to Lambert while Versilov himself came unarmed. It was when he saw her dignified pride in the face of Lambert's insulting threats that he couldn't restrain himself and rushed in. It was only after that that he ran amok. Did he really want to shoot her at that moment? I don't believe he knew himself, but I suppose he'd have shot her if we hadn't interfered.

His wound, although not fatal, still turned out to be grave enough for him to have to stay in bed for a long time. He spent that time, of course, at Mother's.

Now, as I write these lines, spring is outside the windows. It is mid-May. Mother is sitting by his bed. He is stroking her cheeks and her hair and tenderly trying to intercept the gaze of her averted eyes. Oh, this is only half of the former Versilov: this man refuses to be parted from Mother, and I know he'll never leave her again. He even "received his reward in tears," as Makar put it in his story about the merchant; I believe, though, that Versilov still has a long time to live. With the rest of us, he is now as sincere and unaffected as a small child, although he never loses a dignified restraint and never says anything he feels he shouldn't. His intelligence and his moral standards have remained unchanged, while his striving for an ideal has become even stronger. Personally, I've never loved him more than I do now, and I'm only sorry that I have neither the time nor the space to say more about him. Nevertheless, I'll tell one recent episode among many such.

By Lent he had quite recovered and during the sixth week he announced he was going to fast. I don't believe he'd fasted before that for thirty years or more. Mother was very pleased. They started, then, preparing lenten dishes, but rather expensive and refined ones. All Monday and Tuesday I heard him singing in his room "The Bridegroom Cometh," and I enjoyed both the tune and the verses tremendously. During those two days he spoke very eloquently about religion, but then on Wednesday he suddenly broke his fast. Something had irritated him unexpectedly, something that he described laughingly as "an amusing incongruity." Something about the way the priest looked or the way the service was conducted had displeased him, and when he returned home he told us with a quiet smile: "I do love God very much, my friends, but I simply have no talent for these things." That day roast beef was served for dinner.

I know that now Mother often sits down next to him and, smiling meekly, starts talking to him in a quiet voice, sometimes on the most abstract subjects. Now she somehow "dares" to talk to him about those things, although I don't know when or how this happened. Most often she talks to him in whispers. He listens to her with a smile, strokes her hair, kisses her hands. True happiness radiates from his face. Sometimes he gets into strange, almost hysterical states. Thus he may take the photograph of Mother—the one I'd seen him kiss once—look at it with tears in his eyes, kiss it, plunge into his memories, and call us all to him. But, at such moments, he talks very little. He has never spoken of Katerina, never mentioned her name. Indeed, it's as though he's forgotten about her altogether. Nor has he ever said a word about marrying Mother. During the summer there was talk of taking him abroad for a cure, but Mrs. Prutkov decided there was no need for that. Besides, he didn't want to go himself. Now they're planning to spend the summer somewhere in the countryside outside Petersburg.

By the way, for the time being, we're all living on Mrs. Prutkov's money, and at this point I'd like to say that I'm sorry now that in the course of these notes I have allowed myself to make some disrespectful and even scornful remarks about that lady. But when I made those remarks, I became in my imagination exactly the individual I had been at the moment I was describing; and now, as I have finished these memoirs, I feel that if I have succeeded in re-educating myself, it was precisely through the process of remembering and noting down my recollections just as they came. I now no longer agree with many of the things I've written and, specifically, with the general tone and wording of certain passages. Nevertheless, I refuse to change one word or to delete anything.

I said he has never spoken of Katerina. Actually, I think he may even have overcome his passion for her. As a matter of fact, only Tatyana Prutkov and I ever speak of Katerina around here, and at that only in secret. Just now Katerina is abroad. Before she left, I saw her a few times and I've already received two letters from her and have answered both of them. But I'd rather not divulge the contents of this correspondence or repeat what we said to each other during our last meetings before her departure: that is a completely *new* story and, indeed, is still located entirely in the future. There are certain things that I wouldn't even tell Tatyana. But enough on that subject, except for one thing: I want it understood that Katerina hasn't married anyone yet and is now traveling in Europe with the Pelishevs. Her father has since died and she is now one of the richest widows around. At this moment she is in Paris. Her break with Björing was quite sudden and seems to have happened spontaneously, I mean as if it were the most natural thing in the world. But I suppose I'd better say a few words about that.

The morning of the awful scene, pockmarked Semyon, the man to whom Trishatov and his long-legged friend had gone after deserting Lambert, had warned Björing about Lambert's plans. He had done so for practical considerations. Lambert had at first convinced him to come in on the deal with him and, after he had got hold of the document, he'd told him about every circumstance and every detail of the operation, including the final stratagem introduced by Versilov to get Mrs. Prutkov out of the way. At the last moment, however, Semyon, being the most practical man of the lot, had decided to pull out of it. He was afraid that it might lead to unpredictably grave consequences, what with the hotheaded and inexperienced Lambert and Versilov maddened by passion. Indeed, he felt it would be much wiser for him to rely on Björing's gratitude. All that I learned later from Trishatov, although I still don't quite understand why Lambert had to drag Semyon into the deal in the first place, nor can I make any sense out of the relations between the two of them.

The question that preoccupied me much more was why Lambert had gone to Versilov. But now that is quite clear to me. First of all, Versilov knew all there was to know about the persons involved and, secondly, in case of trouble, if anything went wrong, Lambert hoped to be able to shift the blame to him.

As it turned out, Björing didn't get there in time. He arrived a whole hour after the shot had been fired, and by then Mrs. Prutkov's place looked quite different. About five minutes after the bleeding Versilov had fallen to the carpet, Lambert, who had been lying in a puddle of his own blood and whom we'd all assumed dead, suddenly stirred, sat up, and scrambled to his feet. He stared around blankly for a while; then, apparently gathering what had happened, he walked out into the kitchen, put on his coat, and vanished. He did not look at the document that was lying there on the table. I vaguely heard that he hadn't been too badly hurt by the blow on the head: he got away with only a slight concussion and some loss of blood.

Trishatov had rushed for a doctor, but Versilov came to before the doctor arrived. And even before that, Mrs. Prutkov had succeeded in bringing Katerina back to consciousness and had driven her home. Thus, by the time Björing arrived, he found only the wounded Versilov, the doctor, me, and my mother (Trishatov had told her and she'd rushed over although she was still ill). Björing looked around in bewilderment and, when told that Mrs. Akhmakov had been taken home, left without saying a word. He looked extremely uneasy, feeling certain that a scandal would be unavoidable now. He was wrong: no real scandal followed, although there were all kinds of rumors. Although it proved impossible to keep secret that a shot had been fired, the principal facts were pretty well kept from the public. The police released the results of their investigation, saying only that one V***, a family man of around fifty, had suddenly declared his passionate love to a highly respectable lady, who did not happen to reciprocate his feelings. And so, in a moment of exasperation, V*** attempted to shoot himself. Nothing beyond this leaked out, and it was in this form that the report appeared in the press with only the participants' initials. I am sure, for instance, that they never even questioned Lambert. Nevertheless, Björing, who knew exactly what had taken place, became worried. And, to make things worse, just two days earlier he'd learned that Katerina had agreed to a private meeting with Versilov, who he knew was in love with her. That really incensed him, and he had the effrontery to tell Katerina that, after what had happened, he was no longer surprised at all the fantastic rumors that were circulating about her. Whereupon Katerina broke off their engagement then and there. She did so without anger but also without the least hesitation. Her notion that it was somehow "reasonable" to marry the man vanished like a patch of fog scattered by the wind. Perhaps she'd recognized him for what he was even before that, but it's also quite possible that the shock she had suffered radically changed certain of her views and feelings.

But, again, I'd better say no more on the subject.

Of Lambert, let me say that he soon left for Moscow where he got himself picked up for one of his ventures. As to Trishatov, I've been out of touch with him since that day, although I'm still trying to trace him. He vanished from sight after the death of his great friend, *le grand dadais*, who shot himself.

II

I've mentioned the death of the old Prince Nikolai Sokolsky. That dear kind old man died soon after the events just described, although actually a whole month later. He died of a stroke at night. I never saw him again after that day he spent in my apartment. I heard that in his last month he became much more sensible, even somewhat reserved; he stopped being frightened of everything and bursting into tears and, in all that time, never once mentioned Anna. Whatever love there was left in him was directed toward his daughter. Once, a week or so before his death, Katerina suggested that he invite me, hoping it might distract him, but the mere thought of it made him frown. I'm just reporting this fact without comment.

His estate turned out to be in good order, and he left quite a substantial sum of money, two-thirds of which was bequeathed to his innumerable goddaughters. But what surprised everyone was the fact that Anna's name was not mentioned anywhere in the will—she was left out altogether. Nevertheless, I know for a fact that a few days before his death the old prince called his daughter and his friends Pelishev and Prince V. to his bedside and directed Katerina to see to it that, after his death, Anna received sixty thousand rubles. He expressed that wish in clear and precise terms, quite briefly and without indulging in a single exclamation. But when, after his death, the estate was settled and Katerina informed Anna through her lawyer that she had sixty thousand rubles coming to her, Anna laconically refused to accept the money, despite the assurances that this was, indeed, the wish of the deceased. And so the money is to this day at her disposal in a bank, and Katerina hopes that Anna may still change her mind. But I know that she never will because I am now quite close to her. Anna's gesture caused quite a stir and all kinds of talk. Her aunt, Mrs. Fanariotov, who had been outraged over Anna's scandalous engagement to the old prince, now, after Anna's refusal to accept the money, radically changed her opinion of her niece and solemnly assured her of her respect. On the other hand, Anna's brother broke with her for good. As for me, although I visit her rather often, I cannot say that we talk much about intimate subjects; indeed, we never so much as mention any of the recent happenings. And, while she seems genuinely pleased when I come, she always steers our conversation in such a way that it somehow remains impersonal. Very recently, however, she told me she had made up her mind to enter a convent. Somehow, I don't believe she will. I think that telling me that was simply her way of expressing her bitterness.

The one sad sequel that remains for me to tell concerns my sister Lisa. There's real unhappiness for you, and I realize how insignificant my puny troubles are beside her truly bitter fate! First of all, Prince Sergei never recovered and died in the prison hospital before his trial was scheduled to begin. Actually he died before the old Prince Nikolai. And so Lisa was left alone with the child she was expecting. She did not weep and outwardly remained calm and composed. She became gentle and quiet. But her earlier warm impulsiveness seemed to have been sealed somewhere deep inside her. She meekly helped Mother in the house and looked after the convalescing Versilov, but she practically refused to talk and even avoided looking at anyone. She gave the impression that nothing really concerned her, that she was here only temporarily and was about to leave. When Versilov had more or less recovered, she took to sleeping a lot. I tried to bring her books, but she never read them. She grew thinner and thinner. I never dared try to console her, although I often came in determined to do something about her depression. But as soon as I was in her presence, I felt it impossible to get close to her. Nor could I think of any way to start such a conversation. And so it went until a terrible thing happened: she slipped and fell down some steps—not many steps, only three—which was enough for her to have a miscarriage. After that she was ill nearly all winter. Now she is back on her feet, but her health has been permanently damaged. She is still just as silent with us, although she has begun to talk a little to Mother. These past few days, with the bright spring sun shining high in the sky, have kept reminding me of that other sunny morning last fall when Lisa and I were walking down the street, full of joy, of hope, and of love for one another. Alas, what came of it all? Well, personally, I can't complain: a new life has started for me. But Lisa? Her future is an enigma. And today even just to look at her hurts me.

Nevertheless, about three weeks ago, I succeeded in arousing some interest in her by telling her the latest news about Vasin. He had been released from prison. That reasonable man, I understand, gave the most precise explanations and provided very interesting information that fully vindicated him in the eyes of those on whom his fate depended. Moreover, the notorious manuscript turned out to be nothing but a translation of some French material that he had been collecting for his private edification, to be used only as reference for a learned article he was planning to write eventually for a magazine. At present he is living in the provinces. (His stepfather Stebelkov, on the other hand, is still in prison for his involvement in an affair that is getting more and more complicated as time goes by.)

While I was telling Lisa all this about Vasin, she listened to me with a peculiar smile and then commented that whatever had happened to Vasin was bound to happen just as it did. But she was obviously relieved to know that Sergei's statement had not substantially aggravated Vasin's case. On Dergachev and the rest, I have no further information.

I have finished. Possibly some readers may wonder what happened to that "idea" of mine and what's so "new" about this "new life" I'm now living and about which I am being so mysterious. Well, that new life, the new path I have discovered and am now following, *is* precisely "my idea," that very same old idea of mine but in such a completely different form that it is hardly recognizable. But all this cannot be included in these memoirs: it is a different story. My former life is over and a new life is just beginning. However, I must mention something essential: Tatyana Prutkov, my sincere and loving friend, keeps pestering me every day, insisting that I should now enter the university.

"First get on with your studies and when you've finished, there'll be plenty of time for you to think up all kinds of ideas."

I admit that what she says makes me stop and think, but I still haven't made up my mind. One of the reasons I gave Mrs. Prutkov for not entering the university was that I have no right to study when I should work to support Mother and Lisa. She, however, rejected that objection, assuring me that she'd take care of that and that she had enough money to do so until I graduated. Finally, I decided to seek advice, carefully and critically choosing the adviser. My final choice was Nikolai Semyonovich, who had been my guardian in Moscow and was the husband of my dear friend Maria. It was not that I really needed anyone's advice, I simply felt the desire to hear the opinion of an uninvolved observer; I knew he was a rather cold and selfish man, but beyond any doubt also highly intelligent. So I sent him my manuscript, which I hadn't yet shown to anybody, and asked him to keep it secret, especially from Mrs. Prutkov. Two weeks later I received the manuscript back. It was accompanied by a longish letter. I will give a few excerpts from that letter here, for I believe they express Nikolai's general opinion of the situation and may perhaps shed some light on my story too:

III

". . . I can think of nothing on which you could have spent your time with greater profit than on writing these *Notes*, my dear unforgettable Arkady! You have now provided yourself with what we may call a scrupulous account of the first eventful and dangerous steps on the road of your life. I am convinced that by writing it all down you have been able to 're-educate' yourself, as you chose to put it. I won't allow myself, of course, to criticize you, although every page raises questions. A typical example is your keeping the document for such a very long time. But that is the only reservation I will make out of the hundred-odd that occurred to me.

"I also greatly appreciate your trust in me that prompted you to confide in me alone what you describe as the 'secret of your idea.' But I must firmly turn down your request for my opinion of your idea itself. First of all, a letter doesn't afford sufficient space for an answer and, secondly, I'm not ready to give an appraisal, for I must think about it more in order to digest it thoroughly. The only thing I will say is that it is an original concept, which sets you apart from most of the young people of your generation who, instead of thinking for themselves, pounce upon any available ready-made notions. The stock of these notions is, by the way, quite limited and some of them may also be dangerous. Thus, your 'idea' has saved you, at least for the time being, from the ideas expounded by people like Dergachev & Company that are considerably less original than yours. Finally, I heartily agree with the advice given you by the esteemed Mrs. Prutkov, whom I have met but, as I realize now, failed to appreciate as highly as she deserved. It would, indeed, be very useful to you to enter the university. Learning, as well as life experience, no doubt would substantially broaden your horizons in the next three or four years and help you to define your aspirations with greater precision. And if, after graduating from the university, you still wished to pursue your 'idea,' there would be nothing to prevent you.

"Now, although you haven't asked me to, allow me on my own initiative to share with you a few thoughts and feelings that came to me as I read your *Notes,* so striking in their frankness. Yes, I think Mr. Versilov was right in saying that, because of your young years spent in solitude, you could be dangerous. There are many adolescents like you whose natural endowments may turn into either a servile conformity or an unreasoned predilection for disorder. But this predilection for disorder stems, in most cases perhaps, from what is really an unconscious longing for order or, to use your own word, for 'beauty.' Youth is pure just because it is youth. Possibly, in its immature and crazy impulses, there is a longing for order and a search for truth. But who is to blame if some members of the present young generation believe they have discovered truth in notions so ridiculous that it seems incredible for anyone to accept them? I'd like to remark here that only one generation ago, which is quite recently after all, there was no need to pity such daring young people because in the end they always rejoined our educated ruling class and eventually blended into it to form an indistinguishable whole. And if, early in life, they became conscious of the lurking disorderliness and unfairness around them, the breach of dignity in the parental home, the lack of solid family traditions and of a beautiful, fully evolved way of life—it was all to the good because, after having questioned the value of these traditions, they returned to them in full awareness and were in a better position to understand and appreciate them. But today the situation is quite different: there is almost nothing for the young dissidents to go back to.

"Let me try to make clear what I mean by a comparison or rather by a parallel. If I were a talented Russian writer, I would pick my characters from the hereditary gentry because only among that species of educated Russians can be found at least a semblance of harmonious order that could be used to produce an aesthetic effect of beauty so essential in a novel. And I really mean this although, as you well know, I do not belong to the gentry myself. Long ago, speaking of 'the traditions of the Russian family,'* Pushkin pointed out the legitimate themes for the Russian novel, and, I assure you, these traditions are the only things of beauty we have had until now or, perhaps I should say, the only things that have taken on a definite form. It is not that I am so fully convinced of the perfection of these family traditions but simply that at least they provide certain definite forms to serve as bases for concepts such as 'honor' and 'duty.' And it so happens that these concepts do not exist in Russia outside the gentry even in embryonic, let alone definite, form. I am saying all this with the utmost detachment as a man whose only concern is harmony.

"Whether these concepts of honor and duty are just and true is another question. What matters is the *definiteness* of their forms. Also, we ought to have some kind of order, one that is not prescribed from the outside but that evolves from life itself. The most important thing is to have our own order, any order as long as it is our native one! This has long been our aspiration and it will put our minds to rest at last. We need something we have built all by ourselves instead of constantly listening to foreign ideas, repeatedly razing everything to the ground, living amidst flying splinters, and with nothing but piles of rubbish to show for two hundred years of effort. Don't accuse me of

* In sections XIII and XIV of Chapter 3 of his *Eugene Onegin*. [A. MacA.]

being a Slavophile. And if I sound misanthropic, it's simply because it all depresses me so much.

"Indeed, recently the process has been reversed: no longer is human jetsam latching itself on to our elite; instead, whole batches of our best people are tearing themselves away from it and lightheartedly joining the roving packs of the disorderly and the envious. Moreover, it is no longer so rare to find fathers and heads of our culture-bearing families mocking and ridiculing values that their children may still have been happy to believe in. Worse than that, they don't even bother to hide from their children their great delight at their sudden discovery of the right to dishonor that will enable them to satisfy their greed, a right based on a certain species of reasoning accepted wholesale by so many. You must understand, Arkady, that I'm not talking about genuine believers in progress but about our rabble, which now appears so numerous, of whom it has been said 'Grattez le Russe et vous trouvez le Tartare.' And take my word for it, there are nowhere near as many true liberals and genuine humanitarians among us as we have been led to believe.

"But all this is just philosophizing; let's get back to our hypothetical novelist. His position would be perfectly clear: today he would have no choice but to write historical novels because in our time the 'beautiful' type is no longer to be found and, even if there were still some remnants around, they wouldn't be considered 'beautiful' by the standards prevalent today. Certainly, in historical novels, on the other hand, it would still be possible to create a great many pleasing and reassuring episodes. Indeed, the reader might be sufficiently taken in to believe that a scene from past history could take place in the present. And, provided the writer had great talent, such a book would belong less to Russian literature than to Russian history. For it would be an artistically convincing picture of a Russian illusion, but an illusion that really existed until some people decided that it had never been anything but an illusion. A member of the third generation in a three-generation saga of a cultured Russian upper-middle-class family in proper historical setting could be portrayed in his contemporary aspect only as a rather misanthropic and lonely type and certainly a sad sight to behold. Indeed, he'd strike the reader as some sort of freak, a deviation from the line of his forebears, someone doomed without a future. Very soon this misanthropic descendant would also vanish and new, different, and as yet unknown characters would appear on the scene, and in his wake would come a new illusion. But what sort of faces would these characters have? If they were ugly, there would be no future for the Russian novel. And, alas, it wouldn't be just the novel that would be impossible then!

"Instead of looking for an illustration far afield, let me take your own *Notes*. I'll take the liberty of being completely frank and suggest that you look at Mr. Versilov's two families. I don't wish to enlarge too much on Mr. Versilov himself, but, after all, he *is* a member of the Russian landed gentry and comes from an old, distinguished family. At the same time, however, he is a champion of the Paris Commune. He is a true poet, he loves Russia, yet he also denigrates her; he has no religion and yet would be willing to die for something vague that he is unable even to name but in which he believes ardently, as do so many Russian proponents of European civilization of the Petersburg period of our history. But enough about him personally. Let us turn to his legitimate family. His son is not even worth mentioning—it would be doing him too much honor: anyone who has eyes to see knows how this sort of irresponsible fool will end up, dragging others to perdition along with him. But his daughter—if anyone has a strong character, it is Anna! She has a personality of the proportions of the Abbess Mitrofania,† although I'm not suggesting that she may end up as a criminal—that would be quite uncalled for on my part.

"Now, if you could convince me, Arkady, that this family is an exception, an accident, I would be very relieved. But wouldn't it be much more accurate to conclude that many such legitimate Russian families are broken up and become *accidental* groupings, all merging into the general disorder and chaos. In your manuscript there emerges a type of such an *accidental family* and you, Arkady, are a member of that family; this is already a departure from the typical recent literary character who came from a regular, traditional background and had a childhood and adolescence quite different from yours.

"I must confess I wouldn't at all like to be a novelist who

† The Abbess Mitrofania (in the world, Baroness Praskovia Rosen) was tried and found guilty of forging checks and falsifying a will, which involved enormous sums of money. The October 1874 issue of the magazine *Grazhdanin* describes her as follows in reporting her trial: "She has an intelligent and energetic face, serene and calm. When she installs herself in the dock, it is as though she were getting ready to listen to someone else's interesting trial."

Also, in his *Memoirs* A. F. Koni describes her as "a woman of great intellectual power, of a rather masculine bent, possessing great business acumen. In many ways she rejected the traditions and conventions that governed the society within the narrow framework of which she moved." [A. MacA.]

has to deal with a hero coming from an *accidental family!* It's such an ungrateful task, and it can have no beauty of form. Moreover, such types are still in the process of formation and it's impossible to give them artistic polish. It's too easy to make mistakes, to exaggerate, to miss things. At any rate, there's too much guesswork involved. But then what is there left for a writer who doesn't want to write only historical novels and who is fascinated by the present scene? Well, he'll just have to try to guess and expect to be wrong.

"*Notes* such as yours, however, could, I believe, serve as raw material for some future literary work, for a future picture of the present disorder, but written when the period is already in the past. Oh, when the anger has gone and the future is the present, the artist of that future will discover appropriate beautiful forms to convey the chaos and disorder of the past. And that's when your *Notes* will be needed, and they will provide good material, despite their chaotic and fortuitous nature. . . .

"At least some revealing traits will be preserved, traits from which it will be possible to guess what might have been hidden in the heart of an adolescent who lived through those troubled times, a finding not altogether without value because it is out of adolescents that generations are built. . . ."

RUSSIAN LITERATURE
IN NORTON PAPERBACK

Anton Chekhov   *Seven Short Novels* (translated by Barbara Makanowitzky)

Fyodor Dostoevsky   *The Adolescent*
(translated by Andrew R. MacAndrew)
The Gambler
(translated by Andrew R. MacAndrew)

Nicolai V. Gogol   *Dead Souls* (translated by George Reavey)
"The Overcoat" and Other Tales of Good and Evil
(translated by David Magarshack)

Robert C. Howes, Tr.   *The Tale of the Campaign of Igor*

Alexandra Kollontai   *A Great Love*
(translated by Cathy Porter)
Selected Writings (edited by Alix Holt)

Yuri Olesha   *"Envy" and Other Works*
(translated by Andrew R. MacAndrew)

Alexandr Sergeyevitch Pushkin   *The Complete Prose Tales*
(translated by Gillon R. Aitken)

F. D. Reeve, Tr. and Ed.   *Nineteenth-Century Russian Plays*

Varlam Shalamov   *Kolyma Tales* (translated by John Glad)

Aleksandr Solzhenitsyn   *"We Never Makes Mistakes"*
(translated by Paul W. Blackstock)

Ivan Turgenev   *"First Love" and Other Tales*
(translated by David Magarshack)

NORTON CRITICAL EDITIONS

Anton Chekhov   *Anton Chekhov's Plays* (Eugene K. Bristow, ed.)

Anton Chekhov   *Anton Chekhov's Short Stories* (Ralph E. Matlaw, ed.)

Fyodor Dostoevsky   *The Brothers Karamazov* (Ralph E. Matlaw, ed.)
Crime and Punishment (the Coulson translation;
George Gibian, ed.)

Leo Tolstoy   *Anna Karenina* (the Maude translation; George Gibian, ed.)
War and Peace (the Maude translation; George Gibian, ed.)

Ivan Turgenev   *Fathers and Sons* (a substantially new translation;
Ralph E. Matlaw, ed.)